BITTER WATER

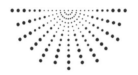

JOHN KING

Water is life's matter and matrix, mother and medium. There is no life without water.

— ALBERT SZENT - GYORGYI

CONTENTS

ACKNOWLEDGEMENTS AND THANKS

I would like to thank my wife, Jan King, for her endless support, encouragement and ideas that often occurred at just the right moment. Sorry this project ended up taking so long!

Thanks also to my lovely daughters, whom I so appreciate – Elizabeth ever kind, helpful and patient. Penny – inquisitive, always aiming to share her knowledge and an absolute magician with difficult or sick animals.

I particularly wish to thank Alan Cocks for his skilful rescue from many unknowingly self-created IT disasters and for sharing his own researches.

Further thanks go to the eagle eyed Robin Phillips, for editorial help. Also to Mia Williamson and Madeleine Tonkinson for patiently reading, for their comments and vast tracts of word processing.

Also to Pattie Ducie for her support and for sticking through the many struggles.

Lastly, to my old colleagues at Broadmoor Hospital and to the patients. You taught me a lot!

PROLOGUE

Many would agree that the world doesn't seem to work for them. Some will point to political corruption and incompetence, environmental threats, or the inbuilt inequities of capitalism in its various forms – even if it is the most successful system we've yet devised. While these factors are all valid, there is another issue, rarely discussed, but affecting most societies – that of **pathologically corrupt corporations**. The fact is that the many are of necessity obliged to use and support these corporations; though the problems they cause are often hidden and resist exposure.

Research by its nature can sometimes lead in unexpected directions. Hopefully, it advances knowledge and understanding, but it can also uncover catastrophes in the making! As researchers, our intention was to shine light on a contentious and difficult issue – that of pathological behaviour in business. We wanted the work to be practical and serve as a help and a warning to potential victims. Never would we have predicted where it would actually lead!

My name is **Andrew Alton**, Head of the International Trade and Development Unit of Croft Management School, Oxford, England. This account follows the work and exploits of a rather unorthodox team exploring this issue head on, though it starts with a young, reluctant economist about to become my research assistant, **Simon Maher**.

In many ways, his journey and enthusiasm was the catalyst that kept us all together.

For many people, the idea of loved and trusted businesses is comforting and usually true. Sometimes though, even well-known and trusted sources bring surprises. The 'LIBOR scandal', the 'PPI scandal' and the 'polluting emissions scandal' are all examples. Even if such episodes are overlooked and forgiven, there remain a minority of businesses that actively thrive by using deception, misrepresentation and theft! The research we undertook considered many such factors in describing seriously aberrant business practice – ranging from weak corporate governance to outright corruption. The connecting thread, in the worst cases, appeared to be serious psychopathology afflicting the most uncaring, brutal and probably sociopathic business leaders. Uncovering this about powerful leaders who had formidable financial and legal 'firepower' was a risky undertaking!

The notion that certain extreme business leaders could have marked psychopathic/sociopathic traits, has gained considerable traction – particularly since the last banking/finance system crash. Our work, therefore didn't focus on minor misbehaviour or sharp practice, but on the extreme exploiters driving pathological, corrupt and criminal businesses. For full disclosure, I should record that most of the research team carried past unhappy experiences at the hands of abusive business. Our research group included the reluctant economist (**Simon Maher**), the academic with a difficult background (**myself – Andrew Alton**), a linguist, a forensic psychiatrist, and eventually, two disgruntled corporate insiders from the USA: **Nick Martin** and **Rob James**. A motley crew perhaps, but in the end we worked well together!

We started by surveying contemporary corporate practice – from corporate governance and corporate citizenship, and then examining the veracity of corporate mission statements, business propaganda and PR. We looked at balance sheet and financial statement irregularities, market manipulations, the murky areas of rogue businesses and overt corporate corruption. It also became clear that digital technology had provided many new methods and opportunities for corporate control and advantage. The creeping commercial (and government) use of algorithms, machine and deep learning, robotics and AI, often seemed unethically used to categorise, control and manipulate subjects.

In the end, the team developed and used the term: 'Business and corporate pathology.' This simply referred to: 'deliberate actions and attitudes demonstrating abnormal levels of greed, deception and self-interest – that lacked concern for the consequences, bringing harm or loss to customers and to the public.' It also captured behaviours and attitudes that would be considered sociopathic in an individual, yet sometimes assumed as normal business practice! It included: serious price gouging, cheating, lying, misrepresentation and other unfair practices.

However, while extremely important – this proved insufficient. To thoroughly unpick the motivations of the most destructive business leaders, their personality style – relationships, behaviour, beliefs and attitudes – needed to be factored in. Of necessity, this included the key classic psychopathic traits.

Finally, we looked to take our research out into the real world – to include those having direct contact and experience of pathologically ruthless business people. These experiences occupy most of this account. Little did we know, just what a can of worms this would open!

Dr Andrew Alton, Oxford, England.

IMPORTANT NOTE

Initially, specific chapters introduce four key members from the Business pathology research team: Simon Maher, Andrew Alton, Nick Martin and Robbie James. Chapters that subsequently take their viewpoint, are exclusively written in the 'first person.' (i.e. describe 'I' and me')

SLOUGH AND OXFORD, UK

SIMON MAHER (THE RELUCTANT ECONOMIST)

Let me introduce myself. My name is Simon Maher, aged 29. A former company economist, living in Slough, Berkshire and currently unemployed. To be absolutely honest, I've never much cared for Slough even from my first acquaintance. The busy confluence of the M4 Motorway, the Great Western Railway, and the endless overhead flights from nearby Heathrow, probably didn't help. I liked the place even less though, after my work disaster. I'll elaborate on that sorry episode soon, but, for the moment, I'll reveal that despite having honourable intentions – the disentangling from my former employer lead to a living hell. It completed my disillusionment with economics, and the need for an alternative direction. Of course, economics has rightly been called 'the dismal science' – known for shaky models and unreliable predictions. Hence today's interview!

Back to my need for a stopgap. I contend that there can be few more soul destroying experiences than being 'processed' by a British 'Job Centre'! The hopeless faces seen there today would probably agree, and the paucity of professional vacancies on their boards, told the same story. Without alternatives though, my life would soon get even more demeaning. By temperament, was more in tune with 'social justice' – but as employment? As a prospective field, it was sadly undermined by corporate money and media hostility. Could I afford to be hitched to such a bandwagon? I still had bills to pay!

I waited nervously in the Job Centre, suspecting things might quickly get problematic. Disguising awkward facts, and there were plenty, never had been my forte.

A fresh faced young assistant headed my way.

"Simon Maher? I'm Finn. Please come to the interview booth."

I gave a brief resume of my situation. Finn's eyes gleamed and he looked ready to pounce.

I tried signalling some of the previous work problems, but showing distaste for certain business approaches, didn't fit expectations. The approved approach seemed one of acceptance and 'total positivity.' I swallowed hard. An awkward exchange seemed certain!

Eventually, the confused 'Finn', remarked, "It seems you weren't in tune with either of your last posts, Mr Maher? For a former company economist, you seem rather jaundiced about business?"

I bit back a clever retort, thinking: *Please give me someone in grown up trousers!*

"You picked that up correctly, Finn. I'm afraid matters eventually got even more complicated than we reached today! Perhaps I can expand, next time," I said, quietly deciding that there mustn't be a next time. I suspected that meeting a tight and predetermined format, was more than either of us could manage today.

Bloody business!

I caught a quick glimpse of myself in the interview booth window – a ragged figure, looking strained and sweaty. The contrast to my previous professional status must seem obvious, and would, itself, raise questions.

"I'll look forward to that," said Finn, his tone belying the words. "In the meantime, I'd like you to complete this quick assessment?"

I did my best with what seemed a rather banal, 'one size fits all' exercise.

Finn looked perplexed and with a shaking head, offered me the benefit of his advice. "If you want another business career in the future, Simon, I'd try and project more enthusiasm at interview!"

I felt sweat form around my collar and referred to our earlier discussion. "Actually, I've very good reasons for scepticism over some corporate 'values' – in addition to what I've already said!"

Finn made a clicking noise with his tongue but didn't enquire further.

With 'box ticking exercise' over for now, I left and hurried back to my new accommodation on the 'Ender Estate.' This former council flat, on the fourth floor of a particularly bleak block, sat behind a stairwell often doubling as an unofficial public urinal. The nearby drab buildings sucked out the light, making the place seem even more dingy. Following the recent wounding of a local youth, police tape festooned the opposite corner – it all seemed quite in keeping with the Ender's reputation!

I held my breath against the fetid odour and climbed the stairs. At the top I could see across the rooftops and stained concrete warehouses to the spring foliage at the town's perimeter. The view here almost reached to my previous accommodation at 'Forest Beeches' – the luxury apartment complex out near Burnham. Those were the days, when I could afford not to worry!

The weathered front door still had old 'Socialist Worker' stickers from the previous tenant. I turned the key, entering with a sigh. Like most people I'd wanted the good life too, but not by abandoning my values like certain companies seemed to expect. Some might think me stubborn, but I wasn't going to trade in my values just to suit under-handed business needs – not then, not now and not ever!

The 'Ender' fomented a toxic brew of problem families, marinated with helpless immigrants, giving local social services much of their clientèle. The postage stamp sized gardens probably contained sufficient junk to fill a scrapper's yard. From the lounge window, I eyed broken motorbikes, rusting washing machine bodies and rotting sofas – some that were probably third hand on arrival! Looking back into the flat's interior its contrast to the comfort at 'Forest Beeches' felt quite overwhelming. I shook my head in despair. *The British version of 'trickle down' economics played out in communities like this. Some kind of trickle! 'Piss down' economics seemed more like it!*

Since leaving for the Job Centre, several new emails had arrived, including one from Nick Martin – my friendly activist contact in New York. In the light of recent developments, his social justice mails had been a lifeline and more meaningful to me than anything I was reading in The Economist. Today, he'd cheerily suggested that I should come over to experience how they did things! Some hopes, now!

I decided to reply to Nick after clearing my mind of the Job Centre interview. Feeling rather pensive, I lay on the sofa, intending to review this morning. My restless imagination, though, wouldn't settle for anything quite so prosaic. As so often recently, my mind followed an undirected spiral of free associations. Soon, I shivered, remembering the recent strange experience on this very sofa. An indistinct but disturbing recall of some kind of an attack from a large blue object – but I could neither place it nor understand the context. Despite formerly rather cheerful and optimistic, I was now beginning to doubt myself. It wasn't as if this was the first or even the second time that this strangeness had occurred! I closed my eyes, and before long the distressing image flooded me again with an uncanny, and worrying sensation.

Hell. Surely I wasn't developing some strange sort of mental health crisis?

A few moments later, the image dissipated, but it had left me puzzled and shaken.

I know that hypnosis can sometimes dredge up difficult memories but this wasn't experienced in a clinical setting – but to me alone in this nasty little flat?

Nothing about either this or the other occasions made much sense. I could only hope it would stop! At the Job Centre I'd partially mentioned some of the circumstances of my job loss and while omitting much, I'd hinted some concerns to their assistant. I didn't, though, reveal their attempts at having me create false analyses of various investment opportunities or the strong hints that, if necessary, they'd deliberately frame this as being my initiative! The subsequent depression that followed my termination was only one of the results.

A snapping sound from the front door startled me. Probably, I'd make more sense of this weirdness another time, so instead I retrieved post from the letter flap. I hadn't even finished a quick scan before my heart started racing. I checked the date, in case of another postal hold up, and re-read it. So, Andrew Alton was offering a meeting any after-noon this week. I just needed to confirm the day. Moments later, I put the phone down after speaking to him - and sighed with relief. The temperamental post hadn't, after all, sunk my chances. Surprisingly, Alton actually suggested meeting later today! I made a brief holding response to Nick Martin and quickly collected up my documents. Anyway, Alton might even find my contact with a published New York activist, relevant. Grabbing my bag, I dashed to the station.

The Great Western train arrived on time. Feeling rather tense and uncomfortable having more time on my hands, I boarded the final carriage.

From recent experience I knew very well what my unoccupied mind would do and scanned my current 'concerns de jour,' for a suitable subject. I chose the forthcoming interview, rehearsed my employment history, polished answers to probable questions and tightened the presentation. All seemed fairly logical, so I looked for a distraction, rather than getting drawn back to the 'sofa experience'! I'd recently taken to setting myself little puzzles rather than fruitless ruminations. Perpetually fascinated by life's big questions, I soon picked over another conundrum.

What is it that most determines the way our lives turn out? Inner elements – genes, cognitive abilities, family experience, beliefs and values, or external factors like education, class, culture, housing, available income etc.

Certainly a strange 'train of thought' for a train journey, I silently quipped, but even so, noticed my strained and questioning reflection in the window. This was surely just a variation of the old 'nature versus nurture,' question – heredity or environment? Knowing that really, the answer was that both are clearly important, I expanded the question to include epigenetics and memes. I pondered where to fit the less scientific elements – metaphysical jokers like 'fate,' 'karma' and 'destiny'? Eventually, I grinned, thinking, *You really are a pretentious twit!*

The girl sitting diagonally opposite me gave a quick look of concern!

Pulling my thoughts away from this morning's experience, I searched for something more direct. The most salient thing right now was: *Decide to change direction. Surely I don't really believe that things are already irrevocably mapped out?*

Like my thoughts, the train was now moving at full throttle. The country outside looked pleasant, if blurred by the speed. My real attention though was busy inside – fighting more ruminations.

I only wanted fairness. Why did everything go so horribly wrong?

No real answers came – just further questions!

Now you're really being neurotic – get a grip!

I once more reeled through the sorry circumstances around my termination!

The train entered a tunnel with a buffeting sound and change of air pressure. I imagined it again, and shook my head -firmly taking myself to task.

Look, life can be complicated, and many things defy reason, common sense

– even your old friend 'cause and effect.' Just accept – that people are often driven by things that they don't fully understand!

I looked around the carriage, resting my eyes on a serene looking young woman further down. Our eyes met and she smiled. How come others didn't seem stressed like me?

Accept, let go and move on!

I stretched, and then looked again. As if to counter my earlier observation, the 'serene young woman,' was now in noisily battling a fractious toddler -previously out of sight! We rounded a bend a little too fast and the carriage lurched. The toddler let out another howl. I knew just how he felt, but I really must keep it together!

I checked my watch, Oxford should be about thirty-five minutes away. Afterwards, we'd all go our separate ways, and probably never think of each other again. Yet an event, like a serious crash, could connect us at a stroke! As the carriage rocked its way onward, I reflected on just how much of life seemed determined by chance and the unforeseen.

That's often true in my experience!

I explored the idea further. Granddad often spoke of relationships which wouldn't have existed without the war. Pop and Nan were a case in point– and their love lasted a lifetime! I moved on to ex-pats – often with little in common but a shared language and a strange new culture. Even so, life-long friendships often formed. I looked at the diversity in this very carriage. The same was surely true for immigrants here.

I was feeling lethargic and in other circumstances could easily have dozed. With only about twenty minutes left, I dispelled sleepiness exploring the new theme of 'unlikely relationships.'

Much that connects people together is by chance or coincidence. The results can really be strange!

I tested this thought with extreme examples I'd read about.

Relationships that develop in crises, like a hostage taking or the shared experience of a catastrophe.

Warped relationships between victims and perpetrators that can occur in abuse cases? The sad relationships of the so-called 'Stockholm Syndrome.' What about PTSD – 'Post-Traumatic Stress Disorder – that I'd recently read about.' Poor souls haunted with traumatic flashbacks, as if on an endless tape loop! That article also spoke of:

... traumatic memories acting like a splinter to the emotions.

... fragments of images, feelings, sounds – even smells, that coalesce into a frightening mental mosaic that can repeat years later!

Hopefully that situation was a rare? Then I remembered this morning's experience on the sofa and started feeling queasy. I looked around the carriage, but everyone here looked quite normal.

Looking for some distraction, I fished another mint from my pocket and checked the country outside. However, my thoughts soon turned to another quandary – the powerful correspondence with Nick Martin, the activist-writer contact from New York and his description of direct action. How could I follow that, now?

Despite everything that's happened, I still want to help to bring about social change. Maybe things went wrong for a larger reason which I don't yet understand? Might today's meeting show another way?

The train entered the city outskirts and stopped at Oxford station. Not long now! I left the train and crossed the station concourse smiling. For some reason I found myself thinking of the catalogue of disasters in Voltaire's 'Candide.' In the story, Dr Pangloss, the optimistic tutor, believed everything happened for the best of all possible worlds. Actually, it turned out to be disaster upon ghastly disaster! I grinned. Things often went that way in my world, too!

I found a taxi for the college campus and as requested we stopped outside the International Development and Ethical Trade Unit. A sign outside reminded visitors that this unit was actually part of the nearby management school. I left the taxi and stood for a while absorbing the honey-coloured architecture. It seemed such a contrast to my bleak and insalubrious part of Slough.

Inside reception, I asked for Dr Andrew Alton and used the waiting time to reflect on Nick Martin's articles that had initiated our correspondence. Might Dr Alton explore similar issues? Certainly, Nick's efforts in New York totally eclipsed my pathetic efforts at activism, and my whole miserable existence in Slough. If at all appropriate, I'd mention Nick's work during the interview. Extracting another mint from an increasingly battered tube, I recalled how my growing appreciation prompted me to write:

Nick, you seem to suggest that the well-being of entire populations are threatened, by bent, unbalanced non-FTA trade deals. Are things really so outrageous?

Apparently they were, but at least Nick fought it! I felt devestated that future collaboration seemed now right out of the question!

It was only a few short weeks ago, that my world had collapsed!

I'd like to think the whole mess resulted from my strong sense of social justice. That really now seemed nonsense, despite the good intentions! My actions hadn't really advanced anything – unless dismissal, the loss of a comfortable apartment and a descent into squalid housing, represented some special kind of achievement! No, nothing whatsoever had been advanced by my sacrifice!

An opening door interrupted my thoughts, and a slim man with a closely cropped beard and a bookish appearance smiled my way.

"Simon Maher? Sorry to have kept you. I'm Andrew Alton. We'll use my office."

I followed Alton down the corridor, noticing smells that I still associate with an educational environment. Not the plasticine and boiled cabbage of first school, or pheromones and the locker room pungency of high school, but that special higher education smell I remembered so well. A melange of photocopied documents, acetone for cleaning whiteboards, stale smoke around the entrances, and other odours I couldn't quite identify.

Abruptly stopping, Alton entered a comfortable though overfull office. He pointed to two chairs facing over a low table and sat down. I looked over inquiringly. Could this be my Dr Pangloss?

"Simon, do sit down. Thanks for coming so promptly. I've now had a chance to check how your CV measures up against the criteria for the post. Very interesting – though I struggled to quite see how your last job fitted?"

It wasn't quite the start I'd hoped for. I swallowed hard.

"Dr Alton, I realise aspects of my CV mightn't immediately seem relevant, and even unusual. As outlined, my qualifications are in economics. My last proper post was company economist and..."

"But it says here that you last worked in a sport shop?"

I swallowed again, knowing that what came next might sound unconvincing – even daft! Why on earth did he start by unpicking the very things that would probably seem the most foolish? Paradoxically, I knew that my gremlins sprung from a wish for fairness, equality and social justice – but Alton couldn't know that and would naturally want to probe. After all, whatever is claimed now, economics isn't exactly noted for its devotion to such things, in the wake of the crash, the associated scandals and a growing collection of failed forecasts.

"You see, Dr Alton, I temporarily took time out in another field, almost hoping to buy some thinking time... after a crisis of conscience."

A grin played over Alton's face.

"Uum... What exactly did your work involve? I mean, your corporate work as a company economist – not the sport shop work."

"Mainly, risk management, statistics/econometrics, development economics – quantitative and qualitative analysis."

"Remind me again – who was that for?"

My cheeks burned. I couldn't very well blurt out the enticements I'd resisted before finally resigning. How I hated bent practice!

"A private equity firm – assessing investment opportunities."

Alton raised his eyebrows quizzically.

I gulped. That little worm in my brain, insisting on fairness again – while simultaneously being self-destructive. At least, that's how others saw it. It's what first enticed me to enter the belly of the corporate beast. A perverse, arrogant hope that with first-hand experience of corporate failures and misbehaviour, I'd surely find ways to counter and humanise it. After my efforts collapsed, so spectacularly, so catastrophically, I can now absolutely see why this failed. Looking back, I'd been hopelessly naive.

"Dr Alton, I'm afraid I became uneasy that we had neither the time nor concern for the little people standing in the way - or for the environment. I very much care about these things. Hence time out in the 'real world', even as a humble 'sales associate'. Researching more ethical approaches, hoping to later write up the experience, and bring 'social justice' to the party"

"Did you succeed?"

I swallowed. Was this the time to tell the whole story? That I'd been pressured to create 'optimistic' assessments, refused and was effectively forced out. No, the implications still weren't clear and this episode had been followed by the second termination!

"Dr Alton, I'm ashamed to say that it took a little time to realise that direct confrontation isn't always the smartest way!"

Alton smiled again.

"So I gather. You do understand what we're doing here? What the research assistant post actually involves?"

I nodded, recalling abstracts of Alton's work. I'd almost cheered aloud reading his monograph; 'Neoliberal Predators.' How he got away with this while nominally attached to a management school, seemed amazing!

"I do Dr Alton, though I'm sure exploring real alternatives must be far more productive than charging head-first at brick walls."

"You haven't explained what you actually did during your stint in the sports shop. Did this somehow fit your commitment to social justice? You know, as outlined in your application?"

"Initially, no. After finding items that were clearly sourced from sweatshops and contrary to stated policy, I took this up with colleagues and tackled management. Later I tried to raise awareness of the implications and exposed several corporate tricks, with other employees in the mall where we worked. Unfortunately, these efforts culminated in me being fired – actually escorted from the premises!"

Alton shook his head and smiled.

"Yes, I bet that made you popular! It's a reaction I know fairly well, myself."

"As time has gone on, Dr Alton, I've realised that social justice means far more to me than economic theories!"

Alton smiled.

"You've probably seen our report on corporations exploiting third world labour?"

"Yes, recently."

Alton abruptly rose and went to a table in the corner. He held up a folder labelled *'Appropriation by enforced privatisation – the West's shame.'*

My heart sped as he passed it over. I scanned the contents, quietly comparing it to my own dismal efforts at education – pushing anti-sweatshop leaflets outside a mall!

"You find it interesting?"

"And how, Dr Alton! I'd never have achieved much through clumsy efforts at direct action."

The interview continued for another hour and a half, before moving to conditions of service. When Alton floated his thoughts on future research, I could hardly wait.

"Your work on privatisation. I find so much worrying about that. In fact, after seeing articles on New York's Indymedia site, I contacted an activist there, writing on the New York scene."

Alton looked up as I mentioned Nick Martin and New York City.

"You seem 'hot to trot,' Simon. Look, we've several other candidates to see, but I should be in touch soon."

Another cab returned me to Oxford station. The late papers had arrived and despite government denials, the Evening News screamed of further cuts.

I settled into the train for the journey back to Slough, replaying our interview. Alton had seemed very receptive, though I hadn't fully revealed the extent of my fall following the 'sweatshop' meeting – or just how disastrous it had been.

Under my shirt felt damp, just recalling the scene!

Raising awareness about the perils of sweatshops to new colleagues was successful alright, but I'd got quite a reputation in the process. An impromptu meeting held in a nearby coffee shop went horribly wrong. I could almost hear the shouts of a colleague that triggered the furore.

"What about us then, Si? Why not talk about that? You reckon most big brands have outsourced to poor countries with cheap labour. Why then are their prices so high and our pay so low?"

I couldn't resist an open goal, but the following session had been more than just spirited – quite a hullabaloo ensued! Other managers later complained I was a major troublemaker, sowing discontent with their staff. Alton though, seemed enthusiastic – even amused by what I said. Of course, he didn't realise that before this dismissal, I'd been generally positive and enthusiastic, but since – deflated, depressed and stuck.

The return journey seemed slower, giving time to reflect. How else could I deal with my own abysmally low feelings? Should I be open or cover up? I certainly had to find a way of explaining my career detour more effectively for other interviews. I undid my top button, overcome by clamminess and a flush of heat. After sacking, I'd sought some treatment, and now saw that my seething anger probably came from time in a children's home – after mum and dad separated. Could such things really be mentioned openly? I looked around the carriage, struck by the apparent normality of the travelling public. Maybe it wasn't surprising that social issues had started to replace economics as my main passion! Nevertheless, they were difficult matters to casually drop into chats, never mind job interviews!

I felt a hand touch my shoulder and looked up. A young, friendly face smiled down and he quickly slid into the seat opposite. It was young Ranjit, from the mall! I snapped out of it and smiled back.

"Simon, hello! We often talk about you and the way you livened things up at "Sports-life! Where have you been, mate?"

"To an interview. How about you?"

"Shopping in Reading. I tell you, the mall isn't half dull since you left. What was all that fuss about anyway? You sure had a big thing about business."

"Only unethical businesses – like the sweatshop thing we talked about!"

"You had that at your previous job too?"

"Can't really go into details Ranj, though it wasn't really that type of work. They certainly had problems with ethics, though. I'd seen my father back-stabbed by a cheating corporation. I suppose that left quite an impression!"

The train started slowing. We'd reached the outskirts of Slough, and I peered over to the woods near my old place at Forest Beeches. We arrived at the station and I said goodbye to Ranjit and reluctantly made my way back to the Ender Estate.

The police tape still covered the opposite corner. I held my breath, climbed the steps and entered the flat with a sigh. First I checked for signs of entry. All seemed well, so I flopped onto the sofa, partly to put off the evening meal preparation, but also for more time to think through my interview. Instead I felt an inner tremor and again was flooded by the strange experience. Oh no – please! Although I'd stated a few things to Alton – there was so much more behind my anxious state.

After the humiliation of my dismissal, I'd consulted a local hypnotherapist. At first, it seemed helpful. I was amazed at my vivid recall of time at the children's home and the strong feelings I'd pushed down about that. The therapist later gave me a disc of hypnotic inductions to practise trance work – and several prepared scripts to put on tape using my own voice. I now think that my further experimenting was a mistake. In retrospect, I suspect a clash with my attempts at meditation. I've since learned, that while meditation is usually very helpful, there can be contraindications. The book I then used as a guide, Keith Perry's 'Meditation Guide for Western Seekers,' warned as much.

Feeling increasingly anxious, I felt around under the sofa. Yes, the book was still there! I flicked through it again, and a passage in the introduction caught my eye.

People with strong anxiety should probably wait until things have settled down.'

Further on, it warned:

'Some may strongly recall times and experiences from earlier in their lives.'

You could say that again! I thought of the big blue object from this morning. I'd first had the experience about three weeks earlier and even thinking about it chilled me. The context was probably using the hypnosis disc, followed by attempts at meditation. The images evoked had been powerful - almost as if memories from several time periods had somehow mingled: The historical memories, those of three weeks ago and the present! I shook my head despairingly!

After I'd calmed a little, I focused on my old children's home again and the memories reappeared. The most striking was of Miki – a young Asian girl there, who became my first real girlfriend. Last time, her image seemed so real! I closed my eyes, focused and it returned as strongly as before. Her young figure seemed almost tangible – though I also sensed danger. I became quite tense and coated in sweat. I'd read somewhere that deep breathing sometimes helped revive memories – and realised that my breathing had taken on a new urgency. I pinched my leg, reminding myself that I was here in Slough. Anything else, was from another time and place!

The children's home was one of a handful piloting the so-called 'pin-down' approach with difficult young people. In the more extreme versions elsewhere, difficult children were subjected to solitary confinement, deprived of furniture, clothing and so on. In our home, the awkward children were instead 'hugged.' In practice this meant they were physically 'held down' until their resistance stopped. Once, I over-heard a visitor being given an explanation.

"Some little devils have virtually no boundaries, until we provide them! In time, this will hopefully get internalised."

Just like last time, a falling sensation had now started, followed by a prickly kind of feeling. A large blue object entered my visual field from the left, but because I sensed this was about to go somewhere unpleasant, I managed to drag myself out of the experience.

Eventually, I emerged from the strange time warp, feeling damp and downright apprehensive. I looked around the room, but it still appeared the same tired, depressing place. I intuitively knew that there was a lot more to come and that I'd have to revisit the experience. For now though, I needed a break, so I scanned the bookcase for a diversion. Then I remembered that I'd recorded an interesting sounding programme earlier in the week. Something to do with privatising third world water. It sounded right up Alton's street!

An hour or so later, drained and helpless, I wiped still-moist eyes.

Their despair totally eclipsed my personal worries and seemed exactly what Nick Martin had meant. Were Western corporations really cornering supplies, and making affordable safe water out of reach? The misery seemed obvious, with haunting images of frail, wasting, children – all for the want of clean water! The programme's presenter was a charity worker and activist named Nina Parenda. For a change, her programme wasn't diluted by the usual corporate propaganda!

This really is what I'd call 'making a difference'!

It was the second time today that I'd felt ashamed of my own thin efforts – pushing leaflets to the disinterested, outside a shopping mall!

I logged onto my computer, intending my usual trawl through progressive web sites and blogs, but instead decided to search 'water privatisation.' I read for over an hour, barely able to digest it all. I'd known something about the problem but nothing of this magnitude. Nina Parenda's facts seemed correct, so why weren't people protesting such an outrage? Why hadn't I?

I read at some of my favourite sites, finishing at New York's Indymedia. Their fascinating material included a new article by Nick Martin, covering anti-sweatshop protests in Manhattan. Nick also drew attention to a forthcoming meeting in New Jersey, about water privatisation. This would feature presentations by international speakers and included an email address. Nothing like it ever seemed to happen here!

Nick often wrote thought provoking articles, and I'd previously forwarded comments and even swapped ideas. Before I knew it, I'd hit the 'compose' button.

Hello again Nick and thanks!

As you know, I usually enjoy your articles, but this one especially interested me. The UK privatised its water some years ago, supposedly to improve quality and help renew infrastructure. Most only noticed rocketing tariffs. You say the absurdity of privatising an essential is being widely rolled out – often where supplies are already insecure. I just saw a powerful programme on ICN on this very issue, by a Bolivian activist called Nina Parenda. Given ICN is an American network, I wondered if you'd seen it too? I hadn't known much about this topic, so would be most interested in anything else you can share and also hearing about the upcoming meeting.

Best wishes and thanks again, Simon Maher – Slough, UK.

With no reason to think any more of it, I clicked 'send' and went off to brew some coffee.

2

MANHATTAN & NEW JERSEY, USA

NICK MARTIN (DEPUTY HR MANAGER AT CANVEY SOLUTIONS AND A PART-TIME ACTIVIST.)

I smiled at reading Simon's response, which was quickly followed by an email from 'A Fairer World' secretary.

'Nick, would you please do the honours, and chair our meeting again Friday evening. We're at the usual place in Hackensack. Thanks Liz.'

I sighed, and peered from the car's side window. Another meeting – another traffic snarl! Outside, the chemical soup west of Manhattan took on a strange glow, giving a polychromatic sunset over New Jersey. Balm for tired eyes perhaps, but a definite red light to deep thinking or breathing!

Concerns about the sky's unnatural colour would have to wait, because my challenge had nearly arrived again. Air pollution would certainly feature at future gatherings, but tonight's meeting was to publicise the issue of enforced water privatisations – particularly in Africa and Latin America. The recent broadcast had caused a flurry of interest and requests for information came from everywhere – even that Simon Maher guy in the UK In fact, I must later remember to forward him some material.

I yawned, rubbing at a stubborn piece of grit in my left eye. If only I wasn't so damnably tired. As the traffic moved I refocused, realising that I'd been singing aloud. I cringed, but then noticed the driver in the next lane banging out a percussion line on his steering wheel and singing with pained intensity.

To hell with it, I thought, and started to belt out, 'A rainy night in Georgia'.

Of course, African water supplies were critical, but things were also dry closer to home and I felt desiccated from yet another day of compromise and corporate bullshit.

Although late in the day, Manhattan's skyscrapers had absorbed the earlier sun and seemed to be still radiating heat. The car's air con packed up a fortnight ago but, like everything else, it needed attention and I was too busy.

I peeled a damp shirt from an extremely hot seat and shifted around. *Next time – leather seats!*

Catching a blurred movement in my peripheral vision, adrenalin squirted from somewhere inside and the blood roared in my ears. I only just avoided a pincer movement by two yellow cabs.

New York! New York! Everyone fighting for the same bit of space!

Although my hands were at the wheel, my attention was really picking over the residue of another tough day at Canvey Solutions Inc. I asked myself, *Do you really want things to be this way?*

Variations on this irksome question came ever more frequently. The inner voice added, *Do you actually enjoy corporate life – everything sacrificed to shareholders and Canvey's bottom line? If not, why be such a hypocrite?*

A smile broke out. It was as well they didn't know about tonight!

The traffic stopped again, this time outside a deli. I imagined the air conditioning inside and mouth-watering fruit salad – melon, pineapple and grapes, and quickly calculated… but, no, better not risk it. My stomach gurgled protest but the traffic moved, injecting more fumes into the street. As I looked up, the late afternoon sunlight glinted from the Chrysler building's happy hat.

Life in New York is a unique blend of pain and pleasure. Though the pain mostly came from work.

Leave while you still have some integrity, the voice added.

Canvey's board chased every profit-boosting, cost-cutting ruse and took every opportunity to keep their workforce fearful. Recently, they'd again warned that attempts to organise would critically damage the business, and lead to redundancies. They expected me to echo the same message. Rumours also 'leaked' that production might be outsourced. The government had made noises around outsourcing, but no doubt they'd find a way around that. The CEO, Dan Farlin, intended to write saying the future was in the staff's own hands. Before long, I was talking aloud. "Some bloody hopes!"

Whether economies from redundancies, outsourcing or some other strategy, Farlin would probably push the implementation to my immediate boss Tom Phelan, and then on to me. I sighed, pushing down growing anger. My speciality was staff selection, support and development – not corporate executions. The notion of plunging families into misery brought a sick feeling of dread.

Brakes squealed and I swung the wheel, dodging a large truck before turning for the Lincoln Tunnel approach. I followed the traffic under the Hudson to Weehawken, passing through an unattractive part of New Jersey. My mind flitted like an insect over decomposing fruit, moving on to fret about soft tyres and cussing the broken sound system before settling on the real issue – anxiety over tonight's public speaking. *What if I screw up?*

I remembered the televised documentary that sparked this meeting. Although I only saw the closing minutes, I doubted the host would have such petty anxieties. She seemed worth a dozen Farlins and a legion of corporate drones!

The car in front turned, and I quickly closed the gap. Moving swiftly forward, I loosened my belt buckle. Now aged forty-three, I'd filled out a little recently – probably the impossible schedules and snatched junk food eaten on the fly.

I glanced at a luxury blonde in the next lane driving a Lexus. To my relief she smiled back. Just this morning I'd noticed that my hair seemed lighter. Sun bleaching or loss of colour? I glanced in the mirror. Were those 'crow's feet'? I didn't like admitting it but I approved of my appearance, and so generally did women – even though relationships often seemed short-lived. Why, I'm not shallow?

I started to build a defence;

That's not vanity, it's just that I...

Brakes squealed somewhere so I refocused on driving and turned the wheel, leaving the drifting to my mind and following the car ahead.

The venue got closer. Disengaging from preoccupations of age and appearance, I dragged my resisting mind to this evening's topic: 'Water privatisation and the developing world.'

Just imagining the hall made my heart gallop and my mouth as dry as a Soweto tap. I chewed my tongue, like a man dying of thirst.

No, not the cold feet thing again. It's only the intro and chairing!

A well-worn script began the futile task of reasoning myself out of fear.

This isn't professional. In fact, with your experience ... it' s bloody ridiculous!

But reason, particularly the finger-wagging variety, never worked. I checked my top inside pocket. A card with handwritten prompts was still there – if unpleasantly moist.

I tried to recall the opening. Instead, my exhausted mind served up a picture of an audience aghast at my spluttering incoherence. I tried to overlay that with a different image of calm self-confidence, and muttered my opening words based on Dr Gerald Davies' internet article.

"Not long from now another war will be propelled by our economic interests. This time, the placards won't say, 'No blood for oil,' but 'No blood for water.' What oil was, fracking is – and water will be tomorrow! The World Bank predicts that two thirds of the world's population will soon have insufficient fresh drinking water. Imagine what that could mean!"

Fumes from the truck ahead sucked into my lungs and the performance was derailed by a bout of coughing. I pulled back and struggled to recall the next sentence.

"It seems a possibility that a mere 15% of the world's population will gain control of 85% of the world's water. Needless to say, the 15% won't be from the undeveloped world! A handful of Western corporations would like to control the multi-billion dollar water market, and it's down to people like us to try to stop it."

The dreary suburbs barely registered as I reviewed my plan. I'd then give a quick biography of Arahti Malli, the main speaker from South Africa. Even that though could be complicated. Many were disaffected after foreign financial institutions had pushed the ANC into hated programmes of privatisation and price hikes. Hopes had once been high though perhaps I should avoid history?

I passed into Hackensack, feeling increasingly weighed down. Life was complicated and my work as Deputy Human Resources Manager for Canvey Solutions seemed barely tolerable, while my other life as fledgling political activist and occasional 'Indymedia' contributor, brought so much more satisfaction. Perhaps Alice, my former wife, was right, my personality – like the iconic Pisces glyph – swam in opposing directions!

I arrived with twenty minutes to spare and patted my breast pocket, checking my introduction notes. I looked for Arahti, mesmerised by the empty chairs, imagining the rows of faces that would arrive.

Eventually, with the introduction done, I nursed a pounding heart, aware of the replay looping through my mind.

Don't be so damn narcissistic.

Arahti voiced genuine fury from the podium. She really was good and I couldn't help but envy her talent.

"A handful of private companies," she intoned, swaying curvaceously, "might soon own our most vital resource."

She mentioned a cholera epidemic after 'commercial rates' were introduced.

I felt almost mesmerised by the sight of her colourful African scarf moving, and as slides of water reserves and statistics played over the screen, a familiar sensation tugged at my eyelids.

Waking suddenly, with my head nodding and pulling the muscles in my neck. I furtively looked around, aware that this wasn't a good look for an attentive chairperson. No-one reacted and Arahti continued her fierce declamation.

You really are a shallow bastard sometimes, I thought, dragging my attention back to thirsty Africans.

"International Water Watch said the disease followed the activities of a small group of Western companies backed by financial institutions, who appeared to want to privatise as much drinking water as possible."

She paused and with eyes blazing, looked around the room.

"It doesn't seem to bother them if the poor, unable to afford privatised water, rely on streams, ponds and lakes contaminated by manure, human waste and deadly pollutants."

The day of corporate overload had taken a toll. I looked down the row at a pretty Latino woman taking notes. For the second time she caught my gaze and smiled back. Something seemed familiar so I decided to seek her out in the coffee break.

I thanked Arahti, closed the meeting's first half and relieved, went to look for the attractive Latino woman. Someone tapped my shoulder. I turned but unfortunately it was an earnest older woman activist I'd spoken with at other meetings. She reintroduced herself as Judy Alton and I remembered her being alarmingly well informed. I fleetingly saw my quarry on the other side of the hall, but Judy stepped into my line of sight.

"Unfortunately, Mr Martin, you understate the seriousness. The latest figures show..."

I nodded, thinking, *Statistical minutiae is the least of my troubles, dear woman!*

Judy finished her correction. She seemed pleasant enough and attractive for her age, but I'd had something else in mind. I looked around, but there was no sign of the younger Latino woman. Sickeningly, it was almost time to start the second half.

I returned to the podium, and caught her eye as I introduced Abdul Farek – an elderly academic from Egypt. As I returned to my seat, she undoubtedly flashed me a smile!

Abdul highlighted the possibility of future water wars in the Middle East, and reminded the audience that as far back as the 1979 Israel Peace Treaty, President Sadat promised no more fighting – except to protect water resources. Soon, the treacly warmth of fatigue captured me and I drifted off again, recalling my Egyptian holiday with Alice. All that shouting and gesticulating of the guards, just because I'd used a zoom lens by the Aswan Dam causeway. Mind you, an unwanted surge down the Nile would create havoc!

I jerked awake with my head nodding again, and found I was looking straight into the eyes of the pretty Latino! Again, a nagging sense of recognition. This really was embarrassing! Abdul's discourse snapped into focus.

"Therefore, it was no surprise that King Hussein also identified water as the one thing that could lead to war."

I shifted position and stifled a yawn – despite genuine interest. I'd get a written outline later and with luck, could still write a decent article. However, Abdul dragged on.

"Former UN Secretary General Boutros Boutros Ghali was even more specific – there could be war over water. Turkey, Morocco and Oman are also worried about water, both for agriculture and for urban growth."

Slides flashed on with hypnotic regularity, intensifying my drowsy feelings.

Abdul eventually finished to enthusiastic applause. I looked down the row to the young woman who smiled again.

With heart pounding, I thanked Abdul for his contribution and formally closed the meeting. Most people drained away into the night, and those remaining clustered around book stands. I couldn't see her and so crossed to the South Africa stand. Arahti had positioned herself alongside and a queue formed. The next table featured the EZLN, also known as the Zapatista movement, and I stood waiting.

I faintly recalled an uprising in Mexico and I flicked through some Zapatista literature to confirm it. I sensed someone come alongside, and when I turned, the Latino woman was next to me. She'd surely approached deliberately, because she wasn't there before. We exchanged smiles and I was struck by a warmth in her eyes and also a familiarity.

She kept eye contact.

"So you're interested in the Zapatistas?"

Before I could answer, she continued, in a clear, soft voice.

"I saw you sleeping in Arahti's talk." She tutted gently. "The chairperson!"

The words censured, but her eyes smiled. She pursed her mouth, and shook her head as if in mock disapproval. I felt completely on the back foot, until the answer suddenly came: *Wasn't she the presenter of that documentary?*

"Sorry", I replied. "It's been a rather a draining day. I'm Nick Martin, by the way."

She gave a wide smile and her hand felt warm.

"Hello Nick, I'm Nina Parenda."

As if anticipating an unspoken question, she added:

"I'm recently over from Bolivia. So, are you interested in the Zapatistas?"

I steered my mind to the 'Zapatistas' compartment, to find it almost empty. Doubly annoying, because she clearly was interested.

"I'd like to know more – and you?"

"Of course, Nick. They're an example to the oppressed everywhere. I visited the Mexican state of Chiapas and found it inspiring. Of course, we had an ELN too."

Her English was flawless, but Chiapas and an ELN. What was that? I tried asking her more about the Zapatistas.

"You haven't read their original postings then?" she asked.

I reluctantly shook my head and her brow creased, signalling that I'd lost credibility.

"Perhaps we can talk another time," she said abruptly.

I sensed things were slipping away.

"Something seemed familiar since first seeing you this evening.

That's why I looked over," I lied. "I'm thinking of a certain television programme on tonight's theme. Was that you?"

She appeared unmoved.

"What did you think of it?"

"I didn't realise the amount of suffering. The programme actually inspired tonight's meeting. Our secretary, Liz Gelder, changed the agenda because everyone felt so concerned."

Nina nodded and a hint of a smile crossed her face.

"I know and I'm happy to be here."

"I'd have introduced you from the platform if I'd realised."

"No, I didn't want that," she replied coolly. "My interest is the children – not applause."

"Can we meet again soon? I'd like to hear more about your work, and more about the Zapatistas."

"Mightn't you fall asleep again?"

I sensed I was blushing.

"Somehow, I don't think so!"

This time she returned a dazzling, full-on smile, reached into her bag and took out a card. She wrote 'Algonquin Hotel' and a phone number in perfect handwriting and held it out.

My mind spun, trying to regain the initiative.

"A great choice for an activist. Weren't the Algonquin Indians persuaded to sell Manhattan to the Americans for some trinkets?"

She pressed the card into my hand, showing no signs of being impressed.

"You should check your facts – it was sold to the Dutch! Perhaps we can meet and talk again. Call me, if you like."

"I will," I replied, slipping the card into my breast pocket behind the still-moist introduction notes. She left and I watched her walk away.

First, Simon Maher's compliment and now this! Things were definitely looking up!

3

SLOUGH, BERKSHIRE

SIMON MAHER

Nick Martin's latest email arrived;

To Simon, my UK brother in social justice.

I read through his message and looked longingly at a poster of Manhattan's skyline stuck to the kitchenette wall. That was something else that couldn't happen now!

I crossed over to the lounge window and my new view – feeling dispirited and chock full of gloomy ruminations. Two and a half months had passed since my dismissal. How could everything have changed so drastically? Ejected from the workplace, losing my apartment and ending up on the Ender Estate, of all places! Why build such monstrosities? There was no answer to be found in the dismal view, the dingy apartment – and still nothing from Andrew Alton!

I thought of the interview and my further reading on post-traumatic stress. Feeling increasingly tense I sprawled onto the sofa and managed to knock something onto the floor. I felt about and located that damned book again. "A Meditation Guide for Western Seekers."

I still hadn't really mastered the meditation thing. Perhaps I should try again because heaven knows I needed some peace and clarity. Surely, watching breaths couldn't be that complicated!

I flicked through the book again, realising I must have originally skipped most of the introduction. A passage there caught my eye.

"Occasionally, some may feel anxiety when meditating or are surprised to

encounter difficult memories or emotions. Experiences can bubble up from childhood, from stressful periods of life – even from neutral times. These may include images, sounds, smells – even temporary changes to the body image. If that should happen, don't worry – it will pass. Similar experiences have been recorded since ancient times. However, anyone with a history of trauma should exercise caution. Certain individuals could be opened to difficult past experience and in such cases, guidance and support from a meditation teacher is advised."

"Great! You mean potentially I could even worsen things?"

It reminded me of the medicine information slips I jokingly called, 'Pharma's get out of jail free cards.' They warned of every conceivable complication – including the very symptoms that would cause anyone to take the stuff in the first place! Still, meditation has a great record and an honourable tradition, so I decided to try again. Propped up against the couch, I painstakingly followed my breaths. In breath – out breath, in and out, in, out...

After a while, something started to work. My shoulders dropped, breath slowed and for a few wonderful moments, my thoughts actually quietened. What bliss! Perversely, my mind then started to air its most stubborn worries! Queues of negative images, stacked like inbound planes to Heathrow. My head now seemed host to the most intransigent of problems. I'd hoped meditation might bring me peace, but oh no – worries whirled like electrons seeking completion!

I tapped my index finger in time, hoping to keep my wayward mind on the supposedly simple task of counting breaths. Instead it delivered a spectacular rant about 'pharmaceutical profiteering'. I noticed that my hands had moved to my chest because, as before, palpitations had started. I slid on headphones and started the 'anxiety' disc that I'd recently purchased from the internet. The accompanying blurb claimed that regular use of the programme may help *"uncover the real roots of your anxieties."*

The leaflet explained that inaudible voices would be whispering separate suggestions to left and right ears – and therefore to each hemisphere. In the background I could hear the sound of a trickling stream and soft bells ringing.

I continued the breathing... in, out, in, out, in, out... until my concentration was grabbed by a loud, disconcerting thought – quite different from the usual mind-chatter.

Maybe your fascination about social justice is just a way of coping with the injustices of your own history? Perhaps you should meditate on that!

I pulled the headphones off, now feeling apprehensive because the image of something big and blue had appeared again – though quickly dissipated. The pattern was becoming quite spooky! The anxiety increased again and it felt as if something was about to take over. Perhaps it was just the build up of stress, but an inner inquisition then started.

Who else could manage to be sacked from a feeble job in a mall? You're not just wasting your education – but your whole life as well!

Life certainly had contracted since discovering the dreadful world of Asian sweatshops while researching my dissertation. The captive young sweatshop girls had really shocked me – though to this day, I'd never quite understood the intensity!

I looked over to the kitchenette wall. Photos of waving factory girls from travels near Bangkok and in the Philippines were stuck under my Manhattan poster. I smiled weakly, muttering, "Now, it's rarely further than Slough High Street!"

My thoughts travelled down well-worn mental tracks, only to slide into empty sidings. This time though, I'd stay with the experience, following each tendril of anxiety to its roots. Something stirred deep inside and the strange blue object appeared momentarily, but quickly slipped away again. Maybe deeper meditation would help. Against normal practice, I'd try it lying down this time.

I lay down, concentrating on inhalations, feeling the cool air against my nostrils. Soon the falling sensation returned. I tried slowing my breaths, but strangely, this seemed to pull me deeper. I started quietly panicking, searching about inside and feeling increasingly frantic. Something from my past was definitely stirring. Had I been defending and avoiding something?

Okay then. Did you ever experience this panic before? What's attempting to come out?

As I dropped further into the experience, my mind answered as though waiting for this moment.

I was fourteen again, frantically kicking and pummelling the rock-hard body in the blue t-shirt and trousers. In desperation I kicked out at Mitch again, catching him in the ribs. I hated the way the huge man had Miki pinned to the floor. I kicked him again and again, until Mitch growled and with a massive arm reached out to pull me to the floor. He

31

placed a hand over my mouth and then rolled onto me, making me feel dizzy. I gasped and brought a knee up, but Mitch's massive body now had us both pinned down. However hard I tried, the mountain of flesh seemed immoveable. I remembered trying to kick and struggle as sweat dripped under my clothing. I choked, fighting for breath, fearing I'd pass out, when Mitch suddenly shifted position.

Was this one of the 'flashbacks' that I'd read about?

Shock and curiosity brought this strange time warp to an abrupt close. Last time, I'd intuited that there was far more to be understood. This time, I put my mini epiphany into words!

Your childhood speaks and at last you listen! You've empathised with underdogs, because you've long been one! The fate of those young Asian factory girls touches you because of what you just relived. Trying to rescue Miki was the doorway to your adolescence and a commitment to helping.

I blew out through pursed lips, trying to absorb the news from my past.

It wasn't as though my time in the so-called 'care' of the local council had been totally repressed. Probably, it's what they call dissociation, that caused this to seem unrelated to the here and now! The memories kept flooding back. Miki, a pretty teenager, was my best friend in the home. That day, something inside snapped. In a total rage, I'd gone for Mitch kicking, hitting – anything to shift that weight from Miki's slender body. Of course, moving a grown man was as likely as an ant shifting an oak tree – but even as my nervous system revived those past sights and sounds, I felt a failure – as if I'd let her down!

The "pin-down" regime lasted about nine months, until stopped by Miki's suicide. Although the female staff had been kinder, I was still glad the home had been closed. I smiled. The writer of that anonymous note to the council never was identified. Somehow, it had just felt like my responsibility!

The computer whirred in the background – primed for action, but I ignored the electronic memory, and focused on my own. Had I complained earlier, could Miki still be alive? Did I really fail her? Perhaps even the questions were more examples of the over-responsibility that had dogged me all through life. In truth, I gravitated to fighting unfairness like iron to a magnet. I opened my eyes again. Did this herald a breakdown? No, but it certainly resembled the Post-Traumatic Stress Disorder issue that I'd recently discovered. The more I thought about it, the more relevant it seemed.

I relaxed, and remembered the Andrew Alton interview, and as usual, one thought led to another. I'd so wanted to abandon the cut-throat business environment for something more caring! I began to chuckle, thinking first of Dr Pangloss, and then my university tutor – an old cynic named Michael Fines. Fines was probably the opposite to Pangloss, though I could certainly use his advice now. I remembered being tempted to change training to a social work course. Fines laughed, claiming social work had effectively been neutered by successive governments, many workers reduced to peripatetic clerks and much of the work de-professionalised. Clients had been rebranded as 'customers' to promote the transition to a more commercial model. I mostly agreed with his observations and hated how, in the public services, the 'dead hand' of managerialism blighted the older more humane practices. Still, was that worse than ending up an unemployed ex-sales assistant?

Shouting came from outside and I went to the window. Below, a quarrel was under way between white and Asian youths. In the background, I heard squealing tyres – probably the estate's persistent joy-riders. I thought about social work again. I'd probably have dealt with kids like those outside. I found this an intriguing idea, even now. A life outside the strictures of business certainly appealed!

Fines claimed management consultants had been brought in to quash professional autonomy, and ensure that the old 'public service' values were replaced by new 'business models.' Professional judgements were increasingly replaced by opaque management models and proprietary algorithms – often pushed by private sector contractors. I chuckled, recalling Fines lampooning the new 'business speak' that social work managers were expected to use with their bemused staff. He once demonstrated this stuff to our tutor group – solemnly pontificating, "First, we must benchmark the service, and then streamline strategies to empower customers by delivering them a one-stop service solution."

He'd loved mocking the 'business first' attitude and the efforts to shift the public from their traditional roles as citizens and retrain them as 'consumers'.

"I wonder," he once asked our tutor group with a wink, "if all the delinquents, the handicapped and confused elderly clients, properly appreciate their new status as customers?"

What would Fines advise me now and what would he think of

Andrew Alton? Neither approved of business at all costs or that every-thing should be a potential profit opportunity!

I snorted, recalling Fines' humour. Still, at least those days offered structure and direction.

"You'll have far more effect as an economist," Fines had said. "As the song says – 'money makes the world go round'."

Funny how I'd ultimately been sickened by the economic world-view and my passion now was social justice!'

I stood up, feeling strangely relieved. Objects looked literally brighter than before and felt like an inner purging. I went to the computer, located a favourite website and found that I read with far less intensity than usual, as if an inner pressure had been released. Ugly sounds filtered in from outside as the youths below traded racial insults. Ironic, how many immigrants lived in this little ghetto – excluded from everything that had first attracted them.

Get real, I thought. *You live here too*!

Moments later I heard the snap of the letter flap. Amazing how a change of circumstances, could alter one's entire mood. After reading the good news from Andrew Alton, I felt that my life was strangely back on track. I checked the inbox, and an email was in from Nick Martin. Was this fate?

4

SLOUGH, BERKSHIRE, UK

SIMON MAHER

Roughly a week and a half had passed since my epiphany. I looked from my window out over the estate, and munched a sandwich. It may be the same depressing view outside, but things had certainly changed for me inside. Somehow since that dramatic eruption of the past, my life didn't feel oppressive in quite the same way. I'd seen the hypnotherapist for what would have to be the last time – though I'd continue with meditation. I told him a little of what had happened. Who'd have thought Freud would be quoted these days? His 'Return of the repressed' idea was interesting, though maybe not as useful as the PTSD model. As I was leaving, he said, "Next time you're in the library, I suggest you look up the word 'abreaction' in a psychology or psychoanalytic dictionary!"

I looked back into the flat and the chaos spreading over the floor. A good half of my books were now boxed and most of my clothing packed. Now it was just a case of tackling the kitchen utensils! I entered the kitchenette, pulled a face at the extent of unwashed crockery and quickly diverted to the lounge to re-read Alton's letter.

It really had been a huge turn of fortune. I pictured Oxford and my interview with another rush of positive feelings. Alton had pushed me a bit but our later discussion was inspiring. The actual interview generally went well and I sensed that the liking was mutual. Therefore, his offer didn't surprise me, but was nevertheless a great relief! I hadn't met such a kindred spirit since Michael Fines, back in the old days. I jotted down some ideas of my own and then looked at Dr Alton's exciting ideas for future research, which covered a very wide spectrum. Was I really soon to be working with him? I only hoped that I'd rise to the challenge. Later, in his letter, Alton went on to mention a variety of mainly US contacts. These included a law agency undertaking pro bono work on important social cases, an array of NGO's, non-profits and helpful foundations. Even the idea I found quite thrilling!

Since the interview, I'd explored more of Alton's publications. Some were accessible online, giving rise to even more excitement. Papers like; 'Resource theft from the undeveloped world', 'Human rights and glob-alisation', and 'Corporate seizure of the commons' I found stunning. Why ever hadn't I explored academic work earlier!

I returned to the window, to look over the estate again. Teenagers preened and flaunted outside the convenience shop. I could almost picture old Mr Singh challenging the under age smokers and drinkers, only to be abused for his pains.

A thunderous rapping noise came from the front door, followed by the sound of running feet. No doubt, kids playing that old favourite; 'knock down ginger'. I grinned, having enjoyed the game myself as a youngster! Anyway, in two days' time, I'd hopefully leave the Ender Estate for good.

I returned to the computer and re-read Nick Martin's mail enthusing about his water privatising meeting. If only we could meet and talk in person! Nick mentioned meeting Nina Parenda and planned further meetings – the lucky blighter! Contact with proper activists was just what I needed. Better still, industry insiders with conflicts of conscience – like me! Surely, others must exist? Still, there should be fascinating times to come, tackling injustices with Andrew Alton.

Returning to action, I went back to the kitchenette to clean and pack my utensils for my move to Oxford...

5

OXFORD. UK

ANDREW ALTON

The door said 'Dr Andrew Alton,' in gold lettering. I entered my office feeling rather flustered. This morning's meeting with Dr Martin Farrelly had threatened to revive old ghosts, and raised anxieties about shielding my history. In discussion, Farrelly added to his earlier lecture, 'Psychopathy in business'! That had proved a little too close to home, given my own background! Still, Martin had raised further excellent points that I couldn't overlook. At the moment, my post seemed secure enough. In fact, with a modicum of luck advancement seemed likely. Yes, pressures to publish did seem fairly intense, but that went with the academic territory. My thoughts were interrupted by a knock and Helen, my secretary looked in.

"About your new assistant Simon's accommodation."

"He's here?"

"No, but apparently he's had no luck with the accommodation leads we sent. You did think that we might have to sort something else out!"

"Thanks Helen. If necessary, we could start Maher off here – on the campus. At least in the short term."

"Does the vice-chancellor know?"

"No, but I think we could help. I feel good about our selection Helen, even if it does make a little extra work for you! I'm also thinking that young Maher might take on some of the donkey work from these

meetings with Martin Farrelly. I think a promising project might very
well shape up!"

"You mean with the forensic psychiatrist?"

"Yes."

Helen left, and I took out Maher's employment file. I felt positive.
Young Maher handled himself well under pressure, though possibly had
a tendency to stick his neck out, which in the current climate – might
need watching. In fact, in some ways, I felt Simon resembled my
younger self from twenty-five years ago! I looked down at the list again.
Yes, given the current shortages, accommodating him here made sense
for now.

I dictated a memo to admin giving Maher's requirements and then
logged onto my home email account. More messages waited, including
the latest email from my mom, Judy Alton. I smiled, and could almost
feel her enthusiasm about a lively anti-water privatising meeting, back
in New Jersey. I pictured her with a real sense of warmth. Mom's
passions had clearly passed through the genes. Great, just as long as
Dad's genes weren't involved! Concern at my relationship to one of
New York's most disgusting, conscienceless, hard-bitten businessmen
threatened my sense of identity. No, please not Dad's genes! After all
this time and travelling such different paths – I'd rather deny any similarities!

A well-worn train of thought started – recounting the painful
domestic mess I'd survived as a child. I almost heard the shouting and
smelt Dad's bourbon fumes. Of course, his creation of 'Marquetcom',
the highly successful PR and marketing empire, gave him many opportunities for what I now knew were highly unpalatable though profitable
practices! Mom hinted my brother Freddy might be following suit.

No, Dr Farrelly's talk of severe personality disorders in business
settings rang some horribly clanging bells. In fact I rather hoped we
could develop ideas together about possible links between pathology
and unsavoury business activities.

I shook my head. Dr Farrelly's words, followed by Mom's contact
had certainly stirred memories. The parental break-up in my childhood
was a grim time. Mom and children leaving, and then her marriage to
David Alton. At least that gave me the opportunity to jettison the Anson
name. Employment in the UK helped keep that aspect of my identity
firmly on the opposite side of the Atlantic. Nowadays, I kept my rela-

tionship to Biff Anson quiet and I intended to keep it like that – even if I did periodically wonder what the old buzzard was up to.

I picked up Maher's file, and remembered his mention of Nick Martin, an activist writer in New York. A quick internet search had me nod with satisfaction. If this was an example of Simon's taste, we should absolutely gel. In fact, he should make a valuable addition to the hoped for 'corporate sociopathy' project with Dr Farrelly.

The phone rang, It was Helen again.

"Simon's just arrived. He hoped he might see you?"

Moments later I was again looking into his rather intense face.

"I understand you had no luck with the accommodation?"

"No, Dr Alton. Looks like B & B tonight."

"After tomorrow, I've arranged for a place to be available on the campus. Tonight we've plenty of space at my home. I'll phone Anne."

"That's kind. You wouldn't believe where I've been living in recent weeks."

"Tell me on the way home. Listen, I've been thinking about our previous discussion on your social justice efforts. Are you still keen?"

"Yes, of course. Why?"

"I'm investigating a new research project with some other professionals – a forensic psychiatrist and a linguist. Thinking of your interests, you could make a good contribution."

With high anticipation of our future working, I closed the office and we went home to Anne.

6

MANHATTAN USA. –
MARQUETCOM'S HEADQUARTERS

ROBBIE JAMES – ASSISTANT TO FOUNDER,
BIFF ANSON

Here in New York, it wasn't only independent journalists and activists like Nick Martin that were affected by that meeting in New Jersey. I could testify that pricked consciences were in the most unlikely of places – including the mighty Empire State building in the heart of mid-town Manhattan.

I looked down forlornly from my window in Marquetcom's sixtieth-storey suite. Anxiety was almost as sky-high as the view!

Nearly a year had passed since I'd joined the legendary PR and marketing firm as an assistant to the founder, Bifton Anson. Things hadn't changed one bit, and despite extensive professional training, Anson persisted in treating me as a humble 'gofer.'

Returning to my desk I re-read my draft report again.

Water privatisation in Latin America – the local impact – represented a considerable effort, but that meeting had only intensified my conflict. I tried including some of the meetings' facts in this report, though Anson would probably hate it all the more. I toyed with softening the text for a few moments and then hit 'undo.' After hearing those life-threatening facts, diluting it wasn't really an option!

Anson's attitude to staff, usually appalling, seemed even more demanding than usual with this project. In twenty-eight years, I'd only known one person approaching this level of impossibility – though Dad was right out of my life now. Since ICN had screened a documen-

40

tary about global water privatising, Anson seemed obsessed – filleting out the suffering and just seeing another business opportunity. Now he'd assembled a consortium hoping to profit from certain water sources in Latin America, and wanted everyone to make this a top priority. I looked at the screen with a feeling of dread. Marketing and PR was one thing, but to deliberately corner one of life's essentials – that was something I could only despise!

Nancy Verey, Anson's secretary phoned through and broke into my thoughts.

"Biff wants to see you ASAP. I think it's about this afternoon's negotiations."

I knocked on his door with a pounding heart, because Anson was almost always critical. When I pushed the heavy door open, I could immediately see that the expression on his unusually large face was tetchy. Anson burped and without looking up, rubbed his more than ample belly and eased the belt out. Nancy once told me a dinner-plate sized steak was his standard fare. Maybe today's was tough, because he burped again.

"Not exactly relishing all the legal jive later," he growled, and poured a measure of antacid.

"Where the hell's Nancy with the coffee?"

My throat tightened as Anson reached for the report and started to read. It had already been returned once, like some errant child's homework. His expression quickly deteriorated, and now looked malevolent. Nancy crept in, putting coffee on the oversized desk and smiled over encouragingly. I knew she also feared Anson – a shared difficulty we'd often discussed. Anson shook his large head as he read and I risked winking back at Nancy. Recently she'd assumed an almost maternal attitude, warning me when trouble loomed. After handing the draft to Anson on an earlier occasion, she'd said, "Watch out," and mimicked his response, "Tidied it up, has he? Hopefully, without the 'bleeding-- heart' crap, this time!"

I'd laughed because she was a talented mimic, reproducing the gravelly southern drawl and the distorted religiosity and racism – so anachronistic in the twenty-first century.

"See, I'm concluding that James is a closet liberal and doesn't even begin to understand business! If God didn't want foreigners paying the proper market rates, he wouldn't favour Christian capitalism. Why else does James think we have the parable of the wise man, investing for a good return?"

"I tried a very different interpretation," she said, "but he wouldn't have it!"

Nancy left, and Anson's scowl intensified. He'd also told her his church in Georgia taught proper values. She'd mimicked him again. "It's the natural order, Nancy. The rich get rich because God rewards them and the poor get what they deserve. The servant who invested money and made it grow got rewarded! Those folk James frets about only want handouts!"

"I mentioned the rich man and the eye of a needle – but he didn't like that!"

I sipped my coffee, wondering how it was possible to drink but still have a dry throat?

Anson paged back, and frowned at the executive summary. He looked up, with the kind of expression that made every cell shrink.

"Liberal crap like this doesn't belong in a business report! You weren't employed as a fucking social worker and I don't buy the bleeding-heart stuff!"

My palms dampened despite the hot coffee cup.

"Nothing I despise more than lefties and whining academics. You know, those that don't take their God-given opportunities, yet try and stop sensible business folk from making things happen!"

My heart raced as Anson suddenly thumped the desk with a fist. His unnaturally large face looked sweaty, red and mottled – like an unhealthy plateful of streaky bacon.

"J D Rockefeller said it right: 'God gave me my money.' See, it comes from him. Put business first and then everything else falls into place. Even the damn government gets that now!"

I nodded.

"Now I've adjusted your language, it's almost passable – apart from the irrelevancies you keep weaving into the executive summary."

"Sorry. It just seemed important we at least consider the social costs."

Anson shook his head despairingly and looked at his watch.

"The meeting starts in ninety minutes. I want a new single page executive summary in the front of each copy – stripped of liberal shit and schoolboy politics. Make it punchy! Incidentally, watch out for a repeat showing of that ICN broadcast. Maybe then even you'll understand why every smart corporation will want some of the action! I don't want us being beaten on this."

If Anson knew I'd been at that meeting!

Eighty-five minutes later, I returned with the revised summaries in my hands but heaviness in my heart. Participants were now arriving so I pulled up a chair alongside Biff's desk and watched as he pressed the concealed button to start recording. The room filled with consortium representatives, their lawyers, plus our boys from marketing and management accounts.

Two hours later, the deal was done. Marquetcom took the major share and would handle PR and marketing. The consortium included Bellevivreau, a US/French water and engineering conglomerate and Thompson Water, from the UK. The necessary legal work would be handled by Mercket-Berthoff Associates. Anson then named a long time associate, Brian Tutch, to manage dealings with the relevant South American officials. Marquetcom would also commission a project headquarters somewhere in South America, probably in partnership with an outside consulting company. He then expressed his hope for further successful water privatisations.

The meeting over, the outsiders left. Superficially, Anson appeared satisfied, though I knew from bitter experience that he'd delegate the details. Someone asked about the South American headquarters. Anson mentioned several possible subcontractors and seemed to favour a Brooklyn outfit called 'Canvey Solutions.'

A female employee from management accounts knocked to request planning meetings but Biff shook his head dismissively and she left. He gave a rather sickly version of a grin.

"Fuck financial modelling. You can handle that, son, I've far better methods… twisting financial balls outperforms any computer tricks. Remember that son. Don't change proven methods!"

Anson's leer came from below his belt.

"On second thoughts, we've some real foxes over in management accounts. Okay, you can arrange that meeting."

This was a new and rather disturbing intimacy. Anson's reputation with women was legendary, but right now a more immediate worry was the second report I'd asked Nancy to pass to Anson, later.

'Water Justice Activists and Privatisation' seemed to me an important angle, but unlikely to find favour.

I returned to my office with more anxiety building. An hour later, lost in thought, I didn't notice Nancy until she touched my shoulder. Her expression suggested that my report hadn't been received well.

"Your face says that he wasn't happy."

"Of course not, but it was what happened next...!"

"Meaning what?"

She took a deep breath.

"Of course, he thumped his desk, raving about 'tree-huggers' and 'that uptight little do-gooder, James' – all the usual stuff. Then it all got quite weird. I went to get coffee but when I returned, he started... well, kind of 'opening up!'"

"About what?"

"Earlier, I'd given him an envelope marked 'private, personal and confidential'. He left it open on his desk."

"What was it, Nancy?"

She looked away, blushing.

"I swear he had tears in his eyes! Actually, something similar happened once before. About three years ago."

She paused, staring into space.

"Matter of fact, he talked then about his ex-wife Judy, and it was about this time of year. I don't think he's really over her."

"Getting back to today?"

"Back to the rant? He likened you to Andrew, his eldest son. Apparently, he's an academic in Oxford, in the UK. I believe he's a politically 'progressive' academic, who has savaged the public relations industry, amongst other things."

"Comparisons to me wouldn't be good news, then?"

"Exactly! Apparently, Judy's forwarded various papers by Andrew over the years. Anyway, seeing your report and then hearing news of Andrew, probably lit his touch paper."

"Meaning?"

"A supposed similarity to what he called, 'his weak-kneed son.' He talked more about the family, and said Andrew usually had his hands full of books but never a baseball bat! He said that the boy didn't understand wealth creators. Then he poured a coffee for me, which is a first, and said more about 'his Judy.' Pulling off a big deal like today was just the kind of thing he'd wanted to share with her but she didn't understand."

"He was right about Andrew's similarity to me with the baseball bat!"

She smiled.

"I just sort of nodded along when he said that their break-up was stupid because Judy forgave him other women, but left over his … 'business ethics'!"

"She sounds a smart lady, but what do you think she was getting at?"

"Not completely sure. An old timer, long gone now, said she was outraged by Biff marketing businesses that used sweatshops. That was apparently the last straw for her and they separated years ago. Anyway, back to today. Biff eventually got really upset, saying that he'd done everything for her and the kids, but they didn't understand."

"He actually said that?"

"Well, I asked a few things, you know to show interest, and he just kept pouring stuff out! The youngest, Donny was apparently about eleven when they broke up, though Donny seems right out of his life now. He didn't seem too worried about that, but certainly seemed upset about 'his Judy.' I think he's an odd mixture of a hard-nosed bully, with a strange sentimental streak. He probably believes he still loves her."

"Any other children? You mentioned Andrew and Donny."

"Yes, a middle boy called Freddy, who runs a big vehicle dealership in Moab, Utah. Freddy's visited here a few times, but I can't say that I took to him. I haven't met Andrew, but Biff really appears to have the knife out for him."

"And he mentioned me being like Andrew?"

"Seems to have made that connection! Here's the thing though, when he went to the toilet, I peeked in the envelope. A handwritten note from Judy Alton, saying how proud she was of Andy's work and she hoped that he'd be, too. She'd enclosed a copy of one of his papers. Guess the topic?"

"Unethical marketing?"

No, it was an academic paper by Andrew Alton and associate. It was called something like: 'Resource theft – enforced privatisation in undeveloped regions.'

Apparently, she later remarried a man called Alton, hence Andrew's name.

When I glanced through the study, water privatising featured strongly! Please be careful Robbie. Don't be seen as the 'bad son'!"

What a shaker! So Anson had both a son and an ex-wife, with the ethical sensibilities and guts to take him on. I wonder what they'd make of today? How I'd love to talk it over with them!

Nancy left and I replayed the conversation until startled by the phone. Anson's voice sounded uncharacteristically subdued.

"I've thought more about that project headquarters and talked with Dan Farlin, the Chief Exec of Canvey Solutions in Brooklyn. Dan's an old friend, so get yourself over there soon. The centre will need specialised staffing so he recommended you liaise with a guy called Nick Martin, their Deputy HR Manager. Go soon – in fact make it your top priority...!"

7

BROOKLYN, USA

NICK MARTIN

Driving over to Brooklyn seemed no way to start the day. I reached Canvey's offices at 8.15am, already disheartened. It wasn't just the traffic or our location in a run-down part of the borough. Staff discouragement seemed contagious and the relentless pressure affected everyone except the perpetrators on the top floor. Time with genuine activists made these corporate preoccupations seem trivial and myopic in comparison. In truth, I'd begun to dread each working day.

I opened my office and checked for new emails. First up was another edict from upstairs:

Any member of staff found misusing Canvey's computer system faces immediate dismissal.

I sighed. Threats but none of my suggestions. How surprising!

Next, a message from our CEO, Dan Farlin:

Nick, please attend a management team meeting at 3pm.

That seemed unlikely to be good news! Next, a note from my immediate boss, Tom Phelan.

Nick, please research Marquetcom, a Manhattan Publicity and Marketing company (you may know of them.) A contract could be in the offing and Robert James – from their office – should make contact soon.

I made coffee and started on the day's business – preparing to fill vacancies in the shipping warehouse. As I could do job descriptions and advertisements in my sleep, my thoughts wandered instead to that New Jersey meeting, to Nina Parenda and what I hoped might follow.

The door suddenly burst open and my boss, Tom Phelan the Director of HR, stood in the doorway with an ashen face.

"What's up Tom? Surely Marquetcom aren't all that bad?"

"Can it Nick – it's not the time for joking. We've an emergency in sales. A young staff member, Tim Mills, flipped out and hit his manager!" Tom's expression had me on my feet and straight out the door.

"Is Mills griping on about the life insurance thing again?"

"No-one would hear him anyway – because he's on the roof! I seem to remember you had training on this sort of thing?" Tom continued as we hurried down the corridor.

"Kurt took the sales team meeting but when he presented the new monthly targets, Mills exploded, hit him and cleared Kurt's desk. He ran up to the roof bellowing like a lunatic. Now he's threatening to jump and won't listen to anyone. Not even me!"

It felt like a cold store as I entered the sales office. No-one was working and staff huddled together drinking hot coffee. In the corner a tearful young secretary was over-enthusiastically comforted by an older colleague. Kurt sat in the corner, his head tipped back and a pad of bloodied tissues pressed to his nose. I ran to the back and opened the door to the stairwell as Phelan followed.

"Can you phone the police. I'll go up alone – we don't want to crowd him."

"Yeah," Tom replied. "I won't have executives assaulted."

"I meant, phone in case we need a special negotiator later!"

I bounded up to the tenth floor, but the door to the roof was stuck. I shouldered the steel bar. It wouldn't budge but the jolt really hurt. Blood roared in my ears and I shouldered it again until finally it lurched open with a screech of scraping metal. The sudden light from outside blinded me and I stumbled and fell, cutting my hand on a strip of riveted metal. I dabbed my bloodied palm on a handkerchief and looked down over the length of the roof deck. At the far end, Tim leant against the slender railings. A fall from this height would certainly smash his cranium like an egg.

Tim hadn't seen me, and I took a deep breath. I'd had basic counselling training, but how could I best proceed? The old training exercises all seemed contrived and inappropriate for this situation. I looked across the rooftop again and then down to the ground. Something else was needed, so I moved slowly forward, calling in a soft voice.

"Can I help you, Tim?"

Mills hunched over the railing, staring down. I called again, but no response.

No strategy seemed relevant, until I recalled that copying – or 'mirroring' as they called it – the subject's posture, tonality, even breathing rate – could help gain rapport with difficult clients. It might be better than nothing.

I slowly moved alongside, but not too close, and mirrored Mills' posture. Unfortunately, this gave me a line of sight straight down onto the executive car park! Mills didn't move. I soon felt nauseous, though managed to synchronise my breath with the rise and fall of Tim's chest so that I could monitor it from the corner of my eye. After about three or four minutes Mills suddenly spoke;

"They really are bastards, you know!"

What the hell – so it worked!

If I remembered correctly, I should then continue to match the subject and then gradually lead him into a different behaviour and hopefully, a different state of mind!

I repeated Mills' words several times.

"Bastards"

Then I tried leading – adding,

"They're absolute bastards."

Mills turned and looked, with tearful eyes in a drawn face.

"Yes, absolute bastards. You people have got absolutely no fucking conscience! Taking out insurance cover. You kept that quiet, didn't you? Sounded great until finding that Canvey is the beneficiary – not our families!"

I wanted to say, 'All the more reason not to end things,' but knew that would just seem sarcastic. Mills was right though, Dan Farlin and Co had absolutely no limits!

Mills swayed over the railing.

"Next we're told our health benefits are being cut."

I noticed blood trickling onto my shirt cuffs.

"The latest rumour is possible outsourcing. You're squeezing us dry. That shit Kurt doles out crazy sales targets! Impossible. Completely impossible! I suppose he gets a bonus for screwing us?"

I nodded understanding.

"You're finding things are completely impossible?"

Mills nodded and seemed to be engaging – unless he was just surprised finding someone from management actually listening.

A car backfired outside the perimeter fence. Mills started, his white hands gripping the railing.

"Anything else getting to you?"

"Debt."

"And?"

Tim sighed and turned – his back was now resting on the railing.

I studied his face. The muscles around his eyes and mouth seemed slightly more relaxed and he'd got back some colour. Maybe voicing his concerns was a relief – even to the Deputy HR Manager!

"My wife might leave. See, Mary finds it all too much... the long hours, the pay, and our debt." Tim's eyes flicked at some invisible thought and his voice tightened.

"Look, I've had enough."

His pupils were like full stops on a face as white as a blank page. This could signal an adrenalin rush and he might suddenly go over the edge. Tim's hands gripped the rail, knuckles white, as if about to swing over. His arms straightened to take the weight.

"Look Tim, I'll call Mary. We'll get her over and sort something out."

Tim's arms relaxed a little and he slowly turned back.

"You mean that?"

I noted his wrinkled forehead and tight lips. Breaking trust at this point could be literally fatal.

"Absolutely. I'll call now. Come down to my office. I'll need your help."

"Don't trick me. There's little to live for. I'll do it, I swear."

We started to cross the rooftop, and I knew how easily he could dash to the railings.

"What's your home number?"

I asked him to repeat the number, to keep him occupied while we crossed the roof. We reached the stairwell without incident, and went straight to my office.

The phone rang – it was Tom.

"The police are here. Shall I send them up?"

"Definitely not. Please leave things with me. Things are currently quiet."

Tim raised his eyebrows.

"Was that Farlin?"

I shook my head, arranging two chairs away from the desk. This certainly wasn't the time to pull rank.

"No, Tom Phelan. I said everything's under control."

I brewed coffee, making small talk and fishing for a strategy.

"Tell me more about what's been happening – then I'll call Mary."

Mills cupped the mug in both hands and stared at the floor. He remained quiet for a while, then shook his head and sighed.

"Now I've hit Kurt I'm finished. I know that. You see, I haven't slept properly for weeks."

Given the recent pronouncements from upstairs, he was probably right to expect little mercy. Nevertheless, their tactics undoubtedly compromised employee health. Hell, I felt that too! I gestured for Tim to continue.

"During the last sale promotion, Kurt insisted we stay late and start early. He's had us in the last three Saturdays, too."

"Did you complain?" I asked, guessing the answer.

"Everyone knows what happened when Matt Zinno tried to affiliate us. It was made real clear, and where's Zinno now? Mary's sick of it and says we've no real life. I'm in debt trying to keep her happy, but I'm sure she's seeing someone else."

I nodded and my sympathy was genuine.

"I come in to the place that causes it every day – and for what? More threats from that bastard. 'You'd best meet your targets Tim. Are you focused, Tim?' Snide shit, designed to humiliate me in front of the team."

I made a mental note to pull Kurt in. This was probably true and they were grinding people into the ground. I then made a decision that almost certainly wouldn't play well with Tom or Dan.

"I intend relocating you – to marketing. Meanwhile, I suggest say twelve sessions of counselling, to get you through this patch. We'll pay."

Astonishment flooded his face.

"I… well, thanks. Yes, that could help."

His eyebrows arched in surprise.

"Treatment will be totally in confidence – though I do have one request."

He nodded.

"Your agreement that the therapist provide a general report to me on the work related factors – but excluding personal material. I mean unreasonable work demands, policies and practices that increase stress. I want to work up proposals for improving our working conditions."

The exceptionally attractive and auburn-haired Mary arrived and it was obvious why Tim might worry about other men. I found the discussion more satisfying than any work time activity in years. Using the training and development budget to fund stress counselling would be a really satisfying strike against Canvey's 'bottom-line' fixation. Far better use than spending on glib trainers, pushing their snake oil solutions, as though guaranteeing personal salvation!

When they'd finished, the couple were smiling and left, hand in hand.

I headed back to sales, to check that their staff were okay. I sped up passing Phelan's door, but he saw and beckoned me in. I speedily formulated a line about our potential liability for stress induced illness, but surprisingly he beamed.

"Hey, good job earlier, and there's more good news. You saw the email about a possible contract in South America? I've heard more and it sounds promising. You'll definitely hear from Marquetcom's guy, Rob James. Keep in touch with me on this one, Nick. We'll probably both be reporting directly to Dan."

What a prospect, I thought, although Tom seemed quite enthusiastic.

"Dan's an old friend of Marquetcom's boss. This could be a big opportunity, Nick. Apparently they want a Latin America operational centre and we might get to handle it. Incidentally, as Mills isn't now a blob on the asphalt, I assume you terminated him?"

"It wasn't quite that straightforward, Tom. Technically, we probably played a big part in what happened, so I'm shifting him to marketing admin for a while. Can we discuss it later? I still have to clear things in sales."

Phelan frowned, but I escaped and rushed to sales and made an appointment with Kurt, who seemed to imagine he was getting an invitation for a 'tea and sympathy' session.

Later that afternoon Rob James from Marquetcom called and arranged a meeting. I felt drained by the time I reached home. I poured a small scotch, and logged on, hoping for contact from my ex-wife. Nothing, and little other post except one from Simon Maher – appreciative comments on my last article and a request for more information.

I grinned at his wish to meet someone like Nina.
Lucky old me. I had an actual date!

8

MANHATTAN

NICK MARTIN

A new day and I walked over to forty-fourth street intrigued by Nina's choice of the Algonquin. From previous comments, she was probably well read and the hotel had well-known literary associations.

"You're already burbling", I muttered.

Nina had presented the water documentary and Canvey's potential new contract was… water privatising! What timing! It almost seemed like some kind of weird cosmic joke! In truth, I hadn't felt so intrigued by a woman as with Nina for ages. Maybe that's why I felt rather keyed up and slightly nervous.

The Algonquin was certainly impressive. I'd been here once before for an after-theatre supper. Maybe I could mention that the famous literary and theatrical group, the Algonquin Round Table, once met here. On second thoughts, superficial name dropping probably wouldn't impress.

She was waiting in the panelled lobby, looking particularly classy, and even more stunning than before. Her face a perfect oval shape and her widely spaced eyes sparkled with life and intelligence. Feeling unaccountably awkward, I ordered coffees.

"Colombian?"

"No, Bolivian!"

"I meant the coffee."

At least our little joke prompted another of her smiles. We talked about New York, and I reminded her of our last meeting.

"I'd like to learn more about the Zapatistas... and about your work. Incidentally, I must say your documentary was superb. If only I'd realised, I'd have introduced you to the meeting for some well deserved credit"

She remained impassive.

"Credit isn't important to me Nick – getting things done is! If that programme helped raise awareness, I'm glad, but now I must get on with my other work."

"Which is?"

"A children's charity for the greater Andean region. We've recently opened a fund-raising mission in New York and there's much to do."

"I imagine so. Tell me more about the Zapatistas."

The coffee arrived while Nina described the uprising in Mexico's Chiapas region. Like Arahti , she seemed a natural presenter if the struggles of the oppressed were concerned.

"You say they descended from the Mayas – the ancients responsible for those incredible temples in the jungle?"

"Yes. Their leader would communicate poetically about various big issues – not just revolutionary material."

I nodded, thinking, *the poetry right here is in your voice!*

"Nick, I assume that – as that group's chairperson – you're not exactly a cheerleader for neoliberalism or for corporate globalisation?"

I grinned.

"That's quite a conversation stopper Nina, but you're right!"

She gave a small smile

"People everywhere can see through it, now more than ever. Their then leader understood and made his communiques very relevant! They're quite celebrated now."

I was struggling.

"You say a mystery man in the jungle wrote to the world about neoliberalism? I'd have thought 'Joe Public' might be too consumed by the latest reality show."

"Not those with a heart," she replied. "He's retired now, but those earlier messages were full of traditional Mayan values – like the harmony between earth and nature. As I said, many were quite poetic!"

She suddenly grinned and her eyes twinkled.

"Of course, the fact that the Zapatista's really understood how the 'neoliberalismo' worked, helped. They exposed the government's sucking up to foreign corporations and the faulty 'Free Trade' project"

Nina clearly didn't 'do' light conversation. She punctuated her speech with expressive hand movements and the deep blue lapis ring on her index finger caught the light as it danced through the air. Unfortunately her superior knowledge pushed me into taking a 'devil's advocate' position. I felt lacking!

"But Nina, Mexico had to modernise. Freeing their markets surely generated the wealth to 'trickle down'?"

Nina flashed me a look of incredulity, and shook her head.

"Nick, where on earth have you been? In neoliberal systems, wealth doesn't trickle down! Like oil, it gets sucked up, from the poor to the rich. I thought everyone knew that now!"

"How about we take a walk in the park?"

"I thought you wanted to hear about the Zapatistas?"

I noted the mock censure.

"Please continue."

"Short version! The name comes from the Mexican revolutionary, Emilio Zapata. Back in 1917 Zapata, and Pancho Villa, fought for every community to have an ejido, amongst other things."

"A what?"

"Communal land – called an ejido. Serious poverty virtually disappeared because poor families could farm it to stay self-sufficient."

I nodded.

"A kind of 'commons' then?' Sounds a good plan."

"Exactly, but by the 1980s, the revolutionary party they founded was hijacked by politicians, free marketers, all the neoliberalismo stooges. They sold out to policies benefitting foreign corporations and the rich, and stabbed their own people in the back."

Her fingers danced again as she replied. Familiar with the rudiments of progressive discussion, I interrupted.

"I suspect I know what comes next. The usual formula is privatising services, push free markets, cut social spending and welfare – except, of course, corporate welfare. Dispossession and poverty for the majority and extreme wealth for a few. Am I right?"

It really was a strange first date, but there seemed no way of changing direction. Was she a socialist, a full blown communist – or what?

Nina beamed.

"Exactly. They privatised the ejidos, and signed up to the North American Free Trade Agreement, which removed subsidies and protections. Big North American corporations rushed to exploit cheap labour. With protection outlawed, cheap imports flooded in, undercutting their agriculture. As you know, since then many US corporations have outsourced to China and India, where labour costs are even less."

"The food got cheaper, though?"

"Not really – there were massive shortages! Historically the Mayans were known as the 'people of the corn.' Unfortunately the chemically raised hybrids from agro-chemical companies killed off the ancient varieties and the prices rocketed."

I shook my head, but she continued.

"So when the Zapatistas marched into San Cristobal, shouting 'Ya Basta,' it touched a nerve, worldwide.'

"Ya Basta?"

"Enough is enough!"

Inside, I reeled through remembered news reports – even school lessons. A wild melange developed as my mind fed in images of maize, Mayan pyramids, breakfast cornflakes, the enclosures and 'highland clearances'. Canvey, Tim Mills, Arahti's talk, even my latest Indymedia article. The central piece of this kaleidoscopic thinking was of course, Nina – her looks, passion and intellect. I thought about suggesting a walk again, but decided it was probably a loser.

"Is your country affected?"

"You bet," she sighed. "We've long experience of multinationals. Things seem better now, though that could easily change. We also know plenty about the power of big money – and of certain intelligence services!"

I threw in a few truisms about trade policy, which sounded flat in comparison.

"How about dinner?" I added, anxious for more time. "What about tonight?"

She smiled, her dark eyes intense and, I fancied, with a certain sensuality.

"Not possible I'm afraid. Maybe tomorrow?"

Her hand touched mine and her level of eye contact felt almost shocking.

"We need people like you, Nick", she said, squeezing my hand. "Would you like to help us make a difference?"

I nodded, unsure who 'we' and 'us' included or what actually was being asked. We agreed to meet at an Italian restaurant on Mulberry Street.

"I'll explain tomorrow," she promised.

I left, buzzing and turned left at Fifth Avenue, continuing to NYC Public Library. Ninety minutes later I pocketed my notes on the Zapatistas. With this I'd make a better impression next time!

I continued to Forty-Second Street, collected pizza to go, and took the subway to Seventy-Second Street/Central Park West. Soon, I walked past the San Remo building on the way to my apartment on Seventy-Eighth Street.

Reaching home, I checked if Alice had contacted. In fact, there was only one new email – from Simon Maher in England. Apparently, he'd shown my sweatshop article to his boss Dr Andrew Alton. It truly seemed amazing just how connected our world was. Simon had attached a short paper by Alton, which could wait until later. I opened a drawer, and took out a folder labelled 'water privatisation.' I scanned two articles and outlines that soon took digital wings to England.

Things felt rather pleasing. Simon's was one of several responses after my last article. Judy Alton, the earnest activist from New Jersey had also contacted saying:

Great job with the chairing. The meetings run more smoothly, now.

Best of all, was Nina's request for help. I smiled. *Still, best not give up the day job, just yet!*

9

COLORADO

JUDY ALTON

There had been endless staggering views! Judy Alton's surprise at the sheer variety of Colorado's landscapes just grew. She'd found this detour to the Colorado National Monument from the old driving atlas. On earlier visits to her second son, Freddy, she'd flown and missed most of this. Originally from the North East, she had the general impression of mountain scenery, whispering aspen trees and fall colours – but nothing approaching this grandeur.

The road ahead climbed a steep hill and then looked out onto a red, orange and purple landscape of balanced rocks and stone towers. Further on was a viewing point and she stopped to look down onto a collection of huge rock spires, known as the Parade of the Monoliths. The colours and textures here were spectacular and couldn't be more different from home in New Jersey.

Soon, it was time to put her foot down for the I70, which appeared the fastest way to reach Freddy in Utah. Closer to her eldest son Andrew, visits to Freddy were infrequent and tended to trigger memories of her married years in Georgia. The rows, Biff's affairs, the tiresome wheeler-dealing and his dabbling in pork barrel politics. In fact, even now she looked back in disbelief on the peculiar mixture of fundamentalism, conservatism and warped religiosity, so at odds with his actual behaviour. Strange, how a long drive all these years later, had her ruminating over whether they could have been better parents.

The car radio played appropriate country music. The scenery and the down-home melodies and lyrics somehow made her even more reflective. After leaving and later divorcing Biff, she'd succumbed to the more civilised charms of David Alton. That relationship sadly was ended two years later by a car accident outside Baltimore. Although painfully lonely, she couldn't seem to risk trying again. Secretly, she wished the visit was to Andrew instead. They were similar in so many ways and unlike Freddy, he'd kept the Alton name.

Soon she turned down Highway 128 towards Moab. The Grand River Valley here was stunning. The rocks and buttes took on a purple tint with the lowering sun. The road followed the Colorado River and the remaining rays turned the flanking tamarisks to an even deeper pink. Despite the beauty, the fact Freddy had so much in common with his father already had her apprehensive. Last time, he hinted at talents with 'creative accounting' and talked endlessly about money. She'd also witnessed a nasty scene with a customer. Might he deal substandard vehicles? She tried ignoring the worries, but couldn't banish the knots inside. There was a certain incongruity about spending so much time on charity activities while feeling like this about one of her own children. It seemed that whatever the mental gymnastics, the problem wouldn't ease.

Finally, she reached Moab and located Freddy's property. Moments later hugging the children, and holding their warm bodies close, the awkward questions subsided. Freddy wasn't home, but his wife, a rather limited though welcoming Mary, invited her in. The home seemed awash with gadgets and technology and Mary played her videos of the children through an enormous television.

Judy left to buy a few items before Moab's shops closed, and continued on to Anson Autos. An attractive, gum-chewing receptionist led her down to Freddy's overstated office. Initially, he looked blank but then grinned. She suspected that he also felt tense.

"Hi, Mom! You finally came again."

"I know, it really has been quite a long while. My, haven't the kids shot up!"

"Certainly have. The business has grown lots, too. I'll update you."

Clearly he warmed to this topic, and instinctively she didn't ask too many questions.

"So, that's business, and how's Mr University Professor?"

She tried to summarise but he took little pleasure in hearing of

Andy's success. He walked her around the showroom, pointing to changes, before taking her outside to the car lot. Old resentments seemed to cloud the atmosphere between them and, however willing, her interest in the vehicle trade soon ran dry.

They returned home, but Freddy quickly excused himself with mention of urgent business. Maybe he found it a strain too. She only knew that a visit to Andy would be so different – if only he wasn't so far away. One day, she'd visit Oxford and watch him parade in robes at one of those graduation ceremonies he talked about.

Later that evening, she took coffee down to Freddy in his den. A low murmur emerged and she guessed he must be on the phone. She waited for him to stop and put down the heavy tray, before realising she could hear through the closed door. At first, it was the similarities to Biff's tone that struck her – but as she tuned in – she could make out some of the discussion:

"Yes… two suitable places in 'The Maze' area. Lots of the park is almost always empty… yes, a remote box canyon." Freddy coughed, and the remainder was difficult to hear. Although out of character, something compelled her to keep listening. He answered another unheard question: "… yes… cross country with a 4WD, avoiding the Hans Flat Ranger Station. Yeah, he knows somewhere too, out by the La Sal Mountains."

Feeling increasingly awkward, she knocked and called:

"Coffee?"

"Have to go. Mom's here."

She opened the door, and he grinned awkwardly.

"Hi, talking with Dad, your favourite man," he said with artificial brightness.

She mustered a smile and put down the tray. Rosewood units lined the walls. She saw a cabinet with a flashy hi-fi and in the far corner, what looked like a short-wave radio. Something made him tense again and he stood abruptly, as though urging her to leave.

"You've really made it cosy here, son."

He nodded but something was strange. She'd learned to trust her intuition and her feelings were often correct. He looked shifty and the discussion was unlikely to be straightforward. Hiding materials somewhere remote? What – hot car parts? It didn't really seem likely.

"I really have to finish some business, Mom."

Visits were too infrequent to spoil, and the rest of the day had passed reasonably.

"OK, I'll say goodnight, son. See you in the morning."

The next day she told them of her moving plans.

"I'm just too close to New York. The area really has gone downhill. Anyway, I've always liked Philadelphia. The cultural life is first class."

He smiled.

"Sounds great, Mom. Once you've moved, I'll visit and make sure you're okay."

She successfully masked surprise. Concern from Fred was almost unheard of.

"Won't you miss your friends?" asked Mary.

She nodded, remembering the group meetings and Nick, the friendly chairperson.

"Yeah, Philly is real cool," said Freddy. "I'll definitely come and see you in your new place."

"I'd like that."

If only it was wholly true.

When the time came, she left with a mother's guilt and quite a heavy heart.

10

OXFORD UK

Andrew Alton's Oxford couldn't be more different from childhood in Georgia or, for that matter, life with Mom and David in New Jersey. I looked back at the monitor and another of Mom's emails, reminding me of the old days. This proposed move to Philadelphia sounded positive, but I found the news of Fred downright disturbing.

My study appeared immaculate – panelled walls and rich chocolate beams that almost looked edible. A European-styled home, at last, even if it had taken years to come! Dad's faux Spanish Hacienda, its garish Mexican colours, brassy furniture, barbecue and sports equipment, never did appeal. Neither had his bullying behaviour. My escape was education and I left for the North East. Ivy League success led to a Research Fellowship in Europe and rapid ascent of the academic ladder. Nowadays, I was only too happy to leave past history in the past!

I went back to working on a piece about coca eradication in South America. Two paragraphs in, the door opened. It was my wife Anne and her face said writing was over.

"I took a call from the new research assistant... what's his name – Simon Mark?"

"Simon Maher."

"Yes. He sounded upset. Said it was urgent and asked if you'd call. I do wish you'd get an extension up here or use a mobile like everyone else."

She passed a note asking me to call my publisher.

"More re-writes, I bet."

I phoned the college, and asked for Simon. So far his attitude seemed promising. I exhaled loudly into the mouthpiece, rather irked by the delay. There was a sudden thump on the line – followed by Simon's voice.

"Hello."

"Andrew, returning your call. You do realise it's Saturday?"

His voice sounded tight.

"Yes, I'm sorry. Look, there's a worrying development that I think involves our work." He sounded hesitant. "Could you come over? It really is serious."

"Hell – if I must! Probably about thirty minutes, traffic willing."

Forty-five minutes and several bottlenecks later, I knocked at the apartment door. Simon's boyish, intense face looked strained and the reason soon became obvious! Furniture was strewn about, drawers out of the filing cabinet and books and papers everywhere. Simon didn't seem naturally tidy, but this degree of chaos was something else.

"Spring cleaning? You should contact an agency!"

Simon managed a small grin.

"Only joking! Obviously you've been burgled. It's a hell of a mess, but why would it relate to our work?"

"Because important material has been taken. I should have mentioned it before, but I'm certain I've been followed. There are other worries, too."

"Hold on. Like what?"

Simon stroked his chin, and looked at the floor.

"I know you warned me, but I'm fairly sure I was photographed and later followed at a protest on GMO (genetically modified organism) trials. Other things have happened several times now. Infected material arrives on the internet and some snail-mail is either particularly slow or doesn't arrive at all!"

"Don't get paranoid, Simon! Look, we all have bad patches! A burglary is shocking, but I doubt that it's related to our work."

"You haven't heard everything, yet. It isn't just this mess, but other things have disappeared, too. Our summary of 'Bellevivreau's' water grabs, for example, and material from the 'Arms to Rogue States' project that I'd brought back to tidy up."

"Gone from here?"

Simon grimaced and nodded.

"I have a bad feeling. A portable telly and some CDs were taken too, but I don't think this was an ordinary break-in. Why, out of everything, would an opportunistic thief, or even a junkie, take an analysis of international arms sales or the activities of a multinational water company? It just doesn't make sense!"

I heard, but didn't answer. Apparently scanning Simon's social policy books, my mind went elsewhere – pondering other recent incidents. For example, the last re-write I'd sent Delavers – my publisher. Aspects might be controversial, but chunks of manuscript didn't normally go adrift in the mail. The next-door neighbour said that someone was tampering with the bins while Anne was out. Apparently, he was no tramp and quickly shifted, when challenged!

"What is it?" he asked.

"Sorry. Just need a moment to think."

The neighbour on the other side casually mentioned a prowler behind our house, while we were out shopping. Could any of this relate in some strange way to recent collaboration with the forensic psychiatrist, Dr Martin Farrelly?

"What's up?"

"Actually, we had prowlers at home. I just wondered if it could relate to…?"

"To what?"

"The joint work with Dr Martin Farrelly and Stephen Grotstein, that I'm sure I told you about and intend to put you onto? Some ideas about so-called 'corporate pathology'. Ideas that might relate to our areas of interest."

Simon's brow wrinkled.

"Remind me again?"

"The almost psychopathic behaviour of certain big businesses, for a start. The effects on corporate ethics if a sociopathic CEO actually heads a business."

"Sounds possible, if controversial!"

"It's certainly relevant in international trade where some really 'cut-throat' deals are done. Interestingly, when we last met, Farrelly also thought that something was wrong. Guess what? He'd also had a break-in and believed he'd been watched."

I couldn't suppress a grin.

"I told him, it sounded unfortunate coming from a psychiatrist. They're supposed to diagnose paranoia, not demonstrate it!"

Simon gave a wan smile.

"Yeah, funny! Actually, I'd really like to join that project."

"Yes, later, Simon. Was the missing material backed up?"

He went to a bookshelf, and located memory sticks hidden behind the books. He held one up.

"Two days ago, and fortunately that's still here."

"Good. Take extra copies from now on. We'll keep one in my office."

"But who'd be interested?" he asked.

"No idea. Maybe it's just a coincidence."

"And the Bellevivreau and arms sale material?"

"Bizarre! I suppose we aren't exactly popular with the business world. In fact, I've recently been pressured to tone things down. Perhaps Bellevivreau hired a private investigator – though that seems extraordinarily far-fetched?"

Simon pulled a face.

"Nah. It's difficult to imagine a big corporate interest being fazed by an academic, a forensic psychiatrist and a linguist."

"I know. We have written critically on various topics, but I can't see business spending money to pry."

"I'd better phone the police before I clear this up," Simon said, looking around the room.

"Incidentally, how did you meet Farrelly?" he added.

"Attending his lecture: 'Creative psychopaths in business'. I've long had questions about certain ruthless business leaders, for personal reasons I'll probably share with you, one day. We talked some more after his lecture and then kept meeting. I've made links to macro issues that interest us that look promising!"

"What does Farrelly do?"

"Heads up a Secure Unit for the Health Authority. They look after mentally disordered offenders. It's the heavy end of the market. Given his clientèle, it seemed a stretch to hear him waxing lyrical about certain chief executives and pathological business behaviour!"

"Sounds about right to me," Simon replied. "Did he name names?"

"No, he was careful, but his meaning was clear enough. The relevant names sort of dropped into your head! Apparently, his managers pulled him in over one paper. Said it was far too political and could bring the Authority into disrepute. He's still keen to pursue the project, though."

Simon whistled.

"I know. Just be a good boy and keep those bad-mad people locked safely away. Dole out plenty of Big Pharma's drugs, though, because they must profit! Ever looked into Pharma's behaviour, and its profits, Andrew?"

I had. I'd also noted Simon's capacity for moral outrage and, meanwhile, my writing called.

"True. Look, I must get back. Keep any further work backed up. You'd better inform college security and the police about the burglary, but try to keep the content quiet, as much as you possibly can."

Back home, I resumed work, wondering what Mom would make of the development. She kept in regular contact, so I quickly checked. Sure enough, a new post waited, saying more about her visit to Utah, and about Philadelphia – but news of Freddy brought a sinking feeling. Even after all these years, the idea of Dad collaborating with younger brother Fred felt quite unsettling. I looked out of the window. Even though I'd long ago given up on any hopes of closeness, Dad's lack of interest still hurt. Saddened by recalling the old man's hard features, I shut down the computer and went looking for more rewarding contact, with Anne.

11

MANHATTAN

ROBBIE JAMES

Another consortium meeting, and more disapproval from Anson. I left Marquetcom's suite with his denunciation burning in my ears:

"We didn't look for lame bleeding hearts, Robert."

More friction, ending in termination, seemed almost inevitable.

I walked up Fifth Avenue lost in a bubble of fear and defensiveness. Several times recently, I'd masked anxiety, by pretending to join in while Anson played hard-ball. Shamefully, that had happened today. I'd actually nodded and smiled as he belittled the consequences for, as he put it:

"Those fucking peasants you love so much."

I felt a gutless coward effectively abandoning my beliefs, and a lack of integrity felt sickening. There was more! Anson was demanding progress on the water project headquarters with this guy, Nick Martin, from Canvey Solutions.

I crossed the road on automatic pilot and then found myself moving towards Times Square. In need of diversion, I entered a music store and made for the listening posts. CDs apparently were passé and the stock had shrunk accordingly. I flipped my way through a sale rack. What was all this stuff? No Bach, Schubert, or Schumann – not even William Schuman. Only contemporary classical – Dallopicalla, Takemitsu, Ligeti, and the like. I moved along to their book section, but browsing in the current affairs section proved a mistake. Material on globalisation, inequality and social issues – were far too close to home! I moved on to psychology, but the personal growth literature there only deepened my sense of failure.

I left with stomach churning and then beat a familiar path to Eighth Ave. Furtively checking behind, I ducked into an 'adult' bookshop, knowing from experience this would change my mood faster than anything. Inside, racks of cellophane-wrapped pink-wetness were piled under huge shelves of DVDs that beckoned lewdly. I went over to a side table holding magazines released from their plastic straitjackets and 'dog-eared' by eager fingers. I flicked through a selection despite knowing my Catholic schooled psyche would later punish me.

I returned home with a well-filled paper bag. Guilt hadn't yet set in, so, hoping to delay the inevitable inner flagellation, I logged onto the internet. Remembering the music store, I entered 'Ligeti' into the search engine and half-heartedly read and listened to samples, while free-wheeling around the day's events.

So that's Ligeti. Interesting music, but not really my cup of tea.

Remembering what else I'd seen, I entered 'globalisation and water supplies', which only deepened my worry. In fact, uneasiness soon mushroomed into anxiety, and felt ready to head to self-recrimination. Recalling something else, I typed in 'Bohemian Grove', and was taken over a hypertext bridge to the odd world of so-called 'conspiracy theories'. As guilt was snapping at my heels, I stayed, following links until midnight.

The articles ranged from plausible, to mind bending and preposterous. I read of alleged cover-ups over the Kennedy assassination, apparently correct claims that the CIA was initially formed around a core of ex-Nazis, while other links took me to the Iran-Contra scandal, to 9/11 anomalies and a phenomenon known as 'Chemtrails'. Eventually, tiredness won, though a tense sleep culminated in a nightmare involving a goose-stepping parade, all dressed in Ku Klux Klan robes!

I woke to light entering the window and the previous twenty-four hours reeling through my mind. With the weekend ahead, there was nothing to do but reflect on last night's odd material. Accounts conjuring up an odd mixture of presidents, top politicians, bankers and major businessmen – a global elite, ritually interacting at 'Bohemian Grove' amongst Californian redwoods. Alleged groups of the elite planning global serfdom by controlling populations with a mix of surveillance, fear and debt – helped by tech corporations, banks, pharmaceutical corporations and the mainstream media. A wonderfully inglorious melange – which was just for starters!

However, I also knew that notions of global manipulation turned up in serious discourse too – even if in more nuanced and academic language. Powerful elites did control the media, and did set agendas out of public view. Populations probably were exploited by energy companies, exposed to pollution in the service of corporate profits. The 'truth' often seemed just as unbelievable as many so-called 'conspiracy theories'!

I sat up, knocking the articles I'd printed off last night onto the floor and, as I retrieved them, glimpsed magazines under my bed that would have horrified Dad. I quickly dismissed the thought, and flicked through the more interesting articles. The militia sites worried me, though I found the material strangely intriguing. Their poisonous rhetoric rang bells from the past. Certainly, it reminded me of my current employer, but also of something else that I couldn't quite identify.

Coffee called so I made a brew. Light was now streaming through the skylight and I settled back to read through more printouts. The first one examined the extreme religious right, and their wish to almost impose a theocracy onto what was essentially a secular society. That would allow their agenda to be portrayed as God's agenda! Some thought they'd already been successful, and relished the approaching 'rapture' –where they could watch the ungodly fry at the coming Armageddon! The next article I picked looked at the ultra conservatives. Many promoted white privilege, male supremacy, and subservience for women and ethnic groups. The most brutal vision of capitalism was championed as if ordained by God! Those with this world-view, said the article, favoured authoritarian methods, punitive social control at home and aggressive foreign policies. They disliked regulations about environmental standards, health, safety or protections for labour. The Government should absolutely favour the elite and their rich friends. This all translated into sweetheart deals for cronies, tax cuts, generous corporate welfare and the aggressive protection of private property. In contrast, the 'masses' should expect surveillance, harsh social control, an emphasis on punishment and incarceration for the poor.

Phew. It actually seemed quite compelling and rang bells. I took more coffee, and skimmed another report exploring the racial supremacists, anti-Semitic groups and other strange groups – who mixed apocalyptic and racist ideas into unholy concoctions. Apparently, the article insisted, these were out there somewhere, only waiting to strike! Some of this predated the massive anti-terrorist mechanisms now omnipresent. What caused these 'cold warriors' to believe a smidgeon of tolerance almost threatened civilisation? How did 'liberal' become so dirty?

I put the article down, noticing my heart was speeding and I had a sense of nausea. Whatever touched me wasn't just Anson. In fact, I found myself thinking of my father, Terry James. A fragment of a memory involving guns, boots and strange visitors drifted into my mind, but didn't cohere. I dressed and left the apartment, hoping shopping might change my mood. For some reason I kept picturing Dad's drunken behaviour at mealtimes. It often involved anti-government rants, the iniquitous private Federal Reserve or the supposed illegality of income tax. All the while, Mom would smile sweetly and keep serving. Perhaps, finding a boss like Anson hadn't happened by chance!

Dad held a view, popular at the time, that people were either 'producers' or 'parasites'. Parasites were found at the top and bottom of society. At the top, a parasitic, corrupt government was in league with finance and the wealthy elite. At the lower level, were lazy, feckless, welfare scroungers. Of course, in those days, there was a large middle class, the 'producers' or hard-working average people.

"What will you be, boy, a producer or parasite?" was his favourite saying. That, and "Don't be such a bonehead!"

Of course, it was Dad's attitude and, later, my sexuality that propelled my escape to the North East and further education. I remembered what Nancy told me about Anson's eldest son, Andrew. It sounded like Andrew also had 'father problems' so, somewhere, there was a shared experience of Biff. I wondered what advice Andrew would have?

Later in the afternoon, I walked through the East Village, mulling over my childhood. As well as hating the government, Dad loathed minority groups: Jews, Blacks, immigrants, welfare recipients, gays, lesbians, environmental and conservation activists – in fact, just about everyone that I felt most in tune with!

How was Terry now? We hadn't spoken in years and he'd be in his mid-50s. Cousin Carl believed he'd moved to Wyoming or Montana, years ago.

Anyway, good riddance! I didn't have to bother now.

At least, that's what I thought then!

12

OXFORD UK

ANDREW ALTON

Oxford traffic is a pig. No wonder they push that 'park and drive' scheme.

Swinging the old Volvo from the exit, I avoided a group of students straggling on bikes, only to head straight into a stationary queue of vehicles. Simon sat beside me, munching from a bag of black pepper crisps.

"Not sharing today?" I asked with a grin.

He proffered the half-eaten bag.

"I'm so pleased to join in with this project. It's just the kind of thing that grabs me. Fill me in on Farrelly and Grotstein, please."

"Well Martin is a shrink," I replied. "So, if you've worries about your mental health…!"

Simon grinned.

"Well, I work with you in probably the least popular outfit in the college, so I suppose something could be wrong!"

"Ha ha. No, they're an interesting pair, although Stephen Grotstein is a bit of an old hair splitter. You know what linguists are! He also regularly flips into lecture mode. Reminds me of someone. I can't possibly think who!"

We eventually turned off the Witney Road, and pulled into the drive of a large house partly hidden behind a laurel hedge. Its tall twisting chimneys said 'listed', though it looked a little spooky.

"What a place," said Simon. "And this is where Farrelly lives?"

"No, it's chez Grotstein," I replied.

We rang the bell until a maid arrived and took us to the drawing room. Judging from the objects on display, Grotstein was probably well travelled and had a fondness for Indian and Tibetan artefacts. An impressive stone Buddha and a dancing Shiva stood on opposite sides of the room and a striking Mandala graced the far wall. The door opened and a wiry endomorph with a grey beard and darting eyes entered, introducing himself as Steven Grotstein. Shortly afterwards, Dr Farrelly arrived wearing an expensive suit. He appeared rather tense.

"Hello Martin," I said. "As agreed, meet my research assistant, Simon Maher. I'm sure he'll be a valuable addition."

Farrelly shook Simon's hand, but continued without further small talk.

"Andrew, you said on the phone you might have been the victim of dirty tricks?"

Grotstein's face was a study in scepticism.

"Probably. Simon's apartment was burgled, and work relating to our task has disappeared. Other things have gone, too."

Grotstein sighed and shook his head.

"Simon also believes he's been photographed and followed. Next door reported someone going through the bins in our house and another neighbour actually saw a prowler at the back. Could we both be paranoid, Martin? You should know!"

Farrelly smiled and turned to Grotstein.

"How about you, Stephen? Anything unusual?"

Grotstein sighed again.

"Sounds far-fetched to me. Look, I thought we'd come to agree a way forward."

The others murmured agreement, and moved into productive mode. I reached into my bag.

"We've brought material from a site monitoring corporate misbehaviour. Simon isn't known yet and he obtained strategic documents from a range of corporations. I've compiled a table charting actions that clearly contradict their corporate mission statements."

A sniff came from Simon's direction.

"Correction, Simon pulled that together and helped to structure it!"

I passed the substantial bundle around.

"Martin, could you briefly review the diagnostic criteria material again? Simon is new to the DSM and, as he'll be collecting data, it's important he understands."

"DSM?" queried Simon.

"Yes," I said. "If we examine corporate misbehaviour from a psychopathology viewpoint, we'll need agreed definitions."

Farrelly looked up from his papers.

"Basically, Simon, DSM is the American psychiatric bible – the Diagnostic and Statistical Manual."

Grotstein snorted. "Behavioural descriptions with its context expressed with static nouns. Commonly known as 'psycho-babble'!"

Farrelly's eyes narrowed, though he continued anyway.

"The manual gives the American Psychiatric Association's diagnostic pointers for different mental disorders. There's also a rival system called the ICD – the International Classification of Diseases."

"It's fairly authoritative then," I said.

Farrelly nodded and passed papers to Simon.

"Here's a summary. Incidentally, the term 'psychopathy' disappears in later editions, and is replaced by APD – 'Anti-social Personality Disorder'."

"I'm worried things could get tricky," I said. "If we produce material implying that certain CEOs and business leaders act like psychopaths or have APD, we won't get far – unless to court for a slander trial! Mind you, your lecture was outspoken, Martin. What was your comment about charismatic narcissists?"

Farrelly shook his head.

"I just said that some 'fanatical groups, cults, and even major businesses seem to be led by charismatic, creative psychopaths or individuals with signs of narcissistic personality disorder'. That was said to a specialist audience. We certainly won't win many friends, comparing highly paid business leaders to extremists, cult leaders, or criminals – however ruthless or egocentric their behaviour might seem to us!"

"Language is always critical," said Grotstein, his domed head bobbing up and down as he spoke.

"You must understand that words set the conceptual framework for the listener or reader's mind – and help give meaning."

Everyone nodded, but apparently Grotstein was just warming up.

"You weren't here last time, Simon, so I'll give an analogy. If the brain processes somewhat like a computer, then consider its operating system as language. Without the help of language, minds just idle, producing random images and memories. Always be careful with language!"

I wondered how to derail Grotstein from giving another lecture and looked over to Simon – but it was already too late. Grotstein was off and his long fingers made plucking gestures, as though pulling words from the air.

"Take sensory rich words, Simon. For example, 'a ripe, red, juicy strawberry'. These words engage the senses, to encourage images and ideo-motor responses, to evoke the appearance, taste and sensation of the berry – do you see? Of course, different kinds of nouns – abstract nouns, intangible things like feelings, concepts and qualities, that help the listener to access their inner resources and memories. That sort of language helps to build beliefs and values – ideal for motivation or persuasion. These things are generally activated by abstract nouns – and are given their unique meanings by the listener. How can you best elicit these? By helping the listener find examples from their own personal experience."

Farrelly shook his head and Simon darted me a look, but Grotstein ploughed on regardless.

"When language is used artfully, for example in hypnotic language like the corporate examples you gave us earlier, the meaning is subjectively accessed and then builds on related meanings. This sort of language provides leverage that's almost impossible to resist. You see, hypnosis isn't only found in the clinic or on the stage – it's everywhere – particularly in advertising! Forgive the double negative gentlemen, but you cannot *not* be influenced by certain language structures."

I made a mental note to find a strategy to short circuit Grotstein – if he tried pontificating like this again.

"Interesting," said Simon, "though I'm not sure how…"

"How it relates to our work?" interrupted Grotstein. "Well, clever communicators use such knowledge."

Yes, just like my father, I thought.

"Not just with PR and advertising," continued Grotstein, as if catching my thought, "but many charismatic and psychopathic leaders have such skills in abundance. By all means, watch their relationships and behaviour like the psychiatrists do, but, above all, listen to their language. Crafty business leaders, advertisers, policy makers, think-tanks, and certain politicians and members of the establishment, play the public, like skilled fishermen!"

Farrelly nodded.

"Stephen's quite right in saying that many intelligent psychopaths are highly charismatic. Sometimes, that can be a diagnostic pointer in itself. The higher levels of politics and some big corporations have plenty like that. Often, it's a case of 'birds of a feather'."

I glanced at Simon, wondering how he was coping with the lecture. Grotstein was now looking slightly dotty – with mildly protruding eyes.

"I realise that language is important, Stephen," I tried, "but surely it must also be about intention and behaviour? The old adage 'follow the money', surely still holds true! It's power and money that nearly always figure!"

Grotstein nodded.

"You need to unpack the word 'power', though! What idiosyncratic networks are activated, in both speaker and listener?"

Everyone exchanged glances, realising that, for now, it was hopeless!

Farrelly handed round a sheet giving the main DSM distinctions.

"I then put my idea to the others. I've put together a sample of a data collection sheet that we could trial when finding useful material. For example, with anti-social corporate behaviour, I suggest recording examples under the appropriate diagnostic pointer. For example, 'lacks empathy', 'doesn't learn from experience', 'short-termism', or whatever the example is. It'll help us to structure the data, for later writing up."

The others agreed to pilot the idea.

Simon still appeared concerned.

"We didn't really get around to discussing it," he said, "but some of us suspect some external interference."

No response.

He persisted.

"Odd things have happened and I, for one, am worried."

Grotstein looked sceptical. Farrelly and I nodded, but as no-one seemed to want to take it up, the meeting wound down.

On the drive back, I was buzzing. Simon broke into my thoughts.

"Certainly an interesting group, but do you think we can actually work together?"

"I know what you mean," I replied, noticing a black four-wheel drive that seemed to follow every time we turned.

"I'm still worried someone is taking undue interest," Simon said.

"Possibly. Still, at least we have free speech, however much Grotstein would complicate that!"

13

OMID (OFFICE FOR MONITORING INTERNAL DISSIDENTS) LONDON

Indeed, 'someone' was noticing far more than just two troublesome academics in Oxford. Since the terrorist disaster in the USA, attitudes towards protest and dissidence had intensified in most Western societies. In the UK, in addition to the ubiquitous CCTV surveillance, new methods of control and containment were being actively developed. Unknown to either Simon Maher or Andrew Alton, their names had been included on a database with thousands of activists and other individuals with known or suspected dissident sympathies. The programme was watched over by a discreet dedicated section within the intelligence services. Of course, the public were far more concerned with finding and tracking real terrorists – than monitoring an 'awkward squad' of lefties, troublesome academics, anti-corporate and anti-capitalist nuisances. OMID – the Office for monitoring internal dissidents – had formed and couldn't be busier.

Potential troublemakers, Maher and Alton had been assigned a medium level 2 rating and placed on the list. An investigative journalist who'd recently penetrated the outer layers of the operation, stated:

"The UK focus includes people whose only wrong doing is criticising manipulations by big business, a self-centred finance sector, big American Corporations, and anyone else questioning the savage 'winner takes all' version of neoliberalism with everything counted, costed and for sale."

While possibly confused conceptually, the journalist was, nevertheless, successfully gagged under new and expanded legislation and the public remained in the dark.

Some of OMID's staff, though, worried that their work now targeted people formerly happy to accept the more benign, social-democratic approach to capitalism. Given the inevitable 'mission-creep', others were soon included on OMID's programme. Suspicion even attached to left-leaning students, those protesting austerity and service cuts, or drawing attention at attempts to offload the deficit or the costs of financial scandals onto the long-suffering taxpayer.

Today, section leaders Dick Hennessy and Frank McGarvey had been summoned to see Director Michael Donaldson The two men waited by the water cooler near Donaldson's office. There'd been rumours of a further expansion of their role, instigated by the Americans. Privately, Hennessy had major concerns, but he was ambitious enough to be discrete.

"I assumed US Security would only want to target proper terrorists," emphasised Hennessy.

"Including the common 'tree-huggers'?"

"Of course, just as we do. I wonder what Donaldson has up his sleeve now?"

"Don't know, but I bet it means extra work."

Donaldson called them in. His walls were covered in maps, studded with coloured pins. It reminded Hennessy of a film set for a wartime strategy room!

Donaldson studied them for a moment. A sharp-faced intelligence veteran, he was married to work and his usual modus operandi was via the 'old boy's network'. Hennessy assumed the new breed of agents weren't at all to his taste.

"Look, chaps, I'll come straight to the point. A change of direction is coming, which, I'm afraid, will increase workloads. As you know, we cooperate closely with our American colleagues, whom, I'm afraid, keep ratcheting up their measures. The US Security apparatus consists of a cluster of agencies. Some are 'invisible' – rather like us. Currently, our coordination with the USA is via joint protocols – a ramshackle arrangement for what should be a smooth and unrestricted exchange of information. In future, we hope to share most things."

"Sir, aren't there dangers?" asked McGarvey. "We already have rumblings from the shop floor. If the civil liberties crowd learn how extensive the sharing is already...?"

"Yes, both good points, but don't pursue them! Decisions have already been taken at the highest level. Your points are understood, but won't be further considered."

Donaldson lit his pipe. Modern conventions on workplace smoking had passed him by, but no-one challenged it.

"I'll get to the crux of it. US Intelligence suspect that their home-grown groups, possibly even so-called 'social justice' groups and other 'issue' groups, might potentially have been infiltrated and could unknowingly provide cover to proper hard-line terrorists. In other words, people masquerading as everyday-issue activists could be wolves in sheep's clothing, as it were, able to strike and then melt back into cover."

"Like who, though?" asked Hennessy. "Let's face it, the 'land of the free' has groups covering every conceivable issue."

"True," replied Donaldson. "So do we, but, as you know, our policies and theirs increasingly run in parallel. Between you and I," he said conspiratorially, "the Americans now pretty well keep tabs on everyone. The private sector are also taking part."

"Business as usual, then – no pun intended! Who worries them in particular?" asked Hennessy.

Donaldson screwed up his face.

"Their picture is quite complicated. Naturally, they have our sort of customers – anti-corporate, anti-globalist zealots. Some single-issue groups like animal rights and environmentalists – sometimes called 'bio-terrorists', to up the ante! Another important group in the US are the militias – that gun toting, weekend soldier crowd, found in virtually every state. Finally, there are the real terrorist groups – Islamist or otherwise."

McGarvey groaned.

Donaldson scowled and continued.

"Returning to our troublemakers, we've now agreed to compile level 2 dossiers on the more 'active' activists and also troublesome academics. These will be shared with the Americans. Regarding our US colleagues, they have three major groupings.

Firstly – domestic activist and protest groups.

Secondly, the armed militias, the neo-Nazi groups, Christian

Patriots and other far right groups – who might potentially migrate to the militia movements."

"That's not relevant to our scene, though," said McGarvey.

Donaldson shot him a look.

"Thirdly, and more worrying – extreme fundamentalist terrorists and other genuine terrorist groups and individuals. Now, personally, I'm not convinced that sharing details about most of our sort of troublemakers is necessary or justified – but those are our orders."

"It does seem extreme, Sir," said Hennessy. "Certainly, they're a nuisance, as we find at every Arms fair, free trade protest and so on, but surely not…"

"What's actually involved, Sir?" interrupted McGarvey, now looking more enthusiastic.

"We already track agitators. I mean how deep do we go?"

"Firstly, more information gathering. Selecting likely subjects and building dossiers," Donaldson stated. "Some will merit further investigation and others full surveillance!"

"What about the proxy server thing?' asked Hennessy.

"Pretty well sorted," Donaldson replied. "Our IT section has modified software developed for paedophiles. Anti-paedophile sentiments and terrorist fears have softened up the public to accept more internet monitoring. Most haven't realised quite how extensive it already is! From now on, the most persistent agitators are cleared for full surveillance."

Hennessy interjected.

"The idea the Americans floated, couldn't that also apply…?"

Donaldson cut him short.

"Very good, Dick, I was just coming to that. We also have individuals who don't wish us well, and you pretty well know who they are. So, yes, we must also be vigilant. In the meantime, get on with preparation for the expanded work!"

Donaldson stood up. The meeting was over.

"Thank you, gentlemen. Please take this forward. I'll need regular reporting and updates."

Hennessy returned to his office and spent several hours prioritising names on the database. He decided to meet team members individually for case allocation and asked his secretary to individually send them through.

"Phyllis, I'll start with Gill Marney, please."

Dealing with Gill was usually a pleasure. Hennessy had high hopes for her future. He knew that having favourites was inadvisable, although she did cross her legs rather deliciously! Oxford and surrounds would suit very nicely.

14

OXFORD UK

SIMON MAHER

After Andrew Alton's warning, I tried not to show strong agreement with the sentiments expressed at the 'Guard our Environment' anti-GMO meeting. It certainly was difficult because they had really committed activists. In fact, some members were present tonight – whom I'd helped to spoil a GMO field trial. No-one actually mentioned that little escapade, although a further trial was set to start in the Wallingford area. Apparently, this involved a 'super wheat' that supposedly had more efficient photosynthesis. A spirited discussion developed. The usual nonsense PR about feeding the poor, naturally, or should I say unnaturally, had been promoted by 'Bio-nutrasynthesis'. Of course, the more obvious answer of just tackling extreme poverty was never suggested by the saintly agri-corporation.

A new girl joined us this evening. She seemed keen, slightly naive, though very pretty. She asked questions that, in themselves, seemed quite perceptive, yet lacking in fundamental understanding. Still, I suppose that not everyone has basic biological and horticultural knowledge.

I spoke with her at the end of the evening. Her name was Gill Marney and she admitted to being a relative newbie about the GMO issue. She seemed easy to talk to and we had a good conversation. Gill knew her stuff about social justice issues and appeared up to speed on the corporate front. In our subsequent chat, she also proved au fait about arms sales, as well as being quite a looker. Interesting! I thought of what Nick Martin had said about meeting Nina Parenda, and grinned. Must keep my mind on the job in hand. Still, if meeting women at an activist's meeting was good enough for Nick – why not me?

15

MANHATTAN

NICK MARTIN

I prepared for another 'date' with Nina, and my mouth felt unusually dry. Brooding in this way wasn't typical for me, but last time I'd been right out of my league. Simon Maher had congratulated me over my little articles, but Nina was a real activist and a proper expert. I felt almost fraudulent in comparison, and that didn't sit comfortably at all. I checked my appearance yet again, wondering whether my previous failed relationships signalled a problem with commitment that women somehow sensed? Marriage to Alice had suffered that way. The green card had been irresistible, but that relationship's failure seemed as painful as it was inevitable.

Given the reputation of British management, I still felt amazed the Americans had been impressed by my HR experience and that I'd landed the Canvey job. The job continued, though the marriage lasted just two years. I'd remained in the USA, staying friends with Alice until her disappearance just over a year ago.

I left and took the convertible. I located parking and walked on to the agreed restaurant on Mulberry. Despite the busyness and subdued lighting, I quickly spotted Nina, with her glossy black hair tumbling over a classic blue suit. She certainly looked stunning, smiling and then complimenting my appearance! In truth, I found her self-assurance just a little unsettling. As we made pleasantries over an aperitif, I asked her opinion of the year's best films.

"I'm far too busy to watch movies, Nick. I like making them, though!"

As the evening progressed, the impression small talk didn't cut it was amply confirmed. Although undoubtedly beautiful and very feminine, Nina's style of thinking had what used to be thought an almost masculine grip and focus.

I was soon burbling again.

"I've never been to South America, Nina. In fact, Simon Bolivar was just a name until recently. Tell me something about your country."

Nina certainly was captivating when animated. It turned out she originally came from Cochambamba, and her description of the infamous water war was gripping. She went further, even making IMF Structural Adjustment Plans sound like a 'who-dunnit'. In fact, from what she said, that wasn't too far from the truth!

"Of course, the sharks moved on to strip other vulnerable countries. You know the pattern?"

"I think so. Let me see. Recommend slashing their spend on health and social programmes, freeze wages, gut labour rights, enforce privatisation and open everything to foreign investment?"

Her dazzling smile made me feel rather dizzy.

"Very good, though you said something similar last time. You'll find I have an excellent memory!"

"Right."

I got the censuring look again and felt appropriately silly.

"No marks for consistency then?"

She ignored my attempts at humour.

"Your country's futile efforts to eradicate coca causes real problems in the Andean region."

"Actually, it's my adopted country, although I do love it."

Food arrived and, passing the salt, her hand seemed to linger longer than necessary. She smiled when I looked, and held eye contact while I struggled to find something relevant to say.

"Cocaine is a major problem, Nina. We have to do something."

She shook her head.

Aromas wafted from nearby tables and my attention briefly wandered. Her facial structure really was exquisite. Never mind producing films – she should be starring! When my attention finally returned, she was in the middle of some explanation.

"... but that's partly because of misunderstandings. In our legend, coca was gifted to the Quechua and Aymara peoples by the sun god."

"But..."

I stopped – after another of her 'looks'.'

"People have used it for thousands of years. Chewed or as tea, the Andean people use it as a mild stimulant to help with hunger, fatigue and altitude sickness. The campesinos are upset by attempts at eradication – because often they have very little else."

Coffee arrived. I held my cup up.

"Some stimulation of our own, I suppose."

She smiled.

"You have to admit, cocaine causes a real problem for the West."

"We're part of the Western hemisphere, too. Following the initial looting, we continued suffering for centuries. Then came the water war, fumigation and eradication."

"Surely the government has the right to stop drugs reaching our streets."

"Do Bolivians, or Colombians for that matter, spray or burn tobacco plantations or fast-food places in the US, because they harm health? Do we insist that land used for tobacco or beef must now be used for cash crops – or else! Do you really imagine that Wall Street or Las Vegas produce 'healthy' products?"

"Hardly a fair comparison!"

"Maybe, but we've been pushed around just to benefit banks and foreign multinationals, for a very long time!"

I felt uninformed, and poured more wine, hoping to move the conversation along.

"Enjoying New York?"

"No, Nick. You asked about my country, so let me tell you! First, our gold was seized by the Spanish. Others then took control of silver and tin mines. Then multinationals came after oil and then wanted our gas. The continent has huge biodiversity and resources. Of course, they'd really like it all!"

I quaffed my wine, not knowing what to make of the evening. Like before, it was certainly an unorthodox date! I was thinking about Britain's colonial grabs when her fingers touched the top of my arm. I looked up into deep eyes.

"You see, coca's almost like a national flower. As tea it gives energy and helps long working hours. Some think it helps digestion and also the circulatory system. The poor mix coca leaf with ash – sometimes their only food. Yet, in Colombia and elsewhere, your government shovelled huge sums to the military and private contractors, to try and eradicate it."

"We promoted alternatives though? You mentioned cash crops earlier."

"Theoretically, but often there were no real markets. Most coca production moved to Colombia and then they were sprayed and fumigated. Your public still knows little of this. In the South, you see, we remember Guatemala, Nicaragua, Chile and many other places."

I nodded weakly, making a mental note for further research.

"People know so little of what's happened in South America," she repeated.

We left the restaurant, still talking. In some ways it had seemed more a tutorial than a date – but what a tutor! As we walked to my car, she slipped a hand in mine, and then stopped and looked straight into my eyes.

"We need help, Nick. Do you care about what I've said?"

My head nodded.

"Would you like to help us bring change?"

My throat was tight. Her eyes seemed dark and troubled, though quite beautiful. I found myself nodding.

"Friends are, of course, important, but we also need practical help too. Are you interested in helping us to make things better? I suspect you probably are!"

"Of course – if I can!"

"You must have many contacts in your work. I've friends in the South who want to help improve things – not just for my charity, but wider too. We need helpful business contacts, IT support and various other things. Perhaps you can play a part? I'll explain more, soon!"

We continued hand in hand to the car. Just now I'd do whatever she asked...

16

BROOKLYN

ROBBIE JAMES

I turned the wheel towards Brooklyn, fuming after further humiliation from Anson. 'A human punch-bag' hadn't been the job description and how I regretted ignoring my intuition at the time of the interview. After discussions with senior Marquetcom staff, I was finally introduced to the big man. With hindsight, I now realised Anson was probably on best behaviour, but my initial response had been right! Nothing in training could have prepared me for the spewing venom of one of Anson's bad days.

Barely noticing the bridge, I instead replayed the latest episode. Summoned to Anson's office only to have my carefully prepared work rubbished. Worse still, my report on global water activism was literally thrown across the office! Surely it deserved a mature discussion, not a bawling out. Anson screaming that he didn't recruit for the Peace Corps and demanding why I wasn't focused on the proposed South American operational centre.

Anson's short list of providers included Canvey Solutions. I drove deeper into Brooklyn to their site. I signed in, was escorted to a conference room and introduced both to Michael Fruell, the Marketing Director, and Deputy HR Manager Nick Martin, who explained that his role was to help gauge staffing requirements. His rather tense face had a surprising familiarity. Before I could explore why, a small team of senior managers arrived to give Canvey's pitch.

They began with the usual corporate fanfare. However, in his section, Martin suggested we be mindful of the social costs and the local feelings. He referred back to Cochambamba, as a 'historical black mark against water privatisation'. I found this quite unexpected and rather startling. Fruell looked highly displeased, shaking his head. Remembering Nina's documentary and our discussion, I couldn't help but nod in agreement. Canvey's other staff stayed right on the business case, but, in Canvey's summary, Martin showed more awareness of the potential impact on the Columbian public. I quite warmed to him.

After the presentation finished, Nick Martin approached me with an invitation to lunch, and suggested a local Italian restaurant. Given Fruell's earlier reaction, I half expected there'd be frantic retractions over the pasta, quickly followed by a hard sell. Instead, soon after we arrived, Martin spoke.

"I suspect we may share a sense of discomfort, Mr James? I noticed you agreeing when I raised concerns?"

"Most people call me Robbie – have done for years."

"No pun intended, Robbie. I didn't try to muddy the water. What I just said was just my intuition."

For a moment, I wondered if this was a test. Could he even be in Anson's pocket?

"The pitch was impressive," I replied, "though we've others to consider."

Martin raised his eyebrows, but something inside urged me to take a chance.

"Okay, you're right, I am worried. It's potentially a money spinner, but I have major reservations. Water's an absolute necessity and privatising caused some real horrors elsewhere."

His response totally took me aback.

"Have you heard about the consequences in South Africa?"

I looked down at my hands, clenched from wrestling with my conscience. I knew that my guard was down and that, from a business perspective, our discussion was all wrong.

"I heard something about it. Yes, disturbing!"

"Singing from the company hymn sheet gets difficult when the song sickens you," he continued. "I've been there more than once. Actually, I'm there right now! We're heading for a reorganisation just to save dollars – and to hell with the workers. Please keep that to yourself for now."

I nodded, but the surprises continued.

"How about you?" he asked. "I sense that something is chewing you up?"

His openness encouraged me to let go, too. One issue led to another, and we exchanged views for over an hour. Nick seemed well informed about poverty, corporate globalisation, and particularly the downsides of water privatisation. That made more sense, when he revealed a friend who had first-hand experience at Cochambamba. It was then we both realised we'd been at the New Jersey meeting.

"I thought you were somehow familiar. It was only my second meeting. Have you been involved for long?"

"Over two years," replied Nick.

We tackled more sacred corporate cows, and then agreed that we would meet again – even if Canvey's bid was unsuccessful.

Driving back to Manhattan, I felt elated. As though something inside had ignited. If Cochambamba's poor and defenceless resisted, why not me? Anson and the consortium didn't care – certainly not about South America's poor. This particular worm could certainly turn and vengeance could indeed be very sweet. I understood there were many skeletons in Marquetcom's corporate cupboard!

Before getting back to the office, a plan had started forming...

17

UTAH/MONTANA USA

FREDDY ANSON

Andrew's younger brother, Freddy Anson, pushed his four by four hard from Moab through Salt Lake City. Briefly stopping at Logan, he then turned into the Canyon Road, and made for Jackson Hole, Wyoming. Despite a touch of irritation at the traffic, he relaxed on seeing the dealerships on the strip leading to the centre.

The town centre looked packed, but the sight of the elk horn arch on the square reminded him to check for his weapon. He reached under the seat and felt the warmth of the Smith & Wesson. Freddy looked up at the last moment, barely avoiding collision with an old-time coach and horses. *Damn tourists, playing at the Wild West!* Eventually, he got through the centre and then punted the accelerator on the road through Grand Teton National Park. The road continued to Yellowstone, skirting the wonderful Jenny Lake – passing the photogenic Teton Mountains, rising straight up from the valley floor. Apparently, named by the pioneer fur trappers in homage to thrusting breasts. He chewed a dry tongue in approval!

Cursing the slow tourists, Freddy exited Yellowstone's Eastern entrance, turning north at Cody and entering Montana. Soon, he saw the described distinctive barn and post-box on the right-hand side. The track led to a farm down a long track flanked with carpets of fringed gentian. At the track's end a large grizzled man wearing a black t-shirt waved him down with a rifle.

"Hi! I'm Fred Anson – looking for Terry James."

"I'm Terry. Come on in, man. Talking on the radio is fine, but I'd rather put a face to the voice."

They entered the farmhouse. Terry propped his rifle behind the door, and motioned to a leather chair. The interior was done out like a traditional lodge, and had moose heads mounted on opposing walls. Freddy sat, weary from the long drive, scanning literature on the nearby table as Terry prepared coffee. He picked up a leaflet; 'Improvised Weapons of the American Underground'.

"Good for kicking the government's ass," said Terry, entering with steaming mugs and a plate of chocolate-chip cookies.

"Here, drink this. I like meeting brothers from out of State. Some buddies are comin' over this evening, so you'll meet 'em before the gathering."

Freddy felt rather in awe. James was quite a name in militia circles.

"How are things over in Utah?"

"It gets sicker all the time. The New World Order is everywhere. Robert's book had it right – the end game is imminent. Big finance might have caused mayhem, but they still pull the strings – even with my car business. In the next-door state, they've abortion clinics, legalised prostitution and gambling. There are gay support groups, and, over in Arizona, Sedona is chock full of new age hippies and weirdos. How much worse can it get – and yet the bloodsuckers want to take our guns as well as taxes."

"Let 'em try," said Terry. "Check on the table again, man."

Freddy riffled through more leaflets with material on 'Firearms', 'Hand-to-hand Combat,' and 'Militia Intelligence Methods'.

Terry rubbed the bristles on his chin, and he looked strangely intense.

"Have you read 'The Turner Diaries', Fred? Bill really spelled out how it'll be. Someone has to clean America up. If not the brothers, then who?"

Terry's craggy face and piercing eyes reminded him of a bird of prey and Freddy sensed he could get out of his depth easily with this man. Reading 'The People's Spell-breaker' and visiting websites was one thing, but James struck him as an 'action man'. Still, Dad had urged him to actively network.

The talk wound down and Terry then went to a rack and selected two weapons.

"Let's see what you're made of."

Terry beckoned, and led him down a wooded track to a practice range. The mountain air soon rang to the sound of shots and the extent that Terry outclassed him was painfully obvious. Shortly after, they returned to the house, some of the Montana Group members arriving ahead of the weekend exercise. Terry introduced him to Frank Dell, Donny McFee and Lee Damson. They struck him as a hard-bitten lot and he could only relax when conversation turned to the usual topics – taxes, gun control and government corruption. They swapped stories over beers – each outdoing the other to prove that America had become soft and rotten. The identified culprits: the liberal media, Hollywood and an overbearing government colluding with the 'New World Order'.

That evening, Terry outlined plans to further connect key militia groups across the country. As Terry put it: "So folk can defend themselves from their own rotten government." Their key task now was updating their communication links. When they'd left, James spoke to him alone.

"Fred, are you ready to play your part – like your Daddy? Biff's a great example."

He nodded, unsure quite what was meant, though he guessed Dad would be pleased.

James fixed him with a firm expression that jolted him from any sense of ease.

"The important things are effective networking, securing our communications, and helping the bro's get the weapons they need. We have a communication specialist on board now – a guy called Zoltan Heltay. I hope you'll play a part helping us find somewhere for storing the kit." He swallowed but, after watching Terry blow those targets away, didn't argue!

"I'll introduce you to Zoltan later. I've an idea how you could play a very helpful part."

It was a suggestion he'd later regret...!

18

MANHATTAN

BIFF ANSON

Biff Anson's out-sized face was a study in frustration, and his nostrils flared in disgust. He held a paper by Andrew Alton: 'Neoliberal policies and water privatisation. Outcomes and future implications.'

Next to the brown envelope was handwritten note, which he read again.

Biff, I hope you're keeping well. I recently visited Freddy and, as you know, he's fine. No word from Donny, but I thought I'd enclose a copy of a new paper by Andy – I hope you'll find it interesting. Trust you're as proud of his work as I am! Regards, Judy.

She must somehow know – but how? He searched for any other explanation because her strait-laced dabbling had led to their break-up in the first place. This arriving right now couldn't just be coincidence – it must be a message? She'd forwarded other materials, but why this rant by the little bleeding heart – now of all times?!

He returned the items to the envelope, put them in the desk and slammed the drawer. Nancy entered with coffee. He waved her away but, as she reached the door, he snapped.

"Get Rob James to come in, right away."

Robbie's perspective – five minutes later

I was by the water cooler when Nancy sidled up.

"The master's calling. Be careful Robbie. He seemed in an ugly mood!"

My heart sped.

"I find him chilling, sometimes."

Nancy nodded, and smiled ruefully as I left.

It reminded me of being summoned to the headmaster. I even managed to stumble as I entered his office. The large face opposite wore an ugly sneer and, seeing my revised report out on the desk, the headmaster analogy seemed about right!

Anson leaned forward.

"Are you suited to a business career?"

I nodded, but no words came.

"Why the schoolboy essays? Do you really think that's what I pay you for?"

I made a fist around my thumb and tried to relax my throat, anticipating my voice would sound choked.

"I was trying to be objective. Some will worry about the human costs. Surely we have to accept that?"

Anson snorted.

"Don't be so stupid – business is business. If people don't take proper care, they've no-one but themselves to blame! You never have grasped self-reliance!"

"To be fair, though, some people's circumstances..."

"I wish you'd get your thinking straightened out! Of course, people have to strive for the American Dream. Opportunities are there, to take or make. Anyone can make it, if they try hard enough. They can be a chief executive – be the damned President, if they have sufficient drive!"

I nodded, while thinking: *Yes, if they're millionaires already and happy whoring for corporate America*, but held back from speaking.

"You really think I had everything handed to me on a plate, son? Look at it this way –actually, we're taking freedom to the people in the South. Later, they'll be thankful for what free and open trade gives them."

Biff's big red face swam in and out of focus, and I felt nauseous. Did people really believe this stuff? Next, he'd be quoting Ayn Rand!

"Bucking nature is where you go wrong. It just doesn't work!"

I fought a paralysis of the emotions, and eventually croaked out.

"In developing countries, any gains usually get made by corrupt local elites, willing to sell out to foreign corporations. That's probably even more true in the undeveloped world. Working for themselves and any overseas business that pays them – not their own people. For example, in…"

As the big fists pounded on the desk, I felt sweat trickling from my armpits.

"Such a child! You really don't get it, do you? Doing our bidding is the whole point! Those you term 'the local elite' have reached the top because they got off their butts and took their opportunities! Made something of themselves while the others didn't! Son, you're either a winner or the other thing, and losers are a waste of space. In nature, weak animals become food for the superior ones. Why should we be any different?"

Anson's face wore a grotesque sneer.

"Frankly, I'm having real doubts about you. Success in business calls for a killer instinct. Do you understand?"

My mouth had gone dry as I searched for something that would speak to him. Could Anson even compute anything other than 'bottom-line concerns'? I sifted through the recent discussions with Nick, for any concept, metaphor or bridge into that cold, cold world. Maybe the perils of Social Darwinism? No, he'd probably only approve!

At that moment, Anson spoke.

"I've read your comments on the support service tenders and am minded to go with the bid from Canvey Solutions. Their CEO's an old friend. Fine-tune some numbers with them."

He passed me some notes.

"Here are some technical queries and suggestions for service specifications. We'll need to locate a centre for running the future South American operations. That needs further study and Canvey's agreement, because they'll provide the staffing. Bring back some answers and then arrange a meeting here between their people and our management accounts."

I turned to leave.

"And I won't require further silly essays. Unless you'd rather work with… or, better still, perhaps 'volunteer' your services to Friends of the Earth!"

19

MANHATTAN

NICK MARTIN

I walked over to the Algonquin Hotel again. Meetings here with Nina had become a regular fixture. We'd dined too, and I'd taken her on to a concert at the Lincoln Centre. I'd have liked nothing better than detouring afterwards to my apartment, a short walk away, but I sensed she'd need to see more seriousness, more commitment to the cause – whatever that was! In a strange way, though, I felt that something long lost was revived just being with her.

Inside the Algonquin, I found Nina sat talking with a highly attractive blonde woman in an exquisitely cut trouser suit. I joined their table and, as I sat, caught an intoxicating and expensive perfume. The woman smiled and then introduced herself as Corinne Flayman, a charity colleague. Nina grinned knowingly, adding that I'd be pleased that Corinne shared the same interests. The woman removed her sunglasses, confirming her stunning appearance. She then excused herself to make a phone call and stepped outside.

With Corinne gone, I told Nina the news about South America, but, against all expectations, she barely reacted – almost as if knowing this already. A disappointing reaction, and having a third party cramp my style certainly hadn't been on my agenda.

"Nina, I'm waiting for you to explain exactly in what way I might help?"

"Yes, I do know. Incidentally, you can speak quite openly because

Corinne is totally in the picture. I wouldn't work with anyone uncommitted. I expect you'd gathered that!"

She gave another dazzling smile.

"You still really want to help, Nick?"

The request that followed was profoundly shocking – even if it would provide a path to spike Anson's guns. For a time, I almost felt disorientated and I later remembered I'd probably been looking into her eyes like some kind of moonstruck adolescent. Despite the objections coming to mind thick and fast, I knew then and there I wouldn't refuse. Modifying Canvey's kit, put by for the operational centre, seemed such an incredible idea. Perhaps her plan was for some sort of 'spyware' installation. I understood that wasn't unknown within industrial espionage. Their idea was that information could be regularly sucked up, and local activists warned of everything planned.

"I almost had the impression that you'd guessed already of Canvey's probable involvement?"

"Nothing really surprises me. You'll find I've many contacts, Nick."

"I'm not quite sure where the new headquarters will be. Robbie said Anson had considered Quito?"

"I don't think so," she replied.

My head spun with the danger, but how could I refuse after she'd described such suffering? She then mentioned a friend who could help with the technical side. It was only later that I realised I hadn't asked how the 'modifications' to the equipment would happen, or who else was involved. I heard myself speak.

"Of course I'll help. The easiest way would be for your contact to take a job with us. The kit could then be quietly modified in our stores. Strangely enough, if we get the contract, it will be me who'll set up and oversee the local base. Strange, because, after our talk, I really wanted to see some of South America for myself!"

The situation's enormity was eased by another dazzling smile.

"Wonderful! Actually, I suspect you will get the contract, Nick. I'm really thrilled the way things are working out."

Corinne returned and looked at Nina enquiringly.

"Nick is with us. He could get Marco a position in his plant, so he can prepare things!"

"How?" Corinne asked.

Her sunglasses were off again and I upwardly revised my opinion of her looks –soon running out of superlatives.

"Easy," I replied.

"As Deputy HR Manager, I could place him in the warehouse. Vacancies come up there regularly."

They smiled, appreciatively.

"Marco knows his stuff," said Corinne. "Don't worry."

Nina looked at me directly.

"You see, if we can know the plans as they're made, so much the better!"

"I guess so, but how?"

"The answer's in your pocket," Corinne said.

"What, mop up spilt water with our hankies?" I said with mock incredulity. "Great thinking!"

Nina rolled her eyes, but a small smile played around her mouth.

"No, you idiot, the cell phone!"

"Put phones in the system boxes?"

"Don't be silly. Look, even as we sit here, conversations, pictures and videos whiz all around us. Mobile links to the internet have been available for years, now."

"Parts of the system may not connect to the internet."

"No, Marco can install miniature devices based on mobile phone technology," Nina claimed. "They broadcast a digital facsimile of processed data. If needed, microphones could even be concealed in the screen assembly. We've looked at your standard flat monitors. Microphones and pinhole devices could easily be introduced. For example, in those small speaker apertures, set into the frame."

I couldn't help but notice, she hadn't for a moment doubted I'd cooperate!

"If the new centre is networked, and that should be standard, we can continuously keep up to speed with their plans!"

In imagination, I was already in the dock, and a prosecutor was summing up. Words like 'conspiracy', 'industrial espionage', 'commercial and intellectual property' rattled about my head and my guts clenched violently.

"I get the idea, but it's highly illegal. I could... we could all be locked up!"

Nina's beautiful face clouded.

"Remember Arahtis' talk, Nick. Lives are at stake. Listen, I lived near Cochambamba and saw what happened when a multinational took over. You said you were impressed by my broadcast?"

I nodded weakly.

Corinne smiled intensely too. I suddenly felt pathetic, as my final resistance drained away.

"Don't worry, Nick. We'll be safe. We're all in this together."

Even as the voice of reason delivered its warning, I knew I'd ignore it.

"I never thought a charity – or any NGO for that matter – would be involved in anything like this?"

She smiled, probably sensing the tide turning.

"The forces opposing us are powerful. We must do whatever is necessary!"

I was adrift, and sensed they could easily run rings around me.

"Look. I know about the power of big business, the links between corporations and government, and the potential for corruption. Which is why we're even having this conversation."

Nina leaned forward, touching my arm.

"Of course. I didn't mean to sound patronising. It's just that some corporations are devious and have enormous resources. As a small, relatively powerless group, we sometimes have to think outside the box."

I nodded.

She continued.

"Who knows what tricks Anson will pull? It's rumoured that some well-connected corporations occasionally get helped by the official intelligence apparatus. These days, that includes private contractors – so we do what we must!"

An impressive argument, that didn't ease my fears one iota. Truth to tell, I felt so entranced by them that disentanglement wasn't even an option.

"In the 1960s, US Intelligence definitely infiltrated domestic activist groups," Corinne said. It's happening again – but now with up-to-date technology and legislative cover. Anyway, putting corporate interests first is virtually official policy!"

What a thought! I leaned back, and looked at the surrounding faces for any signs that we were being observed. In the far corner, a fat man crammed food into his puffy face. Next to him, two well-dressed middle-aged women laughed together. A nearby couple gazed at each other adoringly. It was difficult to see any as potential spooks, but maybe that's how it worked? Taking a long sip of coffee, I fiddled with a sugar packet and weighed the implications.

"Okay, you've warned me, but I'm still in. Others face even larger risks if we don't take a stand. We're just a small group confronting a huge wave. My only experience of surfing involves a mouse and monitor. To mix the watery metaphors even more – we're all in the same boat!"

Both women smiled. Nina reached over and gently stroked my wrist.

"Have Marco apply for a warehouse job," I said. "I'll set up an interview." I winked. "Amazingly, I happen to know already that he'll be successful! I assume Marco speaks English?"

"He's Chilean, but has excellent English."

I left the hotel, strangely elated. The evening hadn't exactly been conducive to romance, but we'd be together again soon.

Three days later, a job application for Marco Gonzalez reached my desk. I only hesitated for a moment, before making up my mind. I wrote 'approved for i/v', and passed it to my assistant for interview. Batch interviews for miscellaneous staff were Thursdays, and the next day I saw Marco's name on the schedule. When Thursday came, I saw the assistant speaking with a well-built young South American who I supposed was Marco. Hopefully, she'd be suitably impressed and I could sign off the forms – 'approved for employment' – without complications. Later, I prepared the way by checking current vacancies with Rick Diego, the warehouse supervisor.

The following Monday, I took Marco down to the warehouse, and made a quick detour into a side room.

"Marco, I'll do what I can to be helpful, but, from now on, we mustn't speak openly. If you need to communicate with me, do it through Nina."

"Actually, my contact is Corinne, though she's constantly in touch with Nina. This is her number."

I took the small card with a number but no name, and slipped it straight into my breast pocket. This, for some reason, reminded me of my first meeting with Nina. Moments later, everyone was 'smiles and handshakes', as Rick Diego was introduced to his new warehouseman...

20

MANHATTAN

ROBBIE JAMES

Two days later, I watched a contingent from Canvey Solutions file into Marquetcom's general meeting room. What a wooden crowd – almost clones of Marquetcom's own 'bean counters.' I felt perspiration on my brow and avoided looking at Nick. Maybe Anson was right – I wasn't cut out for a business career. Still, I did know the importance of being discreet about our relationship, and waited until the meeting was well under way before risking a glance.

We'd continued to meet outside of work, sharing outright scepticism of corporate life and dislike of our employers. I wondered if others felt oppressed by a system obliged to first seek profit, without moral regard for others – or were we just isolated oddities? With most workers now feeling vulnerable and keeping quiet, it was difficult to know.

A bundle of financial projections were circulating, but I felt jaded and instead thought about our discussions at the little Italian restaurant. Privately, Nick and I were as one in hoping that the whole project would somehow unravel.

Recently, Nick had shared another part of his identity – a small-time writer about social issues. Perhaps I should share my secrets, too? As the meeting dragged on, I forced myself to make notes. It seemed so frustrating, being together yet unable to discuss anything that mattered!

Anson's voice boomed, and broke into my reverie.

"Well. So, how will local labour costs be capped?"

I looked up. Anson's face was set into a vicious snarl, and looking my way. Adrenalin flooded because I knew that, to him, squeezing labour was almost an article of faith.

"Sorry," I began, "I must have left…"

"'Your brains at home," completed Anson.

Nick interrupted.

"We thought Canvey would address this issue during local recruitment. Rob certainly raised it in our discussions. I'm afraid the neglect in clarifying this in the draft proposals was my fault."

Anson's face relaxed and he grunted.

"Get it corrected then."

One I owe you!

More public humiliation was avoided, but, after Canvey's team left, Anson bawled me out again, adding:

"You're such an unassertive little person!"

I slunk away to nurse my latest wounds, but resentment was building like a pressure cooker with a blocked valve. Nick had been adamant that, from an HR viewpoint, Anson's behaviour constituted bullying. Redress might be technically possible, but I didn't fancy my chances. I had a plan, though, and now might be just the time.

Later that afternoon, braced for sarcasm or worse, I asked to discuss something with Anson. Perhaps the old man's earlier savagery had drained some poison, because he seemed uncharacteristically benign.

"What's up, son?"

"Biff, I know this mightn't be popular, but after researching the matter, I think we could find ourselves at risk of severe negative publicity by water activists."

His face darkened.

"'No, please hear me out, because I'm thinking of the company. A PR disaster for a PR and marketing business would be really bad optics."

"Continue."

"Activists will always be activists, but shouldn't we play to our strengths?"

"Explain."

"By minimising negative effects ahead of time! We're among the best, if not the best, PR outfit on the planet. So, let's work up such a good advance campaign that whatever is said later will be neutralised. I could make a start. After a generation of charity rock concerts, environmentalism and the climate thing – times have changed. People have changed, too. We ought to get ahead of the game and think smarter!"

Biff quietly stroked his chin.

"Don't tell me you're waking up at last? Okay, but I'll be watching, so don't fuck up!"

"Studying our other PR and media work in depth would really help," I said. "You know – to have it be congruent with the house style."

Anson looked piercingly and his watery blue eyes didn't blink.

"Okay. The public campaign files are in cabinets next door. You've seen some already. By all means study them, but, if you really want to understand how it works, you need to study the raw data they're built from. Those files are here."

He pointed to the rows of black cabinets on the back wall, reached into his drawer and tossed over a bunch of keys.

"The keys are for those cabinets. Seeing you're at last showing some initiative, study the real material. Start with the official marketing releases next door – then come back here and see the real data."

He laughed and shook his head.

"Let's hope that doesn't upset your delicate feelings! Hopefully, I don't have to stress total confidentiality. With the right know how – changing turds into gold nuggets is real easy!"

I gripped the keys tightly, barely able to believe my fortune.

"I'm leaving for the Hamptons and will be out for the next two days. Help yourself and I'll explain to Nancy. Confidentiality is an absolute must. By the way, any government contracts are out of bounds. Keep right away!"

Anson left. Perfect! It had worked far better than I could ever have imagined! I sat a while at Biff's magnificent carved desk – temporarily master of all I surveyed. Nancy had said it was from a French chateau and of sufficient quality to grace the French presidential office! I peered down at the gargoyle-like faces carved into its legs. I'd never properly looked before – probably too focused on the gargoyle behind the desk! I tried the drawers, but they were locked. Below the central panel I found the button I'd seen Anson push in meetings – presumably to start recording.

Marquetcom's prowess at spinning was legendary. Rumour had it that Anson and an inside group had helped 'information manage' many controversial issues over the years. Given Anson's warning about government contracts, that seemed quite likely. I'd recently met one of the insiders – an anthropoid type named Brian Tutch. Tutch had been tasked to negotiate with the South American officials and he struck me as being particularly unwholesome.

I recalled a rumour that PR specialists had been contracted to help boost the 'brand USA' image. I crossed to the black cabinets, wondering if it had included Marquetcom. I unlocked the cabinets, high on anticipation. To hell with it, if possible I'd view the forbidden files, too. From my training, I knew something about the murky origins of state propaganda and its corporate cousin – 'public relations'. The industry was apparently founded by Sigmund Freud's nephew, and his seminal book launching the PR industry was titled... 'Propaganda!'

The drawers of the first cabinet easily slid open and I immediately saw files of a dozen or more household names in pharmaceuticals, energy, and the food industry. Some sections had briefings, apparently prepared for Washington's K Street lobbyists. I sampled some more closely – noting Marquetcom's help to contain the fall-out from several flawed drugs, in conjunction with high-powered law firms – including the one now associated with the water privatising plan.

Another cabinet held work for agriculture and chemical companies – including a project trying to mould the public perception of GMOs. This partnered with European associates, because of fears that European antipathy could damage the industry. Lobbyists had held helpful meetings with British politicians. The next cabinet contained damage limitation work about certain celebrity misdemeanours. Material that, if sold, could probably finance early retirement! I quickly dismissed the thought – publicising personal details had too many painful associations.

The contents of the fifth cabinet were perhaps the most intriguing – and included major government commissions. Perception management strategies to help frame 'the war on drugs' and, later, 'the war on terrorism'. I shook my head, wondering when they'd ever get that war *is another form of terrorism.*

I pulled out another thick file: 'Public perception of coca eradication in Latin America'. So, Marquetcom did handle government contracts! It seemed a potentially useful and rather juicy plum!

I moved next door to see some of the finished, public documents, starting with 'Pharmaceuticals' – which I knew to be one of the most profitable industries. Contrary to their spin, the spend on marketing, PR and admin, including political donations, was allegedly twice that of research and development. How much had come Marquetcom's way? I pulled out several large box files labelled 'Kane & Field Pharmaceuticals'. On the top were advertising layouts for a product called 'Peak-Me'. This sounded intriguing. A product combining an anxiolytic and a performance enhancer, which was designed for 'peak performance' in the workplace. I soon realised that it had run into difficulties. That sometimes happens with pharmaceuticals, but this seemed as good a place as any to get a feel for the house style. First, I read through the public file, before returning to Biff's office and looking through the corresponding 'raw data'.

I spread the papers out over the huge desk – and they were dynamite! Not just the slick marketing, but a systematic plan to invent a whole new health syndrome with the corresponding product solution called – 'Peak-Me'. The preamble quoted research outlining increased anxiety caused by demands for high 'performance' in both the private and public sectors, where presentations and public speaking are often needed. Apparently, this is a major source of anxiety, even of panic, for many. With the general workplace insecurity and feeble union cover, employers were free to demand ever more.

No argument there – I thought.

The marketing strategy cleverly elided the usual idea of 'performance anxiety' as a kind of 'stage-fright' – with the corporate obsessions about measuring and appraising 'performance'.

The briefing notes said:

Nowadays, both individual and team performance is typically evaluated. Contracts are routinely monitored and rated against 'performance indicators'. 'Performance' is assessed at most levels – and workers remunerated, coached, counselled or dismissed as a consequence...

The implication seemed obvious that, in such circumstances, 'who wouldn't have performance anxiety?' It was a fiendish logic. The campaign would actually highlight insecurity, stressing that the modern workplace required 'peak performance' at all times. Hence the development of 'Peak-Me'.

I read through the suggested advertising copy with grudging admiration. Work insecurity would of course be heightened by globalisation and outsourcing. The briefing continued:

In the public sector, considerable stress comes from targets, goals, appraisals, cuts, insecure funding and unending political interventions. In the private sector, competition, enforced or insufficient overtime, loss of healthcare benefits, threats to downsize or outsource, bank crises and the general fluctuations in the business cycle should ensure regular customers.

In fact, I thought, conditions should be ripe for a marketing explosion, potentially covering most of the working community.

I'd probably use it myself! I muttered.

The marketing plan was particularly stunning, and included recruiting well placed medics as 'opinion leaders'. Conferences would be planned where 'product champions' would enthuse – for a good expense package, of course! I looked through the suggested presentation outlines. 'Peak-Me', it said, would:

Address anxiety without drowsiness, cleverly combining anxiolytic effects with properties that boost alertness and performance.

Previously this had been thought unachievable, rather like driving with one foot on the gas – the other on the brake!

I read on, almost in disbelief. We'd analysed many campaigns in training, but building a new syndrome from unnecessary stress was ingenious, in a sick kind of way! Further on were prepared plans for 'awareness sessions', and workplace groups, where 'Peak-Me', would be promoted as the answer. Rewards for the medical 'opinion leaders' weren't mere 'drug lunches' or samples, but far more substantial rewards. Unfortunately, the details and the names of potential invitees were removed.

The door suddenly swung open and my stomach lurched at Nancy's uncharacteristically harsh tone.

"Biff doesn't want anyone to touch those papers!"

I held the cabinet keys up and, seeing the fear in her eyes, shook them from side to side.

"I'm doing a project. Biff gave me the keys and said to continue. Well, his actual words were: 'You may as well do something useful for a change!' He said he'd tell you."

Her face relaxed.

"He must have forgotten. I just don't want to get shouted at again."

"You and me both," I replied, with my most supportive smile.

She left and I continued reading. The campaign was extremely thorough and I thumbed through proposed 'educational programmes', and mock-ups for publication. Another section contained suggested celebrity endorsements.

I went to Nancy's office to find a coffee. She was dealing with a large man with white-blond hair that I recognised as Brian Tutch. I heard her explain Biff's early departure. Tutch growled in response and dislike hit me again, right at gut level. I decided to give coffee a miss and return later.

I continued absorbing the dossier, snorting at what I next read, which seemed surreal and served them right! Apparently, while Kane and Field's lobbyists were pushing for recognition of the new syndrome, they tripped over other lobbyists, essentially pushing further deregulation, 'flexibility' and less workplace protections. I laughed out loud, thinking, *there is no honour amongst thieves and lobbyists.* My notebook filled with examples that I thought could prove useful later.

'Poor old Joe Worker', seen either as a tax cow for milking or else for corporate friends to use and spit out.

I finally reached where everything had unravelled. A multi-pronged campaign was about to launch when clear evidence of kidney damage came to light, and it had to be pulled. This must have been a bitter disappointment. I pulled some key documents together and then headed for the photocopier.

What better insurance, if matters went badly wrong?

2 1

LONDON

OMID

Inside OMID's headquarters, team leader Dick Hennessy hated stopping and resented the interruption. Rather than wasting time with new biometrics kit, he just wanted his busy team outperforming the others. Boots on the ground was what got results, not hi-tec fussing. Still, Donaldson insisted that everyone had to attend this training.

The teams filed into the seminar room to find three civilians waiting, introduced as the 'representatives' from Digisurv. An attractive short-haired blonde woman started the proceedings and began to pitch Digisurv – 'as the leading provider of innovative digital surveillance'. Her speech over, she gave a biometrics refresher – fingerprints, hand geometry, retinal patterns, DNA, voice and facial recognition technology. They knew much of this already, but it soon became clear that the new generation of facial recognition would be the next big thing. This session seemed, at best, one part education to three parts sales pitch, though it soon became clear the decision to deploy the system had been made already. Recognition cameras were already installed at the airport. Immigration officers had long used more primitive equipment to send digital images of faces and irises to a central database via mobile phone technology.

The second speaker, a long-haired techie, discussed the technicalities. Blinding everyone with science, he explained that the software used advanced mathematics and complex algorithms to compare facial images to a notional 'eigenface'. The proposed new system could then potentially interface with digital surveillance cameras in public spaces to help recognise people of interest from stored images on databases. Loud murmuring filled the room. Someone called out that this represented mass surveillance. Others said that, given omnipresent CCTV and the NSA and GCHQ surveillance scandal, things already seemed that way. Donaldson called everyone to order and then a more conventional third speaker described some new live-streaming equipment that could link and cross-reference to databases in real time.

Hands shot up throughout the room, but Donaldson waved them down.

"First, I'd like to explain how we can use this technology."

Donaldson effectively outlined an escalation of their work. McGarvey suggested that, because many organisations were now classed as potential security threats, the priority was surely expanding databases.

"Absolutely," Donaldson agreed.

"This will also be a priority for colleagues in the MIs and Special Branch, but let's be sure to keep our particular focus."

Not to be outdone, Hennessy then suggested linking the new facial recognition data with the existing database of hard-liners.

"We could then instantly identify troublemakers at the usual activist outings – IMF, G8, G20, arms fairs – and track their movements in and out of the country." More murmuring broke out.

"Wouldn't that cross a line?" someone asked. "What about the Human Rights Act?

"Interesting points," said Donaldson. "Remember, the Americans said there's a risk of real terrorists embedding into activist groups, and finding shelter within their networks. Remember, most terrorist groups hate our way of life and see US and UK business interests as legitimate targets! We should follow the American lead and include troublesome activists on the list. Proper terrorists and subversives and dissidents – big terrorists and little terrorists – if you like. It'll only get messy if we aren't sure who's who! Therefore, I want all our anti-corporate and anti-capitalist friends included. Not just as a one-off operation, but an extension of operational policy, approved at the highest level."

Hubbub broke out, but Donaldson waved them down.

"As you know, we have a forthcoming arms fair. The mayor's office and police have agreed the streets to be closed and where the demonstrators will be allowed. The police will manage the route, but I want some of you operating the new equipment, testing whether it indeed recognises our 'knowns'. I'd like others taking new images to extend the database."

Donaldson paused to allow questioning, which was now sounding critical.

"The public are already unhappy," someone said from McGarvey's team. "I monitor many critical blogs. There was fury about children on the DNA database, excessive CCTV intrusion, and anti-terrorist legislation misused to snoop on minor misdemeanours. They're unhappy about protesters being photographed. If the information about live streaming and image databases gets publicised, the anger could really blow."

"Terrorism is a global issue and I'm afraid the new policy isn't open to challenge. Everyone here knows that activist malcontents are a nuisance, potentially undermining our way of life. That is, after all, why we have the section."

Gill Marney, from Henessy's team, put her hand up.

"We might be overlooking something, Sir?"

"Go on."

"Activists sometimes dress up ridiculously at demos – fairies in pink wigs for example. I know this goes back a bit, but the so-called Tutti Blanchi in Genoa, padding themselves like 'Michelin' men. Images like those won't help build a digital database."

Donaldson smiled.

"Very good question, Marney. You'll get the answer at your team briefing. Okay, thanks for coming this morning, everybody. Now let's get on with it!"

Hennessy self-motivated by turning the pressure up and he used the same strategy with everyone else. Back at the team's meeting room, he kept a lively pace.

"I want us moving forward at full throttle. Take care, obviously, but we don't want McGarvey's team getting ahead. I want to see results, images where possible, movements recorded and contacts logged. For a selected group – conversations recorded. You have approval for bugs and taps on level 2s, and key internet traffic to be monitored."

Gill Marney put up her hand.

"The Gov said you'd get back to my question."

JOHN KING

"Yes," he replied.

Hennessy sat on the table looking thoughtful and everyone became silent.

"Let's remember the purpose of this exercise. The service monitors extremists threatening our way of life. In the past, that meant monitoring communists, anarchist groups, and assorted malcontents and troublemakers. More recently, our brief has included activists disrupting business or attacking transnationals or global trade policies. Of course, trade is our lifeblood and, in many ways, protecting strategically important business interests lies at the heart of foreign policy. The expanded task, therefore, fits nicely."

He looked for agreement and then continued.

"Of course, naive people, folk who don't really understand how the world works, might get caught up by surveillance. People obsessed with single issues like... I don't know, sweatshops, or the fate of some obscure crab etc. Recently, these damn people don't just stick to their preoccupations, but can group together. Some almost think of themselves as a 'global social justice' movement. Naive people can easily fall prey to hard-liners."

Dave Chappell, a senior agent, chipped in.

"Surely sensible people see them as 'flakes', Sir."

"True, but more and more 'sensible folks' are being sucked in by propaganda, particularly since the last banking fiasco. When anti-corporate agitators and environmentalists claim that the 'wicked corporations' are stripping the Earth and spoiling habitats, things can get problematical. Cosy, middle-class people, full of TV wildlife programmes, who believe themselves 'environmentally aware' – can get exposed to hard-liners and eco-terrorists. They disrupt business and threaten our values."

Chappell rolled his eyes.

"Surely people know which side their bread's buttered, Sir."

"Historically, when a population gets a sense of grievance, it can sweep things away. Look what happened in the US when the people turned against Vietnam or indeed Middle East adventures! Also, the American angle – the fear that active terrorists could embed within the ranks of extremists and loonies."

Gill Marney held her hand up.

"So, what's our strategy?"

"Good question, Gill. Call it a Trojan horse approach. We want you to cosy up, or, if you like, to infiltrate. Get inside their groups and organisations. Incidentally, that's the answer to your earlier question. You'll know who they are, including the pink fairies, because you'll be with them! The Americans are doing that already. We also need to do the same..."

2 2

OXFORDSHIRE

SIMON MAHER

The 'Business Pathology' group, as we'd tentatively called ourselves, held our third meeting at Stephen Grotstein's home, near Witney, Oxfordshire. As we entered the drive, I peered up at the distinctive twisting chimneys in the oldest part of the house. If I was right, they were extremely old. I looked at Andrew, and said:

"I must ask Grotstein about the place's history."

"You'll be lucky," Andrew replied with a grin.

"He'll challenge your syntax, quibble about the semantics and question your references for the word 'history'!"

"Probably," I said. "I just hope we don't get more lectures."

Grotstein met them at the door, shaking his head. He waived us in, muttering. "Martin's here, but he's in a bit of a flap."

They entered carrying a stack of printouts.

Farrelly was in the library, looking tense.

"Hello, you two! Given what was said the first time, I should tell you before we start that I've also had some documents stolen. Important material, I'm afraid."

"Are you really sure, Martin?" asked Grotstein sceptically. "I lose things all the time!"

"Quite certain," Farrelly replied. He turned to Andrew.

"Actually, it included that material on water privatising you asked me to look at."

"From where?"

"My office in town. Not the Secure Unit, thank goodness, or I really would be in trouble! I've also had a car break-in, though that isn't a first. Nothing taken this time, but I think someone was searching for something – those papers perhaps?"

I momentarily shivered.

"You were given a copy, but those were exactly the same documents stolen from my apartment. Other things disappeared too, though, really, I can't imagine opportunistic thieves bothering. I think this material was targeted!"

"Maybe the talk of sociopaths attracts more of them," said Farrelly, winking.

Grotstein snorted.

"Not exactly psychological, Martin. Pop metaphysics, maybe! Look, are we going to start?"

"I was just joking – but those papers definitely were taken. Something else. I've now received a stiff letter from the Health Authority, pointing out aspects of my contract and asking to be advised of future speaking engagements. It feels like a warning to shut up. Andrew, you were warned about keeping your head down, too?"

Andrew looked at Grotstein before replying.

"Exactly. Look, Stephen, we really do think something's going on."

Grotstein snorted again.

"Martin, I realise psychiatry is on the soft side of real science. Perhaps you've seen too many patients?"

I was starting to think Grotstein was a crusty old bastard, but Farrelly smiled and Grotstein grinned back.

"Yes Stephen, but please let's keep our minds open, shall we? Simon, you were going to share your internet trawling."

I passed the bundles around, though the response seemed muted.

"Not punchy enough?"

"You know what," said Andrew. "I think, to have real impact, we need original work – interviews with experts and victims. I could try to sell the idea to the college, because business schools need a definite position these days. After the corporate and finance sector disasters – many schools talk up the 'corporate responsibility' elements in their syllabus. The business school doesn't exactly love our unit, but we nevertheless come under their umbrella. In the current climate, it might be difficult for them to deny the relevance!"

Andrew winked, and I knew what was coming.

"Even though, for 98% of the programme, they school their students on the finer points of dodging social responsibility and worshipping the bottom line!"

Grotstein sighed before speaking.

"We'll leave you to explore that one, Martin. You've prepared something for us?"

"Yes."

Farrelly pulled papers out from an expensive looking calf skin attaché case.

"Okay, I believe we must refine our parameters. Last time, I sketched out the clinical features of psychopathy or sociopathy, although we ought to now use the current term – 'anti-social personality disorder'. Now, as you know, I work with the most violent, pathological and obviously criminal examples of psychopathy. We're talking, though, about high functioning 'creative psychopaths'. Not the petty thieves and swindlers that come before the courts, but those in expensive suits that inhabit boardrooms, law practices – even the legislature."

I glanced at Farrelly, and then risked it.

"We also have managers that wear some fairly natty suits!"

"Exactly Simon, and I guess I do too... which shows the problem with throwing about stereotypes and pejorative labels! We certainly don't want to vilify the honest, hard-working business people we all rely on. Rather, throw a little light on those clever, conniving executives from certain big businesses and the financial sector. Those who run scams so big, so audacious, that people can barely grasp what's going on."

"Do you think the public has any appetite for it?"

"Maybe now," replied Farrelly. "After the financial upheavals, many are leery of Wall Street, City bankers and finance sector shysters. The sentiment has also spilled over onto politics and parts of the media who seemed complicit. There was widespread disgust about bank bailouts, which some see as the biggest theft in history!"

"If the system favours greed and self-interest, then the high-functioning psychopath's disorder actually gives them an advantage over normal, more rounded people?" I suggested.

"Leading to the age of the psychopath," replied Andrew. "Perhaps we're already there!"

Farrelly broke in-

"Unfortunately, when such types get into positions of leadership or ownership – they can build organisations in their own image. Their employees get stuck with operating a pathological system – just to live!"

I noticed Andrew was nodding vigorously.

"I agree! Where an organisation is led by a sociopath, everyone has to accommodate to their strange moral code, which can engender a kind of secondary sociopathy in staff. Previously reasonable and normal people find they have to justify unreasonable policies. It's often painful both for them and their clients. Relationships between government and public services were affected like that during austerity and cutbacks!"

I interrupted.

"Exactly. After losing my last job, I had to deal with the benefit and housing agencies. It was dehumanising! It felt like an inhuman 'processing'. I doubt that their staff who were normal enjoyed it much, either."

"You have to realise that true psychopaths are qualitatively different from ordinary people," said Farrelly. "However bright or charismatic they might seem, something essentially human seems missing. Unfortunately, under our economic system, being a little sociopathic pays. In the case of big business, it pays profoundly."

Farrelly passed around papers.

"Some researchers claim business is the 'higher-functioning' psychopath's favourite environment. Of course, some also gravitate to law or politics because of the power it gives them over others."

I looked through Farrelly's handout as he continued.

"Ruthlessness, comfort with deception and manipulation often leads to rapid promotion. So, their character pathology paradoxically gives an advantage! Psychopaths can make quick, though often short-term, decisions, without worrying over the effects on others. That's a valuable asset."

"You mean valuable for companies and investors?" I asked.

"Exactly. The focus on short-term advantage suits the economic system admirably. They'll do whatever is necessary to boost annual figures rather than worry about long-term effects."

Even Grotstein was taking notice now. Farrelly, having their attention, ploughed on.

"Actually, you can make a taxonomy of pathology by noticing where in time the subject is most focused. Depressives, poor devils, are usually preoccupied with their miserable pasts. Anxious patients worry about the future. Psychopaths, though, are mainly interested in 'now'. They want what they want, and want it now! Typically, they aren't overly concerned with the future and don't easily learn from past experience. Of course, these both need the ability to reflect."

"Aren't you elevating the psycho-babble too highly?" asked Grotstein.

"You admitted last time, these descriptions are mainly invented by psychiatrists."

"Maybe, Stephen, but just consider for a moment. Having a lack of empathy makes savage budget cuts, lay-offs, outsourcing and similar acts – a breeze! Look at what showed up during the financial catastrophe. Not just outright fraud but a love of risk taking, and also the charisma and persuasiveness often associated with psychopathy. With the focus on short term, their 'solutions' to the problems they helped to create typically involve others losing their jobs."

Andrew's brow furrowed.

"That all rings bells. I once knew someone just like that, rather well. I suppose your forensic unit is the heavy end of the market. We shouldn't lose our focus on the corporate rogues!"

"Exactly. We work with murderers, rapists and armed robbers. These are clearly wrong, but what about corporate raiders? As someone once pointed out, they mightn't kill people, but they sure kill jobs and companies. They don't use knives, but they certainly strip out assets. Executive robbers can happily plunder pensions. Corporate psychopaths might not shoot employees, but happily fire them!"

I was feeling overloaded and put my attention on the Mandala opposite until the sensation passed.

Farrelly continued.

"Consider the psychology of politicians who knowingly manipulate their voters, or the politics of arms sales. It's positively frightening! Did you know the cost of corporate crime in the USA last year was probably more than..."

"Can we get back to these meetings now," interrupted Grotstein.

"Yes, I think that information on the ways sociopaths impact public life should enter public discourse. Many pointers can be found in their language and I planned sharing some useful research with you."

He riffled through his paper and looked momentarily flustered.

"Ah, I've left it upstairs. Excuse me a moment, gentlemen."

With Grotstein gone, Andrew briefly summarised how the 'Corporation' had reached its current status.

"You mean that, originally, they had to prove their worth to society before being incorporated?" I asked.

Farrelly interjected.

"That's right, but quickly before Stephen returns and gives another lecture, can I just summarise where I think we're at? First, we agree that our aim isn't just kicking at certain styles of capitalism or globalisation. Granted, we believe corporate-driven globalisation can be..."

The door abruptly swung open, and Grotstein entered, looking ashen. He dropped into a chair, with a hand on his chest.

"I take it back. Something *is* going on."

"What happened?" asked Farrelly. "You look like you've seen a ghost."

"I saw something alright, but I assure you it was alive!"

We heard a car speeding away.

"Hear that? They're leaving."

"Who?"

"Sorry. Look, I went to my study to find the papers and, as I opened the door, someone pushed me over. Two men dashed to the window and escaped."

"They had a ladder?" asked Farrelly.

Grotstein stared at the floor.

"I'm afraid I got out rather quickly."

"Are you okay?" asked Farrelly.

Grotstein nodded, his hand still on his chest.

"Let's look," I suggested.

We all trooped up to the study and, sure enough, a window was wide open.

"They were dressed in black or dark blue clothing and attacked me as soon as I entered. One was fiddling with the power point, down there. Look, the plate's half off!"

"Shit, probably trying to place a bug... possibly a device using the house wiring."

Grotstein exhaled dramatically, shaking his head.

"Sounds rather fanciful!"

I bit my lip, to stop reminding Grotstein why we were now gathered in his study!

"Nothing outside," said Farrelly, moving back from the window.

Grotstein suggested a nip of scotch and we returned downstairs.

"It's ridiculous. Who'd be interested in us?"

I swallowed before answering.

"I can only think of two possibilities. We released a controversial article about water privatisation – well, it was Andrew really. Big money is potentially involved. I wonder if Bellevivreau, or one of the others, want to monitor what we're doing?"

Andrew nodded, but Grotstein's brow wrinkled. He snorted.

"How?"

"Well, private investigators don't just handle divorces or missing people. Some work for the corporate sector. It's called industrial or corporate intelligence and apparently is a growth industry."

Andrew nodded.

"From a report we saw recently, national security mightn't be the only focus of that listening station in Gloucestershire – or, for that matter, the others worldwide."

"What does that have to do with industrial espionage?" asked Grotstein.

I beat Andy to the answer.

"Information has been known to also reach business – purely for the home team, of course!"

"What's the other possibility then?" asked Farrelly.

"I suppose, the intelligence community itself," I said.

We heard a familiar snort, a presage to Grotstein's reply.

"Don't be absurd. Why us?"

"I don't know."

"In the sixties, there was a scandal in the States mainly about spying on anti-war activists. It's happening again. Even 'greens' and environmentalists have been targeted and ended up on 'no-fly' lists."

"Surely not here though?" said Andrew.

For all his usual disbelief, a pale Grotstein stayed silent.

Andrew sounded irritable.

"Okay Simon, we get that you're clued up on the strange ways of the intelligence services, but, really, why should we interest them?"

"I honestly don't know."

"I suppose we have written some unpopular things? I gather MI5 had more than a million files by the 1980s and, given the recent scandals, it's likely they now have information on quite a chunk of the population."

Dismay descended.

"I don't know about everyone," said Andrew, "but I've had enough for tonight."

Although Grotstein now had his papers on language patterns, he nodded agreement.

I looked around the room.

"Andy and I are attending an arms fair protest next week in London. Anyone care to join us?"

Neither could commit, so we agreed to meet again in a fortnight. Grotstein would then present his material on language patterns.

We left, and returned to Oxford, unaware of anything else.

A LITTLE LATER ON in New York City, an encrypted email report arrived from Klieberman–Boss, the PI company used by Biff Anson for many years. Anson had personally briefed old Jack Klieberman and settled into a large leather chair in his office to read the report – pausing only for antacid.

So, Andrew wanted to fire pot shots across the Atlantic, but two could play that game. This required careful handling. Little Andy might believe himself a hot-shot academic, but this plan was far too important to be scuttled by his activities.

He read on: *More muckraking about water privatisation, and also potentially slanderous nonsense about so-called business psychopaths.*

After another swig, he re-read the transcription.

This needed a decisive derailing...!

23

BROOKLYN

NICK MARTIN

I arrived at the office early, while it still smelt of polish. I scanned my to-do list and then checked for new post. One item in particular caught my eye – a report and note from Dr Alan Simmonds: 'Workplace implications from consultations with TM.'

Pinned to Alan's report was a handwritten note.

Hello Nick. I'm enclosing a report on the workplace implications from my work with Timothy Mills, formerly of your Sales Dept. Thank you again for the referral. Alan.

I pursed my lips and started to read. No-one here knew that Alan had also been my therapist for the past three years.

As agreed, the report contained virtually no personal details concerning Tim's treatment, except to say that his move to Marketing seemed helpful. The focus was Canvey's employment practices. I certainly couldn't argue with the headline findings.

Key issues include workplace bullying and a long-hours culture sustained by messages from top management, which, intentionally or not, accentuate insecurity by encouraging an overly competitive environment.

The examples were extensive. Dr Simmonds stressed that this was a medical/psychological and not a legal view. Nevertheless, he considered that the company could conceivably be exposed to litigation for stress-induced illness. Recommendations followed. Given the prevailing attitudes, incorporating these into something acceptable to the Board, seemed unlikely. I thought of Robbie's 'Peak-Me' story. It would have been eaten like candy, here!

I started to draft a report, with a heavy heart. It felt like my duty, though it would probably be an empty exercise. Worker protections were so feeble that naked exploitation was reframed as 'offering extra opportunities'!

Since meeting Nina, the corporate world was even less appealing. The truth was – I really wanted out. Perhaps helping Marco would be a first step.

I looked out at the unattractive view. The few trees appeared tired and dry. I thought about my own sessions with Dr Simmonds. Recently, they'd been filled with a turmoil that was absent before Nina. The exploration of past relationship failures made me realise just how defended I'd been. In a recent session, I said "I'd previously met the world as if dressed in rubber!" It felt apt at the time, but, on reflection, seemed glib and trite. In Nina's company, I could feel deeply, but also felt unusually vulnerable. As Alan had pointed out, my past relationships with women oscillated between 'distant and brittle' or 'close and vulnerable'. It didn't make much sense – being well educated, travelled, and financially doing well, but sometimes as vulnerable as a child! Alan might talk of 'peeling the layers like an onion', but as everyone knows – peeling onions often leads to tears! I understood therapy, in theory. Childhood conflicts re-experienced within the therapeutic relationship get worked through and hopefully integrated. It was just that it seemed such damn awkward timing, with work so demanding and with a woman I wanted to impress. Had my childhood really been so damaging?

I'd started vigorously refuting this, when the phone rang. It was Farlin's PA – known as the 'gorgeous' Evelyn.

"Hi, Nick, Evie here. Dan wants you in his office at 2.00pm."

Adrenalin pumped. Surely not the Marco thing? No, she'd sounded quite normal and that really would be a security or police matter.

"Thanks Evie. Is it about Marquetcom?"

"You've got it."

I replaced the receiver. The phone rang again, this time it was Nora, my assistant.

"Nick, Rob James from Marquetcom called. You were talking to Evie at the time, so can you please call him back?"

I searched for the number, remembering that Anson was rumoured to sometimes record calls. When I got through, Robbie sounded unusually bright and cheerful.

"Hi, it's good news here! Biff has agreed what we worked up so it's all systems go! Thought you'd like to know."

Despite the bright voice, I felt sure that, really, like me, he'd be dismayed. I jokingly mimed vomiting, while replying brightly.

"That's great! We must meet soon to discuss practicalities. Dan Farlin wants to see me this afternoon. That's probably why."

"How about a working lunch? Say 1.00pm Wednesday, at the usual place?"

I finished up the call, realising that Marco would soon have to act and already feeling light headed with anxiety. What if Dan had somehow got wind of it?

Farlin was an utterly ruthless boss, but – unlike Anson – it was in a disarming, even charming, way.

At precisely 2.00pm, I arrived at Farlin's office. Dan leant back in his chair, looking relaxed and cheerful.

"Come on in, Nick. We heard this morning the South American job is definitely ours!"

He pointed to one of the conference chairs opposite.

"Dan, may I briefly explain something, before we start? You might have heard about an altercation in Kurt's sales team a short while ago? A disagreement about hours and targets, amongst other things?"

Dan's face changed – almost imperceptibly, though I registered a tiny contraction around the mouth and darkening of the eye.

"Before getting to that, Nick, there's something I first want to tell you. I know various rumours have been circulating, but the Board has now decided on relocating our production. A few supervisory jobs will go to the new plant, but assembly will cease in Brooklyn and move to Haiti. The consultancy wing, project management and special services stay. Sales and marketing will be more efficiently handled online. You'll help bring those arrangements about. Now, you were saying something about Kurt's team?"

I held Dan's gaze, but felt winded. The report, critical of Canvey's labour practices, suddenly seemed irrelevant.

"Continue, Nick."

"Sorry, Dan, you caught me by surprise. The thing is, we had some problems so I drafted a report. I think we could be drifting into breach of regulations."

Dan smiled.

"That's what regulations are for. I suspect they'll be academic in Haiti, though – don't you?! This altercation in Kurt's team, I assume we've got rid of the troublemakers?"

"It's just Kurt pushed his people very hard during the recent campaign, and..."

"Good, good," Farlin interrupted. "That's what we want. Kurt's a good guy who's going places."

His face broke into a smile.

"Though maybe not with us! You'll be very busy. Of course, if people wish to relocate with new contracts, they'll be welcome, but I don't somehow think you'll get many takers."

I felt like the ground was falling away and briefly wondered if some physical mechanism lay behind the sensation. It was both an odd thought and experience!

A wide smile spread over Dan's face.

"I'm sure you'll cope."

"When did you plan announcing this?"

The smile became wider.

"Why do we have an HR Department?"

"You want me working on relocation, redundancies and the South American centre?"

"It'll be reflected in your next package. Anyway, our shareholders should be pleased."

Inside, I silently screamed.

It's kow-towing to bloody shareholders that leads to job losses here and exploitation overseas!

I regained my composure and asked:

"And South America?"

"Yes, both I and Anson want you to take the lead in setting up the operational HQ. That will include sorting out support staff and the IT requirements."

"Where, though, Dan? I understand Caracas was mooted at one stage."

"Yes, that was the other thing I wanted to tell you. Caracas was considered, but there's far too much nationalist sentiment and, anyway, it's now become a basket case. Their priorities got very strange and inflation's gone mad. It's too insecure and not a good environment for business."

They used to put their own citizens first, I thought, recalling past comments by Nina.

"Marquetcom considered a number of possibilities – and, ideally, they're considering additional privatisations elsewhere. Bolivia is ruled out because of that damned Cochambamba episode."

Typical Farlin sensitivity!

Dan leaned forward.

"We thought long and hard. Could it be Ecuador – a beautiful country with exceptional resources. Guyana also seemed interesting from an English language point of view, but there are infrastructure problems."

I imagined the map, and tried to anticipate. Paraguay? I couldn't even think what that was noted for – hiding ex-Nazis? Peru? Vast water resources in the Amazon basin, but huge deserts on the seaboard.

Dan spoke again.

"So, we decided together on Bogotá, Colombia."

I froze.

"It's really dangerous, though, Dan? Isn't Bogotá one of the world's murder capitals?"

"It'll be fine. Strategically, it makes sense. We understand that suitable premises are available in an excellent location – the Alvenida Jiminez de Queseda. We've talked with a Realtor there. It sounds ideal, but I'd like you to check it out. You'll need to sort out a task team for later, to help with local recruitment."

I suddenly became aware that I'd slumped, and straightened myself. Dan had moved on and started enthusing about beautiful colonial architecture, but I could only picture gun-toting coca barons and kidnapping scenarios. Dan gurgled on about the climate and year-round spring temperatures – because Bogotá was eight and a half thousand feet up in the Andes. Outwardly smiling, his eyes stayed as cold as ice.

"Spring, Nick, though it's only four degrees from the equator. Imagine that!"

I returned to my office feeling dazed and decided to leave for home.

A hot shower and change didn't help much, but, later on, I met with Nina and Corinne for food on Amsterdam Avenue. I felt battered and sick for Canvey's workers. Nina, though, was surprisingly upbeat about the choice of Bogotá.

"It's not so bad, Nick. We've contacts there. Our Colombian brothers have had similar struggles with plundering corporations."

"It's one hell of a dangerous place. That's all I know."

"Don't worry. We have helpful friends."

She stroked my arm. It was the second time today I'd been told not to worry. It was easy to say, though her touch sure felt good. She leaned over and kissed me and then abruptly stood.

"I'm sorry. As I explained on the phone, I have a meeting. You need to discuss Marco's task with Corinne. See you tomorrow."

I watched her graceful movements as she exited, while Corinne smiled disarmingly.

"Will it take very long to set up the centre?"

I shrugged and told her the day's developments.

"I've been told to move things as quickly as possible. There was one awkward moment when Dan Farlin wondered if local procurement of IT might have advantages. Fortunately, I persuaded him our own was best, because we know everything about keeping it running."

I couldn't help a grin.

"Though, of course, we'll need to know a little more than usual with these particular models!"

It seemed the one bright moment in a rather grim day.

"Dan, my boss, wants me checking out a potential site and has already lined up a local Realtor!"

"I know Bogotá well," she replied. "As Nina said, we have helpful friends."

I felt concerned, because Dan seemed to know lots about Bogotá, too. He said that, of the most precious commodities, like oil, gold, platinum, emeralds and so on, Colombia has sixteen! Maybe he, and Anson, intend looking for other opportunities. Apparently they're old friends."

"Maybe," she replied. "He was right about Colombia's natural wealth, though. Why else have they had decades of conflict?"

"I'd never thought…"

There was something disconcerting about her manner and the way she held eye contact. As we parted, she squeezed my arm.

"Thanks, Nick. We really appreciate your help."

There it was again. Eye contact held just a little too long. Corinne seemed to somehow meld sensuality, studiousness, with faux innocence. Like South America, itself, she seemed more than a little confusing and thoroughly hot!

24

NEW JERSEY USA

JUDY ALTON

It was nearly time, and the planned move felt exhilarating. Philadelphia, as a city, had always appealed. Its atmosphere, manageable size and rich cultural life. The only future drawback to Judy was losing her friends and the local groups. She looked at the card in her hand, and then the jumble of partially packed boxes strewn over the floor. Certainly, her work with 'A Fairer World' and their meetings had played a major part in her life. Even with packing to finish, she'd attended the climate change meeting. Images of freak weather, ozone holes and glacial melt had remained with her all day. The meeting on 'water' had been another highlight – particularly given Andy's recent work.

Judy looked at the card again. She'd talked several times with the pleasant young chairperson, who passed his card – Nick Martin, Independent Journalist. They'd chatted again last night. He apparently now had an assignment that would take him to Bogotá. She certainly didn't envy him that! Returning the card to the drawer, she sighed and then emptied the whole lot into a nearby empty packing carton.

With the removal van due first thing in the morning, the amount left felt quite daunting. She was making a final check of the kitchen cupboards when the phone rang.

"Hi, Mom! How's packing going? Finished yet?"

"Andy. Thanks for asking! No, chaos reigns and it's tomorrow. I'm very excited, though."

"Great! I'm pleased. Philly's a civilised place and I'm sure you'll be happy there. Did you get my letter and the paper?"

"I meant to phone, but what with the move... I'm very proud, though. I already thought as much, but your paper filled in the details. Excellent!"

"Thanks."

"Mind you," she teased, "I worried about these things since before you were born. Still, you've explored it far more deeply. I'm really proud!"

"Thanks Mom, though it was you who woke me up to these things in the first place."

"I'll take that as a compliment. 'A Fairer World' had a powerful meeting on climate change last night. Have you researched that?"

"Yes. Many of the causes are similar to the other things I've written about. Rapacious business has much to answer for."

"I so wish your father could understand that!"

She heard a long exhalation before he replied.

"Anyway, I just wanted to wish you luck. Hopefully, I'll come over and see the new place, when possible. Bye for now, Mom."

She continued checking cupboards and drawers, reflecting that it was typical of Andy to call. Part way through untangling a ball of garden twine, the phone rang again.

"Hi Mom. Just checking you're packed and ready."

It was Freddy.

"Slowly getting there," she replied.

"Does the new place have a pool?"

"No, I'm in one of the old original parts of town."

"A shame. I hope you're getting cabled up this time."

"I hadn't really thought of it."

"You should get some of those curved 3D screens in the new place."

"Possibly, though I don't watch all that much."

"Actually Mom, there is something else. I've a friend moving up your way soon. I'm thinking of coming with him 'cause I've some business in the North East. I'd like to ask you a favour and, of course, to see your new place as well."

"I'll look forward to it, Fred. Is your friend anyone I know?"

"No, though hopefully you soon will. We'll probably be over in about two weeks. I'll explain everything then."

Fred rang off, but she felt acutely uncomfortable about her different feelings about her children. It was a painful discrepancy. She tried to busy herself when the phone interrupted yet again. She answered with a sense of relief.

"Mrs Alton? It's Eddy here from 'Garden State Removals'. Two small changes for tomorrow. I hope this is okay, but we have another part-load quite close to you. We should arrive about an hour later than previously stated. We'll have a new guy on board called Barry Crane. Frank, whom you met before, has took sick so Barry will replace him. Don't worry, he's well experienced and has excellent references."

A LITTLE LATER, several miles away, in Manhattan, Biff Anson took another call from Jack Klieberman of 'Klieberman–Boss Investigations'.

"Everything is arranged. We'll have someone on the removal truck, so you'll get to know everything."

Biff grunted.

"It'll be fine. You've plenty of reasons to trust our work."

"I suppose so. Anything more from England on what the little bleeding heart is doing now?"

"You bet. A report is on the way!"

At the same time in Moab, Utah, Freddy scratched his head. How to summarise Mom's likes and dislikes? He needn't have worried. Zoltan Heltay, the new communications guy, asked some really clever questions. Things he'd never even thought about before.

"I told Mom we'll arrive in about a fortnight," said Freddy. "You'll be ready then?"

"Yes. Judy sounds very interesting, but are you sure she'll agree?"

"Don't worry, I'm her son. I'm sure Mom will do whatever I ask!"

25

LONDON

OMID HEADQUARTERS

Cooperation between police and intelligence about organised crime and anti-terrorism matters didn't sit well with most of OMID. The thought of cops muddying their turf certainly didn't appeal. Hennessy and McGarvey met to discuss the implications. Infiltration of activist groups had made good progress. Everyone agreed police involvement would only cause complications.

"I suppose we should keep rapport with them," said McGarvey. "Police intelligence might sometimes be useful."

A sly grin stole across his face.

"To pinch the old Military Intelligence joke – unless 'police intelligence' is an oxymoron!"

"They get more powers all the time," said Hennessy. "If this does happen, we need to keep silent about really critical operations. Keep them out of it."

When they finished, Hennessy returned to his office.

He was an old-fashioned team leader, believing in individual supervision and debriefing when team members were working under cover. Gill Marney, assigned to the Oxford area, had been pencilled in for supervision this afternoon. A distractingly pretty blonde, Gill usually attracted considerable attention from men. Even he'd sometimes found keeping his mind on supervision difficult and, with locker-room thinking, jokingly wished that 'debriefing' meant something else entirely!

He sorted out papers for the supervisory session. Oxford had a reputation for producing troublemakers, but it was also a top recruitment location. Gill had done very well linking to the young academic, Simon Maher, and through him to Dr Andrew Alton. Hennessy flicked through Maher's file again. Maher was a level 2, with observed involvement with activists and regular sightings at demonstrations. Visits to certain websites and blogs had been noted. Maher had been selected for closer surveillance, particularly given the association with a troublesome academic.

Gill knocked at Hennessy's door and, after preliminaries, they started supervision, reviewing her full and well-written report.

"I'm pleased with the way you managed to link with Maher and the other Oxford level twos, so naturally."

"Thank you, Sir."

"What are the latest happenings?"

She passed over a list.

"These are the local groups. I've added several new names warranting observation. Our friend Maher turned up in another context, too."

"How do you mean?"

"We struck up conversation at a meeting of local 'greens'. I later attended a meeting of 'GOE', and saw him again. Naturally, I asked appropriate questions at their meeting, and that seems to have impressed him. Afterwards, he came over and picked up on several things I'd asked. He seems a bit obsessive, and likes getting the details right! To cut a long story short, he asked me out for a drink."

Lucky blighter, thought Hennessy.

"What's GOE?"

"'Guard our Environment.' A regional group covering Oxfordshire, Buckinghamshire and Berkshire, following local GMO trials. I tried to get involved, because of rumours local activists destroyed field trials."

"And?"

"Nothing was said overtly, though, at their meeting, they drew attention to crop trials near Bracknell and Wallingford."

"It's the sort of activity Maher probably would like," said Hennessy. "We've recorded him at several demos. He's probably a sucker for direct action."

"GOE gave a very slanted view about GMOs and they undoubtedly spread a negative image. Maher seems quite informed about this sort of stuff."

"The Americans are quite exercised over the negative European press on GMOs. We'll do what we can to correct that."

Fifty minutes or so later, he came to the other matter.

"Let's fix our next session, but I also have other news for you. How about supervision at the same time, same day – in three weeks' time?"

"Fine with me, Sir. What's the other news?"

"We plan sending a small observation group to the States to see how they do things. You have been selected to take part. Actually, it's an exchange, so we'll get some of their people, as will the other services. You'll go to New York City."

"Thank you, Sir. What's involved?"

"That's where your writing prowess comes in. There's a need for developing new protocols for joint working with the rather extensive raft of US Intelligence and security agencies. The current arrangements are far too complicated. You probably won't be involved in a great deal of 'hands-on' work, but we will expect comprehensive write-ups and your later participation in formulating and the new protocol. After that, you continue with Mr Maher and Co. in Oxford! Keep going for now, but, next month, you get to bite the 'Big Apple'!"

2 6

OXFORD

SIMON MAHER

My new female friend certainly was intriguing, but I found one thing puzzling – her patchy grasp of some issues. Strangely, Gill often seemed better informed, when we discussed things the second time. Still, I frequently did further research when something grabbed me – maybe she did too? Anyway, she was fun, pretty, and I'd rather started to enjoy her company. Eventually, I discovered that some women found me somewhat intense! Still, following that lonely patch in Slough, meeting anyone with an interest in important things seemed a minor miracle.

I heard a knock at the door and quickly scanned the room. It still wasn't exactly in much of a shape for entertaining, despite attempts at tidying up. There was a brief awkward moment at the door, which I settled by a ridiculously formal handshake. Gill looked both relaxed and alluring, so I quickly steered the conversation to a known topic – GMOs. We'd gone on for a drink together following the last GOE meeting. Given her enthusiasm, I'd mentioned a certain 'pulling' of a crop trial and might possibly have hinted at some involvement. She'd expressed her wish to be helpful and it had somehow just come out! I rather hoped she'd forget, but instead she fixed me with her pretty blue eyes.

"Simon, I've thought more about those GMO trials. Can I come along next time?"

"I don't know. I'd have to check with the others first. I don't usually advocate law breaking, but someone must stand up or damned corporations will control the entire food chain. If allowed, they'd modify plants to make them infertile, and then lock farmers into buying seeds, again and again! The implications are awful! For example, in India..."

I stopped, realising that I was heading into 'breathless lecture' territory.

She grinned.

"Simon, you give a whole new meaning to the term 'crop circle'!" She laughed. "Sorry, but, don't you remember, they discussed all that at the last GOE meeting! Ever heard of 'preaching to the converted'?!"

Of course, she was right, but stopping didn't come easily – so I continued.

"You see, they get hold of varieties developed by the indigenous people, apply a genetic tweak, patent it and then use law to deprive people of their own heritage!"

"That's business for you, I suppose," she replied.

As her face had clouded, I thought, *Talk to her, not at her – you pompous idiot.*

"How about dinner? Not here. I mean, going out?"

She agreed, and, because it was so successful, I suggested a walk on the weekend up to the ancient 'White Horse', at Uffington.

Gill arrived on Saturday looking wonderful – blonde hair freshly washed and her skin looking radiant. The day was warm and inviting and, unusually, 'preaching' social justice or the environment was far from my mind. We started the climb to the 'White Horse', and I wondered how she'd react if I held her hand. At that moment, she spoke, breaking the spell.

"I agreed with what you said last time, about taking a stand. It makes sense to me, so the next time you take out a trial, can I come?"

"Probably."

The slope got steeper and I just hoped the view from the top would impress. She asked more about my research, and then said a little about her IT work. I found the interest genuinely heartening. She asked lots and kept in strong eye contact. People often tried to silence me, but Gill seemed fascinated by my work. Before thinking, I briefly mentioned the corporate sociopathy idea and the possible social relevance.

As we climbed higher, the fields below looked like a giant patchwork, and distant hedgerows and woods showed flecks of gold and red.

It looked quite beautiful and, as the moment seemed right, I slipped an arm around her. She smiled back up.

"It's beautiful, Gill, but will it stay that way?"

"Or end up as a monoculture?" she replied.

We passed some hazel trees and then passed through a turnstile. After reaching the top, we linked arms and stood taking in the rolling countryside. I felt happier than I had for years. A companion, who nourished mind and eye – could things get better? Her hand moved up my back, cupping my shoulder. She stood on tiptoes and I felt a warm kiss against my cheek.

"What a beautiful view."

She pointed back at me, smiling.

"That one isn't bad, either!"

We descended hand in hand but, half way down, she squeezed my hand, and mentioned a work assignment that would take her to New York for a few weeks. Her firm apparently needed help troubleshooting and bedding in a new system in their US premises. It hopefully wouldn't take long, but it was disappointing.

"Sounds quite an opportunity, Gill, but I'll really miss you – especially now! When do you leave?"

"In about a month's time. Listen, you earlier mentioned your boss, Andrew. What's he like?"

I could hear Andy's voice urging caution, though her sympathies seemed obvious.

"Andy? A good boss – hard working, and often with several projects going simultaneously. Mind you, these days, academics must keep publishing to survive!"

"What kind of research?"

"Currently, access to water supplies, water scarcity and the whole privatising mania. The 'joys' of neoliberalism. Andy seems to thrive on big topics. Globalisation, debt in developing countries, international trade policies."

"Not a fan of globalisation, then?"

"Depends on how you define it. Corporate-led globalisation, no. We certainly believe in international cooperation, but not everything focused on profit. Not many vote for that."

A voice inside whispered, *Ease up – you're ranting again!*

As we continued descending, she slipped over on some loose

ground, and ripped a hole in her tights. I squatted beside her, inadvertently appreciating an expanse of shapely leg as she inspected and brushed around the tear. I helped her up with both hands and we hugged, before continuing down, with my arm encircling her waist.

"This idea of sociopathic attitudes infecting business? Surely tarring all businesses with the same brush is rather extreme?"

"Hopefully not, because that's just what we want to avoid. Most business people are decent folk, but some corporate behaviour is corrupt and rotten. Of course, many business people were burnt by the finance sector conmen, too. As someone said, "they played – but we all paid!"

"What corporations do you mean, in particular?"

Andrew's warning came to mind, so I moved things on.

"We hope to explore more about that in a new project, but it's only at an early stage. Listen, there's a protest at the Docklands Arms Fair in London next week. Andy's coming. How about joining us?"

"A fair? What, antique guns and armour – that sort of thing?"

I slipped on some loose stone, sliding into a gorse bush.

"Yow."

"No, a kind of trade fair. Rich countries showing off their best in killing machinery. You do realise we're one of the world's largest arms exporters?"

She flashed a bright smile.

"You're really rather preachy? First, GM crops and now a peace protester. Are you religious, Simon?"

She darted a look, and then grinned, holding her eyes wide open.

"I hope not because I'm afraid I'm only too human!"

The message seemed clear.

"Don't be daft. Just that we claim an ethical foreign policy, but somehow end up selling arms to impoverished countries and they end up being used for repression."

"I suppose it's a big earner?"

"Yes. Politicians sometimes act like arms salesmen. Intelligence services seem to help, too. It truly is a vile trade!"

Gill looked pale.

"Are you okay?"

"Yes. It was just a little more exercise than usual."

They returned to the car, but the drive back seemed strangely quiet.

I stole some glances, but Gill seemed lost in thought and rather distant. She got out of the car and said:

"Yes. I'll join you for that protest. Phone me."

Everything was alright again!

27

BOGOTÁ, COLOMBIA

NICK MARTIN

My first engagement in Bogotá was with Sergio Fontibon – owner of the Realtors bearing his name. My brief was inspecting the potential new office.

Travelling to Fontibons office was a real surprise. I'd almost expected a small, rather ramshackle place, not a city of six million with impressive high rises, fine churches and handsome colonial buildings.

I hailed a cab. Despite his limited English, the chatty driver decided it was his place to teach me the city's system of carreras, calles, avenidas, diagonals and transversals en route. This, he said, should help me to navigate the city. The Realtor's office was apparently located on a large and well-known Avenida.

Clearly a sociable fellow, the driver waved his hands around worryingly while driving and spoke at a shouting pitch. He pointed to notable sights on the way – like the Teatro Colon, Church of San Francisco and the gold museum. As we sped along, he enthused at length about 'La Lechuga', which I later discovered was a religious artefact in gold and emeralds.

The taxi approached La Plaza de Bolivar, only to hit another traffic snarl. I couldn't help but smile at the shouting and honking. The Latin temperament displayed almost made New York civilised in comparison. Once beyond the Plaza, the traffic cleared, the driver quietened down and I could at last mentally prepare for the appointment. Annoyingly, Marquetcom apparently intended sending Brian Tutch to repre-sent their interests. Robbie James had warned me of this person's closeness to Anson. At that moment, the driver started bellowing again, interrupting my preparation.

"*Bogotá es una ciadad cosmopolitia en constante expansion.*"

"English please," I replied.

"Sorry! I say he always growing this city. Many people all party world now."

"I didn't realise!"

"Like you see balls?"

"Sorry?"

"Where balls fight the man? Look there – Plaza de Toros de Santamaria."

He pointed out a bullfighting arena. I smiled, but wished he'd shut up.

"Not my kind of thing!"

We turned into a Transversal, picked up speed and then turned into an Avenida. Shortly afterwards, we pulled up outside a smart office. I paid the driver, and entered Sergio Fontibon's office. Sergio seemed another happy man – full of smiles and handshakes. In the corner was a large muscular man with blond hair that almost verged on white. I recoiled, despite Fontibon's enthusiasm.

"Mr Nick, may I introduce Mr Brian Tutch, from the Marquetcom firm."

Maybe Tutch's reputation, or perhaps my years in HR, had taught me to read people? In any case, my hand was still hurting from Tutch's bone-crushing handshake. *Arrogant Bastard*, I thought, feeling not just dislike, but curiosity at the strength of my reaction. Certainly, he had a dominant, even menacing, persona. I saw why Robbie struggled describing it. Still, for now, we must cooperate.

"Looking forward to working together," I lied. "Hopefully, we'll soon get things moving."

Tutch grunted and smiled. At least I suppose that was the intention, though, truthfully, it appeared more of a grimace.

We left in Sergio's car to view the property.

"What do you think of our city?" asked Sergio. "It's been called the 'Athens' of South America."

"Like Buenos Aires is known as the Paris of the southern hemi-sphere? No, just joking. It's impressive."

Sergio laughed.

"Yes. I suppose we're not very Greek."

Fontibon's English was good, but Tutch seemed humourless.

."Actually, we speak the purest Spanish in the hemisphere. Ah, we're here – the Avenida Jeminez de Quesada."

We pulled up outside a sleek modern complex.

"Maybe you recognise that name from our history?" asked Sergio.

"Sure," said Tutch. "Gonzalo Jimenez de Quesada – the conquistador."

Sergio looked impressed.

"Yeah. Old Gonzo culled some Indians and brought civilisation," added Tutch.

I gulped, hearing Mr Sensitivity's efforts at conversation – *'culled some Indians'*!

Sergio seemed unmoved, though I suspected he was more of Spanish than Indian descent.

Even before reaching the front door, I realised the reason for my rapidly growing discomfort. Obvious really: Canvey and Marquetcom were twenty-first century plunderers, setting up a profiteering operation in a street appropriately named after a conquistador... and I was here helping to facilitate some more!

We entered the building, with Fontibon chirruping over its various advantages as we looked over the accommodation. So far, so good. The building had been freshly decorated, and had desks and other office fittings from the previous occupier available at a fair price. The configuration of space appeared good, and Sergio confirmed computer re-cabling wouldn't be a problem. Downstairs was a secure cellar with several lockable sections – a feature that particularly interested Tutch. Sergio assured us no other property would better suit our needs and twenty minutes later we were back in his office, discussing the lease. With reluctance, I agreed to meet with Tutch the following day to discuss operational details.

"Señor Nick, I'll find you a better-placed hotel," offered Sergio.

He returned having booked a room at the premier 'Eldorado'.

"You'll be more comfortable with meeting Mr Brian there."

I glanced at Tutch, who bared his teeth in return, and I decided against a repeat of the hand-crushing experience.

Sergio drove me to the Eldorado as I mulled over the day's proceedings. The premise's suitability had been an unexpected bonus and, with no need to look further, I should have time for a little sight-seeing. Why Tutch wanted the secure basement seemed odd, but that shouldn't affect the operation or the cabling – my main concerns. Sergio pulled up outside what was an obviously superior hotel that had uniformed doormen. My bags were swiftly whisked away and, in no time, I was channel hopping the television and inspecting the mini-bar. I checked the time and finally was able to do what had been on my mind, all day. I reached for the phone and, after a short delay, heard her voice.

"Nina, missing you! Bogotá's quite a place. I'm impressed. I've changed hotels to the Eldorado."

I outlined my day, including Tutch and the Avenida property. Just hearing her voice raised my spirits.

"The communications should be good," I said, omitting details.

She asked nothing further, but I felt sure the message was received.

"I've been looking forward to talking, all day."

"Me too. Listen, Nick, we've friends nearby, including someone I'd like you to meet. He's a good man and Corinne's friend. You'll find he's a mine of information on the local scene!"

"Nina, remember that Canvey has government IT contracts. Anything jeopardising that won't be forgiven."

"Trust me. Corinne's friend could be very important in the future."

I swallowed. In the past, South America hadn't been kind to so-called revolutionaries and I didn't need more complications.

"Are you still there?"

"Sorry. Yes, I guess so. How will I find him?"

"Good. Go to the Bar Suba at around 8pm tomorrow. It's at Calle 9-12-24. Corinne will arrange everything. Don't worry, he'll recognise you."

"Okay. Really missing you."

"Miss you too! Hurry back, darling."

I felt warmth just hearing her voice and pushed the concerns away. Fatigue washed over me. Bogotá's night-life would have to wait and I decided to stay with the hotel restaurant. After all, there was probably wrangling to do with Tutch in the morning.

I eventually slept fitfully, drifting in and out, and finally woke from a nightmare. I recalled one very odd section. I'd been tied to a tree with Corinne swinging from vines like some seductive Jungle Jane and parrots screaming in the background. A green lizard crawled onto a branch opposite. The creature opened its mouth, which morphed into the equally repulsive features of Brian Tutch.

I struggled down to breakfast, rather disorientated, with the dream still resonating. As my head ached, I added an effervescent vitamin C tablet to a glass of water and then swallowed two painkillers in preparation. My object now was clearly establishing Canvey's lead role over the proposed centre, and minimising operational interference by Marquetcom.

I'd barely finished breakfast when an unexpectedly relaxed Tutch arrived.

In the event, my fears of a clash were an anti-climax. Tutch seemed only too happy for Canvey to have clear operational control, though he said Anson had ideas for other South American projects and would need the basement, under separate lock and key. Adjustments to cover that part of the leasing costs wouldn't be a problem.

"Why the long face?" he asked. "Lighten up and get yourself a woman. That's what I'm going to do."

Tutch grinned and left. I ordered more coffee, relieved about the trouble-free negotiation. So, my day would be free!

Outside was bright and I walked up to the Plaza de Bolivar. Farlin was right – just four degrees from the equator, but still fresh because of the altitude. I checked the Bogotá guide, and made my way to La Zona Rosa to check out the shops and gourmet food displays. Later that afternoon, I took a cab to La Candalaria district, wandering through the colonial streets and browsing galleries. When evening came, I flagged another taxi for the Bar Suba. My grasp of the city's topography was very slight, but the cab appeared to turn back towards the Presidential Palace and then entered a dilapidated area. Desperate street people picked over piles of refuse. Further on, a small crowd huddled together, but the reason wasn't obvious. I quickly wound up the window and checked the door lock. The place radiated menace and despair, reminding me for the first time of Bogotá's reputation. The taxi abruptly passed out of the area and into civilisation again.

Bar Suba stood in an attractive, though narrow, colonial street. Several restaurants lined the road and hunger was now making itself known. I entered the bar, acutely aware that I didn't even know my contact's name or appearance. Despite the low lighting, I checked faces, but there was no response. I decided to wait ten minutes. I could then leave and claim I'd tried!

The bar was stocked with international beers, so I ordered a Heineken and sat at a table. In the corner was a small band consisting of guitar, bass, piano and a bandoleon. The sort of combo I'd associate with the tango, Argentina, and Piazolla. Lost in the music, I didn't notice someone approach.

"Señor Nick?"

A refined face smiled down at me. The man was tall and slim, with the appearance of an academic. He sat down opposite and smiled.

"How did you...?"

"Corinne described you well! I'm Miguel Hernandez."

We shook hands. His English was excellent, which at least gave me some confidence. After ordering drinks, Miguel asked after Nina in New York, and then for my impressions of Bogotá.

"To be honest, Miguel, I kind of assumed my contact may come from a certain group – one with unfortunate past relationships with the government? Despite the on and off peace negotiations, isn't it dangerous openly wandering about?"

Miguel smiled.

"Yes, you're correct. I was with FARC (the Revolutionary Armed Forces of Colombia – a guerrilla group) and, despite the ceasefire and appearances, certain things are still alive. We always had sympathisers here in Bogotá, but I'm still careful. Of course, there were many roles. Not everyone's a foot-soldier."

I nodded, still unclear what I was doing here. Then Miguel said:

"Fortunately, Corinne and Nina see the big picture. See, if your woman's attacked, you fight for her. If your country is attacked, you join the army. But, when the aim is general plundering of the continent – that requires a special kind of fight."

I swallowed a mouthful of beer. As with Nina, I sensed this meeting wouldn't involve much small talk. Miguel enquired about my work for Canvey and about New York.

I tried to respond generally, but he quickly interrupted.

"Don't worry, Nick, I understand. Corinne and Nina have explained everything, including your role in helping. Look, we all think the same way. A local elite working with foreign corporations will strip us out, if allowed. Oil, gold, platinum, emeralds – they'd take everything. See, one percent of our population owns over half the land. I expect you know what that means!"

I nodded. The man smiled.

"And, now, you're coming for the water!"

I tried formulating a response, but Miguel had moved on to food.

"You must try our local dishes. The chef here is very good and a friend."

He recommended 'Puchero Bogatano', explaining the recipe was chicken steak, yucca, arrachacha corn and plantains. Over the meal, he described the more than five decades of war.

"They say it finished with the deal, but there are still homeless families and plenty of kids with no school place. That hurts, Nick – I used to be a teacher."

"Who fought who, exactly? I mean, Nina explained something about it, but back home this isn't exactly front-page stuff."

Miguel stared into his beer before answering.

"On one side, a murderous right-wing paramilitary force in league with the army. The original paramilitary is said to have disbanded, but large chunks still operate and are potentially around for hire. Facing them were FARC – the Revolutionary Armed Forces of Columbia, and a smaller group – the ejercito de Liberacion Nacional (ELN) Many are unhappy at the supposed peace deal. The government is slow in fulfilling its promises and some want to restart. Many are still seen as dissidents."

"Nina mentioned an ELN in Bolivia," I replied, feeling confused and rather concerned because Miguel's eyes now blazed with a worrying intensity.

"Yes. Our brothers in Bolivia had a similar struggle."

The dessert arrived, 'Bunuelos Bogatanos' – a cornmeal doughnut effort. Certainly tasty, but I could feel pressure on my belt.

"How will it end?"

Miguel shrugged.

"Supposedly it has. We've had many past peace processes though and, somehow, there have always been problems. After the 1985 cease-fire, we agreed to re-enter civil society and formed a political party – the Patriotic Union."

Miguel fixed me with an unblinking stare.

"Can you imagine what then happened?"

I managed the last mouthful of Bunuelos Bogatanos, before replying.

"I don't know. What?"

"Two presidential candidates, elected congressmen, regional deputies, local councillors and, in all, three thousand party activists – assassinated! Perhaps you can understand why we neither trust the state nor those standing behind them! It stopped not that long ago – but we'll see! Tomorrow, I'll take you down to visit the heartland. You'll find it very interesting."

I felt a lurching in my stomach. Miguel seemed okay, but I hadn't bargained on mixing with ex-FARC members!

"I planned to visit the museums tomorrow."

"You can do that any time. You have other things to see now, things Nina wants you to understand."

"This is all fascinating, Miguel, and vital for people living here, but I'm on a job for my firm. Even though I hate their plan, I must keep my nose clean. Anyway, that's essential, if we're to have someone sympathetic on the inside."

"Don't worry, my friend. Spend a little time in the countryside and you'll see why your help is so important. Although it's now supposedly finished, if you're to understand the background of 'Plan Colombia' – you have to see something of Colombia itself! I believe you're at the Eldorado, so I'll pick you up about 8.15 in the morning – unless, of course, you'd rather stick with me. I'm going on to Juanillo's, later. Hot Spanish music and a great atmosphere."

"No, I'd like to explore for a while and then head back. Listen, the taxi drove through a very rough area on the way here, which I'd rather avoid."

Miguel smiled.

"Probably El Carchuto. Yes, it's mostly cleared now, but you're better off staying away. There were riots, some time back when they tried moving beggars and squatters out. A 'clean up' financed by local 'businessmen' hired gangs – that allegedly included off-duty policemen. The place used to be a magnet for down and outs, and apparently some street children got executed in the process."

I gulped my last mouthful of beer as Miguel smiled brightly.

"Right. I'll see you about 8.15 tomorrow."

I left the bar, needing a walk and, after Miguel's talk, vaguely checked that no-one followed behind.

It was still pleasantly warm outside. Hopefully, a walk would clear my mind of ex-guerrillas or thoughts of crazed off-duty policemen despatching street children. I crossed the street, passing another busy restaurant. All seemed normal enough!

I walked to the end of the road, and turned into what at first seemed an ordinary residential road, expecting to pass the back gardens of the road with Bar Suba. The flora by these back gardens, however, was of a quite different type. A collection of women in revealing clothing lent against the back fences. One smiled at me and beckoned. I walked on, caught between curiosity and an impulse to turn and look. Feigning nonchalance, I continued walking on, reasoning that I could turn at the next corner and return to the street with Bar Suba. One woman stepped forward. Her skirt was split and, when she leaned forward, a loose blouse revealed an impressive acreage of breasts. She whispered and I awkwardly smiled.

"No thanks," I mumbled and quickly walked on.

Footsteps came from nowhere. A hand clamped over my mouth and I felt a sharp object pressed into my kidney. The assailant hissed in Spanish – his hot breath grazing my ear. I froze, as a hand slipped into my pocket. I thought of pulling my arm back and elbowing him in the stomach, but, before I could move, he pushed me forward and kicked my ankles sharply upwards. My fall seemed to occur in slow motion, but my collision with the ground was real enough. I lay eye level to the gutter, with pain screaming from my knees and ankles. The sound of running footsteps came from behind, but, by the time I'd mustered the strength to turn, there was nothing. I struggled to my feet rubbing a knee with one hand and then my ankle. The woman smiled then spoke in Spanish and mimed some activity. After what had happened, she must be joking!

I felt down to check my pocket.

Oh no! A wad of travellers' cheques and my credit card folder – all gone.

I returned to the street with Bar Suba. Twenty minutes and a taxi ride later, I was back at the Eldorado, negotiating with the hotel to pay the driver, and then calling American Express.

The next morning, Miguel arrived as arranged. The swelling to my knee and ankle had reduced enough to walk, but, when I explained what happened, Miguel only smiled. A more irritating response was difficult to imagine.

"Welcome to Bogotá, my friend!"

"I can tell you it was very disturbing!"

"But could have been worse. More kidnappings happen in Colombia than anywhere – although that's less likely in the city. You're more likely to encounter a criminal using solpamine."

"What?"

"You were safe with me at Bar Suba, but sometimes criminals spike drinks. A tourist drinks, gets disorientated, and then robbed. There are untrustworthy taxi drivers, too, so you were lucky, compared to what might have happened!"

I held back a sarcastic response. No wonder I'd feared Bogotá.

"Come," said Miguel. "You wanted sightseeing, so that's what we'll do." He led the way to a battered, though comfortable, old Chrysler.

An hour or so later, I was taxiing down the runway in a little Cessna, wondering quite how I came to be consorting with an ex-FARC member who openly moved around and had access to an aircraft. Eventually I asked just that. Miguel called across to Luis, the pilot, and they both laughed.

"We operated on the fringe, but, look, we were a real army, with undercover people and our own intelligence."

"Where are we going now?"

"We discussed the disaster of 'Plan Colombia' last night. They still push eradication though. Now it's time for you to see the results. We're heading south to Mocoa, a small town in Putamayo Department."

At the runway's end, Luis turned around for take-off.

"The way we see it, Nick, that wasn't just a billion-dollar anti-narcotics and military assistance plan. By accident or design, it also helped more corporate plunder."

The engine accelerated, and, without further warning, the little plane hurtled down the runway. The nose lifted, Luis banked and, moments later, we crossed what Miguel then said were the Cordillera Oriental Mountains.

He continued.

"Some areas persistently fumigated just happen to have large mineral and oil deposits. Fumigation helps clear the peasants out and makes what's there accessible. We don't agree and I'm afraid the oil people both there and elsewhere have had pipelines bombed many times."

Below, the endless swathe of green jungle had me feel at Miguel's mercy. I swallowed, then said what was on my mind.

"Miguel, I understand about the corporate abuses, but I've also heard that FARC raised funds from the odd kidnapping, extortion and even taxed the drug trade!"

"We did what we must," said Miguel, his face clouding. "We faced powerful forces. The oilmen were happy enough when the military and anti-narcotics programme reached where we're going. Why do you suppose that might be?"

I hadn't expected an aerial lecture and felt increasingly uneasy. Below I saw brown patches dotting the immense landscape and feared the worst.

"To keep Washington and the outside world happy, they outsourced the worst violence to privately-run paramilitary groups."

The talk of executing street children came to mind, but, at that moment, Luis said something in Spanish and the plane began to point downwards.

We landed at a small strip in the jungle. A rather beautiful young woman called Elsa, dressed in battle fatigues, waited in a battle-scarred jeep and quickly drove us away. We passed through a small village called Almenara and alongside the road were fields of shrivelled plants.

"What happened here?" I asked, guessing the answer.

"Coca spraying," said Miguel.

I felt increasingly anxious. What could I do and, more to the point, what should I glean from this? Some kilometres further on we passed more fields with withered stalks pointing to the sky.

"Corn," said Miguel, shaking his head.

We arrived at the small township called Mocoa and Elsa parked outside a large wooden house. An old man sitting on an ornate carved chair welcomed us in. Miguel and Luis started a long conversation, and I stole sidelong glances at Elsa. There was something rather compelling about her in a tight uniform with sleek dark hair peeping from under a beret. She caught me looking and flashed a smile – in that moment reminding me of Nina. In fact, apart from her uniform, there was a distinct resemblance. The conversation abruptly tailed off and Miguel then spoke in English.

"Roja here is the village's head-honcho and has just described a spraying operation that's ruining their crops. It's an operation by a private US outfit called the Arm-Rite Corporation, and it's protected by helicopter gunships."

"I thought help was given to help move growers away from coca?" I remarked, feeling rather out of my depth.

"That was the idea," Miguel replied. "Many entered into agreements for food aid, help with the infrastructure and, most importantly, help to market alternatives. Very little happened. Instead, they get poisoned from the sky."

Roja started another monologue and the others nodded along with serious faces. Elsa suddenly clucked and shook her head. I wondered what was said, but doubted it was good. Talk eventually stopped and we returned to the jeep. As the others climbed in, a beautiful blue and black butterfly settled on Elsa's beret. I touched her shoulder, and pointed. She removed her cap, gently coaxing the butterfly out of the window with little shooing sounds. Elsa had perfect white teeth showing against her nut-brown skin and glossy hair. I couldn't help but find her rather special.

We drove back into the countryside, and my city eyes felt soothed by the green luxuriance. Periodically, we passed more clearings with withered coca. More worrying were fields that Miguel identified as rice, yucca and plantain – shrivelled and dead. Miguel, Luis and Elsa jabbered away in Spanish, but gradually I became aware of another sound behind their voices, though, at first, the others didn't notice it. The sound got louder and louder – a whirring, which seemed to come from every direction at once. The trees ahead began shaking.

"Helicopter!" Luis shouted.

A mist began floating over the treetops and Elsa quickly pulled in.

"Is that coca over there?" I asked.

Luis responded, but I couldn't hear.

"Pineapples grow nearby," said Miguel.

We got out and the crop-duster made another sweep. Off to one side, a sinister black helicopter hovered as though standing guard. The aircraft banked and soon a choking spray rained down. I fumbled for my handkerchief, but what I then saw was shocking. Elsa had dragged a large weapon from the jeep, and appeared to be aiming at the aircraft. I tried to shout, but spray entered my lungs and I choked. At that moment, I heard a noise and saw a flash. I looked up in horror towards the crop-duster. Something had struck it and sheared the tail fin away. It momentarily hung in the air, lurched at a mad angle and then dropped. We heard another explosion and the remainder burst into a brilliant ball of orange flame, from which surely nothing would survive.

"Come quickly," said Luis and everyone ran back to the jeep.

Luis had pulled off his bandanna and tied it over his face as protection from spray, managing to look like some Wild West desperado. Miguel and Elsa seemed delighted, laughing and jabbering as we drove away. I, though, felt sick and terrified by what had happened and its implications. Miguel noticed.

"It was necessary, Nick. Roja explained that the spraying affects their food, but they won't listen. Listen, the herbicide sprayed around these villages is a hundred times stronger than allowed in the USA."

I nodded, temporarily lost for words – the image of an orange ball of flame locked onto my inner eye.

"You see their children get ill and many have skin problems. Fish are poisoned and pets killed. Many chickens and pigs have died too."

During the remaining trip to Mocoa, everyone quietened, but one thought, and one thought only, ran through my mind like a closed tape loop.

I didn't ask for this or even have any idea that this would happen!

28

MOAB, UTAH

FREDDY ANSON'S PERSPECTIVE

Moab, Utah had been steaming hot. At his home, Freddy Anson dabbed his forehead, turned off the short-wave radio and re-read his notes. Several weeks ago, there'd been some alarm when Rick Tucker thought that the Feds might have penetrated their encryption system. Of course, Tucker was only an amateur, but with Zoltan Heltay, the new communications guy, now aboard, their communications should be safe again. The new code Zoltan had issued did seem rather complicated, but most of the guys thought things would be safer that way.

Today was a task that Freddy relished. He started preparing early, filling the cool-bags, piling in beer, food, and extra water containers into the SUV, and then drove to the showroom. The day was hot and airless and the pennants strung around the lot's perimeter hung limply, as they had for several weeks. Customers were already poking around and he could see others in the showroom.

Freddy opened the locked garage and transferred the provisions to a prepared four wheel drive, fitting the cool-bags and other water containers around the boxes he'd placed there yesterday. He then drove out and sat for a while observing the various activities. At the low-ticket end of the lot, a young couple were examining an old Dodge. First the man peered underneath and then gave the tyres the obligatory kick. Fred looked back to the showroom where several interested customers milled around. He pictured the task ahead, remembering that Dad had requested him to undertake this job, just at the time Mom had visited. In fact, at the time, he'd worried she could have overheard their conversation. *Why does she insist on bragging about Andrew? It's always Andy this, Andy that.* Still, Dad had entrusted this task to him – not to a nerdy academic. He couldn't imagine Andrew having the grit to survive even one day in the wilderness!

He surveyed the lot again. It seemed to be ticking over, so perhaps he should leave.

The freshly serviced four-wheel drive started with a gratifying sense of smoothness. He drove off, passing the Apache Motel, full of tourists as usual, probably yearning to tell friends they stayed where John Wayne lodged in his Western days. He turned right, and then headed for Highway 191, already feeling lighter. Business was the paramount thing, though he did love time in the wilderness. Deciding between the La Sal site or the Maze had been difficult, but he and Terry had finally picked the Maze because of the sheer remoteness.

By the time he passed the entrance to the Arches National Park, most other traffic had dropped away and he continued to the I70. Even after ten years, this bizarre landscape still had the power to amaze. Unlike brother Andrew, he was no academic, but found solace in this wonderful terrain. He now appreciated something of the local geology – like the Wingate Sandstone cliffs that towered above those strange chocolate-coloured stone spirals. Beyond, swirls of ochre rock resembled messy blobs of overcooked custard from a drunken confectioner's kitchen. The road climbed a huge mesa and, below, he saw the Green and the Colorado rivers meandering through deep canyons between buttes and spires.

He stopped and looked across territory that was almost devoid of human activity. The air here was clear and he watched red-tailed hawks patrolling their territory.

Freddy turned south towards Horseshoe Canyon, and then pulled in to check the map.

"Should be left about here," he muttered, and selected a track between patches of slick-rock and sandy soil that only supported a few tired Yuccas.

A few hundred yards further on, he pulled into the shade of an ancient juniper and checked in the back. Despite the bumpy track, the contents appeared secure, so he took out a cool-box and sat on a nearby rock to eat a sandwich. The shade here was limited and sitting only just bearable. Fishhook cacti tumbled from a fissure opposite – their purple blooms intense against a creamy background of sand verbena. A noise came from behind and he instinctively reached for the ankle holster, but it was just a mouse scurrying under a nearby juniper. In the far distance, a cloud of orange dust rose as a vehicle crossed a lonely track.

He set off again, aware of the difficult terrain to come, but it should be secluded and allow safe passage around the Hans Flat Ranger Station. Ahead, he saw the perched rock that Terry had photographed and – thankful for the four-wheel drive – edged off the little track towards the two huge boulders. One had an indentation like a mouth and it would probably continue eroding and eventually form a natural stone arch. He steered towards the boulders, grateful for the traction provided by the needle grass, and manoeuvred up onto the slick-rock. The vehicle climbed steeply and, at the top, he stopped to check the map. The aim was avoiding the Ranger Station – overnight permits and a paper trail being the last thing they wanted. Hopefully he could soon turn towards Horse Canyon, and pick the track up again near Bagpipe Butte. He moved off again, and this time the hood dipped down as the rock's surface dropped away to the right. He quickly reversed, but the wheels spun and the rock went into a dangerous drop. He pulled hard left and eased the brake off, slowly inching forward with the vehicle now at a positively terrifying angle. The tyres finally gained traction and, after several sweaty minutes, he levelled out. Was he now too far west?

He looked to the next ridge, and thankfully spotted the bluff looking like a parrot's beak – just as Terry's photo showed. He pointed the vehicle in that direction, picking a route through the pinon and juniper.

Fifty minutes later, he rejoined the main track into the Maze district, having successfully bypassed the Ranger Station. This was probably the country's most isolated wilderness!

The detour had added about an hour and a quarter, but once the storage place was established, an RV could take a more direct route without raising suspicion.

The setting sun cast a blood-red light over the crumbling cliffs of organ rock shale. He pulled over to consult the map again. Three massive rock fins should mark the way. After reaching the fins, he turned right and saw in the distance the massive rock formation called the 'chocolate drops', glowing in the late afternoon sun.

He descended the next canyon – the walls looking like vast banks of

Neapolitan ice-cream in chocolate, pink and cream bands, that seemed to get closer as he descended. Reaching the bottom, he checked the instructions, and drove exactly 0.4 of a mile to where the canyon divided into three parts, and he took the left-hand channel. After about a tenth of a mile, this forked and he took the smaller right bend. Further up, behind pinon and rabbit-bush, he found a concealed entrance to a narrow cave. He was now soaked with sweat and sat for a while watching the swallows performing high above. After a rest, he stacked the boxes well back inside the cave, periodically stopping to listen. A ranger or even a back-country tour coming this far seemed extremely unlikely. Terry was right – they were almost guaranteed solitude and all known sights lay in the opposite direction.

Freddy pitched a tent near the cave entrance, and fixed his meal under spotlight, as dusk arrived quickly. The night that followed was hot and, with a noisy owl and coyotes howling, sleep didn't come easily. At dawn, he heard scrabbling sounds from the edge of the tent – possibly an inquisitive mouse? He woke to sunlight filtering into the open tent and fixed a leisurely breakfast. Killing time here was no hardship as he watched darting violet swallows and white-throated swifts hunting insects high in the cliffs, imagining it as an aerial dogfight. Later, he heard the sound of an approaching vehicle and checked his watch. It was 11.00, the agreed time for rendezvous and, although unlikely to be anyone else, he checked his ankle holster. Moments later, a grey, high clearance four-wheel drive emerged from behind a boulder. Terry James was driving and beside him was Zoltan Heltay, the special communications guy. Terry climbed out, and wrapped him in a bear hug.

"Good to see you again, bro. You've met Zolt?"

Freddy nodded.

"Just once."

Zoltan held out a hand and he gave it his most powerful squeeze.

"You've got the stuff?" asked Terry.

"It's all in the cave. Incidentally, your map was spot on."

"Good. Let's get the other stuff shifted."

Although still early, they soon were soaked from carrying heavy boxes. Terry took an ice box from his vehicle and they drank cold beer and watched a nervous antelope squirrel scamper about.

"No-one saw you come here?" asked Terry.

"Not a soul. How about you guys?"

Terry chewed tobacco and spat on the ground.

"Nah. We stayed overnight in Hanksville and then set off early. Saw some 4WDs parked near the North Trail Canyon. One of them activity outfits, I think, but they was empty. Probably hiking to the Maze overlook."

Terry stood up.

"This shit's hot and needs to rest up for a bit. Thanks to your Daddy, I'll be taking some shiny Koch and Hecklers back to Montana. Zoltan's going with you on the Philly trip – so there'll be plenty of room!"

He nodded, looking side on at Zoltan and feeling anxious, though unsure quite why. Zoltan pointed to another rodent scurrying around.

"Antelope squirrel?" he asked.

"Nope, a grey spotted rock squirrel," replied Freddy. "Fat little son of a bitch."

"What did your Ma think 'bout Zolt stayin' on a while?" Terry asked.

"She's fine. Maybe a little surprised I hadn't mentioned him before – seeing he's such a good friend," he replied with a grin.

He studied the man again. Zoltan certainly was handsome and he wondered how Mom would react. Whatever resentments he had, he didn't want her in harm's way.

Terry grabbed a beer and threw it in a single motion. It shimmered towards him and dropped at his feet on the sandy soil. He twisted the bottle top and it frothed. He took a swig before speaking.

"Where are you from, Zoltan?"

"Originally Hungary. My family came to the US when I was twelve. First we lived in the South, but moved later to New York and then California. Dad was a mathematician and lectured there. Let's see, what else? Besides doing communications, I mainly worked with imports/exports and IT... and I'm single."

"Shit – are you two gettin' married or what?" said Terry.

He looked as Zoltan stretched, pushing his arms over his head and his chest pulled hard against the black t-shirt. The man appeared in prime condition.

"It's okay," replied Zoltan. "Fred just wants to know who's staying at his Mom's place. It's normal."

"Exactly right," he replied. "So, what's the import/export business?"

"Mainly IT and communications kit."

Terry flipped the top off another beer.

"Yeah, but now you're helpin' the bro's fix our communications – aintcha?"

Zoltan smiled.

"Well, you're just about up to the twenty-first century, now."

"Zolt's been over in Montana and got the new encryption sorted. Hell, you've used it. Waddya think?"

He nodded and Zoltan grinned before responding.

"As I said, Dad was a mathematician so encryption comes easily to me. Security in the North East is rough, though, and we think one of the units might have been compromised. That's why I need good cover."

"Hence the stay with Mom?"

"Yeah," said James. "It makes you mad, don't it? You'd think the Feds would have enough on their plates – terrorists hiding out and liberal troublemakers everywhere. They oughta support real patriots, but them boneheads don't know their ass from their elbow!"

Freddy nodded wisely. Schooled early on with the right to bear arms, his response came easily.

"They'll take my gun over my dead body."

"Right," agreed Terry. "Bet you know 'bout government interference, Zolt – livin' with them Communis' sons of bitches. I usually don't hang with European dudes, but you're okay, man!"

James fixed him with a stare.

"Of course, Zolt's a US citizen now, or he wouldn't be with us!"

Zoltan nodded with a tight smile, as James slapped him on the back.

"Let's get the K and Hs into my wheels. You plan visiting your Dad while up in the North East, Fred?"

He nodded.

"Say hi to him, okay? Biff's a good guy –real generous."

Half an hour later, he watched Terry's four-wheel drive disappear behind the boulders and, soon afterwards, they started back to Moab. Ascending the canyon seemed easier, though he knew difficult sections lay ahead. While he still felt uncertain about Zoltan, the man asked sensible things about the business and seemed to know a lot about vehicles. By the time they reached Green River, he felt happier.

"You have to understand, my Mom, Judy, is a hundred percent liberal – or a 'Progressive', as she calls it – God help her! Don't under any circumstances let her know what you're doing, or give any hint of my militia involvement."

Zoltan smiled, his voice steady and firm.

"Don't worry. I'll tell her what she needs to hear."

Freddy looked him in the eye. There was something disconcerting about the little half smile and, despite the heat, he felt a tiny chill. When they arrived at Moab, Zoltan pointed out a coffee shop and suggested a break. They were soon deep in conversation about the relative merits of various SUVs and his concerns forgotten.

"So, we'll leave for Philly first thing tomorrow."

29

OXFORD/LONDON

SIMON MAHER

I scrolled through the message headers until I found Nick's email. With a research trip to the US now possible, this contact seemed more valuable than ever. Our lively exchange on social justice issues became even richer when we discovered a shared love of the Blues. The subject line of his email read:

They don't only trade commodities – sometimes it's lives, too!

I read through Nick's thoughts about our forthcoming arms fair. Apparently, his group had met on this topic, too, and accessed information from the UN Library on global arms sales. I decided to copy down some of the facts, for the 'demo', knowing these sometimes develop into impromptu 'teach-ins', where old hands 'spread the word'. I slipped a note with some key facts into my wallet, thinking – *If I give info about the demo to Nick, maybe he'll mention it in an article?* I'd even recently reconsidered the possibility we might actually meet. Some projects needed research best done in the States, and we were awaiting approval for a research trip. The 'corporate sociopathy' project would undoubtedly be strengthened by direct research using structured interviews. As Andrew wasn't keen to go, perhaps I would and, therefore, might not be parted from Gill after all!

I checked the time, pocketed my compact digital camera and hurried to the station. As agreed, Andrew was waiting, though he looked rather pale and preoccupied. Gill would join us later in London. I looked from the train at the countryside, remembering our day at the 'White Horse' and our discussion about Britain's agricultural heritage. A recent report claimed that lobbyists from an agribusiness giant recently met with a senior government official. I was about to raise this with Andrew when he cut across my thoughts.

"Still looking forward to the US trip?"

I quickly refocused.

"Are you saying it's approved?"

"In principle, yes. George Danton agrees and is sorting out funding. He understands that, if we're to publish, we first must research – so, yes, get yourself a guidebook!"

Wonderful! First, a day of protest and now this! Andrew, though, seemed unusually tense. The experience at Grotstein's seemed to have unnerved him.

"Andrew, I don't want to add to our concerns, but do you remember at Grotstein's I mentioned the possibility of industrial spying. Everyone else seemed rather sceptical."

"Of course, I remember."

"One of the exhibitors at today's fair did exactly that and arranged full surveillance on activists."

Andrew frowned.

"Surveillance? Surveillance of what exactly?"

"Of activists from the 'Campaign on Arms Trading'. I'm involved with COAT so I know it's true. Apparently, Union Defence Systems hired an industrial intelligence outfit, operating from an ordinary suburban home. COAT was well and truly infiltrated."

Andrew put down his paper, and stared.

"You mean they pretended to be activists?"

"Exactly! They put together a database with bio's, National Insurance numbers, criminal records, where available. Everything available for sale!"

"Just as well we know our little group personally."

"Yes, but get this duplicity. They actually set up a front group proving that the arms trade contributes to poverty, whilst at the same time sending encrypted faxes of activists' personal details, to UDS's head office!"

Andrew slumped.

"That really is one for the files."

We arrived at Paddington Station and then continued on to Mile

End to meet up with Gill. She appeared very becoming in her tight denim suit and I felt proud to be with such an attractive woman. She seemed pleased, too, and stood on tiptoes to kiss me. We then set off along a drab East London Street towards the exhibition. It wasn't long before, unexpected, exotic creatures were seen ahead. A man in a pink tutu led a green dog with a ruffle around his neck.

"I hope that's only food dye," said Gill.

At the next corner a group of women holding flowers followed a canvas tank. The crowd ahead was thick with every kind of protester – environmental groups, peace groups, international socialists, church groups and Trots. A man passed them wearing a Zapatista t-shirt saying 'Todos Somos Marcos'.

"Who is in charge of this circus?" Gill asked.

It was difficult to hear over the sound of banging drums.

"That's the beauty of it," I shouted. "There is no single leader – everyone just sort of converges. It drives the police crazy because they don't know who to threaten or arrest!"

The crowd grew by the moment. A new influx from a church group joined from a side street. At the same time, a small group of pink and silver fairies danced down the main road. Anarchists jostled pacifists and the view ahead was blocked by balloons and placards. The exhibition site was still about a quarter of a mile off when word came down that the police were closing the road. Andrew nudged me and pointed at the kerb. A man stood with a tray piled high with swimming goggles.

"Shit. They must be expecting tear gas!"

I turned to Gill.

"Trust you like orto-chlorobenzylidene-malononitrile's sweet fragrance."

She grinned.

"Not only preachy – he's pretentious, as well!"

Her jibe seemed strangely warming.

I pointed over at 'Marie Antoinette' holding a placard showing children with outstretched hands. The caption read – *Never mind cake – give 'em bombs!*

The sound of a samba band came from behind, and I turned to see a pretty blonde with butterfly wings approaching. A papier-mâché missile protruded from her midriff like some giant phallus. We swiftly moved to avoid a collision with young men playing football with a large rubber ball with a globe embossed upon it. Their t-shirts bore the logos of major oil companies and tech giants. I smiled at Gill, rather pleased by the carnival atmosphere, hoping that she was enjoying it too. Perhaps we could dine together again tonight. No sooner did I have that thought than the drumming abruptly ceased and we saw plumes of smoke ahead. The crowd had stopped moving, and then started pushing back. Talking had turned to a fearful murmur as people ahead started surging backwards. I looked over at Andrew, but just then 'Marie Antoinette' turned and her pointy toe caught his ankle. Andy's face contorted with pain.

We were now in the convergence of two powerful currents, as people behind moved forward and those ahead tried to escape.

"Let's cut down here," said Gill, pointing to a small street off to the left.

We pushed through the human tide into the side street. This seemed much clearer, although, further down, we saw police with cameras. Some photographers were set apart from the rest and I assumed these were the press. Maybe later I'd try to engage them with some facts about the arms trade. I silently rehearsed as we moved forward. *You echo government propaganda about an ethical foreign policy, and then stand by while peaceful protesters are harassed. While, yards away, war toys are displayed to tyrants. Remember the 'Scott report'?*

Half way down the block, an explosion erupted with flames and black smoke.

"That isn't tear gas," said Andrew. "They're setting cars alight."

I strained to see what was happening.

"Shit, 'Black Bloc'. Anarchists. They're usually low key in London."

At the end of the street, a water cannon arced into the air, and a small group of men ran up the road. Police wrestled several to the ground, but we were clearly in danger of heading straight into trouble. I looked behind, wondering if we should retrace our steps, but, just then, police with riot shields came around the corner. Another group of police advanced and were snatching individuals. Andrew looked terrified and rooted to the spot. Thankfully, Gill quickly grasped the situation.

"Come on," she said, grabbing Andrew's arm.

We heard the unmistakeable sound of hooves drumming, and mounted police rounded the corner.

"Quickly," said Gill, running further on. She pushed open the door of a small garage workshop, wedged into a small gap in an otherwise terraced street. It was dark inside, but I could make out a servicing pit and hoist. The place reeked of oil and cars.

"This way," said Gill, pushing a side door onto a small alley passing between houses and leading to the next street. We ran to the end and peered up and down the street. To the right, mounted police stood against a barricade. The left seemed clear, but I couldn't see far, because the road curved.

"I reckon if we go left, we'd soon be out of their sight. That's the general direction of the exhibition centre. Maybe we can then approach it from the side."

"Where has everyone gone?" asked Andrew, sinking onto his haunches. "Heck I feel quite dizzy."

"Sit here a moment," said Gill. "I'm just going back to the garage for a moment. I think I noticed a toilet."

Andrew eased himself down into the alleyway and leant against a paling fence under an apple tree from someone's back garden.

"I don't know, Simon, I feel quite odd. Did you see the way the police went for the anarchists? Maybe they were asking for trouble, but I didn't like the look of those truncheons! To be honest, I'm feeling quite off colour today. Perhaps I shouldn't have come!"

Andy wiped his forehead with the back of his hand and definitely looked poorly.

"Wait here, and I'll poke my head out and check."

I looked out from the tiny alley. Unlike the other, this street seemed clear.

I called out. "All clear on the left."

Gill got back, and we moved forward together, rounding the road's curve, and out of sight of the police.

"Just as well we aren't dressed as fairies," said Gill. "With a bit of luck, we'll look like local residents leaving from one of their back gates."

We came to another bend in the tree-lined road.

"I reckon we're about four or five blocks from the exhibition centre," I said to the others.

Shrill police whistles could still be heard above the noise of the crowd. We set off hopefully, but two black cars suddenly drove towards us at speed. Figures jumped out, running towards us.

I instantly knew this was trouble. I grabbed Gill's hand and ran back towards the garage, reaching the curve in the road before realising Andrew wasn't with us. I turned around, but Andy appeared frozen. We watched him dragged off to one of the cars and then quickly ducked back to the alley and into the garage. I was panting and the dank, oily smell stung my lungs.

"What happened?" Gill asked. "Andy just froze!"

"I don't know. He looked terrified and must have completely panicked. He's been under a lot of strain recently because the College have been piling on the pressure. When I mentioned surveillance of protest groups, he seemed really spooked – no pun intended!"

"Let's stay here until it's calmed down outside."

"Good idea."

Gill came close, and slipped an arm around my waist.

∿

Andrew Alton

I FOUND myself jammed between two Special Branch Officers in the back of a Jaguar and couldn't stop trembling.

"So, explain why you are on this road in a temporary exclusion zone?" Sergeant Fowkes, the larger of the two, asked, pointing to the trestles and tapes closing the road.

"Local residents were leafleted, asking them not to exit their back-yards during the closure. So, are you a resident?" he demanded.

I shook my head, gripping the padded armrest hard as the car sped away.

"This is stupid. I'm only here making a peaceful protest."

"So were they," sneered Fowkes as they passed two smouldering vehicles.

The car headed west, I was unsure where, but thought it possibly somewhere in the Paddington area. The second Jag had gone – perhaps it was searching for Simon and Gill.

We entered a barrack-like building, I assumed a police station. I was taken to Mr George Glick, although the interrogation proper didn't start for another two hours. Glick then took me through a maze of corridors to a small side room and then introduced a Sgt Murray and a Mr Vann from 'the special office'.

There was no explanation of what was 'special' or why I was in need of such an interview. I sat on a hard wooden bench as Murray and Vann played tough and soft cop.

The questioning was repetitive and, eventually, I exploded.

"How complicated can you make it? Like thousands of others, I came to protest the selling of instruments of destruction. How do you make that a problem?"

Murray left, and Vann continued alone.

"Dr Alton, we had intelligence about a possible terrorist action aimed at today's defence exhibition."

"Why should I believe that? If true, perhaps you should ask why? You call it a 'defence exhibition'. Do you really believe that defence is the real purpose of most of those weapons?"

"We aren't here to debate politics. The exhibition was completely legal."

"That makes it okay?"

"Dangerous people can use association with activists as cover."

"You don't understand. I'm a researcher and educator at Oxford – not a terrorist."

"We know exactly who you are, Dr Alton."

I momentarily froze.

"Meaning what?"

"You say 'educator'. We understand very well how you use, or should I say, misuse, your position to cause discontent, and undermine business and institutions important to this country – and others."

I felt sick.

"That's quite untrue. I research and write fairly, using validated methodology."

"No, you tell a partial version, Dr Alton. A dangerous version, if I may say so."

Vann leaned forward.

"Some people wish to weaken or destroy our institutions and whole way of life. Sometimes, wrong ideas are even more dangerous than explosives."

Vann leaned further forward, and his proximity triggered unwanted memories. When losing, Dad would shut down arguments with intimidation.

"So, what 'way of life' do I threaten most, I wonder? Rabid consumerism? Corporate plunder? Economic imperialism by debt and bent trade rules? Promoting democracy with bombs? Free market fundamentalism, perhaps – consistently putting profits before people? Perhaps you meanthe surveillance society and attempts to chill free speech? Shall I continue?"

Vann's eyes narrowed.

"I'm asking the questions, Dr Alton. What exactly was your purpose in Lambourn Strete?"

Irritation prickled inside.

"My purpose? Protest, of course, like hundreds, probably thousands, of others!"

"Did you see hundreds or thousands, in Lambourn Street?"

"You know not! We cut through there to get away from the thugs – and I don't just mean the anarchists! Okay, we hopped over the barrier, because – thanks to police tactics – we were in danger of being crushed."

Vann's eyes were impenetrable. He leaned forward again.

"Don't get clever, Alton. That street was closed for good reasons. Just now you said 'we'. So, who were your associates?"

"They aren't 'associates' as you put it. Just my research assistant, Simon Maher, and Gill Marney, a friend of Simon's from an environmental group. She only came along for the ride."

"We believe you're potentially dangerous, Dr Alton. You provide support and encouragement for those threatening our way of life."

"Let me see if I understand," said Andrew. "You're saying I'm virtually a terrorist for opposing the pushing of the equipment of terror – is that it? Anyone with a vestige of awareness knows repressive regimes love that kind of equipment. Probably, there are people there right now, arranging arms sales that may end up in the hands of tyrants and actual terrorists – yet you waste time playing mind games with me!"

"Wasting time, with people who have subversive views and possibly more."

"Really? I understood spooks sometimes act as the lackeys for arms manufacturers, and government ministers sometimes act like arms salesmen. So, this sort of nonsense doesn't exactly surprise me!"

Vann didn't react.

"A known troublemaker with worrying contacts, accompanied by another known troublemaker – possibly two – found in an area specifically placed off limits. Those are the facts."

There was a knock at the door. A female officer entered and handed over a thick file. Vann flicked through it.

"Ah, yes. You've been busy, Dr Alton!"

My stomach churned and hands were wet, with my right thumbnail pressed into my forefinger. *A fat dossier bearing my name – incredible!*

Vann continued.

"You seem to have a problem with the business community, Dr Alton."

"No, not ethical business. Only those treating everything as commodity, who buy political influence and believe they 'own' our democracy and culture."

"You're a cheerful man, aren't you, Alton? The bench you're sitting on. Presumably that made itself, marketed, transported and sold itself? Your breakfast this morning, the transport you rode to London, the car that brought you here – all provided by legitimate business!"

"Perhaps you didn't hear. I've no problem whatsoever with business that keeps to its own domain. I just don't like businesses that corrupt everything, including politics, in an increasingly insane quest for endless profit. I also don't like corporations that are divorced from the consequences of their own actions."

"I think you exaggerate."

"Really? Business is, of course, necessary, but some corporations lack even a jot of loyalty to their own workers, and see the environment just as something to be plundered, or a toilet for their waste."

Vann shook his head.

"Anyway, if you're with the police, or whatever, aren't you supposed to believe in regulations and limits? Isn't that your 'raison d'être'? You probably think that regulations are only for the public. You must be so proud, working for an elite establishment that would spit you out without a second thought. How they must laugh!"

"Wasting your time, Dr Alton. I know what I believe, and what might happen, if people like you had their way."

Vann went out, leaving me to wait alone for almost an hour. When he returned, he asked more about Simon and Gill. I deflected as best as I could, but felt preoccupied by that fat dossier.

"What's in that file?"

"You're not the only one who researches, Dr Alton."

"Can I see it, please?"

"I'm afraid not," said Vann, closing the dossier. He stood up and then spoke pointedly, as if emphasising his warning.

"You can leave now, but, if I were you, I'd think extremely carefully about your activities and associations."

Vann pressed a button by the desk and a female officer appeared. She silently escorted me through a network of corridors until we reached another section of the complex, where the staff were uniformed and passed me over to a regular officer.

We set off again, passing through what I supposed was a charge room, and then a side room with a fixed camera. As I passed by the door, a white adolescent boy was having his hand put onto an inked roller. I waited as the officer unlocked the door, reading a notice urging suspects to give statements and warning against non-cooperation. I felt shocked and angry being here, but what could I do? Complain to the police? They were the police!

The door opened into a lobby. On second thoughts, Vann probably wasn't an ordinary cop. 'Special office', they'd said, but what did that mean?

The officer crossed to the outer door, pressed a button and said:

"Goodnight sir. Turn left for the nearest tube station."

I was summarily ejected into the cool night air of London. I checked my watch and it read 10.15pm.

3 0

MANHATTAN USA

ROBBIE JAMES

I walked over to the agreed restaurant in Tribeca, still buzzing from seeing Anson's confidential files and looking forward to the pleasure of sharing this with Nick. Although it was the hated water project that first brought us together, a genuine friendship had developed. Today, Nick seemed extremely tense and didn't need much encouragement to start offloading. He launched into the forthcoming changes at Canvey and the plummeting of staff morale. As he clearly needed to vent, I held back on the 'Peak-Me' fiasco, and let him continue.

"If only our staff could somehow strike back – although, in the circumstances, 'strike' probably isn't the most appropriate word! The thing is, they've all built lives around Canvey, and now..."

My knowledge of employment law was limited, so I could really only listen sympathetically. After Nick had finished, I tried to describe the 'Peak-Me' episode.

"What I discovered was fiendishly clever. It almost seemed a shame their campaign didn't launch – to see whether..."

"Yes, but there's slick, and sick," interrupted Nick. "So much stress is totally unnecessary. We recently had a guy pushed to breaking point by his manager and almost jump off the roof."

"He has my sympathy!"

"Quite, but get this. When I mentioned it upstairs, they immediately thought the manager was in the right!"

"Bastards! Listen, when we last met, you were leaving for Colombia. How did that go?"

"Very eventful!"

Nick's account made mine seem pale in comparison and I felt rather stupid at hyping it. His mention of Brian Tutch in Bogotá brought me completely back to earth.

"I know just what you mean. He's a ruthless, untrustworthy character, which is probably why Anson likes him."

"Really gave me the creeps," said Nick, with a grimace. "There's something almost reptilian..."

I remembered my own reaction.

"While you were away, I had another bad run-in with Anson. I'd prepared a report on the local impact, with an analysis of probable objections and resistance."

"What did he say?"

"Words didn't actually figure. He threw the report across the office, just missing my head! His secretary is terrified."

"These guys are something else," Nick said, shaking his head. "Mine doesn't throw reports – he's more the ice-cold killer type. Dead in the eyes, although he did manage a little smirk when passing me the news that will make much of the workforce redundant! That reminds me. Do you remember me talking about a guy who'd contacted from England, Simon Maher?"

"The research guy with an interest in water privatising?"

"Yes, him. Simon reckons some of these characters are technically sociopaths."

"Interesting point. Better hope your 'cold killer' guy doesn't discover your writing activities."

"Doubt it's his favourite website! Listen, this Simon Maher guy is coming over soon on a research trip and hopes to meet. How about joining in? It could be interesting."

"Last time you introduced someone to me it was very interesting! I'm still seeing her by the way. We're going to the Rodin exhibition together soon. The one on loan from Paris."

"You really like Corinne then?"

"Of course. She is a little forward, though, if you know what I mean. I prefer taking things slower. What about you and Nina?"

The answer was written all over his face.

"She's very special – and inspiring. I've never met anyone like her!"

The waiter sidled up and served the fancy icecream concoctions we'd ordered earlier. Rain had started outside and I pointed to the window.

"Not again. To think I was sweating in the jungle just a few days ago."

Nick stared out the window stroking his chin, and looking rather distant. I sensed there was some preoccupation or avoidance. Still, I had things on my mind too – important, personal things, I hadn't yet shared. Nick excused himself for the restroom and returned, with a determined expression.

"Robbie, I'd like to share something with you, but it must completely stay between us. Agreed?"

"Of course – though I think we've rather shown our hands already."

Nick paused, and then seemed to cross some sort of internal boundary.

"I really want to be more proactive about social justice – rather than just dabbling with written articles."

"So you've said before."

"Yes, but because of what Nina has explained, I'd like to do more about the matter we're both involved with."

"Of course. That's what kept me writing reports to Anson!"

"No, I mean something more active!"

Nick seemed almost in trance as he described the plan to modify the IT kit.

I listened with mounting excitement.

"Bloody fantastic! I felt that way searching out the 'juicy' files at Marquetcom – I still do! I say, screw the bastards! It does sound risky, though? I thought software could grab screenshots of sensitive material?"

"But someone could discover it. This way, everything will be hidden under the hood, so to speak. The guy helping us is a Spanish-speaking IT whiz. I'm arranging for his transfer to Bogotá as an IT technician."

"Well, you are the HR man, but if things went wrong, mightn't it track back to you? Anyway, what will happen to the info?"

"Not sure. I suppose it gets funnelled to Nina's contacts in Bogotá. I expect they'll ensure things eventually get royally screwed – I don't know, finance, contracts, maybe black PR. Haven't the details yet."

"Physical sabotage, maybe?"

Nick paled.

"Shit. I hadn't got that far."

"Now that we're putting everything on the table, I'll tell you something else. Corinne pumped me, no pun intended, for information on Marquetcom and Anson. Now I've studied his past work and become quite friendly with his secretary – that adds up to lots, including government contracts."

Nick nodded.

"'Birds of a feather flock together.' Let's face it, most politicians are slimy creatures."

"True enough! What are we getting into, though? I don't want to join the prison population."

"We can't close our eyes now. If anything is going to change, people must make a stand."

"It isn't 'people' though, it's us! Imagine charges of criminal damage, or industrial espionage? For all we know, it might potentially be covered by the new anti-terrorist laws?"

"Steady on."

The waiter brought coffee and Nick insisted on paying. Outside, the rain had become heavier.

"Can I offer you a lift?" he asked.

"No, but if you're returning to mid-town, I'll come with you. I need to get something."

I hoped my discomfort was hidden. There was no way I could explain my addiction to doubtful bookshops. As Nick drove past Hudson Park and into Greenwich Village, I felt a familiar surge of adrenalin and desire as we neared Christopher Street.

"Ever visit the Village?" Nick asked. "There are great Jazz clubs."

While it had been a day for sharing secrets, I wasn't quite ready to share how and why I knew it so well. The rain was sheeting down and we passed two men walking with linked arms.

"Guess the sidewalk is slippery."

I knew better, and his innocent mistake only heightened my conflict. We reached mid-town and parted company. Soon I was near the bus station and, moments later, glanced over my shoulder and glided into an adult video store.

31

OXFORD, ENGLAND

SIMON MAHER

I was stunned by details of Andy's interrogation and the stress written over his usually optimistic face.

"You say they had a dossier on you?"

"I know – it's total madness! We've a long tradition of academics questioning power and privilege. It isn't as though I even have much of a history of direct action. Obviously, they won't like my work or politics, but apparently now I'm a major dissident – and half way to being a terrorist!"

"Steady on. We ought to warn Farrelly and Grotstein, though."

"Done that! Farrelly suggests we hold the next meeting at his Secure Unit. No-one can get to us there."

I remembered the childhood visits to mad Aunty Joan, and shivered. We used to visit her at one of those scary Gothic-type county psychiatric hospitals.

"But doesn't Farrelly deal with seriously disturbed or dodgy people – murderers, rapists and the like?" I asked.

"Yes, but they have locks, keys, beefy staff, and the patients are supervised. We won't be in danger."

"I've vivid memories of childhood visits to a relative, so I'm not particularly keen. When is this happening?"

"In the circumstances, we thought later this afternoon!"

I felt a prickle both of anxiety and irritation.

"Heck, Andy! I planned to take Gill out tonight. Why all the hurry?"

"You asked to be involved, remember? Think about it, we've had two burglaries, other strange happenings and now my arrest. We need to agree our strategy."

"We've every right to protest, Andy. Why should we be treated like criminals?"

"Talk about stating the obvious. I think we should take stock and get Martin and Stephen's views. Maybe they'll want to abandon ship. Good news for you, though. The research trip to the States has been granted funding – though not too generous!"

Despite the news, I felt uneasy. Not just cancelling Gill – it was that damn psychiatric unit. It reminded me of parental unhappiness. Visits to Joan were always followed by arguments and, eventually, my parent's separation.

We left for the Secure Unit at 6pm. Oxford seemed congested as usual and the light already failing. Maybe it was just high anxiety, but I noticed a dark Mercedes appear to follow us through Oxford, even though Andrew took short-cuts through the estates. I felt convinced it was tailing, but eventually it turned away.

We arrived at dusk, and just the sign *Huxton Forensic Secure Unit* brought a chill.

A sliding glass door opened to a well-lit reception area. I listened to Andrew explaining we were from the school, doing a joint project with Dr Farrelly, and were expected. The receptionist, a dour squat woman said that, nevertheless, entry procedures must be followed. She pointed down to a line on the floor, and then up to a camera mounted on the wall.

"Martin warned me about this," said Andrew. "It followed a scandal at another unit. Apparently, paedophile visitors brought children on visits – really for the amusement of paedophile patients. A new security regime was subsequently introduced. Martin also has to sign us in."

As if on cue, Dr Farrelly arrived to start the signing-in process. Shortly afterwards, the door slid open to admit the angular form of Stephen Grotstein.

Photo visitors' badges were then clipped onto to our clothing. The receptionist pointed to a compartment that had two sliding glass doors, and then told us to enter what Martin jokingly called 'the decompression chamber'. For a few moments, we were completely enclosed, before the inner door opened and delivered us inside. We emerged into a long corridor, and alarmingly saw unescorted patients freely wandering about. We followed Farrelly down a long corridor and could see into side wards as we passed through.

"My office is on the far wing," said Farrelly.

Passing another ward, I thought I recognised a hunched-up older man, looking extremely angry. I noticed that other patients kept their distance. It was a few moments before I realised it was the swarthy face of Michael Nimes, the infamous strangler, who even now periodically showed up in television crime documentaries. So much for Andrew's assurances about safety!

"We'll go through the day room here to reach the other wing and my office," said Farrelly, as he led us onto a women's ward.

Several pathetic-looking women sat in large institutional chairs. Most smoked and one cuddled a teddy bear. Over in one corner, a woman with lank hair rocked to and fro, lost in her own world. A pale woman with dark rings under her eyes approached Martin. It wasn't clear if she had a speech impediment or just an impenetrable accent.

"Oiv gotta speak wiv you, Doc? Gotta letta from muvva. She's maybe goanna visit?"

The woman grabbed at Farrelly, revealing scars running down her arm.

"Not now, Tamara. I'll see you tomorrow."

"Oi'll finish it, Doc!" She grabbed at Martin's sleeve.

Eventually she released Farrelly, and promptly turned her back on him.

"I'll see you after the clinical team meeting tomorrow."

We escaped, and reached Farrelly's office.

"We thought she was going to hold onto you," said Grotstein.

"Seemed in real a state," agreed Andrew.

"Tamara has a history of impulsive assaults," Farrelly explained. "She has what's called a 'borderline personality disorder' and, before getting a Hospital Order, had made several knife attacks. Poor girl has the usual background – neglect and substantial childhood abuse. She's a self-mutilator – did you notice her arms?"

I nodded weakly. This was exactly the sort of thing I'd feared.

"I thought I saw Michael Nimes earlier."

"Who?" asked Andrew.

"You probably weren't in the UK then," I replied. "Some years back, he was caught following the killing of several pensioners – of both sexes, if I remember?"

"That's right," said Farrelly cheerfully. "Whispering Mick Nimes, our resident gerontophile – now being assessed for transfer to lower security - though everyone knows the Home Office won't agree."

"Why 'whispering'?"

"He sometimes talks in a sort of throaty whisper," explained Farrelly. "There's no physical reason. One of the therapists believes it's some kind of blurring with his victims. They could probably only whisper because of the strangulation. Michael periodically mentally relives the scene, so to speak."

I really didn't want to hear more and felt pleased we'd reached Farrelly's office.

"Let's decide, where we are now with the project," I quickly suggested.

"Indeed," agreed Grotstein. "My view is that the whole thing is growing. We started off by looking at the influence of psychopathy in business, but now we can see the wider, systemic implications. If powerful business interests pull the political strings, where does it start and finish?"

Andrew beamed.

"Exactly, Stephen. John Dewey said it correctly: "Politics is the shadow cast on society by big business."

"Hang on, folks," said Farrelly. "Let's keep things in proportion. We're just three academics and a forensic psychiatrist and in no position to change the world. We have to keep within sensible boundaries."

"Agreed," I replied. "It's certainly frustrating though. Writing papers is all very well, but I sometimes feel that it's either preaching to the converted or splitting academic hairs. Academia sometimes seems a bitchy, competitive little world."

Andrew looked thunderous.

"I'm not thrilled to hear that, Simon. I've had positive responses to our work from all over the world. The material has been quoted and used in education and by activists in a number of settings!"

"Sorry. I didn't mean for that to sound undermining. Of course the work is valuable. I mean, heck – I've been a part of it!"

"Let's review the situation," said Farrelly. "Three different break-ins. Andy had someone snooping around his home and material has gone missing. We've both had strong and unprecedented warnings from our employers. Now you've seen a dossier about you from someone who clearly wasn't part of the ordinary police. Of course, we don't know that these things are definitely connected."

"Personally, I don't think there's much doubt," I said.

Farrelly continued.

"But do we conclude that someone – or, possibly, the intelligence services – have broken into our property and, in the case of Simon's apartment, taken other things, to appear like an ordinary burglary?"

"Good point," he agreed. "A burglary for information maybe, but stealing property doesn't seem likely."

"Highly unlikely," said Grotstein. "Look, shall we get on, or just keep on spooking ourselves?"

Farrelly nodded.

"I agree. Andrew's interrogation was outright intimidation. What we're doing is a legitimate enquiry. I say we continue."

The others murmured agreement.

"The probable effects of severe personality disorders within the business and political elite seems a highly relevant, if controversial, area," said Farrelly.

"Not forgetting their communication styles," added Grotstein.

Farrelly continued.

"It's every bit as relevant as, say, studying, I don't know... the neuro-biology of bipolar disorder. In fact, in terms of the numbers ultimately affected by their activities, far more important. Unfortunately, it touches the interests of a powerful and sometimes secretive elite. It also crosses several domains – criminal justice, economics, psychology, psychiatry, political science, linguistics and moral philosophy, for starters.

"That's why your lecture so excited me," said Andrew. "Extrapo-lating your ideas into economics and geopolitics illuminated so much. The question is, do we just focus on individuals or try to describe the way pathological attitudes become woven into corporate structures – into its very heart?"

"Corporate heart?" I repeated. "Surely an oxymoron! As someone once said, corporations are really just machines for accumulating money!"

"Simon, you claimed last time that corporations might have received help from intelligence?" asked Farrelly.

"It's improper, but some certainly believe so – courtesy of their home countries' long-suffering public. Since the Cold War's ending, intelligence and the military have to justify their existence. The terrorist threat certainly helps. In the US, chunks have been given to the private sector. These days, we don't really know who's doing what."

"Exactly. Which is another reason why I suggested we meet and hold information here, in the Secure Unit."

I looked around Farrelly's office, wondering if the unit's madness was somehow contaminating our thinking. It was possibly a rather odd train of thought. When I tuned in again, Andrew asked:

"Do you see it like that, Si?"

"Sorry, Andy. I dipped out for a moment. What did you say?"

"Actually, I was summarising. So, basically, we all agree to continue with the project. Simon, you and I will continue researching corporate activities – particularly in vital areas like water, food, medicine, environmental degradation, workplace insecurity, etc. Martin, you'll help identify and clarify any links found to both individual and organisational pathology. Stephen will help us to unpick the linguistic legerdemain used to sell the corporate world-view."

Grotstein drummed his fingers.

"Funnily enough, that brings me back to where we were so rudely interrupted last time. If you remember, I was just about to present some findings on language patterns."

I silently screamed *No!* and vainly looked at the others.

"Yes. I suppose we should use the rest of our time together productively," Farrelly replied with a weary voice.

My fears of another lecture were warranted. Grotstein analysed various CEO statements in depth, and then moved on to analyse transcripts from employees, whistle-blowers, shareholder reports – even excerpts from management books and articles by well-known consultants. Funnily enough, his own language also began to seem hypnotic. As terms like 'pre-suppositional frameworks' and 'glittering generalities' glided by, I felt myself getting mildly disorientated, as I watched the goatee beard moving. Grotstein gave examples of so-called covert 'hypnotic patterns', 'yes sets' and 'embedded commands'.

"These patterns are particularly popular in advertising," he said, referring us to several popular campaigns, and also some classic propaganda techniques applied to PR and marketing.

As Grotstein droned on, my eyes swam. 'Disinformation', 'reframing', 'policy laundering', 'sanitising and normalising', 'Orwellian language patterns', 'memes' and...

An alarm suddenly shrilled. Farrelly jumped up and ran to the corridor. Everyone looked helpless, as the sound of running feet came from left and right, followed by raised voices and the sound of a struggle.

I went to the door and looked out. A large black man with dreadlocks struggled with the arm-locks being used by two nurses, while another administered an injection. The man was dragged further down the corridor, bundled into a side room and locked in.

Farrelly returned.

"Sorry about that. We're right next to the 'disturbed' ward or, perhaps I should say, 'the Intensive Care Unit'. One patient just attacked another and then assaulted a member of staff. The poor chap suffers command hallucinations and doesn't realise what he's doing."

Grotstein started again.

"Actually, the concept of command hallucinations resembles what I was saying earlier about the role of 'embedded commands' in modern marketing language..."

"Hell, I'd no idea of the time," I interjected and looked at my watch with what I hoped resembled surprise.

"Yes, extremely interesting, Stephen," said Farrelly, trying to further interrupt by quickly linking Grotstein's 'lecture' to cognitive therapy concepts. It was as if an unspoken agreement to silence Grotstein at all costs had somehow filled the room.

We agreed to meet again in a fortnight.

"Sadly, I won't be here, because of my research trip to America," I said, feeling rather intoxicated by the announcement.

We drove back to Oxford with full heads.

"Did Grotstein mean that some people deliberately use certain language patterns, or that some leaders just have a natural gift of motivating others – Hitler, for example?"

"'Natural gift' – I'm not sure about that! Martin once claimed that high functioning, intelligent psychopaths often rate high in charisma and leadership abilities. You can certainly see good examples in politics. Hopefully, you can follow that up with Dr Gianavecci in New York."

"Absolutely. Incidentally, that Indymedia guy I told you about, Nick Martin, has agreed to meet and says he also knows other people I should meet."

"Good. Please be careful if he's a journo, though. We don't want to find chunks of our work lifted, or find a half-baked account on the internet!"

We reached the college. Andrew pulled in and we discussed plans for the coming week. Deep in conversation, I barely noticed a dark saloon draw up, further back. I felt quite high. Facing my fears of the psychiatric unit somehow felt liberating.

"How safe is New York, Andy? It has quite a reputation."

"Nothing ever happened to me. These days it's all 'zero tolerance'. Apparently, the famous area around Times Square is almost 'Disney-fied' now! That isn't true of parts of Harlem and the Bronx – so use common sense if you go there."

"Got it. Okay, I'll see you Monday."

I left the car and walked down the path towards my quarters.

"Hey, you've forgotten your case."

I retraced my path and Andrew passed over the briefcase with notes from tonight and our earlier meetings.

The badly lit college grounds were dark here from a large over-hanging monkey puzzle tree. The moon was hidden and for the first time I noticed a mist descending. My building looked almost completely dark, although it was Friday evening so most students would be out. I had just passed under an overhanging branch when it happened. Unseen hands went over my face and someone held my arms. I tried to break away, but as my briefcase was snatched away, my legs were pulled upwards and I fell face down. Winded and dazed from a collision with the flagstones, I stayed motionless, hoping to avoid further violence. A car door slammed, and immediately drove away at speed. My knee throbbed, and it was probably several minutes before I recovered sufficiently to struggle up. I replayed what happened, this time prevailing in my imagination – tackling and pushing my assailants to the ground. It was probably childish behaviour that didn't relieve the pain, but generated enough energy to get me back into my apartment. Wiping the blood from my wrist, I took British comfort in a cup of hot tea.

Only minutes ago, I'd questioned safety in New York, yet here I was nursing wounds and wondering how to explain the loss of my case.

I called Andrew.

"Have you told the police?"

"I can't see that would help. Anyway, I thought you'd had enough of them!"

"True," Andrew replied, "but get this. Martin just phoned from the unit. He's heard from the Head of Security – apparently they're friendly."

I sensed this wouldn't be good.

"Apparently, the Estate Warden did a routine sweep around the complex earlier and saw a stationary car with three men, behind the Unit. One was near the wall with what he thought was some kind of listening device. They moved off smartly when they saw him."

"The car... did you?"

"Yes, I asked. It was a large dark car. He thought, a Mercedes."

"This is getting freaky."

"I know. After my London experience, I'm not exactly overjoyed, either. I can't imagine the police lurking around secure units though or robbing someone on a college campus."

"I know. Hell, my wrist aches. I'll be glad to get to New York," I quipped, "It's probably safer there!"

As SIMON WAS RECOUNTING his experience to Gill, the three contractors working for Klieberman–Boss of New York debriefed. One retrieved the tiny device from the recesses of Simon's case.

"That woman was right. The little bastard usually keeps it with him and is an obsessive note taker!"

The second perused the writing, and the third brewed coffee. It would be a long night's work, but their client should be very pleased.

32

PHILADELPHIA

JUDY ALTON'S PERSPECTIVE

Philadelphia had almost everything that Judy Alton had hoped for from the move. The elegant Georgian red-brick in the Society Hill area fitted her sense of style and the cultural life– was a dream. Getting to the Lincoln Centre from New Jersey had always been a struggle. Now, it was only a short ride down Spruce to Broad Street, and the Academy of Music and Kimmel Centre. She believed the Philadelphia Orchestra sounded just as sumptuous as during the glory years under Stokowski or the under-rated Ormandy. The place just felt comfortable and reminded her of her childhood in Boston. Of course, it had its poor areas, but she'd always had empathy with the underprivileged. In fact, it was through responding to a local charity that she'd discovered the local networks – and her sort of people.

Aware of uneasiness at the fringe of her mind, she busied herself with tidying the lounge. She recalled the recent contact from Freddy, which brought familiar ruminations. How congruent was it helping little known charities, yet with such conflicted feelings about her own son? Why children with such different characters?

She made coffee and settled down to look through old photo albums. Andrew, stiff and serious, holding the school prize. Another, of him winning the inter-school chess championship. Donny seemed such a carefree little boy with his curly hair and a winning smile. Then there was Freddy, often pointing a toy gun. Several snaps caught him with a particularly unpleasant sneer. Further on was a photo of him with the bronzed Biff. Both had similar expressions. The photos brought back a horrible exchange, some years back, when Freddy accused her of preferring her other children. In her heart, she knew it was partly true and felt a mother's guilt. She sighed, and closed the album. This conflict didn't ever seem to heal.

Freddy had phoned a couple of days back – ostensibly to check how she was settling in. Concern from that quarter was uncharacteristic. She'd felt wary and uncomfortable.

"You must miss your old friends," Freddy suggested. "Are you lonely?"

"I do miss people," she'd agreed.

"Mom, do you remember me saying I have business in the North East? So, I'd also like to come and visit your new place. I'll probably cut over to New York to see Dad as well while I'm there. Is it okay for me to stay a short while?"

"Of course, when?"

"Hopefully in a couple of days' time."

She'd caught herself wishing it was Andy coming, and busily tried to neutralise the thought, when Freddy said:

"Yeah, and I'm bringing a friend with me who'll be working a while in the Philly area."

"Okay. That's fine."

"Thing is, Mom, my friend Zoltan doesn't know anyone up there. I kinda hoped you could perhaps put him up a short while – just until he gets fixed up."

She'd already intuited from his voice that there'd be more to it, though guilt made it impossible to refuse. So, Freddy and unknown friend were coming to stay – without the leavening quality of Mary and the children.

She picked up another album and went through it from cover to cover. Donny's innocence, Andy's studiousness, and then Freddy! The children were mirrored by their friends. Andy at the chess club with Michael, his main competitor at the spelling bee, who later became his best friend. Donny had many close relationships and apparently still kept contact with old school friends. Freddy, though, always gravitated to the troublesome kids. She'd tried to show acceptance, but his best friend, Alec, was a tough little nut whom she just knew would be a bad influence. Freddy had no

185

desire whatsoever to avoid trouble and was steered by a totally different set of values. A photo of Freddy and Alec together brought it all back. She remembered how unperturbed Biff was after they were caught joyriding. As parents, they were called to the police station, and thinking of Freddy's smirking expression still upset her.

Judy closed the photo album and put on some music. She continued adjusting furniture, while struggling with difficult feelings. Moving upstairs, she prepared the guest bedrooms, knowing that housework could be a meditation for her and making rooms bright and welcoming – a way of expressing love. Friends suggested taking a maid, but, in truth, she liked what these rituals provided.

She prepared the guest rooms, but, as she descended the stairs, the bell rang. She, surprisingly, felt a twinge of anxiety, as normally she liked visitors. She composed herself and answered the door.

"Hi Mom!"

Freddy smirked as he stood on the doorstep. Beside him was an extremely handsome young man in chinos and a black t-shirt.

"Some business got postponed, so we're slightly earlier than expected. Meet my friend, Zoltan."

She shook the young man's hand, mildly shaken both by the surprise and his striking appearance. He had good eye contact, a firm grip and was certainly no Alec!

"Nice to meet you, Mrs Alton."

The voice was American, though with a slight foreign accent and his appearance was like the young Omar Sharif. She welcomed them inside and disappeared to the kitchen to make coffee.

"You're still into that classical music stuff, then, Mom?"

Freddy's voice floated into the kitchen, mingled with snatches of Kodaly's Hary Janos suite.

"Change it if you wish, Freddy."

She returned with the drinks.

"You like Kodaly, Mrs Alton?"

"I certainly do."

She passed Zoltan a coffee.

"It's Judy, by the way."

"Thanks. I like him too, Judy. He's Hungarian, like me, so maybe that's not surprising. We share the same first name, as well!"

"Spooky," said Freddy. "Can we turn it off now?"

She caught up with news of Mary and the kids, but found Zoltan's presence hard to ignore.

"What actually is your work, Zoltan?"

"I mainly freelance in IT," he replied, "I've a biggish contract here, probably lasting about three months. Not here with you, of course," he added, with a smile.

"Where do you live?"

"Many places, Mrs Alton – sorry Judy! Most recently Montana, but, in the recent past, San Francisco and then Atlanta. When we as a family first arrived, we lived in the South and, later, New York City. Listen, I really appreciate you letting me stay a short time. Don't worry, I'll find somewhere suitable as soon as possible."

"You're welcome. You have bags?"

"I'll bring them in. There is a slight problem because I brought a few materials for the job. Is there anywhere I could store some stuff for a while? Freddy said he thought you'd mentioned a shed?"

"Is it valuable?" she asked.

"I guess so, yes."

"Okay, the shed should be secure and you can keep the key. I finally listened to a friend's advice and ruthlessly de-cluttered before moving. She's a Feng Shui nut, so the shed's completely empty!"

He smiled.

"Let the good chi flow, eh, Judy!"

They brought bags in, and a little later she saw them move boxes into the shed. Afterwards, she passed Zoltan the key.

"Freddy, do you plan visiting your father?"

"Possibly tomorrow or the day after. We've local business here first and then I'll probably take the train. You know what parking is like in Manhattan."

She spent a surprisingly pleasant afternoon despite awkward feelings about Freddy. Zoltan seemed cultured and liked classical music. It was difficult seeing him and Freddy having much in common.

"Mom, Zolt might have to pick up something from Baltimore. Is getting there difficult from here?"

Zoltan frowned.

"I'm not sure about that, Freddy. It's just I heard about a good supplier there."

"It's easily reached – DC, too," she replied, but he didn't pursue it.

The next night, she sat listening to the radio – Brendel playing a late

Schubert sonata. The men entered the lounge and Zoltan chose a nearby chair. After a while, he leaned forward, whispering.

"Schubert sensed imminent death. You can hear the anger and then the acceptance."

His eyes seemed liquid, intense and something passed between them. Then the moment was broken when Freddy, without warning, retuned to a rock station. Words caught in her throat, though she bit them back. Freddy looked over, and, realising his mistake, retuned again, but the spell was broken.

She rose early the next day. Freddy came downstairs holding an overnight bag.

"I'll leave straight after breakfast. Any message for Dad?"

"Just hello and tell him Andy's doing well."

"Right. What's study-boy doing now, anyway?"

"Research and editing a new book. Due out in a few months, I understand."

Freddy shrugged.

"Well, I'll leave soon. I'm leaving the Hyundai here."

"Okay, son."

Zoltan began looking through her shelves of discs lining the wall. From behind, he had classic proportions – broad shoulders, long legs and well-cut dark hair. She derailed the thought, feeling slightly ashamed at admiring her son's friend that way.

He turned, catching her eye.

"Seen anything you like?" she asked, catching the irony in her question.

"Lots," he replied. "You're rather fond of Hungarian music, Judy. Dohnanyi, for example. Few people even know of his second symphony. I'm impressed. The Bartok quartets too."

"Love them. People argue whether the Bartok, Shostakovich or late Beethoven are the absolute pinnacle. Personally, I think Bartok's have the widest range and intensity."

"Another Hungarian! I agree. The way he suggests folk music without making actual quotes is amazing. Which is your favourite reading?"

"I grew up with the original Juilliard Quartet recordings."

Zoltan crossed the room, and stood opposite. His tanned face, refined and sensual. She swallowed, catching a faintly sweet, musky aroma – feeling a floating sensation.

Freddy came in with an overnight bag.

"I'm off now, Mom. Back in two days."

He stood in the doorway and she called across the room – unable to move.

"Bye son. See you soon."

Freddy raised his hand with a traditional Indian 'How salute' and left. She turned back to Zoltan.

He smiled, asking:

"Coffee, Judy?"

"Thanks. You'll find the necessary at the back of the kitchen."

She caught her breath. It had been a long time since her name had been spoken so tenderly, but her response seemed ridiculous – she'd only known him a couple of days! She remembered David Alton, but that was all years ago, and more a meeting of minds and values than anything physical.

Zoltan returned with coffee.

"How's the music scene here?"

"Very good," she replied. "Do you enjoy Czech music?"

"Yes. Why do you ask?"

"We have an interesting concert this Friday. Not the usual Dvorak/Smetana, but Fibich, Martinu, and a contemporary Czech composer, whose name I've forgotten. Would you like to come?"

He held her gaze and nodded.

"Yes, very much so. I'm due in Baltimore earlier that day and won't get back until late afternoon. Is that okay?"

"Sure."

"I need to check on stuff in the shed, so I'll call out when I leave."

She registered her disappointment at him being out and also just how quickly her imagination moved from a night at the symphony, to picturing his muscular body naked. She started blushing and began to straighten the room. Half an hour later, he emerged from the shed, and joined her in the kitchen.

"I'm going now, Judy. See you later tonight."

33

OXFORD & HEATHROW

SIMON MAHER

I quickly recovered from the mugging experience, feeling blessed that fortune was now smiling, instead. How helpful that Gill's assignment and my research visit almost coincided! What a godsend that her firm's new system had proved so problematic!

"So, you wonderful man," she'd said kissing me, "it seems that I'll arrive in New York just three days later than you."

I jokingly suggested rearranging dates so we could fly together, but apparently that was a stretch too far. We agreed to each purchase prepaid cell phones in New York and meanwhile I gave her the contact details of my hotel on Thirty-Second Street.

Andrew took the morning off to drive me to the airport, but still seemed very tense.

"I'll phone later, with potential Californian contacts and some corporate watch people. Try to make more contacts because I sense several papers could come from this – maybe even a book!"

"Joint authorship?"

Andrew smiled.

"Talking of bursting into print, I'm still tempted to write about my London experience. I'm sure those were spooks who were using police facilities."

"You're still rattled?"

"I suppose so, yes. Be careful, Si. We don't want to see another dossier – with your name this time!"

"It wouldn't entirely surprise me."

The radio data system cut in with a traffic update – an accident further up the M25. We crawled to the Heathrow link road, making 'check-in' with little time to spare.

The flight was mostly uneventful. The ice near Greenland shimmered, but I wondered for how much longer. I half-heartedly watched a film, and then extracted the documents that Andrew had sent – mainly articles by someone called Karen Sanderson. Karen was a potential interviewee – a former business journalist, who now specialised in uncovering corporate misbehaviour. The trolley came down the aisle, so I took a beer and ploughed through one of her articles. It was another variation on the corporate hijacking of democracy thanks to Washington's plague of lobbyists.

Sanderson's articles covered a staggering catalogue of dishonesty. Halfway through an article, linking dirty air with dirty politics, the pilot announced our run-in to Newark Airport. Outside looked murky and I'd only vaguely noticed the darkening sky, despite flying west. Strong wind buffeted the plane and the cloud and driving rain meant little visibility. I watched in frustration as droplets of rain cohered and skated across the window surface. Maddening, I'd so anticipated seeing Manhattan from above, not a return to London weather! The plane moved in and out of clouds and I could only catch glimpses of fuel tanks and warehouses. The wings vibrated alarmingly as the engines reversed and I gripped the armrest and shut my eyes until we bumped across the runway and stopped. I climbed from the cramped seat, thankful to at last reach the USA safely.

Andrew had stressed the slender budget, so I located the airport bus and settled into a window seat, still itching for a sight of the iconic Manhattan skyline. The bus rattled along for about forty minutes, but, frustratingly, there was little to see. The ground outside sloped upwards and I could only suppose the annoying mound was the west bank of the Hudson River. Eventually the bus climbed a hillock as intense rain beat against the windows. We passed through a rather run-down area, then abruptly descended to the Lincoln Tunnel, to be deposited, seemingly almost from nowhere, into mid-town Manhattan.

I left the bus, battling the torrents of rain and wind that gusted down the city's canyons, driving rain deep into my clothing. The hotel wasn't actually far from the Empire State building. Despite the foul weather, I found the experience intoxicating – the circling yellow cabs, tempting delicatessens, fast food, fast everything and – high above – the iconic 'New Yorker' sign. I continued to brave the wind and struggled towards the hotel on Thirty-Second Street. One structure stood above all others – the distinctive art-deco outline of the Empire State building. Getting closer, the wind intensified, and blew my umbrella inside out. I sheltered in the nearby Plaza, and watched as the spire appeared and then disappeared into low cloud. I crossed over to a deli on the opposite corner and, with feigned confidence, requested a 'bagel and lox'. Picking up my soaked case, I squelched across the road to the hotel's check-in, thinking how unlikely this had seemed, until recently. I climbed the stairs to my room, mumbling to myself.

"Now let's stop dreaming and start things moving..."

34

MANHATTAN

FREDDY ANSON'S PERSPECTIVE

Freddy Anson could see his face reflected in the polished pink marble of Marquetcom's reception. He smoothed and patted his hair, before the pin-up quality receptionist reached him. She smiled like a starlet and he followed behind, and moments later reached Biff's office.

Though Dad's favourite, he could still feel uneasy in his company – even now. The big face opposite smiled and Freddy looked into those watery blue eyes – eyes that, when necessary, could almost impart a physical shock.

"We'll use the comfortable ones, son."

Dad beckoned and crossed to the chairs at the office's far end.

"How's business?"

"Practically rolling in, Dad."

"Good. Unlike Andrew, you at least understand what's important. So, tell me, does Mom like her new place?"

"Yes. She thinks it's great! Zoltan and I arrived a couple of days back. Mom seems happy about him staying on a while."

"I know. I like to keep my eye on things, though don't tell her that."

"Got it. Zoltan's doing the rounds and helping improve communications. He knows a lot about that, and about motors, too."

"Good, though your Mom always has been naive in the ways of the world. She should be careful!"

He didn't miss Biff's face clouding, but knew better than

commenting on anything to do with Mom.

"And the stuff's stored safely?"

Freddy nodded.

"No-one saw you going into that canyon?"

He shook his head, feeling rather like a child visiting the headmaster.

"How is business, really?"

"Given the tightening of credit, okay, I guess. Vans and 4WDs are shifting and we're trying for an RV dealership. Business always slows down when they hike prices."

"It'll change when it suits the right people. Thinking of an RV outlet, you say? Smart thinking! Recreational Vehicles could be useful in quietly shifting the bigger kit to other states. Push ahead with that.

"How do you mean?"

"RVs should have sufficient length for a false floor, for concealing kit, and would look natural around National Parks. RVs go to Utah – from all over."

He suddenly clicked and grinned at Dad's ingenuity.

"Perhaps I should tell you, I already know Zoltan, through other contacts."

Freddy shook his head, wondering what else the old vulture had kept to himself.

"You didn't think that I'd let you take a total unknown to your Mom's, did you?"

The large face took on an odd mixture of grin and sneer.

"You could have..." Freddy tailed off, reading Biff's face and thinking better of it.

"Zoltan might visit me while he's in the East. There's lots to do, though, and he probably won't get back for a while. I expect he told you that?"

Freddy nodded dumbly.

Nancy arrived with coffee and, after she left, they talked business for another half an hour, before adjourning to a nearby bar.

In truth, often he found time with Dad difficult, despite everything they had in common. He looked at women in the bar, while Dad boasted of his business successes, inviting comparisons only where he would be superior. After an hour of this, he made his excuses.

With a hotel situated off Times Square – there was so much more to explore.

35

MANHATTAN

SIMON MAHER

I eyed the hotel phone with suspicion, having heard stories about inflated calls, and Andy's warning that this was an 'economy trip'. Surely simple local calls couldn't cost much?

I dialled the number copied from Nick Martin's last email. Surprisingly, someone answered.

"Hello, Nick Martin."

"Hi Nick. I've just arrived in New York."

"Sorry?"

There was a brief pause, before Nick spoke again.

"Ah, from your accent, I'm guessing it's Simon Maher – right?"

"Right. Looking forward to meeting, when possible. In your last mail, you mentioned possible helpful research contacts and I'd also like to take you up on that."

"I'm originally from the UK, too, so catching up would be welcome. I gather everything back there has gone to the dogs!"

"Pretty well, yes."

"Well, I'm committed tomorrow, but how about Sunday brunch? We've touched on favourite Blues by email, but how about Jazz – or are you allergic?"

"Not sure. I'm open to trying, though!"

"How about mid-day at the Bluenote club, Greenwich Village? Any cab will know it. We can eat, listen and later talk. Also, I've a friend, called Robbie, who shares our interests. I mentioned your visit, and he'd like to meet while you're here. I happen to know that he has very relevant information to your mission. You can't do many interviews on the weekend and I know he's free tomorrow."

"Oh."

"His full name is Robbie James."

He passed the phone number.

"Look forward to the Bluenote on Sunday!"

I crossed to the window and looked out. Rain was still lashing down and the awning of the Korean restaurant below flapped insanely. I sat in a lumpy chair by the window, trying to decide what to do next. Andy stressed that the trip must count, and how hard he'd pushed for the funding. Perhaps this Robbie James guy would see me tomorrow? I dialled his number, with little expectation of finding another person at home on a Friday evening. I was wrong and, equally surprising, Robbie suggested meeting this evening, proposing a diner he knew on Seventh Ave.

Later, I left the hotel, thankful for a slight pause in the rain. My eye constantly drawn to the Empire State building, now illuminated in gold. I'd read the spire sometimes took on different colours – green for St Patrick's day, lavender for 'gay pride', and so on. With no reason to remember either date, I doubted I'd see a change this time. I continued walking to Broadway, watching taxis dart in and out like fish swallowing and discharging their fares – reminding me of a Joni Mitchell lyric. As I approached Times Square, I heard myself quietly humming 'On Broadway' and grinned at the ways of the unconscious. The pavement here sparkled like a starry night. Maybe it just had a high mica content or similar – but it seemed so appropriate for Broadway! I grinned again. My internal jukebox was now playing 'Diamonds on the soles of her feet', which I quickly altered to 'his feet'. I crossed to Seventh Ave and, moments later, found the diner.

A slim and earnest-looking man with neat brown hair and soft blue eyes waited outside. I reckoned him in his late twenties or early thirties. He stepped forward with an extended hand.

"Simon? I'm Robert James, though just about everyone calls me Robbie."

We shook hands and I felt rather puzzled. I wasn't wearing a label saying 'I'm Simon Maher – recently arrived from England'!

"Impressive. How did you know it was me?"

Robbie shrugged and smiled.

"Come on in. They've the best sandwiches in town."

I followed behind, wondering why Robbie would think a sandwich sufficient after a long day and an eight-hour flight, but the answer was soon evident. Waitresses scuttled around with gigantic trays of sandwiches – corned beef, pastrami, pickles and side orders big enough for a family.

Robbie ordered. Many of the customers were clearly Jewish, and I could hear banter that would be unthinkable in Oxford. I felt stuffily British.

"What do you think of New York?" he asked.

"As overwhelming as I expected! I hope to fit in some exploring between business."

"Perhaps I can help. New York caters for every taste."

The 'sandwiches' arrived.

"Nick says you're interested in social justice. Not a fan of bankers or the corporate takeover, I guess?"

"Absolutely," replied Robbie with a grin. "Nick told me you're over here researching the issue. What aspect in particular?"

I smiled, recalling my cramped life in Slough.

"Before joining the academic world, I made some fairly ineffective protests, mainly on the sweatshops. That episode cost me my job and home, but, as a research assistant, I'm now actually paid to explore the big issues that interest me. Currently, what could easily be called cultures of 'business and corporate psychopathy'."

Robbie raised an eyebrow.

"Unethical behaviour is only the tip of the iceberg. We believe that some corporations are almost certainly headed by sociopaths who play out their material."

Robbie looked thoughtful.

"Sounds fascinating, though pretty risky. I'll tell you what, though, my boss is a real piece – completely unethical and a major bully. Nick explained you'd corresponded on water privatisation. That's one of the reasons he thought we should meet!"

"Tell me more."

"Both of our companies are involved in a privatisation project planned for Colombia – and, if possible, even further. I tried raising the human costs, which could be extensive. I provided detailed briefings to my boss... but there wasn't a shred of compassion or understanding. Couldn't get under his radar."

"That's the kind of information I'm looking for," I said. "Inability to have empathy sounds familiar. It probably goes with the type."

"Meaning?"

"Psychopaths, if indeed he fits that category. They have recognisable traits and you just described one."

"I thought psychopaths were... I don't know, dangerous violent offenders.""They can be, but, actually, there's a spectrum. Some wear fancy business suits and run financial institutions," I replied.

Martin Farrelly's voice played in the back of my mind, and I was soon on a roll.

"Yes, some are lawyers, politicians or chief executives! When you think about their actions, don't you ever wonder about their personalities?"

"Yes," said Robbie, "but I hadn't considered that. I'd say my boss, Biff Anson of Marquetcom, could be an excellent example."

Robbie leant forward with a worried expression on his young face.

"Anson has me down as a wimp and despises any second thoughts whatsoever over this water thing. What he doesn't realise is I've found things out about Marquetcom... which, if not skeletons in the cupboard, are, at the very least, decomposing cadavers!"

"You must have a stressful work environment!"

"Nick and I meet regularly over this work. He described your correspondence, so I think I can trust you. I'll tell you this straight out – I don't like Anson or what he does. We'd both love to stop the harm our companies do, but don't quite know how! Nick's girlfriend, who you might meet later, is an experienced activist and a particularly deep person. We've learned lots from her, including that leaving actions to others will never bring change. Look, Simon, if you need first-hand information, I might be able to help."

My fatigue evaporated like mist under hot sunshine. All this on my first evening! Andy damn well ought to be impressed!

"Of course, I still must eat and pay the bills, so if I agree to help, you have to be discreet."

"Of course."

More sandwiches and coffee arrived.

"The thing is, Anson is very canny and probably paranoid. Apparently, he even records staff conversations."

"He sounds a barrel of laughs."

"Just a little!"

The male partner of a nearby couple seemed to take undue interest and I was about to suggest we speak more quietly when Robbie leaned forward to whisper.

"In a minute, discretely look down at the back on the right side. You'll see a guy with a bright red shirt and a particularly broad face. That's Anson's son, Freddy. He came into the office earlier today to see his father."

"A chip off the old block?"

"Yes, and a very nasty piece of work. I've become quite friendly with Anson's secretary and, according to rumours she's heard, Freddy's involved with the militia, out West."

"Militia?"

It clearly meant something to Robbie, but it passed over my head.

We finished eating, and agreed to meet again soon.

I returned to Broadway and retraced my way to the hotel. Only three days until Gill arrives, but what a first day! Andy should be delighted!

36

MANHATTAN

NICK MARTIN

I hunted for painkillers – after waking with the kind of headache that soon dominates one's world. Too much drinking last night and talking too long and late with Nina and Corinne. Still, Marco's handy-work was now achieved – hence our little celebration.

I crawled back into bed, reflecting on last night. I could swear Corinne had been flirting again. I dismissed the thought, and pictured Nina instead – her warmth and her voice, typically talking up the cause of the oppressed. My mind kept jabbering on, as if trying to draw attention away from my headache. I suddenly remembered the brunch arrangement with Simon Maher, and immediately regretted it. After all, Sunday morning usually meant a lie in.

My irritation was sharply interrupted by an insistent rapping at the front door. I quickly sat up. Nina wouldn't knock like that and the English guy didn't yet have my address. The knocking got more aggressive. It was 9.45am and much cooler today, so I slipped on a robe and slippers. Through the front door's spyhole, I could see three strangers outside waiting. I shivered and tightened my belt.

I called "Who is it?", now certain this was no social call.

"Open up, Mr Martin."

I opened the door to the unwanted visitors – two men and a woman. The tallest man bore a certain resemblance to Sinatra. He flashed an identification card at me.

"Security."

They entered before I could even respond.

The card announced CIA and the 'visitor' was a Thomas Morelli. He introduced the others.

"This is Jack Holt and Mary Hume from Homeland Security."

Despite considerable anxiety, I tried to look confident.

"I always thought the CIA handled overseas intelligence matters. Anyway, why so early on a Sunday?"

"Post 9/11, the various agencies are coordinated, Mr Martin. We can indeed act domestically in terrorist investigations."

"Whatever, but why come here? Look, I'm rather unwell this morning – which is why I'm not dressed."

"We understand you have interests in Colombia," said Morelli.

My stomach clenched as I sifted through the possibilities. They surely didn't know about the doctored equipment? No, it hadn't even been used yet. The helicopter incident? I tried to keep a cool expression.

"My firm's business interest. Is that what you mean?"

Holt gave an unpleasant leer.

"More personal, I'm afraid."

The fiery cart-wheeling aircraft filled my mind as my inner voice repeated: *you didn't expect it, ask to be there, or take part.*

You could still be considered an accomplice, came the response.

Without permission, they sat down.

"Mr Martin, travellers' cheques, taken to Colombia by you, were used to purchase fertiliser."

"Fertiliser! Why on earth... no pun intended! Look, I'm Deputy Human Resources Manager for an ITC company, not a farmer! Anyway, I can explain. Unhappily, I got mugged in Bogotá and cheques and a credit card were stolen. I immediately reported it. I'm told this sort of thing frequently happens – though I'm surprised if farmers have taken to robbing!"

"Maybe," said Mary Hume. "Perhaps you also know that fertiliser can make explosives. Your purchase was used in that way!"

My heart thumped under the stress. This whole Colombian episode seemed to be doomed.

"But it wasn't my purchase! As I told you, cheques and my card had been stolen!"

"Anything else you'd like to explain?" asked Morelli.

"Not really. I'd met a business contact for a drink. Afterwards, I took a walk for some air before returning to my hotel. That was when I got mugged!"

"When you say business contact, what kind of business?"

His question caught me off guard and my frightened mind went into overdrive. The agents became very interested and time seemed to stop. I feared I might look evasive, and it could all spin out of control. If I answered truthfully, things might point to Nina and Corrine. Others could be compromised, too. I felt frozen, even as my mind whirled frantically. Miguel Hernandez was part of an organisation formerly proscribed by the State Department. Miguel seemed okay and had spent time and effort with me. Was he really a terrorist or just someone fighting for his people? After all, lies, dirty tricks and propaganda could run both ways.

Morelli spoke louder.

"Explain: 'met with a contact'?"

A hangover certainly didn't help with creativity. I needed something more plausible!

"Someone I met at the Realtors. See, I was in Bogotá, sorting out premises. Someone in their office offered to show me around a bit. Later, we had a drink together. Afterwards I went outside for a wander and got jumped. I only wanted to stretch my legs, before going back to the hotel."

"The name of this person, Mr Martin?"

A blank mind and my heart beat even faster.

"Err... Luis, I think. Don't know his last name."

"You *think* it was Luis. You were taken around Bogotá by someone, then went drinking with them, but *think* they might be called Luis. Luis, who?"

"Umm, I... Look, I'm sorry, I really can't remember."

"The Realtor will know? Presumably they'll know their own staff. The name of the Realtor, please?"

Despite the cooler temperature, moisture was popping out everywhere.

"Exact address?"

"On one of the Transversals named after a famous conquistador. I can't quite remember. Not too far from the centre."

"A little young to have so many memory problems, aren't you?" sneered Holt.

"Maybe. Look, he didn't actually work there. No, actually I met Luis as I left the Realtors."

Morelli raised an eyebrow.

"He was looking around inside and heard me speaking English. After I left, he approached and asked if I'd like his help showing me around. His pay-off was practising his English. He told me he studied Religious Art and wanted tour guide work – hence the need for practice."

The agents remained impassive while sweat trickled from my armpit.

"Okay, Mr Martin. We hear what you say, though it all seems weak and incomplete. No doubt we'll talk again soon. You say travellers' cheques and a card were stolen at the same time?"

"That's right," I replied.

"And you reported the theft right away?"

"Absolutely. I called immediately I got back to the hotel. It's all on record."

"There'll be investigations," said Morelli, "but we'll leave it there, for now. Our advice is to be very, very careful of your actions and associations. These are dangerous times!"

They left and I slumped into a chair, and my first thought was speaking with Nina. I checked my watch.

"Shit – only 40 minutes until the meeting with Simon Maher."

I quickly dressed and downed cereals in record time.

As usual, there was no shortage of cabs, but the actual ride was a blur.

What on earth was that talk about 'watching your associations'?

As we reached Greenwich Village, an even more worrying thought came.

If they check with Fontibon, they'll find he ran me back to the Eldorado, and that there was no Luis! Actually, now I have more time to think, there was a Luis – the pilot who flew me to the south. If that came out, they could accuse me of consorting with known ex-terrorists or drug traders. In fact, they could claim anything!

Fear blocked any anticipations about a pleasurable brunch, music or meeting Maher.

At the Bluenote, I was warmly greeted by an earnest young man.

"The face behind the emails," he said and shook my hand.

After the earlier experience, anyone friendly was welcome. I'd have loved nothing more than to pour out what had just happened, but I didn't really know Maher.

"I'm completely new to Jazz," said Simon. "What's playing?"

"It's a Bud Powell tribute."

"Bud Powell?"

"One of the seminal bebop pianists – quirky, innovative, best known as an accompanist to Charlie Parker. Musically influential, but, shall we say, had health problems."

"Okay. Lead on!"

It was rather dark and the music had started. A table was available and we ordered brunch. Between numbers, I asked about his flight and his first impressions of New York, but was grateful for low lighting and long numbers. A long drum solo worsened my headache, but the pianist emulated Bud's 'sound' and continued with a flurry of notes. From Simon's face, though, it wasn't the ideal initiation.

"Let's move on somewhere else for coffee and to talk?"

We left by taxi, and I asked for the Algonquin. The associations made it comforting.

Progress up the Avenue was slow and, despite the sharp wind, I knew the chill wasn't only due to the weather. When we arrived, for a moment, I almost expected to see Nina – though she and Corinne now shared an apartment on the Upper East Side. Over a warming coffee, Simon asked about the local environmental scene. I made a desultory attempt, but was really re-running the morning's visit.

Maybe Nina would have ideas to help improve my story. Equally, she might be appalled at my amateurish efforts! Simon enthused about my articles. Normally I'd love that, but right now I just wanted to offload about the morning's visit. Maher asked more about the New Jersey meetings and the water privatising issue.

Perhaps it was exhaustion or shock, but, somehow, it just all tumbled out. First, I described my mugging in Bogotá, almost as an onlooker, and then the morning's visit – omitting key details, like Marco and the aircraft episode. It helped that Simon was an intelligent listener with some familiarity with Latin American issues. Apparently, his boss had written fairly extensively about South American politics.

"You can probably understand me taking the offer up to see some more of Colombia, first hand," I said. "It seemed too important to pass by."

"I'd have done the same. But what do you think they meant by the 'watch your associations' comment this morning? Hey, you don't think you might be under surveillance right now, do you?"

"No, they couldn't possibly know we were heading here. If they really suspect my involvement in terrorism, I'd have been lifted this morning. Probably, just a warning tactic."

My words sounded hollow, even to me!

Simon raised his eyebrows.

"My boss, Andrew, was arrested outside a London Arms Fair. They made certain that he saw a fat dossier bearing his name. His interrogator said something strangely similar 'about being careful of associations'!"

"Spooky. Still, I suppose if we activists network internationally, we shouldn't be surprised that they do, too."

Simon nodded.

"I remember mentioning that arms fair, in one of my emails to you. It demonstrated the state's priorities to us. They really put the fear into Andy, just because he protested the killing machine. Why does it worry them, so?"

"I don't know. I suppose they fear that a critical mass might be irresistible?"

I could hear Nina's voice in the back of my mind.

"Perhaps they worry people might properly see – the inequality, the disappearing middle class, a government that seems dedicated to protecting the plutocracy and pandering to powerful corporations."

Simon grinned.

"Never mind Jazz – this is the sort of music I like to hear! If people really got our governments' priorities, they wouldn't accept it. They want overworked people feeling insecure and fearful so they can't think!"

I usually enjoyed the cut and thrust of this sort of discussion but, just now, my head ached. Simon cut across my thoughts.

"Do you agree, or not?"

"Sorry, I'm just trying to make sense of some things."

It all seemed very sobering. Thinking back to the morning's visit, I added.

"Some activists believe that real freedom is shrinking. Perhaps we should assume that's true in our case!"

"I agree, and the more reason for those in the activist community to support one another. Let's meet again soon!"

37

MANHATTAN

GILL MARNEY'S PERPECTIVE

Gill Marney was part of a small team from the UK's OMID arriving in New York City. Her sub-team were discretely transported to their temporary placement in Security's Manhattan 1 office and were then introduced to their Chief, Tom Freison. The meeting included a brief formal welcome, followed by a section overview. Freison discussed the staff complement and their way of interfacing with the many other agencies of the US Security apparatus. Although Donaldson's public-school manner was absent, she found Freison equally impressive. He detailed a similar mission to OMID's back home, emphasised the importance of the two systems running in parallel and highlighted their concern.

"We currently have two main worries," he told them.

"First, the monitoring of domestic extremists. Second, as I believe has been explained to you, intelligence suggests dangerous extremists might attempt to covertly shelter inside more regular activist groups. We're uncertain exactly who or where, and therefore will keep the whole spectrum under observation. In any case, they undermine business and institutions and generally reduce our competitiveness. This we must prevent."

Freison's pep talk was quite rousing and, later, they had a demonstration of the city's amazing facial recognition system. Typically, they'd been first in the technology queue. The team that she'd been individually assigned to, however, were far less impressive, including a sneering, lecherous agent called Jack Holt whose eyes rarely rose above her chest. Holt certainly seemed full of it, and she resented his implication that the Brits were somehow backward and had come to learn the basics. She was relieved when the day finally finished.

As agreed with Simon, she purchased a local prepaid phone, hoping it would be safer. Later, she called him, and just the sound of his voice helped lift her spirits.

"Gill, great to hear you! Not long now. All packed and ready?"

"I'm already here, Simon!"

"What!" he yelped. "I thought we had to wait another two days!"

"Our new system got even more difficult, so my visit was brought forward. Can we meet or are you still busy?"

"You bet. I know a great diner!"

After their meal, they returned to his hotel hand in hand, almost like teenagers. Approaching the Empire State building, she remembered the sad scene from the movie, 'An Affair to Remember', realising that it must have been shot from somewhere near here. That ended poignantly, but this time she was in charge and – after hours putting up with Jack Holt – some romance was surely deserved. The setting helped and even the little lightbulbs threaded through the trees here made it all seem magical. He pulled her close and, at the moment she tilted her head to receive his kiss, a jet passed behind the Empire State building's illuminated spire. She hugged him, wondering for a moment what Freison would make of her behaviour, and quickly pushed the thought away. It was something she might have to work out... another time!

3 8

BALTIMORE & PHILADELPHIA

ZOLTAN HELTAY'S PERSPECTIVE

Zoltan navigated through the suburbs, until he reached the tangle of Baltimore's 'Little Italy'. Soon he became lost, and turned back to a coffee shop on the previous corner to ask the way.

Their coffee was good and he sat looking out at the stone-row houses, drinking and contemplating the task ahead. He asked for another coffee, and requested the directions for Yarrow Street from a rather sinister-looking Italian barista, tinkering with an ancient espresso machine.

"Da Yarrow Street? Izzabouta mile from a here. Wait momento."

The man disappeared to a back room, emerged with a map and then laboriously traced the route with a stubby finger. Zoltan jotted down directions and paid.

Zoltan drove on towards Fells Point, and made for a rather run-down area lying beyond. After several wrong turns, he spotted Yarrow Street and two buildings from the corner was the described lock-up with its faded blue door. Abdul's encrypted message had said a ship-ment had now arrived and was ready for collection. The lock-up was part of an old warehouse, which now consisted of a panel-beating workshop, a motorbike repair shop and several storerooms.

It was now mid-afternoon and the street seemed deserted. He inserted the key into a rusty lock, opened the door and quickly closed a secondary shutter behind him. The lights worked, as Abdul specified.

He looked around the room. Boxes were stacked against one wall and, in the corner, a large suitcase with a carrying harness and several smaller boxes. He carefully picked up each of the small boxes. Satisfied with his inspection, he carried them and the suitcase to the van, relocked the premises and retraced his way through the Baltimore suburbs to Philadelphia and Judy Anson.

∾

JUDY LINGERED IN HER BATH, imagining the evening ahead. Yesterday, Zoltan returned late. She was about to retire when he arrived back, looking rather exhilarated and very handsome. She said her goodnight, but, after he took her hand and tenderly kissed it, sleep had eluded her. Later that night, she'd heard a noise and quietly stepped out of her room onto the landing. He'd emerged from the bathroom with a bare chest and a towel around his waist. Moonlight flooded through the hall window and time almost stopped as they gazed at each other. She wanted him, but words wouldn't come. He smiled and she returned to her room for a restless night.

Judy looked through the water, not entirely displeased with what she saw, imagining her body from his point of view. She drifted into what might have happened if only she'd been more free. She told herself to get a grip, and then vigorously dried off, as though it would wipe her fantasy away. Surely, the charities and a spiritual life was more important and having a man in her life would only complicate it. She dressed and heard a car door slam and saw Zoltan carrying boxes to the shed. He cut quite a figure and she pictured them together at the concert. She finished her make-up, arriving downstairs as Zoltan entered the house. He grinned, raising his eyebrows.

"Wow Judy! You look great!"

The directness of his eye contact brought a delightful lurch to her stomach.

"We should leave soon so you may want to change."

He left to shower and she realised, with a jolt, she'd imagined the scene! An inner voice cavilled, but she decided to ignore it.

So, you're actually human!

Zoltan reappeared in a black suit, transformed into the kind of escort most women would envy.

He linked arms as they entered the foyer, and it didn't seem presumptuous – just the attentive escort. Their seats were good and, despite a programme change, it was marvellous. Smetana's portrait of the Vlatva River, a contemporary Czech piece by Marek Kopelent, and Martinu's wonderful Sixth Symphony to finish. She almost felt like her younger self on a first date, but it was what he said next that she found so thrilling.

"I love the Vlatva, Judy. Not just in Prague, but upstream in Bohemia. I visited a wonderful medieval town on the Vlatva, called Cesky Krumlov. That brought it all back. It was so special, I'd love to take you there."

She swallowed. Did he really say, 'I'd love to take you'?

"It has a Gothic castle with an amazing colourful tower, and bears roaming where the moat once was. The town's packed with fabulously coloured baroque buildings, nestling on an S-bend in the river. It's really quite wonderful!"

"I loved Europe," she replied. "My absolute favourite was Italy: Venice, Florence, Sienna and, of course, Rome. I never got to Eastern Europe, though. You must tell me about Hungary."

The interval bell rang and they returned to the auditorium. He held her hand this time and it felt so right. After the concert, he suggested a meal.

"Pity we didn't see a Hungarian restaurant or you could try our food. Maybe I'll cook at home one evening?"

They settled for Italian. The conversation flowed and he shared an enthusiasm for 'world music'. She tried to steer the conversation towards politics. Freddy seemed almost oblivious, yet Zoltan was apparently his friend?

"Your parents must have lived under communism. Was that awful?" she asked.

"We escaped, so I suppose that answers your question. Mind you, not everything is just and fair here!"

"Of course. Like what, though?"

"Oh, I don't know... weak workers' rights or pushing free market fundamentalism down everyone's throat. That has possibly caused almost as many problems as the horrors of communism!"

"You think so?"

"Ask the globalised poor. Of course, 'free market' fundamentalists are only too happy to do business with repressive dictators – if everyone profits!"

She nodded.

So, he opposed market excesses! Could it get any better?

He held her hand again. *Yes, it could! Let's really test him!*

"It's the word 'liberal' in 'neoliberalism' that I find upsetting," she said. "The only thing free, is the freedom to use money for controlling weaker economies. Then financial elites end up with more power than a country's elected government!"

"Ah, the 'virtual senate of capital' argument. I couldn't agree more."

"I'm surprised," she said, "Freddy doesn't think that way at all. I'm glad you do, though."

His warm hand stroked hers.

"Because I do business with Freddy, it doesn't mean we have the same outlook. You see, I've travelled extensively and some things are so obvious, unless you're blind, stupid or rich enough to keep your eyes closed. I just wish we could change things."

In the restaurant's soft glow, he looked devastatingly handsome.

They returned home and she didn't want the evening to end. Truly, she hadn't met anyone as attractive or sensitive, since losing David. They stood close and he put his arm around her shoulders.

"Thanks for sharing the evening, Judy. It was really special."

They moved close and, as their eyes made contact, she felt light headed. The kiss might have started slowly, but it finished passionately.

39

MANHATTAN

ROBBIE JAMES

Looking at lines on the ceiling didn't really help me to move out of this feeling. I felt an even greater mess than usual. Recently, I'd assembled some sensitive commercial information for Simon and was almost caught. That wasn't the only thing. I also had to admit to a growing attraction to Simon, and that brought more conflict. Anson had been more abusive than usual recently and, as so often at these times, I'd frequented the adult shops near the Port Authority Bus Depot and ended up in the clubs and bars down in the Village. I really needed to understand the pattern. Why did something always knock me off balance? Usually, something external, but sometimes even my own thoughts! It had been like that for years!

Would I ever understand myself, and take hold of the steering wheel of my own life? I went over to my desk, took out paper and started doodling. Following an idea I'd read, I started to map recurrent states of mind and put them into little bubbles. The diagram soon grew in complexity. Biff wasn't the only one to suggest that I was more than a little screwed up – or worse. Perhaps they were right! Certainly, being in my head was no fun place!

I listed difficult recurrent feelings like the article suggested, drawing in connections with arrows and boxes, until it looked like a giant algorithm. Soon, the page filled, so I started free-wheeling, letting my pen and imagination continue in a sort of free verse. After about thirty minutes, I read my ramblings back.

The mental sky starts out clear and bright. The sun of the 'self' shines high in the psyche. Happy thoughts chirp like delighted birds alighting on fresh territory. Colourful ideas radiate like ripples on a lake – but, eventually, those dark thoughts arrive again. Sharp thought-arrows penetrate my shelter, stirring black pools of sorrow. In time, a careless thought enters a forbidden zone, becoming stuck like a tern in an oil spill – covered in stickiness, glued solid and unable to soar. Fearful messages spread through the neural loom like wildfire, as chemicals spill across synapses, and whisper fearful thoughts to every cell. It's time to shut down!

Everything clamps and constricts. Batten down the hatches – a storm's coming! A pinprick of consciousness locks onto its own anxious productions in a downward spiral of constricted thought. The overburdened mind shears night from day, aware only of bad darkness, split from white goodness, as it weaves a heavy straight-jacket of fear and guilt. A one-dimensional sackcloth of memories, bleeding and cut from their context, is recruited to drape the soul and spirit in shame. The mind seeks an escape, but the sticky morass engulfs it, like an animal caught in quicksand – sinking deeper and deeper.

The mind frantically throws up skeins of thought, trying to drag itself from the quagmire, but the thought-loops only catch another branch of the same poisonous tree. Struggling, it sinks deeper and deeper – no vision, no light, no air!

After intense pain and despair, comes a gradual lightening – focus broadens, relaxes and the world of context slowly reappears. Sometimes, though, it can only be prised from one poisonous obsession, by some other grim event, or another black thought that brings further cold stinging winds into the mind-bubble. Often, one thorn is ejected, just to be replaced by another. Then the mental iris contracts, and the inner ear hears familiar whisperings – different words, but the same old tune.

At other times, however, the record can change, bringing sweet and wonderful music. My difficulty was getting control of the process!

I put the pen down and scanned the page's content. Surprisingly, the exercise did give some relief.

I decided to make a call and Simon answered quickly.

"Simon, Robbie here. Wondering how the research was going and things in general?"

"Fine. In fact, I'm just about to visit the UN Library, to look at their material on water privatisation. Fortunate that I mentioned it to Nick, though. Apparently, now you must be associated with a recognised NGO to use the library. Nick put me wise and joined me up to CCW."

"Who?"

"Concerned Citizens Worldwide – a group monitoring corporate abuse in developing countries. Apparently, his girlfriend is involved."

"Good. Listen, how would you feel if I came along? I can be guide and, later, research assistant?"

The line remained quiet and I crossed my fingers. I still felt vulnerable and emerging from that dark place was always difficult.

"Yeah, okay, but I really have to work. As the college is funding the trip, I have to, as it were, 'take home the bacon'."

"Got it! Listen, I've put some material together I think you'll find very interesting. I'll explain more later."

"Great! I'm looking at the map as we speak. How about we meet, say, at the corner of Fifth Avenue and Forty-Second Street and then walk down to the UN building? I want to see something of the place while I'm here."

"Sounds like you're getting the hang of things already. You've suggested a particularly interesting route. Let's meet at the Public Library's entrance and I'll point out some things on the way."

I left my apartment, passed St Mark's Place and crossed to the Astor Place subway. My spirits were beginning to rise and I had no particular reason to notice if anyone followed behind me and into the subway. Twenty minutes later, I was on Fifth Avenue, shaking Simon's hand.

We 'lobby hopped' along Forty-Second Street's finest. Simon expressed particular enthusiasm for art-deco architecture, but the Beaux Art delights of Grand Central Station are worth anyone's time. I showed him the view out over the concourse, the famous oyster bar, and the pin-point lights of the constellation set in the vaulted ceiling. We exited on Forty-Second and made our way towards the Chrysler building.

"What do you think?"

"It all seems weirdly familiar. Probably all the movies set here."

"Probably. You asked for art deco?"

I pointed to the floral patterns on the Chanin building, and Simon smiled in appreciation. He really was quite handsome!

We moved on to the mosaics in the Home Savings of America's lobby, but his strongest reaction was to the Chrysler building itself.

"Those gargoyles are fantastic!"

"Wait till you see inside the lobby," I said touching his shoulder to guide him over the street.

As I expected, it was the marquetry on the elevator doors that impressed him most.

"I never thought I'd see all this first hand," said Simon.

"To be honest, I don't really feel like burying myself in reports. But..." He held his palms up.

I liked Simon – his outlook, accent, looks, and humour. If I could only find someone like that, I'd leave the sleaze behind.

We arrived at the UN complex.

"Where's that sculpture?" he asked. "You know, with the handgun."

"You probably mean 'Non-Violence'? The piece with a knotted barrel?"

We found and viewed it, from various angles.

"A pity its message wasn't taken seriously!"

"Exactly! Incidentally, we're technically not on US territory now. The fact it's a special international zone, apparently, doesn't stop it from being a hotbed for bugging."

Once inside the Dag Hammarskjold library, NGO member Simon Maher and assistant were inducted into the use of UNBIS – the UN Bibliographic Information Service system.

"Let's do a preliminary search on 'water privatisation' and see what it brings up."

"Great suggestion, Holmes," Simon replied with a grin.

The first report, by the Economic and Social Council, was unequivocal.

The right to drinking water and sanitation is part of internationally recognised human rights that should also be a prerequisite to various other rights.

We worked at separate terminals. After a while, I tapped Simon's shoulder, and pointed to my screen:

Article 25 (1). The right to a standard of living adequate for health and the right to water, is a part of the International Covenant on Economic, Social and Cultural rights.

"That seems clear enough."

A po-faced looking librarian scowled in our direction. I highlighted another passage.

The right to water is such that it affects peace and security... growing water scarcity may lead to international conflict.

We worked through numerous reports. To lighten matters up, I started to scribble my guesses of delegates' origin, as they entered. Simon joined in, but it soon deteriorated to suggestions like Narnia, Oz and Mars. Perhaps it was a necessary break in what was grim reading. Over a billion lack access to safe drinking water, and more than two and a half billion lack sanitation. Two million deaths are estimated from diarrhoeal diseases and the results of toxic waste dumping – including the destruction of water catchments and depletion of aquifers.

We moved onto the outcomes of various privatisations. Simon seemed a ferocious note taker and I felt slow in comparison. I scanned over his handwriting... *States must be able to exercise control over water resources on behalf of all their citizens, free of unjustified interference... Water should not be treated as a mere commodity or as consumer goods.*

A group of African delegates entered and I wondered what they made of these reports.

In many countries, privatisation has only worsened water access. It's more expensive and a system of management by exclusion has exacerbated poverty in many countries... water should be affordable to all, regardless of financial means.

I pointed to my notes and Simon leaned in close to whisper his reply.

We finished and left the UN building, almost overflowing with desperate images.

"Maybe I can show you some of the more interesting parts of New York?"

40

MANHATTAN

GILL'S PERSPECTIVE

Gill wiped her forehead, barely able to believe the situation. No, surely not! Involvement in field observations, she'd anticipated – but not here!

The work was mostly familiar. The databases of activists differed little from OMID's expanded mission. At first, getting out of the office was nice, observing things first hand. Today, she'd started out with supervisor Vern Matacic and Jack Holt. Holt was now out tailing a mark. Someone he described as… "That weedy little fag, Robbie James"!

She was sitting with Vern at a café near St Mark's Place, trying to keep calm. Holt called through from the NYC Public Library. Apparently, his target, Rob James, had now linked with 'Simon' – the recipient of the call they'd earlier intercepted. Both were now en route to the UN complex.

"These characters love hanging out together," said Matacic. "James was seen at an anti-water privatising meeting in Jersey, chaired by Nick Martin, and he has since attended regularly. Now he's off with this 'Simon' guy, doing so-called 'research' at the UN. These types now even network internationally!"

She had few doubts that this 'Simon' was, in fact, her Simon, and felt impending panic. Si mentioned someone called 'Robbie' and, even back in England, said that the UN Library was on his agenda. She was aware of protective feelings – feelings that were totally hypocritical. After all, she'd previously fed back several months of information about him – but it now seemed so different!

They entered James' apartment with little difficulty. Matacic picked up scribbled notes left on his desk.

"Shit, you should see this. He fancies himself as a bit of a tortured poet."

Gill scanned through the jottings. He did seem in rather a mess.

She checked with Vern.

"Have I grasped our task correctly? Rob is an associate of Nick Martin, the guy that Jack and the others visited – the one whose money was used for bomb-making materials in Colombia. Rob's company plans to bring in a water privatisation there. Meanwhile, Martin works for a consultancy corporation contracted to run the South American office. James is currently out with this guy, Simon, and says he has information for him. If that discussion happens here, we'll record it. I think you also said he's Terry James' son. How is that relevant, again?"

"Terry James is a well-known militia leader in Montana – and potentially dangerous," replied Matacic. "Incidentally, a good summary, Gill. You've grasped it very well."

"Okay, so his dad is a militia guy and the 'dissident net watch' shows James visiting various 'militia sites'."

"In addition to a range of activist, conspiracy and general whacko sites," added Matacic.

The door opened to Jack Holt.

"I followed him from Astor Place to Forty-Second Street. They then moved off for the UN building."

Matacic moved around the room, examining papers, books and stacks of internet printouts.

"Take a look at these, Jack."

Matacic pointed to Robbie's scribbling.

"This guy's head is so full of shit," said Holt. "Spending a day at the UN would be like kinda light relief!"

They saw piles of jottings on corporate law, corporate crime and a list of Marquetcom marketing campaigns. Printouts about central banking added to the confusion.

Holt appeared perplexed.

"What a fucking magpie! How many pies can one person stick their fingers into?"

'The dissident watch' also recorded visits to conspiracy sites and a large number of gay websites. They fired up James' computer and Holt quickly outflanked its security, going straight to the email section.

"'Look." He pointed to a folder with a few months of messages to and from Nick Martin. Holt read several aloud.

Hi Nick. Attached are pieces relevant to our recent chat. The first is a bit old, but fascinating. Apparently, the EU backed water privatisation globally. That got 'leaked', causing something of a stink. No doubt it'll be redrafted and then secretly rolled out again – giving a new twist to the expression 'business as usual'! Look forward to us 'talking' again soon. Robbie.

Holt scrolled down to another message on the same subject.

Hi again! Found this quote from Fortune magazine, way back at the millennium. "Water promises to be to the 21st century, what oil was to the 20th century – a precious commodity, determining the Wealth of Nations." Well, they are still fighting, the water battle has started and we're on the front line! Look at the attachment. Apparently, the World Bank predicted the private water management business could reach $1,000,000,000,000 soon. Makes you thirsty, doesn't it? Off to drink some water, while I can afford it! Robbie.

"Another happy little researcher!" said Holt.

Gill and Matacic read over Holt's shoulder.

"These idiots are getting tangled up with projects of real economic importance. They need to be watched," Matacic said.

He turned to Gill.

"This guy, Simon Maher, cross checks with lists from your people. Obviously, he isn't important enough to be flagged at a high level?"

Gill prayed her voice didn't tremble.

"I think I may be able to help. I recognised the voice when we intercepted the call. I should do because I spoke with him myself, just two nights ago."

Matacic spun around.

"What?"

"Simon was on my list at home. I built a dossier about him and his associates, for months. He mixes with real anti-corporate types in Oxford! Coincidentally, his research work in the US came up around the same time as my assignment. In a funny way, he's not all bad!"

"The most poisonous snakes often look pretty," said Holt.

You should know, Gill thought, struggling to keep a professional facade.

Holt sneered.

"He's out with bent little Robbie. Is Maher gay too?"

"I don't think so," she replied. "I realised it was my Simon – by that, I mean the Simon on my list – when I heard his voice on the playback. It was a 'velvet surveillance', so we'd spent a lot of time together. Of course, he mentioned this trip, even his plans to use the UN Library. He has various other interviews lined up."

Holt looked at Matacic.

"Sounds like our kind of troublemaker!"

Her heart pounded. Worried it would strain credulity, she then said:

"Perhaps I should mention that we're meeting tonight. See, Simon thinks that I'm here helping to sort out IT problems for an international accounting company. My boss, Dick Hennessy, and Commander Donaldson thought continuing contact, if feasible, could be useful. As you said, 'they network internationally'."

Holt leered and then rolled his eyes.

"Okay," Matacic replied. "That might work out well. Maher may know more about what James and Martin are getting up to. We'll look forward to you telling us, tomorrow…"

41

MANHATTAN

ROBBIE JAMES

Robbie blinked against the brightness as they emerged from the UN Library.

"Yes, seeing more of New York is exactly what I'd like," said Simon. "I'm in your hands."

My mind went off in a quite different direction.

How about a cable car trip?

What, Colorado? Before dinner?"

"Ha ha. Not necessary! Follow me."

We returned via Forty-Fourth Street and rounded the Helmsley building to Park Avenue. I pointed out the polychromatic dome of St Bartholomew's, and then that extraordinary fantasy crowning the GE building.

"You wanted art deco. How about that?"

Simon was fixated by the stylised crown of radio waves and lightning bolts.

"What do you reckon?"

I was struck again by Simon's good looks.

"The whole place has tremendous energy," he answered. "Strangely, I'm reminded of childhood comic books – Spiderman, Superman, and Batman. Gotham City!"

"That's right. Indeed it is Gotham City," I agreed.

"And how it changes character every few blocks."

"You should see the difference between the Upper East Side and Lower East Side," I said.

"Mind you, the amount of sleaze near the bus terminal was something else," Simon replied.

I felt myself colouring. Surely, he didn't know about that.

"Yes, it's quite a town," I quickly replied.

We passed the Citycorp building, and tiny St Peter's church, nestling beneath the supporting columns. A few minutes later, we were looking from a Swiss cable car, swinging over the East River.

"It goes to Roosevelt Island, formerly 'Welfare Island'," I explained. "It once had hospitals, a workhouse and mental asylum, though it's mainly apartments now."

We walked down to the river, to look back across the city.

The return, looking onto Queensborough Bridge with the bristling forest of towers behind, was even more spectacular.

Hearing of his fondness of art deco, I walked Simon down to the Rockefeller Centre. The day was now drawing in and I felt curious to know more about my new friend.

"How about a libation? I know that the 'Village' has really good bars. Many people think it has a European feel."

"Greenwich Village? Actually, I've been already. Nick and I took Sunday brunch at the Bluenote club."

"Yes, but it comes to life after dark."

It was just about light when we emerged from the subway. Simon had heard of Washington Square, still busy with New York University students, dog walkers and the occasional drug dealer. The red-brick row houses on the edge glowed under the last slanting rays. As we turned into Bleaker Street, Simon claimed that parts reminded him of London. The Gothic gables and turrets of the Jefferson Courthouse, now a public library, was even more of a surprise. We emerged at Sheridan Square and, as we neared my old stamping grounds, my heart skipped a beat. I suggested a drink, and we made for a bar on Christopher Street I knew rather well.

As usual, it all seemed loud and very camp. I sneaked a glance to gauge his reaction. Simon leaned in close, in order to be heard.

"Suddenly, I find I'm thinking of YMCA and the Village People. Is this bar what I think?"

Before I could answer, two men joined us.

"Who's she brought in?" said one.

Simon smiled.

"This is Simon, over from England."

"Another Brit, I'm afraid!"

"Love your accent, darling," said the older man.

I turned to Simon.

"What would you like?"

"Thanks. A beer would be great. Listen, something just got clearer. I really appreciated your help today. The thing is, mentioning my girlfriend just didn't seem relevant at the time. In fact, she's here in New York and we're meeting later tonight."

My stomach contracted, with the fear of rejection – a very familiar feeling.

"You did mention someone," I replied. "I thought 'girlfriend' might be a friend who happened to be female. I have many friends like that. Look man, I hope my lifestyle doesn't complicate things. I'm sure we've many other things in common. This aspect of my life is, well… just one aspect!"

"No problem. I only wanted to avoid a misunderstanding. I know it's already been quite a day, but this morning you said you had material to show me?"

"You're right; it has been a long day. I kind of thought that, after finishing at the library and some sightseeing, you'd come back to the apartment. The material is there."

"Impossible tonight. I have appointments tomorrow and a business journalist the following day. Is Friday possible?"

I swallowed my disappointment.

"Yes, that works. Come to my place Friday evening and I'll have the material there ready for you."

4 2

OXFORD

ANDREW ALTON

Life returned to normal, with no obvious repercussions after my arrest. I looked over the notes from last night's meeting with Farrelly and Grotstein, thinking what a shame that Simon had missed it. I'd offered to prepare an overview for the others on the problems caused by privatisation, and was working on this when the phone rang. Simon's voice sounded as clear as if from the next-door office.

"Hi Andy, just making contact. Things okay at home?"

"All's quiet again. Strange you phoning now. I was just preparing some material for the group's next meeting. You'd have enjoyed last night. Stephen behaved quite well, this time. How are things going in New York?"

"Plenty has happened! I've already made some useful contacts and met Nick Martin, the independent writer I mentioned. He's introduced some other relevant folk. I went to the UN Library with one. The guy works for a company that's preparing a major water privatisation in Colombia. Said his CEO is a particularly unpleasant bully. He's quite disgruntled, and offered first-hand information about the project and his boss. I've got other interviews lined up, too."

"Great! You've hit the ground running."

Simon started enthusing about New York, but, before I could respond, my secretary Helen put her head around the corner.

"The Vice-Chancellor wants to see you."

"Listen, Simon, must go, keep me in touch. Helen just told me Danton wants a word right now. Good luck and we'll speak soon."

I set off for central administration, feeling rather cheerful. Following months of work, a study demonstrated a clear growth in poverty indicators after following certain policies. Though the work didn't exactly chime with economic orthodoxy, it was out for peer review. Danton probably wanted an update. In fact, a meeting at this time could be fortuitous – a chance to float ideas for expansion now that the course had attracted additional interest.

His secretary waved me in, but, as I entered his office, Danton's expression shrivelled any sense of optimism.

"Good morning, George."

"Good morning. Do sit down, Andrew. Look, I'll come straight to the point. I'm afraid this won't be good news, but I fear that recent developments will have major impacts on your future work."

"I thought things were going rather well."

"At one level, yes, but, as you know, we're under extreme pressure."

"What, you mean with education increasingly politicised and put under unnecessary pressure?"

Danton pulled the whiskers of his well-manicured beard.

"I wouldn't put it quite that way, myself. The point is, that we have no choice other than to enter into a number of partnership arrangements with business. This is, after all, a business school. The board of governors is committed to business sponsorships and that we under-take more business-orientated research. That's also in line with current government policy."

"We can't all become cheerleaders for big business, George! My unit couldn't conduct our kind of research in big business's pocket."

Danton looked almost shifty.

"I know how passionate you are about that, Andrew, but you're missing the point. As an institution, we're required to show proper business functioning."

"I thought our aim was for academic excellence, not whoring for business." I instantly wished that I'd held back with that one. Rudeness to the VC was hardly skilful management.

Danton looked guarded.

"Andrew, your unit comes under the umbrella of the business school! Please remember that. I understand your point, but, frankly, hearing you talk about business in that way – is worrying!"

"It sounds like you're leading up to something, George?"

"I'm coming to that. I suppose you know many other departments have forged links with business partners, who are now sponsoring some of the bigger projects."

A sore subject indeed and one that infuriated me.

"I know it's a worldwide trend," I said. "Resulting in junk science, useless pro-business propaganda, phoney trials and suppressed information that otherwise might have helped people and the environment!"

"We have to live in the real world!"

"You mean the one that's being destroyed?"

"You sound stridently anti-capitalist. I sometimes wonder if you forget your unit is attached to a business school?"

"I don't forget that, but, personally, I can't always appreciate pandering to corporate needs that are quite so insane. Look where that's brought us! I certainly do support ethical business, but not greedy corporations that wish to own everything – even to patent life itself!"

"Finished?" asked Danton. "No, it's not perfect, but it is the system we live and work in, I'm afraid. Which is why I must now tell you that your unit won't be accepting students for the new year. It continues for now, but will be as a research entity harnessed to business needs – including those of the new private partners."

"What?" I asked.

"As you know, we provide consultancy for Diamond Telecom and their internet subsidiary. A partnering proposal has come from a powerful and influential US company. Association with our school is seen by them as being very prestigious."

I felt as though an abyss had opened up and everything that I valued would soon be sliding into darkness.

"Who is this partner, George?"

"I can't reveal that just yet, because negotiations aren't finalised. I'm afraid there's more. As you know, in this climate, central government funding is tighter. New guidelines are out for research."

Danton picked up a paper on his desk.

"The relevant section says: *'Business orientated research should be encouraged where possible, specifically geared to activities promoting efficiency, sustainable development and which are ultimately beneficial to the UK economy'.*"

Danton's mouth tightened.

"I'm not at liberty to expand, but I'm afraid there have been complaints from more than one quarter, that your work, whilst undoubtedly brilliant, doesn't always meet those ends. Indeed, some believe it's often the opposite!"

"We always try to research with integrity, George, not just dress up corporate wish-lists as research. Enough of that comes from the PR people! Proper research won't flourish, if we're subjected to the whims of a corporate paymaster."

"I understand that, but I see an impasse approaching, Andrew. Things must change and you may have to consider your position."

"Sounds like I hardly have a position any more, George. You know what I've tried to achieve."

"You'd still head the unit if you choose to stay, though, perhaps, from what you've said, you might not find future projects quite so congenial. You could also tutor students from the main business school and we hope to expand our consultancy. I can foresee conflicts there, though, so we'd have to discuss how that would work."

"I'm staggered, George. We've been developing an exciting new syllabus, including Developmental Economics, Human Rights, the preservation of natural resources, security, global development and the politics of environmental protection, just for starters. Relevant issues that should generate a lot of interest. Many want alternatives to the orthodox 'truths' that got us into this mess."

"I'm sorry, Andrew. You have to understand that our core business is moving in the opposite direction. I really am sorry. By all means, round off the papers and the work you've started."

"Young Simon Maher is in the US researching new material."

Danton shook his head, and seemed to struggle.

"I know, I know. You must finish that work. Look, I appreciate this comes as a shock and there's a lot to take in. We've several weeks until next term. Take time out if you wish. We'll talk again soon."

I felt unsteady and short of breath on the way back to my office. I sat for a while, staving off dizziness.

"Everything okay?" Helen asked.

"Guess so. To be honest, no. I've a headache and need to be quiet for a while."

I closed the door to avoid further questions, leaning on the desk with my head in my hands. *What on earth did Danton mean by: 'complaints from some quarters'? Or the part about taking a business partner?* I felt as though my whole world was being re-arranged, without me!

I phoned Anne.

"Hello love. Glad you're in. I'm coming home now because of a development we must talk over. I'll explain in a bit."

I drove home almost on automatic pilot, and tried to consider the options. I could consult my professional association. This almost seemed a 'constructive dismissal' situation? I wasn't actually being dismissed, though, so there was probably little they could do. Could I rally colleagues? What about contacting past, present or even potential students in the hope they'd protest? Probably futile and, besides, I couldn't be seen to be orchestrating it. Anyway, the income from corporate funding would probably dwarf anything my small student intake would generate. Maybe I should take up Danton's offer of time out to consider my position?

Anne was her usual supportive, intelligent self and within two hours I'd taken the first decision. I'd take time out. We sat together on the sofa, leaning against each other. Anne snuggled in, her head on my shoulder.

"Don't worry, Anne, if I can't hack it, I'm probably well placed for something with an NGO or even one of the big charities."

"I'll back you whatever, darling. Who knows, we might look back later and see this as a blessing in disguise."

I called Grotstein.

"Does this mean you'll drop our project?"

"Absolutely not! Makes me all the more keen."

Farrelly was unavailable, so I left a message.

I found the number Simon had left, and checked my watch. He should still be available.

"Simon, it's Andy here."

"Hi. Didn't expect to hear back so quickly. How did the thing with the VC go?"

"That's why I'm calling you. Fairly disastrous, I'm afraid."

"How so?"

I explained.

"Basically, we'll be closed as a teaching unit. Research can continue, but, get this – only to serve business needs and as part of a corporate sponsorship arrangement!"

"Shit! What's happening?"

"Not sure. A combination of the College chasing business sponsorship and new government guidelines for funding, I think. I smell some powerful arm twisting, though, behind the scenes. We probably don't know the half of it yet! I hope you get some good material, Simon, because it's probably our last chance to research with integrity. We'd need to work independently, in the future."

"You're right. This really is disastrous. Please God, I won't return to selling clothes in a mall!"

"As I said to Anne, we're well connected and respected in the field and our work has been well received in most places. There should be openings with NGOs or elsewhere. Anyway, I must stop. Tell me about the rest of your day?"

"Up until a few minutes ago, it had been rather good! Spent last evening with Gill. We had a nice meal and things together."

"I won't ask!"

"I also spoke with that guy, Robbie James, again. We're going to meet soon to discuss his company and the bullying boss I told you about. His company is called Marquetcom and the boss is... it's rather an odd name really – Biff Anson. Apparently, this Anson has a really awful reputation, so his information could be very relevant to our study."

Hearing Dad's name caused a slight nervous system malfunction, tripping on a kind of freeze-frame mechanism. I stared down to the telephone address book on the kidney-shaped table, and then focused on tiny dust motes falling onto the wood. A gnat fluttered across the hall and settled on the table. My throat felt dry and tight.

"Are you there, Andy?" insisted the voice on the other end. I realised Simon had already asked me several times.

Thinking began again, as invisible fingers combed various inner files. Simon's voice continued, but my attention had returned to a terrible argument from childhood. Mom, sobbing about Dad's ethics after Biff had been bragging over besting someone, though it was years before I discovered that the 'someone' was Uncle Mike – Mom's brother!

"Are you there, Andy?"

"Sorry, Simon. Not your fault, but you rather shocked me."

"Yeah, I was the same when you told me about Danton. We've both had a shit time!"

"No, by what you just said," my voice cracked. "You see, Biff Anson happens to be my father!"

The line remained quiet, and then Simon finally responded.

"Bloody hell! Listen, I'm sorry... I didn't mean... are you sure there isn't another one?"

"You said the business is Marquetcom?"

"I believe so. Look, I had no idea."

"I know. Don't worry. Dad and I haven't talked for years. You can probably take everything your friend says and multiply it by at least ten. Guess we gravitated to this field for good reasons, wouldn't you say?"

"I guess so. It's a shock, nevertheless."

"Look, Simon, I'd have to discuss this with Anne, but I just had the crazy thought that maybe I'll come over and join you. Maybe confront the Dad thing. New York isn't exactly my cup of tea, but with everything..."

"I rather like it," he replied. "Still, it would be great to have you here. Let me know what you decide."

I returned to the lounge and Anne brought a coffee. My hand shook as I took the cup. What might this Rob James reveal? It could be very bad.

"You look quite stressed, darling. What did Simon say?"

"He's hit the ground running and made some useful contacts already. One apparently works for just the sort of corporation and business leader we're studying – you know the work with Martin and Stephen Grotstein."

"That's good, dear."

"Yes, but it would be a lot better if that leader wasn't my own father!"

"Your father! But..."

"Of course, Simon didn't realise. I've taken my stepfather's name, since late childhood."

"You said he, your father, was hard-nosed, but a sociopath? Surely he's not in that league?"

"I'm afraid so! He isn't exactly proud of me, either! I suppose we each sum up everything that the other despises. Probably that's why we don't have contact."

"A strange cartoon-like name, Biff. Almost onomatopoeic."

It was my first smile of the afternoon.

"I'd never thought of that. He's certainly no Disney character, though. The name is short for Bifton – a little place in Alabama where my paternal grandparents met. It's strange. I can tell you virtually everything about Mom's family, but almost nothing about his side."

"You certainly talk about Mom a lot."

"Anne, I think I should go and join Simon. Be around what's happening and see what he's turned up. I'm uncertain what my future holds, now. If we're to be corporately controlled – perhaps I can't go on. If this is to be the last project, it needs to be good!"

"I'll back you whatever, darling."

"Thanks. I can also visit Mom's new place. Of course, I'll keep in regular touch…"

43

PHILADELPHIA – MANHATTAN

JUDY ALTON'S PERSPECTIVE

Judy woke, feeling very contented and then reached over to check the space to her right. Light crept through the shutters and she gazed at the nape of his neck and curled an arm over his back and shoulders. Zoltan grunted, so she snuggled in, gently blowing air over the back of his neck.

"Hello, lover," she said softly.

"Hi!"

Her body hadn't felt so warm and alive in years.

"Breakfast?" she asked.

He smiled and nodded.

She made her way downstairs, wondering what the boys would think of this development. Of course, it couldn't last with him being her junior – but it was certainly what she needed right now.

Anyway, I'm not ready to curl up with a shawl and slippers yet. She noticed she was humming the song 'Breakfast in America' as she grabbed the tray. A single daft phrase looped through her mind. "Can I have kippers for breakfast, Mommy dear, Mommy dear?" *Kippers are popular in Northern Europe – but with Hungarians?* Doubtful, still, Zolt was American now. 'Mommy dear, Mommy dear?'

She smiled. What the heck was her unconscious implying? Anyway, she wasn't that old.

She fixed breakfast – cereal, Canadian streaky bacon, hash browns and sausages – and took the tray up.

"Breakfast!" she called.

He was still, but she could hear little moaning sounds. Then he snorted and she realised he was sleeping again. She put the tray down and sat by the bed, watching for a moment. He moaned again before turning and thumping his arm on the mattress. He mumbled, seeming to say something in another language. Nothing recognisable – it sounded almost Middle Eastern. Soon his body jerked and he rolled over, flailing his arm across the mattress and crying out "Abdullah".

How strange? Mind you, as she was discovering, Zoltan was an educated and cultured man. Perhaps it was a phrase from Rumi, or from someone similar? He'd mentioned a love of Middle Eastern literature and poetry. He twitched again, and opened his eyes. She smiled and he grinned back.

"I brought you some breakfast."

He opened his arms and beckoned. "Let it wait a moment."

Afterwards, she lay back, gazing at the ceiling, while he finished the food.

"That was really great," he said.

"Certainly was!" she replied

"You were talking in your sleep, earlier."

His face clouded. "Really?"

"Don't worry," she laughed, "you didn't say anything rude about me."

"I couldn't say anything rude about you!"

"Oh yeah! It hasn't escaped me that, before falling back to sleep, you must have seen how I look first thing in the morning!"

"No wonder I was talking in my sleep then!"

She picked up a pillow and threw it. He bounced it back at her again and then they collapsed with laughter. She felt twenty years younger.

They cuddled and, for the first time in ages, she felt the impulse to update her wardrobe. For years, life had revolved around the children and, later, charities and other causes. Besides her love of music, there'd been little fun or romance.

While massaging his shoulders, the phone rang and she reluctantly made her way downstairs.

"Hi Mom!"

Freddy, of all people!

"Hello, son. Yes, thanks, I'm fine. Yes, he's here now. I'll call him."

She felt her colour rising. Silly, to feel embarrassed, as if Freddy could possibly know what they'd been doing. She called upstairs.

"Freddy for you."

She went to the kitchen, then made her way back to the lounge with coffees. At the lounge door, she heard a muffled conversation. Zoltan was still talking, and opening the door was difficult with her hands occupied. As she put the cups on the floor, she heard him speak.

"I can tell you… no, I can tell you, it's completely effective. You don't need to worry. Yeah, there's more for Utah and Mario will sort out stuff for Arizona... Don't know, I'm concentrating on comms. Yes, Baltimore, DC, New York City and probably New England."

She'd again overheard part of Freddy's conversation – albeit accidentally. The question was whatever was he involving Zoltan in, now?

She entered the room, and Zolt looked up and winked.

"Okay, man. Look, must get on so I'll speak again soon. Yes, I'll pass your goodbye to your mom."

He replaced the phone and smiled.

"Freddy and I still do a little business. You overheard us?" he asked rather hesitantly.

"Not really," she pouted. "Although, as I came in, you were saying something about New England?"

"Eventually. I hope to set up a small distribution network for materials – you know, information technology and communications, and that might involve some travel. No, Freddy sent his love and I wondered if you'd heard – that's all."

She smiled, thinking, *I hope you'll stay a long while yet.*

They'd been listening to music about an hour when Zoltan's cell phone rang. She saw his face change expression as he listened. Zoltan left the room and she heard the back door close. He returned, looking somewhat preoccupied.

"Actually Jude, I meant to tell you that I've also got some business in New York. If I take the train over, I can get a meeting in today, finish things tomorrow and still get back late in the day."

"Must you?" She pouted, though was happy to show him how she felt.

"Be careful, Zolt. It's safer than it used to be, but – you know!"

HASSAN ALRAHMANI ALKOURKOUK, or to use his assumed name, Zoltan, was no stranger to New York City and knew that many Iranian ex-pats lived in the vicinity. Some, like his parents, had fled Ayatollah Khomeni's theocracy, but the US government had been extremely helpful in his family's case.

A cab dropped him near Abdullah Bim Ami's home in Brooklyn. He entered to an embrace from Abdul.

"Hassan – sadikie!"

The greeting and hearing his own name came as a relief. Zoltan might be a workable persona, and he enjoyed being a lover again, but pretending to be with the militia felt exceptionally tedious. A comrade to red-necks, bigots, and weekend soldiers like Freddy Anson, tried his patience. Still, at least Abdul had asked his wife, Afari, to prepare traditional food for later – a rare treat these days.

"How's the world of office supplies?" asked Zoltan.

"Busy."

"I sometimes still dream of home, do you?"

Abdul nodded his agreement.

He tried to start a conversation about home and the old days, but Abdul clearly wanted to get down to business and contradicting the leader wasn't appropriate. After a few moments, Abdul put a hand on his shoulder and looked upwards, as though speaking to the heavens.

"If only we had more like you, Hassan. You are able to blend perfectly with the Americans. Only two others can achieve this."

"I thought we had more."

"No, the network is broad, but has only two like you."

"It's sometimes a trial," he replied. "The militia are mostly primitive and uncultured."

"I understand, brother, because I know how you think," said Abdul. "Strange, we could so easily have known each other years ago. Imagine, we both played in Chehel Sohur Park, worshipped at the Imam Mosque, and knew Istfahan as our home – the most beautiful city in the world! We both speak Farsi and good English, though you..."

"Yes, I speak Spanish, French and I'm a communications specialist. You've said so, many times, Abdul. Why did you call me in, now?"

"Because your training is thorough and your understanding deep. I judge you as having the most ability. If we're to pull off the big blow, it has to be you!"

A voice called from the kitchen. They went to the dining room for traditional food as Abdul had promised – Adass Polo and a delicious Abgousht. Afari, then a tasty Rangeenak for dessert. The dates and walnuts might be Californian, but it tasted wonderfully traditional. After the meal, they withdrew to the lounge.

"Baltimore went well?"

"Yes, we have everything."

"Good, further drops will come later. As I said, I've called you in today because you have been chosen to execute the first attack."

Zoltan nodded, trying to contain feelings that were mostly on the cold side of dread.

"Our preparations will soon pay off – Alhandullellah! Come Hassan, look."

Abdul took them to an upstairs bedroom. He opened the curtains and pointed across the rooftops to Manhattan's gleaming towers.

"The Americans are taken with ideas of Empire. Tell me, what do you see?"

Zoltan scanned the skyline. After One Trade Centre and Park Avenue residential, one structure drew the eye – the still classic lines of the iconic Empire State building. He shook his head and looked at Abdul, who nodded and smiled.

"Yes, that's right! They wish to be a state with an empire! What and where could be more fitting? I now have delivery contracts that regularly take me there."

Planning was finished and, by late afternoon, the Hassan genie was firmly back in the bottle.

He returned to Manhattan and, wandering the streets, the Zoltan persona re-emerged seamlessly. New York still had a certain frisson. He liked the beat of the city and the heady melange of luxury rubbing shoulders with poverty and sleaze. He wandered about in the late afternoon light, passing corporate slabs, art-deco masterpieces and drinking in the unique street-life. Standing outside a glass-walled corporate headquarters, he watched a wisecracking street trader deal handcrafted silver rings. It helped to keep his conflicting thoughts at bay. He couldn't hate the place, and yet he'd just been complicit in jointly planning a disaster! By the time he'd reached the Rockefeller Centre, the light was failing. For some reason one of his dad's stories about the West's machinations came to mind. What plans had been hatched in places like this? How strange that their nation's natural resources, particularly oil, simultaneously brought blessings and disasters.

In the past, his country had the potential for huge wealth, yet, when their first elected government dared to suggest that their own people rather than foreign oil corporations should benefit, everything fell apart. His dad never stopped talking of the coup that overthrew Muhammad Mossedegh's democratic government and installed the Shah – a friend to Western interests. Nowadays, almost everyone knew it had been orchestrated by the CIA and MI6. Were they driven by interests in buildings like these and the finance district? Threats from communism – or threats to oil company profits? After the '79 revolution, their whole world had changed.

Zoltan turned the corner, feeling compelled to look up to the Empire State building, now bathed in a golden halo. He'd seen it earlier from Abdul's home and in a few short hours he'd be up there – meeting with Anson! He felt certain about one thing – his relationship with Anson's ex-wife wouldn't enter their discussions! He continued up Broadway towards Columbus Circle and his hotel. Although knowing he was courting trouble, he couldn't resist turning to look at it again. Suddenly, he was flooded with images of the 9/11 attack, in all its horrifying detail. A sense of dread, usually locked in his mental attic, slithered down into his body and he shivered. Surely, he couldn't be the cause of something similar? The street-lights had come on and it was now bright enough to see the faces of others on the sidewalk. Ahead, a woman in her thirties stared into a shop window. He pictured her throwing a ball to a pretty blonde girl then – without warning – fear took over. The sky went a brilliant white, and both figures simply evaporated! He stopped and peered into the nearest shop window, with tightness gripping his chest, and said to himself: *Remember what hangs on this mission*, but then, as he watched a family pass, their limbs detached in a sort of bizarre slow motion, and their faces liquefied, and turned to ash, which then scattered! He shook his head and the image dissipated. He turned back to check, but the family walked on, quite unharmed. He put his hand over his pounding heart and thought of Judy, until he reached the hotel.

Zoltan slept fitfully and woke early. Snippets of a terrifying nightmare hovered on the fringes of his awareness. He could just about reconstruct an image of being tied to a bed and injected. The image had an uncanny familiarity.

Later, he left the hotel, found a diner and took breakfast, with little enthusiasm. It seemed to him that power everywhere seemed to lie with the heartless and corrupt – people untouched by religion or conscience. Were they even reachable? Yet he was soon to be in the company of a particularly repulsive example.

He reached the Empire State building, and took a lift to Marquet-com's suite, trying to compose himself as it hurtled upwards. Anson seemed the kind of creature whose greed ravaged everything. He'd even suck his own people dry... but did the cure have to be quite so drastic? He thought of all the unseen people who would be damaged – those existing even below the underpaid cleaners, waitresses, single mothers on welfare or the hidden street people who emerged from the shadows to their nightly home on the streets. What had they done to deserve such a fate – unnoticed and uncared for by people like Anson? Yet, they'd die too!

The lift doors opened to the luxurious reception area, done out in pink marble. A sleek brunette looked at him questioningly.

"Sorry, I'm new here. Are you Zoltan Heltay?"

He nodded.

"Follow me, please. Mr Anson is expecting you."

They walked through from the building's core, knocked and then entered Anson's huge office. The view from this height was command-ing. The Chrysler building's helmet glinted and the view extended over Central Park, to the distant suburbs. Recalling the earlier imaginings of destruction, he suppressed a shudder. The figure hunched behind the desk had all the intimidating presence he remembered from their earlier meetings.

Anson waved to a chair opposite.

"Take a seat, son. How are you doing?"

"Okay, Sir."

"And how's Freddy? Sometimes I worry that he isn't the sharpest knife in the drawer!"

He felt unsure how to answer. Intuition said that antagonising Anson was unwise, but then the big face broke into a grin.

"I just meant he's lived with red-necks for years! As I said, most aspects of our business here aren't for Freddy to know. What I say must stay confidential. Okay?"

Anson quickly sounded belligerent, so Zoltan nodded agreement.

"I'm used to being discreet, Sir, although I don't really know the purpose of today's meeting. We last talked about how my networking with the militia might fit with your other interests, so..."

"I know. Hold your horses. Look, I'm mostly funding what we're going to put around the country. It's a substantial contribution, so I'd like to get the most from my investment. Make sense?"

"Of course."

"As you know, material comes into Baltimore for the East. More soon to San Francisco for the West, and New Orleans for the South."

"I checked the Baltimore drop recently."

Biff leaned forward.

"I know. The thing is, son, I'm thinking of doing you a favour. I have other projects in mind where you could play a part."

"Are you going to say more?"

"Later on. I first want to check if you're interested in serious money."

"Of course."

"That's the right answer. Play things right and you stand to make a bundle. More, I bet than you've ever seen!"

"You have my interest."

"I won't go into the details yet. Things aren't quite ready, but we'll talk before long. I'll get back to you, in fact, and an associate will make contact soon. For now, we need to streamline the distribution. I also have a little domestic job, that I'll discuss in a moment."

"As far as distribution is concerned, Mr Anson, we have trusted people, in several militia groups."

"Good. We've sourced materials from another region," said Anson. "Some transfers to New Orleans soon. Fancy the Crescent City?"

"Why not?" he replied. "You'll explain later?"

"Yes."

He studied Anson's face. More money could be useful. Abdul said that circulating funds was becoming difficult. New anti-laundering measures had apparently made getting money to the network difficult.

"We'll revisit this next time."

They spent the remaining time discussing communications, encryption and distribution. Eventually, the meeting was over. He asked the pretty brunette the way to the toilet and she directed him to the executive rest-rooms. The facilities were dressed in marble, too, with gilded fittings. He located a service hatch in the ceiling of the end cubicle, climbed on the pedestal and pushed upwards, almost losing balance. The hatch was stiff, but eventually opened up to a space that should be sufficiently large. He replaced the hatch and, after flushing the toilet, left – noting the lift layout and then departing via the main lobby.

Within an hour, he was en route to Philadelphia and Judy. As the train passed through the New Jersey countryside, he relaxed, oblivious that his new lover was busy cleaning his room.

∼

JUDY NOTICED A BATTERED-LOOKING notebook under the bed and, although disapproving of her own actions, couldn't resist looking. She flicked through and, near the end, found a poem by Rumi, called "Why cling?"

She read, wondering what had made him copy this by hand.

Why cling to one's life?
'Till it is soiled and ragged.
The sun dies and dies
Squandering a hundred lives.
Every instant
God has decreed life for you
And he will give
Another and another and another
Mathnawi V

She closed the book, and smiled, remembering the earlier incident. She was probably right. Such a cultured man. He'd obviously been quoting poetry in his sleep!

44

MANHATTAN

GILL'S PERSPECTIVE

Gill felt in uncharted territory. Divided loyalties brought uncomfortable tensions and a crisis was building inside. Sometimes, she almost wished Si hadn't been so successful in opening her eyes. Before, things were more straightforward, but Si had now engaged her on several levels. They'd known each other for several months now, but, as they cuddled last night, he'd gently stroked her breasts. The timing felt right, and lead quite naturally to lovemaking. It wasn't at all an ethical development – she knew that, and here, in the cold light of day, with Vern Matacic and the revolting Jack Holt, things seemed very different.

Wasn't this virtually whoring for the job? her conscience asked. No. She genuinely liked him. In fact, it was much more than 'liked'!

She looked up to find Matacic looking at her.

"So, Gill, bring us up to speed with Maher and friends?"

She resisted the temptation, but wanted to say:

Here's a news flash, Vern. These are ordinary, ethical people who actually want to do good. As a matter of fact, I love Simon – so get 'up to speed' with that!

Yet she was nothing, if not professional, and quickly calmed.

"Yes, Maher said some interesting things."

What a mess. Let her profession down by a 'forbidden' romantic entanglement, or betray Simon, her integrity and everything he'd helped her to see? She looked for something innocuous to say. They already knew about the email exchanges, so that would have to do.

"Apparently, he corresponded with Nick Martin for quite a time – before coming here."

Holt interrupted.

"Yes, we know. I called at his apartment."

Holt scowled at Matacic.

"You know, the one whose money was used for bombs in Colombia – with possibly more to come!"

Matacic nodded.

"Yes, I remember."

"Anyway," she continued. "Seems Maher and Martin hit it off, and have many interests in common. Martin is also friendly with Robbie James.

"Yes, we saw regular contact, on his computer. Is Martin gay, too?" asked Holt.

"Don't think so. I don't know for sure, but Simon told me he's quite taken with some South American woman. Said she's pretty clever."

"From Colombia?" asked Matacic.

"I'm not sure. Maher's day out with Rob James ended strangely, though. Rather amusing, really."

"Why?" asked Holt.

"As you know, they went to the UN Library together. Simon said the research was very productive. Afterwards, James took him sightseeing around the city. They ended up in Greenwich Village, which was all very pleasant. Then, and this is the funny bit, James walked them around Washington Square and, without warning, straight into a gay bar!"

"You sure Maher isn't a fag?" asked Matacic. "See, I don't care, but information like that can sometimes be useful."

Remembering last night, she shook her head.

"Maybe you've experience that says otherwise," said Holt, leering. "Anything you'd like to tell us?"

"Of course not," she replied. "He's just a pathetic activist, though not totally bad."

"Maybe, but these guys attempt to undermine our way of life. They're usually trouble!"

She nodded, but Holt had only inflamed her conflict. In truth, many things that Si had said over the months now made sense. His outrage over water privatising in poor countries, for example. She now got why he felt so strongly and why it mattered.

"The most interesting thing he said was about his boss – a guy called Andrew Alton."

"What's with Alton?" asked Holt.

"I know Alton," she replied. "I was undercover and with them, when he got pulled during a London protest. Andrew is an academic and something of a troublemaker. We made it pretty clear that we're keeping an eye on him. Alton writes controversial studies, which are difficult for businesses – including some of yours. Alton is American, incidentally."

"Yeah, yeah, so what's the deal?" asked Holt, impatiently.

"I'm getting there. Andrew heads an academic unit, which tutors future troublemakers and also cranks out anti-corporate 'research'. A bit of a muckraker, really."

"Yeah, got it. We have plenty like that," replied Holt.

"Anyway, it turns out his college is pulling the plug on him. New policy is business research should be business-orientated and contribute to the economy. They plan to make that a condition for future funding. Simon said the college is squeezed for funds and will, therefore, seek future business partnerships. Corporate sponsorship really and, of course, the business school is a plum target. Knowing him, I'm fairly sure that Alton won't change or make his work more business friendly!"

"So, what's your point?" Holt asked.

"This is where it all gets weird. Apparently, after hearing this news, Alton got into a spin and phoned Simon here, in New York. Simon, expecting plenty of kudos for effort, told him about meeting Rob James. Said that James reported that the business he works for has a boss with exactly the kind of profile they're researching! Of course, Simon expected a gold star for making speedy progress. When Alton asked about the company and its leader, he blurted out Anson's name. Apparently, initially, Alton went deathly quiet, and then revealed that this example of a so-called 'sociopathic business leader' was none other than his father!"

"Nice one," said Holt.

"Apparently, Alton was so shaken, he decided to take a break and intends coming over. Maybe he plans confronting his father?"

Matacic raised his bushy eyebrows.

"Whoa! Roll over Sigmund? Alton clearly has problems with his daddy! Well done for keeping us informed, Gill. Sounds like we should also keep an eye on Alton, when he arrives."

～

JACK HOLT LEFT the room and returned to his office. Using his personal cell phone, he dialled the office of Klieberman–Boss, and asked for Jack Klieberman. As usual, he wasn't big on pleasantries.

"What do you have?"

"I can confirm that Mr Anson's assistant, Robert James, is indeed treacherous. Also, that Maher's digging the dirt over several issues, including Mr Anson's business dealings, and the Colombian project. James intends passing him information."

"Thanks, Jack, you did well. It'll be reflected."

"There's something more, and it's pretty weird. Simon Maher's boss is a guy called Andrew Alton. Turns out that he's none other than Mr Anson's oldest son! I gather that, when Alton heard they intended to discuss his father's activities, he threw a fit. Now he aims to come over. He isn't Mr Anson's greatest fan. I guess he wants to be on hand for any action."

"Good job," replied Klieberman. "You did well bringing this in. Keep in touch."

Minutes later, Klieberman called Biff Anson.

"Keep a special eye on James. It's confirmed that he's untrustworthy and intends passing information – both commercial and personal... Yeah, exactly... Also, that nonsense our associates forwarded from Oxford... Yes, they're still banging that drum. Incidentally, we now know that James is a faggot."

"Little shit. I've had worries about him for a while," Biff replied. "I could easily chuck him, though perhaps he might still be useful."

"Another thing is, when your son Andrew heard that James planned talking about you and the business, he decided that he'd come over. Not sure what he intends."

"Okay, Jack, thanks. You did real well turning up another useful contact!"

Although he couldn't see it, Klieberman could imagine the contorted grin. The tone was unmistakeable.

"Well, well, well," said Anson. "It just gets better and better. The faggot, so-called assistant, plans bitching into the ear of my lily-livered son. Almost like old times. I'll tell you what, though, Andy will really piss his pants, when he finds I've got his precious job in my pocket!"

4 5

MANHATTAN

SIMON MAHER

I picked up the bundle of articles and sighed. My appointments with business journalist Kate Sanderson and an authority on psychopathy, Dr Gianavecci, had been arranged. Nick suggested another meeting. Robbie had offered his information and, to add to it all, Andrew would be arriving shortly! Meanwhile, an exciting city to explore and, more to the point, an exciting woman wanting attention. Everything seemed such a far cry from the old days in Slough!

I looked down from the hotel window, watching the Korean restaurant below receive a delivery, before forcing my attention back to Kate Sanderson's article on corporate ethics. Sanderson, formerly a straight business journalist, first came to professional attention with a hard-hitting series on finance sector lobbying. She was also one of the first off the block to warn of the sub-prime mortgage disaster that affected countless Americans, and then rippled around the world. Integrating this sort of material with Gianavecci's psychological and psychiatric insights seemed a major task, if indeed such links could be made. Truthfully, in the cold light of day, it seemed almost outside my competence. I read for half an hour, and then left the hotel to refine my questions over breakfast.

Kate Sanderson's office was only three blocks away. She was welcoming, and explained that this poky little place wasn't what she'd been used to in the mainstream business press. Now, freelancing, and with a reputation for sizzling corporate pork, meant a more austere lifestyle. Despite her silvering hair, she was a striking woman and my presentation skills let me down!

"So, what exactly did you want to discuss, Mr Maher?"

I sketched out our group's membership.

"We hope to explore probable links that exist between psychopathology, certain extreme business leaders, and the behaviour of their organisations."

Her eyes lit up.

"Yes, I'm familiar with the concept. You're not the first to discuss it, by any means. Certainly, some leaders fit that description. You should also look at the political, legal and economic context that allows – and even encourages – those behaviours. For example, aspects of corporate law. Of course, the same interests also help to shape legislation and business culture!"

"How?"

She smiled.

"Oh, just the whole red in tooth and claw, Anglo-American capitalism. The Anglo-Saxon model, as our European cousins call it. The current 'winner takes all' insanity hasn't always been quite so extreme. Of course, if you dare question it, you're immediately labelled a socialist, communist or some other word that the public have been conditioned to dislike. I don't conform to any of their labels, which they hate. Our challenge is to develop more human, responsive models."

Kate wasn't just attractive; she was also very articulate. Her analysis went on to mention Leo Strauss's philosophy, to Hayek, Friedman, the 'Chicago boys' and their devastating experiments in Latin America.

"Mind you," I said, "we'd be just as extreme if we reject everything that the system has achieved."

"Exactly. Self-reliance and individualism are in America's DNA and underpin our success. That vitality and creativity are the very qualities needed to settle such a vast and unknown land."

"I agree. Which is why it's so sad if corrupt corporate predators or finance hucksters sully the good things about America and the generosity of its people. Europe certainly misses the old America, the innovations, ideals and generosity, and would like it back!"

She nodded, so I continued.

"Our little group believes the extreme 'profit before people' model requires people with a certain psychology to make it work. Spiritual figures don't usually head major corporations – not necessarily because they lack drive or intelligence."

Someone brought coffee in and, looking up, I was surprised to see that her assistant was male. Old stereotypes die hard and I realised that I'd lost her response.

"Sorry Kate, I missed that. I'd suggested they probably 'had a certain psychology'."

Her intelligent eyes looked at me piercingly.

"I thought we were on the same page. I believe the modern term is 'anti-social personalities'. I assume that's what you meant?"

"Yes, at least with some of the key people at the top."

She smiled.

I continued. "Calling either good entrepreneurs or ordinary business activity pathological, would be quite inaccurate and wrong. No, our focus is when individuals with pathological traits lead a big business or gain political or judicial power and their pathology affects many others. That can lead to a detestable form of Social Darwinism or a sick type of globalisation – the great 'race to the bottom'. Also, to workers being trapped in institutionally anti-social systems, where, well…"

"The shit has risen to the top…?"

Her directness was refreshing.

"Maybe, now I'm getting carried away," I said.

She grinned.

"According to the authorities – you probably should be literally carried away – or carted off!"

The phone rang. When she finished listening, she smiled and said:

"Another phoney front group. Turns out that the so-called 'Centre for Personal Responsibility', who are challenging smoking bans on civil liberties grounds, are actually financed by tobacco. Surely they realise we've seen through that old ploy by now."

I smiled as Kate shook her head.

"Personally, I'd include the whole lobbying culture in your research. All those dollars from oil, communications, energy, pharmaceutical and finance institutions, and suddenly, hey presto – legislation magically appears favouring them. It's completely blatant and everyone knows it stinks!"

I furiously scribbled while she outlined the revolving door between government departments and the corporate world. Half-hearted regulators who move to lucrative jobs in the industries they previously regulated. Former politicians, who later sit on Boards. Even more interesting, a few who leave Boards for political office – shape favourable policies, and then return to corporate life.

"It seems that corporations have become the dominant institutions and are almost untouchable."

"Hardly an original comment, Simon, though essentially correct! Look, I've meetings here for most of the day. Let's go for coffee at my favourite shop and continue the discussion there."

Before I could answer, a noise came from outside, and Kate's assistant entered, looking worried.

"Kate, we've a problem. NYPD are outside."

She went out, and I heard raised voices. Kate then returned with two men, reached into her drawer and handed them a slim file.

"We'll be back in touch soon. Be more careful in future. Libel can be costly and so can using stolen materials!"

"I should listen to your own advice or you'll find out more about slander – first hand."

The older man smirked.

"Don't get smart with us, lady. It's not us who's in bother. As I said, you'll hear more."

They left with one of the officers whistling.

"Morons! Mindless goons who can't even think for themselves."

"Yes, they get everywhere," I agreed. "What was all that about?"

"Recently, documents got anonymously sent showing lobbyists for a private corrections corporation pushing for punitive legal changes."

I understood.

"More prisoners, longer custody, means more business?"

"Exactly! Apparently even criminal law should be a business opportunity."

"Phew! It's getting frightening."

"Let's take that coffee."

We emerged into a crowded street and Kate led the way to her coffee shop. A barista recited a huge range dwarfing anything at home. We found a quiet seat at the back.

"What will happen now?"

She shrugged and smiled.

"Material keeps turning up in my email or the post, just begging to be shared!"

I grinned, and fished out my notebook.

"When your visitors arrived, we'd just agreed how the biggest corporations were becoming untouchable."

"We did. Of course, at first, corporations were controlled by the states and needed to demonstrate that they'd work for the public good."

"Rather different from now," I said.

"Well, then the court made what many consider to be the truly dreadful error of granting so-called 'corporate person-hood'."

A daft image formed in my imagination – an oil company, with derricks for legs and a body like the Statue of Liberty, juggling dollars as it shuffled down Wall Street!

"'Corporate person-hood'?"

"Yes. A landmark Supreme Court ruling said that corporations should have the same rights as people. Clearly, corporate person-hood is just a legal fiction, but, in 1976, they ruled that money used for political purposes is their form of free speech! The idea has since been reconfirmed and controls on spending loosened."

"On that basis, a poor person challenging a corporation has nearly zero 'free speech'."

"Quite so," she replied. "Of course, when corporations were first granted legal person-hood – women, Native Americans, and most African-Americans couldn't even vote!"

"The psychiatrist in our group mentioned that. He also told us of a Canadian researcher, who effectively asked: 'If we're supposed to view the corporation as a person – what sort of person would it be?' Hence, the corporate 'psychopath' sobriquet!"

She nodded.

"Disturbingly, that's often true! Most of us will have heard of conmen, who are usually psychopaths, but, funnily, when an organisation shows similar features and acts it out on a large enough canvas – we can't see it! Deceit is often the norm in politics, and also with a number of corporations."

My pen flew again, as she described the tricks many top executives used to reward themselves, while pretending there are no bottom-line consequences.

"That's how they do it!"

"Absolutely –bilk the shareholders, and simultaneously cut employees' earnings, health benefits, pensions, and so on. Apparently, big auditing firms may have been complicit."

"Yes."

"Of course, that's all small beer to what emerged after the great financial meltdown. You sometimes wonder if executives are paid so extravagantly because of their ability and willingness to deceive and manipulate? Such 'skills' are apparently highly marketable."

Kate left for the rest-room. I needed some mental space and gazed out at the traffic, mentally playing again with Joni Mitchell's lyric – 'shoals of yellow taxi fish'. Sometimes it almost seemed that entire areas just existed for the benefit of big corporations and financial institutions. The 'sea of humanity' - like the real sea. Sprats gobbled up by larger fish who became food for yet bigger fish, who themselves were then eaten by marauding sharks. Who could challenge the corporate sharks? I grinned. It certainly seemed a fishy business!

Kate returned and was soon back in her element. People had said I could be too intense, but Kate was evidently from the same mould. She picked up again, without missing a beat.

"Despite their person-hood, corporations, unlike real people, have no responsibilities other than making shareholders more money. Limited responsibility for their effect on people, or the environment. We live in the bizarre situation where the rights of real flesh and blood people are given less importance than those of the 'legal inventions' that shape their lives!"

"An example?"

"Well, agri-businesses and supermarkets determine food choices for most of us, the actions of oil and chemical corporations affect our air quality. In many cities, the only public space is commercial lobby space or shopping malls. Corrections corporations attempt to shape the criminal justice system, the military-industrial complex diverts our tax dollars, and pharmaceutical and insurance interests distort our health system."

We ordered hero sandwiches and Kate described the slippery manoeuvres that help 'incentivise' Boards.

"Ordinary workers apparently don't need incentives, but executives must constantly suck at the teat in order to keep motivated. They must have different genes?"

THE NOTEBOOK KEPT FILLING. By the time Kate had finished describing the personal financial affairs of 'bought and sold' politicians, their appetite finally seemed sated. Neither had noticed the actions of the man sitting opposite or noticed as Jack Holt checked the image and quietly forward it to the facial recognition database. Holt quickly left the coffee shop, pleased with adding the young Englishman. In any case, Ms Sanderson was already on the database and her vulnerabilities checked.

46

MANHATTAN

NICK MARTIN

I lay in bed listening to rain patter onto the skylight, thankful it was Saturday, and reflected on what had been a truly dreadful week. I'd expected anger about the redundancies, but seeing grown men break down had been extremely disturbing.

I dragged my mind back to the present. Attending the Breughel exhibition would be a healthy diversion; but then I recalled Tim Mills' tearful face. Since the rooftop episode, Tim had really progressed, but he looked now as if he might implode.

The rain grew heavier and a warm bed almost seemed too inviting to leave. Thoughts of Tim's therapy inevitably led to my own. Amazingly, it now seemed to be working. The previous patterns of relating seemed so futile now. The excitement of the chase, followed by fears of emotional suffocation, anxieties about commitment and then a rapid cooling off. Maybe it was growing older, or just growing up, but, whatever, I felt more contented and ready to make a commitment to Nina.

My body needed coffee, but my mind was stuck on Canvey. Their plans would cause misery for many people – but for what? The outsourcing mania seemed everywhere. What was the sense? After China, where next? The depths of Africa?! The middle class de-professionalised and left to flip burgers as corporations outsourced ever more intensively?

The rain grew lighter and eventually I dragged myself out of bed.

After coffee, I felt slightly more cheerful and decided I definitely would visit the Breughel exhibition. Those colourful scenes of peasants and their life had long intrigued me. I poured another cup, and pondered Nina and Corinne's relationship. Corinne's flirty vibes were so different to Nina and it sometimes was a little difficult seeing them as colleagues. I'd recently shown Corinne a plan of the Bogotá accommodation. I unrolled it, and held it open for her to see. She came close, very close, until her breasts actually touched my outstretched arms. I looked at her sideways and she smiled, making no attempt to move, but then neither did I! It was the latest of several little incidents I didn't quite get. Unhappily, I'd recently felt an almost animal attraction, even though messing things up with Nina was the last thing I wanted. I made some toast and then searched through the bookcases. Somewhere was an art book that had a good section on the Breughel family.

Part way through searching, the phone rang. It was Corinne, and her voice sounded unusually urgent. *Synchronicity again,* I thought.

"Corinne – what's up?"

"It's Nina. Nick, she's been arrested!"

My heart rate kicked up a notch. Surely not the doctored computers!

"The security services arrived early this morning. I'm not exactly sure whether it was FBI, Homeland Security, plain-clothes NYPD or what. I was excluded, but, from the little I heard, they seem to think she's used the charity as a front for funding terrorists."

"What nonsense! Everyone knows how devoted she is to children. The very idea is crazy!"

"Can I come over, Nick? I need to talk."

I hesitated for a moment, remembering her soft breasts pressing into me.

"Well, I was just leaving to go out to... yes, yes, of course. Hopefully we can work something out."

I put the phone down. I had heard that, under new legislation, suspects often don't get told exactly why they're arrested. Pushing away inappropriate thoughts about Corinne, I made more toast and then phoned Robbie, but no reply. Maybe Corinne had already tried? Perhaps Michael Gallo, my attorney, could help? Gallo had been excellent over the 'green card' matter. I dialled his office, with few hopes.

"Gallo speaking."

"Michael, Nick Martin here. Didn't expect to find you on a Saturday morning."

"Saturday. Ha, if only! I'm preparing a big case for next week. How can I help?"

I quickly explained.

"Actually Michael, she's much more than a friend."

"I see. Look, I hate to say this, but often it's difficult finding much out in these cases. Even access to legal counsel can be denied. Let me try and I'll get back to you."

The doorbell rang. Corinne entered and said, "Oh Nick," and hugged me. I sensed something pass between us, even as my inner voice urged – *not more complications, please.*

I broke away from the clinch and looked at Corinne. Her eyes were clear and her blonde hair appeared freshly washed. At first, she held my gaze, and then leant forward and kissed me.

"I'm sorry, Nick. You must be so worried. I know how you feel about Nina. Don't worry, we'll sort something out."

"Coffee?" I asked, moving to the kitchen.

"Thanks."

An unhelpful monologue was running in the background. *She's rather irresistible, maybe a little short, but fantastic breasts and lips. I still can't really see her as some kind of charity worker, though Nina obviously rates her.*

I returned with the coffee, to find her arranged on the sofa, that somehow managed to reveal an expanse of highly photogenic leg. It really didn't help!

"It doesn't make sense, Corinne. Mind you, I had unwanted visitors arrive here! Tell me again, exactly what happened?"

She sighed and shook her head.

"There isn't much to tell. We'd had several busy, but successful, days fund raising. Late in the week, Nina met with Senator Monroe in Washington."

"Over what?" I asked.

"Political support is extremely important and Nina always tries to cultivate helpful contacts. US relationships with Latin America have been strained for decades. Some politicians will openly acknowledge that and, like Monroe, want to improve things. Then, last night, she met with Simon Maher, the English guy you introduced. He hoped Nina might have information helpful to his research and had been really impressed by her film. Then, early this morning, agents arrived at our apartment and she was arrested. That's all I can tell you."

"It's mad, though! How could anyone think a children's charity would raise funds for terrorism – especially someone like Nina?"

I sounded choked despite attempts to stay calm.

"I know." Corinne moved closer. "I'm so sorry. You must be really upset."

I bit my lip and shook my head.

It all seemed to happen in an instant. Her arms were around me. I looked down at her mouth, blue eyes, her mouth again – then those amazing breasts. She stood on tiptoes and kissed me. Her lips warm against mine, and her full soft breasts pressing against my chest. My heart sped as we embraced. Now, things seem blurred, but tongues were involved and we somehow made our way to the bed. She was beautiful naked, and the lovemaking was the most intense I'd ever experienced. I lay back afterwards, but was completely taken aback when she smiled, and asked:

"Was I as good as Nina?"

I momentarily froze, unsure quite how to respond. Why ever would she ask such a thing?

I tried to find a tone that could convey reassurance.

"Amazing," I said – hoping to forestall further questions.

Corinne snuggled in close.

"I guess you knew I liked you from the start?"

"Well, I... I wasn't quite sure what was happening."

I looked up at the skylight, watching passing clouds and feeling quite hollow. What, indeed, was 'happening'? It took ages before I'd slept with Nina. She seemed so sweet and gentle and the experience as spiritual as this was physical. Corinne had been a tiger in comparison.

My mind started clearing, and with that came the guilt. As therapy progressed, I realised my feelings for Nina now were the closest I'd ever come to real love. Dammit, it was real love! At least, that's what I'd thought. *How shallow to let this happen!*

I glanced sideways, shamefully searching for justification. *Obviously, she's stunning, but I didn't plan for this, although I've a feeling she just may have.* The argument didn't convince. I wanted a future with Nina, so why let my body do the thinking?

The phone rang. It was Michael Gallo.

"Hi Nick. Not much to report, I'm afraid. Under current legislation, the practice often is to initially cover everything under a heavy security blanket. Anyone in a position to reveal anything useful gets prohibited from speaking.

"What can we do?" I asked.

"Immediately – nothing," said Gallo. "I'll continue asking questions and apply pressure. If there are developments, I'll get straight back."

I put the phone down and looked back, watching as Corrine dressed. I noticed her exquisite and obviously expensive lingerie, but this observation somehow deepened my conflict. What now?

Would she tell Nina – if eventually we saw her again? Surely, we must see her! Anyway, if I were any sort of decent person, I'd simply level with her. Explain it as a mistake that happened under the stress of her arrest. *We were distraught, and sort of came together for comfort. 'Came together' won't exactly help – you moron!*

I continued adjusting my words until Corinne suddenly spoke.

"I've heard of charities accused like this before."

She smiled brightly, as though this conversation was quite normal.

"I wonder if there's anything helpful on the internet," I replied.

I fired up the computer, and searched under 'terrorist and funding', as much for something to do as expecting an answer.

I groaned aloud. The first article I saw said that terrorist groups have increasingly financed their operations through so-called charitable networks and outwardly humanitarian organisations. I continued reading:

Many methods are used to raise and manage funds, including front companies, money laundering and criminal enterprises that involve drugs and arms sales. Other strategies include kidnapping, pirating software, gold and diamond smuggling – even phoney welfare claims.

The possibilities seemed endless and new legislation potentially allowed the authorities to get anyone out the way.

"Could they come after you next?" I asked "I mean, I know Nina was the director, but you worked closely together?"

"Dear Nick, you do worry." She hugged me again, but seemed strangely untroubled.

"You'd better check your funds. How do you know they haven't been frozen?"

"Mmm, you're right, but it'll be difficult until Monday. I can think of other things we could do now, though." She smiled and raised her eyebrows.

"Corinne, I can't. Let's head out for brunch. I gave Gallo my cell phone number. If you like, come with me to the Metropolitan art museum. I want to see the visiting Breughel exhibition."

We left the apartment and walked towards the subway. She reached for my hand and my overstressed mind couldn't come up with the necessary moves to disengage.

I'd work on that later...!

47

LONDON TO NYC

ANDREW ALTON

The stewardess smiled a warm welcome as I entered the cabin. After a surfeit of bad news, at least I'd now have time to just relax. I settled into the cramped seat and tried to focus on the short safety video.

The flight proved exceptionally uncomfortable – worsened by the overhang of a particularly obese passenger in the adjoining seat. I'd hoped to use my time planning, but annoyingly found myself caught up with childhood memories of Biff's intimidating ways. Was this a displacement of the fear of hearing up-to-date news from total strangers. Could a confrontation even become necessary? In fact, the prospect of seeing Mom was the only thing about this damn trip I anticipated with any pleasure.

After landing at JFK, I found the express bus stop. Needing a friendly voice, I called Simon, who sounded uncharacteristically subdued and preoccupied with the recent arrest of an activist he'd met. As the bus passed through dreary stretches of Queen's, I reflected on Simon's story. Apparently, he'd met with an activist he'd been corresponding with. That person had a strange visit from security types and, shortly afterwards, his girlfriend had been arrested. It raised unwanted memories of my own arrest and that odd warning about watching associations. The world really was going mad!

The Manhattan skyline gradually appeared and the bus then passed onto the island, and stopped near Grand Central Station. Although

New York City was familiar to me, it felt rather overwhelming. A case of goodbye familiar spires and quadrangles – and hello art-deco masterpieces, gigantic monuments to corporate power and controlled chaos.

I retrieved my bags, and walked down crowded streets to East Fiftieth and my hotel. Simon waited in the lobby while I checked in and stowed my bags. We headed out to a nearby coffee shop.

"I found your story of the arrested activist worrying, particularly after what happened to me back home."

"Actually, you're 'back home' right now, Andy!"

"I suppose, technically, you're right. I almost feel European these days… an honorary Brit, if you like."

Simon smiled.

"If you like, you mean. We're just the junior partner in the American Empire these days!"

"This Nick character you met… is he on our wavelength?"

"Very much so. Ostensibly, he works for an IT company, but, like us, increasingly became involved with social justice issues! He's a good guy, though the real powerhouse is his girlfriend – the one arrested. She's a charity worker and activist called Nina Parenda. Remember me raving about a water privatising documentary, some months back? That was her work! In fact, I spent the evening with her and a colleague, the night before her arrest! She's exceptionally knowledgeable, and a generally impressive person."

"Not a great way of keeping your head down, though, Si! What kind of charity?"

"A children's charity. You'd really have liked her. By the end of the evening, my head spun and her knowledge of Latin American politics was encyclopaedic!"

The implications seemed rather obvious to me.

"If you were with her, and she was arrested the following morning, how do you know that you weren't all under surveillance the previous night?"

"Well… I suppose I don't. I shouldn't think so, though. Our kind of research mightn't be popular here in the heart of the corporate world, but we're only asking questions and that's not illegal!"

How naive, but I felt too tired to argue. Simon still appeared worried, though, pursing his mouth, as though holding something back. I'd found, with him, that this often signalled a request.

"Andy," he faltered, "I know you're my boss, and that you've had a really long day, but I wonder...?"

I sensed a tedious explanation imminent, and just now lacked the patience.

"You're right. I'm shattered. Continue, if you must!"

He coloured, and I regretted my sharpness.

"You know me too well, Andy! Okay, well, I've sort of let you in for something, though, if necessary, we can cancel. The thing is, on my first evening here, I met a guy called Robbie James. Do you remember me telling you?"

"I do. It was all highly proactive and I was suitably impressed. What have you let me in for?"

"I... I wondered if you'd do the same. I know he's free this evening, because we already had a rendezvous. Rob would love to meet you, if you feel up to it. I'm afraid I said you'd probably agree. I shouldn't have presumed, I know, but he works for your father and has relevant information."

"I may be tired, but haven't lost my memory. Okay, we'll go."

"I know it's been a long flight, but if..."

"What's the matter with you, Si? I said yes! Yes, I'm happy to meet right now. Having already flown half way across the world, I may as well get on with it!"

"He's in the East Village, just a short subway ride."

I didn't normally snap, but these weren't normal times.

"Sorry. I'm wound up over Dad. In fact, over things on both sides of the Atlantic. The threats to our work involve you, too!"

Simon blew out his cheeks.

"To be honest, I've avoided thinking about it. Anyway, I'll call Robbie and confirm tonight."

The apartment was off St Mark's Street in the designated area of the East Village. As we walked from the Astor Place subway, I kept recalling Dad's influence on my childhood. Simon kept prattling about the European atmosphere and I wished he'd shut up. Any other time, I'd enjoy this sort of funky district, but not tonight. We passed a buzzing ethnic restaurant – exactly the kind of place I'd normally choose after plastic airline food.

"You must be starving?" asked Simon, mistaking my expression.

"We can come back later, if you like. Greenwich Village is also quite close and has a good choice. I had an amusing experience over there with Robbie," he snorted. "I'll tell you later, though you'll have to be discreet!"

Simon clearly itched to tell the story, but I felt far too strung up to listen. As if in agreement, a burst of acid hit my stomach.

"To be honest, Si, I'm feeling quite queasy. I'd rather get this meeting done and get some sleep. You must admit, it's a rather weird situation!"

The apartment seemed small and cosy, if partly obscured by a surfeit of books and clutter. Recalling Simon's apartment, he'd probably find it a home from home. Rob was welcoming, but I was dismayed to find someone else present – who he introduced by the name of Nick Martin. Robbie then took a phone call outside and I checked out the bookshelves while Simon and Martin chatted. I'd found that the Brits often judged each other from their accents. I used bookshelves the same way. By that measure, Rob seemed literate and intelligent. My first impressions were of an earnest and very probably homosexual young man. Rob's call suddenly finished, which cut further speculation short.

"Andrew, I hope it's okay if Nick joins us? Nick's a friend who's also involved with your father's water acquisition. He and Simon have already met."

Simon looked puzzled.

"I mentioned Nick earlier at the coffee shop – don't you remember?"

Feeling increasingly unwell, I'd forgotten. In imagination, I spat: *No, it's not okay! Actually, I wish he'd piss off!*

"Good to meet you," I croaked.

"Remember, I explained what had happened to Nick's girlfriend, in the same conversation." Simon looked puzzled.

I nodded.

"Sorry to hear about that, Nick."

I was struggling to keep a clear head.

"Rob, what I'd like is getting acquainted with my father's current activities and maybe hearing what he's like as a boss. I'm afraid our differences have led to a very long-standing rift."

Robbie looked thoughtful.

"This must be difficult for you. I'll fill you in as best I can. Nick knows him too, which is why I invited him."

"If you prefer, I can leave," said Nick. "Maybe, we can talk another time?"

I shook my head, feeling too exhausted to argue.

"No, stay, though my relationship to Biff must stay confidential for now – particularly given the nature of our proposed research. You can probably imagine my reaction when Simon phoned and, well... basically said he'd heard of this business leader, a 24-carat sociopath – who then turned out to be my father! It almost felt like some cruel cosmic joke!"

"Andy. Anyone who knows your work sees your values shining through."

Hearing that helped.

"Shall we make a start?" I said, trying to regain some initiative.

"Could you tell me about his current work and also what he's like as a boss – although, I admit, I'm tempted to stay ignorant!"

Rob's face spoke volumes and he confirmed some horribly familiar behaviour patterns.

After a while, I felt sick. I tried kidding myself it was only jet-lag, but, as the descriptions of Dad's bullying unfolded, I knew it was more. I could almost smell the bourbon and feel the fingers jabbing at my chest again. Tight lumps formed under my shoulder blades and a painful ridge ran down my neck. Eventually, I lost track of the conversation – only realising it when the others looked uncomfortable.

Robbie suggested refreshments and left to do battle with a rogue coffee maker. He looked strained when he returned.

"You know, it's weird how much of this seems familiar. Dad was vicious too. In fact, working for Biff sometimes feels like old times."

I nodded. Robbie might be attempting empathy, but I couldn't face a session of 'whose father is the biggest bastard'?

"I guess vicious is right. Dad ruined just about every relationship he ever had."

I felt Simon's hand touch my shoulder.

"Andy, perhaps we should drop anything to do with your dad as far as the research is concerned? Even highly trained doctors and therapists avoid treating their own families. This couldn't be closer to home!"

It made sense, but I couldn't back out now from finding out more. It was like being compelled to look at a traffic accident – however bloody the mess, or frightening it appeared!

"Thanks Simon, but let's continue for now."

I addressed the others.

"I understand Si's sketched out the plan. We are hoping to collect material on the worst corporate excesses. It isn't that things are better or different in the UK – but almost everything here happens on a bigger scale."

"There's certainly no shortage of material," said Nick with a grin.

The others murmured agreement.

Simon interrupted.

"The idea of the 'psychopathic corporation' has been around quite a while, but Andrew's work, and the multiplying effects of globalisation, amplifies it!"

"Sounds excellent," replied Robbie. "Anyway, let me share a few relevant things."

He went to a unit in the corner, and returned holding a green file.

"Where do we begin? Biff's characteristics are, I think, agreed."

Robbie paused, looking uncomfortable.

"Stop me if I'm too harsh."

"Don't hold back."

He opened the file, coughing nervously.

"Please continue. I have to know!"

I listened to the summary of Marquetcom's campaigns and then the huge Kane and Field project around the 'Peak-Me' product. As the evidence of my father's deviousness unfolded, I began feeling more and more nauseous. I tried telling myself, 'that's just how business is', but my body wouldn't buy it.

Robbie then took out more papers.

"They also took government contracts; usually campaigns at glossing over controversial, corporate-friendly policies. These were high-level, closed projects, led by Biff and an inner circle."

Nick whistled under his breath and shook his head.

"I've some other stuff. Just a minute."

He thumbed the file and looked at me.

"With your UK connection, these might also interest you. Marquetcom took on projects for the agro-chemical industry, for Big Food and the supermarkets. One of your UK supermarket chains heard about it and then consulted for marketing and business strategy. This was some years back and they probably all use similar tactics now. The basic strategy, though, is classic Biff."

"Consisting of what?" I asked.

"Attempts to virtually control the food distribution chain!"

He turned to the file.

"This is how it went. First, the big supermarkets keep up sustained low prices, killing off small competitors and squeezing the others. The endgame was controlling the buying and selling gate and the access to consumers!"

"Control the access?"

"Yes. Consumers would have had few other places to buy and producers few other places to sell to. Then they can massively squeeze suppliers and farmers, who, of course, then have few other outlets."

"Couldn't the farmers fight back?"

"No, once supermarkets control access to customers, they can literally make farmers and food manufacturers pay for that."

"Sounds fiendish," said Simon, "but it certainly rings bells."

Robbie kept reading from his papers.

"Then, pressure planning authorities to approve giant out-of-town supermarkets that have attached parking. That will starve out the small shops."

"True," said Simon. "In many places, big hypermarkets are almost the only option. At least they're cheaper, though!"

"Really? Ever noticed the mark-ups in the small franchises that they've opened in town centres? Even big hypermarkets don't necessarily mean cheaper prices. Marquetcom suggested ways of hiding higher prices. Of course, everyone uses the 'known value items' – or KVI strategy, now."

My stomach sunk. "What's that?"

"Targeting the things shoppers typically use for price comparisons – bread, milk, bananas, that sort of thing. By massively cutting those, the smaller shops have to follow or lose trade. Of course, they can't. If the KVIs stay stable, the public often won't notice other price hikes – so the theory goes. Of course, after concentrating power, they flex their muscles."

"That's just normal business practice, isn't it?" said Nick.

"Staying with the food example, they award contracts to the cheapest growers – typically those with the lowest labour protections and using the most chemicals. Those conditions are forced onto other growers by intense competition and the fear of losing contracts. That ensures that poverty conditions are replicated almost everywhere."

"The great 'race to the bottom'," I said. "A topic we've frequently written about. Look, this is all very fascinating, but can we get back to Biff."

"Sorry, Andrew. So, Marquetcom also took on controversial work from Health Management Organisations, from Big Food, and Big Pharma. They ran cynical and deeply deceptive campaigns, clearly against the public interest. As far as this UK supermarket thing is concerned, their consultancy section seemed very busy. I think a lot has been challenged now, but Biff personally drafted guidelines and suggestions to the project team. You can see it here in some of his notes."

Robbie passed over the file, and I immediately recognised the flamboyant handwriting. After reading a page, I baulked, passing it over to Simon.

"Can you read this out, Si?"

"Okay. I'll read the handwritten suggestions."

I suggest appointing young buyers without knowledge of the product lines – so negotiations won't be hampered by understanding the production difficulties. Move the buyers around regularly, to discourage loyalties to suppliers.

Tie suppliers to strict performance criteria, to minimum margins and rigorous quality control. Demand upfront payments before carrying products, and threaten de-listing if there are difficulties over discounts!

"Here, Andy, you should see these..."

I reluctantly took back the file. Seeing it made it worse.

Charge extra for special placements, e.g. aisle ends or 'eye level'. Insist suppliers bear reduced prices during promotions. Suppliers should also contribute to store refurbishments and advertising!

I'd almost had enough. Some suggestions sounded on the fringe of legality and most were blatantly 'one-way traffic'.

Pass back the handling costs, ensure producers accept the cost of wastage and fund 'buy-one-get-one-free' campaigns.

My hands trembled. Somehow, seeing Dad's thinking laid bare in his own handwriting was profoundly shocking. The thinking was exactly the sort of thing Mom hated and which had led to their break-up.

"Shit! This stuff really happens?" asked Simon.

The group fell quiet and I felt all eyes on me. I felt tainted and beyond my personal threshold. Strangely, I wanted more than anything to discuss it all with Mom. In childhood, she'd shielded me from Dad's bullying ways and an anxiety that the whole adult world could be this way.

The subject had changed and the others seemed quite animated.

Simon joined in and Nick dug for more about Colombia and quizzed Robbie about someone named Brian Tutch. I felt contaminated and burdened with memories. Time slowed and I felt like my mind had been anaesthetised.

"Are you okay, Andy?" Simon asked. "This must be difficult for you."

I nodded, but, in reality, I was struggling over whether I should confront Biff and, if so, how?

"To be honest, guys, with the jet-lag and everything, I'm about done in and ready for sleep. Maybe we could meet again soon?"

Forty minutes later, I was back at the hotel and preparing for bed. Ordinary activities like folding clothes and cleaning my teeth seemed strangely comforting. I was almost finished with the bedtime rituals when the phone rang. The familiar voice of Helen, my secretary at the College, sounded astonishingly clear.

"Enjoying the 'Big Apple'?" she asked brightly. "Hope I haven't woken you?"

"You're okay, but I'm certainly tired. Actually, I was about to turn in."

"Sorry, I won't keep you long. You wanted me to let you know if I heard anything more about the corporate sponsor."

"You've heard something?"

"Yes, I just found out. Strange you being in New York, because it turns out to be a New York business – called Marquetcom. Apparently, they are movers and shakers in PR and marketing and are led by someone called Bifton Anson. The business school clearly believes that they'll make prestigious partners."

I could hardly wait to replace receiver.

"Thanks Helen. I'll get back sometime in the next few days."

I lay down, feeling sick and rather dizzy. Would this be my ultimate challenge?

48

MANHATTAN

SIMON MAHER

As we left the East Village, I felt a genuine sympathy for Andy. After all, my boss seemed a naturally modest man with real humanity, who rarely pulled rank. In fact, I considered him as almost more a friend than a boss. As we returned uptown together, stress was etched on his face. I hoped he could sleep well.

It was about 10pm when we parted company. Still buzzing, I walked on to Times Square, remembering that the street-life here was rather more entertaining than the inebriated youths and students back in Oxford.

I reached the frantic sliver that constitutes Times Square and wandered around the theatre district. In a lane by one of the larger theatres, I stumbled on Sardis Restaurant, though, at first, I couldn't remember what it was famous for. I remembered and peered from outside, hoping to see the caricatures or, better still, a famous face. Instead, I was in front of an attractive girl at a window table. Our eyes met, but her male companion scowled, so I quickly moved on.

The incident reminded me that Gill had anticipated having a long day and I wondered if she'd finished by now. I checked the time, and pulled out my cell phone. Surely, she couldn't still be working?

NEWARK – Gill Marney.

At around the same time, in an unmarked security office near Newark, Gill, Jack Holt and Vern Matacic worked on another taping operation and had now almost completed the transcription of the meeting earlier at Rob James' apartment. The work felt almost treacherous to Gill – but it was, after all, her job.

"This new equipment is seriously cool," said Holt in his typically annoying way.

She swallowed and nodded.

"Brian told Jack we should watch this James guy," said Matacic. He has a bad feeling about him. Apparently, there's a lot riding on that Colombian business."

She nodded.

"That Simon guy has such a plummy accent," Holt said, with a sniff.

"Lord Lefty, with a broom up his British ass!"

She detested Holt, but even that was dwarfed by an overwhelming inner struggle. In the early days, passing information had been easy, but that had all changed since coming to understand, never mind falling for, Si. Now it was more of a betrayal. Si and Andy helped her see many things differently, but an inner crisis was building. They were supposedly 'the enemy', while creatures like Anson were virtually lionised! Of course, a real emotional involvement with a mark had absolutely been warned against in training. All very well, but, unfortunately, she now doubted the moral standing of her work, of her employer, and her employer's employer.

With playback finished, Matacic cracked his knuckles.

"That sure is one little nest of snakes," he said.

Holt nodded.

"Yeah, real flat earth types. They don't get that profitable business generates the wealth that globalisation spreads around the world. It isn't complicated, yet they'd rather undermine someone like Anson, working his butt off, creating wealth."

"Exactly. Real wealth, rather than tom-fool theories," agreed Matacic.

Gill nodded, but held her comments back. Thanks to Simon, she could easily produce a flood of facts to counter their argument.

"I guess you're right, Vern," she said. "Although some of Anson's practices do seem extreme."

"Keeping ahead of the competition, you mean? If someone can think strategically, and sell their skills – why not? Why have our corporations led the world? They jumped into the market and went for it – all guns blazing. When necessary, winners aren't afraid to get their hands dirty."

Her cell phone then rang.

"Oh, it's you... Strangely enough, I'm just finishing now... Yes, quite a day. Unfortunately, more glitches... Okay. Yes, I'm hungry too. I could be there in, let's see, probably forty or fifty minutes... Okay, we'll meet there, then."

What timing! Matacic and Holt looked over expectantly.

"How about that? Simon Maher! Apparently, he's hungry and still high from that meeting. He wondered if we could meet up."

"I bet," said Holt, again leering.

"Are you going?"

"He's hungry – I'm hungry, so I suppose I may as well."

"Yeah, you should," said Matacic. "The more we can find out about these guys the better. He might describe Alton's reactions, and what he plans on doing about it."

"Absolutely," agreed Holt with a wink. "Do your thing, and make him sing. Be sure to tell us everything, now!"

Recalling their previous intimacy – Holt could take a run!

"We'll take you back to Manhattan," said Matacic. "Where are you meeting?"

"Near Times Square," said Gill. "At the top of the hour outside the Paramount building, to be specific."

~

Simon Maher

AT THE SAME TIME, I was killing time wandering around the theatre district, amazed just how many of the shows were also playing in London. I thought about Mom's love of musicals and her record collection. Perhaps another day I should push the boat out and take in a real Broadway Musical. She'd love hearing about that. Maybe Gill would like it, too?

I passed a row of small theatres from Forty-Second Street's heyday, and the restored 'New Amsterdam'. Apparently, they'd been reduced to kung-fu movie houses and porno cinemas until the big clean-up a few years back. Near Eighth Avenue, though, things turned decidedly sleazy and colourful neon signs promised 'adult' entertainment. I checked my watch. It was now almost time, so I skirted the block around Forty-Third Street to the Paramount building. As agreed, Gill was there – shining despite the hour.

"How was work?"

"Okay. Well, to be honest, it was a trying day. Stubborn problems we can't seem to sort."

Gill responded to my kiss, though, close up, she seemed rather tense. Still, a day troubleshooting computers would stress anyone out. We walked up Broadway together and found a diner. Over the food, I asked more about her work, though, in truth, I was more intrigued by her near perfect hands holding the menu than damn computers!

"I appreciate your interest, Si, but must I? I've had more than enough of computers for one day. How did your meeting with Andy go?"

"He had a rough day, too. Robbie shared information about his dad – what he's like as a boss and some of his shitty deals. Honestly, you'd have been amazed, if you'd heard it! It was awful for Andy, though."

"Will he see his father?"

I shook my head.

"Don't know. He mentioned the possibility, though it doesn't exactly sound a fun prospect."

"Has Nick heard anything more about his girlfriend? Nina, isn't it?"

"Yes, Nina. No, nothing, so he was quite sober, too. His work wants him to return to Colombia soon. He really doesn't want to leave before finding out what's happened."

Gill reached over and took my hand. I returned the squeeze, but her face seemed troubled.

"I'm so glad we're here together."

I leaned forward and kissed her lips.

"Me too. It's a cold old world."

I sighed and nodded.

"Like I said, you wouldn't believe what we heard!"

49

PHILADELPHIA

ZOLTAN'S PERSPECTIVE

Now back in Philadelphia, Hassan seamlessly merged with the Zoltan persona. Being with Judy again felt good, although time with Abdullah had reminded him this was really forbidden. Why was pleasure always forbidden? The question always seemed to follow time spent with the leader.

He avoided New York's many temptations, but, after returning, couldn't wait and they'd made urgent love right then and there, in the lounge. Today started the same way, despite Judy being exquisitely made up, and ready to shop in the city centre. There was something about her appearance of being every inch the society lady – deliciously out of bounds to everyone but him! In fact, her acting so contrary to the stereotype was like suddenly discovering that water happily flowed uphill!

Judy left for the shops and he busied himself with breakfast. The afterglow was spoilt by the phone ringing.

"Judy Alton's residence. She's out just now. Who is this?"

A voice on the other end quietly replied.

"Her son, Andrew. Would that be Zoltan?"

"Yes, right."

"Freddy's friend? Mom said you were staying a while."

"Yes. Have you arrived in New York?"

"Late yesterday. Can you tell Mom, I'll come over the day after tomorrow? I guess we'll meet then."

Andrew rang off and Zoltan resumed breakfast. A short time later, the phone rang again and a deep voice growled into his ear.

"I need you here, immediately."

It was Anson.

"Why?"

"I'll explain later, but coming now will certainly pay off!"

"That's quite difficult, Sir. Right now, I'm..."

"If you want business, son, come real soon. Okay?"

The voice demanded immediate compliance.

"I'll call back as soon as I've sorted out transport."

Anson rang off. Zoltan finished his coffee, reflecting that contact with separate family members, before breakfast, seemed quite unusual. Then he penned Judy a short note.

Called away on urgent business and may possibly be away tonight. Some good news, though. Your son, Andrew, called and intends to visit in two days' time.

Maybe, he'd get another 'welcome' when he returned – unless Andrew cramped their style!

A quick call established the quickest way to New York right now was by Greyhound bus and he immediately booked. Departure was imminent and he only just reached the terminal in time.

The bus crossed the Delaware river and sped through the Pennsylvania countryside. His seat was comfortable enough and he checked out the other passengers. Mainly poor whites, several black families and a sprinkling of what he imagined were students. The bus entered the 'Garden State', though at first there was little difference – pleasant, but lacking the drama of the West.

The knocking sound started softly, but gradually got louder. Their driver slowed and then pulled over. For some miles, a smell had wafted through the cabin. Passengers looked at each other accusingly, and fanned themselves as though signalling, 'nothing to do with me'. Eventually, a young couple made their way to the front of the bus with a suitcase and a whining and scratching went with them. People looked at each other with shrugs or raised eyebrows. The couple spoke to the driver. He opened the door and they left the bus, but the voices could be heard through the open door.

"It's right there on the ticket conditions. It clearly says that animals can't travel on the bus. Anyway, shutting your puppy up in a suitcase is cruel."

They pleaded, but the driver seemed unyielding. The couple cleaned up the little dog outside, while the driver spoke to someone on his cell phone. He then climbed back inside. People looked relieved and prepared to continue the journey. Instead, the driver made an announcement over the PA system.

"I'm afraid we have an unscheduled delay, folks, because of a serious mechanical problem. You may have heard a knocking noise, probably indicating a big end packing up. I've called for a replacement bus, which should get here in about ninety minutes."

The passengers exited and most climbed up the turnpike's bank. A group gathered around the puppy and several teenagers climbed a tree. An old man who'd sat opposite on the bus tried engaging with Zoltan about the World Series. With little interest, or knowledge, of baseball, he tried to change topics, but the man persisted, seemingly unable to read cues.

"No," Zoltan countered, "the thing is, I *really* haven't been following the series. Actually, my sport is shooting."

The man raised his eyebrows.

"You don't follow the series, man?"

Most other things had passed him by.

"Don't you wanna catch up, man?"

"Nope, I've never watched it, but I do like shooting!"

His metaphorical bullet finally hit home and the man walked away, shaking his head as if this was incomprehensible!

He scrambled up the bank, hoping to keep an eye open for the replacement bus. Children ran along the ridge, but most people were reading or chatting. Zoltan relaxed, watching the traffic pass as the sun warmed his back. Suddenly, the hairs behind his neck lifted and he heard a voice say:

"Mr Anson will wonder where we've got to!"

He turned and saw a muscular man with blond, almost white, hair squatting behind him. Anson must have had him followed.

The man reached for his hand and gave a crushing handshake.

"Hello, Zoltan."

"Who are you?"

"My name is Brian Tutch. I work alongside Mr Anson and the Marquetcom people."

"How do you know me?"

"Mr Anson knows everyone who visits. Anyway, you've been in his personal office."

Observation was something he did, rather than had done to him.

"You follow people who visit Anson's office? Seems an odd way to do business!"

"Of course not!"

The face, with its dead eyes and flaring nostrils, seemed singularly repellent.

"I neither do surveillance nor run errands, Zoltan. I handle special projects for Mr Anson. We rather hope you'll join us."

A sudden cheer broke out. The replacement bus had arrived and passengers surged forward, scrambling to board. He stood and quickly headed for the bus, though it was soon obvious no-one would respect the previous seating arrangements.

Zoltan found himself near the back, with Tutch sitting behind him. The bus sped through the remaining countryside without a word passing between them until they entered the sprawling conurbation and then crossed into Manhattan. As they approached the bus terminal, he heard Tutch on his cell phone. He finished speaking and said in a throaty kind of stage whisper:

"We'll get a cab from the bus terminal."

He nodded, as it seemed best to discover Anson's intentions. From the cab, he saw the Empire State building and just the sight made his stomach lurch.

If only there was a guarantee that any deaths would be people like Tutch and Anson, it would be so different, but that couldn't be.

The cab turned towards Thirty-Third Street. His stomach clenched as he passed people on the street – people with social networks, friends and families. He tried diverting himself with recollections of home, of training in Afghanistan, Judy – anything to change his state, until the panic subsided. They entered the marbled entrance and were soon rocketing upwards in a high-speed elevator. Reaching Marquetcom's reception, a pretty blonde receptionist then took them to Anson's cavernous office.

Inside, the out-sized head of Anson seemed perched atop the large hunched body like a waiting vulture. Anson managed to somehow smile and sneer, simultaneously.

"Hello, son."

Anson pointed to the chocolate-coloured leather seats by the window.

"Hello, Mr Anson. This is getting like some extended job interview! I didn't expect to see you, so soon."

"I always believe that business should come first. When necessary, I expect my associates to put the job first – whatever that takes."

So, he was an 'associate'. From the corner of his eye, he saw Tutch's white-blond head nodding agreement.

"What job, though, Mr Anson? You didn't fully explain, last time. And why did Mr Tutch follow me onto the bus? I assume that wasn't by chance!"

The broad face grinned.

"Don't worry about Brian."

The big shoulders rocked as he chuckled.

"I didn't want you getting lost! No, Brian manages special projects for us. Anyway, I've interests in Philly. Heck, you're lodging with one!"

He guffawed and the blue eyes watered.

"It was important to me that you came. Brian called by just in case you needed help to talk the decision over."

His muscles tightened, though he suspected that showing anger would only be seen as weakness.

"Well, I'm here without any 'help'."

Anson's smile disappeared and he leaned forward.

"Were you raised proper?"

"I'm not quite sure that…"

"You know. Respecting your parents and so on?"

"Of course. Yes, very much so."

"Good! Then you'll probably get why I'm so disappointed with my little milksop – the disloyal little bastard!"

"I don't understand – disloyal?"

"My son, Zoltan, is a traitor to everything I believe in and have worked for. A... a lily-livered little wimp and enemy to business. Always has been!"

"I thought Fred ran a very successful business?"

"My eldest son, Andrew! The boy's irresistibly drawn to everything despicable – everything weak and pathetic. You and I have worked to secure the network, and to get important materials into patriot's hands. Working for America – right?"

"Sure."

"I've also worked to help so many real businesses, getting them to market. I mean real businesses, that make shareholders money and create jobs. Free enterprise made us the world's greatest country! Yet, somehow, I raised a boy who undermines these things. He attacks privatisation, when everyone knows it brings efficiency and attacks growth from mergers. He denies that free trade allows developing countries the opportunity to specialise, and to grow their economies. He opposes all these things and is completely phobic about profit. He also protests the manufacture and sale of defence equipment. In fact, you could say that Andrew is a one-man industry, for churning out rubbish to complicate things for business – yet does no business himself!"

"I was told his academic work is influential, and gets lots of positive comment."

"Judy thinks so, but the boy's a wimp. Dangerous... a distorter of facts – but now it's got personal!"

"How do you mean, Sir?"

Tutch grinned, as if in anticipation.

"Well, son, we're partners now, aren't we – our little business being somewhat unorthodox! What I'm going to tell you has upset me, personally."

Zoltan looked into the leathery face and watery blue eyes, wondering what on earth could personally upset such a man. He bet it would involve power, money, or both.

"Little Andy has decided to interfere in areas where I've started to work – probably deliberately. We're about to launch a big project, to privatise South American water into safe hands. So now the boy writes papers attacking and undermining water privatisation. It gets worse! He's now peddling the ridiculous idea that certain successful business and political leaders actually have a pathological make-up! A bizarre, ass-first idea that confuses success with illness!"

Anson's face had turned red and his hands bunched into fists.

"Meaning?"

"In his jumbled mind, it's losers who are healthy – like those lazy fucks writing scurrilous crap about doers and achievers. Yet..."

He watched the hands rise and thump the desk. Anson's face now looked puce and his mind automatically served up the moves to outflank an attack.

"So, one of your sons has a rather 'anti-business' outlook?"

"Rather! No, it's virtually a vocation with him! Apparently, he and associates are concocting slander disguised as 'research', branding certain successful business leaders 'sociopaths' and claiming they negatively influence their companies. The cherry on the cake is finding that his assistant is over here, digging for dirt. Apparently, he's colluding with one of my staff, seeking information about Marquetcom and my leadership!"

Anson's face was now an unhealthy purple.

"Apparently," he boomed, "these clowns claim I'm sociopathic!"

Zoltan nodded solemnly – thinking, *quite true!*

"How fucking ridiculous is that? Have I killed anyone? Although, at the moment..."

He leaned forward over the desk.

"Perhaps I should be flattered."

"I still don't quite see how I figure in this, Mr Anson?"

"When we first discussed you working on the North East network and staying at Judy's, she lived in New Jersey. It seemed a good plan, but I'd no idea then that Andrew would turn up. I'm fairly certain that he'll head over to see her real soon. I'd like you to befriend him and find out more. What he doesn't yet know, is that I'll soon be yanking his strings through that fancy College."

"Great move, Biff," sniggered Tutch, his shoulders shaking. "The boy wants to kick business, but, instead, business will take his little College and arrange to kick his ass!"

"I suppose I could try," replied Zoltan – ignoring Tutch. "You're quite right, though, about visiting his mom. He phoned today while Judy was out shopping. Said he'd be over in a couple of days."

"I'd also like you to listen for any mention of my assistant – a treacherous piece of shit called Rob James."

"I don't know how long Andrew plans to stay, though?"

"Neither do I, but I'd like you to keep in touch and report regularly."

"You gonna mention the other matters?" asked Tutch.

Biff frowned.

"I'm not senile," he snapped. "Last time, I said there could be some big opportunities for you."

"Something about New Orleans."

"Maybe later. I'm thinking, further south."

"The Caribbean?"

"No, I've interests in South America. Specifically, Colombia."

"Not a happy place."

"I don't know. You'll like the money. Tell me, does the 'Iran-Contra affair' mean much to you?"

At the mention of Iran, his heart picked up speed as he mentally tracked the information. His family had left shortly before the 1980 war with Iraq. He remembered Dad's shock when details of the scandal emerged in 1986.

"I think so," he replied, uneasily.

"We quietly sold weapons to the Iranians – actually, to them and the Iraqis. A greatly misjudged patriot then had the brilliant idea of using the proceeds to help the rebels fight the Sandinistas in Nicaragua. Those Commie bastards could have easily driven up through Mexico and lobbed stuff at Texas!"

"They sure needed swatting," agreed Tutch.

He nodded, unsure where this was leading.

"Many people still didn't realise that, after the brouhaha died down, the funding quietly continued, this time with drug money. It was a brilliant idea."

"How does that relate to now?" he asked.

Anson grinned.

"You don't think things are any different? As a matter of fact, some of the same Contra weapons are still in use – Colombia this time. There's a better prize than overthrowing a tin-pot left regime, now."

Anson kept heading off in unexpected directions.

"Don't look puzzled, son. Oil and drugs have been the big money-makers. All right, things are flat in the oil trade just now, but it will pick up in time!"

"I don't understand," he said, playing along. "I thought the idea was about eliminating drugs. You know, spraying the coca, alternative development, and so on."

"Yes, but that's not all."

Biff leaned on the huge desk.

"A civil war smouldered there for decades. It's supposed to have ended, but, even so, lots of things are still in place. The Colombian military linked with paramilitary groups, supporting a pro-Western, pro-business administration – cast as the good guys. Opposing them, were lefty guerrillas – the so-called bad guys if you like – called FARC, and the ELN. You see what that meant?"

"No, it sounds like a lot of trouble."

"Maybe, but war provided cover for grabbing rich territory, and a ready market for weapons. There's supposedly peace now, although the trouble lasted for decades."

"I don't think the public has an appetite for more military adventures."

"That's the other beauty of it. Yes, we had troops teaching counter-terrorist strategies and how to protect the pipelines, but much of that became privatised. Private contractors had a free hand to fumigate coca, fly aircraft and helicopters, even to gather intelligence – yet aren't subject to the same restrictions!"

A big grin broke across his face.

"So, if anything goes wrong, Washington isn't directly involved! I mentioned the fumigation programme. Guess where the most popular fumigation areas are?"

It instantly came to him.

"Where potential resources are located, I imagine?"

"You've got it, boy! I tell you, the opportunities are fantastic: private contracts, arms sales, oil interests, drugs, if you want them – and the residues of a civil war to suck it all in."

Anson's face broke into a hyena-like grin. "Perfect! Are you in?"

Zoltan left the Marquetcom suite and, some ninety minutes later, described his encounter to Abdul.

"For once, I agree with Anson," Abdul said. "About the money, naturally, but also the possibility of cooperation with other groups. Before 9/11, most anti-US incidents involved Latin America. I believe in mutual help!"

50

BROOKLYN

ROBBIE JAMES

I joined the Brooklyn train to get over to Canvey's site, feeling somewhat disconsolate. Until recently, I'd enjoyed nothing more than meetings with Nick, but, since the agents' visit and then Nina's arrest, he seemed tense and preoccupied. I wanted to help, but had a nagging fear the authorities might find me interesting, too.

As the train emerged into the light, I looked back towards Manhattan and the mid-town towers, with the Empire State building standing proud. I sighed. Somehow, the trains rocking and snatching glimpses of other lives from the carriage deepened an already reflective mood. Life was becoming increasingly complicated and those in the progressive community felt under attack. It seemed much the same in other Western democracies. According to Simon, the Brits were now developing something of a surveillance state, while in Europe there was a chilling of dissent and growing authoritarianism. Perhaps our little group was unknowingly galloping into danger. Some progressives called the alliance of corporate and political interests a 'corporatocracy' – or soft fascism. There was widespread concern that most opposition was being frustrated, by the authorities, security and intelligence. What Simon witnessed at Kate Sanderson's office, and Andrew's experience in London, seemed further evidence. Maybe I'd been identified as a troublemaker too, and could be under surveillance?

I looked around the carriage. Opposite, a young man was plugged into his i-Pod and aggressive rap leaked from his earphones. On the left, an obese man shovelled in potato chips from a family-sized bag. The rest seemed a rather unremarkable mix of ordinary people going about their business.

I reached Canvey's stop and linked up with Nick. We worked together on the specifications for the proposed Colombian administration centre. He'd heard nothing of Nina and was also awash with gloomy news from other friends.

"Almost anything is discouraged, now," he said. "Just this week, activists in DC got herded into a fenced-off area to exercise 'free' speech in a specially controlled 'free speech area'. Positively Orwellian!"

"Yes, I read about that on the internet."

"You're not still visiting those wacky sites?" Nick asked.

"Occasionally," I replied. "Although, recently, I saw some fascinating stuff on the so-called 'Chemtrail' phenomena. Have you heard of that?"

"You mean chemically treating cash to catch out thieves?"

"No, it's far more interesting. The apparent aerial spraying of the population."

"I heard something, though I can't accept the idea."

"No, really, people worldwide report large trails spewing from aircraft, that are quite different from condensation trails. Looking up, it often appears like a giant aerial game of tic-tac-toe. Eventually, the trails spread, merge and a formerly blue sky turns a sludgy white and dims. Really, you should take a look on the internet. There are endless photos!"

"Now you mention it, I think I've seen something locally rather like that," replied Nick.

"The true believers think the aim is deflecting the sun's energy to help slow climate change, although some claim the sprays are toxic. Others reckon they're weather modification experiments or to enhance military communications."

Nick grinned and shook his head.

"Don't be silly. They're condensation trails!"

"No, these are thicker trails that are often laid down in patterns. As I said, there are masses of photographs and videos on the internet."

"Are we nuts, discussing this?" he asked.

"Possibly."

Nick furrowed his brow.

"The spraying that really does worry me is what I saw in Colombia."

"The aerial fumigation, thing?"

"Yes. People were really frightened, and thought it affected their health. I'm due to go again soon. Talking of which, we really have to get these costings finished."

Late afternoon, I took the long subway journey back to Manhattan. I left the subway at Thirty-Third Street, and noticed two men trailing behind.

It had started raining and, as often after a long day, I was tempted by the adult shops near Eighth Avenue. I could have called at the office, but, instead, grabbed a snack at a nearby diner, returned to the subway and then headed for Nina and Corinne's place. Nick's low state was quite upsetting. I really wanted to help him and I'd always found Nina kind and thoughtful. I wondered if there could be any clues in her apartment that might help explain the real reasons for her arrest. Corinne seemed rather doubtful, though, when I phoned, encouraged me to come over and try anyway!

By the time I left the subway, it was heavily raining, although their apartment was only another two more blocks away. I walked on, absorbed in the reflections in puddles, replaying past conversations, and searching for any possible lead. I sheltered for a while under the awning of a lighting shop, until a passing taxi splashed water all over my ankles. I silently cursed and turned back to take another look at their display. Even soaking socks couldn't detract from a particularly intriguing display. Classy lamps sprouted from the stems of up-lighters. Art Nouveau style pieces with tiffany glass and with coloured mushroom lamps, which looked rather phallic. Many of the lamps were illuminated and I stood studying the various shapes and colours, picturing how they might look in my apartment. The shop window reflected the road behind and, as my eyes moved around the display, I saw two figures sheltering under a nearby gingko tree, who appeared to be looking my way. I set off again, only just avoiding a vast puddle stretching over most of the sidewalk. I paused outside a restaurant window and read their menu. By tilting my head slightly, the road behind was reflected in the glass. I involuntarily shivered because the two men stared again, although they also quickly moved – as if matching my movements! Perhaps Nina's arrest had just unnerved me and, as I reached the apartment, I looked back. No-one seemed visible, so I rang the bell.

Corinne's voice answered and, as I heard the latch releasing, I again checked behind. Still nothing, so I climbed the stairs. She opened the apartment door and welcomed me in.

"You're all wet. Let me take your coat!"

I stepped into the tastefully furnished apartment. Corinne rather provocatively reached for my coat and held eye contact.

"Quite a place!"

"Thanks, we like it. I'm so glad to see you, although I doubt that we'll find anything."

She grinned.

"At least, not relating to Nina's disappearance!"

"I've been with Nick all day today and he's worried sick. I'd hate to leave any possibility unexplored."

"And if we did find something, what then? Who could we tell?"

"Good question. I suppose Nick's attorney, Michael Gallo, in the first instance."

She flashed another of her smiles. I felt awkward, remembering other times she'd come on to me and her apparent disappointment over my reticence. Truthfully, I still had uncertainty over my ultimate sexuality – still, that wasn't a question for tonight.

"Fancy a drink?" she asked, managing both to flick her golden hair and be dazzling with a smile.

I thought, *by any standards, she's stunning but, oh, doesn't she know it!*

I first intuited the evening might get complicated when the lyrics to an old Pet Shop Boys song persisted in coming to mind.

'Which do you choose, a hard or soft option?'

Amazing, the way appropriate songs would always come to mind. I'd had exactly that conversation with Simon, who experienced much the same.

I only realised I was leaning on the drinks cabinet when she brushed against me while pouring drinks. Was that lyric from 'West End Girls', I wondered, as her thigh pressed against me again. I swallowed and pointed to an Art-Nouveau lamp in the corner.

"Strange. I admired a similar lamp in a shop just down the block."

"Yes, that's where we bought it. Would you like another?" she asked.

"A Southern Comfort would really hit the spot."

"So, Robbie, what are you hoping to find?"

"I'm not sure. Anything that throws some light on why Nina's being detained. I don't know... financial documents, letters, plans, strategies for the charity – doubtful contacts? I know it's a very long shot, but, right now, we've few other options."

Corinne passed me a drink and settled on the couch opposite. Although short, she revealed an expanse of shapely leg in the process. I pulled my mind back to the task in hand.

"A great apartment, Corinne. Given Upper East Side prices, you must be doing well?"

"Yes, but we entertain here for the charity – often at quite a high level. We've recently had a Senator and several corporate big wigs, too."

She shifted position and her skirt rode higher.

"Fund raising is all about contacts."

My heart sped. I thought my sexuality was probably settled, but my body seemed to have other ideas. I wanted to be cool, but my voice sounded tight.

"It's the weirdest thing, but I thought I was being followed earlier this evening."

I described my experience. Her eyes opened wide and she looked even prettier.

"Hey, I hope not," Corinne replied. "Maybe we're all being watched?"

"Meaning what?"

"After Nina was arrested, Nick said 'Mightn't you also be under observation?' He even wondered if our funds had been frozen."

"Have they?"

"No, nothing like that's happened. Not yet, anyway."

"Is there any chance the charity could have – even inadvertently – forwarded funds to anything that could resemble a terrorist group?"

"Of course not! Nick asked the same thing. We're focused on helping children because child poverty in South America is critical. What with the recent situation in Colombia, past problems in Nina's country and elsewhere – you wouldn't realise how many kids are without parents. The needs there are huge!"

"I've heard Nina on the subject."

She came and sat beside me.

"We both know of some terrible things."

"Yes, Nick explained some of it to me. Maybe we should take a look around the apartment now?"

She stood up.

"I can't think of anything relevant in here."

"It's superb," I said, looking around the lounge and eyeing their small crystal chandelier.

"Like I said, we entertain. Come and I'll show you the layout first."

She stood beside me, gently holding my arm and steering me around the apartment.

"The kitchen is through here, and the service area, over there. We have another reception room, a dining room, the hall and over here – a smaller sitting room. Above," she pointed to the stairs, "is an office, two bedrooms and third bedroom, currently used for storage."

Strangely, I rather enjoyed being steered around by her.

"Are you also Bolivian?"

"No, from Brazil, but I have lived there. Also, I was in Colombia for eighteen months before coming to the US. Let's start over here."

She went to the bureau opposite, which held a variety of drinks and glasses. The lower compartment stored place mats, chargers, servers and containers for Petit-four.

"I don't think there'll be anything here."

A large curved buffet yielded similar finds, but nothing relevant to our search. We moved on to the reception and dining room, but found nothing of note. In the smaller sitting room, I noticed an address book in Nina's handwriting. The book listed various organisations – mainly NGOs, and addresses and phone numbers from all over South America. I also noted numbers for several political figures and large businesses.

"What's with the business contacts?"

"Some businesses are very ethical and want to help," she replied. "Others like to appear ethical and charitable and we have to play their game. That seems appropriate if it brings in needed funds."

I smiled. As a PR and marketing professional, it was refreshing to see the good guys beat the big boys at their own game. It was just depressing that my employer was so devoted to team 'plunder on regardless'!

"Let's go upstairs," Corinne said, leading the way.

I followed her upstairs, trying to fight an impulse to look, but a quick glimpse at her shapely legs sent my thoughts down paths I'd long thought were closed.

We rooted around the storage room, finding only excess clothes, removal boxes, a defunct computer and surplus books. She moved on to Nina's bedroom. I felt increasingly uncomfortable when she opened drawers, pulling out clothes and underwear. I looked through half-closed eyes wondering if this was really necessary. At the far end of the room was a computer and desk, along with shelving racks and two large filing cabinets. I went over to the desk while Corinne replaced the clothing, and noticed an incomplete handwritten letter.

"I'll tell you what, Robbie, you sort through the papers and I'll come back in about half an hour with a drink to keep you going."

"Okay, but look. Could this be relevant?"

She took the letter from my hand.

"It's a draft reply from Nina to Victor, one of the campesino leaders. She keeps in touch with folk back home. Victor's only a coca grower, but quite influential. He's bright and the others look up to him."

I couldn't quite believe her nonchalance.

"A coca grower! No wonder you're having trouble – writing to coca growers!"

Corinne laughed a pretty, silvery laugh.

"No, you silly. The people just use coca for medical and nutritional reasons. Cocaine's only one derivative and not of interest to most campesinos. That's why they hate attempts at eradication, though Victor's group also opposes extending trade deals. Big foreign money only leads to more plunder."

I nodded.

"I know. The war on drugs preceded the 'war on terror' and they both turned into a boondoggle for the 'defence' and 'security' industries. Could you start the computer for me?"

She booted the computer up, entered the correct passwords, and left. Sitting under the letter, I found a note from Victor. It exceeded my limited Spanish, but appeared to be a request for help. I put the notes down and then searched through the packed cabinets. They contained cuttings and articles – many by Nina herself.

I worked through the papers, noting contact with several organisations who would probably be considered controversial. One promoted political representation for the indigenous Aymaras. Already at the outer fringe of my extremely limited Spanish, I understood 'Un moviemento socialista'. A Socialist Movement. The authorities would certainly love that! Other papers explored the practicalities of returning to pre-colonial, though modernised, social structures. As I worked through the cabinets, I felt a growing excitement.

"We're onto something," I mumbled to myself.

Nina was sharp, even brilliant, but this material would undoubtedly threaten the local elites profiting from foreign businesses and other backers of the 'Washington consensus'.

Certain matters had definitely improved. I noted that indigenous people now had representatives and translators to make government business accessible in the Quecha and Aymara languages. That wouldn't please some! Digging deeper into the cabinets, I discovered briefing papers and translations, presumably in Quechua and Aymara, and Spanish and English. I stopped to read an English translation of a paper tracing the historical plunder of resources – from silver in colonial days to guano and tin. Foreign corporations were poised to plunder gas and oil and were now eyeing the huge fresh water reserves!

Nina's arrest was starting to make more sense. Even if the claim of funding terrorists was rubbish, she'd probably been on a collision course with certain powerful corporations and probably made powerful enemies. I grinned, reading her next comment.

Over 500 years may have passed since Columbus initiated exploitation and genocide in the Southern Continent, but still the looters continue their merry work!

Other files showed contact with trade unions, miners' movements, coca growers, and peasant and community groups – and not only in her native Bolivia! She'd encouraged resistance to an oil pipeline and supported groups in Ecuador, Mexico, Venezuela, as well as Colombia. Probably there were many in energy, mining, water and the finance sectors who'd love to see her off the scene!

I'd become so engrossed that I'd failed to notice Corinne re-enter until she put her arms around me, resting her chin lightly on my shoulder, as I stared at the screen.

"Anything interesting?"

"I think so!"

I felt warm fingers gently knead my neck.

I turned around and looked up. Her eyes and mouth were foreground and I felt a warm sensation spreading around my body.

"What I mean, is… well, she wouldn't exactly make friends in high places, with all this!"

She leaned around, smiling that dazzling smile again, gazing straight into my eyes. I felt flustered.

"I mean, as well as taking swipes at business interests, Nina supports groups that the authorities could call terrorist organisations, if they chose. I reckon that's what happened."

She nodded and leaned against me while she massaged the top of my shoulders. As she rubbed, I could feel the sway of her large breasts across my neck and back. I looked back at her, the blond hair, loose but stylish, and those blue, blue eyes, improbably blending innocence and sensuality. She moistened her lips with the point of her tongue. I turned around and felt her cupping my face with warm hands. She came closer and bent down. Her kiss was warm and sweet, and, for the moment, pushed away any doubts.

"Come on, we haven't checked my room."

She took my hand. I followed, feeling suddenly small and in the grip of an unwanted childhood memory – the stranger in the park who'd held my hand and led me away.

I pushed the image from my mind. I needed to keep a grip, telling myself, *Don't get childlike. Keep it together or she'll think you're either a freak or crippled inside.*

We arrived at her bedroom. Corinne sat on the bed, and leant back on her elbows.

"I wonder if there's anything interesting in here?" she asked.

So, she'd changed into stockings! Surely, her meaning must be clear because the inside of her legs showed. She changed position, providing a glimpse of black lingerie. I felt trapped between the pull of her expectations and the push of my own unexpected desire. I gazed helplessly, and then found myself trance-like, moving to sit beside her. Within moments we were kissing, although she took the lead.

My mind started babbling.

You're the man. Take the initiative. Get on with it.

Something happened. My body seemed to switch on and then take over. Her breasts were soft and incredible. In fact, her whole body was beautiful and my desire was more explosive than I'd ever have believed.

Afterwards, I lay back, feeling an incredible freedom, as though some invisible bonds had been broken – ready to throw off the years of doubt and confusion. At this moment, I sensed things really could be different. I felt altogether different and even just looking around the room, the ornaments and pictures seemed brighter and almost luminous. I sighed and fell asleep.

51

MANHATTAN

ANDREW ALTON

I woke with anxiety gnawing at the pit of my stomach, for a moment unsure of my whereabouts. Light filtered around the edges of the blinds and I sat up to look around the dim hotel room. Then it all came flooding back, including the decision to tackle Dad over the College mess. As soon as I'd heard the news from Helen two nights ago, I knew that a confrontation would soon be on the agenda – and today was the day!

I got up and tried to decide what to wear. Should I match the setting with a business suit, or the softer but smart clothing of an academic? Perhaps I should forget all that and go for holiday casual wear? After all, I was the one who'd been wronged and wasn't in the slightest beholden to the man. Finally, I decided on smart casual wear and breakfasted at a nearby diner. I walked the short distance to Marquetcom's office, looking up to the spire, site of King Kong's imaginary havoc.

"It'll be another kind of gorilla today," I whispered to myself.

The streets seemed overfull with people randomly milling – or at least that's how it seemed. Maybe, it was only stress, but things felt unreal – even faintly ridiculous. I tried summoning up a more resourceful state of mind and entered the Empire State building's famous lobby.

A high-speed elevator sped me up to Marquetcom's sixtieth floor suite. A classy-looking receptionist started her patter, but soon stopped after I announced my identity. My body felt clammy and already jammed between fight and flight.

"Wait here a moment, Mr Alton."

She crossed to a phone and spoke a few words.

"I'm sorry, but Mr Anson hasn't yet arrived. He had an earlier outside appointment and won't get back until roughly 11am."

"Oh hell, two more hours?"

She smiled before continuing.

"However, Mr Anson anticipated you might call and arranged for Rob James, one of his senior assistants, to offer assistance until he arrives."

I sensed someone approach.

"Mr James is here now, Sir."

I found myself face-to-face with Robbie and tried to adopt a neutral expression. Showing recognition could be disastrous. Robbie obviously felt the same.

"Good morning. I believe you're Andrew Alton, Mr Anson's son, over here from England?"

I nodded.

"Yes, that's right. I gather he's not here yet?"

"No. Cheryl probably explained that Mr Anson asked me to look after you, if he should be out. We'll be more comfortable in my office until he gets back."

We left the reception for Robbie's small, though comfortable, room.

"Heck. I didn't expect this."

"Makes two of us," said Rob, busying himself with a coffee percolator. "Good to see you again. Obviously, you've decided to talk –though please keep me out of it. How are you feeling?"

"Pretty grim. There's been another development."

Robbie shook his head when the implications of Anson's sponsorship sank in.

"We agreed about his bullying ways, but getting his hooks into my lectureship and research programme... is truly despicable. Things any better for you?"

"Funnily enough – yes, quite a lot better. I had an unexpectedly good evening!"

"Good, though I feel rather embarrassed that you have such an employer! Mind you, if he knew about our discussions the other night!"

I pointed to the window. "You'd probably end up flying!"

Robbie beamed.

"Normally, that would frighten me, but, today, I think I'd push him out first!"

"His tricks are appalling though," I said. "If he has to misuse an academic institution by commissioning junky, self-serving research – why mine? Do you know if he's involved with any other institutes?"

"Can't say for sure," replied Robbie. "None that I know of."

"It's so vindictive!"

Robbie nodded.

"Yes, well there are many examples of that."

We exchanged examples and tales, for at least another hour.

"Possibly selfish," said Rob, "but it's such a relief meeting someone who understands the ethical dimension. It's just as well that he can't hear this, though."

I nodded, shaping my hand like a mock revolver and touching my temple.

"Mind you, I'm careful with phone or email. Rumour has it that he sometimes even monitors communications! Anyway, coming back to now, can I do anything to help. Those were my instructions?"

"Well, I intend..."

The air buffeted our faces as the door burst open. We sat there, frozen and speechless. It wasn't certain if the ghastly grin had merged with a sneer, or vice versa, but my father had a strange grimace and his face had turned a dirty brick colour. Two security people stood in the doorway.

"You don't think I just monitor calls and emails, do you, son?"

One of the security men put a box on the desk and packed the contents of the drawer.

"You probably think you've been sacked, and your stuff is being packed," Biff proclaimed. "You'd be right, but this won't be released until I see what you've been up to. Understand!"

Robbie's buoyancy had evaporated. He looked shocked and stayed mute as security escorted him out.

Biff stared at me with malevolence. The face was undoubtedly older, but there had been no mellowing.

"You wanted to talk, so come back to my room."

His office was only two doors away, but I felt strangely uncoordinated, and it seemed much further. I followed along, entering an office that was designed, above all, to impress. My last visit was years ago to the previous address on Madison Avenue. I took stock of an extremely large room lined with cabinets, book shelves and, in the middle, a huge carved desk. One end had a conference area, with a table and chairs. The other end – an array of comfortable dark leather easy chairs. It all reeked of power, prestige and money.

"Coffee, or perhaps, bourbon? That's what I'm having."

I remembered his heavy bouts of drinking and the aggressive consequences. My queasy stomach agreed.

"Coffee, thanks."

An assistant called Nancy brought in coffee, and then scurried away without receiving thanks. I knew I had to quickly gain initiative and looked him straight in the eye.

"Was sacking him really necessary? He was only blowing off steam. Everyone does that from time to time."

His face told me that this was a hopeless cause.

"You think so, eh? I've reason to believe our little lavender friend hasn't played for our team for quite a time and I've a feeling you know exactly what I mean!"

He was chilling. Whether it was caused by the words or his expression, the sensations from my abdomen had sent a shock to my diaphragm that restricted free breathing. My throat felt tight to the fear that the old man somehow knew about our recent meeting – and that he had been the prime specimen. I held his gaze and tried to steady my breath – knowing that he'd jump on any signs of weakness.

"I don't know what that means, but I do know about your interference with my workplace."

His face again took on the weird melange of a smile and sneer.

"Investing in your future is a good thing!" he replied.

The old responses were unravelling. I looked at the large frame opposite with the balled fists, conscious of a childhood on the receiving end. Then the dam burst and I heard myself shout.

"So, my future is important. Really, despite knowing nothing of what I've been doing, for years! Why mess it about now?"

"How wrong you are! Unfortunately, your mom insisted on forwarding many examples of your so-called 'work', over the years. Dear Mommy seemed very proud, though I felt differently."

"I bet you did!"

Biff leaned forward. Though it defied nature, any known logic or mechanism, the large head seemed to somehow emanate darkness.

"Actually, you don't understand at all. I loved your mother – still do. I worked my butt off trying to do the best for all of you. You had the brains and could easily have joined me in the business."

"Have you actually read my work?"

"Yes. Airy-fairy nonsense. Your problem is that you don't understand business and never have! It's a dog-eat-dog world, that you just don't get. You have to use your wits. Get in first – or get nowhere."

"Believe that if you want – but I think differently. I believe ethical business is best. Treating employees, customers, suppliers, the environment – even competitors – fairly and decently. That's absolutely possible!"

"Because you're naive and haven't really been in business. Your head's in the clouds, not a real-life business environment."

"I think you'll find my work is widely read."

"You're such a child," he said. "Get your feet back on the ground. Study nature, that shows you how things really are. Does the antelope say to a lion, 'Close your mouth buddy, and ask yourself – will this be ethical?' See what happens when you try to fight nature?"

"Did you ever think that humans may differ from animals? Well, some, anyway! Of course, you wouldn't know this, but people can develop, mature, hold different values, exercise restraint! Anyway, please tell me why you picked my College to mess with."

"Easy. The management school wanted sponsorship. It's a prestigious connection that could do both of our businesses good."

"Why call an academic institution a business? Unfortunately, people like you think everything is for sale or must be a business opportunity."

The big face grinned.

"Because money makes the world go round! Your type doesn't understand market disciplines. I'm doing you a favour – helping you to confront reality."

"How kind! The same 'reality', I suppose, that 'helps' people by making them unable to afford water or the necessary medicines to keep them alive! 'Reality' from the same good old philosophy that turns people into sweatshop slaves just to enrich corporations. The same enlightened philosophy that turns entire nations into debtors, forcing them to hand over their resources to foreigners – even as their own people starve."

"You're a happy little fucker, aren't you? Like I said, you should get into harmony with nature. Remember the lion."

He paused and grinned.

"On second thoughts, forget the lion. The Brits have had their day. Think of the eagle, swooping down to take what it wants. I can imagine your ideas of an alternative. Government handouts for every feckless, lazy individual with their hands held out, I suppose? And the money comes from where?"

I looked at the big head, aggressively stuck forward like some bird of prey and suddenly wanted to hit it – very hard!

"The lion and eagle you so love to talk about, just take what they need. Those I object to, accumulate and accumulate, bloating themselves to the point of damaging others and destroying the environment!"

The big face darkened again.

"Look, I want my investment to produce useful work, helpful to business. The College management wants that and I understand that the British education authorities want it too – though the sooner they get real and privatise the whole damn thing the better. Anyone with a brain knows the rational decisions come from letting the market choose. That's the undeniable truth!"

"As demonstrated in the finance system meltdown, I suppose! Try telling that to people who lost their homes!"

"Look, son, if people make decisions that put themselves outside the market rules – and then complain, that's their lookout!"

I felt rage boiling.

"So, when workers' jobs are sent to Mexico or India, or China, that's their fault?"

"If they price themselves out of work, and make themselves uncompetitive, yes. Unless, of course, you think that corporate boards are full of sociopaths, rather than good businessmen!"

It felt like a punch to my gut. Why would he use those particular words? Fear quickly spread through my body like butter on hot toast. Did he somehow know? Could it just be a response to my comment about ruthless accumulators? I searched for possibilities.

Maybe it was just coincidental. Many psychological terms were now in everyday use – although this hadn't been an everyday conversation!

I studied my father's face. The unblinking watery eyes stared back with no observable change. Surely his words were merely chance?

"Many Board decisions benefit only themselves and a small investment elite. Employees are ground down, people lose pensions and the environment is ravaged. On and on it goes."

Biff shook his head in apparent disbelief.

"I can't imagine the harm you do, working in a unit nominally attached to a school of business administration."

"You're worried that I might humanise it?" I replied.

"The opposite! Human nature means letting the strongest lead and quite rightly call the shots!"

"Social Darwinism is a soulless creed!"

"I've invested in our sponsorship and expect results. I'm not exactly a fan of some of your work."

"Like what?"

"You'll see in good time, but, for example, your nonsense about privatisation. Most things are run more efficiently in the private sector."

I sensed no chink in his armour. We were nowhere near even speaking the same language.

"Efficient for whom, exactly? What about Cochabamba, Bolivia?"

"Blown out of proportion. Distorted by lefties and liberals. I've closely followed the issue of water privatising in South America. More closely than you'd imagine, although perhaps our little friend Robbie has already told you that?"

"I hadn't met him until this morning. You seemed acquainted with our conversation."

He reached into his desk and, smiling, held up a file.

"Yes, I know all about him!"

"Clean affordable water is a human right."

"So is a proper return on investment."

"I don't think there's anything more to say, so I'll go."

"I guess not. Give my love to Judy."

"Do what?"

"Pass my love to your mom."

"I don't have the words, nor a lead-lined container."

I left, exited the suite and re-entered Fifth Avenue's bustle.

My say had been a long time coming!

52

PHILADELPHIA

Zoltan hadn't long arrived back, when he picked up on a call. Andrew got straight to the point

"Hi, it's Andrew here. Is Mom in?"

"No, out shopping, but she'll be back soon. Shall I ask her to call?"

"Just tell her I'm at Penn Station about to get the train over."

"Will do! Listen, call when you arrive and I'll pick you up from the station."

Judy's feelings were written all over her face, after he told her. Of course, that was understandable, but could cause another complication.

Judy cut across his thoughts.

"I'm really close to Andy. I'm so thrilled that you two will meet."

He kissed her, but sensed something else was bothering her.

"The thing is, my love," said Judy, "I don't know how Andy will react to us."

"It's normal," he replied. "Sons should be protective of their mothers and sisters. Don't worry."

He hugged her, and gently kissed her neck.

"I suppose we'll just have to be good or careful."

"Mmm – we'll see!"

The station was busy, but he recognised Andrew from photos around the home. In any case, he appeared as bookish and intellectual as he'd have predicted.

When they returned, Judy lit up. Initially, he felt almost excluded by their intimacy – exchanging news and discussing old times. Had he recently made love to this man's mother? The idea felt awkward, but then he recalled one of Abdul's favourite sayings. 'Anything done for the mission's sake will be forgiven.'

"Isn't that awful, Zoltan?" he heard her say.

He tried to replay their discussion, but had only heard snippets. The conversation had turned to something related to Andrew's work.

"Sorry. I'd just remembered something vital I must do and, for a moment, missed the conversation. I believe it was about education in the UK? Something was said about corporate capture?"

"Yes. Education had been largely left alone in the UK, but the corporate sponsorship thing has gradually, well… you explain it, Andy."

"Until now, my research centred on various corporate abuses, often resulting from corporate-led globalisation."

"You say 'up until now'… that's changing?"

"Yes, and they now want me to support that agenda and produce business-friendly pap and junk research. I really couldn't stand that."

He listened to Judy coo and cluck.

"Of course not, son."

"But, wait, there's more, Mom!"

He immediately knew what was coming and felt ashamed. He'd heard the build-up – the college's acceptance of sponsorship, the sudden intervention of an American corporation… and then came the bombshell!

"Their sponsor is Marquetcom, Mom. In other words, Biff's pulling strings behind the scene!"

He watched the colour drain from her face.

"He's so… so… devious! What's his game?"

"Control, I suppose, and of course the College wants the corporate dollars. Mind you, ever since the Reagan-Thatcher love-in, British governments have been wedded to doing more and more things the American way."

Judy appeared lost in thought.

"I wonder if this might also be about me, darling. He knows how close we are and always did like interfering. Of course, it's also good business!"

Andrew appeared quite consumed.

"I can't be a corporate pawn!"

Zoltan nodded understanding.

"What will you do, then?" she said.

"I don't know. Given the time of year, I can take six weeks leave of absence to think things over. Before all this happened, I'd won agreement for Simon Maher, a junior colleague, to make a US research trip. He's in New York right now."

"Are you researching, too, or just visiting your mom?" Zoltan asked.

"Not sure. Now we know Biff's involved, some odd things are making a lot more sense."

"By the way, I loved that paper you sent about privatising, darling," Judy interjected. "It was superb. I told my friends back in New Jersey about it, including the meetings chairperson, a pleasant young man called Nick Martin. I particularly remember because, apparently, he already knew of your paper."

"You know Nick Martin?"

She nodded.

"Yes. We talked shortly after you sent the paper. I so miss that group."

Zoltan watched as Andrew registered surprise.

"Amazing. Talk about the global village! I met Nick a few nights ago in New York. Simon had already hooked up with him because they'd been in correspondence."

Judy smiled and nodded.

"I also sent a copy to your dad."

Watching Andrew's face, he realised that the French impressionists had it right. Flesh really can take on all those tones!

"Mom! Please tell me that you're joking. No wonder he's being so vindictive!"

She looked chastened.

"Sorry, Andy. I just wanted to show him your progress. I mean, he is still your father."

"But, Mom, he'd hate everything the paper says!"

He'd never seen Judy look so crestfallen.

"I'm sorry, Andy. I felt proud, and hoped he'd share in that. I even hoped you might get through to him. We argued over just these very things, even when you were a baby."

"I was probably pickled in it. Forwarding him that privatisation article, of all things, was a really bad call, though."

"Why?"

"Because we now know that he's behind a water privatisation in South America. He'd just love my paper, in fact he virtually said as much. His interference makes more sense now!"

"You mean you've seen him?"

"Yes, and it was devastating. I was just about to tell you!"

"What happened?"

"Let me explain some other background first, because some very odd things have happened. Recently, I started a new project."

He sketched out his work with Simon, Farrelly and Grotstein.

"Although there's plenty of other work on these lines, we hoped to extend it and show the way that institutionalised pathology infects the wider system."

Zoltan knew what would be coming next.

"Interesting, but why do you think…?"

"However, when I was back in England, Simon phoned from New York. Contacts he'd met had given him information about a business with extremely dubious ethics, lead by a prize sociopath… A certain Biff Anson!"

Her face fell.

"That's beyond belief! Life deals some really strange hands sometimes! So, you came over hoping to find out more?"

Andrew nodded.

"Yes. Simon had already been introduced to one of Biff's employees, who didn't realise he's my father. The evening I arrived in New York, we all met to discuss Marquetcom and Biff's management style. I can tell you, it certainly wasn't edifying! In fact, it was horribly stressful. Afterwards, I returned to my hotel, and my head had hardly hit the pillow when my PA called with news that the mystery corporate sponsor was a certain Bifton Anson."

"You poor dear. Age hasn't mellowed him. How awful!"

It must have been bad, but, despite time in America, Zoltan felt amazed. Such a discussion could never have happened involving his mother – especially in front of an outsider!

Andrew appeared overwhelmed.

"He needs to be stopped, Mom! He epitomises the thought virus of greed, menacing health, happiness and even the planet's future."

Andrew's colour had returned and he now had the bit between his teeth.

"Rationales like 'trickle-down economics' or 'all boats will rise together' just mask gross inequality and get parroted everywhere. After tremendous destruction, it becomes obvious that, while some luxury yachts may have risen, most boats were holed below the waterline!"

Zoltan looked at the bookish, passionate man, fired with ideas. Andrew might be bright, but he didn't know that real change required more than just writing papers.

A well-meaning child!

"These are just the kind of things your dad and I fought about all those years ago. Now what will you do?"

Andrew started pacing, and Judy looked worried.

"I don't know. It can't work having Biff pulling my strings. I might have to leave."

"You can stay here as long as you like. I've plenty of room. Maybe it's time to consider coming home and working in your own country again?"

"I've Anne to consider. There's always freelancing, NGOs, or working for a charity."

"You have to put yourself first, now!"

"Biff's attitudes run contrary to everything I believe in," Andrew said. His senior assistant, a guy called Robbie James, shared some really hair-raising stuff about... I can hardly even say the word... 'Dad', including his treatment of staff. I witnessed that for myself later on, because he sacked Robbie right in front of me. It was almost as though he'd known the contents of our earlier meeting – and no-one held back at all!"

She looked thoughtful.

"He's always been crafty, Andy. In the old days, he used private investigators in all kinds of sneaky ways."

Zoltan thought of Brian Tutch, and filed that away for the future.

"Someone needs to stop him," Andrew repeated.

"Careful, darling. He was always at his most dangerous when cornered."

They continued over a long lunch. Zoltan contributed sympathetically and, by the end of the afternoon, had taken the role of a 'supportive sounding-board'.

"What's your work, Zoltan?" asked Andrew.

"Freelancing, mainly with IT. I've contracts in the North East –

Baltimore, New York City, and, afterwards, New England. May even have something later in South America."

Judy gave a sharp intake of breath, and for a moment he feared she'd accidentally given the game away.

"You didn't mention that, Zoltan?"

"It arrived on my laptop," he said. "It isn't certain, and probably only for a short time. There's plenty to finish here – if I can stay a little longer?"

Her face relaxed.

"No problem," she replied, without missing a beat.

The phone rang and Judy picked up.

"Yes, he's here now. I'll put him on."

Zoltan couldn't hear anything. Andrew frowned, turned his back and mumbled. When he finished, he looked crestfallen.

"Something up?" asked Zoltan.

"What is it, son?"

"I just don't believe it."

Andrew had crumpled like a deflated concertina.

"That was my PA from England. She's seen confidential papers and wanted to warn me. Apparently, they plan axing Simon's post! She saw a report full of business gabble, like 'narrowing the focus to core business only', 'suiting the new business environment', and so on. It seems Simon can finish the trip, and then has approximately two months to write it up – and that's it! If I was paranoid, I'd almost think that Biff had got wind of Simon's plans and has pulled strings!"

Andrew crumpled again. His colour drained and now looked a waxy yellow, apart – that is – from the white knuckles on clenched hands. He thumped the sofa seat, and rocked to and fro.

"Shit, shit, shit! Of course, that's it! When Marquetcom negotiated the sponsorship, Biff would have had access to our ongoing work."

"Sorry, how would...?"

"The feasibility report for our research project – including 'sociopathic markers in corporate behaviour'. We had to submit a protocol for the Research Panel, and register it as part of our output. The theme wasn't exactly popular and we pushed for it on the basis that the school now teaches elements on 'corporate responsibility'. In other words, how to effectively whitewash, or more to the point, greenwash. I shudder to think what Biff would have made of our protocol!"

Judy's face looked grave.

"You don't know for sure, son."

"Feels right though, wouldn't you say?"

She nodded.

Andrew started pacing again.

"Sorry, before I took the call, you said something, Zoltan?"

"South America," he replied. "I'd just mentioned I might soon go there."

"Nick Martin, the guy Mom mentioned earlier, returns there soon, because his firm is partnering with Marquetcom over the water privatising. I just wish we could spike the whole damn thing," said Andrew.

"I'll get more coffee," said Judy.

Zoltan watched her leave, and then pulled his mind back to the discussion.

"You'd like for Colombian activists to take action?"

"I wouldn't entirely rule that out," Andrew replied. "Nick's girlfriend was apparently close to that scene, but now she's been arrested and they've lost contact. Actually, I got scooped up by the authorities at an arms fair demonstration in London, so I know how scary that can be. Just peacefully protesting, but left in no doubt that I'm seen as trouble."

The sound of breaking glass and an expletive came from the kitchen. Judy called out. "Andy, love, do be careful. You're messing with powerful forces."

"I've no intention of getting into their clutches."

Zoltan quickly processed the information. This could be bad news, given the cooperation between the US and the Brits.

Judy returned with a frown and fresh coffee.

"What do you mean, 'seen as trouble', Andy?"

"Not quite sure. It was implied, so even more intimidating. I certainly didn't appreciate seeing a fat dossier bearing my name."

In Zoltan's peripheral vision, he saw Judy shake her head.

"Hang on, son. You said 'scooped up at a demonstration'. I assume it had many people?"

"An almighty crowd."

"Was everyone arrested?" asked Judy.

"I don't know how many. Simon, me and another friend became detached from the main crowd. I was grabbed and taken to a police station. I didn't see anyone else there, though."

Judy shook her head.

"That doesn't sound right to me. If others weren't also being questioned, what's the likelihood that a police station would just happen to have your dossier to hand?"

She's certainly sharp, Zoltan thought!

Andrew sank into his chair, looking pale and pinched. Judy clucked, leaning forward and touching him. Quite an intimate scene, like a mother comforting her infant.

Andrew sat upright again.

"Mom, you're so right! Why didn't I see that? Of course, the chances of my file just happening to be there are, well... almost zero! It's almost like they knew I'd be coming."

You were obviously under surveillance, Zoltan thought, wondering how someone so intelligent could also be quite so slow? At that moment, his cell phone rang and he went outside to take the call. It came from the network, and the brief coded message indicated that something would arrive soon on his laptop. He went to his room to check, and then, as requested, checked the materials in the shed were ready...

ANDREW ALTON

AS THE IMPLICATIONS SUNK IN, Andrew shook his head.

"How could I have been so stupid? I just felt... Well, to be honest, I was quite shaken and wanted out of the place as quickly as possible."

I tailed off, gazing at the carpet as the disturbing puzzle fell into place.

"Unhappily, I only see one explanation! Simon had an activist friend, actually a girlfriend, called Gill Marney, who came with us that day. Only our colleagues on the research project, my wife Anne, and then Gill even knew we were going to the demo. We stayed together, so Gill knew where we were all the time. We thought she was a committed activist, though I suspected Simon might have told her about our work. I warned him to be discreet, but they were getting very friendly."

He looked even paler.

"I can only think she was feeding information back to... whoever."

"Where were you taken?" asked Judy.

"I don't know – I think it was in the Paddington area of London. I'm sure now that it wasn't the regular police... probably security or intelligence, and the link can only be Gill. She suggested we escape down the very side street where I was arrested. Mom, she's over here too, and still very close to Simon."

"Over here?"

"In New York City. Supposedly troubleshooting a new business system for her US office. She's spent time with Simon, most evenings."

Judy shook her head.

"Mom, we absolutely have to keep this from Zoltan. Even if Gill is from Intelligence, we have to respect her position and work around it, for now.

"I'm sure we can trust Zoltan, dear. I mean he..."

"Mom, no. Please, let's just consume our own smoke until things are clearer. It's better that way. Promise?"

A LITTLE LATER, Zoltan returned to the house, satisfied that all was well. The body language in the room, however, wasn't good. Annoying, because Anson's task required him to have a good relationship with Dr Alton. Andrew now seemed fazed and even Judy looked preoccupied. He left for his room, to give them privacy. When he returned, Andrew was on the phone.

He strained to hear.

"Things make a whole lot more sense now. Martin... the break-ins, the missing material. No, I haven't decided. Please can you let Stephen Grotstein know what's happened and check that Anne's okay."

Andrew turned around. He held up a hand, mouthed "sorry" and crept back to the kitchen to hug Judy. Surprisingly, the response wasn't the desultory peck of a preoccupied mother. Zoltan raised his eyebrows and she mouthed:

"Come to my room, tonight."

He nodded, surprised once more, at the way people can respond to stress. They moved apart seconds before Andrew entered. He was already speaking.

"Mom, I'd like Simon to join us. Could he stay a day or two, if necessary? We've so much to discuss and he also doesn't yet know that termination is heading his way."

"Of course, son. I'd like to meet him anyway."

Zoltan returned to his room and fired up his laptop to send a brief something to Anson. He ended his note with, 'more to come'.

So, Alton's junior colleague would soon join them. Things couldn't get any messier…

53

MANHATTAN

GILL'S PERSPECTIVE

Gill loved New York's buzz, except the encumbrance of Matacic and Holt as mentors. Holt she loathed especially and felt sure that, under all the tedious innuendo, he was probably sexually inadequate. Certainly wasn't true of Simon and their relationship had now transitioned into a full-scale affair. Of course, this wasn't professional and dealing with the subsequent emotions had been problematic. One moment, she was being close and intimate with Si and, the next, Holt and Matacic were pumping her for information.

She made her way up Fifth Avenue, delaying Holt's inevitable innuendoes by time in a shoe shop. Gill picked up a pair of classic black patent evening shoes, casually stroking the leather, but actually engrossed in her dilemma. Being around Simon had challenged many of her beliefs. That was almost as uncomfortable as the nagging sense of disloyalty she was now suffering. Previously, she'd classified the social justice community as economically illiterate, frightened to compete and looking back to simpler times. It seemed a 'given' that the world would roll on in the same old way. Economies would grow their way out of trouble and prosperity would continue.

On the other side of the floor, some strappy shoes beckoned, though she was mostly focused on the matter of her changing values. She'd been quite convinced growth was necessary and always good. She'd thought public services inefficient and should be privatised. Now she

asked 'efficient for whom, at what cost, and for whose benefit?' Everything she'd thought solid had been challenged. Did 'free trade' always
work, and for whom was it free? Did our democracy really represent
the voters will or really act in the interest of the majority? Did the
state's so-called 'right hand' – the police, military, prisons, justice apparatus and, yes, the intelligence services – actually serve the people? Why
did the repressive 'right hand' always trump the so-called caring 'left
hand'? Simon succeeded in exposing the flaws and contradictions in so
many of her beliefs – but, even as her old world-view collapsed, so, too,
did her peace of mind!

Gill rejoined the crowds on the Avenue, even more aware that this
sea change in her outlook would eventually propel her into a crisis.
*Why should the taxpayer's resources be used to shut down people with alterna-
tive views or real worries about the future? Is that really what her work had
come to?* She reached Trump Tower, and entered its glitzy interior.
Today it appeared to her like a glossy ashtray and no amount of baubles
could distract her. The truth stared her in the face – this kind of
compromise couldn't continue! When she got home, she'd have to
resign. By the time she'd left the building, she decided to work out an
exit strategy, including explaining everything to Simon. Meanwhile,
she'd try and discover the fate of this Nina woman, who seemed so
important to Simon and his friends.

She reached the 'Manhattan One' office, near the Rockefeller
complex. If she could only locate Nina that would help her credibility
when she finally revealed her duplicity to Simon and Andrew.
However, Nina could be almost anywhere. Some years back, it would
have been more straightforward. Real suspects could be 'rendered' to
cooperative countries – or that place in Cuba. Things had moved on
and now holding sites existed in mainland USA. Government lawyers
had found ways of arguing that the legislation could apply to certain
radicals and domestic extremists. She entered the room to find her
mentors – or in Holt's case, 'tormentor' – already at work.

"Ah, nice Brits," said Holt, suggestively.

"Take no notice, Gill," said Matacic, rolling his eyes.

She wondered about the best way to find Nina.

"So, you guys are already working. What have we got on today?"

"I nearly asked you that," said Holt with a wink.

"Shut up, Jack," said Matacic. "Ever heard of harassment? Sorry Gill,
we're working down in the financial district – solo on this one, I'm

afraid. I suggest you put more time in with the integrated data systems. You'll need to write all that up in your report."

"You said something about dissidents and mental illness the other day?"

They repeated the sorry story with relish.

"Surely that would never be accepted?"

"Probably not," said Matacic, grinning. "Though, 'Political lunacy' might still exist in China. In the old USSR, political dissidents regularly were taken off to mental hospitals."

"Don't forget," said Holt, "that holding camps for terrorists and troublemakers already exist in the Mountain States and the desert South West."

She asked for a further quick demonstration of the integrated information system. Matacic quickly reviewed its workings, demonstrating the 'surveillance database', 'suspect database', 'detainees database' and, finally, the 'international database'.

Matacic and Holt departed, leaving her to play with the system and study the manuals. She decided to go all out, and, in case they monitored online activities, moved to another terminal and booted it up. The name of the woman... was it something like 'Nina Pahenda', though she was unsure of the spelling. She didn't see Matacic use additional passwords during his demonstration. She tried and – sure enough – she was in! With trembling hands, she entered Nina's first name into the international database and immediately struck lucky. Nina Parenda, Bolivian, 38 years old. She noted Nina's birthdate signified Aquarius: *Revolutionary and humanitarian tendencies, and...*

She stopped the internal astro-babble and focused on the screen. She certainly didn't want Holt, or anyone else for that matter, asking awkward questions.

Gill worked down the screen, summarising Nina's interests. Observed connections spanned many activist groups and a variety of political, labour, and community organisations. Contact with anti-capitalist groups was noted and probable support and links with narco-terrorists. Another field in the database described her work with the Andean children's charity, cross-referenced to records of her entry documents connected to a charity mission in New York City. Further down, the comment, *observe after entry.*

Gill opened the surveillance database. Nina's name was also linked with the suspect database. Why? She scanned the related fields – 'prohibited contacts', 'documentary evidence' and a box containing thumb-nail images. She opened one, and saw a refined and rather beautiful face. She passed over the rest and went into another field marked 'critical evidence'. There, in hypertext, was the comment – *contact with RM.* She clicked on this, but a box opened, saying, *ACCESS DENIED.*

She closed it and then tried again – but had the same result!

A noise came from behind. She turned as a female agent named Michelle entered the room and smiled, though showed no particular interest.

She seized the initiative,

"The system is normally much faster than ours at home. My terminal seemed rather clunky this morning but this one works fine."

She quickly minimised the database, and brought up the L-S-F-R-S – the 'live, streamed facial recognition system'. In truth, it was rather amazing. An operator could even select an image from the database, and then cross-reference to live feeds coming from a few key street locations, airport arrivals, the port authority bus station, train termi-nals, subway stations, etc. Occasionally a flag lit, indicating that the system had recognised a known face. In another part of the building, a rotating team monitored sightings twenty-four/seven. Michelle finished rummaging inside her desk. Gill saw she'd picked up a choco-late bar and a box of tights, or 'pantyhose' as they're called here. The woman smiled again.

"Hi, I'm Michelle. We briefly met several days ago. Like to talk with you again soon, but just now I'm late for an appointment. Another long day," she added, holding up the items by way of explanation.

Michelle left. Gill returned to the system and accessed the detainees database. Details appeared of secure holding places, unknown to the general public. She entered Nina's number, which registered a location called 'Camp Ute' in the South West. She noted down the details and a GPS reference.

She worked on the system manuals, but mainly puzzled over how to explain this mess to Simon. What if he didn't or couldn't accept her explanation? Subject to the UK's Official Secrets Act, the consequences would be far more severe than just her career ending in tatters. She took her mind off the prospect by jotting down an overview of the system for her report. What if Si was so appalled at her duplicity that their relationship couldn't survive? Still, she couldn't continue like this. That much was clear.

As the day wore on, her turmoil heightened. Late morning, Matacic and Holt returned from down-town and Holt unloaded further torrents of innuendo and nonsense. *In-your-endo – creep* – she thought, and was instantly disgusted with herself for following Holt's ways. She just avoided an unwanted late job in New Jersey, on the pretext of continuing her report for London.

Simon quickly answered her call. She kept her voice bright, reasoning that calls from here may be routinely monitored.

"Si, our time here is galloping away. There's only just over two weeks left, so we need to make the most of it. Are you free later on?"

"I've been thinking the same," he replied. "It's kind of weird you phoning now. Andy just called, inviting me over to his mom's place in Philadelphia. Apparently, he has important news and wants to talk, so I planned on taking a train later this afternoon. Strange, because I was literally about to call and ask you to come. His mom is apparently very welcoming, but I'll phone first to check."

"Well, I've the weekend off. Are you sure it will be okay?"

"Absolutely, Andy likes you, but, as I said, I'll call him. Let's meet at Penn Station – 4.30pm, by the ticket line."

She rang off. Replaying it through the ears of a listener, the conversation could easily be understood as her following her surveillance task. She penned Matacic a note and then logged off and left with hope and fear in equal measures.

54

MANHATTAN

SIMON MAHER

I continued walking up Fifth Avenue, quite puzzled by Andy's call. He sounded stressed, which seemed understandable enough, but why all the urgency? My planned meeting with media analyst, Norman Solnick, had been postponed, so I filled in time browsing in a nearby book store. America sometimes seemed so contradictory. I puzzled over the sheer quality of progressive writing that coexisted with downright weirdness and bigotry. I moved on to their guidebook section. Andrew had talked about the contradictions and beauty out West – like 'anything goes' Nevada, right next door to 'uptight' Idaho – and all within a short drive! I'd love to see it. I left the bookshop, with a mind full of cowboys, red-rock canyons and cacti. Still, with appointments and interviews ahead in San Francisco, maybe I could return overland.

I certainly felt excited at the prospect of time with Gill, and seeing Philadelphia, the original seat of government. Perhaps we'd see the major sites? I then remembered promising Gill that I'd specifically ask permission for her to join us at Judy's. I skirted Herald Square, and paused in Macy's entrance to phone – wondering if Macy's was really bigger than London's Harrods? I'd duck in afterwards and compare.

A woman's voice then answered.

"Hello, Mrs Alton? This is Simon Maher, Andy's co-worker. Is he there?"

When Andrew arrived, he sounded rather edgy.

"Andy, can I ask a favour. I hope it's okay, but I've asked Gill to come with me. We'd like time together. Would that be okay with you and your mom?"

The line stayed silent.

"Are you there, Andy? Is that okay?"

There was a groan, and his voice croaked back.

"I don't believe it!"

"I thought you liked Gill. I know it's a bit cheeky, but…"

"No. Gill is one of the main reasons we need to talk. That and, I'm afraid, more developments from back home."

"What about Gill?"

I felt anxious, sensing bad news. Maybe all that 'para-linguistic' guff Grotstein spouted really meant something. He'd once told us that voice tonality carries and evokes emotion, almost better than anything else. He finally choked it out, but Andy's outpouring was the last thing I expected.

"But, Gill was with us during the whole arms fair thing," I countered. "Remember?"

"But replay it again. Who found that passage off the side street? Who, other than Anne, Farrelly and Grotstein, even knew that we were going?"

I felt sick.

"They seemed to know just where we were!"

My mind flowed to all points of the compass searching for alternative explanations.

"But, I met her at an anti-GMO group."

"Now you're being naive. Remember how surprised you were when she didn't always seem up to speed with issues and you had to fill her in. Think about it. Why was she so uninformed about a lot of things? Single-issue activists are quite rare these days because most can now see how things are interconnected."

My mind went into overdrive – part defending Gill, and another part sniffing out facts that smelt distinctly 'off'. Deeply in thought, I'd drifted into Macy's doorway, obstructing the exit. An obese woman hissed at me like an irritated goose.

"What timing, Andy! I'm due to meet her soon at Penn Station!"

The line went quiet. When he spoke again, Andrew sounded more collected.

"Okay, let's keep cool. It's probably best that you continue, but keep it zipped over the weekend – yes, I did mean your mouth! Try to hear things as if through Gill's ears, before speaking."

"Okay, got it. We discuss important things alone and keep as natural as possible."

"I'll fix it with Mom. See you later this evening."

I felt sick at being so easily duped. I'd fallen for Gill, but she'd deceived me. I wandered into the enormous Macy's store, but took little in.

Perhaps we have it wrong, I tried. *Oh yeah,* said another part of my mind. *You want to be fooled again?*

She waited by the ticket line, looking gorgeous in a smart business suit, if rather tense. We hugged, but my body felt tight. I felt sure my eyes would appear veiled and she'd notice something was wrong! When I looked into her eyes, though, something was already happening. She looked away and, trembling, spoke.

"Simon, we'll soon be in a crowded carriage. I have to tell you something first, before we leave."

"Let's have a quick coffee."

"Have we time?"

"If we go right now."

We found a nearby coffee shop. Her speech seemed pressured as it all tumbled out. Hearing her confirm everything Andy had suspected was deeply shocking. Time seemed to slow while she explained her former role and then her change of heart.

"So much has changed since meeting and then getting to know you, Simon. Nothing seems the same at all."

I couldn't suppress a smile, despite the seriousness.

"God bless Jung and synchronicity!"

"Sorry?"

I relayed the conversation with Andy.

"When I phoned Andy to check about you coming, it all came out. Apparently, something Judy, his mother, asked caused them to rumble your role in the arms fair experience. I felt completely shocked, but we decided to go ahead with the visit and see how you behaved!"

"Si, I just had to tell you right now. This moment has been building for quite some time. I think you now know how I feel for you, but it isn't only that, you silver-tongued devil. I now really believe in what you are doing!"

"Really, huh?"

My relief was short-lived, as the details ebbed back – Andy's arrest, the operation at Grotstein's and the rest.

"But why? Why did you do it?"

"It was my job, Si. Believe it or not, I once had a bright career. You probably notice I'm using the past tense! My appraisals were excellent and the future looked good. Also, I shared the view that activists were mainly troublemakers, and a potential threat to order and prosperity."

"And now?"

She grabbed my hand and squeezed it.

"Ever considered teaching? You certainly changed my outlook."

"Thanks for the vote of confidence! It's funny you mention teaching because Andy said there's more news from the College. I gather our future could be in jeopardy! I almost wonder if Andy's heading towards a constructive dismissal scenario. I'm not cut out to be a corporate cheerleader either!"

"True," she replied with a grin. "There's something else I must tell you… something that will interest your friend, Nick."

I suddenly realised that we'd lost track of the time and checked my watch.

"Hell, look!" I held up my wrist. "It leaves in five minutes!"

By the time we hurried back to the platform, the last carriage was disappearing.

"Oh no. Would you believe it! We'll have to wait for the next."

We exited on Seventh Avenue and found another diner. Sat in a quiet corner, Gill told me more about her disillusionment with her profession. I stroked her hand, remembering how I'd been when conventional economic theory started to die for me. This must be even worse!

"I still need to protect our operational details – and those of the American agency," she said, forcefully.

Strangely, I now felt even closer. I'd had other girlfriends, but none I felt so strongly about since Miki, at the children's home. I squeezed her hand again.

"Of course. I understand you have to disengage professionally. Even so, I don't think the state's security apparatus should be turned on law-abiding citizens. I so admire you taking a stand like this!"

Gill nodded.

"It sounds crazy now, but I can only tell you that, from the inside, we construed it as a threat to national interests. If you'd had our training…"

I winked.

"I know. I reckon that John Dewey, or was it Coolidge, had it right, when he said something like: 'the business of government is… Business!' The thing is, who were you really serving?"

She stared down at the table.

"I can now see that it wasn't the public – in the way we thought."

"Yes, the interests of the rich and privileged, so often get to be called 'national interests'."

I noticed how her mouth was now tight and recalled the distress when your beliefs crumble – I'd experienced it. I gently stroked her cheek.

"I can't tell you how much this means to me."

She gave a rather wan smile.

"Thanks. I feel I've been so blind and stupid. I struggled for months, reading around the issues we discussed. At first, to speak more convincingly at meetings – and to you! A case of 'know your enemy'!"

I nodded.

"But, as time went on and I thought through the issues, I realised you were usually right. So much just to benefit a limited elite, with enough crumbs to pacify the rest. I'm amazed… appalled, really, how I didn't see it before."

I stroked her back.

"You and millions of others. Selective reporting and a diet of trivia, doesn't lead to an informed, participating democracy!"

She laughed.

"You're a wordy, pompous ass – even when trying to be nice!"

"Sorry… leopards and spots!"

I leaned over the table and kissed her.

"That's more like it, Mr Serious!"

I checked my watch. The offices would soon turn out and this place would fill.

"You said something earlier about having something for Nick?"

She rested her chin on cupped hands and stared at the table.

"I can't believe I'm saying this. Look, I had the opportunity to access the system to find out Nina's location. So, I did!"

"Fantastic! Nick feels he's completely hit a wall."

"Potentially, it's very dangerous, though, Si. Any blunders could point straight back to me."

"Got it, but Nick's a sensible guy. Let's talk it over with Andy, but don't worry, no-one will blunder."

"The legislation can now more or less capture anything!"

"You'd be wrong to think that we don't realise that. People like us could easily be wrongly trapped."

I saw her relax. 'People like us' had found its mark.

"I'm still anxious about this weekend, though. In fact, that's the understatement of the year!"

As predicted, the diner soon filled. The waitress refilled our coffee and Gill twiddled with her spoon.

"Don't worry, darling. Andy's very understanding. We well realise that when phrases like 'national interest', 'security' and 'patriotic duty' are thrown about, that drives and influences everything. You should hear our friend, Stephen Grotstein, the linguist, on the topic!"

"And what drives you, Simon? As usual, you're getting all abstract on me!"

I cupped her face in my hands.

"What's driving me now, is your pretty face. Driving me mad! Come on, or we'll miss another one!"

We descended into the depths of Penn Station.

"Apparently, the original station was a superb landmark building that was buried by the concrete remake of Madison Square Garden."

"Remake?"

"Yes. Yet another classic building, ripped down for development."

"Not another rant, Simon – our next train is almost due!"

The journey was uneventful, though Gill's tension visibly mounted as we got closer. She looked pale and, when our taxi from the station pulled in, held up trembling hands.

"Don't worry. Let me talk with Andy and his mom first. Andy has a very understanding nature. Incidentally, apparently, a friend of Andy's younger brother is staying too. His name is Zoten or Zoltan or something like that. I don't know how long he's here for."

She puffed out her cheeks.

"He mustn't under any circumstances get to know of my professional identity. Come on. Let's face the music!"

The door opened and we were welcomed in by Mrs Alton and Andy.

I hadn't known what to expect, but, in the circumstances, they seemed impressively natural.

While Gill went to her room to unpack, I briefed the others on what had transpired. At first, they were both understandably doubtful. I tried my best to reassure them.

"No, she's completely genuine. I'm not just saying that because I want to believe. Revealing her change of position was incredibly difficult for her."

"Could be a double bluff?" said Andrew.

"She came right out and told me. At that point, I hadn't said a single thing about your suspicions! She voluntarily opened up and just laid the whole thing out. No, it's genuine, alright. We talked at length and she explained how the change has been building for some months. Everything we said made sense and eventually she just had to make the change. She's obviously shaken rigid by her decision. Of course, this puts her whole career on the line – particularly her input about Nina. Incidentally, Gill is adamant that her other identity, or, rather, former identity, is for our little group only and absolutely mustn't be discussed with your house guest."

"Don't worry, I'll smoke if she's genuine," said Judy.

"Mom, she's a professional. They're probably trained to bluff and counter bluff!"

"A woman's intuition trumps any training, Andy!"

They laughed and, at that moment, Gill entered the room.

"Where is this Zoten guy, then?" asked Simon.

"Should be here soon. Incidentally, it's Zoltan," Judy replied, spelling his name.

Everyone tried to talk normally, but inevitably there was some awkwardness. I searched for a way to loosen things up, when Gill spoke.

"I expect Simon probably explained certain things while I was unpacking. Before I say anymore, Andrew, I want you to know how I regret what happened on the day of the arms fair. It was my job, but please know how sorry I am now – particularly the way things have turned out."

Andrew smiled, but I suspected that convincing Judy would be key to Gill's acceptance. Judy peered through narrowed eyes while Gill continued.

"The time with you two really affected me. I've had to reconsider…

well, really almost everything. Nevertheless, I'm deeply sorry for my part in the situation."

"It's okay, Gill – we understand." Andy touched her shoulder.

"It's been a wake-up call for us all and a warning of just what we've been up against. You know, a number of things occurred over the months. Were they all down to your agency?"

Gill sunk down into her seat, looking small and vulnerable. I sat beside her for support, as she outlined the actions relating to our group, without compromising names or secrets. I encircled her with my arm, as if warding off any attack. Eventually, Andy summarised the situation in his usual organised way.

"So, basically, the arms fair thing, trawling through the detritus of our homes, and the attempted bugging at Grotstein's was down to your lot?"

"Former-lot," I corrected. "Several other things happened, though."

"Exactly," agreed Andrew.

"So, the break-in at Farrely's, at the campus apartment and the mugging – wasn't from your agency?"

"Absolutely not. You'd changed the evening of the Grotstein rendezvous, so that mess-up was accidental. Before Zoltan arrives, can I just repeat again that he absolutely mustn't know this! Not only could I be skewered by the Official Secrets Act, but my US hosts must be protected and respected."

"I'm sure Zoltan's very trustworthy, and we have..."

Gill interjected in a steely tone.

"No, Judy, I really mean it! Look, I now really believe and respect what you're doing. I intend passing the coordinates for Nina's location. You possibly don't realise quite what that opens me up to. I'm sorry, though, unless that request is respected, I can't help any further!"

The room fell silent. I spoke first.

"I think it's only fair that we..."

Judy cut across.

"Of course, we understand, dear. I didn't mean to seem thoughtless."

"So not everything in Oxford was down to your old firm," repeated Andy.

"Perhaps more than one agency was involved?" suggested Judy.

"Two sources of surveillance?" asked Andy.

"I don't know, but you really must be careful," said Judy. "When you forwarded that water privatising study, my first thought was... you could easily upset some powerful people!"

"The same material that you then forwarded to Dad," said Andrew, with a mock scowl. He suddenly sat up straight, tapping the top of his head.

"Hey, that's it – Dad!"

"Meaning?"

"We should wise up. We know he uses investigators. Robbie said that he records people, and so on."

"He's certainly had opponents and competitors investigated in the past," said Judy.

I grasped the implications.

"That would certainly explain Marquetcom approaching the College and pulling strings."

"Clichés apart, I think you could be right," said Andrew. "Talking of College, Si, I'm afraid there's something else. You may prefer to hear this privately?"

"Go ahead. It seems like it's a day for letting it all hang out!"

I took a deep breath, almost expected some allegation of impropriety, but the reality was even worse.

"They're axing my post... why?"

"'I can only repeat what Helen said," said Andrew. "Mainly, lots of business jive like 'Restructuring, and refocusing academic content in line with the new objectives' – that sort of thing. I suspect that the knives are well and truly out for us!"

I felt battered from a roller-coaster of a day. Barriers to the woman I loved were disappearing – but, so too, was my job!

"So, I'm to be sacked again! Will you stay on?"

Andrew sunk in his chair.

"I don't really know. I'll go back to clear things up, but I can't see me as a corporate cheerleader – certainly not for Dad!"

I couldn't help grinning, which caused Andrew to scowl.

"Have I missed something, Simon?"

"Sorry. I used the same expression earlier. I just had the crazy image of us decked out with pom-poms! Sorry – put it down to stress!"

Andrew grinned, though the lighter atmosphere didn't last.

"I said earlier to Mom, how I'd love Biff to be stopped in his tracks. It's bad enough that our relatively comfortable lives are inconvenienced, but when the most vulnerable people are damaged... As far back as I can remember, he's either messed things up for Mom or played dirty tricks on competitors. He now seems at an even more destructive stage."

THE FONT DOOR gently closed and Zoltan crept upstairs. Hopefully, no-one had heard. The device secreted for Anson's assignment functioned well as he listened to the unfolding conversation coming from downstairs. The next voice was unknown and probably Simon.

"I certainly get why you'd want to stop him. Rob and Nick felt the same."

"If only we could work out how!" said Andrew.

Simon cut in.

"Anyway, I reckon Gill has had enough for now. By the way, Judy, we hoped to see a little of Philadelphia. Perhaps you could make some suggestions?"

In Zoltan's judgement, this seemed a good moment to 'return'. He crept downstairs, noisily opened and shut the front door, and entered the lounge. He smiled at Judy, and extended a hand to Gill.

"Hello everyone. I'm Zoltan Heltay – friend of Judy's other son, Freddy, and a temporary house guest. Good meeting you all. I hope you'll find Philadelphia as welcoming as I did."

55

MANHATTAN

NICK MARTIN

A slack Sunday evening and I already dreaded the week ahead. The only relief was a brief delay on my return to Bogotá, because of redundancy complications – but that was hardly a cause for celebration.

Robbie had taken to calling in most evenings since his dismissal, something that caused its own problems. Previously, he'd seemed a gentle kind of guy, but, since his dismissal, he seemed positively obsessed with thwarting Anson's plans. I made a sandwich and searched for some other things to be unhappy about. Tim Mills' suicide really was a blow, after his earlier progress. Another Colombian trip would mean a break in my sessions with Dr Simmonds at this critical time. The main thing, of course, though, was the ongoing silence around Nina. In any case, that wretched episode with Corinne might scupper everything.

I crossed to the bureau to read Michael Gallo's letter again for perhaps the fifth time! Gallo said that new rules allowed for a complete information blanket with detained suspects. His letter talked of 'indications' that her status might be 'indeterminate', whatever that meant! He said it could also be that her detention was discretionary, or evidence shaky. It 'might' also mean the opposite – that evidence was even more serious! In fact, 'could', 'may' and 'might' figured a lot in his letter – but then lawyers always did seem tricky! It wasn't so long ago that government departments played around with 'service standards', 'complaint policies' and had some semblance of accountability. Recently, though, the state seemed quite relaxed at showing a naked fist and dancing only for its corporate paymasters. I picked up a book, but it was hopeless – my mind was far too busy spreading manure. Instead, I decided to focus on the real issue – Corinne and her recent revelation.

Corinne had kept in contact and remained seductive. I'd discussed the situation with Dr Simmonds and finally had a straight talk with her over what had happened between us and my feelings for Nina. What she then said was shocking and I replayed it for the 'umpteenth' time.

She laughed, saying:

"That isn't a problem, Nick, you silly! It was only sex. I believe that, when passion calls, you should follow the lead. It's only energy following its natural course."

"You don't understand, Corinne. I love Nina."

"I know. She loves you too. She told me."

"She said that?"

"Yes, but that doesn't have to stop you and I being lovers – or Nina and I, for that matter."

"What are you saying?"

"Of course! We both enjoy the closeness of a physical relationship with those people we like. I love the way my body wants to merge, if I feel loving towards someone. I give to them, they give to me, and I see nothing wrong in that. Nina, I know, feels the same way!"

Something big must have registered on my face, shock or amazement – but she just continued to smile sweetly.

"It isn't a problem. In terms of an eventual long-term commitment, it will almost certainly be with a man, for both of us."

At first, I'd been aghast. The whole notion jammed my mental switchboard. Corinne as a latter-day hippie, making it all sound open, liberated – even inevitable. My inner voice, though, wasn't so easily persuaded. I admit it was me who'd put Nina on a pedestal – treating her almost like some spiritual being. I even felt awkward the first time we made love, but her unasked-for beatification was, after all, of my own doing – a product of my own mind!

I'd picked over this issue ever since Corinne told me, and today was no exception. Why should sexuality and spirituality always seem antithetical? What if they're the same stuff, or 'energy' as Corinne would put it – but configured differently?

What a crock of New Age bilge, came my initial response, but the issue had set off a degree of introspection I hadn't experienced since my late teens. Anyway, beyond the given frameworks of family, culture, and religion, what did I actually believe? Maybe, at some higher level, so-called whores were really saintly, while self-appointed moral guardians were just trainee spiritual accountants. Who really knew! Wasn't the world already overflowing with moral conservatives and zealots, lacking even an ounce of compassion or generosity! Maybe Corinne's values came from somewhere different. She said that, despite some differences in outlook, she and Nina had been occasional lovers. Corinne's general promiscuity seemed to have few limits. She really believed, if she could give and receive 'energy,' as she put it, and both parties enjoyed it, why not? Her talk of 'energy', though, seemed to me like warmed-over phrases taken from a tantric yoga manual!

I picked up a framed photo of Nina, and looked at her sensitive face. Why should someone having her drive and passion be sexually restrained? Surely, just yet another unexamined assumption? Are the repressed generally creative and giving? No! Apparently, some psychoanalysts suggested that the freeing up of sexuality could actually promote creativity? Mind you, a true Freudian might conclude that Corinne demonstrated 'polymorphous perversity'. I grinned, thinking, *You're beginning to sound like Dr Simmonds and as pompous as Simon! To hell with it*, I thought. *I love her – I think she loves me, so why let this interfere? After all...*

My ruminations were interrupted by the bell. I pressed the answer, and called out.

"Who's there?"

"It's Simon. May I come up?"

A moment later, I let in Simon, together with an attractive woman I didn't recognise.

"Come in."

Simon looked a little uncertain.

"I hoped to see you earlier, Nick, but I've been away in Philadelphia, staying with Andrew and his mom. This is my girlfriend, Gill Marney, who's also over from England. Happily, she had a business assignment here, at roughly the same time as my visit."

"Good to meet you, Gill. Knowing Simon, I expect we'll share interests!"

Simon smiled as he touched my shoulder.

"Funny you should say that. As a matter of fact, you've one big thing in common already... That's why we're here."

"You've heard something?"

"Kind of, although we have to explain a few things first," he replied. Let's go out. We passed a nice looking diner around the corner."

A few moments later we were huddled over coffees, in a quiet corner of the diner but I could hardly contain my frustration as they described Gill's circumstances. Apparently, Gill worried that we could be bugged back at the apartment. She was still concerned emphasised, and then re-emphasised, that her information was for our group only. I listened patiently.

"Yes, but what about Nina?"

Simon looked at Gill awkwardly.

"Gill used her position to find Nina's whereabouts."

The words echoed around my head.

"Why not just tell me straight out?"

"Because it potentially puts Gill at risk. Remember, not long ago you were questioned about Bogotá. We don't know who is monitored and couldn't just blurt it out on the phone."

Gill nodded.

"I have to be careful, Nick. Actually, we all must."

Inside, I felt like screaming, *Please get on with it!*

"Gill, you must have lots to weigh up. Do you think other colleagues have changed their outlook?"

"I don't know," she replied. "Occasionally people make remarks, but there are systems to prevent those sorts of conversations from happening."

"It's great that we're all working on the same side now, but getting back to Nina's location?"

"I mustn't risk discovery, Nick. Poking around with your lawyer or, worse still, setting off to try to find Nina would almost certainly go badly wrong."

I felt I'd shake her by the throat if this continued much longer.

"What do you suggest?"

The phone rang again. This time it was Robbie, and I barely choked back an impulse to shout at him.

"You're outside the apartment. Come back to the diner just on the corner. Yes, that's the one. Simon and his girlfriend are here, though it isn't exactly a party."

Robbie soon arrived, looking tense. I hoped he'd quickly realise the timing was bad and leave.

"Sorry about your job," said Simon, "I suppose getting away from Anson is at least some consolation?"

"Yeah, though unemployment's a lousy occupation – no pun intended. I've walked in on something?"

Fortunately, he grasped the situation and gave Gill the assurance needed. It was just as well, as I had no more tolerance for delay.

"You were about to tell me about Nina's location!" I held Gill's eye. "Please. I really need to know!"

"Promise not to act without discussing it with me first!"

"Agreed," I replied – while thinking, *We'll see!*

"Nina has been accused of channelling funds to groups in South America – groups designated by the State Department as terrorist organisations, or with those connections."

"Rubbish," I said.

Robbie nodded.

"Yeah, though I did see lots of evidence in her apartment of contact with activists. Her articles alone would upset certain interests."

"I'm sure that's true," said Gill. "Andrew's work is 'popular' in the same way!"

"So we now realise," Simon said ruefully.

"Please, please, please, Gill! Tell what you know of Nina's whereabouts?"

"I used a different workstation to access the information, but that really won't fool anyone. In any case, a colleague came in while I used that computer."

"Totally understood," I said. "We'll be the absolute essence of discretion. I really do get it."

Gill scraped her bottom lip with her teeth.

"Okay. Well, it seems Nina was placed on a surveillance list for quite some time. Specific allegations have been made, but I was locked out of those records, so didn't learn exactly who said what. Something must have moved her into a more active classification, but I couldn't get the critical information. Initially, she went to Camp Albert down in Arizona's Superstition Mountains, but was later moved on to Camp Ute, in southern Utah – near the small towns of Monticello and Moab."

"We checked with Andy's mom," said Simon. Monticello is a small town in the back of nowhere. Judy knows the area, because another son, Freddy, lives nearby."

I was already flicking through the internet maps.

"Utah, you say."

We gathered around the map, looking on as Gill's manicured finger roved across it.

"Here it is, just south of Moab on the 191 – near the Colorado/Utah border. Judy says the whole area is quite spectacular, though very isolated and hot. The coordinates match the La Sal Mountains – about here. That's a bit higher, so it could be a bit cooler. She hasn't seen anything like a camp, though, so I expect it's well concealed."

In my peripheral vision, I saw Robbie's head shaking, and he whistled under his breath.

"Unbelievable! My Cousin Carl lives on the edge of Moab. Amazing!"

At last, I felt a flicker of hope.

"Are you in touch with him?"

"Not for quite a while, though we were close as kids. I could always visit and I have the time now."

"Can I come? Actually, I must come!"

Gill paled and I caught her eye.

"We won't do anything stupid! I just need to be near and get a fix on the area."

"I'm not exactly happy, but I suppose visiting Robbie's cousin gives some cover," she said. "Please don't mention my involvement to anybody."

She bit her lip.

"There are some other things I think you should know. Nick, you've already come to notice because of the Bogotá bomb thing, so don't give cause for further suspicion. You also need to know that the guys staffing the camp won't mess around. Camp security has been outsourced to a private company. They'll want to prove themselves and won't get bonuses by being soft!"

"Got it."

"Robbie, can you check about a visit, and me coming?" I said. "Say I'm a friend, keen to see the wonders of the West after years living in the North East!"

"Will do!"

I passed the phone over.

"No time like the present!"

The call was short and to the point. Robbie smiled as he put the phone down.

"It's all good. Carl's happy and his wife, Myleen, is cool too! When do you want to leave – tomorrow or later?"

"Actually, tomorrow might very well be possible. I'm owed time before the next Colombia trip. As Deputy HR Manager, there must be some benefits!"

I called work, and reminded Tom Phelan that I'd been promised a break before Colombia. The timing suited and Phelan was unexpectedly positive.

For the first time in weeks, Robbie lightened up too.

"It'll be great to get out of the city. Your apartment's been like a second home! Pass me the phone, please."

Robbie located the countrywide view.

"We could fly to Denver, hire a car and drive west, or fly to Salt Lake City and then drive south west. Alternatively, Las Vegas. What do you think, Mile High City, Sin City or Mormon Central?"

I stared at the map. "How about driving the whole way? Having lived here for years, I've actually seen very little."

"It's one hell of a way," Robbie replied. "I can see several possibilities, though."

He studied the map.

"How about Philly, Columbus, Indianapolis, St Louis, Kansas City, Denver... down the I72 to Grand Junction and on to Moab?"

"Let's stay overnight at Andy's mom's, so Andy can be involved," said Simon. "Perhaps the brother living in Moab might help?"

Gill sighed. "Robbie."

"Uh huh."

"I'm afraid security also has an interest in you!"

"Oh hell!"

"I can't say more, other than you're under watch."

Robbie stayed silent and his face paled.

"More drinks, everyone?" I asked. "Seems we must learn to live looking over our shoulders. Do you agree?"

The others murmured agreement.

"So, let's leave early tomorrow for Philadelphia. Then it's off into the wild unknown...!"

56

PHILLADELPHIA

ZOLTAN'S PERSPECTIVE

Zoltan's mind hit the buffers and closed to further questions. He shivered, and returned the phone to his pocket. Odd, every time he heard that guttural voice, it brought an upheaval that couldn't be challenged!

Light flooded into the bedroom, projecting strangely comforting shadows of leaves on the wall. He mentally traced the pattern until feeling a little more collected.

The sound of the front door closing reached upstairs. Zoltan went over to the window, opening it onto a bright Philadelphia Saturday and the sound of children playing. A blue sky looked inviting and sun caressed the treetops. He watched Judy and Andrew walk to the corner and then turn. He went downstairs and out onto the porch. The air felt warm and even the birds sounded contented. It was the kind of day families might picnic together and normal people would pursue their hobbies – but there'd be nothing like that for him today. He sighed, and returned to the kitchen. After getting that call, and with the others out, he had no choice but to fine-tune his mission.

First, though, it was breakfast. Separating some bacon rashers, he stood over the hob-top as it cooked. Perhaps the smoke triggered something, but, as the bacon sizzled, he felt uncomfortably aware of violent images in the background. His body squirmed to the truth that had seeped into every part of his body – that what lay ahead now actually felt repellent! He served the overcooked flesh and then cleared the debris away – imagining the steps to come. First, transporting the materials and setting diversions. Now even this seemed fraught with problems. He mapped out the steps onto paper in a kind of flow chart, marking problem areas with an asterisk. As taught in training, he opened and closed his eyes several times until an eidetic image had formed. Then he applied a rubber to the paper until all was erased and shredded it into the toilet bowl. He watching until every confetti-like scrap had entered into the swirling vortex. If only his fear could be dispersed so easily!

Preparedness was now second nature, so the phone call had been puzzling. His group were drilled relentlessly at their training camp in Gereshk. At the time, he'd developed heightened states of focus and awareness and was able to register the slightest crinkle around someone's mouth or the subtle changes of skin colour that indicated a change of emotion. He could see the tiny micro-muscular movements that preceded an attack and could sense the hairs stand behind his own neck. Really, he needed to regain those skills that had flowered so readily in the quiet desert landscape. Here in busy Philadelphia, though, things weren't quite so easy. That wasn't the only problem, either. His attraction to Judy and the jitters over the mission certainly weren't part of the plan. Neither had he anticipated being pulled into her family's problems.

Zoltan tidied up and rinsed the plates. Physical preparation was all very well, but what if he now recoiled from the task's essence – disgusted at being the potential cause of a huge loss of life? He sat down. *And what if you yourself aren't prepared to die?* Questions that sent shivers throughout his body.

He went outside and warmed his back in the sun until feeling a little better. The pretty back garden was secluded and he pottered for a while. To any onlooker, he'd be enjoying the garden, cleaning leaves between thumb and forefinger, and prodding the soil with a fingertip. As he passed under the pergola, the sweet perfume of roses brought back memories of Istfahan's gardens and less complicated times. Finally, satisfied that he was alone, he finished with the garden and quickly slipped into the shed.

Inside, everything looked untouched and a fine coat of dust coated the boxes. He sat on a crate, reviewing developments – his affair with Judy, Andrew's arrival, Simon and girlfriend and, of course, Anson!

The old suitcase sat opposite. Its wrinkled surface almost resembled a topographical map – the Rockies perhaps or even Afghanistan. He muttered aloud.

"We're both veterans, but I'm afraid this will be your final trip!"

Abdul said that around eighty-four suitcase nuclear devices had disappeared after the demise of the USSR – although some experts thought it was more a case of dodgy Soviet paperwork. He shook his head, because part of the reality was right there in front of him! These so-called 'experts' didn't agree on much. Some thought that a bomb would probably be just be a radiological dispersion device and not really so dangerous. That was certainly true in 1996, when Chechnyan rebels left a device of Caesium 137, wrapped in dynamite, in Izmailovo Park. The authorities nevertheless leapt into action, even though 'dirty bombs' were just a firecracker compared to a proper nuclear device. Abdul had been astute with the plans. This would be far more effective detonated up high, to overcome the shielding from other buildings. With Marquetcom's headquarters as the source, their link to Anson was doubly useful. In fact, a more appropriate place seemed hard to imagine! He grinned, though his mood only lightened for a moment. Soon, his heart pounded again and sweat coated his forehead.

These jitters had got worse since his last visit to Utah. He sat and spun increasingly frail webs of justification that didn't really work. After all, there were many others like Judy and her son – decent individuals with good values. Was he really going to bring about such indiscriminate destruction?

He was busying himself by checking the crates' fastenings, when the strange inner experience happened again! An overwhelming image of a devastating explosion grabbed his breath, firing off salvoes of adrenaline. At first, the image was stationary, but it quickly gained an almost filmic energy and motion. Detached limbs spattered blood and whirled through the air. In his mind, he could hear screams, smell the dust and acrid smoke, as block after city block fell to the blast. He shook his head and went to the tiny window, hoping light from outside might lessen the horror in his head. The anticipatory guilt was a corrosive acid – that burnt his soul. He unclenched his fists and tried to calm, but the lull was derailed by yet another terrifying image – a crowd transformed to ashes and blown away by the wind. He anchored himself on the crate, dredging up memories from travels, the training, and from Abdul and the network – anything to give justification to the horror.

We've been so often attacked, he reasoned, *someone has to hit back.*

Looting by the 'Ansons' of this world was even helped by Western governments. Yes, they shed some crocodile tears at G8 conferences, but then they continued supporting their stinking, predatory corporations. Abdul was right, the people must share responsibility for their governments' actions. The West had to be made to think, so cease undermining yourself, or resisting God's will!

Birdsong filtered in from outside, reminding him of a kinder world. He breathed until the panic subsided and crossed to the window, running a finger around the frame. No rain had penetrated, so he returned to the box and slid a finger underneath. It was dry and everything was well sealed. A leak here would be disastrous – nothing should happen here on Judy's doorstep. The conventional material was needed for other locations. Anson and the weekend soldiers were welcome – it should make ideal bait. He returned to the house and scrubbed his hands before making a sandwich. Afterwards, he went into the lounge and checked that the listening devices were still properly concealed.

The front door opened. Judy and Andrew were back.

"Coffee?" he called from the kitchen.

"Thanks, Zolt. Yes, for me."

Further murmuring came from the hall.

"Same for Andy?"

The others entered the kitchen, Judy, bright-eyed, excited and – by the look of the bags – with shopping. Possibly a feminine response to having the two most important men in her life, under the same roof – but potentially telling! Last night had been a close call. He'd crept into her room and they eventually fell asleep in each other's arms. As he was about to leave and turn the door handle, the bathroom door closed further down the corridor!

"Shopping spree?" he asked, pointing to the bags.

"You bet. I'll show you."

Don't' – he screamed inside. *Uninvolved women don't show their new clothing to strangers!*

The situation was saved by the telephone ringing, but she was beaten to it by Andrew. He strained to hear, but needn't have bothered. When he returned, Andrew was smiling broadly.

"That was Simon. He'd like to come over, bringing Gill, Nick and Rob James too. Apparently, they plan driving south and want to stay the night."

"Of course. Anyway, I already know Nick!"

"Apparently, they've heard of something interesting down in Utah," Andrew said.

"Good."

Zoltan tried to mask irritation at yet another interruption.

"I think you'll like Nick," said Andrew. "He's in IT, so you'll have that in common. Robbie's amusing and Simon and Gill you've met already."

"I also know Utah."

"Of course, your friendship with Freddy."

Zoltan chatted for a while, before retiring to his room, wondering whether the device would be necessary, or if he'd be included. He listened as Judy and Andrew wrestled with the same question.

"I already told Zolt, about Nick's girl being arrested," came Judy's voice. "These things are happening everywhere, now."

"I don't know, Mom. I think we should be cautious!"

"I've been involved with most of these issues since before you were born! Zoltan is definitely one of us, I'm certain. He's been involved in progressive issues both in California and the south. He was picked up and questioned over those Occupy Wall Street protests a while back."

Zoltan expected her to be challenged, but it seemed as if – mission accomplished!

After the other visitors arrived from New York, he listened from his room while they discussed his presence. Nick and Judy already knew each other from the New Jersey meetings and Nick and Robbie seemed accepting of her reassurances. Gill agreed he already knew about Nina, but stressed that her name or involvement be completely left out. Judy pointed out that Zoltan knew the area because of his involvement with Freddy, so the trip couldn't be hidden from him. They agreed, and Judy then came upstairs and asked him to join the others.

Once downstairs, he realised that his input over many discussions had clearly paid off. In Judy's words, he was quickly accepted as 'one of us'. Gill, perhaps, had reservations and seemed more cautious, but the others were 'touchy-feely' liberals, quick to welcome someone into their circle. His social justice interests were, of course, warmly welcomed and, for now, he could comfortably sit back and listen.

"Good seeing you again, Andrew," said Nick. "I still feel embarrassed turning up on your first night in New York."

"It's okay really. I've heard about Nina and I hope your lawyer gets to visit her. Everyone agrees she's very special. Her programme certainly rattled some cages. Si raved over it, didn't you?"

"Inspiring!"

"I saw it too. Fantastic," Zoltan said, to everyone's obvious approval.

"Yeah," said Nick. "Another lawyer told my lawyer that he'd heard rumours of a holding camp for 'terrorist' suspects and extremists – somewhere near Moab or Monticello, in Utah. Of course, these days, being an extremist just means having alternative views. Andy, do you think your brother in Utah could help, at all?"

Andrew's face clouded.

"Maybe I should explain about Fred."

Andrew hesitated, and looked at the floor.

A glowing reference wasn't expected. Judy looked tense, with a firmly closed mouth. The description was accurate and, in many ways, Andrew could also have been describing their father. With Judy appearing so stressed, he spoke out.

"Freddy might be more focused on money than we are, but no-one can deny that he provides well for his family. By the way, I've often passed through Monticello. Seemed quite a nice little place."

The others looked expectant.

"Didn't see anything like a holding camp there, though."

Robbie nodded.

"Yeah, I never saw anything like that either. Mind you, tracks go west into red-rock country or east to the La Sal Mountains. A camp could literally be anywhere. It's so odd, Andy, us both having relatives in the same small town."

Andy nodded. Zoltan also knew the area far more intimately than he dared reveal.

"Won't the two of you draw attention?" asked Andrew. "I'm already worried we might have come to the authorities' notice!"

"I agree," said Gill. "Poke around too obviously, you could be picked up!"

"We could avoid asking by having a hand-held GPS unit," suggested Nick.

"All those military welfare dollars did produce one useful thing then," quipped Robbie. Everyone laughed.

"Fred could help with that," said Zoltan. "His vehicles mostly have GPS."

Zoltan also noticed Judy's sharp intake of breath and she touched Andrew's arm. Something told Zoltan to let things take their course.

"Why don't you go with them, Andy? It's time you and Freddy had contact. You're both old enough to put past differences behind you now."

He assessed the implications. If Andrew joined the expedition, that would stop Anson's surveillance brief, and he could be alone with Judy. Creeping around in the night might add a certain frisson, but he preferred how it was before.

He suggested to Andrew.

"Freddy certainly could benefit from what you teach!"

"A nice thought, but he's never shown the slightest interest."

"People mature."

Judy looked enthusiastic. He suspected she'd think that a good mother meant having a united family.

"Go on, Andy, it's only for a few days!"

Andrew bit his lower lip.

"I suppose it's possible. Is that okay with you two?"

"Fine with me," said Robbie. "Okay, Nick?"

"Great!" replied Nick. "We'll have some good conversations en route. I really enjoyed some of your written stuff that Simon sent!"

Zoltan noticed a worried glance pass from Andrew to Simon.

"What's with the face?" asked Simon.

"I've been wondering what could cause interest by the authorities. Recalling your break-in on the campus and Nick's remark about good conversations. The stuff you sent Nick – it didn't include the 'Belle-vivreau' report, did it?"

"Only the water privatisation summary and a few other references."

"Yeah, that reached me at the right moment," said Nick, "Just when Canvey were getting up to their armpits! I say 'right moment' now, though, at the time, it felt the worst possible time – though it forced me to take a stand. Nina, incidentally, was very impressed."

Zoltan noticed Robbie's mouth opening like a stranded fish.

"You discussed 'Bellevivreau'?"

"Yes. Why?"

"Just that Biff brought Bellevivreau into the water privatisation consortium. Marquetcom and Bellevivreau are the major players, with two smaller companies, one British and one French. We discussed so much that first night, I probably didn't mention it.

"Bellevivreau sounds French," said Judy.

"Well spotted, Mom. Formerly known for their aggressive practices in Africa. Now US owned."

335

Zoltan saw Simon pale – something else was coming. Simon's voice was tight.

"Andy… on second thoughts, I did make a passing reference to Bellevivreau. Not the big dossier we worked up, just a few facts about the African activities. If you remember, our exchanges at the time were mainly over water privatising."

Andrew continued looking tense.

"Don't worry. Activists are always communicating to each other about various corporate activities."

"You say that now, Si, but remember it was you that first warned us of activists being monitored. You, who thought the theft of that material seemed fishy. You, who said intelligence services could even serve commercial interests! Remember that Echelon thing, and the monitoring of key words?"

"Sorry, Andy, I just had my academic hat on and didn't think of that."

In his peripheral vision, he saw Gill subtly nod.

"Gill, have you ever heard of that, from an IT perspective?" Zoltan asked.

"Not really, although electronic communications are easily monitored. I've heard the rumour that businesses might have been helped, but they'd be huge corporations. I don't know if it's true."

Simon exhaled loudly.

"Remember that quote? 'The business of America – is business!'"

"There must be thousands of emails mentioning big corporations every day," said Judy.

"Which could potentially be tracked," added Gill.

Zoltan looked around the room. Now, it was getting interesting.

"I'll never forget that dossier with my name," said Andrew.

"I suppose any of us could have been selected for observation?" Robbie whispered.

"Potentially, that's probably true," replied Gill.

Robbie looked sweaty. Clearly, something had touched him.

Andrew pursed his lips and whistled.

"The land of the free? Let's start by getting new 'prepaid' cell phones, which might be less traceable. If it's okay with you, Mom, we'll stay overnight and then share the drive?"

"Of course, son. No shortage of room here."

"Simon, you may as well continue with those planned interviews in San Francisco," said Andrew.

"I hoped you'd agree. The psychopathy expert I arranged to interview, Dr Gianavecci, had to reschedule. Amazingly, we're both going to be in San Francisco at the same time. His secretary called and we've arranged an alternative meeting."

"Great."

"No, it gets even better. A conference in San Francisco in two days' time, called: 'Neoliberal policies – the real legacy'. All the big hitters are presenting, with sessions on labour rights, sweatshops, 'fair' trade, well actually on most big issues, including perils of social media, data mining and our new digital overlords! Apparently, they're expecting a big crowd from the south."

"Southern USA?" Judy asked.

"No the global south – the undeveloped and developing world."

"Ah, that's what I thought."

"McVittie will dissect the IMF/WTO/World Bank trio, or what's left of it. Alex Veitch will discuss Albert's Parecon model, Frank Rossi will talk on the 'sell-out' of the corporate media. Sounds a really great programme!"

Zoltan felt sure what would come next. They'd debate all the issues he'd mentioned. The following discussion was indeed brilliant, but he excused himself and returned to his room. His preparation had worked and, despite Abdul's warnings, the sexual relationship hadn't dulled his senses – if anything, he seemed even sharper! He forwarded an encrypted message to the contact in Wilmington, saying conditions weren't fully ready. The message would pass through two other contacts, before reaching Abdul. In the morning, he'd send word to Anson and warn him about Bellevivreau.

Late that night, he made his way to Judy's room, quietly entering her unlocked door. She was undressing, and looking quite gorgeous. He sat, savouring the moment.

"Didn't you enjoy the discussion?" she asked. "You left rather suddenly."

"Sorry, just really tired. Yeah, they're a great lot."

"Not too tired, I hope. Could you bring a bottle of water up, first?"

He gently pushed the door open a crack, but everything seemed quiet. He paused, and crept into the hallway. A floorboard creaked as he gently released the handle behind him. The landing seemed dark, but empty, so he turned towards the stairs. At that moment, a door further up the passage scraped open. He turned, as the moon emerged from behind a cloud, throwing light into the shadowy areas. Gill was leaving the bathroom and, for a moment, they faced each other at opposite ends of the hallway. Had she seen him exit Judy's bedroom? He involuntarily stiffened when she looked at him with what seemed a little half-smile, and raised her eyebrows. He smiled back, willing her to keep quiet. Another cloud covered the moon, and they continued on their separate ways. He could kick himself for being so sloppy. Perhaps he'd try and say something diverting in the morning!

PHILADELPHIA

NICK MARTIN

After the previous evening's conversation, it was hard to get to sleep and the others seemed high about the forthcoming trip, too. Eventually, waking early, I decided there was time before breakfast to take a brief look at the historical area.

I walked up Ninth Street to Walnut, and then crossed to Penn's landing. The sky was overcast and the Delaware's surface impenetrable. The first tourists of the day had arrived. Parents with clothing for every weather, excitable children, and obese folk in outfits that shouted 'vacation time'!

I turned away from the Delaware, navigating by guidebook, and walked to the improbably named Olde City and Elfreth's Alley. According to the book, this was America's oldest residential street. I didn't expect to be impressed, but it was, in fact, an attractive cobbled street with pretty houses and wrought-iron gates.

I walked back towards Independence Hall, but crowds were already building. History seeped from the red-brick Georgian buildings and I half expected to see docents in historical costume. I battled crowds at Independence Hall, although I'd hoped to see where Jefferson and the others drafted the Constitution. The queues were impossible, so I crossed for the Liberty Bell, but found the same story.

Frustrated, I struck off towards the city centre, intending a quick browse in Reading Terminal Market. Passing an attractive coffee shop, I decided to take on some fuel. A waitress, catching my accent, decided her role was listing Philadelphia's sights.

"You should climb City Hall tower," she said, "and then do the museums. The Museum of Art was where Sly ran up those steps in 'Rocky'."

"I didn't realise films were made here."

I was perhaps also slow in noticing the old black Chrysler Imperial pull up opposite and someone record my image. The shop's almond croissants were particularly delicious, so I ignored the Chrysler and ordered another. Just then, my cell phone rang. It was Michael Gallo.

"Hi, Nick. Just catching you up with the latest. I applied to see Nina, but it was rejected. Apparently, there are several levels of detention and she's been placed on the most serious. Even attorneys can be excluded."

"Hell! What else can be done?"

"I'm in contact with several colleagues in the same boat. We intend to appeal, but that takes time."

"I bet."

"Something else... a colleague in San Francisco had an experience with a Syrian friend of someone similarly detained."

"Go on."

"The guy somehow found out where his friend was held, and tried to make contact. He landed up in big trouble. I mention this in case you should have ideas of that sort. Let's continue my way – the legal way."

"Chance would be a fine thing. We don't know where she is – remember. Anyway, what was your lawyer friend's name?"

"Mark Alming. Why, are you planning to go to the West Coast?"

"No, but I've a friend flying there later today."

I noted down the name in my little pocketbook.

"I'd advise him to be extremely careful in the current climate. Bye for now, Nick."

I stared into my espresso, picturing Nina's face. The call had been quite depressing and I decided to give up on the market. As I got up to leave, the black Chrysler pulled away.

At Judy's, the others were up and preparing for the trip. Spirits seemed high, but, after Gallo's call, I couldn't match their mood.

"Could you take Simon to the airport?" asked Andrew. "And we'll buy new cell phones. We could hit the road, as soon as you get back."

The trip to the airport was surprisingly easy. Simon seemed excited about the conference, and gabbled on about the key presenters. As I reflected later, that's probably why I forgot to pass him the lawyer's name.

Well, I couldn't have predicted what would happen!

58

PHILADELPHIA – COLORADO – UTAH

ROBBIE JAMES

I settled into the hire car and checked the road atlas, glad to have a role, at last. Soon I must find alternative work, but, for now, I had purpose and companionship. The others knew little of the South West, and would hopefully look to me.

The next sign announced, I95 – direction Baltimore.

"We can pick up the I70 at Baltimore and then stay with it almost for the whole way. Where did you put our new phones?"

"In the trunk," replied Andrew. "We'll hand them out later.'"

"I haven't been out of New York City in ages," Nick said. "Robbie, run through that route again?"

"Right, will do. Columbus, Indianapolis, St Louis, Kansas City and on to Denver. From Denver, we continue through Colorado, before turning south to Utah. The bad news is that it's a hell of a long way, and we probably won't get any further than Indianapolis today."

"Apart from the car race, it's a rather dull place, isn't it?"

I knew the standard jokes.

"Yeah. Known as 'Indiano-place' or 'Napsville'." I laughed. "Still, it should beat sleeping in the car."

As predicted, it was dark when we arrived. The motel was only eclipsed in blandness by a nearby diner. In the morning, 'Napsville' proved accurate enough, despite our proximity to the Union Station complex.

As usual, I felt the outsider, needing to prove my usefulness.

"By the way, Andy," I asked. "Did you check with your mom, in case Gill sent a message?"

"Phoned from my hotel room... nothing as yet."

After breakfast, we rejoined the Interstate, driving west as far as St Louis and taking a brief detour through the city centre. I knew it well, guiding them to the old river-front district between the Eads and Martin Luther King bridges. By now I'd adopted a tour guide role, and described how cotton and ore used to be dragged up from the Mississippi to the factories and cast-iron warehouses. Andrew wondered where the St Louis Symphony performed, but, when reminded about the remaining distance, insisted that we depart right now. We left, with eyes fixed on the soaring Gateway Arch, until it melded with the rear horizon.

The road seemed interminable, but eventually we rolled into Kansas City. I was fully into guide mode now, pointing out the sights.

"I didn't expect to see art deco out here," said Nick as we passed the City Hall.

"Pity Simon isn't here. He had quite a thing about it."

I pointed to the Union Station.

"You can still see a pock-marked wall, after a 'Pretty Boy Floyd' shoot-out."

We argued over whether to look, but Andrew settled the matter by literally putting his foot down... on the accelerator!

"Continuing the Prohibition theme," Andrew quipped, "we agreed that the driver has the final decision. You'll have your turn later, but I say we go all out for Denver!"

I felt my spirits flag with my temporary leadership role fast eroding, yet somehow I couldn't challenge it. Things always seemed this way!

We rejoined the I70, and headed west. Lawrence seemed pretty, Topeka grim and then there was Abilene.

"Wild Bill Hickock was Marshal here," I ventured.

"Westerns were never my thing," replied Nick.

"Nor mine," agreed Andrew.

We passed into Colorado and, for a time, the plains were endless.

Eventually, I took my turn at the wheel.

"It's so boring! So glad we've cruise control. Have you noticed all the rubber chunks on the roadside? If I were a tyre, I'd get tired too, peel off and take a nap."

"I thought Colorado was mountainous," said Nick, ignoring my attempts at humour.

"Not this side," I replied. "Keep your eye on the horizon, though."

Sure enough, where the sky met the plains, other shapes appeared. Soon the profile of down-town Denver appeared as the plains gave way to the immense bulk of the Rockies.

We reached Denver earlier than expected. Andrew took the wheel again, negotiating the city grid, as Nick read from a guidebook. He suggested a quick drive past the Museum of Western Art.

"Apparently, it was once the city's premier brothel!" No-one responded, and we turned into Cherokee Street and proceeded down Colfax Avenue to admire the Capitol building.

"Do you know why it's called 'Mile High City'?" asked Nick, his head in the guidebook. "It's nothing to do with in-flight delight."

"Go on, tell us," I replied.

"When you get to the thirteenth step," Nick said, pointing to the Capitol, "a plaque states that you're now exactly a mile above sea level."

"Talking of mile high, or maybe high miles," said Andrew, "I say we push on into the Rockies."

He pulled over and asked for the map.

"We could stop at Idaho Springs or Georgetown – perhaps even Dillon or Vail, if we make real progress."

Andy's dominance was getting irksome. After all, it was me who knew the territory!

"Vail is far too expensive," I said authoritatively. "It caters for the super-rich, with some of the best quality ski snow anywhere."

"Perhaps you'll have a new career as a travel guide," said Nick with a grin.

Sometime later we pulled into a motel in Glenwood Springs. The sky was dark and we appeared to be down in a canyon. I caught a whiff of sulphur. Nick looked over, wrinkling his nostrils.

"Hot springs," I said.

"Shit. I thought we'd arrived in Hades," he replied.

"No, that'll probably come later! Has anyone checked with Judy in case Gill's called?"

"I'll do that from the room," replied Andy.

I was still unpacking when I heard a tap at the door. The visitors were Andy and Nick, but their faces said this wasn't a social chat.

"You two look cheerful. What's up?"

Nick spoke first.

"Gill's sent a message. Judy called from the cell phone we gave her. Hopefully it will be safe for limited contact."

Nick touched my shoulder.

"Not good news, I'm afraid, because I know you and Corinne are friendly. Gill has discovered that Corinne has links to the agency hosting her visit. This probably means Corinne has fed them information!"

"She... she's... no, surely not. I don't believe it!"

"Afraid so. Gill doesn't have hard details. It sort of came out tangentially – a comment from one of her mentors. Gill said that asking questions or showing too much interest would have given the game away."

I felt winded and sat back on the bed. For the first time since puberty, I'd felt a new sense of certainty about my sexuality – though I was probably just being used. The closeness was probably an act on Corinne's part. Already, memories of other betrayals were stirring. Nick's voice seemed to come from miles away.

"You're as white as a sheet!"

"Because, I thought we were close, Nick. If Corinne's been feeding stuff back, that will certainly include information about me."

Nick exhaled, and shook his head.

"What has she said about Nina, more to the point? Let's not forget why we're on this little jaunt!"

Andrew chimed in.

"Mom passed on something else."

"More good news?"

"Apparently a private security company has won the contract for the camp's domestic services and security. It's designated an official military site. Orders authorise the detention of anyone caught in the area."

"Detention in the camp?"

"Yes, under the provisions of anti-terrorist legislation."

"Potentially, that could trap cross-country backpackers, hunters – well, anyone really."

"Apparently any unauthorised person, without evidence to the contrary, will be deemed to be trying to aid or abet terrorists or terrorist suspects. Remember, the definitions are kept fuzzy. Even representing attorneys are affected."

"Basically, they could potentially stop, even disappear, anyone they don't like," said Nick. "It's dangerous – positively Stalinist. Michael Gallo told me the same thing!"

I was still reeling from the revelation about Corinne.

"Great! So, the person we thought was a friend was really spying on us, and now we're up against privatised thugs who'll do anything to justify their contract."

Nick touched my shoulder.

"Steady on. Don't go wobbly this early in the trip. Andy, did your mom mention the security company's name?"

"I'm not certain. I was quite shaken by the news. It sounded like Amright or Armright."

"Oh shit, not Arm-Rite?" asked Nick, spelling the name out.

"You know them?"

"Yes, down in Colombia. They ran a spraying operation that also shifted indigenous people out of their own territory – seemingly for the benefit of certain corporations."

"That's a rather loaded comment, Nick."

"Possibly, but they certainly seemed brutal with local communities. Really, they're mercenaries, now with domestic contracts?"

"Yes," said Andrew. "If I remember, private security contractors were first used domestically in the New Orleans cyclone episode."

The others left and I retired for a hellish night – worsened by the sulphurous reek. Of course, things looked bad for Nina, but, if Corinne was passing on material, we could all be investigated. My life had aspects that even I didn't like considering, let alone the security services doing a clog-dance on! One fear particularly sucked my energy like a hungry leech. Could they apply underhand leverage. Heaven knows, there was enough material!

In the morning, there was a tap at the door. Andrew and Nick stood with bags in hand.

"Let's go find your cousin," said Andrew.

"After breakfast though," added Nick.

The local diner served Western breakfasts, including specialities new to me. A blowzy blonde in a greasy overall greeted us.

"Hi y'all. What are ya taking?"

I checked the board and ordered the cactus omelettes, which proved surprisingly tasty.

"What's this cousin like?" asked Nick.

"Carl? He was a little wild as a kid, I guess. As a teenager, he fought a lot. Actually, he was closer to Terry, my dad, than I was."

"It was like that with me and Freddy," said Andrew, draining his coffee. "Come on, let's hit the road."

"My turn driving," said Nick.

We entered Utah, and took the river road to Moab. Outside was a stunning, almost cinematic, landscape.

I took a little comfort that I was able to name geological features – the spires, arches, hoodoos, buttes and mesas.

"I remember seeing this in a *National Geographic* magazine," said Nick. "I assumed the pictures were enhanced, but actually you couldn't improve on this."

Eventually we reached the small town nestling between red cliffs – Moab, at last.

"Robbie, where is Carl's place?"

"Just out of town, on the 191. The same road we'll need later for Monticello. What about Freddy? Shall we contact him now, Andy?"

"I'd rather wait. Let's get to Carl's first."

As we passed through the ranch-style gates, anxiety took over. This could potentially be disastrous. Carl and I got on well as kids, but things got strange when details of my sexuality leaked out. In those days, Carl had a reputation as a joker. I hoped with every fibre that he'd changed.

In fact, Carl appeared to have matured and he welcomed us warmly. Maybe it was fatherhood or learning to deal with customers, but he'd certainly changed. I had quite fond memories of his wife, Myleen, and we shared the experience of growing up in Flagstaff. In those days, Myleen had been a bubbly, uncomplicated girl, rather in awe of Carl and his antics. She'd stood by him over several episodes of joyriding – even after his reputation had been mired from the time in a youth correctional unit. Myleen had maybe gained some weight, but was still pretty and clearly devoted to Carl and young Wayne.

We were ushered into the lounge and Myleen left to get us drinks.

"Good to see you again, man," said Carl. "You never seem to leave the smoke."

I introduced the others, and Carl then showed us around the property. Judging from his small fleet, business was good.

"These trips you do, what exactly are they?" asked Nick.

"Basically, small groups for experiences off-roading in the wilderness. We also hire vehicles out to more experienced drivers. They have to be good, though, because some of the trails go over slick-rock, and have scary drops."

"Who built them?" asked Nick. "Off-road enthusiasts?"

"No, this area's been prospected for years – copper, radium, vanadium and uranium. Many tracks are very old and primitive, so experienced drivers come for thrills. We also get photographers looking for unusual angles on Castle Valley, The Arches and Canyonlands."

"Do your vehicles all have GPS?" I asked.

"Of course – it's standard. Some people want to see the back reaches of Canyonlands National Park, and getting lost is easy there. The Park's 'Maze' district is probably the most remote area in all of mainland USA! Incidentally, what do you guys want to see while you're down?"

"I couldn't explain it on the phone, Carl, but I've left my job. It got too stressful, so I need to blow the city fumes away with some nature."

"Yeah, his job was a killer," said Nick. "I know, because our companies shared projects. I fancied seeing the area, too. Originally, I'm from England and Andy actually now lives and works there – though he started life as a 'good old southern boy'. Isn't that right, Andy?"

"Hardly," said Andrew, grinning. "He means my childhood was in Georgia, though I've lived in Europe for years. What we've seen already is spectacular. It couldn't be more different from Oxford, where I work!"

"You betcha," said Carl. "We don't get too many pro-fessors down here!"

Later, Myleen came in with a tray and a big smile. She'd always been a good cook and our conversation slowed to demolish southern fried chicken that would have had the Colonel reaching for his chequebook. Mid-way through the meal, Andrew's cell phone rang and he excused himself. He returned, looking tense.

"Anyone in particular?" I asked.

"It was Mom, wondering if I'd seen Freddy yet. Look, I may as well slope off this afternoon to get the Freddy thing done. I know how keen Mom is. It's probably best done alone. I'll ask him about a kitted-out vehicle."

"You need a vehicle?" asked Carl, looking puzzled.

"I've a brother here," said Andrew. "Fred Anson. He has an auto dealership on the other side of town."

"Anson Autos, by any chance?"

"I believe that is the name," Andrew replied.

Carl's mouth tightened.

"You know it?"

"Probably best left," said Carl. "Let's just say I had trouble with a clocked jeep."

"Clocked?"

"You know – the mileage turned back. Listen man, don't feel bad. I use another supplier now. There ain't no single family that don't have a bad or crazy member somewhere. Ain't that right, Robbie?"

I nodded. Hopefully, Carl meant his own teenage brushes with the law.

Myleen returned with coffee.

"I'll see you all when I'm done at Freddy's?"

Carl's friendly face nodded.

"Yeah, good luck there, bud. I might take the guys out on one of the short trails later. Help them wind down. Incidentally, if you need a jeep…"

"Thanks," replied Andrew. "Actually, things have been rather strained between Freddy and me, so asking might, you know… kind of 'break the ice'."

59

UTAH

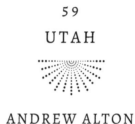

ANDREW ALTON

I pulled over to check the sketched directions that Carl gave me. Take the next turning left for two blocks, and the dealership should be on the next corner. Navigating provided a brief diversion from emotions that were difficult to label. My relationship with Freddy never was easy, with Dad so obviously favouring his middle son and Freddy taking advantage! Truthfully, I didn't really like either of them, yet when Mom hinted that Biff may have possible business links with Fred, I'd felt betrayed. Was I resentful or just envious because Dad never bothered with me? Deep in thought, I almost missed the entrance and had to swing around in a wide circle.

I pulled up outside the dealership, surprised by its sheer size. The lot had eye-catching bunting around the perimeter and clearly seemed busy. I entered the reception, wondering if Freddy had changed much. A pretty, gum-chewing young woman in reception looked up and smiled. I asked for Freddy, she deftly shifted the gum with her tongue, and responded.

"I'm sorry, but the boss has today off."

I gave my details and was soon navigating to her hand-drawn map.

Freddy's home was about a mile away, down a long drive and protected behind a large motorised gate. It opened automatically and Freddy's home came into view. I thought – *Oh no! Not another faux hacienda like Dad's old place!*

I parked, and Freddy came out, followed by Mary and their two children. His face showed genuine surprise as he bounded down the steps, and pumped my hand.

"Hey Bro, what brings you? We thought you lived in England?"

Fred introduced Mervyn, aged ten, and a daughter, Tammy, eight. Neither child seemed the objectionable unruly children I rather expected.

Freddy guided me inside.

"Come on in. Could you use a cold beer?"

I took perverse pleasure that Freddy's décor was every bit as unsubtle as I'd imagined. He led me to the lounge and we settled into huge leather armchairs. At least he had some rather nice western-themed bronzes, including a cowboy on a bucking bronco, reminiscent of the Wyoming state trademark. Freddy noticed my approving glance.

"An original – good huh? Cost me 7k! So, Mom says you're a big time academic in England. Are you here researching, or just aching to visit your brother?"

"Pretty close, Fred. I'm down with a couple of friends from New York. We all needed a break and, because they're city types, we wanted to see something of the old Wild West – and, also, so I could call by! Actually, I did want to ask you something business related. Do you by chance have a four-wheel-drive for hire with GPS, good for off-roading? I'll explain why, the guys are interested to see Indian petroglyphs. We want to look around without getting lost!"

Freddy smiled.

"Sure Bro, no problem. Don't worry about payment, consider it a gift. I reckon my business is considerably more profitable than the academic game! Call by the lot first thing tomorrow, and I'll have it ready. Where will you look – Newspaper Rock?"

"Not sure. One of the guys has a relative living here who seems quite knowledgeable and has maps. We understand there are Anasazi Indian ruins. Possibly even undiscovered sites."

"Surely not researching that now? Mom mentioned you've written stuff critical of businesses managing water supplies. Those Anasazi dudes are long gone now, so I'm afraid that you've missed out on that one!"

"No, it's just interest. The water thing that Mom mentioned is important, though."

"Guess I'm with Dad on that. I say we ought to let experienced corporations do what they do best."

"You mean taking over, controlling vital resources and selling them back to the people, over the odds?"

"See, there you go! No, I'm talking about managing things properly and generating a healthy profit! Dad reckons you never really got what proper business is about."

"Freddy, there's business – and then there's funny business. I remember what Dad's style of doing business did to Mom!"

Mary brought in a tray of sandwiches and more beer. She smiled sweetly.

"It's gonna be great for you boys catching up again."

I dredged up a grin and nodded.

Mary sat down, smiling.

"Tell us about Anne and your place in England."

I realised, with some discomfort, that I'd barely thought about England. Partly the pace of developments, but also the vast landscape down here had got into me. The crowded little island, the rain and traffic, almost seemed a different life. I tried to sound enthusiastic and was half way through describing Oxford when a large SUV towing a trailer arrived in a cloud of dust. Freddy and Mary faced me and didn't see it. Two men approached the front door, and were greeted by Mervyn. Before I could speak, the boy burst into the room.

"Daddy, Uncle Terry and Lee are here."

My brother's face clouded.

Freddy stood to greet the two, and Mary went for more beer. I judged the younger, ginger haired man to be in his thirties. Apart from a small beer belly, he looked a typical tough red-neck. The older man was in his mid-fifties, dressed in black. His appearance was rather magnetic, with a tanned and weather-beaten face, grey-blue eyes and a strong jaw. He projected a 'don't mess with me' attitude.

"Let me introduce two friends," Freddy said.

He pointed towards the older man. "This is Terry James and, over there, Lee Damson. Meet my older brother, Andrew. He's a paleface, 'cause he's just over from England."

"Pleased to meet you, bud," said Terry, giving an exceptionally firm handshake. "You work with them Brits?"

"Yes, political science at Oxford. I head a section focusing on trade, ecology and social justice."

A daft, almost loopy grin crossed the face of the ginger red-neck.

"You ain't one of them... what they called... eeeunivarsity Dons, are ya?"

"Well, I'm a fellow of..."

"Cos we got lots of Dons down hee-ar," interrupted Damson, with a snigger. "There's Don McKenzie at the garage and Donny Smith who ranches over at..."

"Shut up, Lee!" interrupted the older man. "Sorry, bud. He's a real bonehead sometimes."

"Do you ranch in England?" asked Damson.

"Bonehead," said James again, shaking his head and smiling.

"Well, England's quite small and people don't have ranches. Maybe small farms."

"How about militias over they-ar?" tried Damson. "Which outfit do ya go with?"

"Sorry?"

Terry James's face grew dark.

"Take no notice. We have kinda civil defence groups, sometimes called militias. We was talking 'bout it earlier, that's all. Lee kinda gets things stuck in his brain. He's a regular bonehead, 'aint-cha, boy?"

They certainly were a strange pair.

"I believe the Brits have some kind of volunteer army called the Territorials, Lee, though I don't know much about it."

The older man frowned and his face indicated that he didn't want it pursued.

I inquired about their work, and James explained that he ranched in Montana but had other interests trading classic cars, and occasionally did business with Freddy. Damson was a local with business links to Terry James, that sometimes took him to Montana.

I excused myself because several beers had led to the inevitable. On the way back, I passed several opened doors and couldn't resist peering in. Much seemed over the top, and the place was awash with gadgets. Mary was still in the kitchen. I stood for a moment outside the lounge, wondering how to raise our past difficulties – knowing Mom would be thrilled if I said we'd patched things up. Perhaps, after the visitors left, I could make an effort.

Voices filtered through the door.

"Where do you plan putting them?" I heard Freddy ask.

"The hide," came James's voice. "We're heading there now. Probably stay overnight."

"Right," said Freddy. "Listen, I really should spend time with my bro. I'll message you real soon."

The talk moved to gossip about someone called 'Frankie' and, when I entered, James and Damson were already on their feet.

"We're leaving, bud," said James.

"Don't let my visit interrupt," I said. "I can wait elsewhere, if you need to talk business."

"No, it's cool man – we're done," replied Terry.

Damson grinned awkwardly as they left the room. He watched them leaning on Damson's pick-up, talking, wondering why Freddy dealt with such people – and why so evasive?

Freddy re-entered with a frown.

"You do much business with them?"

"Not really, Bro. They sometimes trade classic car parts and I buy stuff from time to time. It's funny you were asking before about off-road vehicles. That's our other shared interest. We've made trips out together, exploring remote canyons and such like."

Something else was smouldering. The question stuck in my throat, but it was 'now or never'.

"Mom had the impression that you and Biff might be doing business together. Is that right? I'm just being curious!"

Freddy frowned again.

"Can't be that curious, Bro – seeing we haven't spoken for years! Dad talked about investment opportunities in the South West, but we haven't found anything as yet."

"Aren't you're the lucky one? My work looks at business and investment internationally, yet I never hear from him."

"To be fair, Andy, I gather that your career specialises in bashing business!"

I could feel the old anger igniting. As words were rising to my throat, I calmed myself, reasoning that this was just classic sibling rivalry stuff that wouldn't get anywhere. While Freddy was undoubtedly a chip off the old block, it was best to keep things cool for Mom's sake!

But Freddy was on a roll.

"No, it's true! Dad says you never understood business!"

I focused on my breath – one of Anne's favourite yoga techniques – and let it wash over me. Resentment continued to move in my mind in big sticky images as Freddy recited a string of business successes. Memories of Biff and Freddy playing baseball, Dad buying Freddy's first car, funding his first business and bailing him out – several times! I started to give myself a pep talk to keep the 'lid on'.

You wouldn't really want that sort of relationship with Dad or the compromises required, I reasoned. *You made the right choices for you, so just keep it cool and keep it friendly!*

Freddy was mocking and triumphant.

"Maybe you're right, Fred. There's an old saying – 'those who can, do, and the others teach'! Maybe I wasn't made for the rough and tumble of business. Anyway, tell me, how is your business doing now?"

The question obviously pleased him. Even so, I couldn't quite bring myself to enthuse over tales of outflanking competitors or outlandish mark-ups. I remembered Carl's tale of the clocked jeep, but kept quiet.

I stayed for another hour and a half of chat and food, until the atmosphere between us was almost reasonable, and then returned to Carl's. His house was already in sight when my cell phone rang and I pulled over to take the call. Simon's voice came through, clear, and he sounded excited.

"How's it going – any developments in Utah?"

"We're heading out to look tomorrow. I just had a rather grating meeting with brother Freddy – the first in years. How about you?"

"San Francisco's great and the conference presentations – first class. I picked up some fascinating material on big finance tricks since the last crisis. Veitch has agreed an interview tomorrow, over lunch."

"Well done. We need leads and contacts. Presumably you haven't forgotten we'll probably be looking for alternative employment?"

"Of course not, misery! The only downside here is a rather intimidating police presence."

"At the conference?"

"More around the site. Some activists used the occasion for demonstrations. After a session on corporate malfeasance, a group took to the streets. Certain corporations were publicly named. Then the 'robocops' arrived – you know, with the sticks, padding and visors."

"Protesting against corporate criminals is a crime now?"

"Exactly! And, just like home, public money is then used to silence the public. It's heavy. They're trying to virtually criminalise dissent. Apparently, several people associated with the demo were taken, and sort of 'disappeared'."

"Disappeared?"

"Seems a few key protesters were pre-selected and then 'snatched'. That's the only word I can use! They also took pictures of everyone."

"Where are the 'snatched' people now?"

"We don't know. Some were penned up, photographed, DNA taken and then released. Three or four were driven off, though."

The London Arms Fair flooded back.

"Be careful, Si, and call back soon. Evenings are probably best for contacting me. I mightn't be in a position to take a call if we're... you know! Hey, you don't think the arrested guys from the demo went to one, do you?"

"What a horrible thought. No, they were only protesting!"

"But, if they were pre-selected?"

"I don't know. Be careful. I'll call back soon."

I started the car and pulled out. Half way down the block, the phone rang again. I pulled in, expecting to hear Nick or Robbie, but it was Anne.

"Hi, darling, I talked about you only half an hour ago. You must have picked it up on the airwaves! How are things?"

"Fine, Andy. Missing you and wanted to hear your voice. There are a couple of other things, but what do you mean, you just mentioned me?"

"You won't believe it, but to my brother Freddy and his wife. I just visited. In fact, I only left five minutes ago!"

"You're right, I am surprised."

I filled her in on the visit.

"To be honest, we barely kept from one of our old-time rows. His wife seems a good sort, though. She had the knack of appearing, just when we were about to throw punches! A good woman's worth her weight in gold – I should know!"

She laughed.

"You old smoothy! There were two other things. A fat-looking envelope turned up from the College. Also, Martin Farrelly called. He's had a break-in at home and some research material taken. The Health Authority has forbidden him to speak publicly on the corporate psychopathy thing and wants him to drop it altogether. Of course, he won't, but he thought you should know. I said you'd be back soon, but I'd pass it on when we next spoke. I didn't give him your cell phone number."

"Thanks, darling. Looking forward to seeing you soon. Incidentally, the scenery here is quite spectacular. I must bring you over some time."

She rang off and I sat quietly.

Really, I wanted to speak with Mom. Perhaps it was Anne's call, or just needing to talk after the time with Freddy. Anyway, she'd want to know. I took the phone, and dialled the companion cell phone I'd bought in the name of Anne Alton, and gave to Mom. At the time, it just seemed a basic security manoeuvre, but, suddenly, I wondered why. Why on earth give my mother a phone registered in my wife's name? The number dialled out, and I decided not to pursue the thought!

No response. Nothing. Damn, it must be turned off. I waited for the voice-mail to cut in. Still nothing. I felt uneasy. Had something happened? Against better judgement, I dialled the land-line and it picked up after five rings.

"Mom?"

"Andy! How are you?"

"You didn't answer the cell phone?"

"Sorry, darling. I had a little accident about half an hour ago."

"Are you okay?"

"Yes, fine. I meant an accident with the phone. I took a bath and had it on the side in case you called. Some soap had been there and it was slippery, and…"

I shook my head. After the earlier thought, it wasn't an image I wanted to follow.

"Okay, Mom, I get the idea."

"I planned to replace it later this afternoon and then call you."

I described the visit to Freddy, softening the tense moments, and then the call from Anne. Strange how I still found her voice a comfort.

"Nick and Robbie were out in a jeep seeing local sights while I was with Freddy. We've been made very welcome."

We talked for a short while. I suddenly remembered we were on the land-line and wound the conversation down. What lay ahead now – hopefully some of Myleen's food! Mom's voice had at least made me feel more cheerful.

Several hundred miles away, a recorder deactivated. The coordinates briefly showed on the screen, before being sent to the printer…

6 0

MANHATTAN

GILL'S PERSPECTIVE

After Si left, Gill only had her placement with US Security to help ward off a growing sense of loneliness. Before leaving for San Francisco, Simon told her that, despite the buzz, Manhattan can get very oppressive. How true, and she also began feeling homesick. Today had been particularly trying, and worsened by Holt's incessant sexist banter. She was working on her report for London when Holt's head came around the corner and he winked.

"What have you been up to? The chief's asking for you, babe."

She made her way upstairs, uncertain what to expect. Tom Freison was the equivalent of Donaldson back home, similarly tall and distinguished, if considerably less formal. They'd talked on several occasions, and she found him altogether more impressive than Holt and Matacic. He was also enthusiastic about the exchange.

She knocked and then entered Freison's understated and ordered room. He pointed to an empty chair and, after pleasantries, asked for her impressions, so far. She returned the enthusiasm about the US/UK exchange.

"Good to hear. I'm glad it's useful. Vern tells me, though, that synchronicity has struck again?"

"Meaningful coincidences? Not quite following you, Sir."

"I meant, it's rather handy… you being in New York and a guy turns up you'd been observing in England – followed by a second one!"

She sifted through the words, but her stomach was already churning. This was a paranoia-inducing environment at the best of times. Hopefully, he wouldn't know the full extent of her struggles.

"Anyway, since you told Vern about that cosy family get-together in Philly, the local office there has kept an eye on Alton's mother. Turns out that she's hooked up with the local activists. Of course, our people already have agents in local groups. After all, Philly was the nation's birthplace and some crackpot might try to make something out of that."

She nodded, wondering where on earth this was heading.

"I'm told that some of your 'friends' are on a little cross-country trip. Andrew Alton phoned his mother this afternoon and the call was intercepted. Two other people of interest, Nicholas Martin and Robert James, are with him. Guess where they are?"

She knew only too well and tried to adopt an expression of mild interest, remembering the old adage, controlled breathing means a controlled voice!

She exhaled slowly, and shook her head.

"I really don't know. Alton mentioned wanting to see more of the real America while he's here. I also heard Rob James say that, since being canned, he wanted time out of the city. I thought it was just idle talk."

"They're in the south of Utah, Gill. Doesn't that strike you as a coincidence that the same Nick Martin, who formerly consorted with Nina Parenda and whose 'stolen' money went for bomb-making materials, turns up just down the road from where she's being held?!"

She looked for a plausible answer, as anxiety curdled her stomach. Was Freison about to accuse her of collusion, or divulging secrets? She reviewed recent developments at speed. To keep credibility with Matacic, she'd divulged aspects of her Philadelphia visit, as part of continued surveillance of Simon and Andrew – but she hadn't mentioned Utah. Looking up to the ceiling, she hopefully gave an impression of 'the penny dropping'.

"Ah, I think I know! Andrew has a brother – called Freddy Anson. I believe they said that he lives in… I think it… was… Moab in Utah. Do the intercept coordinates match, by any chance?"

"As a matter of fact, yes, they do."

"That must be it then. What makes you believe Martin and James are with him?"

"Alton mentioned them in his call."

Freison picked up a piece of paper and studied it for a moment.

"He said that James and Martin were out on a jeep trip. What did they have to say about this Freddy Anson guy?"

"Not much. He's a businessman, like his dad, though there doesn't seem much love lost between the brothers. I remember a conversation where the mother seemed keen that they patch things up."

"I see. What about Maher – the one you observed?"

"Away in San Francisco for a few days – interviewing 'experts' there, though I haven't the details. I gathered an anti-corporate conference is on at the same time. The prospect of time with socialists and trouble-makers seemed to excite him."

"That figures! There's also something else."

"Yes, Sir?"

"Tom or Chief will do – you're not in London now! Philly discov-ered that the mother, Judy Alton, has a house guest who is also of inter-est. They've been observed out together several times."

"What, dating?"

"They seem close. The man is Zoltan Heltay – now an American citizen, but born in Hungary. We think he might have militia associa-tions in the West. Heltay's a computer and communication specialist."

"I briefly met him that weekend."

Her mind moved quickly. Freison said they 'seemed fairly close'. She remembered seeing Heltay leave Judy's bedroom, in shorts and t-shirt. *Close indeed!* She recalled Donaldson's briefing about possible penetra-tion by hard-line terrorists. Freison had reiterated the same concern when she first arrived.

"Where is this going, Chief?"

"It's more a case of where you're going. Matacic said that the Alton woman made you welcome?"

"I guess so."

"You may as well make yourself useful while you're here. I'd like you to visit again, so get yourself another invitation. Discover what they're up to in Utah, because it seems like they'll keep contact with Alton's mother. Secondly, please keep an eye on Heltay. What is he doing in the North East?"

She nodded thoughtfully. It was a good question.

"My nose tells me something is 'off' with the whole group. Think about it! Martin, who is close to Parenda and with questions over the Colombia bomb episode, works for an IT/consulting company that has an important Colombian contract. Robert, 'Robbie' James, who's been ratting on one of the city's top businessmen, turns up at Anson's ex-wife's home and then goes on "holiday" with Anson's son. Alton, as you well know, is an extremist academic – anti-corporate, anti-globalisation and probably an anti-capitalist troublemaker to boot. He's Anson's son, but bears him a grudge."

She had to acknowledge, summarised like that, it didn't sound good.

"We know, from visiting his flat, that James and Martin were in regular email contact and oppose water privatising, as did Martin and your friend, Simon Maher."

Surely that was it, but no, Freison continued.

"Robbie's father, Terry James, is a known militia leader, suspected of anti-government planning and actions. Then, for good measure, this Zoltan Heltay character turns up. In the meantime, your mark from the UK, Simon Maher, is off with tree-huggers in San Francisco! Find out everything you can about this lot. It might soon be time to clip Mr Maher's wings. We haven't yet decided."

She nodded, seeking to find an appropriate expression. Her stomach felt knotted as she picked her way through a veritable thicket of implications. In the back of her mind, her mother's voice recited:

'Oh what a tangled web we weave…'

61

SAN FRANCISCO

SIMON MAHER

San Francisco was everything I'd hoped for and more – beautiful and exciting, but it also had a hard underside and, at night, it wore a very different face! I'd taken a cheap hotel room in the notorious Tenderloin district. In contrast to the glitz of the finance district or Nob Hill's affluence, this gritty, run-down area seemed distinctly threatening after dark.

I left the hotel, and stepped into the night. According to the map, walking to North Beach should be fairly straightforward. Outside seemed unexpectedly busy and, although adopting a purposeful gait, there was no avoiding the sheer number of characters begging, soliciting or hanging about in the street. It was my second introduction to the hidden homeless and dispossessed who congregated nightly – with simply nowhere else to go.

I walked tall with squared shoulders and an inflated chest, trying to discourage trouble. People loitered outside all-hours shops and fast-food joints, begging and drinking. Further on, two women with absurdly short skirts leaned suggestively, near a porn DVD shop. I slipped a few quarters into the hand of a beggar and quickly moved on. Although undoubtedly intimidating, I felt strangely ashamed, avoiding the victims of poverty, racism and class in the world's most unequal society.

I crossed the road, moving in the general direction of North Beach, while reflecting on the conference. Today's presentations really were superb – particularly those by the South American contingent and Frank Rossi's seminar: 'Are the media unwitting propagandists?' I smiled. I'd once been called a social justice propagandist. Others said less gently – 'a sanctimonious prig'! I was just being enthusiastic, and never did understand how people could be lukewarm about important matters. I walked on, looking left and right, replaying Rossi's presentation. He essentially seemed right, the mainstream media had been absolutely in lock-step with the business elite, and spent decades promoting the most regressive social, economic and political architecture supporting market fundamentalism. Nothing else got space!

Two large men in leather motorcycle gear approached, but passed without incident and I went back to mulling over the day. Rossi claimed that, while totally critical of Islamic fundamentalists, the mainstream media mainly ignored 'market fundamentalism'. He maintained our 'democracy' was actually shaped by PR, spin and outright propaganda. How lucky I was meeting him in the food hall, chatting as we waited in line. Even better, Rossi had read and enjoyed papers written by Andrew. An invitation to join him for drinks at Vesuvio's tonight was the cherry on the cake.

I continued on to Geary Street, passing through a small theatre district. Then turned into Union Square and walked down Stockton Street, noticing a well-built young man in denim jeans, jacket and t-shirt look interested and then seem to follow behind. I turned right at California Street, looking for a short-cut, but, after reaching Grant Avenue, it almost seemed as if I'd stumbled into some strange portal to the Far-East. The narrow streets here were crammed with Chinese, Korean and Vietnamese shops with Chinese signage and eastern-style buildings, including pagodas. Even the telephone boxes had an oriental twist. A pungent aroma hung in the narrow street as I passed oriental grocers and restaurants. I stopped to look inside the next shop window. Chopsticks, pewter dragons and lanterns, piled next to bamboo models and plaster Buddhas. I became aware of high-pitched voices and looked up to see that I was blocking an elderly Chinese woman and her two young companions. As I pulled back to let them pass, I noticed the same well-built young man in denim and a military-style crew-cut, staring with interest. I moved to another window, this time full of herbal preparations, and, as I looked into the reflection, the man continued staring intently. We seemed to be the only Caucasians – and then I remembered San Francisco's reputation as a major gay centre. It wouldn't be the first time I'd been the object of interest – most recently, that amusing episode with Robbie James.

I turned into Waverly Place, passing three Chinese temples on the way. The towering Trans-America pyramid loomed high over the tangle of buildings, and I couldn't stop framing imaginary shots of this huge chunk of Americana. I so wished that I'd thought to bring my camera tonight! I turned back around, and the young man quickly turned away. Strange, because it wasn't as if this was a known gay area like The Castro!

I decided to take a more circular route to Vesuvio's, discretely keeping him in view using shop window reflections. Sure enough, despite occasionally crossing the street, the man continued to follow. Eventually, I reached Columbus Avenue, passing Vesuvio's and the City Lights bookshop. I continued a few yards further for a glimpse of the bright lights of Broadway, and then returned to Vesuvio's bar.

The place was completely packed, but I quickly spotted Frank Rossi sitting with someone that I'd seen at the conference. I waved and then joined them. Frank introduced his companion – Dario, from Colombia. They were apparently discussing the Zapatistas from Mexico. Frank explained that these were the modern-day descendants of the Mayas. I remembered that, back in Philadelphia, Nick Martin enthused about them, too! After several desultory attempts at joining in, I congratulated Frank on his conference presentation and tried to steer him back to 'propaganda and the media', but Rossi seemed distinctly 'off duty'.

"Did you know that Kerouac and the original Beatniks used to hang out in here? Even Dylan Thomas visited when in town."

I nodded. Hearing tales about fifties Beat culture would certainly be fascinating. Better still, Alan Ginsberg and the early counter culture movement that hung out next door in the City Lights bookshop. However, I was here on a mission.

"Frank, in your talk, you said that propaganda is almost as widespread in democratic states as in totalitarian regimes."

He seemed mildly sozzled and reluctant to pick up the bait.

"Hey, Simon, you need a drink!"

Dario called out for three more Buds.

"Thanks. Did I get you right, about propaganda, though?"

"Yeah, it's jazzier, wears a corporate logo, but, yeah, that's true –it's just better integrated. Democracy should listen and learn. It supposedly rests on people power. To coin a phrase, the Greeks had a word for it – 'Demos', the people, and 'Cratos', power. The thing is, our privatised, slick propaganda supports corporate and elite interests and helps to shape public opinion... though most don't realise that!"

"Isn't that a bit strong, Frank?"

"Not really. Another beer?"

Rossi placed the order and continued.

"No, state, corporate and elite interests are often one and the same, now. We saw that with the great bank bailout. Corporate-friendly states protect the interests of their funders. The media are usually complicit, which is unsurprising – because they are powerful corporations themselves!"

I nodded encouragement, happy to have ignited Frank's engines.

"They influence with business-friendly 'op-eds', slanted documentaries and so on. Legions of PR specialists create this garbage, and ensure that corporate-friendly values get spread. Instead of saying that the infrastructure and services we've all paid for will be given over to private interests at knock-down prices, we're told that we're being given more choice!"

"I couldn't agree more, Frank."

"Periodically, we export 'democracy' down the barrel of a gun because it will be business friendly. It's almost a 'democracy franchise', like opening a new fast-food restaurant."

Rossi was a terrier with the rat of corporate propaganda. I started to wonder if Rossi himself might be a practitioner of the dark art and couldn't help but grin. The beer had obviously hit the right spot!

"Still, at least we have free press and media."

"But do they serve democracy? It's mostly privately owned and concentrated into fewer and fewer very rich hands. Just because a little competition remains, it doesn't mean there's real diversity. Whose interests do you imagine plutocrat owners promote?"

"Their own, I guess, and big advertisers?"

"Exactly! So, a 'consumer society' and the 'everything is for sale' approach is presented as the only authentic way of living. Personally, I believe the opposite is true."

I nodded. Frank now had a full head of steam.

"Freedom of the press means freedom for a small group of media owners to promote their own agendas. Actually, it's a hidden form of censorship."

"How?"

"Shaping public opinion and filtering news! You'd be surprised what gets left out if it threatens certain business interests. Many views won't be heard at all. Look at what eventually emerged about the Iraq war! Yet, for ages, you only found that kind of information from a tiny handful of independent journalists and bloggers."

I nodded. It was true!

"Journalists who try to be independent get quickly yanked back into line – or they don't work. Self-censorship is quickly learned if your livelihood's threatened!"

I remembered my time at the mall and started to share the experience, when something pulled my attention to the bar. Despite a mildly beer-fuelled state, I felt someone's gaze, and my attention was drawn near to the bar's entrance. Although the room was crowded, I saw the man who'd followed me earlier. Definitely the same man, in a denim jacket and trousers, a crew-cut and black t-shirt, perched on a bar stool. There was something menacing about his appearance and powerful build. Gill once said that she could sense a spider in the room – and now I knew what she meant. The man quickly looked away and lifted his glass to drink.

I asked Dario about the Colombian media scene and, while pretending to stretch, sneaked another look. Unquestionably, it was the same person. His presence could be coincidental, but, after that creepy feeling of being stared at, I doubted it. Rossi, though, was in full flow.

"The media's become lazy and has come to depend on government and business for information. For example, those pre-packaged government press briefings, or 'embedded' journalists in the military. In return, they select and shape news and commentary within acceptable – and often helpful – parameters. Powerful elites, corporations and government in bed together, sharing the trough in a blatantly undemocratic love fest... when really we need un-spun information, not controlled by giant profit-making corporations... You see, really we should... What the hell is up, Simon?"

'Crew-cut' was talking into his cell phone. I caught his gaze again, and our eyes met. I recalled the 'disappearing' conference delegates. When I looked back, Rossi frowned.

"If you disagree, Simon, do feel free to say so."

"Sorry, Frank. No, I'm absolutely with you, but something distracted me. Wait a moment, and then please be discrete. At the table closest to the entrance, you'll see a young muscular looking guy with a black t-shirt, denim jacket and a military haircut."

Rossi looked discreetly. Dario also.

"It sounds paranoid, I know, but I'm certain he followed me across town."

I described the man's behaviour.

"You've been marked," Rossi said.

"This isn't football!"

"Perhaps you didn't hear, but several activists were pre-emptively arrested by security, and never returned to the conference."

"I heard," I replied. "Snatched from demo's. Unnerving, because I planned joining the water demo, tomorrow."

"No, these guys were grabbed way before the demo's. We heard of several people who had experiences like you just described," said Dario. He leaned forward, his voice now barely audible.

"I feel that I saw that guy back at the conference. I'm not completely sure, but I think so."

"It's a strategy. Pre-emptive arrests of people they think could cause trouble," said Rossi. "Started at a G8 in Miami some years back and has been refined. Sometimes, they shadow activists they plan pulling, to get them off the scene."

"What's the hype about this being America's most liberal city?"

Rossi grinned.

"Did you look down Broadway?"

I'd certainly walked the few extra steps and looked. I assumed Frank was thinking of the neon strip, touting sleazy clubs and porn emporia.

"Yes, I saw that. To be honest, I thought at first he was a gay guy on the prowl."

"I shouldn't tell him that," said Rossi, smiling and shaking his head. "No, this really is a liberal city, but we're now looking at coordinated action, aimed at freezing domestic dissent."

"So I gather," I replied.

"Any action can be smeared as anti-American. You mustn't mess with corporate 'free speech', despite their dollars having almost smoth-ered yours."

"Right on, Frank, but my immediate worry right now is what to do?"

"I'll sort this out," said Dario. "Let me walk back with you."

"I think I know what you have in mind, but I've another idea," said Rossi. "The organisers booked me into the St Francis. It's a great hotel, especially if you're a Dashiell Hammett fan, but I wanted time with our Latin American visitors, like Dario here – so I'm staying up in the Mission, instead."

"What's that – some kind of hostel?"

"No," laughed Rossi, "I'm staying with friends in the Latino area called the Mission District. It's named after the city's oldest building, the Spanish Mission Dolores, dating from the 1770s. There's bags of room, so come with us. That should throw them right off the scent."

"I'll tell you what," said Dario, "Frank, you get a taxi, and Simon and I will walk up to Washington Square and see if he follows. Bring the taxi along the edge of the park in about 10 minutes, and we'll jump straight in. That'll outfox him!"

Dario looked at Rossi and the older man nodded his head.

"Seems like a plan!"

We finished our drinks. Rossi was busy describing Alex Carey's distinction of Grassroots and Treetops propaganda. In the circumstances, his words buzzed over my head like busy gnats, but Rossi wasn't put off.

"It's rather like Herman said, give the appearance of consent and sufficient diversions to capture the public's attention, and certain programmes will sail through unnoticed. With sufficient tittle-tattle, street crime and sport, the public won't notice any legalised theft. Like a conjurer – provide enough diversion, and anything goes. It's the old Roman 'bread and circuses' routine, all over again."

I tried to look interested, but my focus was really on an escape. Rossi seemed unstoppable.

"Ask the public if they want good education for their children and a reasonable safety net for the poor. They'll say yes every time, but, by the time the think-tanks, lobbyists and corporate media have done their best, they'll beg for sky-high medical costs, education fees and savage welfare cuts. They'll say astronomical military spending, the gutting of environmental protections and tax cuts for the super-rich are their hearts' desire. I think we…"

I interrupted.

"Frank. I can't tell you how interested I am and how I agree with you, but right now I need to get out of this fix. Can we continue later – at the Mission?"

Moments later, I walked north up Columbus Avenue with Dario. It might have just been anxiety, but a daft childish ditty ran through my mind. A moment of private madness under stress.

Steppin' out with the Colombian on Columbus
gotta show my control and trust
just a walking and a talking
keep it smooth and don't be baulking
or 'Crew-cut' will guess that he's been sussed.

Now we were standing up, I could see that the Colombian man was tall, wiry, with a powerful aura of 'keep your distance'.

"Walk on towards Washington Square," said Dario.

The area had an Italian character. I pointed to a restaurant and we stood by the window, pretending to discuss the menu. Sure enough, 'Crew-cut' appeared and then followed. We watched his reflected image cross the Avenue and then stare into a shop window. We continued up to the square. Then the Colombian whispered to me and we separated. As instructed, I turned left and entered the park while Dario kept walking ahead. The glow of the street-lights soon disappeared and my heart hammered seemingly out of control. I gingerly moved forward, imagining the probable fallen branches and dog mess. A moment later, I heard a snapping sound from behind and spun around, casting my senses out into the darkness like a fishing net and staring with wide-opened eyes. Something may have moved – I wasn't sure. Still no Dario! I only knew that I was alone and feeling vulnerable! Perhaps 'Crew-cut' had called colleagues, to prepare a snatch. They were probably closing in right now! This would be an ideal place and now we've played right into their hands. A noise came from the right, sounding like the crack of a branch under foot. *Where the hell was Dario?*

I edged sideways, away from the sound and, through the branches, saw the faint halo of a street-light. The trees on the square's edge seemed blurred and I realised that one of San Francisco's famous fogs must have rolled in. Another noise came from the right, so I turned abruptly left, reasoning that anyone shadowing would also have to turn. I walked a dozen steps further and paused – but heard nothing, so I moved off again, funnelling all my awareness to hearing, straining to hear approaching feet. Maybe now I could risk circling back to the main road. I set off, but stopped abruptly. *Hang on, they could then radio for a car to come and then scoop me up – especially now that Dario had disappeared.* Banks of fog were piling into the park and it seemed thicker by the moment. I moved forward and then tripped over a park bench, painfully catching my leg on the bench's base. I stood on one leg, nursing a painful shin and biting back a moan. Suddenly, I heard a dull thud, and a brief eerie moan. Almost immediately, Dario appeared.

"Quickly, back to the road," he said, grabbing my arm.

"Where's 'Crew-cut'?" I asked.

"Resting for a while!"

I felt like a blind man, but Dario somehow kept his sense of direction and soon had us back at the road. Traffic was light but, miraculously, the next vehicle approaching was a taxi. Rossi peered from the passenger window and we waved back. The fog seemed a little lighter here, although billowing swirls obscured the hills and higher buildings.

We scrambled into the taxi.

"Garfield Square – the Mission," said Rossi.

The taxi turned and we were soon moving along Vann Ness Avenue.

"That fog came from nowhere."

"Yeah, we're used to it," answered the driver. "You sound British? I thought you guys had plenty of fog?"

"Not quite like that!"

It thinned and I could catch glimpses of the characteristic wooden houses as the taxi sped along. The driver was right to predict that the fog wouldn't reach the Mission. Eventually the cab slowed down in what was clearly a Latino area. The billboards were in Spanish, and at one place huge murals covered several walls.

"What's with the paintings?" I asked.

"Their heroes. Mainly Latin American politicians," the driver replied, "although there's a beauty of Carlos Santana, on the corner of Twenty-Second."

"Another time," said Rossi. "Stop here, please."

We pulled up outside an unassuming wooden house – seemingly the only Caucasians around. I worried that my accent would stand out like a hearse at a wedding.

Rossi knocked and, while we waited, I realised that mention of Santana had triggered 'Black Magic Woman' inside my head.

The door opened and a large Mexican woman waved us inside, and hugged Rossi and Dario.

"Hi, Frankie, did ya kill 'em today?"

"Hopefully, Elisa! Meet Simon. He's an academic researcher from England, here for the conference."

The large woman squeezed my hand and shouted out something in Spanish. A large man with a huge moustache joined us.

"Simon, meet Esteban. He and Elisa are old friends of mine, from way back."

The man gave my hand an extremely firm squeeze, and patted my shoulder.

"Welcome, friend."

Frank spoke rapidly in Spanish and then explained.

"I've told them what happened. They're fine about you staying."

"Come, you all must be hungry," said Esteban, ushering them into the kitchen where Elisa had obviously been busy. Our arrival coincided with the evening meal and, soon, she ladled out large portions. I was introduced to three daughters sitting around the table. The smallest, Solana, giggled, switching between Spanish and English as she chattered with sisters, Paloma, and the eldest, Melosa.

"Esteban and Elisa have Zapatista contacts," Rossi said.

"True," agreed Esteban. "We support them. Mexico has a long history of '*mal gobierno*'."

I looked questioningly.

"Bad government," explained Dario.

They seemed pleased by the interest and, for the next half hour, described the realities. I'd already heard some of this from Nick – NAFTA, the North American Free Trade Agreement, the uprising at San Cristobal, and the attack on the communal '*edjidos*'. With help from Rossi, they explained the difficulties of the peasantry and the introduction of intensive agribusiness farms. I just wished Andrew could be here to hear it. It was probably like Nick's description of coca spraying – experience made all the difference.

Elisa served something tasty and, while I ate, the eldest daughter, Melosa, flashed sparkling eyes my way. She was undoubtedly pretty, but I was missing Gill and had no wish for complications. Over the meal, they all discussed history – the repeal of Article 27, the ejidos and NAFTA – pushed by foreigners, oligarchs and the *neoliberalismo*. It sounded like these things were regular talking points. Melosa smiled my way again and, I thought, gave a little wink. With zero experience of Latino girls, I had no idea of what, if anything, that could signify.

"We didn't actually live in Chiapas," said Esteban, "but we have relatives there and support the Zapatistas. Everywhere could use a little Zapatismo – even here in the Mission!"

They all roared with laughter. I grinned, wondering what I could possibly contribute to the conversation. Esteban wore an expression of mock solemnity, as he lightly pounded the table.

"We need another Pancho Villa. It's still all about *'tierra y libertad'.*"

I must have looked blank.

"Sorry, Mr Simon, 'land and freedom'. Their leader shouldn't have had to hide out in Lacandon's forests, like some fugitive!"

Esteban poured tequila.

"We need an autonomous, Zapatista-style municipality, here in the Mission!"

Dario shook his head.

"I agree, but, be careful what you say, friend. Strange things are happening now and freely speaking isn't safe any longer. After all, that's why our friend Simon is here."

The meal wound down and then Elisa showed me to the room where I could sleep. I was still wondering what to wear, when Dario stuck his head in.

"Can't risk going to your hotel, so you'll have to manage without your stuff for now. They might know where you were staying, so it's better this way. Incidentally, I'm next door, so you may hear a little noise."

Dario winked, as Melosa's head appeared around the door, and flashed a brilliant smile.

Lucky blighter, I thought, as they closed their door. The subsequent imaginings were infinitely more pleasing than the tumultuous dreams that followed...

62

UTAH

ROBBIE JAMES

I stared into my cereal bowl, aware of rising anxiety. Early this morning, we'd visited Anson Autos and Freddy handed over a jeep with satnav. I'd enjoyed being the unofficial guide, but the trip was now over, leaving just uncertainty. Nick's excitement at being close to Nina seemed palpable, but what could we really achieve?

Last evening, Nick called Michael Gallo, without mentioning his whereabouts. Gallo had researched the background context to our situation and told him of a little-known set of government programmes that had allowed the quiet development of domestic holding camps.

"Nick, run Gallo's information by me again," said Andrew.

"Hang on," he replied, checking his notes. "He said the Department of Defence and the Federal Emergency Management Agency (FEMA) had plans for containing major civil disruptions. Apparently, the Rex-84 thing he mentioned was a plan to cope with refugees from war or Central American disturbances. Apparently, that's been updated – the old military bases closed and quietly prepared as potential detention camps."

"Bloody hell!" I said.

"There's more," continued Nick. "An associated plan gives the military authority over the civilian population in the case of a major emergency. That morphed into a 'Civil Disturbances Plan', Gallo believes, that authorises government agencies to target 'disruptive elements', though the definitions of that seem very loose. Anyway, everything is on the books and ready!"

"Don't we know it," I said.

This was all very sobering and, as we sipped coffee, I mulled over the implications. The camps existed, some were operational and detentions technically 'lawful'. Despite Myleen's cheerfulness and the treats coming from her kitchen, everyone seemed downbeat. Even the blueberry pancakes barely raised the mood.

Andrew spread out a map and we huddled around. The coordinates appeared to centre on the Manti La Sal National Forest, near the La Sal Mountains. Everyone stared at the paper, but someone had to name the issue.

"We've no real plan or strategy," I said. "I'm really worried."

The others were silent.

"Not to mention, the Arm-Rite goons."

Nick looked tense.

"I know. I'm sorry, but that isn't going to stop me looking."

Andrew nodded.

"Naturally. We haven't come all this way just to sit on our hands."

"It looks like we should proceed down the 191, then turn east at La Sal Junction," I offered. "After that, I'm not sure."

"Hopefully, we'll zero-in with the sat-nav," said Andrew. "Let's make a start."

The traffic was quite light. We turned at La Sal Junction and the sat-nav directed us down a narrow country road. The country here was wooded and pretty, though not as dramatic as before. We drove for some miles, but saw nothing resembling a detention camp. Andrew drove at a steady pace, but, as we entered a particularly sharp curve, a Hummer suddenly appeared, moving dangerously fast and pulling a long trailer. It recklessly charged towards us and I braced for a collision. As we swerved, I saw a young red-neck driving with an older man beside him. Andrew pulled hard into the bend, blinded by dust, and braked as the Hummer swept past, showering us with grit. The rear of the trailer disappeared in a wake of orange dust. We braked hard and a protruding stick caught in the wheel arch as we stopped.

"Bloody idiot!" said Andrew uncharacteristically.

Nick jumped out and took a quick look.

"Just a scrape – nothing to worry about."

I felt shocked and couldn't speak.

Andrew looked pale and whistled under his breath.

"What an idiot. Mind you, I thought that yesterday."

"How come?" asked Nick.

"It was really quite strange. While visiting Freddy, the young guy driving and the older man turned up in that Hummer and trailer. The driver was Damson. Lee Damson, I believe. An odd young man, who asked about Britain's Territorial Army – well, actually, he asked about British militias, and asked if I was involved. That's what the older guy, Terry James, explained. He said I should ignore Damson – a regular 'bonehead'. Damson certainly struggled to grasp that we don't actually have militias!"

I could only listen with mounting alarm. Surely not! Someone named Terry James, who called people 'bonehead'. Not that 'Terry James' – not my father? 'Bonehead' boomed inside. It was one of Dad's favourite expressions and, like most people in Terry's world, I'd heard it often enough!

Nick was still cursing.

"The stupid jerk could have taken us all out."

Andrew nodded.

"Anyway, when I returned from a comfort break at Freddy's place, I heard them mention delivering a load to the La Sal site. Seems strange, bringing car parts right out here!"

"Car parts?" repeated Nick.

"Freddy said they trade in classic cars parts. You look pale, Robbie. Really a close call, huh?"

I felt shaken, but didn't want to trade 'worst father' comparisons with Andrew.

"Yeah, way too close."

We drove off again. Further on, the forest got thicker and had small tracks leading off on both sides. Periodically, red and white road signs appeared, looking like out-sized barcodes.

"I wonder where those clowns went," said Nick.

"Don't know," replied Andrew. "Strange place for a car dealer."

I noticed the odd roadside markings had petered out.

"I wonder if those signs somehow point the way. Since the last crossroad, they've disappeared."

"You're right," replied Nick. "Actually, the sat-nav's been silent for several miles. Maybe something got dislodged, when we skidded?"

"No, it's still on. Maybe they use some kind of signal jamming

375

around these places? I think we should turn back. This doesn't feel right."

The road ahead had narrowed, and now appeared more like a logging track.

"I agree. Let's turn back," said Andrew, backing for a tight three-point turn. At the next crossroads, he pointed to one of the little red and white signs.

"Left or right?"

"The coordinates looked closer to Mount Peale, so I reckon north. Turn right," I said.

"I agree," said Nick.

The terrain ahead looked hilly and wild.

"The La Sal Mountains," I informed the others. "Further up, you can ski. Doubt if anyone comes this way, though."

A few miles further on, we climbed a steep hill. As we slowly rounded the bend and came near to the summit, a barrier flanked by a guard box blocked the road. Andrew stopped, and then quickly backed up.

"This must be it. Hopefully, no-one saw us. Let's skirt further round by foot and see what lies beyond that ridge."

He backed down the hill and, about a hundred yards further on, we could see a small gap leading through the trees.

"Let's try in here."

Andrew edged the jeep between trees, finding a natural way into the forest, and made passage between trees until shielded from view. We set off on foot, keeping roughly parallel to the roadside. After a few minutes, a vehicle approached, so we moved deeper behind the tree-line. Two army trucks and a people carrier with tinted windows swept by, bearing an 'A-R' logo.

"Shit. That looked serious," I said.

"You noticed the 'Arm-Rite' logo?" asked Nick. "They're basically mercenaries. Ex-marines and security types. I guess some executive order allows them to operate on US soil."

"We recently discussed that," said Andrew. "Let's try and get over the ridge."

The guard box was close now, so we pushed further back into the trees and then struck off in a wide arc. Ahead was a rock outcrop and the sound of voices from the box gradually became muffled as we climbed the ridge. From here, the camp was spread out below, behind two high wire fences and complete with watchtowers. It included a variety of buildings – new and old. Detainees moved around in the grounds, though seemed outnumbered by the armed guards. The trees had been cut back from the perimeter on three sides of the camp, revealing a track, but, at the far end, the ground was still wooded and appeared to drop sharply away. After a few minutes, we observed as a jeep drove slowly around the perimeter, parked and then waited for a period before returning.

"And Nina's stuck in there," said Nick, shaking his head.

I perched on a nearby rock and wondered what kind of people were inside. Perhaps they were also innocent, but what might they expect from mercenary contractors? It all brought recollections of Guantanamo, Abhu Graib and the network of black CIA prisons. In fact, the only things missing were hobbled captives in the infamous orange boiler suits.

"What now?" I asked.

"I don't know," replied Andrew.

"Let's work our way down to the far end," said Nick. "The trees come closer to the fence there. Maybe we can get a better view."

"Bad idea. How do we know they don't also patrol outside? I mean, if they really think the inmates are dangerous, security will be high."

Nick nodded.

"True, but I don't see an alternative."

We picked our way through trees and boulders to another outcrop of rock half way around and then watched the camp for movements. After about a quarter of an hour, a jeep swept the perimeter again, stopping a few minutes before slowly returning. We waited about forty minutes and saw the pattern repeat twice.

It was now late morning and more detainees wandered in the open exercise area between the watchtowers. The camp could potentially hold a large number, but currently appeared to have limited inmates. Below, we saw what were probably dormitory blocks and other buildings with unknown functions – including a smoking chimney. The thoughts that engendered were, hopefully, ridiculous, but rather chilling. We sat in silence until finally Nick spoke.

"All that is missing are the swastikas."

"Let's not get carried away," said Andrew. "The system obviously thinks it's under threat and, with terrorist attacks both here and

Europe, who can argue? It's still the home of the free – well, notionally anyway."

The jeep patrol returned, and afterwards we gradually moved towards the camp's far end. The ground here sloped sharply away and the brush came close to the outer fence. So far, we hadn't seen an outside foot patrol and the regular jeep run should have about another eight or nine minutes until its next transit. Everyone crawled further around, staying low and keeping behind the brush. The slope here was actually more acute than expected, and I had to lie on my stomach, clutching clumps of grass and small shrubs as we inched our way around. I glanced at Nick, and his sweat-soaked face grimaced back. The soil here was bone dry and finding a foothold proved difficult. On the other side of the fence, a small number of exercising detainees moved in our direction. At first, it wasn't clear, but, as they came closer, Nick muttered, unable to contain his excitement.

"Look," he hissed, "that's her. That's Nina."

"Are you sure?" I whispered.

"Yes."

"I'd like to wave," said Nick, "but…"

I grabbed at Nick's arm, but simultaneously lost my footing, and started sliding face down the steep bank. I scraped my nose, and stones scratched my arms as I hurtled down the slope. My foot then hit something immovable and I slewed violently, and started rolling. I felt excruciating pain, a flash behind my eyes and everything went blank.

The sensation was like opening my eyes underwater, without goggles. Blurry shapes came in and out of focus to finally coalesce into the sight of boots on orange soil. My head throbbed, and then I remembered taking that tumble. Strange, I didn't remember either Andrew or Simon wearing big lace-up boots. The ground was very dry and I smelt the dust. I tried to turn my head to look up, but a sharp pain gripped the back of my neck. Hands hooked under my arms, pulling me up.

"Thanks," I said looking up to thank them.

A suntanned, square-jawed, stubbly face stared back.

"Sorry, who are…?"

Another man dressed in fatigues stepped forward, to take my other arm. He had an Arm-Rite logo on his chest.

"You're coming for another little hike, buddy. Don't worry, we'll soon have your friends."

More hands grabbed at me and I was dragged back up the hillside.

I guessed I must have passed out again as I was pushed onto a bed. I grabbed at the bedding, trying to see my assailant, but the pain in my neck was eclipsed by a light behind my eyes.

A voice said:

"Someone'll be 'round later, buddy."

The door clanged and everything went black.

63

UTAH

ANDREW ALTON

I watched in horror as Robbie slid down, helplessly grasping at clumps of dry grass. He picked up speed and, as his right leg buckled, he rolled and collided with a boulder. We watched him lie there, quiet and immobile.

"Shit, we'd better get down to him!" said Nick. "I only said that *I'd like* to wave. Of course I wasn't going to, but the idiot grabbed at my arm!"

"I saw it," I replied. "Let's go further on, where it isn't so steep."

We worked our way across, holding onto the stems of bushes, and keeping as close to the ground as possible. It became less steep and should soon be possible to pick our way down to Robbie.

Voices came from lower down, and we scrambled to hide behind a nearby tree.

"Look," I whispered, and pointed to a small group of Arm-Rite guards advancing towards Rob.

"Shit. So, there are outside patrols!"

We watched as five guards reached Robbie. Crouching low, we moved on behind a screen of bushes, and watched as he was pulled to his feet and dragged away.

"Let's work out what to do later. No sense in us all ending up inside."

"Right," agreed Nick.

"Did they only find Robbie because he fell, or somehow know we're here?"

"Good question. Another one is, what's our quickest way out of here?"

"If they do know we're here, the last thing they'd expect is for us to head their way."

"Have you banged your head, too?"

"I meant shadow alongside – out of sight!"

Nick shook his head.

"That's crazy. Falling into the path of a routine patrol might have just been bad luck – or maybe not. Perhaps there's electronic surveillance around the camp. I mean, that isn't unlikely."

"I agree," I replied. "And whether electronic or video, the sooner we're away the better. Let's move further down, and then curve back around the hill to the jeep."

We stayed crouching low, moving down the hillside, dodging behind trees – slipping, sliding, jumping over fallen branches and rocks. Voices came from behind. We sped up, skidding down the hillside. When I judged it time to head for the jeep, I dug my heel in and veered left. Fear sucked energy from my body, and my legs felt heavy and spongy. Nick struggled to keep up. Oddly, for just a moment, the memory of my interrogation in London seemed strangely more real than this brightly lit hillside in Utah. More sounds came from behind, but the ache of a stitch in my side didn't even match the 'trapped in treacle' sensation in my legs. I eventually arrived back at the jeep, dove in and started the engine even before Nick closed his door. I reversed, grazing the jeep on a boulder behind and, with wheels spinning in the sandy soil, spun it around to face the road.

"Let's hit it back to Carl's!"

"And say what about Rob?" asked Nick.

"Ask me another…!"

6 4

PHILADELPHIA

GILL'S PERSPECTIVE

Gill felt uncertain quite how Judy would receive her, so the French-style kiss to her cheek was quite a relief. Judy seemed without rancour over the part she'd played in Andy's earlier problems. She therefore decided to simply level with her just why she'd invited herself for another stay. Judy was philosophical.

"So, they want you listening out for news of the boys. I suppose it's no more than I'd expect. They really are sweeties, aren't they? Thank goodness you're with us now."

They talked together over the lunch preparation.

"Thanks for being so understanding. Do be careful when contacting the boys, though. My office knows they're in the Moab area and tracking communications is very sophisticated now!"

Judy's face dropped.

"What's wrong?"

"What you just said. An accident happened with the cell phone Andy gave me. It slipped into the bath! He tried to make contact and eventually had to use the land-line. I later bought a replacement phone, but…"

"Calling from… you know?"

"No, he'd visited Freddy and it was difficult. He'd just finished, wanted to talk and knew his visit would please me."

Of course, I knew most of this from the conversation with Freison.

"So that's how they know the boys are in the Moab area. They'll now have a confirmation of coordinates from close to Freddy's place. Did either of you mention any plans to locate the camp?"

"No."

"I'll file a something and nothing report later this evening."

"Actually, Gill, I wanted to mention this evening."

"Yes."

"Remember Freddy's friend, Zoltan,"

"He's still here?"

"Yes. The thing is… well, he's invited me to a concert tonight. He's actually a rather lovely man and, well, explaining that we're friends, to Andy… felt rather awkward."

I recalled him exiting Judy's bedroom.

"I see. Well, he is rather hunky."

"Just a little!"

She remembered Freison's briefing. Simon's boss's mother, unknowingly, with someone possibly linked to the militia movement. It all seemed far from her usual routine.

About an hour later, Zoltan arrived home. His expression was briefly guarded, though he quickly recovered and shook her hand warmly.

"Gill, I didn't realise you were coming."

"Judy offered another stay. As I've pretty well finished in New York and didn't see much last time, it seemed a good idea. To be honest, New York was getting overwhelming and I wanted to be here for when the boys get back. Simon finishes in San Francisco soon, and will join us."

"Great, isn't it, Zolt?" said Judy, smiling.

"Absolutely," he replied, with a grin.

She caught an almost imperceptible quaver that any untrained person would miss.

"About this evening, Judy?"

"Yes, it turns out that we're both classical music lovers. Kissin is in town – Bach, Mozart and Schubert. Missing that would be such a waste."

"I understand, although I'm more an Andreas Schiff girl."

"You like classical music?"

"Of course."

"Help yourself tonight," said Judy, pointing to the music-laden shelves. "I'd ask you to join us, but I already know it's sold out."

"Don't worry, I'll be comfortable here."

She returned to her room, two rooms from where Zoltan slept. She smiled, *at least, where he was supposed to sleep!* Their earlier nocturnal encounter on the landing hadn't been mentioned.

That evening, she felt some pangs of loneliness, watching from her room as they walked away hand in hand. If only Simon was here! She left her room and stood a moment outside Zoltan's door. Could he be more than they knew? Despite the decision to eventually resign, she couldn't just overlook the possibility of infiltration. His bedroom door was locked so she retrieved picks from her room. The lock turned, but the door still wouldn't budge. He'd obviously used secondary wedging. But how did he re-enter – and how could she? She'd have to keep cool, because any sign would show her hand.

Returning to her room, she forwarded a brief encrypted report. Half an hour later, a worrying message arrived. *The 'travellers' have found their target and the little fag is now held inside.* From the language, she reckoned this was from the loathsome Jack Holt. The message ended, *Please report on Mrs A's reaction and plans, and about the house guest – whatever that takes!*

She could almost see his leer.

Her cell phone rang. It was Simon. An anxious voice described the events leading to his unexpected stay in the Mission district with Frank Rossi.

"At least I'll get to spend more time with Frank. He's such a fascinating guy! Tomorrow, I'm taking time off the conference to interview Dr Gianavecci."

"Who?"

"The psychoanalyst that I wanted to interview in New York. He's here, too."

"Be careful, Si. I'm so looking forward to seeing you!"

She put the phone down, kicked off her shoes and replayed the conversation from a listener's perspective. To anyone monitoring, she was obviously just continuing the surveillance. Of course, what she'd really wanted to say to Simon was, *Get the hell out. Dario is absolutely right and you're in danger!*

She knew their practice of sweeping up known troublemakers ahead of protests. It rather sounded as if Si had been marked and she remembered Freison's comment. If anything did happen, there'd be little assistance from the UK government. They were on board and probably trying out similar techniques. Damn, there was no way of warning him, it all felt so frustrating. Given all of the institutional paranoia, her communications might well be monitored. She remembered Michelle at the office, carefully sounding her out. Over several discussions, Michelle hinted that a few selected agents were unhappy with the extent of domestic spying. Michelle had wondered if the same was true in England.

Given that either Simon or the others could need future help, she resolved then and there to seek Michelle out, on her return to New York.

65

SAN FRANCISCO

SIMON MAHER

I awoke to sunlight streaming into the room. The Mexican décor gave the room an unexpected lift. I blinked, searching for something familiar, and then the previous evening returned in a rush. I groaned, climbed out of bed and looked out over a small back garden and a blue sky. There seemed no trace of last evening's fog. Still, they said it rarely reaches this far. I remembered last night's call to Gill, wondering why she sounded so reticent? Something wasn't quite right!

Noises came from next door, interrupting my thoughts. Probably Dario and Melosa getting dressed – or something! *How did he get away with it?* I'd have thought Latino parents would be particularly strict. Maybe this communal thing had more benefits than I'd realised!

I breakfasted in the kitchen with Dario, though Melosa had disappeared. The younger children, Solana and Paloma, chattered happily as Elisa brought more and more food. Next, Frank arrived and then Esteban joined us, sitting down heavily and leaning his elbows on the large wooden table.

"What are you going to do now, my friend?"

The bushy moustache bounced with each word and his eyes twinkled.

Frank looked up and grinned.

"Be careful how you answer. He's trying to marry off Melosa!"

I recalled the creaking bed, but decided against it.

"Actually, I have a meeting on Nob Hill, so I'm skipping this morning's session at the conference."

"I haven't been up there in ages," said Esteban, spooning in another mouthful.

"I plan joining the 'Water rights are human rights' march later, Frank, but I certainly don't want those people on my tail again!"

I was hit by a disconcerting possibility.

"Heck! I just remembered something. My girlfriend called last night and I mentioned my interview with the doctor later today. If the call was intercepted..."

Frank looked up from his plate.

"What's with this Doc guy?"

I outlined the project and the people we hoped to meet.

"So, you think corporate bosses with psychopathic traits can introduce similar behaviours into their business? I guess that figures," agreed Frank.

"Possibly. Politics, policies and services get infected in the same way!"

"Like the way that sadists in the military can cripple new recruits," said Frank.

I nodded.

"There are several folk in the Bay Area I hope to see. Dr Gianavecci is a psychoanalyst and acknowledged expert on personality disorders. We had a problem linking up in New York, but he also had business here, so we rescheduled."

"A happy coincidence."

"He sounds quite a rarity, Frank. An analyst also versed in social psychology who connects his material to the wider social, economic and political matters. I'm certainly keen to hear what he has to say!"

Esteban laughed aloud, shaking his head.

"I think these types of men are often crazies and just like to complicate things. I say keep life simple."

"You could be right," I replied, "but the meeting's been arranged."

"If this Doc normally practices in New York City, would the spooks even know where he is in San Francisco?" asked Frank.

"Good point. We're meeting at the Rupert Centre for Psycho-political Research. Incidentally, Frank, they publish some excellent stuff that exposes the underlying frames and assumptions of right-wing propaganda."

"It's my field – remember! It's a two-edged sword, though, because you can do exactly the same exercise with left-wing propaganda. Maybe you could change your venue, to throw anyone interested off the scent. The Pacific Union Club, for example?"

"But I can't very well say, 'by the way, Dr Gianavecci, if we meet at the Rupert Centre, we might get interrupted by security goons and then later show up on "no-fly" or watch lists!' I'll just have to chance it."

The venue was a fairly short taxi ride and I felt thankful that Elisa insisted on me staying tonight. We stopped high up on California Street and the views went right across the city to the blue waters of the bay. No wonder it was popular with the well-heeled.

I entered an impressive lobby and asked for Dr Gianavecci, wondering if he could add much about psychopathy to what I'd already heard from Dr Farrelly. A humourless older woman with severe black-framed glasses escorted me to a beautifully furnished room and a dapper little man with a crimson bow-tie. He rose, offering his hand.

"Good morning. I'm Alberto Gianavecci. I understand you're part of a research team exploring the issue of psychopathic disorder in business."

"Thank you, Doctor Gianavecci – yes, exactly!"

"Alberto will do fine. I know we analysts have a reputation for strict formality, but we aren't in session and you aren't a patient."

"Thanks. I'm not really sure where to start?"

The little man sat ramrod straight in one of the well-upholstered chairs.

"I assume you're familiar with the basic features of the anti-social personality?"

Gianavecci wasn't threatening, but I had difficulty with analysts – apparently common with lay people. *Would I be transparent to the analyst's gaze?*

"Well, having read parts of the DSM, I've a basic overview. The psychopaths' capacity to lie, cheat, manipulate and their lack of remorse, for example."

"Ah, the behavioural descriptions so loved by psychiatry. Are you familiar with the psychoanalytic model, though?"

I shook my head.

"The fact they lie so well indicates a degree of psychological integra-tion in their 'self–structure'. Sadly, this is generally anchored around the 'primitive grandiose self' from the narcissistic period, serving the pleasure principle."

I nodded, playing for time, as he continued.

"Unhappily, this type of 'self' is often infiltrated by primitive and aggressive impulses. Many psychopaths aren't just parasitic and exploitative, but also sadistic, and can't authentically invest in others or take in love. It's almost as though others are just objects, or represent food to them."

I swallowed. This wasn't quite what I'd expected.

"Sorry, represent food? You mean that other people are... well, like a commodity to be used?"

"Exactly. Very good! You find this trait throughout psychopathic behaviour. A spectrum from sadistic killer – to small-time con-man, right up to the glib, charming, but utterly ruthless politician or business leader. Typically, they merely use others."

I nodded understanding. This was getting interesting.

"Ted Bundy or, in your country, the fascinating case of Dennis Nielsen, fit the public's image of psychopaths, but these are just the extreme manifestations. To better understand, you also need to consider the other dimensions."

"Sorry – the other dimensions?"

"Yes. Superego pathology and object relations."

I shook my head. Surely, Gianavecci was deliberately being obscure now?

"You mean 'object relations' is a psychoanalytic term? I thought you just said psychopaths relate to others as objects?"

Gianavecci smiled.

"I'm afraid our terminology is sometimes rather unfortunate – a case in point! Think of subject and object in grammar. We mean, does this person have the ability to relate to others, or the 'object', in depth – or do they only think of themselves?"

I nodded understanding.

"With psychopaths, there's always lack of concern for others. Little awareness that the other has their own wishes and needs. Others are like masturbatory fantasies, used just to fulfil the psychopath's needs. Remember, we not only mean outward behaviour, but also how others figure in the psychopath's mind and feelings."

"I see. Certain politicians, bankers and business leaders come to mind! And the superego thing?"

"You probably know the 'superego' is the mental structure, roughly corresponding to 'conscience' and, in psychopaths, is seriously compromised. There's no moral responsibility, little or no capacity for guilt, only pervasive dishonesty, lack of concern and responsibility."

"Sounds the ideal equipment for the captains of laissez-faire capitalism, then!"

Gianavecci frowned, and shook his head.

"Don't jump to conclusions. There are many ethical business people and some fine business philanthropists. In fact, this building is from such a person. But, yes, late finance-capitalism or, as some call it, casino capitalism does benefit such types. Ruthless, greedy behaviour is lauded by shareholders, the media, politicians and brings massive financial rewards. In that particular, our friends from behavioural psychology are right – rewarded behaviour expands, whether appropriate or not."

There was no other sound but a ticking clock and I suddenly felt cold.

"Maybe that's how it gets perpetuated? Clever psychopaths rise to power and then shape the system to their own advantage?"

Gianavecci stroked the side of his face, and looked deep in thought.

"An excellent thought, Mr Maher, which deserves proper consideration."

"Thanks, though I can't really take the credit. A forensic psychiatrist I know suggested something similar. He also thought that certain politicians and media owners can be similarly afflicted?"

"Increasingly, they come from the same small pool, represent the same interests and employ similar approaches. I mean, lying, deception, coercion, dishonesty and fear."

"So, what distinguishes a violent psychopath and, say, the higher functioning characters in the political or business arenas?"

Gianavecci paused, stroking his bow-tie.

"Both have compromised superegos and a limited capacity for object relations, but violent criminals also have primitive aggression filtering into their 'self-structure'. In many ways, though, in their superficiality and empty inner worlds, they are frighteningly similar. How else can the power elites running things ruin the planet or let half the world starve?"

I now felt distinctly odd myself. Discussing a violent psychopath in the same breath as a slippery MP, Senator or Congressman seemed extreme. Surely, Gianavecci must be overplaying it?

He sensed my concerns.

"You have to be selective. There are fine politicians and also many committed business people. It's also about the inner reality of those seeking power over others – not their behaviour alone. What kind of psychology is required to negotiate away the jobs of thousands, while lining your own pockets? Or crafting policies that will decimate other economies and the lives of people in far-away lands – just to profit yourself and your cronies? What kind of psyche deceives employees and effectively steals their pensions? What mindset sets lobbyists to facilitate price gouging for pharmaceutical corporations or war profiteers?"

"But surely," I asked, feeling increasingly uneasy, "there are good, committed politicians?"

The little man's eyes twinkled.

"Yes, I already agreed that! Undoubtedly, there are shining beacons, though, sadly, many who start with high ideals get corrupted – bagged by lobbyists or misled by those especially glib sociopaths who often fill think-tanks, and fashion their quasi philosophies to justify inequality and greed. To anyone informed, such ideas show a limited psychological development – though, unfortunately, many are fooled. I'm sure you've heard the arguments. Tax cuts for the super wealthy will benefit the poor by 'trickle down'. Or deliberately manipulating fundamentalists by pushing ideas that God blesses by giving wealth, while poverty is his punishment."

"They say that?"

"Yes, and more. Much of it showing the sociopathic trademarks of superficiality and lack of empathy."

"How pervasive is this?"

"You have to question the environment created in an administration, when even a head of state is persuaded to accept what we now think were fabricated or distorted 'facts' like 'The Gulf of Tonkin incident', that can indirectly lead to slaughter. Or information suggesting that advance knowledge of the Pearl Harbour attack may have been deliberately withheld – or that the attacks on Hiroshima and Nagasaki went ahead despite the Japanese wish to surrender."

"Really?"

"It's not certain, but some say so. Many things are uncomfortable to contemplate. One of your most revered leaders, Winston Churchill, once said, 'I can't understand the squeamishness about using poisonous gas against uncivilised tribes.'"

Gianavecci went to a bookcase, and returned with a leather-bound volume. He searched inside, then read aloud:

I do not admit that a great wrong has been done to the Red Indians of America or the black people of Australia... by the fact that a stronger race, a higher grade race has come in and taken its place.

"Again, Churchill's words."

Gianavecci replaced the book and sat down.

"How should the governed understand such unqualified glorification?"

I shook my head.

"I don't know."

"Sadly, the public thinks of a Ted Bundy or Jeffrey Dahmer, but can't see the prevalence of sociopathy in high places... for example in war."

"Now you use sociopathy. I thought we were discussing psychopathy."

"We're talking severe personality disorders," replied Gianavecci.

"Meaning what?"

"Pathological patterns of thought, attitudes, beliefs and behaviour that endure for a lifetime, and are structured into the personality. Patterns that are now well recognised, whether they are termed 'antisocial personality disorder', 'sociopathy' or the older and more pejorative term, 'psychopathy'. There are various other personality disorders."

Gianavecci shook his head and now had the bit between his teeth.

"Some distinctions remain useful. By psychopaths, we often mean stone cold, remorseless predators. The sociopath may have major holes in their conscience or are under socialised. They are often fatherless or have been treated cruelly. A true psychopath seems qualitatively different – almost as if born different. Genetic factors, abnormal amounts of neuro-chemicals or brain abnormalities can also be relevant, particularly involving the frontal lobes."

"I see."

"I recommend your project also consider the effects of secondary psychopathy also."

Farrelly had said the same.

"In other words, where ordinary people end up replicating pathological attitudes because of environmental pressures."

"For example?"

"Out of touch politicians who push welfare cuts that actually fund tax cuts for the wealthy, or bank bailouts that end up in bonus-payouts. Subsequently, the everyday people, the clerks and administrators tasked to run 'cut-down' services and justify heartless policies, can eventually start mirroring the attitudes of the politicians and policy makers. They have to, to survive! Their masters use job insecurity, intensive supervision, privatisation, outsourcing and bring in outside management consultants. They build systems that will only attract emotionally autistic staff, or those desperate enough to defend the dirty work – even to themselves! Similar situations exist in the private sector."

Gianavecci had started giving examples from the current corporate environment, when the door knocked. The pinched-faced woman entered and passed him a message. Gianavecci shook his head.

"Sorry, Simon. I've a patient in crisis in New York and must make some urgent calls."

He reached into a briefcase and pulled out a diary.

"I'm here for two more days. If you wish, we could finish the discussion late afternoon Friday. I was about to say where I think lobbying fits into your idea."

The appointment was made and Gianavecci followed the woman from the room.

I found my own way out, replaying the discussion. So, this wonderful building came courtesy of a business benefactor. Gianavecci was right – indiscriminately demonising the business community would be foolish and only weaken our case. The material must be fair and balanced.

Walking over to the edge of the hill, I looked over the city and then back to Coit Tower and Fisherman's Wharf. Suddenly, I envied tourists their playtime. Perhaps I could take the afternoon off and join the water demo, later? I hailed a cab for the Mission, deciding that, after the slog with Gianavecci, searching out those murals was rather appealing. I'd get a cab to the Civic Centre and join the demonstration later. A camera was a must for the murals, though, so I returned to Esteban's. Elisa answered the door, but looked pale, not her usual ebullient self. She seemed lost for words, but I'd stepped over the threshold before seeing the men waiting in the front room. I immediately recognised one as 'Crew-cut' from the previous evening.

"Welcome to the West Coast," said the eldest – a grizzled military type with hard eyes. He waved a badge at me, reading *Jeff Mason, FBI*.

My heart thundered.

"Who's he?" I asked, nodding at 'Crew-cut'.

"We ask the questions, Mr Maher, and you give the answers. However, on this occasion, I'll tell you my colleague here is Vincent Berry from the Arm-Rite Corporation. I'm not at liberty to introduce my other colleague, but you might know that the security agencies now cooperate closely."

Nothing really made sense. The character who'd followed me came from the mercenary group that Andy mentioned in our phone call. In the daylight, he appeared a powerfully built, square-jawed individual with a pasty complexion. A plaster covered the left side of his forehead. Berry then moved forward, sticking his face close, giving off a foul whiff of halitosis.

"Your buddy, the other night, will regret it."

I stepped back sharply, before addressing Mason.

"Why let a private corporation harass an overseas visitor? What happened to civil liberties?"

"Don't be ridiculous, Maher. Private corporations have helped for years, including in the 'war on terror'. You should be more temperate, my friend. You could soon find yourself Arm-Rite's guest."

"I'm not your friend and stuff Arm-Rite because I plan flying out in a few days. Anyway, why are you in a private home? These are good hospitable people."

Mason shook his head.

"The 'good people', as you put it, have links with the Zapatista group and likely connections to Colombian narco-terrorists."

He grinned and continued.

"They also like hosting troublemakers. As for flying out, you'll probably be on a 'no-fly' list."

"So, I attend a conference, which is critical of certain policies and the excesses of corporate power, and I'm suddenly some sort of terrorist?"

The third man spoke for the first time. He had a swarthy appearance and a rumbling voice that came from his boots.

"You can call me Mr Woods. We already know that here, and also in your own country, you tried undermining the business affairs of a US and a US/French corporation. Then you associated with someone under investigation for connections to terrorist actions in Latin America – and also someone currently detained for the same reason.

We've also talked with your friend, Mr Rob James, who told us of your busy times together in New York."

"Talked with James? What do you mean?"

I felt my composure crumbling, but Woods remained inscrutable. The deep voice continued.

"Yes, James. The pretty boy who previously worked with the company you tried to undermine. The company run by your boss, Andrew Alton's, father."

I felt lost for words. If only Frank and Dario would return and help me escape – but I knew the idea was born of desperation. Anyway, they'd still be at the conference hall, and would then march to the Civic Centre. I should be with them!

"Time to go, Mr Maher," said Mason.

"The Presidio or the Island?" asked Berry.

"Island," replied Woods.

Mason and Berry advanced towards me and I knew resistance would be futile. Moments later, I was wedged between them as Berry drove the big Chrysler. I felt helpless. The Island – what island? Not Alcatraz, surely? No, that once housed criminals and closed years ago. Excursion boats visited every day!

The car left the Mission, went through the Castro, and clipped the edge of Haight-Ashbury before turning right along Oak Street. We entered the artery of Market Street, to the financial district, and finally turned to the quayside. Ahead, the sparkling water of the Bay faced Oakland and the immense span of the Bay Bridge. How I yearned again to be a simple tourist. Berry drove to the waterside, close to where the Sausalito ferries departed. Further on, we climbed down some stone steps and joined a waiting motorboat.

"Is it too much to ask where we're going?" I asked.

"Sure," replied Woods pointing to the Bay Bridge.

It certainly was impressive. I'd read it spans eight miles. The first section rested on a small island.

"We're viewing the bridge?" I asked sarcastically. "How about a tour of the bay?"

"No, my friend. We're taking you for a little rest on Yerba Buena Island. You've been such a busy boy!"

The boat roared away and soon the bridge soared overhead. I could see that it did indeed rest on a little island. The boat started rocking in the wake of a passing freighter, as it navigated to the far side of the island. We stopped at a deserted naval station and the boat tied up. I looked back towards the city and the Embarcadero. A lone seagull was hovering above. It squawked forlornly, banked and disappeared. Only moments ago, I'd been yards from the conference and like-minded friends. Now there was just the unknown! Light slanted down onto the city and, in any other circumstances, the view over to the finance district and the famous hills would have been particularly special. Further round, I saw the Golden Gate silhouette and Alcatraz in the foreground.

Mason and Woods clearly knew their way, though we were quickly joined by three naval ratings. The group entered through the now deserted naval station, passed through a gateway and then took a rocky path further around the island. Ahead was a rocky bluff but, as we came closer, I saw a tunnel like a devouring mouth leading to a subterranean complex.

"Where are we?" I asked, though I needn't have bothered, because no-one spoke or answered!

66

UTAH

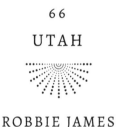

ROBBIE JAMES

I dabbed my face on a small towel. After New York, the extreme dry heat here seemed overwhelming. The initial processing in the camp had been quite cursory – marched to the stores, a tape passed around me and then a regulation dark blue trousers and top issued. I was then escorted down a long corridor to a tiny suite, with a bed, table, chair and a small unit with drawers. An even smaller L-shaped area contained a basin and toilet. Before I could ask, the escort muttered, "You'll get food soon," turned the key and left.

I rolled up my trousers to inspect my knee. The tumble down the bank certainly was violent and I saw the blue tinges of what would surely later be a spectacular bruise below my knee. Muscles in my right leg had been pulled – in fact, my whole back ached. I gently sat on the unyielding bed and pulled my legs up to lie down, but, as I lowered myself, a tightly packed wave of pain shot up my body, causing a flash behind my eyes.

Noises came from outside. A key rattled in the lock and a guard entered with a tray – hamburger, fries, cola and an apple.

"When do I see someone?"

"Can't say. I'm just bringing food. The regular guy for this gallery is sick today."

The door closed and I started to eat, though it was lukewarm and unappetising. The cola, presumably an unknown cheap brand, had an oddly dark flavour and bitter after-taste. I put it back on the table and carefully swung my legs back onto the bed.

I looked around. The room was small and had a smooth, plastic sort of appearance. The surfaces were curved, and without protrusions of any kind. High on the back wall, a small rectangular window let in daylight. On impulse, I got up and balanced on the mattress to tap the window. As I expected, it was some kind of thick plastic material. The set-up reminded me of a documentary I'd seen about a unit for disturbed adolescents. That had similar plastic windows, and curved surfaces with nowhere to tie a fixing. As my lace-up shoes had also been taken and replaced with 'slip-ons' – I presumed they expected suicides or self-harm. I lay down again, but my head throbbed. I shifted around, trying to avoid the pain, and eventually slipped into a troubled sleep.

When I woke, the room looked darker and the light was failing. I must have slept for hours! The bitter taste lingered and I wondered if the cola had been drugged. I teetered on the threshold, drifting in and out of sleep, but, when I fully woke up, the light seemed stronger and brighter. How could that be, because, only a short while ago, day was giving way to evening?

The key turned and a guard carried in a small tray with an egg muffin and coffee.

"Eat and wash," he said. "I'll be back in about 20 minutes to take you for your first interview."

I still couldn't understand how time had moved backwards.

"What time is it, please?"

The man looked at his watch.

"Nearly 9.30."

"In the evening?"

"Of course not. It's 9.30 on Thursday morning."

The guard abruptly left. So, I'd been out of it for most of yesterday afternoon and all night. Something was in that cola – I had no doubt about it. I suspiciously eyed the coffee, though it smelled fairly normal. I took a small sip – it tasted okay and I was thirsty. I heard more foot-steps and then the key turned. Two guards stood in the doorway and one beckoned, so I followed them down the corridor and stood by the exit. One fumbled with keys attached to his body with a lanyard. When the door eventually opened, I was momentarily blinded with the brightness. I followed the first guard and the other positioned himself behind me, although, with two enormous wire fences encircling the enclosure, his caution seemed rather superfluous. In any case, the outer fence had been festooned with looped barbed wire and, beyond, stood several large watchtowers.

We crossed over to another long and low building. Other similarly dressed detainees stood around outside, talking. The lead guard unlocked a door and we proceeded down a passageway, knocked at the third door and entered. At the far end of the room, three men were behind a desk. I was motioned to sit. The first appeared powerfully built, with a swarthy complexion and an unusually deep voice.

"Good morning, Mr James. I'm Mr Woods, from an agency with an interest in your activities. On my right is Mr Dick Riley from the Arm-Rite Corporation. Arm-rite provide housekeeping and security at Camp Ute. On my left is Dr Farrow, one of our psychological specialists."

I looked at the three. Woods, in particular, appeared inscrutable. Riley wore a dark uniform and had a mean, pinched, rat-like face. Farrow wore a white coat and the deep pan of his forehead suggested that he was the brains of the trio. They remained silent – almost compelling me to speak first.

"Why have I been brought here?"

No answer.

"I was out hiking and stumbled across this place. Actually, stumbled is the correct word because I slipped down a bank while walking around the perimeter. What is this place and why am I here?"

Eventually Woods spoke.

"As I told your friend, we ask the questions."

A wave of anxiety hit me. *Nick and Andrew hadn't been caught too? Maybe it was just a try on!*

The one called Dr Farrow cleared his throat and smiled.

"Mr James... Robbie, we know this must be difficult for you and we'd like you to be treated well. You only need to be cooperative."

I nodded, quietly pinching my leg, willing myself to be careful and not reveal anything important.

"How exactly did you come to be hiking around the camp's perimeter?" asked Riley.

"I'm here on a break from the city. I know the general area from years ago. I was out driving and decided to try a new track for a change."

"Yes, yes, all very convincing," said Woods. "Why then did you bring the English guy and Dr Alton?"

"I… I, well they… I don't know what you mean."

"You think we're stupid? I'll ask again, why are you here?"

Dr Farrow gave a smile that said – *Trust me. I only want to help.*

"Cooperation, really would be in your interest, you know!"

"We… I wanted to search for petroglyphs, because I'm interested. I know of some beauties further west, near the Maze, and thought it might be worth looking here. The Indians might have found cooler air in the hills. You'll know what I mean if you've seen the Mesa Verde ruins. Ever been there?"

"You're here to give answers, not pose questions," said Woods. "You said 'we'. … we wanted to find petroglyphs. Who does 'we' include?"

"I told you, I once lived in the area. My friends must have scooted off after I fell and you picked me up."

"Did you enjoy your journey here with Dr Alton and Mr Martin? Of course, you've seen rather a lot of Mr Nick Martin in recent months, haven't you?"

"I know him, if that's what you mean. I ought to. Our respective companies have been jointly involved in a project, so we saw each other frequently."

I pinched my leg, trying to keep focused.

"Of course you did. No doubt that explains why you travelled in a car together for several days. Obviously, the ideal setting for business discussions! I suppose we should gloss over the fact that you'd already been dismissed from your employment. Shall we put it down to 'devotion beyond the call of duty'?"

It felt like running up to an abyss with no way of stopping. His words echoed around my head.

"Why not just tell the truth?" said Farrow.

"What authority do you have pressuring me like this?"

Riley looked at Woods, shaking his head.

"What have we here? James, you'd better believe that we have authority to do whatever is necessary. Pack in with the ridiculous questions!"

Woods leaned forward.

"Your friend, Mr Martin, has outstanding issues relating to terrorist activities in South America – as does his girlfriend. In such circumstances, do you have any idea of the scope of our powers?"

I shook my head, feeling sick, wondering if I'd soon find out, but the inquisition abruptly stopped.

"That's all for now, Mr James. We'll talk again soon."

Woods must have activated an unseen buzzer, because the guards re-entered almost immediately.

My head was so full as I crossed the enclosure that I almost forgot to look for Nina. I couldn't see her, but – nevertheless – I looked about the grounds to familiarise myself with the layout. The building containing my room was actually quite close to the main entrance, but making a dash for the gate would be hopeless. The lead guard fumbled for his key and, at that moment, the inner gate opened to admit a black Lexus. As the guard engaged the key and moved it around, I watched the vehicle slow just inside the gate. My guts lurched as I shaded my eyes to help me see more clearly. I felt sure I saw a familiar figure beside the driver. I closed my eyes, and opened them wide again. I could swear that I'd just seen Brian Tutch! The Lexus moved off, heading towards what I assumed would be the main administration building. A guard's hand pressed against my back and, when I turned, the door was open.

"Hurry up, man. There'll be plenty of time for dreaming, later…"

67

UTAH

ANDREW ALTON

I sped down the hill, to rejoin the road leading back to La Sal Junction. I checked the mirror, but saw nothing follow behind. Nick pressed his face to the window, looking upwards.

"Are you thinking what I'm thinking?"

"Probably! I wondered about a helicopter?"

"Me too. I also wondered if they'd found our vehicle and tagged it with a device. Although, to be honest, I only just thought of that!"

"Gallo was quite right then," said Nick.

"What, that the bozos running these places can detain anyone found outside."

"Surely there must be a different response for some innocent hiker to someone trying to stage a breakout?"

"I suppose so," replied Nick. "Gallo was perfectly clear they'd be hard-line over security. I looked on the internet and people have been squawking about these places for a while. Even after skimming off stuff from loonies and conspiracy nuts, there's certainly enough to worry about."

We reached the junction. I turned right towards Moab, and put my foot down.

"Like what?" I asked.

"Interrogation methods, for example. Some very tough things happened off US soil. Might the same happen domestically?"

"Like what, exactly?"

"I don't know. Keep positive. No sense in torturing yourself."

I heard a small gasp.

"Sorry. An unfortunate choice of words!"

Traffic was light and, after several miles, I pulled into the shade of a large overhanging bluff.

"We need a plan. What to say to Carl and Myleen, for a start."

Nick shrugged. "I've been pondering that, all the drive."

"I suppose we could say we were searching for old Indian sites, and came across a concealed military facility. Robbie got lost, and then was picked up and hauled in for questioning. Can't think what else we can say."

"Carl is his cousin, though," replied Nick. "He mightn't just sit back. He struck me as a bit of an action man!"

"I know."

We continued in silence and then pulled into Carl's drive, refining our story until startled by a tap on the rear window. I turned to see Myleen's smiling face and wound the window down.

"Hi boys – had a good day? I bet Rob's still browsing in that book-shop? He was always one for the books."

I swallowed, thinking these are country folk, with no inkling of terrorism laws or the current threat to activists. I opened the car door.

"Not actually the bookshop, Myleen. I'm afraid there's been a little problem."

Concern spread over her good-natured face.

"Come on in. I'll get you boys a coffee and pie, and you can explain."

We followed her in and gave an edited version.

"Heck, boys, Carl won't be real pleased. He's out with a photography group and should be back in about two hours. I'll get youse more to eat while you wait."

She bustled off to the kitchen.

"I must get Freddy's jeep back soon," I said. "In fact, I might as well head over there now. He'll probably get one of the sales guys to run me back."

"You don't think we'll need it anymore?"

"We know the way now. The roads aren't that bad, so we can take our own. Why, you want more excitement?"

"Funny," replied Nick. "I'll wait for Carl, but now we'll need a plan both for Nina and Robbie."

Myleen reappeared with sandwiches and small talk. She really seemed a helpful, friendly girl and I felt awkward eating again, only to quickly leave.

I drove to Freddy's dealership, pausing outside to compose myself. It was too hot to sit for long and it didn't help that I had absolutely no idea what to do next. Several customers were browsing inside, and staff were busy hanging banners and razzmatazz for a new promotion. The pretty gum-chewing girl was on reception again and showed me down to Freddy's office. Freddy sat behind an oversized desk. Framed sales awards lined his walls and it all seemed designed to impress. Fred really was a 'chip off the old block'. He looked up, with an almost genuine grin.

"Hi, Big Bro! Good to see you again! Take the weight off and tell me how you got on?"

"The 'great outdoors' was invigorating!"

"And those Indian scratchings, petrocliff things... find any?"

"Petroglyphs... not exactly. I unexpectedly found some other things, though."

"What... a mountain lion?"

I felt trapped, tense and with almost non-existent options. Freddy grinned again, and I made a sudden and possibly rash decision.

"No, I saw something that looked rather like a military facility – out by the La Sal Mountains."

"Oh that – yeah."

"What do you mean, 'Oh that'?"

"Yeah, I know. East at La Sal Junction, go way down and then head into the mountains. I believe that some folk with Japanese backgrounds were interred there in the war. I'm not sure. So, you didn't find them petro – what did you call 'em? – in the hills?"

"Petroglyphs. No, it's more a case of what we lost!"

"Shit, the jeep went off a track?"

"No, it's outside, and thanks again. Incidentally, there is a little scratch that I'll pay for. No, it's rather more complicated."

Freddy's eyebrows arched and, in that moment, his cold blue eyes resembled Dad.

"You remember, I came down with friends? The thing is that, when we stumbled across that camp place, it seemed quite intriguing, so we decided to take a hike around the perimeter and see it properly. Anyway, a friend, Robbie, Robbie James, got unlucky and slipped down a bank at the bottom end. It turned out goons were outside patrolling. They picked him up and now are holding him!"

Freddy put his feet on up the desk and leaned back.

"And you can't just turn up and demand him back, right?"

"Exactly."

"As it happens, I do know a bit about that place."

Freddy walked to the window. He looked out into the yard, clicking his tongue.

"When you visited the other day, two guys called Terry James and Lee Damson turned up. Do you remember?"

"Yes. I believe you said they came from Montana, and were trading classic car parts."

"Right. They had parts for someone in town and other stuff for an old guy out in the mountains who specialises in restoring classic Caddies and Buicks. Anyway, the old guy mentioned the camp place, on a previous trip."

Freddy turned around and stared intently.

"I'm going to tell you something else, Bro, but you have to keep it close and quiet. Do you understand?"

"Okay."

"I have another connection with those guys."

Freddy paused, before speaking with unusual intensity.

"We're dedicated patriots."

"Sorry? Don't quite get you."

"Our government is corrupt and on the take. I don't just mean propping up the Wall Street scum – I also mean taking our liberties and guns. With the extended rulings about eminent domain, they can already grab properties – almost everything!"

I understood that, generally, Freddy's interests didn't much extend beyond new car models, so this outburst seemed more than a little surprising. Eminent domain – the legal power to take over property, if the authorities demonstrated that increased employment and tax revenues would result. I felt amazed that Freddy was even aware of the controversial rulings. In fact, it was the most serious I'd ever seen him. Most things were either jokey or concerned business.

"Sorry Fred – how exactly are you patriots?"

"Only patriots can protect our freedoms now. I'm talking about the militia movement. Terry and Lee are with the brothers in Montana and I serve here. Liberties have been eroding for ages. That camp is a threat and just one of many. You see, the Federal Government is in bed with the bankers and probably the United Nations. Eventually, they'll declare martial law!"

I didn't know whether to laugh or keep a straight face. In league with the UN – hardly! What a hoot! Little brother Freddy, the car salesman, spouting conspiracy theories. What I did know, though, was that this wasn't the time for debunking or alienating him.

"The militia, huh? To be honest, Fred, I don't know much about it."

"I have plenty of material at home I can show you. Many outfits have been around a real long time and they have their ears to the ground in most states. In fact, they know more about what's going on than almost anyone. See, the Federal Government has sold out and we must be ready. They're preparing more camps like that, but you won't read about it in the media. That's owned by big business – just like the government."

I was almost glad to be sitting down. Hearing Fred lament the corporate-owned media was so unlikely, it almost seemed hysterical – like finding myself in a parallel universe!

"I thought you were like Dad and all for big business?!"

A triumphant grin stole over Freddy's face.

"Actually, Dad is quite a big supporter."

"Yeah, I know he's helped you out a few times."

"Of our movement."

"Sorry? Dad supports the militia?"

Freddy had a daft grin plastered all over his face.

The situation was getting ever weirder. Dad was undoubtedly a racist, and had sympathies with the extreme right, but he wasn't stupid. What could be in it for him?

"You really got me there, Freddy. I'm amazed! Supporting the militia? I always thought that was more of a rural thing?"

"It's an everywhere thing, Andy. Like I said, we must be prepared, but Dad can be generous."

Fred's words reverberated. Dad contributed to these cowboys – why?

Freddy sat up, his grin fading.

"What do you mean, 'generous'?"

"I guess it isn't for me to discuss Dad's business."

It was too late. Freddy had now clearly moved on. His face assumed a rare and improbably serious expression.

"So, how are you gonna get your buddy out?"

"Exactly! I suppose I shouldn't have involved you, and don't want to put anyone at risk, but I don't really know anyone else down here."

"Which motel are you staying in?"

"No, we're with a guy called Carl Willets – Robbie's cousin. He lives just out of town, on the Monticello road."

An odd expression passed over Freddy's face.

"Do you know him?"

"Yeah, we once had a little run in… an argument over a jeep. That's not it, though."

Freddy perched on the edge of his big desk, shaking his head thoughtfully.

"What then?"

"Something kind of struck me when you said the name Robbie James."

I nodded, puzzled.

"Well, Terry, Terry James you met a few days back, is related to Carl Willets. Carl is his nephew. Terry knows Carl and I don't get on, but keeps in touch, anyway! I've only known Terry a short while, but he did once mention having a son called Robbie… not very enthusiastically, as it happens!"

My cogs were now spinning. Robbie mentioned the militia movement during the drive down and apparently had big problems with his father. Come to think of it, Robbie seemed rather odd when I'd mentioned Terry after the near collision.

"You're wondering if Terry and Robbie could be father and son?"

"With the Carl connection, I'd say it's a near certainty!"

"Sounds possible," I replied. "Might that help?"

"Dunno. Terry hates anything the Federal Government does with a vengeance. I tell you what, Bro, he'll arrive home soon. I'll contact him tonight and fill him in. Let's talk again tomorrow and see where it's all at?"

"Thanks Fred. I do have another worry, though. We believe the authorities can and do monitor communications of anyone arousing their interest. You know, with your militia thing…?"

Freddy grinned.

"Don't worry, that's all covered. Zoltan's my friend, remember!"

There was a knock and the gum-chewing secretary came in. She bent down to Freddy, whispering something with a practised intimacy that I found rather worrying. Still, if Freddy was foolish enough to play away from home, that was his business.

He abruptly stood up.

"Sorry. A problem with a difficult customer that needs immediate attention. Gotta go, so call me early tomorrow. I'll have spoken with Terry and I'll fill you in."

I drove back, with Freddy's comment about Zoltan Heltay still reverberating. *Surveillance wouldn't be a problem because Zoltan was his friend! What did he mean?* The light was fading and, deep in thought, I almost missed Carl's turning. The house lights were on and Carl's jeep stood in the drive. I wondered how Nick had explained Rob's capture and put the Zoltan mystery out of my mind.

I entered with trepidation, but the atmosphere seemed surprisingly light. Nick and Carl drank beer and Myleen, was, as usual, busy with food. Carl held up a bottle, and beckoned.

"How did it go? I assume Robbie stayed with your brother for the evening?"

Clearly Nick had waited for my return. I shot him a questioning look.

"Andy, I haven't explained about Robbie yet. I thought it best to wait, so we could talk it all through together."

"What do you mean?" asked Carl, looking quite unconcerned.

"Grab another beer, Carl. There's been a problem, I'm afraid. Rob has been detained."

"Shit. What's he done now? This ain't no liberal area. I thought that's why he'd moved up East!"

"No, nothing like that... it's more a case of being in the wrong place at the wrong time."

Myleen brought food in and we sketched in the bare bones of the development for Carl.

I expected a knee-jerk response – storming the gate with a crowd or something equally stupid, but Carl seemed unexpectedly thoughtful.

"Actually, I do know 'bout the place, but was sworn to secrecy and haven't told no-one, not even Myleen. This could get very serious."

"How do you mean, 'sworn to secrecy'? Is this generally known about?"

"Yes and no. Old-timers might remember the internment of Japanese-Americans on the same site. A few might also know a small caretaker staff visited periodically. Few would know that it's now opened again, though."

"Say more.'

"I've a buddy, Craig Thomas, who works for the security people."

"The Arm-Rite Corporation?" asked Nick.

"Yeah, that's right. Apparently, they shipped their whole workforce in for security reasons, but some fell overboard and had to be replaced. Craig went through all kinds of hush-hush security checks and signed, what was that thing… closure contract? I think it was called."

"Probably, a non-disclosure agreement," I replied. "Obviously, he didn't take it seriously with you though!"

Carl chuckled.

"Craig and I go way back. We've been best buddies all our lives, but I did take it seriously, and haven't mentioned it, until tonight."

"Could Craig help? Maybe getting messages to Robbie?"

"Don't forget Nina," Nick added.

"I dunno," replied Carl. "Depends how safe it would be? I mean, generally speaking, he'd do anything to help me."

Carl grinned and then started chuckling.

"See, as kids, we was both handfuls. When we was reported for joyriding for the third time, they never realised who it was who actually drove. Craig got away with it and no-one found out. He owes me big time, though he'd probably help anyway."

"Really?"

"We can soon find out. I'll call by after we've eaten."

A superb aroma heralded Myleen's southern fried chicken with collard greens, sweet-corn and banana fritters. I was half way through, when my cell phone rang. Freddy was on the line and I took the call in the hall.

"Hi Bro! The parcel we discussed arrives tomorrow. Suggest you call by at around 3pm."

"Will do. Thanks – looking forward to it."

So, Terry really was Rob's father and had agreed to return tomorrow. Now, there was just the little matter of explaining all this to Carl and Nick…!

68

PHILADELPHIA

JUDY ALTON'S PERSPECTIVE

After being lonely for so long, Judy could hardly believe someone so right was, not only in her life, but actually under her roof. Attraction to Zoltan came quickly, but realising it could be more had sneaked up. In fact, it was only now that she could admit it to herself, let alone to friends. The happiness was only marred by realising that, with their age difference, the bubble must surely burst. With the others away in Utah, at least they could be open again and she'd preferred honesty.

They sat together, discussing her developing adoption by Philadelphia's activist community. Typically, Zoltan was attentive and also well informed about the issues. He sat on the floor in front of her, supported by her knees, and massaged her feet.

"Sounds as if you've located groups addressing most of the big issues," he said. "What about dissidents and political prisoners?"

"Don't be so silly, Zolt – we're not the former Soviet Union!"

"I meant international groups, like Amnesty International. Anyway, don't be so sure, because some things are getting to look familiar. Maybe we don't like opening our minds to that."

"Ridiculous."

"Think about it, though. Activist groups infiltrated by intelligence, public spaces placed out of bounds – protesters penned up in spaces laughably called 'free speech' zones – and the stupid law enforcement doesn't seem to see the irony! The population routinely spied on, and who knows how often that leads to full surveillance? How do you know those meetings you attend aren't infiltrated by some or other government agency?"

Judy sighed.

"I don't. How do we know who anyone is? Maybe you're a government agent!"

He grinned.

"Hardly! You didn't answer. Do you think anyone..."

Her cell phone rang. She picked up, expecting Estelle from 'Water Justice'. Instead, it was Andrew. He spoke quickly, updating her about Robbie's capture.

"How awful for him. Are you and Nick safe? Please be careful, Andy. Strangely enough, Zoltan and I were just discussing freedoms. He thinks they're disappearing – the freedoms, I mean. Little did we know people are disappearing as well!"

Andy's voice suddenly became muffled and she tapped the phone with her palm. Before replacing it, she heard Andy whisper "...can you be overheard?"

"I'm not sure. Why?"

His voice was now almost inaudible, and she could only distinguish a few words – "Has Fred mentioned... has he... said about Melissa's?"

"I can't hear you, son. The phone is cutting in and out. Speak louder!"

His voice returned at normal volume.

"Mom, I need to speak to you when you're completely alone and can't be overheard! If I call back later, can you arrange that? If you can be overheard now, just signal a time, without giving the game away."

"Oh Andy, I'm afraid the line is going odd again! Okay, I'll search on the internet. It'll probably take a couple of hours – you know what I'm like. Speak later, and please be careful."

She replaced the receiver and Zoltan looked over questioningly. She felt so thankful for having his support – particularly now.

"I gather it was Andy. Why so worried?"

She explained the developments and watched him register the news. He held her hand while she talked.

"Such an odd coincidence? You'd only just mentioned the support of dissidents and I laughed at you! Now we learn that Robbie's been detained. I can hardly believe it! Maybe we don't know everything about Nina, but Robbie's a real newcomer to all this – such a nice young man. So, he didn't like Biff's ethics, but that doesn't make him an extremist. I really hope the boys stop poking around now."

"What else did Andy say?"

"Not much. The line was really odd and I couldn't properly hear. Andy mentioned a girl's name and something about her possessions. Patricia's or Melissa's – something like that. I don't really know what he was on about?"

"You mentioned an internet search?"

"Yes. Apparently, they've problems with the GPS. He wondered if there could be helpful FAQs."

A puzzling development! Being evasive with him didn't make sense. Zolt knew they were in Utah, and he was the only other person here. Perhaps Melissa was someone in the UK, and Andy was awaiting information? Zoltan wrapped his arms around her, and she leant into him as he stroked her back.

"Remind me to give you another session on the internet."

"Thanks. Poor Robbie! Whatever can we do to help?'

"I don't know. This is just what I meant earlier. The 'thought police' have arrived – even while we preach freedom and democracy to everyone else!"

"I wish Gill would soon get back."

"Yes, she'll be back soon," he replied. "Look love, when Andy called I was about to say I've a job on the other side of town. Probably take about three or four hours – maybe a little longer. Listen, try not to worry. Maybe, we could go down to Utah later and see if we can help?"

As she looked into his eyes, she felt flushed with warmth. How wonderful and supportive he was!

Zoltan left. She tried music, but concentration was difficult. Andy said he'd call back soon, and was clearly worried that someone could listen. What if the house had been bugged?

It felt a little over the top, but she decided to take the call outside – just in case. She rooted around in the kitchen drawer, having put the spare shed key here, after the second copy turned up again. Her hand felt around bulbs, buttons and oddments of cutlery until she located the right shape. It had been a surprising find, because she genuinely thought Zolt had the only copy, but this was the only other key with the distinctive triangular top. After the moving chaos, mislaying it was understandable.

Outside was pleasantly warm, though no doubt it would be fiercely hot in Moab. She bent down to enjoy the scent of pinks on the path to the shed. If only Andy was definitely safe and Robbie back with the others, things would almost be perfect!

As she unlocked the shed, her cell phone rang. Andy's voice sounded uncharacteristically brittle.

"Mom, are you alone?"

"Yes, love. Zoltan's out on business. I couldn't hear properly earlier. What was it you asked?"

For the first time since Zoltan came, she looked around the shed and then sat herself on a crate.

"Okay, Mom, this will sound weird. Hopefully, the pay-as-you-go phones will give some protection, although anyone listening in will already know this. You see, Freddy lent us a rugged jeep with GPS. After Robbie's problem, I returned it to him. You may even be pleased by this, but I was so shaken over Robbie that I decided to share the bare bones of what had happened with Fred."

"I'm so glad you're talking again."

"I know, but here's the thing. Freddy already knew about the... you know, place... because, wait for it, he's apparently part of a local militia unit! They're legal, but take a real interest in what the government gets up to."

"I'm amazed, Andy. I thought, other than business and his off-road-ing, that Freddy had few other interests."

"Yes, but, that's not all. He also hinted, no virtually said, that someone that we both know supports them, too!"

"Now you really have shaken me. As you know, that person does nothing for nothing!"

Even thinking of Biff made her tense.

"Incredible, isn't it? Anyway, I'd only just taken that on board when sunshine boy put two and two together, and realised that a militia member he's acquainted with in another state was none other than Robbie's actual father!"

"Good Lord!"

"He's now told the guy about his son. Given the militia link and our need for discretion, I warned him to please be aware of possible surveillance. Here's the thing, he made the strangest reply, saying 'don't worry, because Zoltan is a friend'. It was as if their communications would be secure because of help from Zoltan!"

"Well, don't forget that Zolt is an ITC expert and also Freddy's friend. I think these folk go in for soldier games on weekends, but otherwise don't harm anyone."

"But why would... you know who, help them? What could they possibly have in common? Mom, I'm thinking about your safety. I know Zoltan seems a good guy, and our kind of person, but..."

"Hang on, Andy, I just realised something. When you called a couple of hours back, you whispered something that I couldn't quite hear. It sounded like you were whispering a girl's name who had something you wanted. I thought you said Patricia's or Melissa's, but I now realise..."

Andrew cut in.

"That what I said was 'militias'. Yes, I hope you didn't tell him?"

"Well, no... though he was here when you called and could see from my reaction that something important was said. He asked, and I described our rather strange conversation. I told him that you'd asked something about a woman – but the line was bad. Sorry, Andy, I just didn't get it."

"I understand. Where is he now?"

"On a job on the other side of town."

"Doing what, I wonder? Have you seen or heard anything that even hints at the militia thing?"

"No, nothing at all. He just does his IT work. As a matter of fact, I'm out in the shed, sitting on boxes of his equipment, right now."

"What?"

"I let him store some equipment. There are several crates of materials and a large old suitcase. I gave him what, at the time, I thought was the only shed key, but I found the duplicate a couple of days back."

"What's in the boxes?"

"I haven't a clue, Andy. Computer parts or communication equipment, I suppose."

"Have a look."

She crossed the floor to the suitcase and ran her hands over it. The case had a harness contraption, so it could be either carried by hand or as a backpack. It had an unyielding layer under a soft exterior, which, judging from the weight, was probably metal, and an unusual out-sized lock. Maybe it belonged to his parents and originated in Hungary? She went over to the crates, pulling at the lids, but they were sealed and nailed shut.

"Nothing to see, Andy. The crates are locked or sealed tight."

Light suddenly entered the shed, and she was flooded with adrenaline.

"What are you doing, Judy – can I help?"

Crouched over boxes, she hadn't heard anyone approach. Her heart thumped so hard, she felt dizzy and blood roared in her ears – she barely recognised the voice. She brushed her hair back, before turning.

"I arrived back early."

Her shock was tempered by relief, but also shame. Gill smiled quizzically.

"Sorry, you startled me."

Tampering with someone else's property seemed almost unforgivable. Her mom would have been horrified. A faint squawking noise came from the floor. It was her cell phone and she quickly picked up.

"Mom, Mom, Mom... are you okay? Please answer!"

"Sorry, Andy, Gill just got back from New York and surprised me. Regarding your other question, no – nothing to see."

"Okay Mom, bear in mind what I said and be careful. I'm seeing sunshine boy later today. I'll stay in touch."

"Judy, could I have a quick word with Andy?"

She passed the phone.

"Andy, Gill here... Hi to you, too... No, she'll put me in the picture in a moment. Listen, have you heard from Simon? ... Oh really...? Yes, I'm worried. Apparently, he was tailed and said that several conference attendees had been pre-emptively arrested... Yes, exactly, in advance of demonstrations... No, he didn't say, but since he's been silent and doesn't pick up... Okay, talk again soon."

Judy felt anxious. Andy and Nick in danger. Robbie arrested, and now Simon had gone off the map. She said her goodbyes to Andy and returned to the house. Gill's expression increased the foreboding.

"Damn, I so hoped Andy might know something. I didn't want to worry him about Simon. Believe me, I do see the irony that it was me, of all people, telling him!"

Judy nodded.

"How did it go in New York?"

"Okay, I guess. I've pretty well finished my work and negotiated a few days leave with London. You know what? I'm tempted to try and find Si. I fancy San Francisco and we could certainly use some time together."

"Couldn't showing too much interest give the game away? I should talk, though, because I'm thinking of going to Utah! Not that there's a great deal I can do."

Gill seemed preoccupied.

"Actually, something unexpected happened today. A little while back, I discovered a local colleague who was uneasy about the degree of domestic surveillance. She sounded me out today – for the third time! At first, I stayed fairly non-committal. I even wondered if I was being tested."

"I wouldn't be surprised."

"This colleague wondered that, apart from constructing vast data banks, what actually happens to the data from the domestic surveillance programme. I said that some at home wondered the same thing. I mean, why dossiers on political activists and academics?"

Judy listened intently. Friends asked a similar question, as had she and Zoltan earlier today!

"Anyway, I lunched with this colleague. She'd heard various rumours, even the very unlikely idea that an element in the intel community itself may have turned rogue, and might misuse the material to persuade key figures."

"You mean blackmail?"

"If you drop the fancy names – I guess so, yes. Powerful figures – politicians and so on – could be targets."

"Blackmailing what?" Judy asked.

"Anything from financial irregularities and kickbacks, to sexual behaviour."

"Sounds murky."

"It would be! She even implied that work supposedly abandoned might be resurrected."

"Like what?"

"I don't know for sure. Look, perhaps I shouldn't say more. I only hope she's wrong. I'm certainly looking forward to the West Coast though and seeing Si!"

6 9

MANHATTAN

BIFF ANSON'S PERSPECTIVE

Biff finished lunching in his office as usual and then crossed to the window to look down. Rain beat against the glass as he watched the tiny figures below fight a mainly losing battle with a vicious wind that hurtled down the streets. Nancy phoned and, a few moments later, showed in the wet and bedraggled Brian Tutch.

"I bet the Utah weather was a bit different?"

Tutch's white-blond hair appeared soaked, but his face was deeply tanned.

"Sure was. It's baking!"

"What else is cooking down there?"

Tutch sat heavily in a leather chair and then stretched before speaking.

"Mostly going to plan. The Arm-Rite arrangement is working fine. Incidentally, Dick Riley will keep us briefed on our little friend, Rob James! Arm-Rite themselves are certainly sitting pretty. A juicy contract will probably extend to other facilities."

"After our little investment, they should be cooperative," replied Biff. "I always tell my people – pull the money string and everything else follows! I knew in my bones that this domestic detention thing would develop into a growth industry."

"True," Tutch agreed. "Like Colombia – the sky's the limit!"

"Did you warn Freddy? I don't like the idea of Andrew and Co. poking around?"

"Apparently, they borrowed one of his jeeps for their little outing. When Andrew returned it, he revealed Rob James' capture to Fred."

"Hope the boy keeps quiet about our other business. Fred can be a little slow sometimes!"

"Nah. He's reliable."

"More kit is available for Columbia, despite the 'final' truces."

"When are you thinking?"

"Dunno, Brian. Soon, I hope, but there are complications. Canvey's guy, Nick Martin, has been caught up in this Utah fiasco. As he's crucial to the Bogotá office opening, we may have to wait a short while."

"And Zoltan? Are you bringing him in on it? When I spoke with him outside Philly, he was a bit antsy."

"Zoltan's okay, Brian. He's already forwarded me useful information, but, yeah, we'll bring him in. I told him, if he plays his cards right, there'll be big money – but no details yet."

"But will he cooperate?"

"That's another reason why I wanted to see you. Visit him and make a small investment. Ask him – and put $50k in his hand to help with expenses. My instincts are usually right!"

Tutch departed, and Biff returned to the window. The view stretched over mid-town and Central Park, to the top of Manhattan with the East River on the right and the Hudson to the left.

He dialled out.

"Jack Klieberman, please."

Fifteen minutes later, he'd arranged a second line of surveillance in Philadelphia. He smiled and rubbed his hands together. *Perfect. Total information awareness.* He grinned. *Well, if the government can try it, why not me?*

He called Nancy.

"Get Mark Finkelstein in."

Moments later, Robbie James's replacement entered. There'd be no 'bleeding-heart' nonsense this time – he'd ensured that.

"Mark, chase up Canvey and find out when Nick Martin returns from his vacation. I want to speed up the opening of the Bogotá centre. His vacation may need shortening! Brian will visit Bogotá soon to check on progress."

UTAH

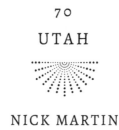

NICK MARTIN

I looked up and down Moab's main street, enjoying some alone time, at last. Carl and Myleen were undoubtedly decent, hospitable people, but, after New York, the country way of life felt so limited. Sure, the outdoor activities seemed great, but the shallows of the cultural life made me breathless! Anyway, I'd felt uncomfortably attracted to Myleen and, although I'd never act on it, it wasn't appropriate for a guest. It must be that redhead thing again!

I mooched about, checking out the local shops and, after finding a general store, stocked up on food, chocolate, two torches and water, and stowed it in the car's trunk. Further along the street, I found a bookshop – presumably the one Myleen mentioned. I wandered in and the elderly assistant gave the customary 'Hi'. Their selection was surprisingly wide, so I looked for publications about the local area. Tucked next to coffee table books on the nearby National Parks and the Colorado plateau, I found a small section on local history and geography – which included several self-published books. I flicked through a chapter outlining the history of mining, confirming much of what Carl had said. Apparently, many tracks originated from several waves of prospecting, although those had mostly petered out after the uranium explorations of the 1950s. I picked up an older publication with yellowing pages, concentrating on South East Utah's history. It said that, though Moab was founded in the late 1800s, it didn't really gain much in size until the uranium boom. Further on in the book, a wartime photo took my eye. The section was discussing the internment of Japanese-Americans – something I'd only vaguely known about, but a black and white image appeared strangely familiar. The text described a camp in the desert South West that hosted several hundred internees – mainly from the South West, but included an overflow contingent from San Francisco.

I looked at the photo again and, underneath, another – from the air this time. Although in black and white, it also looked familiar. My heart sped as I studied them more closely – the curve of the ridge, the watch-towers and mountains behind. Undoubtedly, this showed the camp near the La Sal Mountains – now named 'Camp Ute', and currently home to both Nina and Robbie. The gateway was now bigger, but, apart from several new buildings, much seemed the same. The aerial shot showed the road from Monticello and the smaller road leading up to the main gate. At the far end, I could see where Robbie had taken a tumble. Below that was another small road or track. In fact, networks of tracks extended all over the area.

"Can I help?"

I hadn't noticed the storekeeper approach. The voice sounded old and he startled me.

"Hi. You've quite a range. This interested me, on internment during the war, because I want to write a piece on that."

"Ah yes. Them Japs was wicked monkeys. Did terrible things to our boys in the Pacific."

"So I believe, although the internees were already citizens here. I'm from the UK and we did the same with people of German background."

"They're all the same and it served 'em right. Them Japs was on the wrong side, yet, until recently, they were the ones ending up with a miracle economy!"

"The camp place, is it still here?"

"Oh yeah, it'll still be here. I believe they had a small maintenance gang visit occasionally, just in case. If there's trouble and they pour over the border, we'll need to put 'em somewhere!"

The old man began to laugh, his bony shoulders keeping time with the wheezes.

"These little roads here… are they still open?"

"Yeah. See, that whole patch around the camp is part of the State

Forest. They take good care of the roads and tracks – 'cos it's regulations. In any case, the forests are pretty well opened to logging companies now. They probably keep 'em directly away from the Camp, though."

"So those tracks here on this aerial photo would probably still be open?"

"Yeah, I'd bet on it."

"I'll take the book, thanks."

"Okay. We have large-scale maps by the counter."

I left the bookshop with the book and a map. Dismissing unwholesome thoughts about Myleen, I drove off, but stopped almost immediately to cool off with an ice-cream. I slurped noisily, trying to prevent the top-heavy ice-cream sliding onto the map. The camp was unnamed on the map and discretely termed a military reservation, but the spider's web of tracks could be seen throughout the forest. Might there be alternative ways in and out?

I got back before Carl and Andrew. Myleen was, of course, busy in the kitchen and the rich glossy auburn hair tumbled over her shoulders. I showed her the book and map, trying to keep my mind on the matter in hand.

"I found that bookshop you mentioned."

"Oh, that's good. How about I fix something? You must be hungry?"

The front door slammed and Andrew and Carl entered, looking rather pleased.

"Hi guys. I found something in town that might just help. If I'm right, we could approach the camp from the other side."

"Good," replied Andrew. "We have news, too."

A phone rang and Myleen brought it in.

"You left this in the lounge, Nick," she said leaning over and passing the handset. Her auburn hair fell from her shoulder, almost brushing my cheek. For one tantalising moment, the well-proportioned breasts were at eye level.

"Is that you, Nick?" came the familiar voice of Tom Phelan.

"Yes, Tom. I'm on vacation."

"I know and I'm sorry," he replied. "Thing is, Nick, we're having very strong pressures from Biff Anson. Dan says you must shorten your time away. They want you opening the Colombian office as soon as possible. I'm afraid I can only manage for you to be out for four more days."

"Shit, Tom! That really isn't on. I mean, what if I had a parent die, or something?"

"Nick, Nick, you know better than that! We're talking about Dan Farlin, so it wouldn't make a scrap of difference. Looking forward to seeing you soon!"

71

SAN FRANCISCO

GILL'S PERSPECTIVE

Gill finished packing, thankful that Freison and Matacic accepted she could finish for now in Philadelphia. Zoltan was now back, and she'd only managed a quick glimpse inside his room. Finding a copy of the Koran proved absolutely nothing. As he'd stubbornly remained in, she couldn't even check the shed, so it would have to wait until after her return. London agreed, so she'd negotiated time in San Francisco until the others returned from Utah.

"Of course, we'll expect your final report to include descriptions of operations on the West Coast," said Hennessy.

What a surprise!

From the air, the views were astounding, although the baked golden landscapes of central California actually came as quite a surprise. She passed through San Francisco's airport with little effort and, apart from the pressures to upgrade, the car hire was as painless as Judy had predicted. She flew down the freeway from the airport until reaching the exit to Cow Palace stadium. Suddenly, the road filled with sports fans, hooting and weaving between lanes. The car ahead slowed and a skinny teenager mooned into his rear window. She gunned the accelerator and quickly lost them.

The towers of the city centre appeared, but she had little idea of where or how to start the search for Si. Maybe the discussions with Michelle from the New York office would pay off. Following quiet exchanges on the increased public surveillance and the potential dangers of whistleblowing, Michelle had passed details of a friend and San Francisco agent, Fiona McBain. Michelle was quite definite that Fiona had similar views and would be certain to help, if necessary.

Reaching the city centre exit, Gill immediately saw a sign for the conference centre. She made a snap decision to start there and, if necessary, leave contacting Fiona until later. Parking was available close to the venue, but she couldn't resist a quick walk in the sunshine to the waterside. She watched ferries crossing to Tiburon and Sausolita, and tourist boats in the bay. Maybe, after finding Simon, they'd take a boat trip. The huge Bay Bridge came quite close here, and she could see that it rested on a small island, and continued on to Oakland. The water looked an inviting deep blue, but she'd read it was dangerous and never warmed. She turned back towards the city and the ferry building – a centrepiece to the hills spreading out behind. The guide she skimmed on the flight had warned about the Bay's dangers and also said that the ferry building's tower had been modelled on the 'La Giralda' bell tower of Seville Cathedral.

She left the sunshine and hurried back to the conference centre. Although the final day, a fair crowd was still in attendance. After purchasing a day ticket, she found an assistant eager to help.

"Yes, I do know Frank Rossi. He's doing a seminar in the Wells Fargo room. Starts in about fifteen minutes."

Gill scanned the faces in the lobby. Earnest middle-aged people, latter-day hippies, environmental types and youngsters with nose jewellery and provocative t-shirts. A few months ago, she'd have classed them as potential troublemakers, but, now, she felt the warmth of kindred feeling. Perhaps it was being in love? Whatever, she certainly didn't want to remain with the 'cold warriors'.

She found the Wells Fargo room. The seminar wasn't due to start for twelve minutes and, other than a large bearded man fiddling with a digital projector, the room was empty. She approached him, though he didn't look up.

"Are you Frank Rossi?"

"I certainly hope so, otherwise a phoney will be taking my seminar. Who's asking?"

The man stood up and turned around. She found herself looking into a strong face, with blue eyes, freckles and curly brown hair.

"Are you joining the seminar?"

"Not exactly. I mean, I'd like to, but I need to ask you something."

"I do a Q&A section towards the end."

"It's personal. Look, I believe you know Simon Maher?"

The man gave nothing away.

"I'm his girlfriend. It's a long story, but we're very close."

He stared intently.

"The thing is, I just got in from the East Coast. Simon and I have been in regular phone contact, but now he seems to have disappeared. The last time we spoke, he mentioned being followed and said he was now with you and trying to keep a low profile."

Rossi nodded.

"Yeah, he mentioned you. I'm sorry, but the news isn't great!"

"Why? Do you know where he is?"

The audience were filing into the room. A woman from admin approached to check if things were ready. Rossi asked for a jug of water and a glass. He turned back, with a concerned expression.

"I'm Frank. Simon may have told you that a few attendees involved with various spin-off demo's, got arrested? Generally, it's been the usual harassment, but several have well... kind of 'disappeared'."

She knew only too well what he meant.

"Look, I have to start in a couple of minutes, but I do know that Simon has been grabbed by the authorities. If you try and interfere, you'll get into plenty of hot water."

He looked around. The room was now almost full and already people were standing at the back.

"If you want to join us, I can talk when this is done."

"Thanks, Mr Rossi, but..."

"As I said, it's Frank."

"Thanks, Frank, but I feel I need to do something more active."

Rossi paused, and then scribbled on a piece of paper.

"Look, we stayed with friends called Esteban and Elisa, in the Mission District. They made Simon welcome, but then the authorities arrived and took him, which is bad news, too, for the family. Perhaps they'll remember something they didn't tell me. This note asks them to help all they can. I'll return about 6.30 this evening, so we can talk again then. Sorry, but I have to start now."

She shook his hand. The paper had an address and a message almost certainly in Spanish.

She left the conference centre with a knotted stomach, and returned to the waterfront. Despite Rossi's news, the bay sparkled and the view to the far shore looked even more attractive. Further around, a container ship headed towards the Golden Gate and the open sea. She sighed at the beauty. If only they could be together, sharing the experience.

She decided to try the Mission address before contacting Fiona. Returning to the car, she fiddled with the hire company's free map and tried to trace a route around the one-way systems. She set off, grateful for the air con, because the steepness led to an unintended 'white-knuckle' ride. Maybe the circular route had been a foolish idea, even though it had passed many of those classic Victorian wooden houses.

Soon, she was thoroughly lost and pulled in to a local store for directions. A black woman customer took hold of the map before the assistant could even reply. The woman had a 'deep southern' accent, and stabbed at her map with a pointed finger.

"You is 'ere, honey. On dis road 'ere. Where you want?"

She repeated the address that Rossi had given.

"Dat's easy, sweetheart. Three blocks down Folsom. Den take a left, an' den you's there. Dis right 'ere is Potrero."

The assistant winked. Gill thanked the customer, bought a Hershey bar, and drove on to Garfield Square. She fixed her hair in the mirror, silently trying out various introductions. Latino children played in the street and looked her way. She knocked at the door of the wooden house and a pretty young girl opened the door.

"Is Mommy there?"

Almost immediately, a large Mexican woman came to the door.

"Can I help?"

"I'm looking for Elisa and Esteban Ecoves."

"My, another English person! Esteban, come!"

A paunchy Mexican with a huge moustache came to the front door and she quickly proffered Frank Rossi's note. He read for a moment, smiled broadly and pulled open the door.

"Come in, friend. I'm Esteban and this is my Elisa."

Gill followed them into a large kitchen, decked out with very bright tiles. Elisa motioned to a bench behind a large and well-worn table.

"So, you're Gill. Frank says you're the English girlfriend of Simon, the nice young man who stayed with us – before the trouble."

"Simon phoned me in Philadelphia and warned he might be in trouble. Could you please tell me exactly what happened?"

"Frank's a good friend," said Esteban. "He's helped our people and many others through his work and teaching. Frank always stays with us when he's in town."

She nodded, fascinated at Esteban's moustache bobbing up and down as he spoke.

"Frank brought your friend back a couple of nights ago. Apparently, several people had already been snatched. Simon met Frank and a friend for a drink, and they realised he was being followed. They kinda feared he might be next. Anyway, the next morning, he went off to see a doctor – something to do with his work. I think he was like a shrink, or something like that. We expected him at the end of the day."

"But he didn't return?"

"Late in the afternoon, three kinda spy-guys turned up."

"How did they explain themselves?"

"They didn't. They showed a badge, and told us they'd wait because we had a security suspect staying here. We argued, but they said we should shut up because we were known sympathisers with… what did they say, Elisa? 'Prescribing groups'?"

"Probably, 'proscribed groups'," said Gill.

"Yeah, something weird, like that."

"They mean prohibited organisations or terrorist groups."

"They should talk! All we've ever done is to support people fighting for their families, their livelihoods… sometimes even their lives!"

"So, what happened?"

"They hung about until Simon knocked at the door."

"That's all? Anything that might tell us where he is now?"

A pretty young woman had entered the kitchen moments earlier and drank a glass of fruit juice. Gill assumed she was another daughter.

"They discussed whether to go to the Island or the Presidio," said the girl.

"How do you know that, darling?" asked Elisa.

"I was sewing in the room off the hall and heard them."

"This is our daughter, Melosa," said Elisa.

She extended a hand to the pretty, sparkly-eyed girl.

"What does that mean? The Island or Presidio? I don't know San Francisco at all?"

"Dunno really," said Esteban. "I mean the Presidio is a big park – well, actually – a military reservation, though mostly open to the public, now."

"And headquarters to the US Sixth Army," said the girl. "There's also a military cemetery and museum."

Elisa, raised her substantial eyebrows.

"I didn't know we was so interested in the Army, baby."

The girl gave a pretty, liquid laugh.

"Of course I ain't, Mom, but one time school took us. Two houses from before the big earthquake got rebuilt there. We had local history, civics and stuff at school."

"Are military buildings there?" Gill asked.

"Seems Melosa knows more than me," said Esteban with a proud smile.

"What about 'the Island' – any ideas?"

They looked blank.

"There are several islands in the Bay," offered the girl. "I can get a map."

She returned with a map of Metropolitan San Francisco and the Bay Area, and everyone huddled over it.

"There's Angel Island," said Esteban, "which is like a State Park. I believe it had a POW camp in the war, but it's open to the public now, so that don't seem too likely."

"What about this one?" asked Gill pointing to the unlikely named 'Treasure Island'. "It says 'US Naval Station'?"

"Used to be," replied Esteban, "but that went a few years back. The developers moved in and built a marina. Then there's that little island under the Bay Bridge, attached to Treasure Island. His stubby finger pointed to Yerba Buena Island. Yeah, it seems connected."

"Treasure Island's man-made, from infill," said Melosa.

"The Navy have moved now."

"There's the Isla de los Alcatraces," said Elisa. "That's Spanish. Alcatraz means the island of the pelicans." Elisa shook her head, before continuing. "It had a famous old prison, Gill. Have you heard of it?"

"Yes... Machine Gun Kelly, Al Capone and other infamous characters. I thought that was closed years ago?"

"It was," said Melosa. "Though tourists can visit by boat."

"Sounds unlikely, then."

She knew they were genuinely unable to say more, but they were warm, friendly people. In her heart, she'd rather stay here, drinking coffee and listening to their melodious voices discussing San Francisco or Mexico. Searching around a strange city, with few clues, was daunting. In about four hours, Frank Rossi would return. He seemed knowledgeable and said he often came here.

Elisa seemed to read her mind.

"You're welcome to wait. Frank should be back early evening. Maybe he'll have more ideas. You can stay overnight, too, if you like."

Remembering the traffic and those hills, it was tempting.

"Thanks, Elisa. Yes, I'd like to come back this evening, but, for now, I think I have to discover more about the islands and Presidio."

She left Garfield Square, heading – she hoped – towards the Presidio, but soon became hopelessly lost. She pulled up and found her note with Fiona McBain's details – in her own writing, as Michelle had requested. Apparently, Security had two offices here, Burlingame near the airport and a down-town office in SOMA – the South of Market area, near the old US Mint. Apparently, Fiona was typically based there. She also had Fiona's home number and decided to try that first, knowing only too well the flexible hours worked by agents. After four rings, a woman's voice answered.

"Who's this?"

"Fiona?"

"Sorry, who are you?"

She smiled. Old habits die hard. Fiona would have inbuilt caution – it couldn't be otherwise.

"I'm Gill Marney from the UK. I think you might have heard of me? If possible, I'd like to talk."

"Where are you?"

"Totally lost in my car! As I pulled in, I saw a sign saying Dolores Street and I'd just crossed Twenty-Second Street."

"Good. Continue driving in the same direction. On the left between Seventeenth and Sixteenth streets, you'll see the Mission Dolores. It's an old Spanish building and there's a sign. Wait by the entrance. I'll be along in about fifteen minutes."

Fiona abruptly rang off.

She stopped at the Mission building and took up station by the entrance, watching the world go by. It was pleasant enough waiting in the sun, but she was soon joined by a rather handsome man, probably in his early forties. She noticed him steal several glances, before speaking.

"What did you think of it?"

"Yes, very impressive," she replied, hoping that he'd leave.

"Pity about those Indians. Who'd have thought measles could be so serious!"

"Yes. It's hard to imagine."

He didn't seem discouraged.

"Did you see the thickness of the walls?"

"Yes, but I'm from Europe. We're used to old buildings."

"Thought I recognised an accent. Can I buy you a drink?"

A tall athletic-looking brunette in her thirties approached them. Somehow, she knew that this would be Fiona.

"Kind of you, but I'm meeting somebody."

Fiona made her introductions and they left together, leaving the man looking seriously put out.

"Reckon I arrived just in time. If I'm not mistaken, that guy was trying to hit on you. We'll take your hire car up to Balmy Alley and talk."

Fiona gave directions and they ended up back quite near Elisa and Esteban's. It was clearly a major Latino centre, and awash with murals just like Si described. They walked on and Fiona pointed out shops that had Salvadorian, Nicaraguan and Mexican connections. They entered an attractive-looking coffee shop.

"You obviously know the area well."

"Yep. The service likes to know what's going down. Some people have connections to Central American movements and down in the southern cone, too."

"Yes, I can imagine that would interest them. Your friend Michelle in the Manhattan 1 office felt sure that we would be of similar mind. I believe you are also worried about quite where things in the Service are heading?"

Fiona returned an uncomfortably piercing stare.

"Say more."

"Would you share your perspective first?"

"You're wondering if I'm with internal investigations – trying to set you up?"

"It crossed my mind."

"Okay, I'll tell you what I think," replied Fiona. "Yes, Michelle did speak about you. Yes, I care that a service supposedly devoted to national security wastes time infiltrating social justice groups or spying on concerned citizens legitimately questioning bad policies. That doesn't help security and probably does the opposite."

Gill grinned.

"Some of us back home think the same – even though in a unit doing just what you described."

Fiona briefly played with her coffee spoon, before speaking.

"There's a sprinkling of colleagues around the country who think like that."

"There's a splintering?"

"No, that's too strong, although it's funny that you ask that. There are rumours of a group that has very different priorities."

Gill leaned forward.

"Your friend, Michelle, hinted at whispers of a possible rogue grouping, though I'm not sure I grasped how that might work?"

Fiona moistened her lips, reminding her of a cat.

"More a case of what they might be pursuing. Perhaps we'll discuss it later. It's just that I can't pretend to be blind and deaf anymore."

Gill decided more with gut than mind that Fiona could be trusted.

"You sound rather like my boyfriend, Simon. Si is somewhere here in San Francisco – at least, I think so."

"Say again? You *think* so?"

She poured out the story, omitting that Simon was previously a mark.

"He sounds a good guy, but your story illustrates just what I mean. 'Good people caught up in bad policies.' I didn't join the service for that!"

"'Caught' being the right word," Gill said. "He's totally disappeared!"

Gill held her cell phone out.

"Look, the same number and it works perfectly – but not a word."

Fiona looked thoughtful.

"Our offices took an interest in that conference and took some key protesters off the streets for a few hours. We've had our own quiet schism. Putting activists onto 'no-fly' lists was controversial and our Burlingame office got pulled into that one. Some colleagues were very unhappy, though we also have plenty of hard-liners."

"Sounds familiar," replied Gill.

"Colleagues elsewhere in the country report that local activists are being almost viewed like Soviet-style dissidents. There are rumours that some have been identified as likely candidates for detention in a future emergency."

Gill listened, thinking of the optimistic, idealistic country of the

'American Dream' – formerly loved the world over. Had it really been so damaged by those terrorist atrocities? Where was questioning and proper journalism?

"What happens now locally if someone really falls foul of the system?"

"There are short-term facilities. Potentially, someone with the wrong label could, if necessary, be taken there and then, later, moved to one of the holding camps."

"Heck! Where is this local facility?"

"It's not part of my brief, but I believe a small facility has opened on Yerba Buena Island."

She exhaled and felt mixed emotions – few of them comforting. At least this was something tangible. Melosa said they mentioned an island.

"What's it like?"

"I'm not sure. You've seen the Bay Bridge – the long one going over to Oakland?"

"Yes, I saw it from down near the ferries."

"Its first span touches down on a little island. That's Yerba Buena. It formerly housed a naval station. That's now derelict and the place is mostly open to the public, but they kept land back further around and tunnelled a small complex into the rock. It's out of sight on the other side of the island."

"Could he be there?"

"From what you're saying, yes, if it's only a couple of days since he was picked up. Of course, that's if he was picked up."

"How do you mean?"

"Well, you never know what men are getting up to."

"Sounds like the voice of experience."

Fiona gave a rueful smile.

"Don't even go there," she winked. "I'm probably turning lesbian for good reasons!"

"Could you find out if he's there, Fiona? I've agreement and authority from London and New York to liaise with local services during my trip out west."

"Probably best to lie low for the moment – that makes things easier. Are you staying with the Mexicans around the corner?"

"They offered and seem nice people."

"Listen, they do great desserts here. I'll order if you like?"

Soon, she ate the most exotic ice-cream ever.

"I'll see what I can find out. Let's meet this evening and I'll tell you what I've discovered – if anything."

She nodded and Fiona reached over and stroked her arm.

"Try not to worry. I'll pick you up from the Mexicans' place around 8pm."

After they finished, she drove Fiona back to her car, feeling slightly uneasy. What was that stroking her arm all about? Unbidden, an adolescent memory surfaced – usually locked away. Still, she needed all the help she could get and it was California!

After leaving Fiona, she decided to soak up the atmosphere and explore the area. She found more murals, finding them strangely affecting. Not long ago, she'd have prejudged anyone involved in Latin America's struggles, but she no longer felt like that. She studied the faces on the street and, other than the obvious dealers, saw poor working folk, careworn stressed people – even a few happy faces, despite everything. With Simon, she'd gained another perspective on those who resisted. As he'd said, why should they accept that their homelands should be a happy hunting ground for plunderers, footloose capital or corporations wanting cheap, unprotected labour? Who decided the people in those murals or others were wrong? Wasn't most of it down to an accident of birth?

Gill returned to the Ecoves's home. The family were sat around the large kitchen table, with the younger children busy with homework. Young Solana seemed a charming child and Gill found herself thinking about motherhood.

"Do you eat tortillas in England?" the child asked.

"Well, you can get them, but they're not so common. We like fish and chips, or should I say fish and French fries."

"Oh." The child opened her eyes wide and wrinkled her nose. "Fish and fries," she repeated.

Elisa put her arm around the child and pulled her close.

"Solana, have you finished your homework, darling?"

A knock came from the front door.

"Probably Momma," said Elisa. "She said she'd come this evening."

She left the kitchen, and returned moments later with a smiling Frank Rossi.

"Hi everyone! Hi, err, wait a moment... Gill. Have I got it right?"

She nodded and the large man sat beside her.

"How's your search going? Any news on Simon?"

She quickly reeled through the implications of her answer. Rossi was instinctively easy to trust, but also the kind of person her office would love to hate! Revealing Fiona's identity would be unprofessional, and could jeopardise her position. Anyway, she needed her help.

"Well, apparently Melosa heard the men mention two possibilities, but I haven't found any more out, yet. Maybe tomorrow?"

Esteban asked about today's conference. Rossi was upbeat, and took them through the day's programme.

"Any more arrests?" asked Gill.

"Didn't hear of any," he replied. "Mind you, today was more about celebration and future plans."

Her mind stayed on Simon, as the talk drifted on to Mexico, the Zapatistas and political changes in South America. Rossi's understanding of Latin American politics was extensive and she was soon out of her depth. Discussions in the office were simplistic and usually had a good guy/bad guy storyline. The background scenery might change, but, if you thought deeply enough, the real imperatives were usually elite and commercial interests. Later on, Elisa beckoned and showed her where she could sleep.

"Your Simon stayed in this room."

She'd ensured that Fiona's later arrival wouldn't be a surprise, and explained someone from her firm's West Coast office would be collecting her. She asked for tonight's recipe, and Elisa giggled and asked about British food. Explaining her limited cooking prowess to an earth-mother type seemed rather embarrassing. She mumbled something about forwarding her traditional British recipes later.

A knock at the door and Fiona was shown in, now dressed in softer clothes. It was only then that she realised quite how attractive the woman looked. When she eventually got into Fiona's car, she could hardly wait.

"Did you find anything out about Simon?"

"Let's go for a drink and I'll explain."

Fiona proved to be a confident driver and they were soon on Dolores again, driving through the Mission, but Fiona then turned at Seventeenth and entered a quite different area. From the bars and single-sex couples parading, she guessed that this must be the Castro and, sure enough, they sono passed the Castro theatre. Fiona glanced over, grinning.

"There's a good bar down here," Fiona said, parking with the kind of seamless proficiency Gill never managed.

Several women stood outside hand in hand, but Fiona led her inside. The light then dawned. Surely Fiona wasn't intending some kind of move? She recalled Si's experience in Greenwich Village. She'd laughed when he described it, so maybe this served her right!

The bar was crowded, but the area at the far end had free tables.

"Just a little place I sometimes visit. You can drink or have coffee and snacks down here."

They found a table and Fiona left to get drinks. It was quieter here and the main action was up near the bar and the dance area. A noisy crowd was in and the jukebox played soul music very loud. She couldn't see a single man, but several women shimmied and hugged on the small dance area and she noticed a couple sneaking kisses in a dark corner.

Fiona returned with coffees and potato chips.

"About Simon...?" she asked pointedly.

"Yes, of course," sighed Fiona. "I called by the office earlier this evening and, as expected, he is over at Yerba Buena. That facility is only equipped to hold people for a limited time, so he'll probably be moved on, soon."

"Hell. I really need to see him."

"Impossible, unless I were to formally introduce you as a British agent over on an observation exchange."

"Not a problem. London told me to plug in to the system as much as possible. It's grist to the mill for helping our systems to integrate. My brief was learning the way things are done here and US agents are on exchange back home – doing the same."

"But, Gill, if you just turn up, Simon might realise you're an insider."

"It's rather late for that, Fiona!"

"You haven't?"

"He was my mark, and... it just sort of happened. Hearts act strangely, sometimes. Often, we forget that, in this occupation."

Fiona squeezed her hand, and kept eye contact.

"I'm certainly well aware of the ways of the heart, Gill."

The woman's warm hand kept stroking hers, and she felt strangely unable to retract it. After all, Fiona was the key to her contacting Simon. Even so, she couldn't deny a rather strange excitement.

Fiona removed her hand.

"Come on, I'll take you home."

As they drove off, she felt her job was further unravelling.

"What will you do, when you get back?"

"To be honest, I guess I've had enough. Really, I want 'out' and to change my direction."

They'd stopped at traffic lights, but, even in the dim light, she could see an expression of incredulity crossing Fiona's face.

"And you think they'll just let you walk off into the sunset, hand in hand with one of your marks, and information of unwarranted public surveillance? I don't think so!"

Her stomach lurched, although Fiona had only articulated the rumbling fear that had been around over recent days. Deep down, she knew it was laughably naive to think it could be so easy.

The car pulled up outside Elisa and Esteban's and a little tension drained away. Somehow, when Fiona said 'I'll take you home', she wondered if she'd meant... She registered the hint of disappointment, but quickly buried it.

"I'll enquire tomorrow about a visit to the island. You'll need identification and they'll almost certainly check with New York and London first."

They looked at each other. The woman's hand squeezed her upper arm and then, almost in slow motion, leaned forward and kissed her cheek, saying, "Try not to worry. I'll pick you up in the morning."

Gill left the car and went to the front door. When she turned, Fiona smiled, waved, and accelerated away. Well, tomorrow would be a new day!

7 2

UTAH

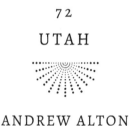

ANDREW ALTON

I shook my head and couldn't help sighing. The circumstances certainly seemed stacked against us. In fact, the possibility of assistance from Carl's friend, Craig Thomas, seemed the only glimmer of hope. At first, I'd assumed our host was a typical hard-drinking red-neck, but, although no intellectual, Carl proved surprisingly sensitive. Terry James, of course, was a more daunting prospect... and then there was Freddy!

I drove over to Freddy's home on the edge of town, fearful about what they might cook up and aghast at how rapidly things had changed. Until recently, I'd had an international reputation, generated cutting-edge research and was a valued part of the College. Now I seemed to be caught between rampant business interests and a pro-business government that wanted to extinguish anything exposing that unholy alliance. Dad apparently manipulating my career in the background and, meanwhile, we were in the hands of Freddy and his militia friends!

Though not usually given to talking to myself – in the privacy of the car, I muttered, "Could things possibly get any weirder?"

Two cars, and the Hummer we almost collided with yesterday, sat in Freddy's drive. As I walked to the door, young Mervyn came out, calling, "Uncle Andrew" and then ran inside, shouting.

"Daddy, it's Uncle Andrew. Uncle Andrew's here!"

Mary came out to greet me.

"They're in the lounge."

He went there and found Freddy talking with Terry James.

"Hi Bro, come and join us. Mary – more beers please!"

Terry James extended a hand.

"Hiya, bud! I gather you've been up country with my boy and he's now in trouble."

"Yes, Terry. Fred probably explained it. While looking for Indian rock drawings, we unknowingly stumbled into an off-limits military facility."

James snorted.

"Indian rock drawings? No shit! Indian cock drawings would be more his style. Ain't that right, Fred?"

Freddy smirked.

"Right, Terry, from what I remember!"

"Rob's sexuality mightn't be the most important thing right now, Mr James."

"Mr James, eh?"

His weather-beaten face broke into a grin.

"Call me, Terry. I was only joshin' 'bout him being a fag. He had a difficult time as a youngster. We ain't seen each other in years – so I wouldn't know if it's true now."

From what I gathered, Robbie mightn't be totally sure, either!

"Anyway, Rob was arrested, grabbed really, from outside this secure place out in the sticks just east of Monticello. We were just curious and walked the perimeter. Unfortunately, Rob slipped down a bank, right into the path of a patrol."

Terry looked thoughtful.

"Thing is, bud, we do know about this camp and several others like it. I believe Fred explained how we come to know?"

A sheepish look crossed his brother's face.

"You mean the militia thing? I'm afraid that's mainly a closed book to me."

"Mom says you hate government corruption," said Freddy. "I would have thought you'd be in favour!"

"Possible that we've similar ends in mind, but different ways of getting there," I replied. "Actually Terry, you were close to the camp yesterday, when we nearly collided with you and the young guy driving."

"That was you guys drifting across the road, was it? I expect Freddy told you I sometimes trade classic car parts. We had a delivery nearby."

"I don't really get the militia thing. What are you trying to achieve? Surely Waco and the Ruby Ridge episode showed that government agencies no longer pussyfoot around. I don't know the full background, but I thought, following the OK City bombing, anyone classed a dissident is truly put under the microscope!"

"That was just a frame up! Everyone knows that kid had a chip in his head! Those bastards plan to bring in martial law. Troops go out doin' so-called 'homeland exercises' and the government legal shysters have virtually disabled 'posse comitatus'."

Mary entered with a tray of beer and biscuits.

"Posse what? Are you boys talking cowboy films again?"

"'Posse Comitatus' is the law stopping the military from domestic policing," I explained.

"Anyway, how could you possibly know their intentions?"

"We got our ways," replied Terry.

Freddy gave his brother a broad wink.

"What can you do?" asked Andrew.

"We sure won't stand by and let the Washington weasels sell us out. Or they let the UN march in."

It felt difficult not to laugh.

"Hardly likely," I replied. "Surely their main worry is political instability, particularly since the finance sector scandals. Corporate America and the elite running things worry that people might wake up and demand something better. No wonder they're almost phobic about activists."

"Now you're just bein' naive," said James. "Them New World Order bastards are shaping up for a complete takeover. You oughta get yourself educated."

"Maybe we should stick with Robbie's problem," I replied, certain that James senior wasn't someone to trade any kind of blows with.

"Rob may not have been my ideal son, but I can't stand thinking of him held by New World Order goons. Listen, we also took a look around the outside of that camp. All I can think of is that maybe we could cut a hole in the back fence, at night."

"I think there are lights around the perimeter. We've no idea about electronic surveillance or if the power could be cut."

"Yep, that makes sense. Freddy, do any of the local bro's work for the power authority?"

"I think so. I'll check it out."

"We must keep this to ourselves," I said.

James shot a dirty look at me and shook his head.

"We won't be advertising it, bud – don't be stupid! Now, was it just you and Rob who travelled down?"

"We have another friend, called Nick Martin. He is with a different corporation to Rob, but they worked together on a joint project."

"Why isn't he here?" asked Freddy.

"Probably in town getting supplies. As I told Fred, we're staying at Carl Willet's place."

"My sister's boy," said Terry.

"Carl has a friend, actually working at the camp. They've been life-long friends and I understand he owes Carl a big favour. We believe he'll act as a go-between, so hopefully we'll get a line of communication with Rob."

"That's good," said James. "Carl always was a good kid."

"I think he's an asshole," said Freddy.

"He just don't like your ways. Anyway, you have to bury the hatchet now."

"So, all we have is Carl's friend, my idea of disabling the power supply, and your idea about cutting the back fence. It isn't really much to go on!"

"We've plenty of muscle, don't forget. We could get a crowd down to make a diversion."

"Would protesting outside – raising local awareness, holding meetings and so on, help?" I asked.

"Nah! That wouldn't play," replied Terry. "When it suits, the government can always play the anti-terrorism card."

Things were progressing from strange to downright bizarre, as far as I was concerned. Was I really seeking common ground with a potentially violent, back-woods militia man?

"I guess we should take another look," said Terry. "Locate the best spot to make entry and tackle the power supply. We could blow it, if necessary."

James seemed serious, but something about him also seemed rather unhinged. I felt reality sliding, remembering the warning in the London police station. Surely, we weren't seriously talking about destroying government property?

"Perhaps it's too early for drastic stuff?"

James's lip curled.

"Let's test the contact with Rob first," I suggested. "He might have useful information on the camp's layout."

Surprisingly, Freddy agreed.

"I reckon Andy's right. Let's wait until we hear back from Robbie. Meanwhile, I've remembered Tank McCullough, from our county group, works with the power people. I'll see him tonight."

I looked around the room, again noting Freddy's taste for the over-stated. The place looked like a tacky showroom for the furniture industry and I quietly shuddered.

"I'll get back to Carl's place and we'll work on getting word to and from Robbie. Freddy, you see this 'Tank' person. I suggest we meet early tomorrow morning and go out and check the best entry point."

James's mouth curled again.

"Don't appoint yourself our leader, Mr University Professor. It's my boy inside!"

"Of course. I was only trying to help."

I was also thinking of Nina and antagonising James wouldn't help her.

"Okay. Let's meet here at 4am, to get there around dawn, when it's light enough not to fall about and dark enough to give some cover," said Terry. "Are you carryin', 'cause I've no doubt those guards will be vicious mothers."

"Sorry? You're asking if I have a firearm? No, that's not my style!"

James looked incredulous.

"Now you're bein' a bonehead!"

Returning to Carl's was a relief. He'd finished earlier than expected and had his hands around a streaky bacon hero. Myleen fussed with coffee and more sandwiches.

"Could we talk with Craig and try to work out a plan?"

"I thought the same," replied Carl. "That's why I called in on the way through. Craig's back on duty tomorrow morning. Apparently, Robbie's been moved from what's called the 'admissions' unit to the main living area."

"Will that make things easier or more difficult?"

"Dunno. Your guess is as good as mine."

"We plan taking another look at the camp early tomorrow."

"Be careful. I'd come, but I've a group of photographers bound for Castle Rock. I hope Fred won't use a clapped-out jeep!"

"Look, he's sorry about that misunderstanding, but, as your uncle Terry said, for Robby's sake, you need to put that behind you."

"I guess so," he replied, with little enthusiasm. "Let's go talk with Craig."

The house was only a short drive, just inside the city limits. Craig appeared a friendly, uncomplicated man and Patsy, his wife, came from a similar mould as Myleen, I decided, while eating a slice of her carrot cake.

"We understand Robbie's been moved."

"Yeah. New folk get processed in a unit near the main gate. After a couple of days, they're moved to one of the main buildings and get their own room."

"What are the other buildings we saw?"

"An activities block, the privileges block, the interrogation block, the special treatments block and a hospital wing. There's also administration, stores, and the boiler room."

"We noticed the chimney... it gave us the creeps."

"You've got conspiracy fever, man," said Carl. "You should have heard the shit Robbie came out with, the night you arrived."

"I can imagine," I replied. "That 'special treatments' block... what's special and what's the treatment?"

"We ain't sure. We're told very little at my level. Apparently, there's about like twenty separate agencies making up US Security services – and private contractors like us. I was told all that during training. I've seen the really top-level Arm-Rite people enter the 'special treatments' block, but, generally, it's the psychology people and some outside security folk. That's all we know, except for rumours."

"Rumours?"

"Some of the guys reckon some people can leave in pretty bad shape."

"Great! Will you have any contact with Robbie's block?"

"Yeah, it's lucky really. The gallery I care for includes his room."

"Gallery?"

"Yeah. There ain't no Mona Lisas, though! It's what they call them big corridors with rooms coming off. Blocks have four galleries – like corridors – that run the length of the building and join another corridor at the end. We get to look after about a dozen rooms each. Like I said, my gallery includes Robbie's room."

"Have you talked with him?"

"No, he was being transferred as I finished my shift. I'll see him in the morning, though."

"What if they realise that you know of him?"

"I'll warn him not to let on. I mean, most inmates come from out of area, so they probably won't expect it. Some come from outside the USA! Most staff come from out of state, too. There are only a handful of locals. I think it's policy to avoid them."

It was our first bit of luck. I quickly assessed the situation. Should I also mention Nina? I decided against it for now, reasoning that Nick might have strong views.

"Is there a relevant policy, for if a guard recognises an inmate?" I asked.

"Yeah. We've lists of stuff... called... er... Yes, that's it, called 'security protocols'. We have to study 'em, and then get tested by supervisors. It says there, that you've gotta declare it right away."

"You're not gonna, bud, right?" asked Carl.

"Course not! What you take me for?"

"Okay," I said. "When it's safe, discretely tell Robbie that we're okay. Find out what's happening and see if he has ideas for getting out. We'll come and see you... well, when is best?"

"Tomorrow's early shift, so I'll be back around five."

"Thanks Craig," said Carl. "We'll come then."

Back at Carl's, Nick had returned from shopping. Between mouthfuls of Myleen's food, he tried to extract as much as possible.

"So, he didn't mention Nina? Are you sure?" he asked for the third time.

I drew a deep breath and tried again.

"I get that you're worried, but I made the best decision I could. If Craig gets caught, it will blow communication with Robbie, but at least shouldn't draw attention to Nina or us. Let's see how that works first."

"I guess so," said Nick, sighing. "It's been a very long time, though."

"I know. With tomorrow's early start, I'm going to turn in now."

"I agree, who knows what's going to come next...?"

73

SAN FRANCISCO

GILL'S PERSPECTIVE

Gill woke early and remembered Si had also slept in this very bed. If only circumstances were different and they were just a normal couple on vacation, eating, sightseeing – making love!

She heard people moving about the house, so she dressed and checked her identification and passes. If Fiona had any success, they could be needed later.

In the kitchen, Elisa was busy preparing the children for school.

"Hi Gilly! Ready for some breakfast?"

The youngest girl looked at her and smiled.

"Fish fries," she said giggling.

"You don't have fish and fries, darling."

"You eat fish fries in England."

"Yes, some people do – a lot!"

"Come along, Solana, darlin' – or you'll be late for school."

Esteban joined them, a smile just about visible under the enormous moustache.

"What's our lovely English lady doin' today?"

"Good morning, Esteban. Looking for Simon again with the person from our West Coast office."

"Ah, the pretty lady from last night?"

Frank Rossi entered the kitchen. The children greeted him and, moments later, Dario the Colombian activist joined them. Rossi seemed in good humour.

"Morning, Gill. That was one of the most successful conferences, ever. Too bad you couldn't come."

"I know, Frank. Simon would have loved it all, too!"

Rossi pursed his lips and shook his head.

"Yeah. That's a real worry. I'm sorry. Any new ideas?"

"No, though I've linked with someone from our local office who'll try to help. Eventually I'll have to bite the bullet and talk with the authorities. Tell them I know he was taken from here and ask why they'd hold a British citizen."

"Doesn't sound a real smart plan," said Dario. "You'll just get your face put onto the system. It'll all be legally sewn up, you can be sure of that."

Frank's bonhomie evaporated and he shook his head. Esteban looked doleful, and even Elisa blew out through pursed lips. Their reactions seemed appropriate enough, even though she knew things they didn't.

"You'll need a good attorney," said Frank. "I may be able to help."

"Thanks, Frank. Let's see where I get to today. I'll get back to you, if necessary."

"Okay sweetheart, I'm here for another day. We'll talk later."

Whilst drinking a second coffee, there was a knock at the door and Elisa showed Fiona in. Her heart sped as her mind replayed the kiss.

Fiona grinned.

"Hi, Gill. Ready for hunting?"

Moments later, they were in her car.

"So, did you succeed in getting me in, Fiona?"

"Call me Fee, everyone else does. Yes, I've permission to take you to the island – but, did you think that Simon's reaction might reveal the nature of your relationship and blow everything?"

"Well, I shouldn't think... I mean, Si's pretty quick on the uptake."

They stopped at red lights. Fiona had a sort of misty expression as she returned her look. She felt strangely confused and had an odd floating sensation in her abdomen. Fiona drove another half block on and pulled in.

"You know, Gill, I've an idea that I think could help. I hope it doesn't freak you out. The thing is, I actually prefer girls – something that isn't a great secret in the Department."

"Well, it is San Francisco!"

"Yes, though that's over-hyped. Look, if you pretended, shall we say, to be with me, they'll draw contrary conclusions about your actual relationship with Simon. Do you see what I mean? Could Simon pick up on that?"

In fact, even she was struggling. Suddenly, Oxford, London and England seemed an awfully long way away.

"I... I don't know Fiona, sorry, Fee. I'm not sure that I can carry..."

They'd had nothing similar in any training scenario. She felt flustered and the idea seemed dangerous, though oddly exciting. An inner voice argued that this might be the only way of seeing Si that didn't either worsen his position or endanger her own.

"C'mon," Fiona touched her shoulder. "I won't bite. Didn't they stress in your training the importance of behavioural flexibility?" She grinned. "Sometimes, it's the difference between success and failure."

"I need to think. It's a strange idea."

"Okay, but we only have this morning. I've arranged with Betty Sampson on the island for a visit early afternoon. Betty used to be a girlfriend, and we're still friendly. I've also turned up some more information that I have to tell you. Let's have coffee and I'll explain."

Fiona pulled into the traffic, with practised ease.

"Actually, we've the morning to kill, so I'll take you up our famous hills, en route."

The steepness was frightening and, at one point, the descent felt so acute she actually worried the car might flip. They drove down the serpentine folds of Lombard Street, which Fee claimed was the world's most crooked street.

Remembering one of Si's monologues, she said, "Surely that would be K Street, Washington?"

"Nice one, Gill! Anyway, let's have a few holiday moments while you're here."

Fiona headed to Fisherman's Wharf, but it was heaving with tourists. They strolled around anyway, admiring the boats and shops.

"What about that coffee? You said you had something to tell me?"

"Yeah, let's go. Tell you what, how about some really special tea? I'll take you to one of my favourite spots."

She involuntarily gripped the armrest as Fiona drove down Russian Hill. It was a literal white-knuckle ride, and she only relaxed when they turned towards Pacific Heights and headed towards Haight-Ashbury.

For a moment, she thought Fee might be making for another Castro hangout, but she turned towards Golden Gate Park.

"I love this place," Fiona said, flashing a full-on smile and making eye contact a little too long. "See what you think."

They entered the park, pulling up under an exceptionally large tree, and Gill looked into its branches, wondering if it could be a Sequoia. She stole a quick glance at Fiona, and registered warm sensations in her abdomen. Sunlight entered the window and the light lit Fiona's hair and the milky skin of her arms. Before thinking, she'd reached over and touched the woman's soft cheek. Fiona leaned over and kissed her on the lips as time seemed to slow. The outside world receded as she concentrated on the warmth on her lips, wanting it to continue. Far away, an inner voice asked what she was thinking of. She ignored the thought and rested her head on Fiona's shoulder. The woman took her hand, gently squeezing her fingers and she closed her eyes, focusing on the sensation. Moments later, a car drew up and she heard the sounds of excited children.

"See," said Fiona, "that wasn't so difficult. You'll do fine this afternoon."

They walked across to the Japanese tea garden. It was beautiful and somehow its tranquillity dispelled anxiety over what had just happened. Apparently, this was a Zen garden, and it aroused her curiosity to discover more. Fiona took her hand and they wandered through the paths, passing bonsai, cherry trees and pools of carp.

"Let's take that tea."

She nodded. The garden was beautiful and she would really prefer to stay within its peace, but she remembered Fiona had something to tell her before the visit. Inside the tea house, they found a secluded table.

"You wanted to discuss something?"

Fiona's face looked quite serious.

"Remember, I hinted yesterday that a group with rogue tendencies may have formed?"

"Yes."

"It's worse. Word is that this grouping might have re-initiated certain programmes that we all thought had been banned!"

Fiona's tone increased her foreboding.

"I've learned more, and it isn't good news."

"Does this affect Simon?"

"Maybe. To be honest, I don't know."

"Don't mess around, Fee. Exactly what do you know?"

"He'll be transferred to a facility in Utah, the day after tomorrow."

"We haven't much time then. What sort of programmes? Something experimental? Michelle, your friend in New York, hinted at something similar."

Fiona nodded.

"By some quirk of history, Simon is heading to the same facility used as an overflow for Bay Area Japanese-Americans in World War Two."

"What happens there now, Fee?"

"I'm not really sure, but have you heard of mind-control experiments?"

"Not really. Only the CIA's infamous MK Ultra and the various spin-off programmes. Rumours of trying to create so-called 'Manchurian Candidate' controlled subjects and assassins. But I thought that was mostly apocryphal – isn't it?"

Fiona shook her head.

"I've also heard talk of bio-chip implants, but surely that's fantasy? Look, we also have advanced surveillance technology, but calling it mind control is surely far too strong?"

She looked around the tea-room. Most ordinary people would consider the state misusing their taxes that way incomprehensible.

Fiona continued.

"Since the development of the so-called 'non-lethal weapons', everything has become vastly more complex. Vortex technology, radio frequency weapons, tune-able microwaves and so on. Then, there are also the very low and ultra-low frequency devices that impact mood and general functioning."

"Now you mention it, Fee, we had an episode at the Greenham Common air base in the UK, a few years back. Women peace campaigners were camped outside the US air base, which, at the time, had nuclear strike missiles. Women became ill and nauseous. Some now think that microwaves or some kind of directed energy weapon might have been responsible. But how does all this relate to Si?" she asked with a sinking feeling.

Fiona reached out, taking her hand again.

"Further research and testing seems to have started again. This time using new spin-offs from existing developments like extra-low frequencies, other RFs, magnetic fields, lasers, thermal guns, and ultrasonic acoustics. These are probably from certain black budget programmes."

"What's their aim this time?"

"We believe they are developing technology to map the biological signatures that correspond to various moods, thoughts and behaviours. With that, they could almost read what's happening inside a subject. Even more worrying, are attempts to control subjects through implantable devices. Of course, they need subjects for experimentation."

Gill shook her head, feeling incredulous.

"You mean microchips and so on?"

"I think so. We may find out more from a friend, later."

Gill looked around the tea-room. The place was getting more crowded, with – of all people – a crowd of Japanese tourists! She looked at Fiona, remembering resting on her shoulder, earlier. Now she felt tired and confused. Was it really only a few months ago that she was doing what she thought was patriotic work and had a secure career path ahead of her?

"What's the place in Utah, Fee?"

She looked around at the Japanese tourists with a horrible feeling she already knew the answer.

"It's called Camp Ute, near a little town called Monticello, down in South East Utah. They have a landing strip, so they'll probably fly him over."

"How would I get there?"

"You wouldn't! If you turned up, it would really blow things. Think about it!"

"I have to help Si. After what you just said, I can't just abandon him."

"And you can't just turn up in Utah. Maybe he'll be excluded from anything like that – him being a British national and so forth. Look, we have to leave now for us to pick up your photo card and clearances."

They returned to Fiona's car. She settled into the seat, fleetingly wondering what being another woman's girlfriend would actually be like. Although her own thought, it shook her. She reassured herself that it only happened because of the need to protect Simon.

"Our office is near the Old Mint in what's called SOMA – the South of Market district."

They skirted Haight-Ashbury, passing more of the Victorian

wooden houses she was coming to love. After reaching Market Street, they pulled into an unmarked car park. Fiona swiped her card-key and then entered the building. Fee seemed well liked and 'high-fived' her way down a long corridor. The ambience was very Californian and miles from London's formality, and even New York's seriousness.

"We have to see a section head," said Fiona. "A guy called Mack Nestroy. He'll check you out and, afterwards, we'll go to the basement and get your temporary visitor's card."

They reached Nestroy's office and entered. He greeted her by name and asked to see her UK papers. Nestroy had clearly already done his homework and, after some questions, smiled broadly.

"So, Ms Marney, US/UK cooperation seems to be going well. I gather that we've managed to pick up someone who was formerly on your watch?"

"Correct, sir. It was all rather complicated, at first. Maher came on a research visit, at roughly the same time I arrived for the exchange. London authorised me to stay in touch. It had been what we call a 'velvet' surveillance."

"I know, we've talked with them. How do you intend to explain pitching up at a secure military site?"

"Fiona explained that to Betty Sampson, Sir. You see, I'd stayed in close contact with Maher in New York and, fortunately, had said how I'd like to visit the West Coast. I'll explain my coming to San Francisco partly as a personal interest thing, but, also, hoping to see him. When I went to the conference to find him, I discovered from Frank Rossi, he's a fan of Rossi's work, that he'd stayed with the Mexican family. After the family explained he'd been taken, I followed it up with the authorities. As a special privilege, because he is a foreign national, and with the 'special understanding' between our countries, I'm being allowed a brief visit, under Ms McBain's supervision."

Nestroy beamed.

"Very good. Keep thinking like that, Marney, and you could be an agent." He sniggered. "Oops, I almost forgot – you already are!"

As they left, Fiona reached out and they left hand in hand. Nestroy called out. "Trying something new, Fee? I may have to give Betty a call."

Fiona turned and grinned.

"Don't get jealous, Macky boy. Anyway, it'd probably give you a heart attack!"

"Hope you didn't mind," said Fiona, when we got out. "Anything that shows distance between you and Simon could help."

Strangely, she didn't mind. There was something both reassuring and exciting about wandering about hand in hand. There'd been that incident at boarding school, but nothing since – despite thoughts in private moments!

"People here seem very relaxed about things," she replied.

"I guess they know me well. Unlike the old days, we're now allowed to be open about these things – because then there's nothing to pressure or blackmail. It isn't like this everywhere, though."

Fiona led them down to the basement photographic studio and, shortly afterwards, Gill pocketed her temporary ID.

They ascended two levels.

"I'd like you to meet and talk with my friend, Marji. No-one's sure the place isn't bugged, so I've arranged for us to leave for coffee."

"Wait here," Fiona said, disappearing into a side office. Moments later, she emerged with a rather dowdy blonde – probably in her mid-fifties – and they left for a coffee shop on Folsom Street.

"Marji is like us, and Michelle, who you met in New York," explained Fiona. Part of a small, discreet network of agents unhappy about being misused."

Marji looked like an overworked suburban housewife, although Gill knew better than going on first appearances.

"Good meeting you, Gill. Fiona explained you've a friend heading for Utah, and asked me to outline a few things."

They settled at a table at the back of the coffee shop.

"Marji is our expert on mind control," said Fiona. "That's why I thought you two should meet."

Marji had a world-weary expression and appeared unlikely as an expert on anything. She sucked at her lower lip, before starting.

"How much do you know about this, Gill?"

"Fee asked the same question and then talked about issues like 'non-lethal weapons' and 'implantable chips'. I didn't know much, but it all sounded rather sick to me. Intelligence gathering and surveillance is one thing, but literally getting into someone's head...?"

"I agree," said Marji, "but they're all at it. For example, Scandinavia is considered enlightened, but I read reports claiming one Swedish region had all the elderly that come into residential care routinely chipped. Apparently, they also ran a similar programme for individuals entering police custody and hospital care. I've seen x-rays of objects embedded at the base of the skull, in the brain, the nostrils, even the chest cavity."

"Yuk."

"Yes," continued Marji. "We suppose that these may have been primitive experiments to get what was then termed 'radio-hypnotic intracerebral control'."

"You mean agencies put them inside people?" asked Gill, shuddering.

"Oh yes," continued Marji. "There have been experiments with cochlear implants – to send signals to the fluids in the inner ear to simulate a voice, also implants to send other impulses by bone conduction. They've even tried implants in false teeth! The big goal was to secretly communicate to brains and minds, from a distance."

Marji periodically shook her head, and punctuated her comments by blowing through pursed lips. She probably appeared slightly loopy to any onlooker. A waitress brought coffee and, for the second time today, Gill contrasted the normality of the setting with the utter weirdness of their conversation!

"How widespread is this?

"Well, we've also tried neuro-magnetic experiments, mainly in a prison population. Similar attempts have probably occurred in many other places – particularly, the former USSR. The really big advances have been more recent – since the success at fusing organic molecules and chips."

"I'm not big on science, so what's the point?" asked Gill.

"Merging biological proteins with computer chips, to allow neural interfacing, which opened the field of bio-synthesis."

Marji's words hung in the air, and she frowned, catching the general incomprehension.

"Sorry, I mean letting chips and brains communicate."

"Spooky," said Fiona. "I'll get us some cake."

Gill watched Fiona's tight jeans crossing to the counter, but Marji was on a roll.

"You see, the early experimental programmes like MK Ultra and Monarch used crude pain, sensory deprivation, radiation and drugs. The early programmes developed the work of the Nazi scientists, brought here at the end of the war during the notorious 'Operation Paperclip'."

Fiona returned, carrying a substantial chunk of cake and a knife.

"I got the last chunk of the coffee walnut, we can share." She started carving and I remarked that the walnut pieces almost resembled brain sections. Marji still ploughed on regardless.

"Of course, these were black budget projects," she said. "Later programmes experimented with implanted transmitters and electrodes. Unfortunately, these led to health problems. Basically, certain microwave and electromagnetic pulses tend to fry human tissue."

"I was just going to suggest burgers," said Fiona, "but I've rather gone off the idea, now. Well done, Marji!"

Marji wasn't about to change tack.

"Yes – 'well done' is exactly my point! Even at low intensities, microwaves cook tissues, resulting in fatigue, memory loss, tumours, and so on."

"Great," said Fiona.

"Anyway, we believe two big programmes may be under way. There are persistent rumours of attempts to develop a large mind-control programme using extremely low and ultra-low frequencies. This could potentially affect the mood and malleability of entire populations."

"Surely not?" Gill protested. "Sounds like science-fiction."

"Well, the Senate discussed the issue in the late nineties. The fact that 'Command Solo' planes broadcast subliminal radio frequency messages in Bosnia and, later, Iraq is a matter of record. The fringe conspiracy community claim domestic tests happen with the rash of microwave towers that we now see everywhere – not to mention the nasties many believe associated with that HAARP programme in Alaska. Perhaps such people are nuts – but maybe not."

She paused while the waitress put down more coffee.

"Far more worrying," continued Marji, "is work on a new generation of injectable organo-fusion chips, which are barely detectable. Their goal is data-harvesting, bio-medical telemetry and neuro-surveillance – either from computer to brain or operator to brain. The more imaginative, speculate chips could be implanted under the cover of drug trials or even vaccinations. It's rumoured that the 'holy grail' – 'surveillance and control by a chip to satellite link' – has already been achieved. Given advances in miniaturisation and, particularly, nanotechnology, it could become virtually undetectable. My information, though, is that things remain in the experimental phase and can still go radically wrong."

"But what has this to do with Simon?" Gill asked.

"It's more a case of what we believe might be happening at Camp Ute," said Fiona.

Marji nodded, and resumed.

"As I explained, we're a small, like-minded group from various parts of the country. Unfortunately, following several attempted whistle-blowing incidents, Directors have been alerted to the discontent and networking has become more difficult.

"And Camp Ute?"

"We believe the South Western sector has a rogue element – specifically centred at Ute. There may be another in the North East."

"A contact that I have in New York City mentioned something like that," said Gill.

Marji continued.

"Some of the wild men, and women for that matter, may have 'gone native', or at least, 'gone private'. We believe the Ute group collaborate with private contractors – the 'Arm-Rite Corporation'. The whisper is that they're quietly continuing with illegal mind-control research, and experiment with detainees."

"No! Surely, they wouldn't mess with a foreign national?" Gill said. "Simon's only an academic researcher and social justice activist. Okay, he pokes around in areas that might upset some, but that's still just about lawful."

Fiona raised her eyebrows.

"So, why did you take him on as an assignment?"

The simple question cut to the heart of everything and sent her into a spin. When Simon once said that intelligence appeared to have some-times prostituted itself to business, it had shaken her, and raised many disturbing questions: did governments really serve up things to powerful business interests and then harass anyone questioning? The old axiom, 'follow the money', now seemed more relevant than ever. Before meeting Simon, she'd somehow left her own role out, but that convenience no longer seemed possible.

"Good question," she replied uneasily. "I believed in what I did then, but as time has gone on, I..."

She took a breath and continued

"Look, I know Simon's on a database shared with the US, but surely they couldn't... they wouldn't include him in that sort of experi-mentation?"

"They're a rogue group," said Marji. "Hopefully, they'd keep off for the reasons you say, but you must be prepared."

"Does the administration know what is happening?"

"That's the sixty-four-thousand-dollar question", replied Marji. "Will we ever know? Are we ever told the truth? Look, there are so many black budgets now, and so many agencies, that you have to wonder if any one person knows it all! It isn't surprising it's out of control."

"What's the worst that could happen?" she asked.

Marji's expression wasn't encouraging.

"You really want to know?"

She nodded.

"The more primitive microwave experiments altered the blood-brain barrier. As well as depression and disorientation, there could be serious consequences, like cancer, leukaemia and so on. Newer methods avoided much of this. I saw an air-force paper recently, though, claiming it's possible to create a virtual reality by combining acoustical, optical and electromagnetic fields, to give the illusion of an outside voice."

"That would be almost like creating a psychotic episode!"

"Exactly. Their major goals, though, are to find ways to control the public mind and, secondly, controlling individuals so that they could undertake espionage, or even assassination."

"The old 'Manchurian Candidate' thing?"

"Exactly! For example, in our field, mind-controlled 'activists' could provide ongoing feedback. There'd be less need to infiltrate!"

She felt exhausted, as if an abyss had opened up before her. Where her work once seemed patriotic, she now saw a service out of control and working in ways that almost seemed inhuman. She'd almost heard enough and just wanted to see Simon. Thankfully, Marji spoke.

"Guess I must get back. Good luck, Gill. I'll see you soon, Fee."

Marji left, but Gill felt drained and unable to react when Fiona reached over and stroked her hand.

"Don't worry, we'll find a way."

She wanted the reassurance, but it all felt hopeless. She looked at other customers – talking, laughing and supremely unaware of the nature of the dark intrigues playing out on the edge of their precious worlds. A family group entered the shop with children, balloons and party hats. A little boy ran to their table, offering his balloon.

"Thanks, but we have to go now, sweetheart," she said, wondering for the second time today if she'd ever have a child.

They left to the sound of children playing, and returned to Fiona's car.

"Time to go," said Fiona, again pulling out with a confidence she'd never mustered.

They drove to the entrance of the Bay Bridge – towards Oakland. Looking back, she could see the financial district's towers and, behind, the city spreading over its famous hills. Ahead, the Bridge touched Yerba Buena Island, where they exited and followed a road around the island, reaching a guarded barrier to a military area.

"This used to be a Navy station," explained Fiona, as a guard checked their papers. "Most of it has been returned to the public now, though they'll know nothing of where we're going."

They continued rounding the headland, and eventually reached another guardhouse.

"This is it," said Fiona, squeezing her hand.

They walked through an abandoned military post and then Fiona took a path up towards a bluff. Further on, an entrance had been tunnelled into the rock. They entered and her papers passed inspection without incident. The space inside seemed surprisingly expansive and split into two distinct passages at the far end. A guard led them into the right-side passage, where they passed offices, a canteen and various service areas.

"You are seeing Betty, right?" asked the guard.

Fiona nodded and the man knocked on the door of what would probably be a large office.

"Come in," called a voice.

They entered, and a well-built woman rose, crossed the room and hugged Fiona. They then appeared to kiss on the lips, though she wasn't certain.

"Gill, this is Betty Sampson."

"Hi, thanks for seeing me!"

Betty had a firm grip, dark hair and a broad and attractive face.

"I gather we've got something of yours?"

"I believe so. A certain Simon Maher?"

"What's the story?"

"I had Maher under observation as part of my assignment in the UK. He trusts me completely. Maher's an academic who's over here researching. It so happened that the timing of our trips coincided. Odd, though handy, because, with my office's permission, we've kept in touch. I gather he's been up to his usual behaviour?"

"Yep. We had a convention of socialists, tree-huggers and assorted troublemakers. In the process of overseeing this, we pulled in a few troublemakers, including Maher. That database from you Brits is proving quite useful. The East Coast have stopped several and now we've scooped up some troublemakers. Your guy apparently likes to tread on important toes?"

Gill managed a grin.

"Like I said – it's business as usual."

"Cute, no?" said Fiona, putting her arm around Gill's waist.

Betty smiled wryly.

"Haven't completely lost your taste then."

"Still seeing Barbara?"

"Yeah, but she's cool," replied Betty with a knowing smile.

"This one's mine, for now," said Fiona, drawing her closer.

Gill pinched her forefinger between thumb and middle finger, silently urging herself to 'act it well for Neville's sake'. Even so, it seemed surreal.

Deep in Mother Earth – as bait for two lesbians. This must surely be a first for the Service. Even so, she registered a certain frisson when Fee pulled her closer while Betty's eyes roved over her body, with barely concealed interest. The air seemed thick with sexuality. If a situation like this got out of hand at home, she could hardly imagine the thicket of disciplinary procedures. Surely things would be the same here?

"How shall we play this meeting with Simon?" asked Fee?

The tension subsided a little. Betty retreated, perching on the edge of her desk and looking thoughtful.

"I guess, keep it formal. I'll come down with you and set the framework. Fee, you'll stay to help supervise the visit."

Betty called for a guard and they retraced the way to the entry area, but this time turned into the left tunnel. They passed about ten rooms, and the guard paused at the last door on the left, and produced a ring with two large brass keys attached to a lanyard. She was surprised the place lacked fancy electronics and the keys resembled those in high-security facilities at home. The guard fiddled with the keys, and swung the door back.

Simon sat in a small chair facing the opening. As he took in his visitors, his pale face showed both shock and stress. She fought for a neutral expression and tried to gauge his current state and level of awareness. How could she warn him against blurting everything out and ruining their chances? Almost without thinking, she reached for Fiona's hand and held it tightly. It was only later she reflected that, though adrenalin might speed the reflexes, it compromises foresight.

"Gill!" "Simon!"

They spoke simultaneously.

Fiona had the presence of mind to quickly squeeze, and then drop her hand.

"Don't worry, Ms Marney, it's okay. Seeing your friend here must be a shock. You'll soon be back outside."

Fee extended her hand to Simon as Betty introduced them.

"Hello, Mr Maher. I'm Betty Sampson, the Officer in Charge, and this is Ms Fiona McBain – Security. She'll supervise the contact session."

"It's a 'contact session', is it?" asked Simon.

"Your friend from the UK has been given the privilege of a short visit," said Betty. "A rare privilege, I can assure you – reflecting the special relationship between our countries."

Simon rolled his eyes.

"What particularly... not that old 'coalition of the willing' thing? The 'triumph' of Anglo-American casino capitalism? Maybe you were thinking of Britain's role as a US airstrip and listening station?"

"Leave it at that, Mr Misery," said Betty. "Ask yourself whether distortions like that help, or worsen, your situation. I'll leave Gill in your tender care," Betty said, giving Fiona a knowing smile.

Feeling quite so out of her depth was unusual. She looked at Simon. He appeared tired, but alert. She mouthed to Fiona, "Is there surveillance of the cell?"

"No," she replied, but pulled a small pad and pen from her bag.

"The guard's probably outside," she whispered. "Write down anything important."

Simon appeared perplexed. She took the pad and wrote.

Fiona is helping. She doesn't agree with harassing activists and I trust her. She's known in the service to be gay, and is playing at an interest in me to help mask my relationship to you. That absolutely mustn't come out.

Simon nodded and mouthed... "hence the" and then clasped one hand with the other.

She nodded.

"How do I get out?" he mouthed.

Fiona took the pad, and scribbled. *You can't. You're being moved to a holding camp in Utah, in two days' time.*

A wave of emotion swept over her. As if reading her mind, he reached for her hand. She instinctively looked for signs of surveillance. *Men are such proprietary creatures*, she thought.

Fiona winked at Simon.

"She's supposed to be mine, remember," she mouthed and grinned.

She was still affected by Marji's information and berated herself for not agreeing a warning to Simon. Maybe she shouldn't create more worry – he already had enough. She looked into his strained face, quickly realising there was no choice. She turned to Fiona and mimed an injection. Fiona's eyes narrowed and she nodded.

Simon shrugged, showing his incomprehension.

She took the pad and wrote.

We believe the camp in Utah is experimenting with medical methods of control and compliance. Don't agree to any medical intervention or treatment.

His face showed little change as he wrote back. *What do you mean, 'medical'?*

Gill took the pad. *Not sure*, she wrote. *Could be chemical, electronic or even implanting chips.*

Oh, he scribbled back. *Chips and no fish! For a moment I thought you might mean pain and sensory deprivation. Is this legal?*

Probably black budget – off the books.

You can't stop this?

We've no influence, and neither can we reveal our position.

Fiona took the pad, writing. *We'll do what we can to help. I've a sympathetic colleague in the region. No names at this point.*

Gill looked at Fiona, allowing herself a brief flash of hope. Fiona winked back and held a finger to her mouth. Gill willed Simon not to mention Andrew, Nick, Robbie or their mission to find Nina. Surely, he'd have realised, when Fee mentioned Utah?

Fiona returned the pad and used paper to her bag. Soon after came a knock and a guard put his head in.

"Wind up in two minutes."

The door closed again. She threw caution to the wind and stood up, holding her arms out. They hugged and kissed.

"I'll come to Utah," she whispered. "We'll do everything possible."

"I love you," he replied.

She remembered the past injunctions about sacrificing personal needs for the job. *To hell with that,* she thought as they kissed again. How she'd wanted to hear those words.

Fiona made a cutting motion with her hands.

"Guard's coming," she mouthed.

She looked at Si, aching to say: *Andy and the others will try to help.*

"Bye bye, love," she whispered. "Hope to see you soon. We'll be exploring everything possible."

The keys rattled and she sprung back as the door opened and the guard beckoned. She wanted to turn, waive or blow a kiss, but knew how it would appear. She stood straight, as she and Fiona made their way back to Betty Sampson's office. It seemed the longest walk of her life and like a nail piercing her heart!

74

PHILADELPHIA – UTAH

ZOLTAN'S PERSPECTIVE

Zoltan laid out the breakfast table. Judy should be down soon and then he'd make the suggestion. He would offer to take time out and accompany her to Utah, before the next Colombian trip. He heard her in the lounge and, moments later, she entered the kitchen in blouse, panties and shoes.

"So, you realise I like you like that then?"

"Darn it, Zolt, don't be so silly. I've lost something. I had a black skirt last night that 'somehow' got taken off downstairs. Have you been tidying again?"

"Guilty! Folded on the chair in the corner. Stay here a moment – I've a suggestion."

She sat opposite and it would be a rare man whose mind didn't go off track.

"What's up, sweetheart?"

"I know how worried you are about Andy and the boys and that you wondered about Utah?"

She nodded.

"I've a gap in my schedule, so why don't we go together. Maybe I can help?"

She stood up, threw her arms around him and they hugged.

"Mmm! I knew I was right moving that skirt!"

He carried her into the lounge and gently put her on the sofa. When they'd finished, he suggested she check the flight options while he consulted the driving atlas.

"Good idea," she replied. "It's a really long way. Better flying and then take a hire car from the airport. I'll call Freddy."

He studied the atlas.

"I suspect Denver's our best bet. Closer than Vegas."

He noticed her voice tighten as she spoke to Freddy. The relationship always seemed difficult. Freddy agreed, but she still seemed uncomfortable.

"Actually, Zolt, I could pack in no time. If seats are available, what say we leave this afternoon? It'll give more time there."

"Works for me."

The journey to the airport was smooth and, even with a recent spate of security alerts, the boarding was surprisingly trouble free. The 'city of brotherly love' quickly disappeared and, as they levelled out over the rural landscape, he recalled the recent encounter with Anson. Fifty thousand dollars certainly was a nice sweetener, but did he need more involvement with these people or to be winging off to Colombia? He glanced at Judy and she smiled back, clearly still delighted by his offer.

The flight passed quickly and he felt her hand touch his.

"We land soon."

The captain announced their destination, banked almost immediately and started the descent to Denver.

Speeding down the I70 later, he decided the pale blue Buick hire car had been a good choice. It was a road he actually knew rather well and he declined Judy's suggestion to view the Colorado National Monument. They snacked on food brought from the airport and drove without stopping. Even so, the sun had started setting as they passed Grand Junction and turned into the Grand River Valley.

"Perhaps we should have used Salt Lake City instead," he said. "A bit shorter."

"Far too po-faced for my liking."

The La Sal Mountains glowed under the last rays of light, as they followed the 128 beside the Colorado River, finally making Moab at dusk. Several vehicles stood in Freddy's drive and he recognised one as belonging to Terry James.

Mary greeted them and Judy hugged young Mervyn. Mary took them to the lounge and said:

"There's a surprise inside for you, Judy."

When the door opened, they saw Andrew, with Nick, Freddy and Terry James. Judy embraced both sons, successfully masking the problem with Freddy.

Andrew beamed.

"Hi Mom, I came straight over when Fred explained you were coming."

He extended his hand.

"Thanks for bringing Mom down, Zoltan."

"I hope we can help," he replied. "At least I know the South West fairly well."

Zoltan noted a slight reservation in Andrew's voice. Had Freddy leaked something about the militia connection? He certainly had the potential to be loose lipped. Perhaps Andrew disliked his Mom being with a younger man – or maybe any man!

Freddy joined them.

"Mom, meet Terry James – Robbie's dad. I do a little business with… Oh, what the heck… Andy probably mentioned our other connection."

Judy raised her eyebrows.

"You know – patriots serving with the militia?"

"Yes, I was a little surprised, but I'm sure you'll explain it to me."

She extended her hand to the grizzled man.

"Pleased to meet you, Terry. I so hope we can find a way of helping Robbie! Are there any developments?"

"I'm not sure this is really for the ladies," said James.

"Don't be silly, Terry. If my boys are facing danger, I want to be involved. After all, you're here helping your son. I've lived too long in civilised places to accept any old-fashioned sexist behaviour!"

Judy had a steely aspect that Zoltan hadn't seen before and he found her sharpness rather shocking. Generally, people were respectful to Terry, but, surprisingly, the weather-beaten face broke into a grin.

"Sorry. Just didn't want you in any danger. We went out near the camp early this morning and getting him out will sure take something."

"He's right, Mom," said Andrew.

"Double wire fences, watchtowers, armed guards – and possibly electronic surveillance."

"There's one good development, though," said Nick, who'd been silent until this point. "Robbie's cousin has a friend who works at the camp and he'll help."

"Yeah, they're due here, when Craig finishes his shift," said Terry. "Maybe then we'll know which way to jump."

Mary bustled in with coffees and an enormous plate of cake.

"Drinks for everyone? I just heard a car... probably Carl and friend."

She looked at Freddy.

"Please keep things cool with Carl. He is Robbie's cousin, and Terry's nephew. Don't set Mervyn a bad example."

"Okay," said Freddy, with a curled lip. "We don't want him thinking that people can walk over him, though!"

Mary left the room.

"You shouldn't take no pussy-whipping," said Terry, through a pinched mouth. "Carl's a good boy and his friend is helping."

Zoltan read Freddy's face, knowing that this could go one of two ways. At that moment, the door opened to Carl and Craig – followed by Mary.

"Food will be up in about an hour," she announced. "I'll leave you all to talk."

Carl introduced everyone to Craig, and then went to Freddy with an extended hand.

"Hi man. I reckon we should get over our little misunderstanding for Robbie's... well, for everyone's sake."

Freddy managed "Uhuh" and shook hands with an awkward grin.

"Anything new happened?" asked Andy.

Zoltan joined the others in a half circle around Carl and friend.

"Craig's put himself at risk for us," said Carl, and the serious expression on his good natured and normally carefree face was unusual. Craig also seemed an uncomplicated country boy and picturing him as guard, however thin the workforce, was difficult.

Craig coloured.

"Hello everyone! Well, Robbie's doin' fine, although the interrogations or 'special treatments' won't have yet started."

"What are 'special treatments'?" Zoltan asked.

"Don't know for certain," Craig replied. "Some folk have them and some don't. The guys say folk sometimes return... well, kinda different."

"Different how, son?" asked Terry. "You mean Rob will come out playin' baseball, marry a fine woman and raise a dozen children?!"

Craig coloured up and looked nervous.

"No, Sir. I just meant sometimes they seem upset, and are kinda different, later."

"Poor Robbie," said Judy. "If only we could do something!"

"Let's pool ideas," said Andrew.

"We saw a double fence, patrols, watchtowers with lighting rigs and probably a video surveillance system. Is that right, Craig?"

"Yes, Sir. There's a unit by the reception area near the main gate. Screens are monitored 24/7."

"Okay," continued Andrew, "let's throw our ideas in the pot and see what comes out. Just get creative and we can evaluate them later."

Terry's face darkened and he pushed out his jaw. He turned square on to Andrew and Zoltan knew what would happen next.

"I told you before, don't try takin' over!"

Annoyance flashed in Andrew's eyes.

"Sorry. Like I said before, he's your son. We only want to help."

"Don't forget that two of them are held now," said Nick.

The jaw softened a little as James shook his head.

"We've a difficult task on and them bastards won't make nothing easy."

"All we've thought of so far," said Andrew, "was cutting the power supply to get around electronic surveillance, although I bet they'll have backup generators?"

"Yeah," replied Craig. "A big diesel unit behind the monitoring room."

"Any other ideas?" Andrew asked.

"Diversions," said Freddy. "Maybe, fire or explosions?"

"Terry and Nick, what do you think?"

"Yeah, we had the diversion idea," said Terry. "We should blow them mothers sky-high and that's the truth."

"I contacted Tank, at the power authority," said Freddy. "A sub-station feeds the camp. It's next to that guard house and barrier at the top of the hill."

"We know where you mean," said Nick. "We saw that on our first visit."

"Something else is worrying me," said Judy. "We still don't know what's happening with Simon and haven't heard from Gill. In fact, Zolt, when we pulled in for gas near Grand Junction, I tried contacting Gill while you were answering the call of nature. I left a voice-mail, so hopefully she'll get back any time."

"Yes, Mom, but that isn't relevant to now, is it?" said Andrew. "Even if, heaven forbid, something happened to Si, he'd hardly be coming here!"

Zoltan looked over at Judy's sweet-natured face and tempered his sense of irritation.

"Hang on, Judy. You called Gill from the service station? Why do you imagine that calls aren't monitored?"

"I can't see that, Zolt. Not with our new cell phones."

"Yes, but you left Gill a message? Can you be certain she isn't being observed? Incoming calls can be tracked too!"

Judy looked crestfallen. As Judy's cell phone rang, Zoltan said, "That'll be Gill," feeling certain about the caller and content.

Judy was making the 'concerned' noises women often make when exchanging personal news. Then she went quiet, and he sensed something important was coming. She said, "Oh no" and "surely not", and then finished.

Her face looked quite pale.

"What is it, Mom? Was that Gill?" asked Andrew.

"It was about your colleague, Simon. You may have to eat your words. Apparently, he's been picked up by authorities in San Francisco and, contrary to what you said, probably will come to Camp Ute!"

Andrew looked pole-axed

"Weird," Zoltan said. "You only just mentioned Gill the moment before she called."

"Call it feminine intuition. Incidentally, it wasn't Gill."

Zoltan bit his response back – his guess was wrong!

"Who was it then?" Andrew asked.

"I'm not sure. Some woman. Said she's a friend of our friend on the West Coast. Then... and this part really was bizarre... then she said that Mahler will perform in two days' time at a tent in Utah! How she could possibly know I love Mahler, I've no idea!"

"I thought Mahler was a long-dead composer?" Andrew suggested. The meaning seemed obvious and Zoltan was surprised he had to explain it.

"That's right – a particularly wonderful composer who died about 1911."

"So, what's the name of the game, Zolt?" asked Freddy.

"I think the message is fairly clear. Look at the names," he said, spelling them out – Maher and Mahler. "They are almost the same, except for missing the letter 'l'. The word 'tent' most likely refers to the 'camp' idea. Therefore, Simon will come to a Camp in Utah, or Camp Ute, in two days. I suspect that's what Gill's friend is telling us."

"That sounds 'way out' to me, Zolt," said Freddy.

"I get it," said Judy. "I didn't get all the details at first, but intuitively knew it referred to Simon and that he was coming. Then the person said, 'Space in the West Coast hotel was limited, so he's nipping over to Utah.' She repeated that twice. It struck me as a really odd statement."

"Got it," said Nick with a big grin. He crossed to the table and held up the local history book and a map from the book store.

"That phrase, 'Nipping over', gives it away. You see, apparently Camp Ute was used during the internment of the Japanese, the Nipponese – or 'Nips' as they were called in pre-PC days. It's all in this book."

"Eh?" Freddy said.

"The Japanese," said Nick. "The camp was used to intern Japanese-Americans during the war. According to this book, a contingent came here from the San Francisco area. Gill's friend is telling us there are only short-term facilities in San Francisco and referred to the historical connections with the city from the time of internment."

"And, also, that he arrives in two days," said Judy, agreeing with Nick's interpretation.

"So, what do you suggest?" asked Terry. "You just wanna hang around for two days, is that it? Them bastards may have Robbie's brains on the table and his balls in a jar by then!"

"No, Sir," said Craig. "The build-up to intensive processing happens over a period of time."

A snort came from Nick.

"We shouldn't rush," said Andrew. "If Si does soon arrive, we'll only get one chance – if that!"

"Before the phone call, we were pooling ideas," said Nick. "I remember a movie where the previous day's surveillance tapes were played, in order to conceal the real current events. Could we do that, or is it too far-fetched?"

The others looked doubtful, and waited for Carl to comment.

"I don't think they routinely record to tape, so I doubt there are past tapes to get hold of. They use digital cameras on a wireless connection. If you tried mocking something up it would need to come from the same angle and I don't see how that's possible."

467

Their faces were grave, but, to Zoltan, the answer seemed obvious.

"Have you got your field manuals handy, Fred?" asked Terry.

"We could easily solve the camera problem," Zoltan interrupted.

The others looked up expectantly.

"How, Zoltan?" asked Andrew.

"Zapping them shouldn't be difficult."

"Zapping?" repeated Andrew. "Would remote controls really help?"

"No, lasers, like the pointers you probably use in lectures – unless that's too modern for old Britain. Far more powerful, though. Hang on, while I get something from the car."

When he returned, the group seemed more animated and Andy was speaking.

"It certainly sounds better than spraying camera lenses, like they sometimes did to speed cameras in Britain."

Zoltan held up a black tube not much bigger than a pen.

"The point is to dazzle the camera's sensor. I have these for communication purposes."

"Would they reach the cameras, Zolt?" asked Judy.

"They use what's called 'collimated light' – a precisely focused beam that doesn't lose brightness as it travels. If the atmosphere is extremely dense, the effectiveness could be reduced, but on a clear day or night, beams even from a modest unit reach a long way."

"Can you achieve more with more powerful units?" asked James.

"You bet! They're rated from class 1 to class 4. Class 4 units can burn, blind, and even cut through metal!"

"Yeah, fry the bastards," said Terry.

"Please! We only want to help to get Robbie and Simon out," said Judy. "Nothing violent."

"You keep forgetting Nina," said Nick.

"No," replied Andrew. "After Craig gets communication with Robbie, we can establish contact with her – hopefully by Robbie himself."

"Yeah," said Craig. "I'll do my best."

"We still gotta sort out what happens next, even if this camera blinding thing works," said Terry. "I thought cut the power. Throw a stick or two at the generator."

"Then what?" asked Nick.

"Then cut a hole through the fences at the back."

"A problem, if you've only one of them laser things, 'cos there's more than one 'ol' camera," Craig reasoned.

"Don't worry. I'll sort that out," said Freddy.

One thing seemed quite obvious to Zoltan now. He certainly had the group's confidence.

"There's still the possibility of thermal imaging," said Andrew. "Apparently, some cameras can also sniff out heat signatures. Look, we can't attempt anything for at least three nights. I suggest we call it a day now and everyone ponders on what's missing and how to improve the plan. Can we meet again tomorrow evening?"

"Good idea," said Nick. "The others have work tomorrow."

Not even Terry dissented and, shortly afterwards, Mary called out dinner was served.

Spirits seemed high throughout the meal, but Zoltan sensed a forced jollity – an unspoken agreement to accept his laser suggestion, whereas it was screamingly obvious the plan was fraught with problems and probably unachievable. He sat beside Judy, and enjoyed her bare foot caressing his ankle. Andy sat opposite. Hiding their affection this way seemed ridiculous. She'd been widowed for years, divorced for more, and her sons were married. What was the problem?

75

UTAH

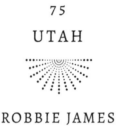

ROBBIE JAMES

I woke up with the gripes, which felt like a mixture of hunger, fear and anger. Remembering the last time, I doubted there'd be an edible breakfast. It was probably like the private prisons, which had made the news recently. Some corporate drone probably calculated minuscule savings through sourcing low-grade supplies and serving small portions!

I washed and dressed. It was about 8am, but the air was already warm, approaching hot, and I soon sunk back on the bed. Clanking sounds came from outside – perhaps a new shift had started? Moments later, keys rattled and the door opened. A well-built man approximately my age, with an improbably friendly face, entered and pulled a chair up to the bed. The degree of his eye contact was unexpected and something almost seemed familiar. The man extended his hand.

"Good to see you again."

"Sorry, we've met?"

The man adopted a slightly pained expression.

"A few times, actually. I'm Craig... Craig Thomas, Carl's best friend. You know, Cousin Carl."

Unbidden, my mind reeled back years, to a leaner, tighter face.

"I remember now, we did meet a few times... but, well... if I remember, we both had our troubles in those days!"

Awkwardness and adrenalin hit me fast. That had been around the time that news of my sexuality had leaked. Carl and Craig had their own problems with the joyriding thing, though Craig seemed the kind of happy go-lucky person I'd like to have known better. After the problems came out, I'd developed what I've since realised was depression – keeping myself to myself – and we'd veered off in different directions.

I shook Craig's hand and, for the moment, banished the old ghosts.

"What are you doing here?"

"Shouldn't I ask you that, man? I work here! Most staff come from, like, out of state. When some left, I took the job. There ain't much work out here. The thing is, I look after the rooms on this gallery."

"Like this one, you mean?"

"Yeah. I'd been unwell for a bit, so I didn't see you earlier. I'm gonna talk real soft now. There ain't no surveillance of rooms yet, though it's bein' discussed."

This was a surprise, but not as much as Craig's next comment.

"See, I saw Carl last night. Met your friends, Andrew and Nick, at Fred Anson's place. Your dad was there, too."

I replayed it.

"Dad at Andy's brother's place? I don't get it. I haven't seen him for years!"

"Careful. If they knew we was talkin' like this, I'd probably get locked up too. They're real big on security."

"Of course, but Dad?"

"I think Freddy trades car parts with him. When Andy returned Freddy's jeep, he levelled with him about your situation. They got talkin' and Freddy then clicked that the Terry James he knows is the same Terry James you know!"

"Shit. Dad's not exactly my greatest fan. You know, since that trouble years ago. We didn't keep in touch after I left home."

"Yeah, but when he heard you was in trouble, he came right over. He hates pretty well everythin' the government does, including this place. Anyway, you ain't been forgotten. They're all workin' on ways to help."

"I expect everything's sewn up on the legal front."

"Yeah, but maybe they wasn't thinkin' legal ways!"

"Fuck! We'll all end up here!"

Craig tapped his shoe on the tiled floor and his open face wore a grin.

"Nah, don't be like that. Your friend Nick seemed worried too. Apparently, he has a lady friend in here."

Craig leaned in and his voice dropped lower.

"He hopes you can talk with her and get news out through me. You know, about how she is doin' and stuff."

"I haven't seen anyone here, so far."

"Yeah, but that changes from today. You're now ready for what they call 'association'. You'll get time for outside exercise later this morning."

"Right. You said they're working on finding ways of getting me out? How will I know what's happening?"

"Cos I'll tell you. I'm responsible for all the rooms on this corridor. The rules allow me to talk. See, if you were considering hurtin' yourself or even endin' things, I am allowed to talk you out of it, and such like. Anyway, man, it's real good to see you again, although I wish it wasn't here. I'll bring you breakfast in a bit and you can go outside for association, at ten."

"The food's real crap here, Craig!"

Craig smiled broadly, showing a good set of white teeth.

"Ain't that the truth? We get the exact same swill."

Craig left and I amused myself watching a bug make its slow passage from one side of the small cell to the other. Craig later returned with a cool plate of greasy cholesterol surprise, and promised to return at the start of 'association'.

The wait seemed interminable. Even allowing for the tumble, my body felt tight and sore, everywhere. I had other worries too. Were my fellow captives actually terrorist suspects? Also, the question of how I'd contact Nina?

Eventually, the key scraped into the lock and Craig beckoned and spoke quickly before we reached the door.

"Let me explain here, 'cos talkin' ain't allowed on the gallery. You'll go outside and can move about and talk with the others. Over on the west side of the camp, you'll see two buildings. That's the privileges area. They have better rooms and stuff for people who are, like, cooperative. Their sleeping quarters get locked off during daytime, but you can enter the smaller building and use the pool table, library, coffee machine and that."

"I haven't exactly got a pocket full of change, Craig."

"Sorry, yes, you get a couple of tokens each day."

I held my hand out for the two plastic discs.

"You don't get 'em if you're bad," said Craig with another wide smile.

"What sort of people are here? I don't want to get assaulted or something."

"I ain't told the details. Far as I can tell, they mostly seem brainy or liberals like yourself, and some ancient hippies. They seem more worried about inmates who have them weird Eastern names. They're held over in the high secure block, on the east side. You'll see it, with the extra inside fence and little windows. That's where they keep them real bad guys."

We walked down the corridor and then Craig opened the door onto the outside exercise area. I blinked at the brightness of the light and stepped outside and took in the surroundings. Left, to the privilege block and, right, the high secure area. In between lay several accommodation blocks and, beyond that, a building that Craig said was the 'special treatments' block. The exercise area extended to the northern perimeter, where I'd taken a tumble, and beyond lay the La Sal Mountains.

I stepped forward into the exercise area. About a hundred or so other inmates gathered about in small groups with approximately two men to every woman. I walked the perimeter trying to catch anyone's eye, when someone called out "Robbie". I turned and it was Nina and another woman. They waved, and I went to join them. Although it hadn't been long, Nina had obviously lost weight. We hugged, but, when I looked more closely, the skin of her oval face now seemed taut over her high cheekbones. Although tired, her eyes seemed as intense and intelligent as before.

"Robbie, how on earth did you get here?"

"I'll explain shortly."

I looked at her companion – a large-boned woman who appeared in her early fifties. She had clear blue eyes and streaks of grey in her otherwise blond hair.

"Let me introduce Diana – Diana Kirkbride from San Francisco."

I shook hands, wondering where to start.

"Diana's from CDD – Citizens Demanding Democracy," she explained. "Their mission is raising awareness of the political fornication with corporations. I completely trust Diana, so you can speak openly."

I filled Nina in with the details. My dismissal from Marquetcom, Nick's hunt for information on her whereabouts and then the breakthrough.

"Please keep completely quiet about that."

"Of course! How is Nick?"

"Hit very hard when you were taken and got quite depressed. His attorney tried getting answers, but the responses were as clear as octopus ink."

"So, you came down together to look?"

I described our trip and the inclusion of Andrew, Simon's boss.

"Yes, Nick had described Andrew's work and I briefly met Simon, the night before I was taken."

I allowed myself a small smile.

"I became the unofficial tour guide during the drive down. The others are city slickers, although Andrew's brother, Freddy, settled in Moab some years back."

"Where is this Moab place? I've heard guards speak of it. I always thought Moab was mentioned in the Bible?"

She continued before I could answer.

"You'll find it's a very odd set-up in here. Mainly people from the activist community, but there's another group, over there," she pointed, "with Middle Eastern or Asian origins, who supposedly have links to banned groups."

I looked across to the low building with its high double fence and loops of barbed wire, and shuddered.

"Sorry, returning to your question. Moab is a little town in South East Utah, set in spectacular country – if you're a tourist. Red-rock canyons and pristine wilderness, but, for any escapee on foot – forget it! We stayed there with my cousin, Carl, on the outskirts of town."

"Why are you here?" asked Diana.

"Apart from rolling down a bank into the arms of a patrol, I don't know. Maybe involvement with anti-corporate causes? I worked for a real bastard, who, as Nina knows, is busy buying up water supplies in South America. Unfortunately for me, he discovered that I wasn't exactly on board. We now believe that many people with a history of opposition are kept under surveillance."

"Undoubtedly," said Diana.

She looked around the exercise area.

"Almost everyone on this side of the camp has been involved with some or other protest. They clearly know an awful lot about us."

I thought about what I'd found in Nina's apartment. Then there was the issue of Corinne!

"What do they now claim about you, Nina?"

She sighed and, as she prepared her answer, I watched a hawk circling on the thermals high above. There then came the whine of an aircraft, and its sound rapidly grew until I saw a small jet flying in low against the mountains. Sunlight glinted on the fuselage as it dipped below the tree-line. I heard no sound of distressed engines or a crash, which could only mean a nearby landing strip.

"You didn't know about the strip?" asked Nina, responding to my expression.

"No, though, as most people don't fall into the arms of a patrol, I assumed they fly people in?"

"Mostly, though some occasionally come by road," replied Diana.

"Sorry, the jet took me by surprise! I'm still confused about what happened with you? Corinne spoke of wild allegations of charity money helping terrorists?"

I tensed even saying Corinne's name, but Nina didn't react. Maybe she still didn't realise the betrayal and I decided to leave it like that for the moment.

Nina smiled.

"It's mad, I know. That's what they say now, although I'd probably drawn their attention for a while."

"How do you mean?"

"Uncle Sam has intervened in the south, for years. They like keeping an eye on anyone who suggests a different way of doing business – literally 'doing business', so I was probably due for trouble. That documentary marked me out as a troublemaker and they certainly don't like my contacts."

"Yes, any real challenge to corporate interests gets you in their sights," said Diana.

"But I suspect it was my involvement with the Senator that sealed it for me."

"Corinne mentioned meeting a Senator. Was it for fund raising?"

"Initially, yes, though eventually it became more. They like to see our relationship as being Senator Monroe's little mid-life crisis. Unhappily for them, his 'crisis' wasn't just physically expressed, though they certainly used our affair to stir up conservatives. No, the real problem was his change of heart. He later spoke too openly about me and our discussions."

"Strange, Richard having the Monroe name," said Diana, "with you championing independence for other nations in the Americas."

"Corinne said the same thing!"

My heart sped again, at the mention of Corinne.

"What's with Monroe's name then?"

A flicker of a smile passed over Nina's face.

"Well, the original Monroe, of 'Monroe doctrine' fame, was the US President who basically declared that only the US could play in the western hemisphere. It should be kept as a site of influence for the United States."

"To be fair, he warned off further interference by the Europeans," said Diana.

"And your Senator Monroe?" I asked.

"There are some personal aspects I want to keep private," she replied. "Put it this way. As people age, they typically get more conservative in their views and attitudes. Just occasionally, the opposite happens."

"I don't follow."

Two guards walked the perimeter close by, and she paused for a moment.

"Senator Monroe had always been known for a conservative, pro-business outlook. He was influential and could be relied on to go the 'right way'. Trouble is, no-one bargained on the effect of him becoming a grandfather."

Diana nodded agreement, but I still didn't understand.

"Richard contacted me after seeing my documentary and wanted to help. He actually came down to Bolivia to meet me. Over several visits, he progressively became more and more of a champion for our charity. In fact, it was Richard who suggested a mission in New York."

"How did he react to Bolivia?"

"That's what frightened people in his camp. He saw things for himself, and was repelled. Seeing suffering children, followed by personally holding his first granddaughter, helped him make the connections. You see his Katie, his daughter, married a Bolivian boy. Then, of course, there was his relationship with me."

"You mean you..."

"I said I'll keep some private. They have both my body and photos, safely locked away!"

"Monroe was pressured?"

She nodded.

"He's from the Bible belt, remember."

"And the thing about the charity funds supporting terrorism?"

"All nonsense. Yes, some has gone to organisations that aren't exactly cheerleaders for corporate exploitation, but every cent was to help children in the South."

"We mustn't draw too much attention," said Diana abruptly.

"We'll go into the privilege building for coffee, and you follow in about ten minutes. Keep it low key and watch what you say. We suspect it's fitted out electronically."

I watched them disappear inside and then walked the fence-line across the compound, close to the 'special treatments' building. The sun was warm and I sat in the shade of a pine tree. Across the open area, I noticed several guards congregating and one seemed to point my way. A sound came from behind, and then the crunch of boots on gravel. I turned and saw the door to the special treatment building swing back. Three guards emerged and wheeled a trolley up to the small hospital wing. A still figure lay on the trolley with a turban-like swathe of bandages to the head. Two guards stepped across my line of vision and then the trolley quickly disappeared from view. I shivered as a crow flew overhead. Its black and mocking cry made me feel even more hollow and alone…

CALIFORNIA – LAS VEGAS – PAGE. ARIZONA

GILL'S PERSPECTIVE

Gill negotiated the Tioga Pass from Yosemite, thinking about yesterday's events. Refusing Fiona's invitation to overnight at her place had been unexpectedly tricky. She wrestled her attention back to the road and the task ahead. Resisting the entrance to Mono Lake, she turned right onto the 395, down through the Owen Valley towards Bishop, passing High Sierra Nevada's peaks. As Si wouldn't arrive at Camp Ute until tomorrow afternoon, she reasoned that the drive would give a taste of the West and avoid any complications with Fiona.

Yosemite Valley had certainly been spectacular, but the queuing Winnebagos backing up to view two black bears basking in the sun had set her back. She hurried through Bishop and Lone Pine, only stopping to look at Mount Whitney's peak and check the route. Her next task was to contact Fiona's friend in Arizona.

She studied the map, deciding that missing out Las Vegas looked almost impossible. Perhaps she'd overnight there as Nevada seemed too sparsely populated to be choosy. The most direct route appeared to be through Death Valley to avoid the long dog's leg down to Barstow. She shook her head almost in disbelief. If back in Oxford or the South Bank office in rainy old London, the idea of driving through one of the hottest, driest and loneliest places on earth would have seemed absurdly fanciful!

Just after Cartago, she joined the 190 heading towards Death Valley.

The transition from green to arid was sudden, but it brought unexpected beauty. Subtle pink, gold and brown tones reflected from the nearby Panamint Range. The sky dazzled as she passed the huge sand dunes lapping at the feet of the pock-marked Grapevine Mountains near Stovepipe Wells. From Death Valley Junction, she passed Furnace Creek and the old Borax works, turning towards Zabriskie point, to view the badlands and look over salt flats blurred by heat-waves.

She reached Las Vegas late in the afternoon. Neon signs winked at the gullible as she drove down the strip, passing ever more improbable fantasy-lands. Crowds thronged around casinos and, as the traffic slowed, and she could hear the 'pot-pot-pot-chink' of a big slot machine win gushing its pay-out. She turned the car and drove back down Las Vegas Boulevard, passing fast-food joints, drive-ins, motels and wedding chapels to the intersection of Main and Fremont Streets – commonly known as 'glitter-gulch'. She stopped to stretch her legs and take in the technicolour wonder. After this interlude, she saw a relatively quiet diner and decided on a quick pit stop before hitting the Interstate again. Their menu straddled fast food and something better, so she ordered a chicken dish and retrieved the scribbled address from her bag. It read *Sheryl Harrison, Marble Canyon Drive, Page* and a phone number. She consulted the map and checked the time.

Page was shown as a small town near Lake Powell and the Glen Canyon dam. On paper, it seemed an odd place to station an agent, although she knew potential targets were routinely monitored now. Sheryl apparently also had duties involving the Navajo nation, though quite why seemed a mystery.

Her order arrived: chicken on a bed of lettuce, piled onto a tower of watermelon and garnished with tomatoes – as tasty as it was odd.

She traced the route to Page, estimating the distance, and decided that pushing on seemed just about feasible. Twenty minutes later, though, she was still in traffic and bathed in multi-coloured neon from a giant casino. The road abruptly cleared and she was suddenly disgorged onto the I15.

By the time she'd reached Kanab, near the Utah-Arizona border, the sun was sinking and the remaining rays reflected blood-red from the cliffs surrounding the town. Eating in Vegas had been the right choice, as she decided to continue on to Page. Further on, she was amazed to see what looked like gigantic walls of Neapolitan ice-cream, beyond the sage-brush. This must be the area on the map called Vermillion Cliffs.

The light had all but disappeared, but, as she passed over a ridge, she blinked in disbelief at the large body of water and marina. This must be Lake Powell, but to see a marina right out here seemed almost surreal. The road dipped down onto the Glen Canyon dam and then entered Page. A little further on, she stopped at a café and, over cake and coffee, looked at Sheryl Harrison's name and number again. She somehow pictured Sheryl as a faux cowgirl type – all designer jeans and chic boots.

She left the café and, a little further along, saw the neon sign for the Marble Canyon Motel – just as Fiona had described. After booking in, the old man on the desk showed her to an upstairs room accessed by an exterior staircase and veranda. She unpacked, dialled Sheryl's number and, when answered, said as agreed:

"Your parcel from California has arrived."

"Thanks," said a quiet voice, and then put the receiver down.

She lay on the bed, flicking through tourist brochures, until hearing a tap on the door. She opened it to a slender woman with glossy black hair and dark eyes.

"I'm Sheryl."

The woman entered unasked, and quickly closed the door behind her. She looked part-Asian, reminding Gill of a documentary she'd once seen about the Eskimos. Sheryl went to the dressing table and sat down on the stool.

"Fee told me about your situation. From England, right? I'd like to go there one day."

"It's often cold and grey – quite unlike here. I'm Gill by the way."

The woman nodded.

"Did Fiona explain where I'm headed?"

"Yeah. Said you could need some assistance. If it ends up with your friend on the run from Ute, you'll need all the help you can get!"

The woman shook out her long hair and smiled.

"Fortunately, we've no shortage of hiding places."

"Sheryl, why are you stationed right out here?"

"To keep an eye on the dam, because potential targets are now monitored. Also, as I'm sure you noticed, I'm part Navajo and we're right on the edge of the Navajo Nation. The agency likes having its finger on *Diné Bikéyah's* pulse."

"On what?"

"Sorry – Navajo-land, in our language."

"I never even realised such a place existed."

"Oh yes, and, with over 27,000 square miles, it's bigger than at least ten regular states. We also have a tribal Council at Window Rock, near the New Mexico border."

"All new to me. Why would they want 'a finger on the Navajo pulse'?"

"Probably paranoia for a start! I guess there are historical issues and debts between our peoples. Someone had the clever idea that terrorists might make contact, or even embed in disaffected groups. Either for support or to make common cause."

"Yes, I've heard those arguments before, though it seems unlikely, right out here. Could you really help if things went badly wrong at Ute?"

Sheryl cupped her chin in her hand, and nodded. She wore several elaborate silver and turquoise rings and appeared very attractive.

"Fiona thinks your friend will arrive tomorrow afternoon."

"So I believe. Some other friends are also trying to help, but I don't yet know if there is any workable plan. Hopefully, I'll discover more tomorrow."

"Ute isn't really all that far. You hop down Highway 98, cross Monument Valley and then pick up the 191 to Monticello. To answer your question, I can easily arrange for shelter if anyone has to lay low. It's really quite restful here."

"Why do you say that?"

"Fee told you of rumours that they're messing with heads at Ute?"

"Yes, though they're unsure whether this is legitimate, black budget or even a rogue splinter group."

"Good summary."

Sheryl fished in her bag for some paper.

"You have my land-line number and this is my personal cell phone, which I keep with me at all times. Call me if you need help."

"Thanks."

"You're welcome. Power-crazy attitudes have screwed our people since Kit Carson's time!"

"As a matter of interest, has anyone of concern contacted the Navajos – or is it just the typical paranoia?"

She cocked her head on one side, and stared at the ceiling.

"Not really, although we did have a Hungarian guy poke around a few months back."

"How do you mean?"

"Ever heard of the Navajo code talkers, in the Second World War?"

She shook her head.

"Apparently, our language is so complicated they used it as a basis for constructing military codes for fighting the Japanese."

"Really?! I'm afraid news of that didn't make it to our cryptography training."

"Yes, Navajos were recruited to help build codes for the Marine assaults in the Pacific."

"And the Hungarian guy?"

"He came down to Window Rock looking for information about the code talkers. Apparently, he was researching an article. Of course, he didn't realise much is still restricted, because of the military tie-in. That's why I was alerted."

She rolled her eyes and grinned.

"He was quite a looker, though!"

"I don't suppose many come right down here. As a matter of interest, did you get his name?"

"I was introduced to him as if working for the tribal Council. The guy was real friendly and went by the name of Zoltan. That's how I know he originally came from Hungary, because I remarked on his name. He's a US citizen now, though."

Gill took a deep breath, wondering about the likelihood of some other handsome man named Zoltan prowling around the South West – with a particular interest in secure communications. The odds seemed depressingly low.

77

SAN FRANCISCO – UTAH

SIMON MAHER

I finished doing some press-ups and sat back on the bed. Gill's unexpected visit had been a lifeline, but the little underground room got more claustrophobic with every day. I knew people had been incarcerated in pits, prisons and castles since the beginning of time – scratching names on cave walls, dungeons, and Gestapo chambers. In comparison, I'd only missed my freedom for five days and at least had electric light and food. In fact, the greasy hamburger and fries were making their presence known at this very moment!

I lay down, but once again the strange sounds started. At first, it sounded similar to a stationary London tube train. Then it moved to a low-pitched rumble and I started to feel nauseous. The tone deepened and seemed to resonate with my organs until I almost expected my stomach to flip its contents. It deepened again until virtually inaudible, though I could now feel a pulsing inside my body. My heart sped up and the surrounding air seemed hot and prickly, as though alive with some invisible energy. This was, I think, the fifth occasion and each time I'd fallen into a deep sleep and woke feeling drained. I could only imagine that the room was near a powerful transformer or something else related to the electrical supply.

My eyes closed and consciousness started slipping away. The energetic turbulence got even stronger and I remember thinking... *if... could.... open my eyes... I'd... see... my... trouser... legs... flapping...*

I woke to the sound of rattling keys. My eyes felt heavy and sore and, as I struggled awake, the sound of the word 'obey' hung in the air. The sound gradually dissipated and, when my eyes opened, three guards were next to me. I shut my eyes again, trying to replay the experience. The sound came from… was it in or outside my head? I wasn't absolutely certain and, in that moment, wondered how Martin Farrelly, or Dr Gianavecci would describe it.

Hands roughly pulled me onto my feet and I was taken to the main entrance hall and then back through the other corridor. We stopped outside a door and knocked. A female voice called "Enter".

It was that Sampson woman, again!

"Hello, Mr Maher. How are you feeling?"

"I don't much care for the hotel! My head feels like it's been stuck in a hair dryer. There's something weird about that room. You should get the electricians to check it out!"

"Then you'll be pleased to hear what I'm about to tell you. You're being moved to another location. I can't tell you exactly where, but you'll certainly have more light and space."

"When will this be?"

"Right now, Mr Maher. Not everyone gets to fly right over our city. Enjoy!"

She looked back at her desk.

"You haven't explained why? What's your authority for this?"

She looked up, smiled, and waved, almost regally.

"All perfectly legal. Goodbye from San Francisco, Mr Maher. Enjoy your flight."

I was taken down the corridor, through the sliding doors, and outside to the barricade and guard box. Sunlight at last! We turned right and took a path around the bluff to a black helicopter on a levelled area. I was pushed into a seat beside two other individuals. The rotor started to whirl and, without further word, we took off, heading over the city.

I felt queasy, looking down onto the financial district's towers. The helicopter traced Market Street and then flew over the huge needle of the Trans-America pyramid. Below, I saw the hills, Pacific Heights and then the green swathe of Golden Gate Park. We then turned towards the red 'coat hanger' of the Golden Gate Bridge, crossed the water and flew over the golden grass of Marin County. The helicopter followed the curve of the bay, finally hovering above a landing strip.

"San Pablo bay I think," said one of my new colleagues. "We must be in Napa County by now. I believe there's a naval station near here, so why not just drive us over?"

The other man grunted acknowledgement as we descended. Below us sat a small white jet with no livery or other markings. The helicopter set down alongside and we were instructed to board.

"That flouts 'the open skies treaty'," the man next to me said. "I fly, and can tell you that all aircraft should have markings."

We left the helicopter and, as I climbed aboard, I heard a flat southern drawl.

"Hello again, Maher."

I was face-to-face with the crew-cut-wearing Vince Berry, from the Arm-Rite Corporation.

"Things jest git better and better fer yew," he sneered.

I passed without replying, gratified to see that he'd lost an upper tooth since our last meeting. The engine started and, within minutes, I looked down, first onto brown grass and then the green mosaic of the central Californian fruit farms. We continued east or south east, and the terrain became drier and the vegetation sparser. Suddenly, a large expanse of water appeared within a landscape of red rocks, cliffs and unusual flat-topped hills. I caught my neighbour's eye, an overweight soft-faced man in his fifties. I nodded to the window, and raised an eyebrow.

"Probably Lake Powell in Utah," murmured the man.

I mouthed "thanks". The engine tone altered and we began descending. Below were great fissures in the land, and canyons with thrusting stone needles. The terrain then became greener as we flew over hills with mountains behind, and manoeuvred into a narrow valley. The pilot had difficulty aligning with the strip, because the approach was so tight. The ground rose abruptly and we bumped over the tarmac and stopped. Two jeeps and a people carrier waited at the strip's perimeter.

Vince Berry and the others hurried us off into a carrier that also held guards. Berry joined a jeep leading the way, while another followed behind. We set off, through a network of what appeared like forestry tracks. Behind, we could hear the jet preparing for take-off again. The track climbed steeply, beside an enclosure with very high fences. Eventually, this joined a more substantial road, passed a raised barrier and entered the camp. We were taken over to a small building close to the gate. I looked around and saw various other buildings, watchtowers, a microwave tower and a further section separated off by additional double fencing. Inmates walked freely in the grounds, while bored-looking guards provided oversight.

Once inside, our small contingent were separated and I was sent to a side room and told to remove my shoes and outer clothing. An issue of dark blue casual clothing and slip-on shoes followed – at least it wasn't the notorious orange boiler suits!

A guard handed me a large transparent bag of property seized from Elisa and Esteban's place and passed me an inventory.

"Sign for your stuff to go into storage."

Guards arrived to escort me to another building. One of them opened an outside door with a large brass key attached to his belt by a lanyard. He had an unexpectedly kind expression and an open face.

"Don't worry. Things here ain't so bad. I'm Craig and I look after this gallery. Generally, new folk start on the admissions section, but, because you had initial processing in San Francisco, you've come straight here... at least for now."

We walked half way down the corridor and stopped by one of the doors. At that moment, the outer door opened and I was momentarily blinded by the brightness. When the door closed, a rather familiar figure walked our way.

Craig looked up and smiled.

"Hi Robbie! Finished afternoon association?"

I was speechless. Our eyes met and struggled to make sense of it. Last that I knew, Nina was in a camp in Utah and the others had left to search. Something must have gone terribly wrong.

"Robbie, what on earth...?!"

"Why are you here, Simon?"

Craig pushed a room's door open, waiving me inside. Standing near the door, I could hear Craig whispering.

"Hey, man, I told you, there are cameras at both ends. You can't socialise here. The new guy will be out for association in a couple of days, but, for now, you'd best tell me how you know him."

I couldn't hear more, so I inspected my new living quarters. It was certainly no hotel, but a definite improvement on San Francisco, and had natural light coming from a small window high on the back wall. I looked around the small ablutions area in the L-shaped space, and then lay down on the thin mattress, reflecting on my new situation. Sleep came quickly and I was woken by the door opening and Craig carrying a tray. The sun was low in the sky. Craig switched on the light, passed me a tray of greasy, unappetising food and pulled up a chair.

"You must use the same crap caterers as San Francisco... looks disgusting!"

The young man grinned.

"You're prob'ley right! Listen, I've talked with Robbie and he explained your situation. I'll try to help. Can't say too much, but you have friends doin' everything possible."

"Sorry, I don't understand."

"I've met with your colleague, Andrew, his mom and Nick Martin, too. They're stayin with Bobby's cousin, Carl Willets. Robbie was with them, too, before he got caught prowlin' about outside. See, Carl and I have been, like, best friends, for years."

He faltered and his face had a sheepish expression.

"I owe Carl big time and he's asked me to help."

"I... I'm amazed. How do I know this isn't some set-up?"

"Guess you don't. You're gonna have to trust me. See, I'm puttin' my head on the block, even talkin' like this."

Craig's eyes were open and had no hint of veiling. At the level of gut and intuition, I believed him.

"I have to leave for a staff brief now, but I can pass messages from and to your friends. You'll soon be allowed out for exercise and then you can check all this with Robbie."

"What happens now, Craig?"

"Keep cool. They'll see you soon for initial questions. You'll be better off if you can seem helpful."

"And, then?"

"I must get to that meetin'. Just keep things cool."

The door locked behind Craig, but a sense of hopelessness had descended...

UTAH

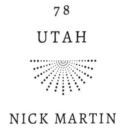

NICK MARTIN

I scratched at my head in frustration. Tom Phelan had now instructed me to return in three days' time, after which I had to return to Colombia. Unless something was decided tonight, I wouldn't even get to play a part in helping Nina.

I unfolded the large-scale map again onto the guest room floor, impatiently smoothing it out with the back of my hand. Forestry tracks surrounded the camp like a network of veins or arteries, and I tried visualising it from above. If we could somehow spring the three captives from the bottom end of the camp, we could use these tracks to avoid the main road.

Andrew entered the room.

"Are you still staring holes in that map?"

"I think these small tracks might be our best way in and out."

"The others have arrived, so you may as well bring it down."

I followed Andy to the lounge. Judy and Myleen served drinks and slices of Myleen's trademark Pecan pie. It had only been an hour since we'd tackled a plate of her Tex-Mex, but I couldn't resist it. In the lounge, Terry James talked with Freddy and Zoltan. In front of them were three laser pointers mounted on what looked like telescopic sights. Carl wandered over, but his smile soon became a yawn.

"Sorry... we started at dawn with some photography freaks."

"Don't worry. I thought Craig would be here, though? I hoped he may have..."

Before I could finish, the door opened and a smiling Craig entered, and headed straight for the Pecan pie.

"Sorry, guys. A hold up with one of the kids. Gee, Myleen, please give this recipe to Patsy."

I interrupted him, mid-mouthful.

"Craig, did Robbie mention Nina?"

"Yes, he's on my gallery, remember."

"Yes, but did he say anything about her?"

"I was about to tell you, but leaving this pie..."

He munched another slice.

"Yeah, Robbie saw her in association. He says that she's well, but don't like the food much. She 'ain't too optimistic about leavin' any time soon."

I nodded, encouraging him to expand, but Craig continued munching.

"Mmm, this is real good! No, Rob reckoned what he'd thought after searchin' her apartment was probably true. They don't like her contacts and reckon they work against the national interest. She was quite def'nite 'bout her charity work bein' straight, though."

"Anything else?"

"Rob said they're mainly protest kind of people. He seemed glad they aren't, like, crim'nals."

"I meant, about Nina?"

"Yeah, one other thing. Robbie wanted me to write it down."

He took out a wallet, and pulled out a half-page of lined paper. Andrew stood right alongside.

"Yeah, Robbie gave me a message right after he saw your other friend."

"Sorry – other friend?"

"Yeah, the new guy, Simon, who arrived on my gallery today. Three new inmates came and I got this guy called Simon Maher. Seems he's a friend of Rob!"

"Hear that everyone?" called Andrew. "Simon flew in a day early. He's in the section where Craig works."

Craig slipped the paper back into his wallet.

"Yeah, so we got three of you folks with us now," said Craig.

"How is Simon?" asked Judy. "Did he seem well?"

"Uh huh. Looked okay, but haven't really had a chance to talk, yet."

"This might complicate everything," said Terry. "I don't want that."

Craig nodded cheerfully, as if news that could possibly lead to everyone's incarceration was an everyday event. When the others resumed talking, Craig turned to me.

"Gettin' back to Rob's message, he apparently wrote it after talking with Nina. He suggested that you talk about this with Andrew. Craig slipped a piece of paper out of his wallet.

"I didn't really get it, but I'll read the message."

The hemisphere's doctrine lives on. Please talk with him personally. He might very well hold the key to our way out.

The room went quiet and I looked up to puzzled faces. Andrew held out his hand.

"Can I see that?"

Andrew stared at it for a moment, then folded the paper and put it into his pocket.

"We'll ponder that one further."

"Yeah, I don't get it either," said Judy.

I felt the hot prickling of anger. Andy was so controlling! If Nina had sent a message, Andrew had no right taking over – it was primarily my concern. I caught Andy's eye, and was about to 'toast' him, but he returned a look that said 'Please wait – I'll explain soon'!

"Some of us have been busy while you guys was playing games," called Terry. "Ain't that right, Freddy?"

"Yeah. Our guy at the power company can throw the power if we tell him when. It'll be either a night or an early morning job, right?"

The others agreed.

"The generator would cut straight in," I reminded them.

"Obviously, son," said James with a penetrating look. "We'd fix that too."

"We agreed to compare notes this evening," said Andrew. "Anyone have any other ideas?"

"This is probably silly," said Judy, "a movie a few years back – I can't remember the name. It was set in Las Vegas and involved a casino robbery. They did something extraordinary to shut the electricity down."

"I remember," interjected Zoltan. "Used an electromagnetic pulse. The military might have a sufficiently powerful unit, but, as far as we're concerned – forget it. Anyway, like Nick said, there's still the problem of the generator."

"I thought I was being silly. In fact, I can't help thinking that most of what we've dreamt up is unrealistic. Since that fateful September day, billions have been spent heightening security."

"Yes, yet our defences were supposedly outflanked by a few extremists with box cutters. Not exactly high-tech," said Freddy.

Judy's outburst had hit home though. I'd battled a similar pessimism and all the 'gung-ho' talk only worsened it. We were surely just fooling ourselves!

"I must admit, I feel the same," I said.

Everyone appeared silenced.

"We don't really know what we could be up against. For example, could they call up a helicopter with a thermal imaging camera?"

"Do they have one, Craig?" asked Freddy.

"Don't think so. Planes fly detainees and official visitors in, but I ain't seen no helicopter."

"When it comes down to it, we mainly have a problem with fences," said Terry. "Now you either get under fences, which means digging, or through a fence, which means cutting, or over a fence, which involves climbing or flying."

"Or they leave through the gate," said Andrew. "What are the regular movements in and out, Craig?"

"Well, food and supplies arrive, usually around 7am. The new shifts arrive at 7.30 in the morning and 4.00 in the afternoon. Specialists and the psychology people pretty well work normal office hours, as do admin. Folk from different security agencies can visit at any time and, generally, we aren't told who or when they're coming. Other than that, there is just them religious visits."

"What are those?" asked Judy.

"Regulations say detainees can see a Minister of Religion. Them Arab guys and others in the isolation block get a Himang, or whatever they're called."

"Maybe an Imam," said Judy. "Meeting the spiritual needs of Moslem detainees?"

"Yeah, that's it – an Imam. The others have two or three different Christian Ministers, mostly on Sundays. They're allowed an assistant, 'cos people get real nervous about coming in. Detainees have a right to see a pastor of their own church."

"The Reverend," said Freddy and Terry simultaneously.

"Robbie could ask for a visit and Steve could slip him cutters or something," said Freddy.

"What are you suggesting?" asked Judy.

"Steve Claybury is a member of our local group, and a certified Minister."

"What church?" asked Andrew.

"It's called 'The Right Hand of God', I believe. Am I correct ,Terry?"

"Yeah."

"Can't say I'm familiar with it," said Andrew.

Judy's face clouded.

"I've heard of them. We'll talk later, son."

Freddy glared at his mother, and threw his brother a look.

"Anyway, Steve's generally known as 'The Reverend'."

A sneering grin passed over Freddy's face.

"Though not because of his godly love of the Federal Government."

"Damn right, son," said James.

"If we created a big diversion at the bottom end, and had something to distract the guards on the gate, maybe Rob could leave with 'The Reverend'," said Andrew. "I mean, walk out the front gate with him."

"Wouldn't it be better if he walked out as him?" suggested Judy.

The room fell quiet.

"Not with you."

"Where do the visits take place?" asked Judy. "I doubt if many would ask for a minister from the 'The Right Hand of God'. No social justice activists would anyway, I'm fairly sure of that. Where are religious visits held?"

"In a little outhouse near the main gate," said Craig. "They don't want the public wanderin' around secure areas. Them Imam guys get driven straight down to the special block. Couple of guards hang about outside until they're finished. I still don't get your idea, though?"

Zoltan grinned.

"I do. 'The Reverend' spends time with Robbie. Later, Rob hits him and the Rev takes a dive and has a little sleep. Meanwhile, Rob puts on his clothes and leaves."

Judy beamed.

"We're on the same page."

"And the guards at the gate?" asked Andrew.

"Maybe Steve could give them a little something," said Freddy. "Hey, how about dosing some of the girl's carrot cake or Pecan pie?"

"Only with something safe," said Judy. "There's far too much violence around already."

"It isn't only Robbie, though," said Andrew. "There's Simon to think about too, so 'The Reverend' would have to take an assistant."

"I was thinkin' of bringin' some ladies to, err, well to 'see to' the guys on the gate," said James with a smirk.

Judy's face clouded.

"Shouldn't we keep this as quiet as possible? The more people in the know, the more chances it will go wrong."

"Mom's right," said Andrew. "But the religious visit idea seems worth developing."

"I suggest we combine it with diversions," said Zoltan. "Get everyone looking at the far end, while the real action's elsewhere."

I held up the map.

"I think I mentioned the forestry tracks last time. They're shown on this map and, as far as I can tell, still open and usable."

"Correct, son," said Terry James. "We looked around the area, before this happened. Yeah, them tracks are still there."

Andrew turned to his brother and Terry.

"How long will you need to sort this out with Claybury? There's also the matter of something to help the gate guards take a rest. You know, I can hardly believe I'm even thinking this way!"

"You can't be a wuss, with them a'holes," said James. "I don't want them cutting off my boy's balls, before he even gets to use 'em proper. I reckon we should get most things organised in a couple of days. Me, Freddy and Zolt have some other ideas for diversions, ain't we?"

Zoltan picked up a larger laser unit and grinned.

"Freddy has a friend who works in the ice-cream place," said James. "Dry-ice looks great in the right light!"

"But what about Nina?" I demanded. "Why we came in the first place – let's not forget!"

Things seemed to be slipping away and she hadn't even been mentioned.

"I've got to get back to New York, the day after tomorrow," I continued. "No-one has discussed helping Nina with any of this!"

"That's quite a problem, cos Nina ain't on my gallery," said Craig. "I don't even know the guys on her block."

"It wouldn't be convincing if Nina requested that pastor," said Judy.

"Exactly," I replied. "That's what I'm saying. We've no plan for her and I soon have to leave!"

"I think we may have to concentrate on Robbie first, for practical reasons," said Andrew. "Nina's message might be signalling that things are more complicated. I've an idea I'll discuss later with you, Nick – and you'd have a key role. If I'm right, and hopefully we'll get a message through Craig to confirm, you'd still be helping even after leaving here. I'll explain later."

Freddy stood up.

"Yeah, I agree. Otherwise, things get too complicated. Look guys, we must get back. Mary's cooked us a meal. Are you ready – Mom, Zoltan, Terry?"

"Let's meet again tomorrow evening," said Andrew. "Same time okay? Craig, can I have a quick word?"

I looked at Terry, half expecting him to challenge Andrew again – even willing it, but Terry was in deep conversation with Zoltan. The meeting had ended unsatisfactorily and I still felt furious with Andrew, who was now talking with Craig. I caught Andrew's eye, but he coloured and looked away. I nevertheless joined them, hoping to force a response.

"Hi Nick," he said. "I was just coming to find you. Look, I'm sorry. I know just what you're thinking, but I was actually taking special care for Nina's sake. Freddy isn't known for his discretion and Terry's a wild card. We absolutely have to get a message back through Craig."

"What the hell did you think I was going to do?"

Craig stepped forward, holding both palms up in the air.

"Whoa guys! Hang on a moment. There's somethin' else. Robbie asked me to keep this back from the others and only wants you two hearing it. Apparently, Nina got very close to a political bigwig called Senator Monroe and believes it's a large part of why she's being held. Seems that folk didn't appreciate their bein' involved. Nick, she wants you to go and see the Senator. Apparently, he has important information that could help gain their release. Rob asked me to read the message out the way I did, and see if anyone else understood it."

"No, I don't think so, although, Andy, you had some idea?"

"The good Senator was certainly where my mind went," said Andy.

"That thing about the 'doctrine for the hemisphere' for a start. Also knowing the public opprobrium and pressure Monroe received after criticising certain corporate practices!"

I looked at the country boy's simple, puzzled face, painfully aware that our only conduit was a flawed vessel.

"Craig, please keep this strictly between the three of us or it could make things far worse for Nina – and dangerous for me."

"You bet. Robbie made that clear already. I won't do anything to make things bad for him or his friends. I got my reasons."

"Thanks. So, tell Robbie 'message received'. Will he see Nina tomorrow?"

"Bound to run into her in association – unless, of course, they start him on special treatments."

"Ask him for more information to help me to meet the Senator... an address for a start. Brief us tomorrow evening, because I leave the next day."

I caught Andrew's eye. Craig was probably more used to baseball discussions and his usually carefree face looked stressed. I sympathised. How much easier my life would have been, too, if I hadn't attended that meeting in New Jersey. If I hadn't met her... No – unthinkable!

I watched Craig leave – momentarily envious of those with simpler lives and, possibly, simpler minds. Still, if Nina thought that meeting the Senator might help... I'd do it!

79

UTAH

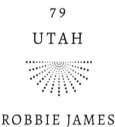

ROBBIE JAMES

The key rattled in the lock, and my door swung open. Craig brought in the breakfast tray, but, from the smell, I had no doubt about its contents. Craig's normally carefree face look worried.

"Why the long face? Heavy night, or did we share the same breakfast?"

"Yeah to both, actually."

I tried to force the greasy breakfast down, as Craig described the plan with 'The Reverend'. The idea of them working to get me out was rather touching, but that was tempered by the ridiculous-sounding plan.

"And the message from Nina?"

"Yeah, I'm just getting to that."

"Look, if Simon and I ask for a religious visit, together, that won't sound convincing, seeing that he's from England and unlikely to know of that church?"

"That's what Andy's mom said. They reckon it's best to level with the authorities, via me, that you two know each other. I could say you've suggested that Simon joins you in a visit – cos he's upset. What was that word Andy used, 'feign', yeah that was it. Simon could feign needin' support, and I'd alert my supervisor that you two know each other."

"I'd be surprised if they aren't onto that already," I replied. "They seem to suspect that we'd come together. Hey, you didn't confirm that, did you?"

Craig's frozen expression couldn't be misunderstood.

"Hell, Craig, why did you do that? If they get interested, and poke around my background, they'll find Andy and Nick are staying there! Promise me that you'll warn them to move asap."

"Sure, Robbie. Sorry man, I ain't used to all these complications."

"Okay. Returning to this plan – what about the gate guards?"

"Your dad had some ideas. Slippin' 'em some laced food was mentioned."

"Shit, if it's up to Dad, everything will get violent. Someone will get hurt or die or something."

"Uh huh. I also passed that strange message on, like you asked. Didn't mean much to anyone. Later, I spoke with Nick and Andrew, like you said. Only Andy understood. Nick says, yes, that he'll do whatever helps. They want you to talk with Nina and get an address and any other info that helps Nick meet with Senator Monroe. Problem is..."

Craig bit his lip.

"What's up?"

Craig tapped his toe on the tiled floor. Then he stood up, looking as if he'd decided something.

"Shit, man, you're getting me nervous."

"The thing is, you'll have to talk with Nina this morning, and tell me at lunchtime. See, I've been told you're going to 'special treatments' at 3.00 this afternoon!"

"Your face says that isn't good news... more questioning?"

"I guess so. Just I've heard people sometimes find time rather difficult there. You may return real soon, or they might keep you a while. There's no real way of knowin'."

"Shit. Not yet another turn of the screw! I'll speak to Nina, and let you know at lunchtime. I mightn't even be able to speak, later!"

"Nah. You'll be okay, man. Listen, gotta go. Back in an hour, for association."

I must have dropped off, and woke up later in a sweat. In a dream, I'd been tied to a medieval rack, in a canvas tunic with a hood. Something bad was about to happen. I struggled up, supporting myself on my elbows. I looked down, half expecting to see dislocated legs, but my sheet somehow tangled around me like a straight-jacket. I kicked it away, and fanned my face and chest with my hand. Outside, the sound of unlocking doors echoed down the gallery. It seemed so frustrating – Simon only three rooms away, yet we couldn't communicate.

My door opened and I followed Craig to the exterior door and exited into the light. I blinked and then looked towards the special treatment block, half expecting to see another bandage-swathed figure, but no-one was there. I scanned the enclosure. To the left, a small stand of pine trees and, underneath, I saw the familiar shape of Nina and her new friend, Diana. They waved and I wandered over to join them.

"Why the happy face?"

"Tell you in a moment. How are you two?"

"I've had better vacations," said Diana. "They should definitely fire the cook!"

"Couldn't agree more! Listen, my friendly guard, Craig, just told me something."

"I wish we had someone 'on side'," said Nina.

"Yes, ours sucks lemons for breakfast," agreed Diana. "Says we can confide in her with about as much conviction as a teenage checkout girl!"

"Craig was with the others last night. Andrew and Nick 'got' your message and Nick agrees to visit Monroe. Unfortunately, he's being forced to return to his workplace early and has very little time left. He asked for an address, for Monroe, and any advice on how best to approach him."

Nina bit her lower lip and looked uncertain.

"Tell Nick to be careful. Richard Monroe's basically a good man. He's as trapped by upbringing and culture as any of us, but he basically has a good, open heart. When he recognised injustice, he was brave enough to help."

"That's good to know."

"Things have since been made very difficult for him. It's been made clear that they'll bring him down, if he doesn't cooperate. Imagine, being from the Bible belt, and accused of having another woman. Even worse, one held because of alleged terrorist connections."

"Okay, so it's vitally important that Nick's careful, but how can he contact Monroe? What should he do?"

"I don't exactly know how we can use it, but Richard has evidence of corruption so huge, it has the potential to cause major problems. I don't think he even knows where I am yet, though I'm sure he'll want to help.

It's possible that he could pull certain strings so hard that we could be released! In fact, that's our only real hope."

"You think so? Craig described a madcap rescue plan they're working up.

The women's faces wore disbelief as he described the plan with 'The Reverend'."

"I know... it sounds really crackers. Dad's been with the weekend soldiers for too long. Getting back to Nick, where exactly can he find the Senator?"

"Politicians are in recess, this time of year. Monroe lives in Nashville, Tennessee."

"You did say it was the Bible belt! What's the address?"

"The mansion's in the Belle Meade area, at 250 Ritterman Drive. Kay, his wife, knows about me. I believe she's currently elsewhere, although they're still married. Incidentally, please ask Craig to say to Nick that most of this happened before he and I got close. Also, if he needs to press any buttons, Richard is very close to his daughter Vivien and his granddaughter. You see, Viv married a Bolivian boy and they live there now. Knowing that might help oil the wheels if things get sticky, but it all needs care. Nick has those skills, which is why he's so good in HR."

"The Senator has material on what exactly – corruption in the administration or involving corporations?"

"Often, the same thing," she replied with a smile. "You're pretty well on the right track, but I think Nick will fare best as an 'honest broker' without preconceptions. Look, in a moment, I'll go to the toilet in the privilege leisure area. I have a pen and paper, and will pass you a note that Nick can give Richard, to help with introductions. When you leave, shake my hand and be ready to receive it."

I nodded, but there was something else that had burned in my guts for too long. I brushed the sweat from my forehead.

"What about Corinne? Could she help?"

"She isn't in a position to do anything. From what I understand, they're not implicating her with this nonsense about sending funds to disapproved organisations. I always handled the finances. For the moment, she's allowed to get on with running the charity, and I'm thankful for that."

I saw no visible change. No indication that Nina knew or suspected Corinne. I almost felt relieved that I wasn't the only one 'taken in'.

"Do you miss her, Robbie?"

"I thought we'd be back together in just a few days!"

"Your assistant?" asked Diana. "Given the way things are going, you might see her here, sooner than you think!"

I nodded, thinking, *Not bloody likely!*

"This rescue plan. Should they hold back and wait to see what comes of contact with the Senator?"

"I think so, yes. The odds on that plan don't seem high, do they?"

"The words 'clutching' and 'straws' come to mind. They could all end up here."

"Exactly," agreed Diana.

"I'll pass that back to Craig at lunchtime. I mightn't be up to it, soon."

"Why, feeling poorly?"

"No, but Craig told me I'm going to 'special treatments' this afternoon. He doesn't know if I'll stay a while or come back. What do you know about it?"

From their faces, it wasn't good news!

Nobody's quite sure what's involved," said Nina. "Not everyone by any means gets sent, but we haven't cracked the code for selection, yet."

"Any idea what happens?"

"No, it's weird. Some folk go and quickly return, sometimes the next day. They seem a little vague, but get back to normal in a day or two."

"And the others?"

"I can't answer that. We don't know, because we don't see them again!"

"What, not at all?"

Diana put her hand on my shoulder.

"Bound to be a simple explanation. Probably, they've used certain interrogation techniques, and don't want the others having advance notice."

"Nice try, Diana. If that were true, no-one would be allowed back again."

They both fell silent.

"Let's have that coffee," I said. "Just one thing, if you see anyone who's been and come back, point them out to me."

Moments later, we were in the privileges block, sipping plastic cups of the murky brown water, which masqueraded as coffee. The women introduced me to several detainees. First, an older activist from San

Francisco – a white-haired friendly man with an institute monitoring alleged corporate corruption, who had 'coincidentally' investigated a corporation with known links to senior figures in the administration. I also met environmental activists from Wyoming and a couple from Denver whose particulars I quickly forgot. Then, all too soon, it was time to return. I shook hands with Nina, curling my fingers over the piece of paper, like a professional conjurer. She caught my eye and smiled sweetly.

The morning had passed all too quickly and I waited to hear Craig serve lunch. The women had identified two acquaintances as being former 'special treatments' visitors, but I'd deduced little. They seemed normal enough. I told myself that rumours flourish in an informational vacuum, and there was little sense working myself into a state. The sound of clanging interrupted this reverie, and then Craig entered with the tray. I was about to joke that all this junk food would bring the return of our teenage pimples, when Craig quickly spoke.

"Did ya talk with Nina? What should I tell Nick?"

I passed him Nina's note and the other information. Craig scribbled down the key points.

"She considers the 'Reverend' plan far too risky. It's definitely best to wait a while, until Nick contacts Monroe," he added. "Make sure you pass that on, Craig."

All too soon, Craig left. I tried to relax, but knew that the next footsteps would be to take me to 'special treatments'. My mind unhelpfully drifted to my adventures in the Village and the porno bookshops. I even superstitiously wondered whether my past behaviour had somehow brought all this about. How I longed for my apartment, a good bottle of wine and some Chopin on the hi-fi. A bug scurried across the floor and disappeared into the safety of a ventilator grill.

At least it had its freedom!

80

UTAH

ZOLTAN'S PERSPECTIVE

Zoltan gripped the wheel as he bounced over the track's ridges. Finding a perfect hide so close to the camp and landing strip had been a master-stroke. He approached the hide and nosed the vehicle down a barely visible track beside a rocky outcrop. Finally, he manoeuvred to the rear of the bluff and backed up to the crevice, which formed a natural entrance to the store.

Balancing the torch on some boxes, he pulled the camouflage away, unlocked the door and entered. He temporarily put the torch on a cool-box, wiped the sweat from his face and made his way to the cabinets at the far end of the chamber. Propping the torch on another nearby box, he removed the bags of powder from the cool-boxes and stowed them in the empty cabinets. He returned to the SUV, repeated the process and locked the cabinets. Now for phase two. Zoltan picked up one of the long crates. Though the short shoulder-launching variety, the missiles were still weighty and, after moving six cases, his shirt was mottled with sweat. He also took three laser pointers mounted on scopes from another cabinet. Promising these was the only way he'd avoided Freddy's involvement – though he mustn't know that! He tidied up, locked the store and replaced the camouflage around the entrance. The odds on anyone finding this place were almost zero, but security came as naturally as breathing!

He retraced his way back to the track – the vehicle's suspension now riding low, and he felt every ridge. This area was prohibited and placed completely out of bounds. No aircraft were due in today and he was almost certainly alone. Even so, he took the next turning right, and headed north for about three miles, zigzagging through a network of former logging tracks. He reached the landing strip's perimeter, and then took another track down a small valley, to a low building unobtrusively hidden behind a stand of pine trees. Department of Defense signs warned against trespass. He backed to the entrance and began the backbreaking task of unloading. Afterwards, he again checked the additional boxes of cocaine, tugging at their fastenings. Everything seemed secure, so he wiped away the sweat and returned to a visibly higher vehicle. He returned to the camp via a different network of tracks, joined the main road and proceeded to the main gate. At the barrier, a guard stepped forward to salute.

"Good afternoon, Major."

Zoltan returned the salute and the barrier swung up. The gate then opened and he drove to the main administration building, and bounded up the steps. The friendly blonde at reception smiled.

"Hi Gerry! Can you let Colonel Forest know I've arrived?"

"Sure thing, Major Heltay."

Moments later, he entered Forest's comfortable office, shaking hands – salutes now dropped behind closed doors.

"Delivery is ready for shipment, sir."

"Good job, Major. It must be roasting outside."

"I'm used to it now, Sir."

"I don't have to emphasise that, apart from Dick Riley, this operation must be kept from Arm-Rite's people, at all costs – particularly as they'll be on the receiving end in Colombia."

"I'm no fan of mercenaries, Colonel. Especially those doing the bidding of jackals like Anson."

"The Administration were mad ever involving them!"

Forest's blood pressure was written on his puce face.

"Capitalism proves its superiority daily, but that shouldn't mean we just casually hand over key parts of security to a corporation! The private sector has its place, but nesting inside the US Armed forces? I don't think so!"

Forest shook his head, his face changing from puce to plum.

"Diluting military traditions just to serve business – seems mad. Typical of politicians, though!"

He knew this was one of Forest's favourite themes.

"I know, Sir. Intelligence is going the same way. Since the New York disaster, we just hand more and more to the private sector. Everyone knows capital's loyalty is only to itself. Where will it all end?"

His face now took an even deeper colour.

"Leave things to the professionals. Remember Iraq? Private contractors shot up cars for sport, killing locals and children for amusement. Videos played on the internet and you know what that did to our reputation! Not answerable to the US code of Military Justice, or even Iraqi law! No, Zoltan, I'm afraid that legitimate force belongs to the state. That's another reason I don't like those militia weekend soldiers running about. By the way, any more developments with them?"

"Apparently, they like the new code I gave them. Makes them more secure in their communications. I've passed over that information to the army's intelligence and security command (INSCOM). Do you still plan hitting them? Terry James has now arrived to help Alton's crowd."

"If James Senior is stupid enough to mess with a secure facility, perhaps he should experience it inside!"

"Probably," Zoltan replied. "Anyway, I'll let you know when their rescue effort is planned... possibly Sunday evening. With Claybury off the scene, they'll almost certainly try to enter the bottom end. I'll go one side and make sure James is on the other! We'll use laser dazzlers on your cameras and dry-ice 'smoke'. I agreed with Anson Senior we'd keep his idiot son, Freddy, out of harm. I think it could prove useful to also keep the other son, Andrew, free for now?"

"I agree. He'll stick around all the while we have his colleague, so we can keep track of him. Dr Alton has an international reputation. Holding him now would just court trouble."

"Nick Martin leaves soon for Nashville. Parenda's attempts at coding her request were fairly flimsy."

"Yes, we'll come back to that later."

"And James's son, Rob?" asked Zoltan.

"I wanted to discuss that. He's currently at 'special treatments' and may be a candidate for the full programme. I'd like you to help. According to Dr Farrow, Robbie has a vulnerable profile. Farrow says he tries to strengthen it through taking an 'activist' identity and then linking with others. Robert has what's termed 'identity hunger'."

"Meaning?"

"The boy has diffuse boundaries, and needs an all-consuming cause to give his identity some structure. Robert probably believes he's found that by becoming a 'social justice activist'. Formerly with one foot in the corporate camp and the other with the activists probably makes him ideal for the programme. Farrow thinks he'll probably implode and become highly malleable."

"How do I fit in?"

"Later, in his treatment, I'd like you over in 'special treatments' to help with his testing. We'll first give him commands to delete recognising you. If he still does, we'll merely say you've been arrested and detained."

"Sorry?"

"Stage it as if you're another detainee, being given the privilege of visiting him. My bet is, we can force memory deletion and override."

"I see. Anson wants me in Colombia, soon. Has Tutch visited here recently?"

"About five days ago. Spent time with Dick Riley. Two of a kind as far as I'm concerned. Outsourcing any part of an operation like this only risks security!"

"I'm with you on that."

"The pigs supping the DC troughs would turn the entire armed services over to some lousy corporation, given half a chance!"

Zoltan nodded, realising that Forest's favourite hobby horse was just about to gallop.

"Imagine answering to accountants, or getting military strategy from a PR Department, or focus group? Lobbyists are probably working up more privatisations as we speak!"

"What about that English guy, Maher, from San Francisco? I heard him in action in Philly. He's probably the most devoted activist of this lot. Latches onto issues like a terrier with a rat."

"So I gather. He's a UK national, which makes things slightly more difficult. There's another complication as well. The British agent who shadowed him might head this way. If so, she'll probably link up with Alton and his brother. We can't have her here. San Francisco was just about credible, but access to a second secure facility could blow her cover with Maher. In fact, I'm not sure what to do about Maher. We'll discuss it later, but she is a definite complication."

He quietly recalled their nocturnal encounter on the landing outside Judy's bedroom and agreed. She was, indeed, a complication!

81

UTAH

ANDREW ALTON

I made the most of time with Mom at Freddy's place. I even surprised myself with Freddy's children. Mom, of course, loved time with her grandchildren, but I hadn't expected to enjoy it. I kicked a ball around the yard with Mervyn, feeling quite amused by his teasing.

"Dad says you're a boffin, Uncle Andrew, but you can't kick a ball!"

I went into the kitchen for a drink. Mom was there, looking preoccupied.

"Hi, darling! Has Mervyn made a footballer of you, yet?"

"Some hopes! Can you please do a second coffee? I suppose I really ought to call Anne again, soon."

"Good idea. I was just coming out to tell you that Gill just called. She's en route – probably about three hours away. I gave her the directions to Carl's place. I didn't think it fair for her to try and update us with Freddy present, and certainly not with Terry. She's already put herself at risk for us."

"Good decision, Mom."

Mary entered the kitchen carrying several shopping bags.

"Y'all staying for a meal?"

"We're expected over at Myleen's," I replied. "Honestly, I can't pick who's the best cook. We've been completely spoilt!"

She blushed.

"You smooth talker. Wish some of it would rub off on Fred!"

"Please explain our prior invitation? We're here tomorrow evening."

"Sure, I'll tell them."

We drove the short distance back to Carl's. I sensed – the way that you do if you're close to someone – that Mom had something on her mind. Carl's house was in view when she eventually spoke.

"What do you think of Zoltan, Andy?"

"I don't know. He seems a clever guy with lots of experience under his belt. Why?"

She stayed quiet. As he pulled up, he looked sideways at his mother's still attractive face and she was blushing.

"No, it's just that I find it good having company again. Not half as nice as having you here, of course – but, someone at home, makes me realise how long I've been alone."

We entered Carl's place and I mulled over her words, and decided that I shouldn't expect her immunity from the moods of women at a certain age.

"Where is he now?"

"Not exactly sure. Trying to source some equipment, I think."

I felt uncomfortable, but it had to be asked.

"Remember that little chat we had about the militia? Has Zolt said or done anything since, to suggest involvement? Unlikely, I know, but thinking of his connections to Freddy...?"

"No, nothing. They just got friendly through business dealings, that's all."

Marvellous smells emanated from the kitchen, but I went straight up to the bedroom. Nick was sprawled out studying the map again.

"You'll wear that thing out."

"Don't worry. I'll leave it behind for you. I still can't believe I'm going for cosy chats with the Senator, while you all get down to business."

"It isn't like that. You'll still be doing what you came to do – helping Nina! Listen, Mom just took a call from Gill. She's due in a couple of hours, and has information."

We heard a car arrive and I went to look out the window. Zoltan was back.

"I wonder where he's been? I'll go down to have a chat before Gill arrives."

"I'll join you soon."

I went out and continued across the landing. Looking down to the entrance hall, I saw Mom hurrying to the front door. Unusually, something made me stop and continue watching. I heard the sound of the front door. Then the porch door opened to Zoltan and he grabbed Mom, pulling her close, and she in turn embraced him. They edged into the hall, kissing with the kind of passion that a son shouldn't watch. At first, I froze, and then quickly stepped back and retreated down the corridor to the bathroom. I locked the door, and perched on the bath with a galloping heart. I told myself this was an absurd reaction. Mom was an adult with a perfect right to a new relationship. Somehow, this wisdom didn't lessen my reaction one iota!

8 2

ARIZONA

GILL'S PERSPECTIVE

Gill woke to the sun's first rays struggling through the unwashed curtains of the Marble Canyon Motel. She was still drying from a shower, when her cell phone rang. Fashioning a robe from her towel, she picked up to hear Sheryl Harrison's voice.

"Gill, I hope I didn't wake you? Listen, I've been thinking. There are things I'd like to discuss before you go. I can get to you in about fifteen. Is that good for you?"

"Yes, of course. See you then."

She dressed quickly and then looked at the map and guidebook. As Sheryl mentioned, the road leading on from Page skirted the Hopi Indian reservation. Sheryl talked of the Hopi people's existence last night, and their life 'dry farming' what were basically barren mesas. Sheryl said that historically the Navajos had forced the Hopis off the fertile pastures, back to their old wintering grounds on the mesa tops. Man's tendency to dominate others seemed universal.

The recollections were interrupted by a tap at the door and, when she opened, Sheryl quickly entered.

"So, you're leaving for Utah this morning?"

"I guess so. A shame when there is so much to see, particularly as I'm never likely to pass through here again."

"How about breakfast?" Sheryl asked. "The diner's just down the road."

They passed relatively green gardens, in contrast to the arid terrain behind the town. In the diner, Gill chose cereals, omelette and ate while quietly admiring Sheryl's silver and turquoise jewellery.

Sheryl noticed the attention.

"They're mainly Navajo, though the delicate bracelet is Zuni and this," she said pointing to a ring, "is Hopi."

"Beautiful. I love them."

"If you weren't so pushed for time, I'd suggest a side trip to the cultural centre on the second mesa. You'd find jewellery and other crafts there or, better still, buy direct from the Hopi villages."

"But you're right. I don't have the time and you wanted to discuss something?"

The woman's face showed uncertainty.

"Actually, it's more that I wanted to bat some things around with you. Our little network has its own communication channels, but, stuck out here, I don't get much chance of talking with the like-minded.

"What is on your mind?"

Sheryl stared into her plate before answering.

"I'm troubled at the way our agency is used. Also, that similar things are happening with intelligence communities throughout the developed world!"

"Wow. You really have got some major stuff bubbling! Do you mean the way that the CIA, MI5, Russia's SVR and so on, mirror each other?"

"True, but more than just that. For example, the way that the terrorism focus gets used to justify massive spending, which always seems to gush into certain pockets. The way terrorist threats lead to curtailed civil liberties – almost everywhere. The same seems true of fears of pandemics."

"And your point about intelligence communities?"

"That their, or should I say, our information often seems misused – a fig leaf for justifying certain things. Intelligence as an industry and the excuse for massive boondoggles for certain corporations."

"Like what?"

"Massive outsourcing, for a start. We now have huge recruitment fairs, because so many functions have been put out to the private sector. Typically, more than a hundred and fifty firms gather to poach staff with an intel background or government security clearances."

Gill shook her head.

"I didn't realise it was so extensive."

"Yes. Not only back-office jobs. Intelligence analysts, doing threat analysis and counter-terrorism work for overseas undercover projects. Of course, private contractors were involved with numerous abuses in Iraq, including the infamous interrogation techniques. Meanwhile, they field armies of lobbyists, fishing for more and more contracts. Behind them, are the companies providing equipment for surveillance, data mining, logistics and so on. You Brits are notorious for increased surveillance."

"Maybe something to add to my report. Where are we going with this, Sheryl?"

"Many that our service now tries stifling endlessly talk of cooperation approaching collusion between government and big business. That's obviously true with the finance sector, oil and pharmaceuticals, but it seems true with defence and construction, too. You know the score – hype the enemies, justify more defence spending, start wars, knock things down and then award contracts for rebuilding! Ever questioned intelligence's role?"

She drained her second cup. Simon certainly had suggested these things, but she hadn't expected to hear this from a colleague!

"The friend now heading to Camp Ute discussed much of this with worrying clarity. When wound up, he'd speculate about us almost having a global class war. A small international elite that craft laws and policies to siphon off what's left! These types lack any loyalty to nationality, race or religion, but do seem to recognise and cooperate with one another. A kind of 'birds of a feather, flocking together' phenomenon."

Sheryl raised her eyebrows.

"Simon reckons that, as well as having a lust for power and wealth, the so-called one percent probably have a shared pathology. A sociopathic world-view that includes the greed, callousness and a general absence of conscience that helps them outflank those with a more normal morality."

Sheryl wrinkled her brow.

"Your boyfriend has some interesting ideas."

"I know. I'm still not sure where we're going with this, though?"

"Mightn't the same be true for the intelligence? If elements of the business world are debased – what if rogue elements have also embedded in intel, with goals far removed from national security?"

She found the notion chilling.

"Your friend in San Francisco hinted about something like that. What do you think?"

"One thing seems for sure. The so-called elite couldn't care less about the needs or struggles of ordinary people! Could a shadow intelligence group outside the genuine intelligence service have developed, to service the needs of such people! See, half of our expenditure now goes to private contractors. Appointments are made secretly, with minimal oversight. Even the bidding for contracts is classified!"

Gill swallowed. Surely this was only wild speculation about the US scene? She sipped her coffee as Sheryl continued.

"There are indications of a splinter group, who work with private intelligence firms. The Arm-Rite people at Camp Ute are a case in point."

It hadn't been quite the start to the day Gill had anticipated. She stared at the delicate turquoise ring, while trying to take it all in.

"You really like that ring, don't you? Look, I can easily take you up onto the mesas. I'm well known there, so you'd probably get a good deal."

"Thanks, but I really do have to leave soon. To be honest, what you said has blown me away. Freelancing intel assets, out of control and for sale... what a truly disturbing prospect!"

"That's the picture that's starting to emerge."

Gill recalled the briefing back home on facial recognition equipment and the contracts for databases. The industry really did indeed seem to be spinning out of control. For example, the new sound-recording surveillance cameras, the private security firms doing security tests on the Underground. Once there was a time when even private prisons seemed unthinkable. She looked up and found Sheryl studying her face.

"Perhaps I'm losing the plot, but I just needed to bounce this around. What do you think?"

"Search me. To be honest, now I could believe almost anything."

For some reason, Sheryl seemed relieved.

"It's been good talking. Guess we've both suffered having no-one to share with. Don't forget, I'll be glad to help if you get any problems."

"Thanks Sheryl, but I really should leave now."

"Keep in touch. Can I recommend a small detour to the Navajo National Monument en route? You'd probably also find Monument Valley impressive."

Despite wanting to see Lake Powell for the last time, with house-boats nestling under red cliffs – she set off. The seventy miles over the Shonto plateau flew by and soon she joined US-160, driving towards Monument Valley.

Bizarre rock formations sprouted from a landscape already over-whelming in its extremes of shape and colour. Ahead, some tiny figures stood by the side of the road. One held a sign and she pulled in beside three Navajo children with embroidered velveteen dresses and tradi-tional silver and turquoise bracelets. She took a photo and pressed some dollars into the hand of the eldest. Further ahead, the rocks formed even more extraordinary shapes and, passing over the next ridge, she looked down on Monument Valley's famous Mittens – their rock 'thumbs' pointing skyward. Beside the Mittens were enormous cliffs, jagged spires and towers rising from blood-red soil.

Spurred on by Simon's imminent arrival, she resisted the visitors centre and, shortly afterwards, crossed the state line to Utah. After about twenty miles, she passed a bizarre sandstone hoodoo. It resem-bled a man with a giant Sombrero, standing on a ridge with purple-tinted hills behind. From the map, this could only be 'Mexican Hat'. It seemed remote enough to risk the phone, so she pulled in and called Judy. With trembling hands, she quickly resumed the drive. Si's early arrival really was a surprise. She put her foot down and, after about two hours, saw signs for Moab and pulled in to check the final directions for Carl's place. Opposite, a large wall of rock had partly eroded, leaving a window-like hole of golden stone framing a deep blue sky. She crossed the road for a closer look and heard a low-flying jet. The noise grew progressively louder until a small white jet screamed overhead.

The regional airport was about 20 miles north, so this could only be more unfortunates bound for Camp Ute. Thirty minutes later, she reached Moab's city limits, and turned into Carl Willet's property...

8 3

UTAH

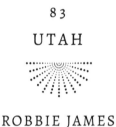

ROBBIE JAMES

Neither Nina nor Diana's reactions seemed reassuring about what might await me at 'special treatments'. I lay on my bed listening for the footsteps to take me. Through the high window, I could just about see a branch of a nearby pine tree and watch a blue jay preen. A welcome diversion, though unlikely to be the bluebird of happiness! Eventually it flew away, leaving me with the dreaded sound of approaching feet. The door opened. It was Craig, together with three guards.

"C'mon buddy… it's time to go," said Craig, with a smile and wink.

"I'm quite happy here," I said, feeling sick with apprehension.

"Move it," said the largest guard.

We walked down the corridor, and exited the block over to the squat building where I'd seen the figure on a hospital trolley. I caught a whiff of hospital-type smells as we entered – strong disinfectant and bodies. It seemed odd, because Nina had pointed to a dedicated hospital wing elsewhere.

"What happens here?"

"You'll soon find out," replied a guard.

We stopped outside a door and the lead guard fiddled with keys and opened it.

I'd expected some sort of interrogation, so it was surprising to find myself in a room similar to the one I'd just left. They pushed me inside.

"This is your room. Wait here."

They left and I looked around. Apart from a kind of bulkhead behind the bed, it seemed similar to my old room. The bed had the same thin mattress and the high Perspex window above looked identical. Luckily, I could see a branch of another tree, now backlit against the strong afternoon sun. Several metal anchoring points were set into the floor on either side of the bed. I went into the ablutions area, which also resembled my last room, apart from a grille high on the wall attached to a small duct. Maybe for air conditioning, though it certainly wasn't working!

After about an hour, I heard feet approaching and stop outside my door. I was then escorted to a room further down the corridor, where Dr Farrow and two others were waiting. The guards left, and Farrow motioned to a seat in front of his desk.

"Hello again, Mr James. Welcome to the programme."

"Dr Farrow, right?"

He nodded and I took the opportunity to scan the room. At one end was a large and complicated extending chair, rather like a dentist's couch. Above it hung a large flat screen, suspended from the ceiling by heavy-duty fixings. On one side of the room were cabinets and bookcases and the other had a trolley and a variety of what looked like medical equipment.

"Yes, I'm Dr Farrow. This is Tom Land and Ms Wendy Shipton, who are assisting. We'll work together to get things straightened out."

"I am already quite 'straightened out', thanks."

Farrow smiled, shaking his head.

"With the greatest respect, I hardly think that 'straightened' is the right word, do you?"

I didn't even know them and already they were making allusions.

"What does this 'programme', as you put it, involve?"

"Do you remember the earlier conversation, when it was explained that we ask the questions. Reflect for a moment and you'll see the wisdom. However, I can tell you that the first stage involves some psychological testing."

"I held down a perfectly good job and have nothing wrong with my psychology, thank you. After all, I'm not imprisoning people who are just out walking!"

"Yes, 'held down' is past tense, Mr James. We're familiar with your attitude to your past employment – and how and why you lost it. Just as we're aware of your exotic tastes in printed material, your internet habits, and the odd company you keep. What was that again – 'Nothing wrong with my psychology'?"

"Perhaps you beat your wife. Maybe you're a paedophile."

I tried to stop because things often went this way. First, failing to defend myself and, later, lashing out – usually, self destructively.

"I was trying to say that interrogating innocent people isn't exactly healthy. You know, 'people who live in glasshouses, shouldn't throw stones'!"

Farrow didn't react and his assistants stayed impassive. He pointed to the other side of the room.

"Please sit in the big chair over there, Mr James. If necessary, we can call for assistance, but I'm sure that won't be necessary, because there's nothing to worry about."

"What, with you happy jokers pulling out my teeth, or something?"

"Don't be silly. Teeth won't be involved at this stage. Just a small psychological assessment. You'll see some pictures and your body might want to react."

"What? You're going to put some damn instrument around my genitals and show me loads of filth?"

"Penile plethysmography won't be involved. Exotic as your tastes undoubtedly are, you're not a sex offender – unless there's something you'd like to tell us? Please sit on the couch."

I crossed the room and sat down. It indeed seemed more of a couch and Tom Land pedalled it down until almost flat. The female assistant pulled a crown-like attachment from the ceiling, complete with leads and pads, and gently attached the array to my head. Farrow attached sensors to other places on my body and Land then put headphones on my head, and secured me with straps across chest, hips and just below the knees. Farrow then crossed to a small box and did something. The screen lit up and white noise flooded the headphones. I noticed that the sound was more pronounced in the left can and realised that Land had misplaced the headphones, missing part of my right ear.

They retired to the far end of the room, and images started playing on the screen. The first was a school playground with children playing. A forlorn, weeping child was off to the side of the main group. With my right ear, I could hear Land ask Farrow.

"What exactly are we recording?"

"His idiosyncratic patterns to various stimuli. We want to find the places in the electromagnetic and auditory spectrum where his internal processing can be compromised or manipulated."

"I don't quite understand?"

"The sensors pick up activity in various biological systems, and can map how incoming information interacts with his neural structures to produce thoughts and emotions. This can all be displayed mathematically. When key states of mind and emotions are active, we map and record them. Then, following chipping, we can recognise key states, or indeed create them with RNM."

"Sorry Doctor, RNM?"

"Come on. I know it's your first time, but do get yourself up to speed. Remote neural monitoring!"

In my left ear, someone was wailing, "I want my Mommy," which did nothing to ease the shock over what I'd just heard.

Farrow fiddled with his control box. Soon, images rotated like a regular slideshow. A tranquil woodland scene showed spring flowers and my body relaxed, while "Claire de Lune" played. Next, a graveside scene with a close-up of a widow's face wracked in grief, and the sound of uncontrolled sobbing. A giant close-up of anonymous female genitalia was followed by a tropical beach scene, with turquoise sea and palm-fringed sands. For a while, I thought I'd detected the pattern, and braced for something difficult, but the next image was of meditating monks and the delightful chimes of what I knew were tuned crystal bowls. The image then suddenly changed to a shocking picture of the self-immolation of a monk – probably in some horrific protest.

The procession of images continued, I guessed, for at least ninety minutes. There were pleasing moments, happy children, snowdrops, tables overflowing with food. They were more than eclipsed by other images – pornographic shots of homosexual coupling, terrorist bombings, mutilations and body parts, wounded animals and the horror of 9/11. After hearing what Farrow had said, I tried to control my reactions, but they seemed outside conscious control.

Eventually, Farrow killed the screen. Land undid the sensors and headphones, and pedalled the couch upright. Shipton removed the sensor array from my head.

"Okay, you can return to the other seat now."

I struggled across the floor, surprised by how weak and wobbly I actually felt. I sat with as much dignity as I could muster, but quivering sensations had migrated from my abdomen. I realised that I was close to tears.

"That's all for today," said Dr Farrow, "but we'll see a lot more of you. Return to your room, for now."

Almost immediately, the door opened and the guards reappeared. Before my legs could respond, hands pulled me to my feet and I was escorted back to my new room. The door firmly clanged and I heard them leave.

I lay back, reviewing all that had happened. A click came from the small washing area and then the whisper of air conditioning started. A moment or two later, I heard a deep humming, which then changed to a lower and lower pitch, until barely audible. I instinctively reached over my head to the dome-shaped bulkhead behind the bed. As my fingertips approached, they encountered a sensation like static electricity and I guessed the metal would be vibrating. My hand confirmed it and rested on the curved metal. My eyes were closing by the time I concluded that it must be air conditioning. I was aware of my other hand flopping onto the bed as I rolled onto my side, drew up my knees and fell into a welcome blackness!

84

UTAH – ARIZONA – ARKANSAS – NASHVILLE, TENNESSEE

NICK MARTIN

I rubbed my shoulder and gripped the steering wheel with my left hand. This drive seemed far longer than I'd imagined. Increasingly, it seemed that I'd have to leave the rental car in Nashville and then fly back to New York. I committed the landscape outside to my memory's hard drive. With the others possibly finishing the rescue, it might be as much as I'd have!

Leaving Utah, I drove the unfortunately numbered US-666, through the old Wild West town of Durango. Turning south to Santa Fe, I joined Interstate 40 into Texas, passing through the yellow soil country near Amarillo and overnighting in Oklahoma City. I resisted visiting the National Cowboy Museum, and instead pushed on into Arkansas and Little Rock – still unfairly associated with historical race disturbances. Eventually, I saw the improbable shape of a pyramid on the horizon, and shortly afterwards crossed the Mississippi into Memphis.

Continuing on was a tussle, as my mind cruelly listed sights like Beale Street, Sun Studios, Graceland and the Civil Rights museum, even as I hit the accelerator, spurred on by a sign: *Nashville 200 miles!*

I motored through the gentle hills of Central Tennessee until the volume of traffic, more than anything else, signalled Nashville's outskirts. I pulled over to remind myself of Monroe's address. Resisting my curiosity to discover what a 'honkytonk' actually entailed, I followed Broadway to West End Avenue and Belle Meade and the Senator's home.

The mansion certainly was impressive, with large exterior columns and a deep verandah. As luck had it, the gate was open already. Monroe should hopefully be back this time of year. I walked up the drive with anxiety in my stomach, silently rehearsing an introduction that I hoped wouldn't cause alarm or lead to my rapid ejection. I rang the bell, slightly surprised by the lack of security. The door opened and I was face-to-face with an elegant middle-aged woman, unafraid to let her hair show silver.

"You've brought the papers over for Jack?" she asked, with a smile.

"Sorry. We might be at cross purposes. My name is Nick Martin and I understood this is Senator Richard Monroe's address?"

I continued despite her bemused expression.

"Sorry to call unannounced. Normally I wouldn't dream of it, but it's absolutely urgent that I see him."

"Sorry, young man," she said in an appealing southern accent. "You're too late. The Senator moved about three weeks ago. I believe he's out near Old Hickory Lake. Wait a moment."

I stood in despair until she returned with a piece of paper and a map.

"From your accent, I guess that you're not from these parts?"

I nodded as she opened out the map.

"Look here, near Hendersonville. Look for Lavinia Row down by the water. His place is called Gallant House –I'll write it down. Lots of country music stars have moved out there as well. Nashville's so busy now."

I thanked her, and made my way back to West End Avenue. I pulled in to take stock. The light was failing and finding an out-of-the-way lakeside address in the dark didn't seem realistic, though, after such a trip, deeply disappointing. I'd try again in the morning and make excuses to Canvey. Mechanical breakdown, illness – I'd think of something because, heaven knows, they'd had their pound of flesh from me.

I retraced the way to Broadway and found a parking space in a side street. Further along, neon signs winked and live music poured out from several bars. Even from the sidewalk, the sounds from Tootsie's Orchid Lounge impressed, so I entered and ordered a beer. Country music remained a mystery and, though I'd heard of terms like 'Western swing' and 'rockabilly', the distinctions weren't at all clear to me. The band inside were a rather motley-looking group – two pretty girls, one the singer and Dobro player, the other on fiddle. The band included a skilled guitarist, a much older steel guitarist and a quiff-wearing, gum-chewing country boy on upright bass. With a country twang to match the heartbreak lyrics, the singer's voice had a particularly haunting quality. Part way through their third number, a pretty blonde with a corkscrew perm approached my table and pointed to the empty seat. I nodded, and watched her trim legs in tight cowgirl jeans and boots fold neatly under the table. When the number ended, she looked over and smiled.

"Hope you didn't mind, but it's really crowded tonight. What do you think of the band?"

I smiled back.

"Good, though I'm new to country music. What's the style?"

"Oh, contemporary. The singer with the Dobro is my twin sister, Natalie."

They started playing again and I watched her sway to the music. They took a small break, and she smiled winningly.

"I'm Josie. Where are you from?"

"New York City. I'm Nick Martin. You're a local?"

"Been here for nearly three years, now. We're originally from Gatlinburg, on the edge of the Smoky Mountains. I sang earlier tonight too – down the road at Robert's."

"You sing too?"

"Yeah, we performed together for years, as 'The McCluskey Twins'. Mom and Dad were keen country music fans. Nat and I love each other, but eventually decided to find our own voice."

We chatted a few minutes, and were then joined by Natalie. Apparently, they weren't identical twins, though that wasn't immediately apparent.

"Where do you plan to stay tonight?" asked Natalie.

"Don't know. I was supposed to meet someone tonight, but couldn't find the address. It was a business visit, so I guess I'll try again in the morning."

"What part of town?"

"Turned out he'd moved to somewhere called Old Hickory Lake. I didn't fancy finding it in the dark."

"The Lake? No way!"

Natalie shook her head and looked at her twin.

"Just that we're goin' there in the morning. Mash Stenton, the record producer, has a place by the lake. We might be recording soon."

Maybe the folklore about twins and telepathy was true, because they said, as one:

"You could stay with us?"

"Really! Are you sure?"

Both girls were remarkably attractive, though I knew I shouldn't spoil good fortune with silly fantasies. Natalie returned to finish her set and, between numbers, Josie chatted about Nashville and country music, reeling off the names of stars who were now living at the Lake.

"Of course, that don't stop rubber-neckers," she said with a pretty tilt to her head. "They run tours past quite a few of the stars' homes."

"What's the recording deal?" I asked.

"It's for Natalie and her band. I'm going to give support." She gave a delightful wink. "Though they may think another chick would give it more punch."

The set finished and Natalie returned to the table, carrying her shiny Dobro. A tall man in Western clothing sidled up, hoping to chat. She quickly dispatched him and touched her sister's arm.

"Phew, I'm beat. Let's go?"

As we walked to the door, I felt a warm hand slip into mine. I traced its owner and Josie grinned back.

"We're in the West End, near Vanderbilt University."

Moments later, I waited in my car, looking to follow their Dodge.

The two-bed apartment was cheerful enough and Southern Comfort made for relaxed conversation and not only about country music. The girls' general outlook was unexpectedly liberal. After the hand-holding thing, I wondered how far that extended? Later in the evening, Natalie picked up her Dobro and Josie joined on guitar. They sang country and, later, Blues which suited Josie's husky voice even more and was rather reminiscent of Rory Block. Following the impromptu jam, they talked about life, music industry politics – even the state of the world.

"It's all money, money, money," said Josie. "I'm so glad Mom and Dad showed us other values, like kindness and caring for other people."

Natalie made her excuses and went off to bed, but Josie stayed, surprising me even more with her views on social and foreign policy. As an experienced HR man, I should never have judged this book by its cover.

Alcohol was starting to affect my clarity, though it was difficult not to ponder the task ahead. That Monroe could somehow bring about Nina's release seemed to me a thin prospect now. Of course, if it happened, Nina would probably want to thank him in person, but she couldn't visit him at home given the controversy. It seemed a long shot, and probably just the booze talking.

"Josie, I've a friend who was, shall we say, having a relationship with someone here."

She smiled and nodded.

"She might need to visit, to kind of talk things through, but couldn't risk visiting his home and..."

Josie responded immediately.

"Sure, she can stay here. Meet him here too, if she likes."

"That's very kind. It's probably unlikely, but..."

"Another drink?"

"Thanks, but I'll need my wits in the morning. Do you have a spare blanket for the couch?"

"Sure, can get a couple, though you'd find it warmer in there."

She pointed to her room and winked.

"Sometimes, I like company."

I grinned, lost for words, grimaced and shrugged.

"The thing is, I was kind of involved with her too. Still am. It's all sort of complicated."

She nodded understanding, and left to get the blankets.

I still felt awkward in the morning as she sprang into the lounge following a shower, her damp hair bouncing like freshly coiled springs.

"Sleep well?" she asked brightly.

"Yes. Look, about last night. I just... it's just that, I..."

She gave an unexpectedly dazzling smile.

"It's okay. I don't often get let down. I get that you're still involved and I admire that in a man. Don't worry, the other offer's open if your 'friend' needs a place."

Natalie emerged from her room, freshly made up and looking extremely appealing. She saw the blankets on the couch and looked at her sister with raised eyebrows. After breakfast, I took a quick shower and, when I re-entered, Josie was explaining the problem of my 'friend' to Natalie. I phoned to reserve a late flight to New York. Then it was time to go.

I followed the girls' old Dodge on the surprisingly short trip to the lake. We passed obviously expensive properties, some modelled on antebellum mansions. The girls slowed and pulled over and I joined Josie at the roadside.

"Okay, we're here," she said, pointing to a fork in the road. "That's Lavinia Row. You should find the house down there."

She pushed a card with a written telephone number into my hand, encircling me with a surprisingly tender hug and kissed my cheek.

"Here's our number. Come back tonight if you miss your plane." She grinned. "Maybe I'd get lucky then! Just joking, but do stay in touch if you like and keep that cute accent. Gotta go, 'cause we're due in a few minutes."

She gave a little wave and they drove off.

I took the right-hand fork and, moments later, found Gallant House. A high brick wall ran around the front of the property. Behind, a row of large willow trees with branches reaching over the wall. Presumably, the property beyond ran right down to the lake.

I pushed a button and waited beside some impressive wrought-iron gates.

Shortly afterwards, a woman with a strong Latino accent answered.

"My name is Nicholas Martin. I've a message for Senator Monroe and need to talk with him."

"Hold on, please."

She returned a few moments later.

"He's busy. What's it about, please?"

"Please tell him that I'm a friend of Miss Parenda. I have a message from her and urgently need to talk."

She left and then returned again, asking, "Are you from the press?"

"No, definitely not."

"He says that, if it turns out you are, he'll consider this unnecessary intrusion and proceed accordingly."

"We've a friend in common – a friend who's in big trouble!"

After another pause, the gate opened inwards. I silently rehearsed an introduction, fearing it would sound trite or implausible.

I climbed the steps and the door opened. As expected, a Latino maid or housekeeper stepped forward. She looked to be in her mid-thirties and shook my hand confidently.

"Good morning. I'm Juanita Martinez and I keep house for the Senator. He's waiting in the library and wants me to take you there."

I followed her in and we eventually stopped outside an impressive large carved door. She knocked and a voice called, "Come in".

A distinguished-looking man with silver hair sat by the window in a deeply upholstered burgundy leather chair. I recognised the Senator from television, although the trim body, taut tanned face and blue eyes appeared even more striking in person. A powerfully built younger man sat in the corner of the room. Monroe stood up and extended his hand.

"Good morning, Mr Martin. I'm surprised, though intrigued, by your arrival. This is my personal assistant, Mr Graham Houner. I'm given to understand you've had communication with Ms Parenda?"

Monroe's handshake was firm. I reached into my pocket for Nina's message and noticed Houner quickly move his hand – probably to a concealed holster. His manner shouted either past or current secret service. I passed Monroe the scrap of paper and waited as he read and then re-read it. I'd looked often enough myself, though much was written in what I assumed was Spanish.

"Nina asks me to trust you. You have your driver's licence?"

Monroe scrutinised it for a moment and handed it back.

"So, when did you see her?"

"I haven't, for months."

"I don't understand." He waved the piece of paper. "So, how did you get this?"

"Via friends. Look, it's no use us wasting time. I don't wish to be rude, but is Nina's safety important to you?"

A sadness passed over Monroe's face.

"I should certainly think so, Mr Martin – otherwise an awful lot has happened for no good reason. Graham, would you mind leaving us for a while."

Houner got up. "I'll be next door, Senator."

I moved the chair, closer to Monroe, whose eyes were on the message again.

"Nina's been detained in a camp in Utah. Did you know?"

The Senator looked up, and shook his head.

"I'm afraid it isn't as simple as that, Mr Martin. You probably know that we'd become rather close, which, shall we say, has been used against me. What's your relationship with Miss Parenda?"

"I guess we're close, too."

Monroe nodded.

"I see. You probably also know her colleague, Corinne?"

I felt a stab of guilt, hearing her name.

"Yes. But did you know Nina is detained in Utah?"

He sighed and shook his head.

"I knew from Corinne that she'd been arrested and what's been alleged. Unfortunately, certain pressures have been applied, forcing me to withdraw from closer involvement, for now."

"I guess your supporters aren't the kind that accept anything but a totally regular personal life."

"That's true, but there's more to it. You noticed the Spanish sentences?"

"Of course."

"You may not know that my daughter, Katie, married a Bolivian boy, known to Nina. Some months back, they moved to Bolivia because of his work with a bank. Through her many contacts, Nina heard rumours of plans to kidnap bank officials. A group believed the bank aided socially-harmful projects for foreign businesses. In the note, she apologises that she was unable to get word to warn me of this, before her arrest."

The Senator now looked strained and rubbed his forehead.

"Sorry to hear that, Senator. Making an ethical living can sometimes be a real struggle, these days. I can vouch for that."

"What do you do exactly, and how did you meet Nina?"

"I'm happy to answer, but first can we agree on this? We both have interests in common and powerful forces ranged against us. Can I suggest completely putting our cards on the table, acknowledging the risks for the other and respecting any confidences shared."

"Having served on the Senate Intelligence Committee, I do know a bit about confidences!"

"And I have friends risking incarceration or worse, trying to help."

"I also have much to lose, so we can certainly agree on discretion. I ask you again, Mr Martin, how did you get involved, and who are these friends you refer to?"

It took me about twenty minutes to sketch out the history of my disillusionment with corporate life, my first encounter with Nina at the New Jersey meeting and the subsequent meeting with Robbie James, Simon Maher and Andrew Alton.

The Senator whistled under his breath.

"That's quite a story, son, but I get where you're coming from. I need a bourbon. Will you join me?"

"Thank you, yes."

"So, the four of you went to Utah, to find Nina?"

"Three of us… Simon went to San Francisco on a research trip. He was picked up there by the authorities, and recently transferred to the camp in Utah. Senator, can I check my understanding? I gather that, recently, you've questioned the status quo, in a way that puts you outside the party line?"

"Call me Richard, please. In my life, I've promoted conservative values – for example, hard work, self-reliance, law and order, free enterprise and balanced books. I know liberals like to portray conservatives like me as ruthless and money obsessed, but that isn't true."

This wasn't what I'd expected. Still, all credit to Nina – Monroe didn't seem the typical sell-out politician. He took another large sip of bourbon and continued.

"Of course, there are good businesses and corporations that create wealth, jobs and prosperity, but others that are content to strip out everything – even to help nuke other economies. What we see so often now isn't real conservatism – it's corporatism! I first met Nina just before her television programme aired and I've since been down to the South and witnessed what some of our corporations are doing. It made me sick and, you know what, there are many other conservatives like me. I know of things that are just plain wrong."

"Which, Richard, might be the key to helping. Nina believes you know some potentially damaging things and pulling the right strings hard enough could force their release. Not only for Nina, but also Robbie James and Simon Maher, too."

Monroe puffed out his cheeks, strain clearly written on the still handsome face.

"Certainly, I know things, but after speaking out against certain sacred cows, and since our affair emerged, the squeeze has really been put on me! Issues like unfair and bent trade deals, the courting of corrupt regimes, life-threatening levels of corporate profiteering – but discussing these and even more serious matters is strictly taboo!"

I nodded.

"I understand. I've lived a double life too – though not at such an exalted level! What could Nina mean by revealing 'things which could facilitate or even force their release'? I mean, with respect, most activists – and even well-informed members of the public – are well aware of one-sided trade deals and corporate profiteering."

Monroe poured another generous glass of bourbon.

"I need more time, Nick. Come back tomorrow. I have to think through the implications and work out the safest conduit for the information."

"Richard, I'm supposed to return to work in New York, tomorrow. In fact, I've a flight booked later this afternoon."

"Cancel it. Go sick or something. I have to be really sure about this. Let's meet again at ten, tomorrow morning."

Monroe was someone who clearly knew his own mind, and arguing seemed futile. Moments later, I heard the clunk of the gate close behind and I returned to Josie and Nashville.

85

UTAH

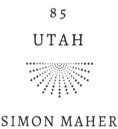

SIMON MAHER

I lay on the bed, watching dust motes dancing in the late afternoon sunlight, deciding that being without reading material was really quite appalling. I puzzled about yesterday's surprise encounter with Robbie and his subsequent disappearance from the gallery. 'Gallery'. What a ridiculous expression! I remembered when Rob guided me around New York City and spoke of the Gallery district in Soho, if I remembered correctly? It had been nothing at all like London's seedy 'Soho'.

The only bright spot was Craig saying I'd join 'association' tomorrow. Another odd expression, like something from a Victorian boarding school. Craig's other information seemed more worrying. The daft plan with 'The Reverend' had now been put on hold, while Nick tried something in Nashville. Rob's father, though, still wanted action and was known to be a 'hot-head'.

I heard approaching feet, although it wasn't a meal time. Moments later, Craig opened the door with two Arm-Rite guards.

"You've an interview now," said Craig, standing in front of his colleagues and giving me a wink. I followed them down the corridor to the enclosure and then over to a long, low building. I scanned the area, looking for Robbie or Nina, but saw no-one familiar. I was taken to a room and found three people waiting.

The powerfully built man with a swarthy complexion pointed to an exposed seat in the middle of the room. It was that character from San Francisco!

"Sit down, Mr Maher. We trust that you enjoyed your flight. I imagine it was a little different to Oxfordshire and merry England!"

I felt anger igniting.

"Surely, you don't expect me to respect this nonsense. As you very well know, I'm a British citizen, abducted in San Francisco, held in an odd underground bunker by some dyke and brought here against my will. Presumably, now you're 'Herr camp-commandant'?

"Don't try to be clever, Maher. I will only tell you that I'm Mr Woods, from a security agency with an interest in your activities."

I weighed up the others – a nasty-looking individual with rodent features, and another character in a white lab coat. Woods noticed my glance.

"My colleagues here are Mr Dick Riley representing the Arm-Rite Corporation, who provide security and other services. On the left we have Dr Farrow, our psychological specialist."

"There must be quite a call on his services. This can't be a healthy occupation!"

"Good you've got a sense of humour, although we don't do funny here!"

"Only funny-peculiar! Look, I want to leave. I've got other things to do."

"Perhaps you'd like to tell us the current whereabouts of Dr Andrew Alton –your boss, the well-known troublemaker."

"I don't recognise your description. Dr Alton is a fine man who merely says the way he sees things. Have you actually read his work? Anyway, presumably you have his Oxford address?"

"It's more his current address in Utah we'd like you to share. Apparently, he's not with his brother."

"I don't understand! I'm here to do research and intend to take the results back to Andrew in Oxford, as soon as this nonsense stops!"

Dick Riley took a large intake of breath. His face wore a sneer, but, before he could speak, Dr Farrow did.

"Cooperation really is in your best interests, Simon."

"You think I should accept your attack on one of the best academics and straightest men I know – just because he holds a mirror up to business sleaze and the corporate-state?"

"Save the lectures, Maher," said Riley.

"We're inviting you to help your own situation," said Woods. "If you don't, I can virtually guarantee that, by close of play tomorrow, Robert James will have given us the information, anyway."

The words rattled around my head. The implication was that I could save Robbie by squealing? Sorry, but I was damned if I'd betray Andrew and assist in his capture. In any case, these people did what they wanted, anyway.

"I repeat, I haven't a clue what you're talking about! I've been in San Francisco, remember, and don't know where anybody is in Utah. I can give you Andrew's Oxford address, if that helps."

"Okay," said Woods. "We'll leave it at that for now. You'll meet with Dr Farrow's team in due course. Let's just remind you a little of why you're helping us, and what needs to be straightened out."

Woods framed his evidence in a chilling fashion, cataloguing the same issues as were mentioned in San Francisco: 'Associating with people with suspected links to terrorists, giving aid to terrorists and undermining national economic security.' Much the same patter and, like the names, total nonsense. What was it with these people? Farrow would no doubt be assisted by Mr Timber or Miss Plantation! Still, at least the interrogation had been brief – for now!

The escorting guards arrived. As we crossed the open space, I looked out for Robbie or Nina, but without success.

So, they already knew Andy was down here and must be actively searching.

Back in my room, I felt full of foreboding and it seemed ages until I heard the sound of clanking cutlery. Eventually, the door opened and Craig brought in the tray. He appeared incongruously unruffled!

"Phew, what a day. We had this long training meeting and, right now, I really want to get off."

"Thanks for reminding me, Craig. Some of us are heading for nowhere!"

"Sorry man. Thing is, I've to meet the others at Carl and Myleen's tonight."

"Good, because that's just what I want to discuss. This is most important. Please tell Andy he must move from Carl's straight away and also to keep away from Freddy's home."

I explained to him what Woods had said.

"I suspect they'll soon find out about Robbie's cousin."

"You mean with Robbie being in special treatments. You're prob'ly right."

"So, tell Andy I said he must move immediately. Tell him tonight. It's very urgent, Craig. Please don't forget!"

86

UTAH

ANDREW ALTON

The great outdoors had never figured much in my past and this was my first ever time in a camping store. I avoided eye contact, but, on the other side of the shop, Gill was getting plenty of attention. I looked at Freddy's list again and picked up a small camping stove. Recalling Myleen's cooking, I shook my head, and pictured Anne's expression at hearing I'd even stepped inside such a place!

"Can I help?"

The young assistant had come from behind. I put the stove back and showed him the list.

"Actually, I'm new to camping. I'll be with friends, but need my own equipment."

Being shown the options was a strangely interesting glimpse into another world. We went outside and the assistant demonstrated self-erecting tents with spring-loaded frames.

"Watch this," he said, throwing it to the ground. It righted itself and then instantly self-erected. I showed appropriate surprise, listening as the young man breathlessly reeled off the pros and cons before adding his recommendation.

Forty minutes later, I pushed a loaded trolley to the car and drove the few hundred yards to the coffee shop. Now that Nick had taken the car, I'd hired a replacement and the neat green Toyota seemed a winner. As arranged, Mom waited inside and also seemed under scrutiny by several men. I realised, with another shock, how attractive she still was. In fact, recent events conspired to unfreeze her image as being 'just Mom' .I remembered her embrace of Zoltan and the disapproval that flooded me.

She looked up and smiled.

"Hello, love. I can heartily recommend these blueberry muffins. Did you have success with the equipment?"

"Yes. Gill received a lot of help, too!"

"I bet she did! Behave yourself out there, won't you?"

"Don't be silly. Actually, I was thinking, when this is all over, I'd bring Anne over to see the area."

"Great idea! I was only kidding, by the way. Gill's very pretty, but she has her head truly screwed on. Anyway, she's really in love with Simon."

"Did you find that motel up the valley, you mentioned?"

"Yes."

"Perhaps I should say the same then – watch out for Zoltan!"

She coloured.

"I'm quite a big girl now."

"Mom, I feel incredibly awkward mentioning this, but I accidentally saw something a couple of days back."

She smiled and nodded. "Go on."

"It was when Zoltan got back. I happened to be on the landing about to come downstairs. I looked down when you went, well… when you ran to the door to greet him."

This time she paled, staring at the table before making eye contact again.

"I see. Andy, darling, I'm getting on and I'm human. What's the problem?"

"I don't really know. I'm sorry, Mom. I just don't want you getting hurt. There was also the rather strange remark of Freddy's I told you about. There could be things we don't know about Zoltan. Incidentally, where is he now?"

"With an old friend in Grand Junction, darling. Don't worry. We've talked about everything. In fact, I've talked more openly with him than with anyone outside the family, for years. He's intelligent, cultured and completely shares our values. You know how important that is to me."

"But you don't really know his background or exactly why he came to the North East."

"I know he came from Hungary as a child. His dad was a mathematician and the family then moved all over the USA. Perhaps he's continuing the same pattern. He's got various contracts in the North East, now. Anyway, I thought you knew all that?"

"It did raise a few questions, you travelling here together."

"Zolt wanted time off. Besides, he knows the South West and thought he might help. What you're really asking, is whether there's something between us? The answer is, yes, we've become close."

"So, this motel up the valley...?"

"Yes, we'll share the same room. Since David died, yes, I've had male friends, but no romantic attachments. That's a lot of lonely years, Andy."

"It's your life. I just want you safe and happy."

"I know, and thanks. Now, explain the plan to me again. After Craig's message from Simon, you and Gill will lay low by camping in the back country. Zoltan and I should also avoid Freddy's place for now – though I can't imagine the authorities would want us. What happens then?"

"Everyone meets up in two evening's time at Anson Autos at about 8.30pm, after they close. Hopefully, by then, we'll have heard something from Nick."

"Got it. Now, how about trying the blueberry muffins?"

Fifteen minutes later, I pulled in at the crossroads, where Freddy and Gill were waiting. Gill came over.

"Follow Freddy," she said, climbing in beside me.

Freddy's dark blue vehicle passed through Moab and then joined the road to Monticello. Freddy turned left at La Sal Junction and they were back on the road that eventually led to Camp Ute. Gill's account of her conversation with Sheryl Harrison was so fascinating, I almost overshot when Freddy suddenly turned left down a small track. I recognised the general area from the first visit – after we'd first gone beyond and behind the camp, and had to turn back.

"Keep what I told you away from both your brother and Zoltan," said Gill. "They're both unknown quantities."

She flashed a sideways glance.

"Yes, I do see the irony that it's me telling you that!"

I smiled.

"Mom talked a bit about Zoltan earlier. What do you make of him?"

Her brow furrowed.

"Apart from his obvious good looks, I don't know. There's something I can't quite put my finger on. Perhaps years in the business or maybe feminine intuition?"

I wanted to hear more, but really this was Mom's business.

The small track wound through the trees and I figured that we must now be about quarter of a mile from the main road. The trees thinned out at the edge of a small clearing. Freddy then pulled up and walked over.

"I reckon this should be good," he said.

"I agree. Close enough to help with any actual rescue and also we won't be seen in town, if anyone's looking."

"Foresters have logged for years, but they stopped here at the edge of the military area," said Freddy. "This is well back from the road."

They unloaded both vehicles and Freddy stayed to help with the tents.

"Stick to the gas cooker," he said. "Avoid wood fires because of smoke. I'll leave now, and I'll see you both Tuesday evening."

"Is it safe?" asked Gill. "You know snakes and bears and things?"

"Keep an eye out for rattlers. There is a small mountain lion population, but it's sparse and they avoid humans. I think you should be okay. The main snakes to avoid are up there on the hill – about three miles away."

He pointed to a spur above the tree-line where we could make out the outline of a watchtower.

"Don't worry," said Freddy. "From up there, you're sort of down in a hole, surrounded by trees. No way you could be seen. Okay, I'm off now. See you Tuesday."

We watched Freddy's vehicle disappear into the trees and were now effectively alone. It was a rather disconcerting thought and I busied myself with the bedding, and then levelled off a space for the camp-stove.

"So, we're further east and south of the camp," I said. "Nick reckons there's a whole network of tracks and trails through the forest. I suppose we can explore that later, in case we need a quick getaway."

I went back to the car to retrieve the large-scale map Nick had found so interesting. The back seat was empty, though I could have sworn I'd left it there. It wasn't until after an exhaustive probing under the seats that I remembered taking it back into Carl's last night.

"Damn," I said, walking back to Gill. "Completely stupid! Let's brew some coffee. Fancy one?"

She nodded agreement.

I turned the gas tap and lit a match. Nothing!

"What the... now what? That sales guy said you turn this and then light the damn thing."

I took out a coin, engaged it in the hatch for gas canisters and removed the flap. Empty! When I looked up, she was grinning.

"The guy said the canisters went in there. Who'd expect it would come without any?"

"You did say you weren't familiar with the great outdoors!"

"Hell! I'll have to go back and pick up some canisters and another map."

"And another large water container while you're at it and half a dozen Hershey bars, please."

"Okay. Expect me in about two hours."

The drive back was uneventful. I resisted the temptation to call in at Myleen's, even though she'd almost certainly offer something to eat. The assistant was off duty at the camping shop, so complaining seemed futile. I picked up gas cannisters, more water and a map, and made my way to the provisions store, congratulating myself for thinking of insect repellent and more sunscreen. Moab was a small town, but with the prospect of days under canvas, it suddenly seemed a major centre of civilisation. I returned to the car with growing reluctance, and started the return.

Shortly after the city limits, I caught up with a large tanker. Stuck behind, I took stock of our current situation. It seemed the authorities knew I was in the area. I'd done nothing illegal, so I should be safe, but Simon's detention showed otherwise and already I'd been forced to camp in the wilderness. Ahead was the prospect of a madcap rescue plan, co-lead by an unhinged militia tough guy. Unless, of course, that folly was stopped by the efforts of a disgruntled colleague on an alternative 'mission-impossible' with unclear objectives, dependent on negotiations with an unknown Senator! I groaned, shaking my head. The worst gambling addict in Vegas wouldn't bet on those odds!

I was so preoccupied with our dilemma and keeping a safe distance, I almost missed the turning to La Sal Junction. I swerved, briefly leaving the road, kicking up gravel and dust. Although clear of the tanker, there was now another car that must have previously been in front of the tanker or I'd have seen it. I eased back. Probably, a forestry worker or a courting couple – unless it was heading for Ute, which seemed unlikely.

I'd felt a sense of unease for a little while before realising that the car in front was the same model and colour Buick that Mom and Zoltan drove down from Denver. I edged closer, realising with mounting concern that, from behind, the driver resembled Zoltan. After another mile or two, all doubt had disappeared. It was Zoltan – even though it made no sense! There was no way of reaching Grand Junction from here and, besides, he should already be there. I touched my head, checking for the cap I'd bought at the camping store. Although it looked stupid, with my anglicised complexion, I'd be in trouble without protection. I took my foot off the accelerator and dropped right back, praying the cap and change of car would stop recognition. Mom definitely said Zoltan was with a friend in Grand Junction – so either he'd lied or there was a change of plan. Maybe Zoltan was trying to make contact? Perhaps Freddy had given directions and Zoltan was bringing a warning. Maybe Mom was in trouble or had an accident?

I again noticed the red and white signs with the barcode type marks. In about three miles, we'd pass the turning to Camp Ute. If Zoltan continued ahead and then turned down to the clearing, he was obviously looking for us. I dropped even further back, but the sense of foreboding remained. As we approached the turning leading to Camp Ute, a small convoy exited to join the main road. I slowed to let them cross and two jeeps, a truck and a people carrier turned towards me. I reflexively touched my cap and straightened my sunglasses. As they passed, I looked down, but when I looked again, the blue Buick had turned and joined the road leading to the camp. I pulled in to the side of the road, heart racing and wiped the sweat from my face. Might Zoltan have misunderstood the directions? Surely, though, with the military vehicles he'd have realised this wasn't the right way?

My hands did the thinking and I quickly swung left and followed. The road curved and the Buick was already out of sight, but, as I rounded the next bend, I saw it in the distance. Beyond the next ridge and curve, I remembered, was the barrier and guard box. I climbed the hill as Zoltan's vehicle reached the top and disappeared from view. I hit the accelerator and the Toyota sped forward. Just before reaching the top, I slowed and found the gap where we hid the day of Robbie's capture. I parked well behind the trees, and then skirted the road on foot, keeping well behind the tree-line until I neared the installation. I could now see the main entrance and the Buick waiting by the barrier. Two trucks left the camp and were undergoing some sort of a check. Zoltan had left the car and was chatting to a guard. When the trucks finally moved, he returned to the Buick. The guard then saluted and the barrier opened. A few moments later, the main gate swung open and he disappeared from view. I sat on the ground, feeling almost breathless. Nothing made sense. At the very worst, I'd feared his possible involvement with militias – but never this! I returned to the Toyota and drove back to the crossroads. Instead of turning towards our camping place, I turned right and then took an old forestry track. I walked back through the scrub until I could see the main road again and watched. No activity came from the camp, so I lay on the ground, staring at a blue sky, and wondering why the skeins of fate had formed such unfathomable knots.

I drove back to Gill, still perplexed. I turned down the barely visible track to where I'd left the two tents, but no Gill. I checked her tent and she then emerged from the trees, with a grin.

"You were a lot longer than expected, so I waited in the trees until certain it was you. Did you get the gas and map?"

"Yeah, I'll get them in a minute. Sit down a moment. Something unbelievable just happened. I'm afraid our situation is even more precarious than we thought…"

8 7

UTAH

ZOLTAN'S PERSPECTIVE

Zoltan drove to the administration block, wondering why he'd been called in again. Last time, Forest mentioned involving him with Robbie James's processing, so perhaps it was that. He bounced up the steps to reception and asked the receptionist for Colonel Forest.

"Hello again, Major Heltay. The Colonel's over in special treatments just now, but should be back soon. He suggested you wait in his office."

He followed her down the passage.

"Make yourself comfortable. He shouldn't be much more than about thirty or forty minutes."

He sat relaxing and then looked around the room. The large office had a seating area one end and a connecting door and large wall mirror the other.

Bookcases and filing cabinets covered the rear wall. Zoltan checked his appearance in the mirror and then looked through Forest's book-cases. The first contained military journals, US Air Force special briefing papers, procedures and administrative manuals. The next unit was crammed with psychological tomes and journals, and military clas-sics, like Sun Tzu's "The Art of War" and Klauswitz was on the upper shelf. Next to another bookcase, he saw a trolley that surprisingly held a small amplifier and speakers. An old-fashioned reel-to-reel tape recorder appeared connected to the sound system. Odd, because he wouldn't have taken Forest for a musical type.

He went to sit down and then saw, on the other side of the desk, a thick file labelled *Major Zoltan Heltay/Hassan A.A.* It surely wasn't left here by chance. It made sense that Forest might access personnel files of camp staff, but his connection here was far more peripheral. He took the file to one of the comfortable chairs and began to turn the pages.

To suddenly see his photo aged nine would have been surprising at any time, but here, in a file at Camp Ute, was quite a jolt. Sequential pictures at different ages were stuck on the inside of the file cover. Regular photos went to about age twenty and appeared less frequently thereafter. The child in the early pictures appeared dazed and had an oddly blank expression. He moved further on in the file and was amazed to see a picture of his parents, taken in Iran. Someone really had an interest in the family, but the accompanying text was even more shocking. So, Dad had worked for the Americans at the time of Prime Minister Mohammed Mossadegh's ousting in 1953. From what he read, Dad may even have received orders from Kermit Roosevelt's staff. He shook his head in disbelief. Dad had always said that Mossadegh's election was the best thing that had ever happened. At last, someone insisting their own resources should benefit their own people – instead of foreign corporations.

He worked his way through the file. Dad was clearly an American asset and, after the Shah's installation, the family were protected by the dreaded SAVAK, the secret police – allegedly trained by the CIA. In 1979, when the Shah fell, the family were flown to the USA just before the American Embassy hostage episode and the coming to power of Ayatollah Khomeini. Further on, he saw Dad's written permission to include him in an exclusive children's training programme, for development as a specialist operative. The papers recorded periods of special training with a Dr D and Dr W. The plan was for him to continue with lessons in Farsi, Arabic and French, as well as normal schooling. His "control", it said somewhat enigmatically, would be Dr Herman Gunther. He continued reading. The next sheet mentioned a period of special training in St Louis and a photo showed a small group of children, looking extremely miserable.

Something was stirring inside. His heart sped and he experienced tightness in his chest just reading Gunther's name. An image of a man with icy blue eyes and wearing a white coat came, but then dissipated just as quickly. He squeezed his hands together and walked to the mirror, as though the reflection would somehow verify his reality. After several deep breaths, the experience stopped almost as soon as it had began – and his breathing returned to normal. He picked up the file again, noticing gaps and missing entries. Further on, he found some happier times, like graduation from West Point. In 1986, he'd been sent to Afghanistan to help the Mujahideen establish secret communications for fighting their Soviet occupiers. The file detailed several visits to Afghanistan, including stays in training camps, where he was encouraged to forge tactical connections. They were right, of course, because that was how his links with several cell members was first made. He returned in the mid-nineties after the Taliban emerged.

He shuffled through the papers, looking for references to that trip, and for anything else about the choosing of the Zoltan persona.

Without warning, the interconnecting door at the far end opened and Mr Wood and Dr Farrow came in.

He snapped the file closed.

"Hello, Sir. I was asked to wait here. Apologies for the file, but I assumed it was left out for my benefit. Anyway, as I'm the subject, I guess there's nothing new."

"Colonel Forest is tied up for the moment. Well, was there anything new?" asked Farrow.

He paused. Seeing his life laid bare like that had made him rather queasy, but there was no point saying that.

"I hadn't fully realised the extent of my father's allegiance to the United States. Up to his death, Dad always talked positively about Mossadegh."

"He was a fine operator – as are you."

"Thank you. I still don't quite understand… I mean…?"

"In a moment. Did anything else strike you?"

He remembered the image of the man in a white coat, but something stopped him from asking.

"My parents agreeing to special training. To be honest, can't remember all the details."

"And the time you spent with Dr D and, later, Dr W?"

"Strange. I can't remember much about it, except I think there was intensive language training. I recall being homesick, but, then, I was a kid."

"Yes," said Farrow. "But, apparently, an exceptional student. Doctors and trainers were very proud of you."

"What was all that about the 'control', Dr Herman Gunther?"

"Ah yes," replied Forest. "Dr Gunther was director and controller of the programme and took a particular interest in graduates. Anyway, back to current business. Robbie James isn't exactly tight lipped and we have a special task in mind for you. I'll explain soon."

"However, best practice states that special operatives must have periodic reviews," said Farrow. "Just to ensure things are as they should be and training doesn't need updating. That's why we've called you in."

Farrow went to the trolley with the sound equipment, firstly turning on the amplifier and then the tape recorder.

"I'd like you to hear something that you might find interesting. Actually, this is Dr Gunther's voice, although the man himself died in 1991."

Forest pressed a button on the recorder.

At the first syllable, Zoltan felt chilled and could only passively listen. That guttural voice seemed to grip his mind. Strangely, he felt he both knew the voice, but also didn't really know it in the slightest! As he focused on the words, the rest of the room receded – and the voice became the centre of his attention.

"Your colour is Friesian," the voice repeated. "Your colour is Friesian. Your colour is Friesian. Now, feel the support in your back and legs, now! And, as you feel the sensation of your feet supported by the floor – stay quiet, just so. So, sit and sew – sew the following together."

He was dimly aware of Forest and Dr Farrow leaving by the inter-connecting door. The voice continued.

"Because sowing is important. We sow the fields to grow the crops, just as I am sowing right now. So…"

AT THE SAME TIME, next door, Woods and Farrow watched through the two-way mirror and listened on a small monitor.

"What made you concerned?" asked Forest.

"His implant reports biological signs of distress for a couple of months now," replied Farrow. "The worry is that the compartments to his personality we installed might break down and he may gain recall.

Of the eight children in that photo with Dr Walther, five are dead... one of a brain tumour, and four suicides."

"What exactly was the training?" asked Woods.

Farrow stayed silent for a moment before answering.

"It's a bit complicated. Gunther was a German scientist/doctor brought over under Operation Paperclip after the war and he wasn't squeamish about extreme methods. You see, when mental splits are created, they're usually walled off with a protective amnesia. One sees that with the so-called multiple personality disorder. With that, usually, each segment of the personality, known as an 'alter', is unaware of the others. Sub-personalities can take different names and even take over for a time. What we see here, though, was designed much more purposefully!"

"Doesn't that screw them up, though?" asked Woods. "Make them unusable?"

"Usually, a multiple personality develops spontaneously after extreme childhood trauma," replied Farrow. "This was engineered far more cleverly. If a spontaneous recall of programming emerged, for example, if he were captured or some clever therapist dug around. Then backup programmes would kick in, including appropriate false memories to protect the basic programmes from discovery. That would certainly be a severely disorienting experience."

"Based on this afternoon, how do you think he's faring?"

Farrow looked at the recordings, which were still spewing out of the machine onto the table.

"The implant recorded a spike when he looked at the child group photos, but he recovered very quickly – in fact, almost instantly. I think things are hanging together."

Woods nodded understanding.

"You guys have done some weird stuff over the years. After that MK Ultra thing got public, I don't know how you continued getting away with it. How long did all that go on?"

"Years, and followed by Bluebird, MK Delta and Artichoke. Research never really stopped – things just got more sophisticated. The early programmes that freaked people out were crude: electric shocks, trials with LSD, chemicals, hypnosis, experiments with electrodes. Things are far more sophisticated now. Chip implants, microwave techniques, RF and electromagnetic tools."

"And after the ban?"

"Black budgets are a boon, as you know! Our friend over there experienced an exceptionally wide range of sophisticated treatments and trainings. That's why he can successfully pass himself off, not just with the Islamist cell, but with the militia too. He becomes so absorbed in each identity, that there's barely any inner conflict. Dissociation is a very useful phenomenon."

"How do you mean?" asked Woods.

"Each part of him stays cleanly separated from the other. One minute, he's a fanatic, the next a red-neck, and then it's back to partying with the activist girlfriend. When centred in one personality, he really believes in it. Let's hope that the romantics are wrong in thinking that love has the power to overcome everything."

"Is he up to doing the Monroe job?"

"I think so, yes. I've seen him several times recently after his talks with the Colonel. From that and what I've seen today, things are still holding together."

"What's happening now?"

"The hypnotic conditioning Dr Gunther added to the other processing is so powerful that Zoltan can't resist. Gunther is in there now giving him some fresh programming."

Woods raised his eyebrows.

"That's why I brought the sound equipment in... with the old stock tapes of Gunther's voice, and digital technology, we can clone virtually anything from a sample. It's called 'voice morphing', so the old guy can say whatever we want from beyond the grave! When things turn to ones and zeros, there's no limit."

In the next room, Gunther's 'voice' was giving an address at Old Hickory Lake near Nashville...

88

UTAH

ANDREW ALTON

A sudden breeze rustled the leaves. I stirred a steaming mug of coffee
while Gill drank.

"I just don't know what the hell to make of it. I mean, I clearly saw
guards saluting and then Zoltan drove in!"

Gill nodded. I guessed she was busy inside, running various scenarios. I tried again.

"I just don't get it. After Freddy's remark, I'd worried about possible
militia involvement, but never even considered a military or security
connection."

"Zoltan must be from US Intelligence, and has infiltrated the militia," she replied.

"That laser dazzling plan – surely he must have told them in the
camp. I wonder how Freddy and Terry James, who actually do support
the militia, figure in this? Did Zoltan plan on letting some of us get
caught, all of us, or what?"

Gill's usually attractive face looked troubled.

"We haven't enough information to figure it out yet, Andy. Which
means keeping quiet, until we do."

"We're supposed to all meet at Freddy's dealership tonight –
remember?"

"Of course, but…"

She broke off as a jet's roar fragmented the peace and we pushed back under the cover of trees. Moments later, a small white jet passed over the far tree-line.

"Off to get more poor devils," I muttered. "I wonder what the implications of this are for Mom?" I asked.

To my surprise, she snapped back.

"Don't tell Judy about this, yet."

Her voice had a steely authority I'd never heard before.

"Seriously, Andy! I can't just close my eyes to the dangers and I haven't formally resigned yet. I'm going to tell you something that you must keep to yourself."

"Of course."

"I was told both in London and New York that US Intelligence has concerns about hard-line terrorists embedding and hiding in other organisations. That's one, though only one, reason why activist groups are being infiltrated. Embedding within militia groups is another possibility. They thrive on anti-government sentiments, as you know."

"But I actually saw Zoltan entering the camp and he was clearly no stranger."

"Never heard of double agents? He probably is an intelligence colleague, checking out militias, but I can't let us take the risk."

I smiled.

"You sounded very authoritative just then – positively scary!"

"Sorry Andy, but I do have devolved authority to act in situations that threaten national security. Some things get stamped into us for good reason!"

I nodded understanding.

"I hope we hear from Nick before this meeting. I'm worried Terry will get restless."

Gill didn't reply and appeared preoccupied.

"Andy, I think we should move – right now!"

I spun around.

"What have you seen?"

"No, think about it. Freddy led us here, and he and Zoltan are friends. Freddy won't yet know that hiding our location from Zoltan is vital!"

Of course, she was absolutely right.

We packed immediately and I again demonstrated total incompetence with the tents.

"We could find another logging track," she said.

"I've another idea. Carl talked about the Abajo Mountains – a bit further on. He said it's green and cooler – rather like here. He sometimes takes groups if they need relief from the heat. Apparently, it's threaded with tracks too, so hopefully we'll find somewhere suitable. It will also avoid returning here in the dark and our lights possibly arousing interest."

She grinned approvingly.

"We'll make an agent of you, yet."

We made our way back to Route 191. This time, I swung the Toyota left towards Monticello. The windshield soon filled with the Abajos.

"Carl said they're locally called the Blue Mountains. There are good canyon views, but it's generally less visited than the other areas."

I turned right onto a dirt road and we started climbing. After several miles, we turned down an old logging track, which seemed noticeably greener and more lush. Despite years in Europe, the memories were seeping back and I identified maple, aspen, box elder and pockets of service-berry and snow-berry. We passed through a scarred area and I remembered Carl's mention of uranium explorations. It soon became green again, with pine and oak. The track suddenly curved and ahead we saw the rim of a substantial canyon and red-rock country far below. On the left, the trees gave way to meadow.

"Looks good here. What do you think?"

We erected the tents, brewed coffee and walked over to the canyon's edge. In the distance, we looked down onto a chaotic jumble of red-rock wilderness with some of the most inhospitable territory to be found anywhere.

"We won't have cell phone coverage out here," I said. "That'll be a problem if Nick tries contacting us with news."

"True," she replied. "We can try calling him this evening, when we're closer to Moab."

"What are those?"

I pointed to miniature trees by the rim.

"They look like something from a garden centre."

"Natural bonsai, Ponderosa pines, I think… probably extremely old."

"I find bonsai quite unsettling. Growing things should be allowed to reach their potential, not be deliberately stunted."

Gill gave exaggerated and solemn nods of agreement.

I grinned.

She spoke.

"So, you're starting to think like an agent and I'm getting all wordy!"

I smiled. Gill generally kept her humour in reserve. Still, if it was ever needed…!

"Let's plan how to best handle tonight…"

89

NASHVILLE

NICK MARTIN

I took the road to the Lake and back to the Senator's mansion. Given Nina's plight, I almost felt guilty that the previous evening had been enjoyable and the McCluskey girls so welcoming. Josie would have been more so, but the episode with Corinne still rankled and another slip would be unforgivable.

The girls claimed my phone impression of someone too feverish to travel was Oscar-worthy! They whooped and whistled when I finished. I found the performance rather satisfying, too, although Tom Phelan didn't seem pleased.

"Not up there with your singing," I said, "though I'm glad you enjoyed the cabaret!"

Anyway, given everything else happening, Canvey could go to hell!

"We'll be singing together again a lot more soon," said Josie. "After that meeting over at Mash's place, I'm joining the group, so now they'll have three chicks out front."

The girls were undoubtedly fun and I remembered the tender kiss Josie planted on my cheek.

The area around the lake was sprinkled with outstanding real estate, as I discovered through taking several wrong turns. Eventually a young girl on a push-bike showed me the way back to Lavinia Row and I arrived with three minutes to spare. Juanita met me at the door and escorted me straight down to the library. Richard Monroe sat ensconced in one of the rich burgundy leather chairs. His assistant, Graham Houner, was again present – which I found disappointing. There was something about Houner I didn't entirely trust, but, separating reason from a vague feeling, wasn't easy. Monroe rose, extending his hand and looking as if sleep hadn't come easy.

"Sleeping well, Nick?"

"It's not easy, is it?"

We made a little small talk about Nashville. Discussion was difficult and I knew that, for me, Houner's presence was the sticking point.

"This is a particularly lovely spot, Senator. Could I see something of the grounds while we talk?"

"Sure, good idea. Graham, would you continue with those papers? I don't know how long we'll be."

Houner had little choice, so we left from the rear of the house and wandered down to the lake. Monroe perched on a recently fallen tree facing the water.

"A big wind came through a few days ago," explained Monroe. "I must get this mess cleared up."

"Not the only thing that blew into your life this week!"

He smiled ruefully.

"I don't quite know where to start with this. You asked yesterday, Nick, if I could pull some levers. I tried last night, though I don't yet know the outcome... either for Nina, you or indeed me."

"Meaning exactly what, Senator?"

"My guess is, that they'll be released, but that afterwards you'll be marked men and women. I can't give any guarantees for your ongoing safety, so I'm going to do something else."

"Thanks, Senator. I understand the risks."

"Forget 'Senator', just call me Richard. I'll tell you some of what I know, which might hopefully bring about their release, and explain why it could also put you at such risk. I suggest you make copies of what I tell you – both audio and written. Keep them in secure locations, both as insurance and negotiating chips."

He pulled a silver digital recorder from his pocket.

"This might help. Take it with you after we've finished."

"Thanks. What about Houner? Is he trustworthy?"

He raised his eyebrows and shrugged.

"I don't know. I always thought so, but it's difficult to be sure of anything now. He's been with me about a year, but, since spending time on the Intelligence Committee, I know that anything is possible."

I looked out over the lake and several pleasure boats, then back over the lawns to the house. The grounds looked enormous and I couldn't see any neighbouring houses from here. As Monroe said, anything was possible.

"You're making me anxious, Richard."

"With good reason. Some things are very dangerous to meddle with. Although real democracy is increasingly nominal, most people still believe that, at the end of the day, the great public calls the shots."

"You mean despite the overwhelming evidence that both parties consistently sell out to special interests," I interrupted. "It's truly amazing, I know."

Monroe stared at the ground, apparently lost in some private memory.

"Yes, more now than ever. Of course, we have many good people, but a considerable part of the elected body are time servers or corporate fixers... and a screen for the darker forces that really pull the strings."

It was an unexpected outburst from a conservative politician.

"I know that, in survey after survey, what people want is fairly straightforward," I said. "Genuine protections in the workplace and for the environment, a more level playing field and less corporate control. What they get is the opposite – year after sorry year!"

Senator Monroe nodded.

"Yes, although it's more complicated than it appears from outside. Many, both in the House and Senate, are undoubtedly busy feathering nests rather than helping the ordinary man and woman. They continue to serve wealth and privilege, follow the party line and pocket the rewards. As for challenging the forces that really shape things – it's not in their interests and, anyway, many are clueless."

A strange intensity was written over Monroe's face, as though things were now somehow out of his control. Was he really saying these things in front of a recording device?

"How long have you felt this way about colleagues, Senator?"

"Richard, please. The shameful answer is a pitifully short time. In many ways, Nina helped me wake up."

"Darker forces shaping things," you said. "A 'shadow government'? I thought those ideas were the old chestnuts of conspiracy nuts, incapable of proper analysis? Could any of this help with Nina and the others?"

Monroe nodded.

"I'm in rather a unique position, Nick. I used to genuinely believe most of the same things as colleagues. Don't get me wrong – as well as the dross, there are still good and dedicated people doing their best. But, what I've seen recently, coupled with my Intelligence Committee experience, caused the curtain to drop – and what is behind is extremely ugly."

He shook his head.

"Despite the various scandals, most people still believe that the main institutions – the courts, law enforcement, press and so on – work for them and generally conform to the Constitution's ideals."

"You may be overestimating public gullibility, Richard."

"You speak as an informed activist, Nick, which makes you dangerous to the powers I mean. Much of their grip relies on a sick world-view and sometimes on outright criminality. They're vulnerable to exposure by people like you."

As we sat on the fallen tree trunk, I looked at the white, bunched knuckles of the man beside me, wondering about the effects on his health.

"In recent years, my political colleagues have helped to deliver the media into fewer and fewer very rich hands – and a consolidated media is more easily controlled. You've probably noticed the unanimity in pushing corporate agendas and also the diminished coverage of proper investigation and real journalism. They fear that the number of people thinking like Nina and your colleagues will grow, you'll network, and reach a critical and unstoppable mass."

"That's happening in parts of the global south, particularly Latin America."

Monroe nodded.

"I know, and some in power are getting rattled."

"All that talk about 'powers behind the curtain'? With the greatest respect, I never expected to hear Wizard of Oz metaphors come from a Senator. There are some really crazy ideas out there already. For example, some militia groups apparently believe the Federal Government is in league with the UN to secretly undermine the Constitution. Eventually, foreign troops could march in, supposedly to save us from ourselves... that kind of thing."

Monroe smiled and shook his head.

I continued, trying to draw him out.

"I've heard some of the theories. Networks of international bankers who conspire behind closed doors. Semi-secretive groups like the Bilderbergers, Trilateral Commission or the Council on Foreign Relations, who pull the strings. The notion that we're really just a faux democracy – a facade to pacify the population. Or accounts that the rich and powerful meet under the Redwoods at Bohemian Grove, and plot our futures between occult rituals and bouts of pissing under the trees together. I assume you weren't referring to that?"

Monroe smiled.

"Of course not, although, strangely, much of that is true, as far as it goes. No. I'm referring to the dark and hidden elements I became familiar with through committee work. I'm now even more familiar, since speaking out."

Monroe sighed and gave an odd, piercing look.

"The thing you need to know, Nick, is that relatively small parts of the intelligence service seem out of control. The tail is wagging the dog. Given that sections of intelligence work have been passed to private interests, the inevitable has happened."

"Like what?"

"A rogue element appears to be up for sale and collaborating for gain. Given that we've pushed the private sector into everywhere, preached increased efficiency and the superiority of 'for profit' organisations – perhaps we shouldn't be surprised. In fact, in some ways, it's a logical development! The end results, though, might potentially be awful – blackmail, drugs, arms running and all manner of evil."

"Is this widespread?"

"That isn't totally clear, though there seem definite hubs of rogue intelligence activity in the South West, the West Coast and in the North East, particularly around New York and Washington. The latter group works with dubious lobbyists and appear skilled at blackmail. They also appear to have done lucrative work for certain corporations. My worry is that they could initiate their own operations."

"So, the characters we tangled with, or that Simon encountered in San Francisco, might they...?"

Monroe nodded and his eyes were ablaze. I intuited that he felt relief to be talking.

"Might they have a foot in both camps? Absolutely! And talking of camps, that place in Utah has definitely been infiltrated."

"Hell, what a mess! Intel already has a reputation of being a law unto themselves – allegations of black budgets, drug running, and so on?"

"All true, but this is worse – imagine a criminal group sheltering inside intelligence, allied to business interests, and able to use market freedoms to coordinate a web of deals. In an extreme scenario, their operations could even cross international boundaries – and effectively be outside of control."

I was struggling to keep up with Monroe.

"So, basically, Richard, you're describing a group of agents who might have gone freelance!"

"Exactly. Nominally, still part of the service, but actually acting like entrepreneurs."

"A criminal element embedding in the most secret part of the state. Mind you, what with lobbying and sleazy donations, some might argue that's pretty well what we already have."

Monroe laughed.

"Including you – right? Even so, Nick, there's a difference between buying influence or, as some say, 'buying democracy' and actual acts of blackmail, smuggling and assassination."

Senator Monroe stood up and we walked the few yards down to the lakeside. He stood, staring out over the water for a few moments and sighed.

"Beautiful, isn't it? Who knows how much longer I'll see it? Anyway, let's move on as quickly as possible, so you can all disappear."

"Richard, is there any back-up contact that I, or the group, can contact if, for any reason, you should become incommunicado?"

He nodded sadly.

"The FBI have a section chief in their down-town Nashville office called Toby Maynard. You can find their number in the book. I completely trust Toby, and he shares many of my concerns. We've talked extensively. You see, few people are really in the know, and it's complicated by turf wars between the various agencies. You can trust Toby, though."

I watched a motorboat approaching from the far side and, for a moment, my anxious mind created machine-gun fire and bullets spraying over the lake. The boat veered harmlessly away as the Senator slowly walked to the water's edge.

"Unfortunately, the history of our intelligence services overflow with anti-democratic activities. Domestically, that includes spying on the population and suppressing dissent."

"Our colleague, Simon, claims that's now very widespread."

"True! Ever hear of the 'Cointelpro' programme in the mid-seventies and the stink that caused? With just a fig leaf of new orders, the infiltration of domestic protest groups is currently more extensive than anyone imagines. That's just the tip of the iceberg, though. Intelligence frequently dabbles in other nations' affairs. Then the undercover operations, like grooming of 'economic hit-men' that help plunder third world countries – siphoning off their wealth in the direction of certain favoured corporations. It's known that they can organise the overthrow of democratically elected governments if certain interests want it and would benefit. Whatever is claimed now, assassination may not have been unknown!"

"When you put it together that way, it's scary. What's the 'economic hit-man' thing that you mentioned?"

"Yet another creation of the hidden forces. Some years ago, a courageous individual emerged after years in the role, and whistle-blew on the whole seedy scheme."

"Which is what, exactly?"

"Intelligence grooms potential operatives and places them into corporations who trade internationally. They typically push big, expensive engineering and superstructure projects – dams, electrical supplies and the like. The hit-man usually has economic credentials and their job is to create reports advocating projects requiring enormous loans. They create dodgy financial reports for corrupt leaders that tempt regimes to look good for their home audience. As long as they can cream some off for themselves, such leaders either don't realise or care if their country becomes entrapped in crippling debt. The resulting loans are also conditional on using Western corporations for the projects – which is why you see the same old names crop up."

"What happens then?"

"They work up loans that will eventually almost bankrupt the economy. Then the regime is manipulated into giving up control of more resources, or pressured for favours – like military bases, or swinging UN votes. Later, 'rescue packages' from the transnational financial institutions arrive – usually with conditions, like enforced privatisations – opening up opportunities for further rounds of profiteering."

"A bit different from the 'no strings' bailouts the finance sector demanded for themselves, last crisis!"

"Quite so! Usually, most of these shenanigans are kept hidden. If things go wrong, all the public notices is that certain regimes are mysteriously toppled or leaders die in strange circumstances. Except, of course, in serious situations where the military get sent in – often for reasons that make very little sense to Joe Public!"

"That really happens, Richard?"

"Of course."

"What kind of corporations do these guys get placed in? Might I have heard of them?"

Monroe stayed silent for a moment, and then appeared to decide something.

"Some have become quite well known in recent years – big engineering firms and oil services like Flaherty-Hamerson, in Houston, or Gidderson Construction in San Francisco. You say you're based in New York City?"

"Yes, with Canvey Solutions. We provide IT and a range of managed business solutions. I'm their Deputy HR Manager."

"You may have heard of a corporation who've been involved in the penetration of a number of vulnerable markets. The intel operative linking with them is a ruthless piece of work called Brian Tutch, should you ever run across him. The corporation he often uses is Marquetcom – headed by another nasty piece, called Bifton Anson." Monroe gave a penetrating look. "Be extremely careful, Nick. This information is potentially dangerous and should only be used as last-ditch insurance for self-protection."

My heart was hammering and I struggled for control, but could see no point in complicating matters further.

"I'll look out for them. So, Richard, you're indicating that factions in intelligence have been involved in some really bad stuff – to put it mildly."

"That's only a fraction of it, Nick. There have been allegations over the years of drug running, assassinations and, of course, dirty tricks against dissenters and progressive leaders. It truly is a dreadful record of manipulation and deception."

Monroe's shoulders were riding high and he shook his head.

"A further worry relates to biological weapons. I intend suggesting a further committee investigation."

I nodded.

"Supposedly, we're signed up to a convention against the manufacture, stockpiling or use of biological weapons."

"I know."

"With the terrorism threat, close links have been sought with the pharmaceutical industry. The intention was both to have antibiotics ready, but also help in detecting bio-threats. Big contracts were awarded, but there was a further reason. Can you guess it?"

"Because of their experience in handling biological materials?"

"Yes, but there are two sides to that particular coin. See, technically it would be easy for an experienced pharmaceutical company to help the development of a bio-weapon capability. I'm talking here of the 'freelancers', not the administration! For example, do you know what's possible with a gram of anthrax?"

I shook my head.

"About a trillion spores, representing approximately a hundred million lethal doses! I'm ashamed now of what I let pass by unchallenged – but no more! They have no inhibitions about... well, about corrupting pharmaceutical programmes and university research departments. Some of the deadliest pathogens known are grown and have even been revived in Pharma and University labs."

I recalled Robbie's account of Marquetcom's connections with Kane and Field.

"So, theoretically, this rogue group could develop a private franchise for this sort of thing – totally off the books?"

"That's just where I was going. As I said before, they may be doing business for themselves now. I don't know who'd be their customers, but certainly not our Department of Defense!"

"Could they set up a threat and then demand money?"

Monroe rubbed his lower lip over his teeth, and then looked skyward.

"I can't imagine they'd go that far, although information is limited. Getting intel on intel is something new."

"I see."

Monroe bent over and threw a pebble, which bounced over the lake's surface.

"Meanwhile, they continue with official government business – information gathering, spying, covert action, disinformation and the rest of it. We think they are probably numerically few and only concentrated in a few distinct regions."

"What a nightmare!"

"It gets worse."

"It couldn't!"

"There's been a long connection between intelligence and organised crime. The mob sometimes did the dirtiest jobs."

"Oh."

"But there's an even more worrying area."

"More worrying?"

"In contradiction to standing orders, it seems that research into 'mind control' has resurfaced. Controlling and directing the 'public mind' has long been a goal. The big concern, therefore, is that the rogue grouping may have access to mind-controlled subjects, prepared over many years. That's quite a formidable resource!"

"Not the old 'Manchurian Candidate' thing?" I asked. "I thought that was just a spiced-up Hollywood fantasy?"

"I'm afraid not. I can't say more, but various extensive programmes continued over the years. They were never going to give up on anything potentially so useful."

"How are subjects selected for testing?"

"In the covert, though 'official', programme, they experimented with prisoners, mental patients – even runaway kids fell prey. This time, word is that subjects come from the first category."

Relief washed over me. "You mean felons in the prison system?"

"I assumed that at first." Monroe looked increasingly uncomfortable. "Unfortunately, this time, it may include those detained under other legislation."

I felt my world closing in as Monroe's words snapped into focus.

"You don't mean... not Utah?"

The Senator nodded and his face looked pained.

"I'm afraid 'fixing' people by technological means appeals to them."

At the moment of hearing the loud crack, I thought, *clay pigeons.*

"What was that?" I asked, and turned to Monroe for an explanation. Richard's body, though, was already falling, and the trickles of grey matter and blood on his designer polo shirt finished expectations of a reply.

I quickly looked up and frantically scanned the lake's surface. Near the centre, a yacht leisurely moved forward. I heard the sound of two motorboats that seemed to come from different directions. Neither could be seen because of stands of trees obscuring the view. I stuffed the digital recorder into my pocket and then crouched, placing my palm on Monroe's shirt, and feeling for a heartbeat. Nothing, although my own heart pounded and sweat trickled under my arms. I felt a stickiness on my hands and wiped the blood and shards of bone onto the grass. Giving into fear, I then ran across the lawn towards the house. Before I could enter, the back door opened and Houner rushed out, brandishing a revolver. My mind sped, though nothing made sense. The Senator was facing the lake when shot and Houner in the mansion.

"Are you okay?" shouted Houner. "I heard a shot and when I looked out, Richard was down."

I felt confused and shocked.

"What are you doing with that gun?"

"I'm not just an assistant," yelled Houner, starting to run towards the body. "My job was also protection."

I ran into the house as an ashen-faced Juanita came to the window with hands held up to her face.

"I heard the shot. What happened, Mr Martin. Is the Senator...?"

"I think so. Houner's gone to investigate and I came to ask you to call 911. Listen, Juanita, this is important."

Her eyes were already filling and a trickle ran down her cheek.

"Juanita, just before it happened, Richard asked me to do some things – very urgent and important things. If I'm delayed, these things won't happen. When they arrive, please don't give my name, so I can do what Richard asked. If I get caught up, it'll be too late."

She nodded tearfully and left to phone, though I had little confidence that she'd taken this in. I headed to the front door and, right under the CCTV screen, found a button for the motorised gate. Moments later, I was speeding towards Nashville...

90

MANHATTAN

BIFF ANSON'S PERSPECTIVE

Biff Anson preferred giving commands to the time-consuming matter of negotiation. Occasionally, however, it seemed a necessary evil. He moved his gaze from mid-town, back into the room and to the opaque eyes of Brian Tutch.

"So, what do you suggest, Brian?"

"I think we should immediately develop alternative ways of shifting the stuff."

"Young Fred accidentally sparked another idea. Large items could be moved around, hidden inside modified recreational vehicles. Utah's crawling with them."

Tutch fell silent for a moment.

"It's a hell of a run, though. Other than remoteness, the other advantage of Utah is having a totally off-the-map airstrip for sending material to and from Colombia. Dick and the Arm-Rite boys could arrange it. If necessary, we could maybe diversify. Perhaps ship stuff to Cartagena, and then forward overland. Zoltan could help guide through a direct shipment?"

"Funny you should mention him, Brian. While you were getting back from the last run, I heard from Dick, at Ute. Apparently, Zoltan's been given, shall we say, a 'special' mission!"

"Meaning what?"

"You remember the Senator Monroe problem? The way his poor bleeding conscience caused him, and others, so much pain?"

"Yeah. It's crazy that a formerly straight-thinking guy can 'lose it' so late in life. We could do without the complication."

"Exactly, although it isn't only his conscience that's bleeding, now. The episode with the daughter's husband appears to have flipped him right out. He recently called Ute, and threatened to spill everything unless they release that damn Parenda woman that he messed with. Get this, though, he also demanded the release of our favourite choirboy, Robbie James, and also Andrew's assistant, Simon Maher."

"They told him to take a jump, right?"

"Not quite. Monroe made it quite clear that critical information would escape, one way or another, if his demands weren't met. He had plans in place to ensure it."

"Fry the fucker!"

"Yes. Given everything Monroe knows, and the authority from his former time on the Intelligence Committee, that indeed was the decision we came to. Refuting evidence from almost anyone else would be less troublesome, so shutting Monroe down was vital."

"Zoltan will do the necessary, right?"

"I believe so, but I'm concerned for Judy."

"She'll be safe. Listen, I haven't seen you for a while, so didn't get to explain about things back in Philly."

"Is she okay?"

"Sure. Maybe a little too okay."

"You're not making sense. In what way, 'too' okay?"

"Everything's fine. Just that they could be getting friendly. Out together, hand in hand... that sort of thing."

Biff's fist hit the desk top.

"Shit, Brian, why didn't you tell me before?"

"Because, from Philly, I got the stuff moved to Utah and have only just returned. That's what I was saying earlier. Utah's one hell of a hike."

"But it is the ticket to a safe airstrip."

"Correct. We've another concern as well. Dick Riley says Colonel Forest has certain reservations. Forest is apparently a real traditionalist and gets really fired up over private sector involvement in military or intelligence work."

A sneer broke across Biff's big face.

"He'd pee his pants if he knew the full story! Brian, you should return and work our investment. Make certain that Dick ensures this Forest guy doesn't mess up. Also, if Judy's down in Utah with Heltay, I don't want more complications."

UTAH

SIMON MAHER

With no books, computer or company, time alone in the little cell certainly dragged. I sat down from having been on tiptoes to peer at a nearby pine tree through the high window. The blue jay had been a real treat, followed by a stunning bird with a bright yellow head and black body. I'd check the name later, with Craig.

I thought again of the rescue plan. It seemed completely flaky – almost a guarantee of trouble. As I mulled it over, I heard sounds coming from outside. The key rattled, and the door opened to a grinning Craig.

"Good news, buddy. You're gonna go out for association. Then you can find Nina, your buddy's girlfriend. She's a good-lookin' girl – Latino, real attractive. She's gotta kind of pretty oval face and…"

I cut him short. Nina's broadcast had made such an impression I reckoned I'd recognise her, even without our brief meeting in New York.

"Yes, we've met. Have you seen Robbie?"

"Not since he moved off this gallery. Dunno how long they'll keep him. Maybe he'll return later. Sometimes that happens."

Outside seemed intensely bright, and it needed time to adjust. I rounded the building, looking for the pine tree, hoping to see the blue jay again. Small groups of detainees were interacting right across the area. A few hundred yards away, I could see three men talking and decided to introduce myself. As I got closer, I realised it was two men and a woman. One beckoned and, when I arrived, he extended a hand.

"Hello there! We haven't seen you before, so I guess you're new? I'm John Farras from San Francisco."

I shook hands with the others.

"Millie Vincent, also from San Francisco. I hear a British accent? Hey, I bet this place wasn't on your tour itinerary?"

"Not exactly, no!" I scanned my surroundings. "A guard told me we're in Utah near somewhere called Moab. That's all I know."

"Right," said the other man. "I'm Paul Zacher from the next-door state. I often pass through these parts. We're south of Moab just neat Monticello – on the road south to Arizona." He pointed to the mountains. "Those are part of the La Sals."

"But why are we here?"

"Because it's one of the loneliest, most inhospitable areas – probably, second only to Death Valley. If you were to escape, there's nowhere to go, though I'm sure you've seen the fences!"

"I meant, why hold us in the first place?"

"Everyone here threatens the status quo in their different ways," Milly suggested.

"Do they actually think we're terrorists or subversives?"

"We know our crime," said Farras.

"Our group researches anti-democratic trends. We had a project underway on how legitimate inquiries are de-legitimised by the pejorative use of the 'conspiracy theory' label."

"Don't quite get you, John?"

"The way that term is used in academic and media circles... there's almost a conspiracy about mentioning conspiracies."

"A conspiracy to deny conspiracies?" I repeated slowly.

Farras raised his eyebrows. Maybe I looked as confused as I felt.

"Yeah. Haven't you noticed how quickly debate gets closed down by the charge of 'conspiracy theory'? It effectively stops academics or the mainstream media following certain issues – or even raising them in the first place."

"Yes, I have noticed that. Although many things that are given that label do seem fairly hair-brained!"

"Yes, but how did the knee-jerk reaction come about? Who benefits when legitimate inquiries are derailed – especially, as we found, when the crimes are on the largest scale?"

"Interestingly, we found that some of the most outrageous conspiracy theories are actually promoted by intelligence, just so their colleagues can easily undermine them," said Zacher. "You wouldn't believe how many journalists are also plants."

"Sorry? You're saying intelligence has plants in the media?"

"Absolutely," replied Milly. "Disinformation is a key activity."

"I don't get it. Why peddle theories, only to knock them down?"

"Because it closes off entire areas of inquiry, making them seem absurd. Investigation is thwarted and the public discouraged from asking big questions or challenging received wisdoms – 'received' being the operative word. Often, people these days will preface ideas with, "Please don't think I'm a conspiracy nut, but mightn't…'"

"Issues still seep out, though."

"Maybe a few celebrity scandals, but do the really massive conspiracies against the working population? The finance scandals transferred huge wealth, which must have taken huge covert and coordinated activity… otherwise known as 'conspiracies', though no-one dares to say it! Take the truly vast amounts that went missing from the Pentagon or were stolen in Iraq. People don't say… obviously fraud and theft, but apologetically mumble about 'conspiracy theories'!"

"Who benefits from 'conspiracy' being the 'kiss of death?'" I asked.

"That's what we'd turned to when we suddenly found ourselves in here," Millie said. "Of course, officially peddled 'conspiracy theories' are different. Decades of hyping security threats so that our taxes can be funnelled to cronies in the military-industrial-intelligence complex, for example. Now, we're told that shadowy terrorist groups threaten, so we must continue a 'war on terror'. They paradoxically claim to protect our freedoms – by destroying them!"

"And continue feeding the same military-industrial-intelligence complex," added Farras. "Simon, these are golden days for arms pushers, war profiteers, and manufactures of surveillance equipment."

I swallowed, and looked over the compound to the mountains. After days of solitary confinement, their intensity seemed almost too much. I scanned the exercise area. Small groups were spread all around the compound, but no Nina. I looked at the branches above, wondering about hidden recording devices.

"Can we be overheard?"

"Don't think so," replied Zacher. "Though, let's face it, we haven't said anything they don't know."

I suddenly felt exhausted. This was fascinating, though almost too much. I needed air and scanned the grounds again. Still no Nina.

"What do people generally do in 'association'?"

"Pretty much what we're doing now," replied Millie. "Talk and exchange ideas unless, of course, they're over in special treatments."

She pointed to a low building on the far side.

"There's also a 'privilege' area, attached to the privileges block over there. You can get coffee and they have some games. Did you get tokens for the coffee machine?"

"No," I replied, as I strained to make out a pair leaving the privileges area.

"The guard on your gallery usually gives them out," said Millie. "They're pretty stingy though. They probably imagine we'll use them as alternative currency!"

I nodded.

"I heard that an activist friend of a friend is here. Nina Parenda, originally from Bolivia."

"Yeah, we know Nina," replied Millie, casting an eye around the enclosure.

"She's over there, look," said Farras, pointing to the privileges block.

I saw her leaving with another woman, and looking much thinner than I'd remembered.

"I must see her, so I'll catch you folk another time. That conspiracy about conspiracies idea, really is something else."

I walked towards the women. Nina and her companion hadn't seen me and were heading for the far end of the grounds. I sped up, but, at that moment, someone grabbed my shoulder from behind. I spun around, squeezing my hands into fists, but it was only Robbie.

"Hello again, Simon. Out for association now?"

"First time," I replied. "More to the point, you're out of that special treatments place."

I noticed a sticking plaster around his nose.

"Shit, they didn't beat you, did they?"

"Not physically. No, I've had a sinus problem for years, that's all. Apparently, they cleaned it out for me while I was kind of anaesthetised, for a test."

"What kind of test?"

"Oh, really weird stuff! They wired me with sensors, and showed pictures. Another time, I had what they called a 'neural exploration' while I was out. Goodness knows what that was about? Looking for a terrorist gene or dissident brain structure – or something!"

"You haven't lost your sense of humour, then?" I grinned. "Remember that day we cracked up in the UN Library?"

A look of puzzlement passed over his face.

"Sorry?"

"You know, the day you helped me at the UN Library, in New York? You showed me around on the way there and afterwards. Remember, the cable car to Roosevelt Island?"

Robbie looked blank.

"We went for a drink at the end of the day, to a bar in Greenwich Village."

"No. We met in Philadelphia for the first time, at Andy's Mom's home. Then you went on to San Francisco. So, you've been to New York? What did you think of the place?"

Nina and her companion had disappeared from view. So, for a moment, did my grip on reality…

92

NASHVILLE

NICK MARTIN

My hands shook on the wheel as I sped towards Nashville. The same hands that were formerly covered in Monroe's blood, bone and brains. That horrific image kept on running, making everything else something of a blur. My mind played a pitiful mantra. *What now, what now, what now?*

The question looped around, but nothing came. By the time I'd reached the Briley Parkway junction, I'd made a decision – I'd just have to trust Toby Maynard's help. Firstly, though, I'd return to Josie's place.

My inbuilt direction usually worked well, but today it deserted me. Suddenly, the traffic seemed wayward, the directions confusing and signs to Vanderbilt University – completely missing. I checked the mirror again, worried that a black Chrysler, which had followed for some minutes, might be tailing. It turned away and I dabbed my forehead, pulled in and took some deep breaths. Soon I was back on Seventeenth Avenue and turning into Ellison Place, thankful to at last recognise something. I parked and walked to the girls' apartment with the weight of the digital recorder in my pocket, the only crumb of reassurance. Even before pushing the bell, I somehow knew that no-one was home. Strange, how empty buildings seem to radiate their emptiness! I found an outside tap and quickly washed my hands. With my right hand still questing for the recorder, I returned to the car and headed back down-town. I spotted a convenience store, and I pulled in.

I smiled at the young female assistant, picked up sandwiches, a notepad, jiffy bags and a pack of cheap pens. I paid and asked if I could quickly check their directory.

"No smart phone? I believe we still have an old directory," she said. "Welcome to Music City. You're new here?"

"It shows then?"

She smiled and disappeared behind the counter, and bobbed up with the directory.

"I need the Fed-Ex depot," he explained.

Another customer took her attention and I quickly flipped through the pages. Sure enough, the FBI office was openly listed in Polk Place. I busted the packaging from the pens and quickly scribbled the address and phone number. I thanked her and, with the *what now* mantra playing again, returned to the car to consider my options.

As I hadn't yet called the others, would Terry James try to push that insane rescue plan? I picked up a pad and started writing, trying to make an outline of Monroe's words. With access to a computer, the contents of the recorder could be stored on some memory sticks. In fact, I must do that and, if necessary, copies of the audio file could potentially then be sent anywhere. For the first time, I felt slightly easier.

I pulled into the traffic until, further on, I spotted a parking lot with spare spaces. Nearby, was a computer shop, which amazingly had an old-fashioned internet café attached. I purchased a clutch of USB devices and also a slot of internet access. Once out of sight, I took the recorder's contents, copied it onto the devices, and made sure anything incriminating was deleted from their computer before leaving. Later, we could set up 'cloud' storage. I doubled back to hide the devices in the vehicle's trunk, and then walked on to Polk Place.

The FBI office was upstairs and apparently shared the big old building with several commercial businesses. I climbed to the third floor and, with a mixture of anticipation and anxiety, asked for Toby Maynard.

"I'll check. Your name please?"

Answering was reflexive, but, even so, I could have kicked myself.

"I'll get him."

Almost immediately, the door slid across the aperture and snapped shut. I spun around to grab the handle and then pulled at it. It was no good, hands held onto my arms almost before I realised anyone was even there. I was bundled down the corridor by two substantial agents and into a side room.

"I gotta say, Tommy, this really beats it," said the older one, shaking his head.

"We're asked to find a suspect, and he suddenly turns up at the front desk, asking for the chief!"

I was pushed behind a desk. Tommy nodded, and grinned at the other man.

"Certainly is different, Dave. Shame, I fancied a trip out to Old Hickory."

I rubbed now sore wrists, incredulous at my own stupidity.

"The strong-arm tactics aren't needed. I voluntarily came to see Toby Maynard."

"You'll soon see him all right. Meanwhile, I'm David Rantz, field agent and this is Tom Dyter. We'd like details of your movements throughout today."

I knew denial was pointless. Juanita must have collapsed under questioning.

"Why do you think I'm here? I was by the lake when it happened."

"When what happened, exactly?"

"The reason that we're here – the Senator! Forensics will find plenty of evidence on me, but not of a firearm discharge. Ask Houner – he saw Richard go down!"

"It's 'Richard', is it?"

There was a click, and a middle-aged man with silver hair, gold-rimmed glasses and a sharp, intelligent face looked around the door.

"I'm back, David. I understand Mr Martin has come to see me. I'll take over here, but I need you to fetch Mr Houner from the mansion."

Rantz and Dyter left, and the man slotted himself into their place.

"I'm the section chief, Toby Maynard. I gather you're Nick Martin."

"Correct. Senator Monroe mentioned you as someone who might be helpful, just before it happened. I never imagined that these circumstances would lead to our meeting."

The keen eyes fixed him as Maynard nodded.

"What circumstances, Mr Martin?"

"He mentioned you as a possible source of help. Richard said you'd become friendly and discussed matters of mutual concern. The same things we discussed today, when he was attacked."

"And now you're caught up in his murder."

"The last thing I ever expected or wanted. I don't like politicians, but he seemed a decent human being."

Maynard nodded sadly.

"Yes, one of the best. Why were you visiting him at Old Hickory Lake?"

"Does that matter? Isn't finding the killer rather more important?"

"Perhaps you don't understand. You are all that we have!"

"You surely don't count me as a suspect? I was right next to him and the shot definitely came from the lake. If I did it, I'd hardly just wander in here voluntarily, would I?"

"Probably not. Houner was watching from the house and saw it happen. Besides, we already know the shot matches a high-powered rifle. You carried no such thing, although Houner does report that you suggested walking in the grounds!"

"I wanted to talk in confidence and Houner kept sticking around. It was the second time I'd called and I couldn't think how else we could talk privately."

"Does the name Nina Parenda mean anything to you, Mr Martin?"

"Of course. She's a charity worker and Richard was... err."

"Yeah, don't worry. I know they were close and that it caused considerable controversy. Nina's a great gal. She opened my eyes to many things, too."

I swallowed hard, trying to keep calm.

"I know. I'm also a close friend – which is why I'm here!"

Maynard's eyes opened wide. "Go on."

"Nina was taken in for questioning in New York and effectively disappeared."

"Yeah, so I believe, but, by then, Richard had to withdraw and I didn't hear anything more."

"I can't say how, but we got wind of her location. A detention facility in the wilds of Utah."

"I don't think Richard knew that. Of course, by then, the party officials were all over him and there were marital complications. Still are, although the poor bastard's past all that now! You said 'we' got wind of her location. Who's 'we'?"

"Friends. Two of them are now locked up as well!"

"What a mess! Why visit Richard, though?"

I looked at the sharp, questing expression on his face, and realised that Maynard wouldn't buy any nonsense.

"Nina was picked up over false allegations of funnelling charity monies to terrorist groups, but we think certain parties wanted her off the scene. Nina hoped that Richard's knowledge of, shall we say, certain corrupt practices and the threats of releasing this information might ease their release. That was the purpose of my visit."

Maynard looked astonished, as I continued.

"Richard described the issues Nina had in mind, and told me that you had discussed similar things. He said you were extremely concerned."

Maynard leaned back, his face pale. He puffed out his cheeks and whistled.

"Did Richard act on it?"

"Apparently, he did – last night. I assume his assassination was the result."

"You can't have proof of that, I suppose, or what he said about me?"

"As a matter of fact, I do! He warned me that, even though Nina and my colleagues could be released, we'd be at major risk afterwards. His idea was to record the information as protection."

I pulled the silver digital recorder from my pocket.

"He suggested I write down the details of our conversation and then make multiple copies of it and of this recording, and stash them somewhere safe. I already have," I lied.

Maynard pursed his lips, momentarily at a loss.

"The cloud, I suppose. Smart move. Let me listen to the recording. We have to cover things procedurally, so I'll hear it while you're in the lab."

"Lab?! Why?"

Maynard rose and crooked his finger.

"Come."

I followed the chief down the corridor. Maynard entered a code on a keypad and then we descended to the floor below. As we walked down another passage, and paused at the fourth door, I realised the office's true size had been concealed by the surrounding businesses. The door opened and my nostrils filled with a complex blend of aromas, that combined to give the odour of spinach marinated in disinfectant. Inside the small lab, two men and a woman were at work.

"Stephanie, please screen Mr Martin for firearm use and run it over to Gass Boulevard. When you've finished, bring him back to Interview Room One and I'll see him there."

Maynard left and Stephanie swabbed my hands. She was a stunning woman and I felt mildly ashamed at thinking that rubber gloves would be an insult to her touch.

"What is this test?" I asked.

"I won't be doing it. We used to do basic things like that here, but, as the lab is closing, pretty well everything is now done at the TBI Forensic lab on Gass Boulevard."

"What will they do?"

"A gunshot residue analysis."

"A what?"

"You see, when the primer ignites, it leaves residues of heavy metal. Certain combinations of lead, barium and antimony are unique to gunshots."

"Then they'll be disappointed because I don't have a gun. I've never had one or even used one."

After swabbing, they checked something with my shoes and I was then escorted back to the same interrogation room. Maynard was staring at the silver recorder and mini-headphones on the table before him. Eventually he looked up.

"Houner watched from the window and had a clear, side-on view. His statement confirms that you had no weapon."

He picked up and held the recorder.

"Now I get what you were doing. As Richard said, we had many such conversations."

"What can be done?"

"Not sure. Have you ever been to Arizona?"

"I don't think so, although apparently the camp isn't far from the state line. Why?"

There was a tap at the door. Stephanie entered and passed Maynard a folded piece of paper. He scanned it and then looked up.

"No signs. The wonders of spectrometry and microscopy, eh!"

"If you say so. What about Arizona?"

"You asked what can be done. The thing is, I'm not the only one concerned. After Richard's explanation, you'll understand why. A few of us who are worried have our own private network. That's how I know about your colleague, Gill Marney. Perhaps, I should say, my colleague as well, because I gather she's shared her other identity with you."

My heart sped. Matters were taking another odd turn.

"Gill? I don't understand..."

"As I said, those of us concerned by these things keep in touch. On her way to Camp Ute, Gill contacted Sheryl, a mutual friend in Arizona, who has a similar outlook. Sheryl offered support and shelter, should your group need it. It's very isolated there."

"You'll stay quiet about this?"

"I've considerable experience at sniffing out bad 'uns, and I believe you! Apparently, Richard wanted me to help you, and I will. Gill is on the same team and, as for Nina, we met several times while she was with Richard. In fact, I give her part credit for opening my eyes – so, yes, of course I'll try to help. In the meantime, you will have to stay alert and keep an eye over your shoulder. You might find Sheryl very helpful. Gill has her details."

"Can I leave soon?"

Maynard looked at his watch.

"The local police should arrive in about 15 minutes – and we'll jointly work the case. At this point, there's nothing against you, so there shouldn't be a problem. They'll probably point out that you might have guided the Senator down to the waterside to give an open shot, so they might want you contactable for further questioning. Given Richard's status and security implications, I'll take the lead and manage the contact."

"I see. This idea of guiding him into the shot, I'd have had to have been particularly courageous. We were literally side by side when it happened!"

"Just telling you that's how folk like us think. Where are you staying tonight? Would you like me to suggest a hotel?"

"I'll probably be with friends I've made locally. I've been there the last two nights."

Maynard peered over the top of his spectacles.

"I'll need their name, address and phone number. Incidentally, take my card."

He wrote another number on the card.

"The top number is the office, but you can reach me on the second number any time."

I hesitated as Maynard waited for the address. Somehow, saying 'I stayed in the apartment of some sisters I met in a down-town honky-tonk' didn't sound right! Maynard peered over his glasses, but my mind was blank. I felt like a wayward student called to the headmaster. I blurted out.

"I'm fond of country music and stayed with a friend who's trying to break into the business."

A huge smile broke across Maynard's face.

"Great… what style, traditional or this cross-over stuff?"

"Western swing," I replied, instantly regretting the answer and hoping I wouldn't have to elaborate.

"Who's your favourite…?"

Someone knocked at the door. An agent put his head in.

"The police are here to see Mr Martin, Chief."

Somehow, with imminent embarrassment and a mind blank about 'Western swing', time with the local police seemed like light relief!

93

UTAH

GILL'S PERSPECTIVE

Gill soon discovered that dressing in a one-man tent was quite a feat. When she finally emerged, Andrew had already dressed and was searching in the Toyota's trunk. The more time they were together, the more she liked him and understood Si's affection.

"Andy, could you use your cell phone to try Nick? I'd rather avoid being compromised should someone be listening in."

"Makes sense," he agreed.

She walked over to the canyon's edge, and gazed at the wilderness below. The sun would soon set and the sky was graduated from indigo at the horizon through various shades of blue to green to the palest lemon, above. The red-rock country glowed a rusty brick-red. She sighed. England's green fields could never offer anything like this.

"Let's go," called Andy.

By the time they'd wound through the Abajos' tracks to the main road it was time for headlights. Passing the turning to La Sal Junction, she wondered what Si would be doing at Ute. A little further on, Andrew slowed and then pulled in.

"I'll try Nick, though, by now, he may have given up on us and called the others."

She watched as Andy called, illuminated by passing car lights.

"Hell. Nick must have the damn phone turned off. We might as well continue."

They entered Moab's limits and found their way to Anson Autos. The complex was dark except for one lit office on the side nearest the road.

She felt rather sorry for Andy. If his description of Freddy was correct – they really were chalk and cheese! Judy, though, seemed just the kind of mother she'd have chosen.

"Coming in?" asked Andrew, jolting her into the present.

As arranged, a side gate had been left unlocked and they then moved towards the light. Inside, Freddy was talking with Terry James and Carl stood beside a disconsolate Judy. Even so, she was soon enveloped in one of her hugs.

"No Zoltan? Where is he?"

"I don't know," Judy replied, looking pained.

"He visited a friend yesterday in Grand Junction, but didn't return. This is so unlike him. I understood he was helping his friend over a difficult IT problem."

"Shall we make a start?" called Andrew.

Terry broke off his discussion with Freddy and scowled.

"Hang on," said Freddy. "I'll get everyone coffee. The showroom machine isn't too bad."

Freddy left and Terry James sidled over.

"Gill, you're in the IT game. Zolt shouldn't take this long on a job, should he? It could really screw things!"

A sour odour filled her nostrils and she wished he'd move.

"Sometimes you just have to carry on to get it sorted. His friend may have been working on a tricky project," she replied, regretting the facile explanation.

Freddy returned, balancing polystyrene cups on a board and handed them around.

"I just said to Freddy," announced Terry, "that I'll wait one more day and then I'm gonna go for it, even if Zolt isn't back. Getting the boys to provide a diversion isn't a problem."

"What about that chaplain person we discussed?" asked Judy "Have you spoken with him?"

"'Fraid The Reverend's gone to ground."

"Anyone heard from Nick?" Gill asked. "We were out of range!"

No-one had heard and disappointment filled the room.

"The more I think about our rescue plan, the more doubtful I am," said Andrew.

A muttered "wuss" came from Terry's direction.

"I dunno Ter," said Carl. "Actually, it does seem a long shot. Them guards is nasty bastards."

The door opened and Craig entered, looking unusually animated.

"Howdy folks. Sorry I'm late. They sprung another of them training meetings on us."

"What news?" asked Judy.

"Robbie's been out for a brief period of association. He ain't back on my gallery yet, but Simon saw him and had a quick word."

"And?" pressed Judy.

"He said Robbie seemed kind of spaced out and had plasters round his nose. He was a bit confused. Simon was worried 'cos he didn't remember the time they spent together in New York."

"See," began Terry. "If we keep waitin', he'll be completely fucked!"

"Don't worry, Terry. It's sometimes like that when folk have been at 'special treatments'. He prob'ly missed some sleep."

At first, Gill couldn't identify the source of the ringing, but eventually Andrew extracted a phone from his pocket. He nodded to an unheard communication, and a succession of expressions passed over his face.

"But you're free, at least for now?" he said. "No, he's AWOL. I can't say more at the moment. No, that's amazing, I can hardly believe it. Yes, I understand, we'll keep it brief. You're okay though? Right, got it – I'll pass you over."

Andy's arm reached in Gill's general direction, proffering the phone. She looked around, momentarily uncertain, but Andy waived the phone until she took it. Nick's voice was urgent on the other end.

"Gill, I'll make this quick, I'm on a public line…"

"You met the party," she interrupted.

"Yes. He intervened, though it's the last thing he'll do."

"He wasn't too pleased at you turning up?" she ventured.

"No, he's dead! Let me finish because it's imperative I'm on for the shortest possible time. Certain parties have negotiated, but, because of potential dangers for everyone concerned, you are being given a key role in the release."

"I don't understand."

"Because of information given by the party I visited, we're now all at risk. There is an expectation that you'll take oversight of certain aspects of the discharge. You're asked to be physically present at the actual release."

She could only assume the strained circumlocutions were for security reasons, but it certainly wasn't clear.

"I'm not sure what I…"

He cut her off.

"Have to go. I fly back first thing in the morning and I'll explain everything when I arrive. Could you, Andy or, perhaps, both of you pick me up from McCarran Airport, Las Vegas? I'll arrive at 11am and you are then directed to proceed straight on to the camp, alone. I'll explain later."

He was gabbling.

"Just wanted to warn you and also to stop T from launching that madcap operation. Tell him release looks imminent, but nothing else."

"Yes," she answered. "I'm sure one of us can collect you."

Remembering Sheryl Harrison at Page, she added, "Probably me".

Nick rang off and she looked at six expectant faces. Good news maybe, but also new complications.

"Nick, from Nashville. Successful negotiations and developments."

She looked at Terry.

"They're being released within 48 hours. Nick flies back in the morning and I'm requested to pick him up in Las Vegas."

James looked stunned – even disappointed. His eyes narrowed.

"They're just gonna let them walk? What the fuck – I don't get it!"

For the second time tonight, the door unexpectedly swung open. This time with Zoltan wearing a wide grin.

"Hi folks, hi Jude! Sorry I'm late, everyone… first a business screw up, then a breakdown and finally a faulty cell phone. Why do difficult things come in threes?"

94

UTAH

SIMON MAHER

Keys rattled in the door, waking me with a start. Craig entered with the breakfast tray.

"Sorry man. It's the same old shit, though the coffee's not so bad this morning."

I stretched and sat up. Usually, I was up well before Craig arrived, but a strange humming had disturbed my sleep.

"You look happy. Any news?"

A grin broke across Craig's face.

"Yeah, as a matter of fact, there is. I heard from the others last night that your friend Nick's pulled something off. You may be leaving soon!"

I put down the greasy bun.

"I can't eat this. Tell me what you know?"

"Not much more. Nick's flying back and Gill will pick him up in Vegas. Top brass want to see you later, so something is up."

"When might we go? Do you know?"

"Don't know nothing else. Listen man, I gotta finish servin' breakfasts. See you later."

Craig picked up his tray and the door clunked closed.

I sat on the bed, trying to absorb the news, but it had generated even more questions. How would we leave? Where would we go? What restrictions would there be? After more rumination, I stood on my tiptoes, peering out at the tree. This had become a way of punctuating my days. Another of the yellow-headed birds had settled on a branch again, but my weight became too much and I fell back onto the bed. I rubbed my toes, determined to get another sighting and flexed my feet like a novice dancer. By the time I tried again, the bird had flown, but a very loud noise filled the air as the white jet flew overhead. Maybe we'd be taken somewhere by jet?

Lunch came and went, but still nothing happened. Eventually, I heard doors bang and approaching footsteps. The door opened and Craig entered with three accompanying guards, an unconvincingly serious expression on his face.

"Mr Maher, you have an interview. Go with the guards and I'll see you later."

As the exterior door opened, I could see inmates from the other galleries exiting for afternoon association. We crossed to the administration building, and opened a door onto a corridor. The guard entered another code and waved me into a side room. Robbie was inside and gave a daffy grin.

"Wait here," said the guard, and closed the door.

Robbie shook his head and rolled his eyes. The plasters around his nose had gone.

"Hey Simon – what's happening?"

Clearly, things still weren't right. I checked myself before answering, thinking, *If this room is bugged, showing any foreknowledge could implicate Craig.*

"No idea. Ever been here before?"

"No."

"You had me a little worried yesterday when I mentioned our day out in New York, and you didn't seem to recall it. You were just having me on, right?"

He looked strangely vacant.

"No, we met for the first time at Andrew's mother's in Philly. Andy's your boss, isn't he?"

My stomach clenched. Something was terribly wrong.

"You know he is. We drove down together, remember?"

He cocked his head and concentrated.

"Yeah, I know that. Don't remember us being together in New York, though. I work for a really cool corporation there, called Marquetcom."

I felt sick. It almost seemed as if part of Robbie's brain had gone missing. An inane grin spread over his face and I fought an irrational impulse to slap him.

"Maybe we'll get prizes for cooperating," said Robbie.

I nodded, hearing approaching footsteps. The door opened. This time, Nina entered and sat opposite.

"What's happening?" she mouthed.

I shook my head, mimed a camera and then cupped my ears, like some party charade. She nodded.

"What's up with you guys?" said Robbie.

I smiled and shook my head.

"I think we should probably just wait quietly," I replied.

All we needed now was someone with a disabled memory shooting their mouth off!

I caught Nina's eye. She'd definitely lost weight, but appeared alert. She glanced at Robbie.

"How was it in 'special treatments', Rob?"

He grinned inanely.

"Aw, okay, I guess. They've a really funny picture show over there."

Robbie gazed at the ceiling. She wrinkled her forehead and I raised my eyebrows in response.

The door opened again. The same three guards arrived and escorted us further up the corridor to a large office. I immediately recognised the individual previously introduced as Mr Woods. Next to him was Dick Riley of the Arm-Rite Corporation and a white-haired stranger.

We were seated opposite their desk and I glanced around the room. The walls were lined by bookcases and cabinets and the far end had a large wall mirror.

"You're probably wondering why you've been sent for?" said Woods.

He looked directly at Nina.

"I suppose you think you've been terribly clever?"

I saw a tiny smile cross her face.

This appeared to seriously put Woods out.

"You might soon want to change your mind about that."

"Why are we here?" I ventured.

The white-haired man replied.

"You'll leave here towards the end of the day. First, though, there are some things you have to understand."

Woods interjected.

"Listen carefully to what Mr Tutch says if you want to stay safe!"

Tutch nodded and his unnaturally white hair bounced with each movement. The light eyebrows and lashes almost gave the appearance of a mulatto.

"It's a while since I've seen you, no?" Tutch said to Robbie, whose face had contorted in a very disturbing grin. Robbie looked up to the ceiling, showing the whites of his eyes.

I looked over to Nina and her face showed disbelief. Robbie almost looked like he'd been wired into an unseen power socket! His mouth gaped open and his face took on an expression of gormless simplicity.

"No, Sir, I don't believe we've met."

A smile, or something more disturbing, played over Tutch's face.

"You people should be careful. Troublemakers often make people very angry. Nevertheless, we've decided to be real helpful."

Tutch leaned forward, looking directly at me.

"Andrew's father, Biff Anson, will act as your guardian angel – until your future gets clearer."

Nothing made sense. Robbie sat with his chin hanging down and parted lips.

"Anson of Marquetcom?" said Nina. "'Guardian angel' – I hardly think so. Anson certainly won't do us any favours!"

"Well, that's where you're quite wrong, little lady," replied Tutch. "We want you to keep in close touch with Mr Anson's organisation. You'll be helped with anything necessary. I'll also be in close touch."

"Why?" I asked.

"For very good reasons," said Dick Riley. "We want an eye on you. Be very clear that we can pick you up any time you misbehave."

"Misbehave! How quaint! It's not us who are shredding the Constitution or acting as thugs for a plutocratic elite," said Nina – her face white with anger.

"Shut up and listen!" said Woods. "If we let you leave, we want you effectively supervised and with a point of contact. I expect you'd also rather not have an agent tagging along every minute of the day?"

"This is crazy," I reasoned. "Marquetcom represents everything that we find morally reprehensible."

"Morally reprehensible," mocked Riley, shaking his head. "You people are such children."

"Mock all you like, but I can't imagine Andrew taking directions from his father."

"It's a little late for that," said Tutch. "Daddy is already pulling the strings at his college."

"Not content with privatising everything, you want protesters privately controlled too?" said Nina. "What's your logo? A blindfolded ostrich with its head stuck in the tar sands?"

"Don't get snippy with us, lady," said Riley, his lips thin in a rodent-like face.

"But, this really is mad," I protested. "I mean, what's the plan for us? Seminars on the caring heart of corporate capitalism and the wonders of privatisation? What do we do in the meantime?"

"Marquetcom are a highly trusted service provider and contractor," said Woods. "Your choice is simple. Continue your business, but regularly report to Mr Tutch at headquarters, or you'll be supervised in other ways that, I guarantee, you'll find extremely disagreeable!"

"Meaning what?" I asked.

Robbie's body twitched and he leaned forward, drooling from the corner of his open mouth.

"When will I see Mr Biff again?" he asked, showing as much maturity as a four-year-old.

"What have you done?" I asked.

"Just be concerned with what might happen to you," said Riley with a sneer.

"He'll recover in a few days," volunteered Woods. "Of course, if you're uncooperative, he might just have a relapse. Keep a low profile, and you're absolutely prohibited from discussing any of this outside."

"So, we're to head to New York?" I checked.

"We'll get to that in a moment," replied Woods. "The girl, Gillian Marney, who hung around with you. We're prepared to have her represent your group and she'll oversee your release. Given the time she's spent with you, we've few illusions about her real outlook, but she's the only one with no record of trouble-making. That's why she was able to see you in San Francisco, Maher. If she doesn't get you back to New York and regular contact with Mr Tutch here, she'll experience severe problems getting home and probably in her future career."

"What about our colleague, in Nashville," asked Nina. "Is he alright?"

"You'll find out soon enough," replied Woods. "For now, return to the same room and, later, you'll get your clothing and other belongings. Remember, keep completely silent about everything. We can easily have you picked up again, and that really would be final."

UTAH – NEVADA – UTAH

GILL'S PERSPECTIVE

Early morning and Gill made preparation to collect Nick. Andy struggled awake, assuring her that things would be fine, if only he could have the small box of books from the trunk!

Typical academic, she thought. *Even in the wilderness, books come first!*

She left the Abajo campsite to the 191 and turned right, in the direction of Blanding. At Bluff, she joined the 163, heading for Arizona, and soon passed the ludicrous rock formation at Mexican Hat. It still wasn't clear to her why Camp Ute were insisting on her involvement? Amazing they didn't suspect she'd changed sides! Surely, that large woman on Yerba Buena Island expected that she'd head for Moab?

Nothing, though, could spoil the extraordinary sight of Monument Valley, its buttes and pinnacles, as she entered the hauntingly beautiful Navajo tribal lands. This time, she pulled over to really take in the amazing formations erupting from sand and blood-red soil, certain that it would be engraved in her memory for ever. What had the Navajo lifestyle been like before being broken by the white man's greed and treachery? The thought reminded her of Sheryl, and she fished in her bag for the number. Sheryl answered almost immediately.

"I expected your call. Where are you now?"

"About two and a half hours away, I think, and it's now 6.30am. What do you mean, 'expected my call'?"

"Meet me at the same diner and I'll explain then. Got to go – see you later."

Sheryl's caution was understandable. Was anywhere safe now?

Gill passed the Navajo National Monument. She hurried down almost empty roads, skirting the Hopi homelands, and reached Page at the predicted time. Sheryl waited in the diner, entering something into her laptop. When she looked up, it was obvious something was troubling her.

"I'm aware you're on your way to pick up your colleague, Nick. Unfortunately, I've some bad news he'll need to know."

"What's happened?"

"Nick was helped by an FBI colleague in Nashville I know and trust, called Toby Maynard. Afterwards, Toby and I spoke briefly. Nick had requested his help to transfer information to Ute. At one point, Nick apparently left a recording of Monroe's digital recorder with Toby. He probably downloaded a copy onto to his laptop. Unfortunately, Toby's charred body was found in his apartment last night, following a fire. Nothing was salvageable and the laptop was gone. Toby was a damn good guy and an important part of our circle."

"Of course, I'll explain to Nick on the drive back. What an awful shock!"

"He'll want to know because Toby was very helpful."

We ordered coffee and I couldn't help my eyes slipping down to those turquoise rings and bracelets.

"I see you still like them?"

I nodded, fascinated as Sheryl undid the clasp of a bracelet and then passed it over.

"A small souvenir of the Indian lands. I hope it's lucky for you."

"Thank you so much. I really wasn't expecting that!"

"You probably wouldn't have time even for the trading posts. You asked on the phone why I expected you. I expect you guessed I cut you short because it's safer?"

Gill nodded.

"Last time we met, I mentioned us having our own network – people like Toby."

She nodded again.

"Before he died, Toby called and told me that Nick would fly to Vegas – it's quicker, and that one of you would collect him. He also said to Nick that, if necessary, I'd help your group to hide, down here."

"Did he also tell you that I'm supposed to play a part in their release?"

"Of course. Toby was in an awkward position, acting as intermediary between Nick and the rogue group. He apparently told them that Nick had multiple copies of the information from the Senator. He understood that the information was of national importance and included copies of a digital sound file that, if necessary, could at any time be spread right over the internet. During the discussions with Ute, Toby was ordered to immediately encrypt the material, and told that he didn't have permission to listen to it! Toby played 'honest broker', stressing that Nick had additional copies and processes in hand for a wide release, if the group should be harmed. Of course, that threat didn't save Toby himself. Clearly, the rogue group are rattled about these further copies, though, or I'm sure that your entire group would be dead already!"

Sheryl's warning reverberated around her head.

"I suppose they'll monitor us? I mean, if the information from Senator Monroe was strong enough to force a release, then…"

"Probably, and you have to play a part in that!"

"Nick told me he'd explain when we meet. We'll call in on the way back."

"Please do," said Sheryl. "Also, please ensure that Nick changes his clothing."

"Do what?"

"Certain radio frequency identification (RFID) tags can be very sophisticated, now. You know, those little anti-theft tags that stores sometimes put in clothes? New miniaturised types can include a tracking capability. Toby's colleagues may have attached something to Nick's clothing.

"Got it. Okay, I guess I'd better shift now and, Sheryl, thanks for everything." She rubbed the bracelet. "And I absolutely love this!"

The virtually empty roads and landscape were so strikingly different from home. She crossed the Glen Canyon dam, and the road climbed a hill overlooking Lake Powell and it's unlikely marina. The cliffs and those odd flat-topped hills lying behind were more impressive than anything that digital trickery could ever manage. In the distance, she saw black clouds clinging to a mesa – bringing a rare downpour to the finger canyons that drained into the lake. Further on, she passed Vermillion Cliffs again and crossed the Kaibab plateau to the I15, which led to the city. Giant billboards had suddenly sprouted from the roadside, boasting extravagant shows and signalling the start of Vegas. It seemed no time before reaching McCarran Airport.

Nick was already waiting and gave her a hug! She passed him a note explaining the need to change clothing. They found a suitable clothing store and, fifteen minutes later, he pushed a bag of clothing into a nearby trash can. The trip back seemed quicker with company. It was now her third time down these roads and she feigned nonchalance while he enthused about the landscape.

"Makes me realise how rarely I got out of the city. Had no idea what I was missing."

"England is beautiful, but this landscape seems so much bigger than everyday troubles," she said.

"The trouble is – ours are a bit more than everyday!"

Eventually Nick's experience in Nashville tumbled out. She winced at Monroe's talk of 'intelligence' corruption, and then the horror that happened next. He, in turn, was startled at Sheryl's friendship with Toby and shocked to hear of his death.

Nick, did you glean anything about this odd demand that I supervise the release?"

"No, just that Ute were quite definite about it."

"I'm amazed they haven't now realised that I'm with you guys. I suppose they must assume I'm continuing my surveillance brief. You say Monroe advised you to make copies of his information. Did you?"

"Of course."

They were close to Glen Canyon dam by the time he'd finished the whole story, including the interlude with Josie and Natalie. Maybe because of her training, his naivety astounded her.

"You secreted handwritten notes and a USB device in the apartment of some singing twins you happened to meet?"

"Yes, but, before visiting Toby's office, I called at an internet café and sent the audio file to myself in NYC, to a new account and to Mom in the UK. She's computer savvy and will copy it to a separate folder and delete the email."

She could feel her face drain.

"You heard Simon discuss communication surveillance? I'm shaken! It could easily fall into the wrong hands."

He coloured, and looked away.

"Actually, I didn't hear Simon talk about that. Look, I had to do something and it was the best I could think of."

"And the original recording?"

"Here." He rummaged around in his pocket and pulled out the silver device.

"I also put copies onto a clutch of USB devices, which I bought for all of us!"

We rolled into Page, finding a half-full diner, but no Sheryl. Half way through the chicken fajitas, she arrived, looking strained, and mouthed:

"Has he changed clothing?"

"Yes, everything is clear. Meet Nick, who's back from Nashville."

"I'm so sorry to hear about Toby. I almost feel if I hadn't…"

"Don't go there, Nick," Sheryl replied. "Toby wouldn't want it, but this certainly demonstrates what you're up against!"

Sheryl shook her head and Gill guessed something else was coming.

"Gill, Toby said… you were instructed to encourage the others to return to New York City and that any help necessary will be provided by Marquetcom."

Nick groaned.

"Yes," Gill agreed. "It's quite crazy. Marquetcom is led by Andrew Alton's father. I got to know Andy a lot more while we were camping. I can't see him…"

Nick interjected.

"My company partnered with Marquetcom in a project. They really are slippery bastards and his father is one of the most unpleasant pieces of humanity I've ever had the misfortune to meet. The whole idea is absurd!"

"Toby said Richard Monroe had told him that Marquetcom often shows up in dubious settings."

"Meaning?"

"Ever noticed how the same handful of corporations always turn up," asked Sheryl. "Ever heard of 'economic hit-men'?"

"No." "Yes." They replied – simultaneously!

Sheryl looked at Nick and grinned. "Tell her."

Nick started.

"Richard explained it during our discussion. Apparently, economists or engineers previously groomed by intelligence persuade leaders of developing countries to take vast loans for big infrastructure projects that they really can't afford. These guys work in a handful of corporations and, to outward appearances, are an ordinary part of their workforce. The loans are contingent on awarding contracts to these same corporations. The 'hit-men' know very well that the debt will be unsustainable."

"So, then their resources come under the control of our corporations," interrupted Sheryl. "Either they'll owe favours or will be unable to resist future demands."

"Exactly," Nick continued. "The 'hit-men' give bent, wildly optimistic figures 'proving' the need for various projects. Huge dams, with little purpose, glitzy new airports, when there isn't even the most basic healthcare – that sort of thing! Of course, these contracts mean huge corporate profits and also payments to the corrupt local politicians that facilitate it."

"Why are you raising this now?"

"You need to understand that Marquetcom has been heavily involved. They've been up to their gills with the dark side of the intelligence world, for years – for example, with placement of economic hitmen. Richard Monroe mentioned a rogue faction was partnering with the private sector in the North East. He indicated that this was Marquetcom. The main interface between the rogue group and Marquetcom is a corrupt intelligence agent, named Brian Tutch."

Suddenly, the situation made more sense to Gill. They were to be put directly under the eyes and control of the North East franchise.

Nick aired another worry.

"Richard Monroe said Tutch has been involved in the 'economic hit-man' business in the past. Maybe that's what he's up to in Colombia."

Fascinating though all this undoubtedly was, Gill suddenly caught sight of the time.

"Heck, Sheryl, time's getting on. We really have to go."

"Yeah. You'd best move. You have my number. Remember, if you need assistance or to lie low, I can probably help. Call me."

They sped towards Monument Valley in silence. She imagined possible scenarios, and guessed Nick was doing the same. Even so, Monument Valley worked its spell and we briefly stopped at the small visitor centre. The great volcanic cores of the 'Mittens' were closer here, and the land sloped, giving unobstructed views over this elemental landscape. On the terrace, a group of young Navajos drummed and chanted. Apart from amplification and a jeep down in the valley, it could have been another age.

This time, Nick took his turn to drive. As they went through Bluff, hand-woven Indian rugs and jewellery were out for sale, but there could be no stopping now. They neared Monticello and the turning into the Abajo Mountains. Fifteen minutes later, the vehicle nosed into the clearing and Andrew emerged from the trees – a book in hand and a wide grin on his face.

"Glad you're back alright. Whatever you did, Nick, it seems to have..."

She interrupted.

"We've very limited time, Andy. I need to reach the camp and be done before the light goes."

He looked puzzled.

"Okay, coming. Oh, you mean how will we fit everyone in? We can take your car, as well."

"That isn't it. We have strict instructions and aren't in a position to argue."

"I could follow behind and wait near the turning."

"And if they hold you? You aren't the one holding the sensitive information. Look, Nick will explain. You should both stay, but I must leave immediately."

Her heart hammered throughout the drive. The red barcode-like signs appeared and then the turning to Ute, which Andy pointed out on the way to their previous site. She followed the road for several miles, climbing two hills. At the last summit, the road curved and she saw a barrier and guard box. Ahead were the fences and buildings of Camp Ute.

A guard approached the car and she lowered the window.

"Why are you here, Ma'am?"

"My name is Gill Marney, from a United Kingdom government agency. I have a meeting with your Mr Woods and I'm expected."

"Hold on a minute, please."

He returned to the small wooden structure and she saw him pick up a clipboard. He returned with another guard.

"You have ID?"

She fished around and extracted the card from the Foreign Office – only to be used in emergencies. He inspected and then returned it.

"Derek will come to show you the way."

The sallow, spotty Derek got in and her skin crept as he sat in the passenger seat. The gate swung open.

"Take a right, and then head for the admin block over there," he said, pointing to a long, low building. Her heart beat even faster. What if she was suspected? Would she even get to see Simon?

She suppressed a shiver and, bracing for the unknown, followed Derek to the entrance...

96

UTAH

JUDY'S PERSPECTIVE

Judy woke to find an arm curled over her body. She slowly turned onto her back, and gazed at Zoltan's sleeping profile. How lucky, having a man so sensitive and attractive. He'd certainly made up for his brief disappearance! How typically unselfish, to battle on in Grand Junction, trying to exhume his friend's equipment from an IT graveyard! Of course, he couldn't have risked calling on a land-line after his cell phone had spluttered. How could anyone have doubted him? She swivelled her head in the other direction to look at his gift again, sparkling on the bedside cabinet. A pretty new watch. What a wonderful man!

She took a shower and, by the time she'd returned, Zoltan was dressing. He smiled, and her heart skipped. Outside, the extraordinary rock formations glowed in the late afternoon sunshine. They'd been so lucky finding this little motel looking out over Castle Valley, even if the rooms seemed a bit undersized.

"I wonder how Gill and Nick are getting on. I wish we knew what was happening."

"Nothing like what just happened here, I hope," he replied with a grin.

"Certainly not," she said, pursing her lips like some maiden aunty. He laughed and hugged her.

"I'm going into Moab," he said. "Pick up a few bits before the shops close. I might briefly call on Freddy at the dealership and check that

Terry isn't doing something stupid. It's frustrating that we don't know what to expect. Will they be released later today, tomorrow morning, can they travel freely or have restrictions?"

"You could probably sum it up by saying we don't know very much," she offered brightly.

He picked up her damp towel and playfully flicked her.

After he left, she busied herself in the small suite, remaking the bed and tidying up. She went to the wardrobe to pick clothing for this evening. He'd probably take her to the small restaurant on the edge of town, again.

She rummaged around for her travel bag, and managed to dislodge the chinos Zoltan hung up earlier. The balance must have been off, because they slithered into an ivory pool of material at her feet.

"Drat it, Zolt," she said aloud, although he wasn't generally the sort of man she had to tidy up after. She picked the chinos up by the legs and gave them a small shake before returning them to the hanger. Two pieces of paper fluttered from his pocket to the floor and, curious, she picked them up.

Her smile drained as she scanned them for a second, and then a third, time. A receipt for a Swiss lady's watch from Hoster's Quality Jeweller, Rivergate Mall, Nashville – and a guarantee stamped with yesterday's date. Feeling weak, she took the receipt and guarantee and sat on the bed. Nothing made sense. Zoltan was in Grand Junction yesterday helping a friend. It was Nick who'd been in Nashville, and he was hardly off buying presents. She picked the watch up again, staring as though willing it to give an answer.

A tap on the window startled her and the watch dropped from her hands onto the bed. She looked up and Andy's face was pressed to the window. He mouthed 'hello' and mimed turning the key. She waved back and went to the door. Moments later, he entered and looked around. He mouthed 'Zoltan' and pointed to the bathroom door.

"He's in town, picking things up at the shops. He said he might call in on Freddy. What's with the cloak and dagger stuff?"

"Sorry. I didn't mean to startle you."

"We're all on edge. What's the news from Nashville? I assume Nick is back?"

Andrew nodded.

"Yes, he's outside now checking on things. He'll join us in a moment."

"Andy, what's going on?"

She looked at the sensitive, drawn face of her eldest child, suddenly certain that whatever was bothering him would be bad. He went over to the dressing table and pulled the little stool over and sat next to the bed.

"Remember when we talked in that coffee shop in Moab, Mom, and you explained your feelings about Zoltan. You wanted me to be happy, although I think you knew that I had reservations."

"Yes."

He rested his fingers on the back of her hand, and looked pained. She suddenly wanted to change the conversation, even knowing that it was irrational.

"I don't think he's all he seems."

"Andy, Zolt's the best thing that's happened to me in a very long time."

He slowly shook his head and she felt her stomach sink. She was already back, hearing about Biff's affairs. Obviously, he was about to tell her something similar.

"You saw him with another woman?"

"No. Nothing like that."

The next few minutes were a blur as he explained. She listened, picturing Zoltan's drive to Ute, the guard's salute and Andy and Gill's subsequent move to the new campsite in the Abajos. Her hand touched something on the bed and she picked up the watch and handed it to him.

"Very nice, but I'm not sure..."

She passed the receipt and guarantee, and watched as his face passed from confusion to understanding.

"A present, to make up for his unexpected absence. I take it you noticed..."

Andrew nodded. There was a tap at the door, and he let Nick in. Even before asking, she knew that clutching at straws was silly.

"Hello, Nick. Can I ask something? Did you by chance buy a watch for Zoltan in Nashville?"

His expression answered before any words.

"Sorry, no. It wasn't that kind of trip."

Andy passed the watch, receipt and guarantee to Nick without speaking. Nick stared, and looked lost in thought.

"But, why, Andy? I suppose he must work for Military Intelligence in some capacity – but why Nashville? I assume you didn't see him there, Nick?"

"Perhaps that isn't the right question," said Nick. "Perhaps, it's more a case of what else was in Nashville? The answer: someone with information that could lead to the release of our friends... and now that person is dead!"

She felt physically sick. Nick had just articulated what her frozen mind was trying to avoid.

"You mean that Zoltan could be the assassin?" whispered Andrew.

"But, why send Zoltan when Nick knows him, and was actually with the Senator? Surely that would be far too risky."

"It could also be an advantage," Nick answered. "If the killer had to show himself, to get into position to take the Senator out – familiarity could help. He could pretend, for example, to be bringing urgent news. In uncertain circumstances, that might just make a vital difference."

"I don't know," said Andrew, shaking his head. "Then he'd have to kill you too, so that doesn't make much sense. The point now is, how do we to handle contact with Zoltan, without showing our hand?"

Her stomach clenched at the words, 'handle contact', remembering their earlier lovemaking. Surely, the person she thought so clever and sensitive wasn't a killer. Surely, he wouldn't be lost to her! Life couldn't be so cruel!

"Being so close to their release, we can't do anything now" replied Nick. "We'll just have to act normally."

"Look, Mom, he was extremely well prepared. You couldn't possibly have known. Other than that one hint over possible militia involvement, there were no clues. To be honest, I couldn't have pictured him as a militia convert, either."

"Andy, we endlessly talked about the things that are important to me – actually, to all of us. Zolt seemed so committed. Normally, I'd pick up on anything phoney straight away!"

"Perhaps that's what being a professional means," Andrew suggested. "To fool us all this time – he must be good!"

Her mind resisted the implications, even as she toyed with the possibilities. Andrew comforted her with an encircling arm.

"We must get back to the Abajo camp, Mom. If things went okay, Gill and the others could be back soon. I think we'll just have to play things straight, and not let Zoltan know what we've discovered. Incidentally, I've now changed our rental car to a blue Kia."

She nodded, lost for words.

"We'll be in touch, very soon."

They left, but it wasn't until the tears rounded her cheek that she even realised she was crying. Trembling, she lay on the bed and sobbed into the pillow.

UTAH

GILL'S PERSPECTIVE

Gill stood beside Derek at reception, as someone was informed about her arrival. The fear kept nagging – was this really an elaborate trick. Any moment, would she be escorted to a cell and the news forwarded to a grateful Donaldson in the UK? The receptionist finished talking on the phone and smiled.

"Mr Woods and the others are ready, Ms Marney. I'll show you down."

Derek grunted and left. The receptionist exited through a half door cut flush to the counter and Gill followed her down to a large office. She pointed towards a seating area with comfortable chairs, and left. Four men waited, their faces tense and expectant. At the end of the room was a long mirror next to an internal door.

"Please sit, Ms Marney."

They were seated in horseshoe formation, reminding her of the promotions panel back home. She sat as directed and the man immediately opposite spoke first.

"I'm Basil Woods, a senior officer of the security service that's hosting your placement. To my right is Colonel Forest, military liaison, then Dr Farrow, head of psychological services here at Camp Ute and Mr Dick Riley from the Arm-Rite Corporation, who provide logistics, security and hotel services for the site."

"It seems an impressive facility, Sir – though hardly a hotel."

"That's just an expression, Marney – meaning the on-site provision of food, security and other practical services. Let's get down to business. We've talked with Tom Freison in New York and your superiors in the UK. You've managed extremely well keeping an eye on this brood, while continuing your observation placement."

"Thank you, Sir. You probably already know that I collected Nicholas Martin from Las Vegas this morning. The one who went to Nashville."

"Yeah, we know," said Colonel Forest.

"Apparently, Martin was told you'd deal with me because I was the only one without a known history and not under active surveillance. Hopefully they'll continue buying that, which potentially lets me play a useful role, at least in the short term."

"Why else do you think you're here?" asked a sneering Dick Riley.

She ignored Riley, having taken an instant and instinctive dislike.

"Exactly, Gill. We want your help ensuring that they get back to New York City," said Basil Woods. "Consider those as your orders, made under delegated authority from your commander."

"What actually is the plan?" she asked – already knowing the answer!

"It isn't convenient for Freison to have a crowd of civilians cluttering up his office. Not good for your group either. However, there are real areas of concern with this bunch. We need to keep them and their activities under observation."

She knew that clarifying this was pivotal.

"When you say 'your group', Sir, please understand I was merely continuing my brief of watching UK troublemakers, who'd regrettably allied themselves with your home-grown troublemakers."

She saw no disagreement on their faces.

"Obviously," replied Woods, "though you'll work under our direction for the time being. Of course, you must realise that, here, our intel works closely with certain approved services from the private sector. Isn't that so, Mr Riley?"

Riley's face wore a smug smile as he nodded.

"Another private sector associate you're probably familiar with is Marquetcom, in New York City. This corporation has done exceptional work in the past. Of course, we realise that Biff Anson is Alton's father and know about the tensions between them. Nevertheless, however odd this may seem, Anson and Marquetcom will be providing a 'guardian angel' function to the group in New York by meeting their needs. There are reasons, important reasons, so please make it absolutely crystal clear that they must cooperate. Alternative facilities for detention exist and, if necessary, other arrangements will be far more intense."

"Sir, I thought that they had information of national importance, which they were threatening to misuse – to manipulate matters their way?"

"Exactly, Marney, exactly. We want you being especially vigilant. I'm sure you understand the primacy of protecting information flows. The Parenda woman, who will be released with the others, had a relationship with Senator Richard Monroe. What you won't know is that Monroe had gone bad. He'd mixed in strange circles and was in danger of almost swallowing socialism! We've watched him for some time and Parenda appears to have really gotten to him. Monroe lost the plot and, by then, was spouting disinformation and lies. We've reason to think he'd also divulged sensitive intel within the relationship – you know, as part of their 'pillow talk'!"

"Gone bad?" she questioned.

"Monroe had previously been an exemplar of decent conservative values, so the change shocked everybody. Privately, he even started agreeing with some of the left-wing horrors in Latin America. The fact his daughter married a Bolivian probably didn't help.

"Damn near Commies," spat Riley.

"So, Nick Martin will have heard disingenuous disinformation and lies from Monroe before he died. We gather he recorded material on a digital recorder. Release of this material would undoubtedly endanger national security."

"You must realise," said Dr Farrow, speaking for the first time, "the balance of Monroe's mind was almost certainly disturbed when spouting this stuff."

"Why do you say that?"

"People sometimes get disorientated and vulnerable, when losing their belief systems. Whatever voodoo the Parenda woman put out seems to have really messed him up. The party was then turning against him and his marriage had been busted."

Woods nodded in agreement before he spoke.

"The other worry is that, although formerly serving on the Intelligence Committee, Monroe oddly seems to have turned against the intelligence community. He'd even made ridiculous allegations about former colleagues. If there's something that can't be tolerated in a fight against terrorism, it's having a divided house or leaks about sensitive operations. Apparently, Nick Martin made copies of this rubbish and we need to stop it! Unfortunately, he's put unknown mechanisms in hand to release the material in the event of something happening to this group!"

"Otherwise, we'd quickly loosen their tongues," sneered Riley.

"Please try to find out more," continued Woods.

It didn't require her stomach curdling to know this was the last thing she'd wanted to hear.

"Of course, Sir. They're a bright lot, though, so I can only do it subtly."

"There is something else," said Dr Farrow.

"You'll find the young man, Robbie James, even odder than usual. He's not a robust individual and, I'm afraid, suffered a minor break-down under stress. You'll probably find him rather childlike and forgetful for a while, though that should wear off. We tried to help and, as a matter of fact, provided minor treatment for a long-standing sinus condition. Even so, during standard testing and interrogation, he... well, I guess, in lay terms, he 'blew a fuse', although I don't anticipate long-term harm."

"So, to recap," said Woods. "Your task is promoting... no, ensuring, their return to New York. Second, try to discover what Martin's done with this nonsense from Monroe. Third, the 'group', including you, are to regularly report to Marquetcom's office in New York City. That will be handled by an agent named Brian Tutch – one of our people!"

An almost inaudible snort came from Colonel Forest.

"Return to New York and liaise with Brian Tutch at Marquetcom's office," she repeated. "Okay. I can guide, encourage and keep my ears open, but, if I push too hard, it'll give the game away."

"Naturally, we realise that," Woods replied.

Four heads nodded and it seemed to be accepted.

"When do we leave?" she asked, noticing that the light was fading.

"They're collecting clothes and effects as we speak," replied Colonel Forest.

"Incidentally," interjected Woods, "the latest RFIDs, with tracking, are concealed in their clothing."

"I've heard Maher mention such things, so they could expect that."

Woods nodded. She followed him and Riley as they left the room. Her heart pounded as she coached herself not to overreact at seeing Simon and hoped he'd understand!

They stopped outside a door and she held her breath to help calm her heart. The door opened and she looked at Robbie and Nina, giving Simon only a passing glance. Woods addressed the others.

"This woman, your friend, has been given instructions that you must follow. Please remember, that you could be picked up in a blink, so be careful. Don't cause any trouble or spray your collectivist, socialist poison around, outside. You won't find us tolerant."

Woods turned to Nina.

"Consider yourself especially lucky. Return to your work for the moment, but children's charity work means just that, and, indeed, only that. Anything else will be viewed extremely seriously – particularly anything that threatens national interests. Do you understand?"

Nina nodded, but, even after incarceration, she had fire in her eyes.

"Presumably, by 'national interests', you mean commercial, corporate interests?"

"You're already on a tightrope, Parenda. Don't get clever or even think of unhelpful dabbling in Colombia. I know you understand what I mean! While, of course, we know nothing about it, perhaps you should ponder your former lover's fate."

Her face drained, and she stared at the floor.

"We don't want to see you people again," sneered Riley. If we do…"

Guards arrived and waited by the door.

"Time to go," said Woods.

Gill looked on as the others collected plastic bags of belongings, and the group followed the guards back to the vehicle. She climbed behind the wheel and retraced her way to the gates. They exited the camp, passing the barrier and guard box, before anyone spoke. Simon next to her, and Nina and Robbie in the back. Simon reached around, rubbing her back and somehow finding where painfully knotted muscles and nerves were radiating tension throughout her body. She smiled and, raising an upright finger to her lips, mouthed, "They may have bugged the car while I was inside. We'll change it, and also your clothing".

Simon nodded, turned around and silently mouthed the message to the others.

They reached the main road, half expecting a tail. She glanced at her watch, which read 7.15pm. The road back seemed completely empty and the headlights lit endless trees, accentuating their isolation. Simon's hand caressed her shoulder. She willed herself to postpone an embrace and continue driving to the Abajo campsite. Eventually, they bumped down the remaining distance to the tents she'd left hours earlier. Andrew appeared with a large torch and they saw another car in the headlights.

"Maybe Andy asked Judy to hire another car."

She parked and Andrew opened the door and helped her out. She ran around to the other side as Simon jumped out and fell into his arms. From inside, a drooling Robbie called, "I'm hungry", in a whinnying, childlike voice…!

98

UTAH

ZOLTAN'S PERSPECTIVE

Zoltan sunk into his seat, shocked. Hearing his worst fears confirmed wasn't the ideal way to have his competence in bugging confirmed. At first, he heard Judy's voice, insistent and quite certain: that 'he's definitely one of us'. Her tone gradually becoming hesitant as she absorbed Andy and Nick's deadly reasoning. Holding onto that receipt because of the damn guarantee seemed such a shockingly amateurish error, and stark proof why cultivating that storyline always was a potential disaster. Of course, the relationship itself was his other big mistake.

Woods had called to inform him that Gill and the others should be back at Andy's camp, leaving his way to Ute clear. He called Woods back, and described what he'd just heard.

"There's no real choice now," said Woods. "Bring her here!"

He drove back to Castle Valley. The motel car park looking across to Parriott mesa was now almost empty. He circled it on foot until opposite their room and, hidden behind a convenient tamarisk, looked in. The curtains were still open and he watched Judy packing. Even in what must be a state of agitation, she was a fine-looking woman and he felt sadness about the turn of events and what could have been.

He entered the main lobby, and smiled over at the tired-looking receptionist. She nodded back and he continued down the hall to their room. It was irritating that this motel didn't follow the usual format, with doors out to the parking area. He calmed his breathing, and moulded his expression to near normality. When he entered, Judy beamed at him.

"Hello, darling. Get what you needed?"

There was barely a flicker betraying that anything was wrong, though he had to consciously relax his jaw. How did she get so good?

"Yeah, I put some stuff in the trunk. Listen, I've been thinking. We might as well get back to Philly, now that we're done here."

She smiled and pointed to the half-packed bag.

"I've been thinking the same and guessed you'd agree. In the morning, or were you thinking of tonight?"

"Why not tonight?"

She slipped into the bathroom and he started packing, taking the opportunity to slide his hand into the pocket of the cream chinos – the focus of the earlier attention. His fingers found them and he pulled out the receipt and guarantee. He resisted the urge to crumple the offending papers and returned them, folded the pants and placed them in his travel bag. No use crying over spilt milk! He patted the Heckler and Koch, knowing he'd need it later this evening.

The bathroom door bolt slid open and Judy came out.

"Jude, I think we should call Andy and the others to tell them of our plan. They might even have the same idea, but we still have to return the vehicle to Denver airport."

"On the same page again," she replied. "I was about to suggest the same."

He listened while she calmly spoke to Andy, betraying nothing of the shock that she must be feeling. Killing her seemed such a pity!

"Won't that make things more complicated," she said and he watched her little dimple moving as she spoke. Soon, he'd never see it again. Her voice remained steady, though he noticed one hand gripped the phone while the other nervously picked at the bedspread – the same hands that had stroked and caressed him a few hours earlier.

"Okay. Perhaps it's better if you explain," she said and held out the phone.

"Andy reckons we should all have a quick meet first. Here, have a word."

He took the phone and said hello.

"Hi Zolt, Andy here. We agree that we should all get out while we can. I'd like a quick meeting to plan and agree our immediate strategy.

As it's quite complicated, we need to all be singing from the same hymn sheet. Can you make it over here?"

He wanted a reason to refuse, but it might raise suspicion. He'd already put together a story to explain Nashville.

"Okay, that sounds a good idea."

Andrew gave directions.

They drove through Moab in silence. As they passed the turning to Freddy's home, he saw her look up the road. She stayed quiet afterwards, and he guessed she was again having conflict about Fred.

"I so hope Freddy hasn't drawn the authorities' attention."

"Probably not. Anyway, it's mostly academic now. They're out and we're about to move on."

They passed the turning that would take them to Ute and continued on to the Abajos. Judy directed him to the small track Andrew described and eventually they saw the tents and vehicles. He extinguished the engine, and the others emerged from the trees. Judy climbed out and hugged her eldest son, and then Nick and Nina. Gill and Simon wandered over hand in hand and then Robbie ambled up and stood beside him.

"I stayed in Moab for a while, as a kid," he said somewhat mindlessly.

Farrow predicted that he'd implode under stress and he certainly looked the worse for wear. When he'd joined Farrow and Forrest in 'special treatments' to assist the testing, Robbie hadn't recognised him. They said his condition would reverse and, sure enough, here he was talking again – after a fashion. It was really quite remarkable.

"Okay everyone," called Andrew. "We're done here. Let's agree our way forward."

"I have to return as quickly as possible," Nick said. "My boss is steaming. The fact that I called in ill means nothing to him, so Nina and I must fly back."

"We'll take the car back to Denver, and then fly on to Philly," Zoltan offered. "Judy's had time with Fred and the kids, so there's no need to stay longer."

"We'll do that, too," said Andrew. "I can't face that long drive now."

Simon murmured something to Gill.

"What do you think, Si?" Andrew asked, "Good idea?"

He sensed that Andrew might manoeuvre to protect his mother.

"Yeah, we may as well go."

Zoltan was silently rehearsing explanations about Nashville, when he felt hairs behind his neck lift. He sensed someone come from behind, a split second before an arm crooked around his neck. He tried to turn, but it was too late – the arm contracted in a scissor-like motion and, at the same time, the others rushed him. The arm's pressure increased until he choked horribly. He kicked backwards, but couldn't make contact. More hands pushed him to the ground and he felt the Heckler & Koch tugged from its holster. A partly folded tent was put over him. He kicked out again, but still couldn't connect and then felt a rope encircle his ankles. He pulled up his knee and kicked again, but the cord now cut into his ankles. Several hands rolled him over, face down. The tent then completely covered his body and was probably tied using the guide ropes. His face was touching the ground. He gasped through the material for air, and the smell of canvas and dissolving dust filled his mouth with a bitter taste.

Although sound was muffled, he heard a voice.

"Throwing it into the canyon is probably best."

Sweating under the canvas, he could only hope that they meant his pistol!

"'Mine got caught on that ledge," came a voice. "Mine too."

"Judy, you brought exactly the right size," came Nina's voice. "I see a new career as a personal shopper!"

He flexed his body to make space like some chrysalis in the canvas covering.

So, it was clothes that had disappeared into the canyon. Judy had brought changes, but how did she know to do that?

"Is it loose enough?" came Judy's voice.

"Yeah. Probably take him at least ten or fifteen minutes to get free," said Andrew. "Should be a nice long walk, though."

Zoltan heard the sounds of them leaving. He'd been face down about ten minutes, when suddenly all hell broke loose. A roaring came from the direction of the canyon and, for a moment, he thought some freak weather event was just about to add to his troubles. His ear was close to the ground and a vibrating sensation travelled through his jawbone to the side of his head. He twisted over, resting his chin on the ground as light started penetrating the canvas package. The noise and the rush of air that flapped at the loosened canvas was almost over-whelming. It could only be a helicopter.

Eventually the noise stopped and hands unpicked the temporary shroud. As the ropes unwound and canvas peeled back, he rolled onto his back. It took a few moments to adjust to the moonlight, torches and the faint glow from the Bell Huey's cabin. A helicopter now stood where their vehicles had been until a short time ago. Standing over him were two men in Arm-Rite uniforms and, next to them, the rat-like features of Dick Riley.

"Not sure why you're snoozing when Mr Woods is waiting?"

He sat up, rubbing at his ankles where the rope had bitten. His tired mind tried to formulate a clever response, but wasting wit on a corporate dope wasn't worth it.

"Obviously, waiting for my chauffeur!"

The guards helped him into the helicopter and the Bell took off, shining a powerful searchlight below. He now saw that they'd been on the rim of a canyon with an almost sheer drop to the desert country below. The pilot extinguished the light and flew towards a glow that could only be Camp Ute. Within minutes, they'd set down at the small airstrip and taken the short drive up to the camp.

Woods was waiting in Colonel Forest's office.

"It didn't go according to plan, then?"

"Afraid not."

He described what had happened at the Abajo campsite.

"The only way I could have got away was literally to take them out. Who knows what may then have happened to that recording!"

"Shame!" replied Woods. "I had things to ask that girlfriend of yours. Any ideas about their immediate plans?"

"Martin talked about getting back to New York as soon as possible. He's under pressure from his employer. Andrew Alton planned to accompany his mom back to Philly. He'd only just suggested that, when they rushed me. I didn't hear from Gill, Maher or Robbie James."

"We've now exchanged one James for another."

"How so?"

"Terry James was caught earlier this evening, poking about outside the camp!" Woods broke into a rare grin.

"We've brought him in for a closer look!"

"I saw that he wasn't present. So, they decided to keep him out of the loop? Probably a good call on their part."

"Probably. In the meantime, you must get back to the North East."

"I know. There's stuff at Judy Alton's. I need to move fast."

"Which is why you need to get back to the airstrip now – as a passenger on the white jet, tonight!"

"Right."

"We haven't totally discarded the possibility that, at some point in the future, you might resolve the problem with the Alton woman. Explain your visit to the Camp as a bona fide agent, but one who'd come round to their way of thinking and wanted to help. We'll see how they behave with Brian and the boys at Marquetcom. In the meantime, there are other tasks. Sit at the table."

Woods pointed to the corner of the room. Beside the table was the small trolley and the tape recorder he'd seen last time.

"Dr Farrow has something he'd like you to consider. The headphones are more comfortable. I have to go next door and will be back soon."

The sick feeling started even before the headphones had covered his ears. Woods flicked a switch and, moments later, the guttural voice intoned:

"Your colour is fresian... your colour is fresian."

After Woods entered the adjoining room, Dr Farrow was bent over a small recorder, amplifier and monitor. Frustration filled his face.

"The connection is fluffy... I can't hear a thing!"

He twisted the knob backwards and forwards rapidly, but still no sound. Farrow grabbed a can from a shelf and gave a blast of compressed air. Still nothing!

"I'll try more jacks," he said, pulling leads from the back of the amplifier. "Stone age kit," he muttered, messing about with the leads. At first, they resisted reattachment, but sound suddenly blasted from the speakers.

Dr Gunther's digitally processed voice was giving out instructions.

"...must be added to water supplies in Putumayo, Colombia, as directed by Mr Tutch. On return, meet your contact in Brooklyn and tell him you're ready..."

99

UTAH – ARIZONA

SIMON MAHER

I sat beside Gill in the front and periodically looked behind. The increasingly inane comments from the back felt troubling. Robbie lay curled up on the back seat and I wouldn't have been surprised to see him sucking a thumb. Andrew drove the vehicle ahead, but suddenly applied the hazard lights, stopped and jumped out. I wound my window down.

"We hadn't actually finished agreeing our next moves," he said, "when Zoltan arrived."

A noise suddenly interrupted the quietness of the forest and a light descended from the sky near their former camp. Everyone froze.

"A helicopter... they must have tracked Zoltan and then sent a rescue," said Gill.

"Let's make this quick. I was about to suggest that we travel in separate groups. That's even more of a good idea now," said Andrew. "There are several different ways back to Denver. We could choose separate routes, and then pick up onward flights."

"Craig thought they didn't have a helicopter," Nick said.

"From what you said, Craig, bless him, was low in the pecking order, and probably wouldn't know much," suggested Gill. "I bet they can access whatever they need!"

I looked over at Robbie, who leaned on the wing with a vacuous expression.

"Something is really wrong there," I said. "He looks ready to fall apart. I can't see him surviving in New York."

"We could look after him in Philadelphia," suggested Judy. "Get him back on his feet."

"We could try," said Andrew, looking doubtful.

"I've another idea," said Gill. "That helpful colleague in Page I told you about offered help. She knew that Ute inmates can end up in a sorry state. At the time, I was worried about you," she said, looking at me.

I smiled, wondering when we'd ever get some time together.

"I can't take more time out," said Nick. "Not if I still want a job."

Nina nodded.

"I'm the same. Corinne has carried the load alone, for a long time now."

Paroxysms of coughing came from behind.

"Robbie needs time to get himself back together," said Gill. "Sheryl could help and may have some other helpful ideas."

The idea made sense, to me, and, in any case, I couldn't bear to be parted so soon.

"I must get back too," said Judy. "I've some hard thinking ahead."

"Leaving Gill with all the responsibility isn't fair," I said, looking at Andy. "How about if I help out? You can stay with your mom and I'll join you in Philly as soon as possible. We've lots to discuss, as well."

A knowing smile played over Andrew's face.

"Okay. That makes sense."

"Haven't you all forgotten something vital?" asked Nick, reaching into his bag.

At that moment, a noise started, and a small light climbed into the night sky. After a moment they saw a searchlight beaming down.

"Shit!" said Nick. "Hope they don't head this way."

We stood in silence until it was obvious that the helicopter had moved over the canyon.

"As I was saying," said Nick. "Everyone should have their own protection." He dug into his bag, and emerged with a fist full of USB devices, and handed them around.

"Simon, will you hold one for Robbie. I won't give his out just now."

People were concealing devices as Gill spoke.

"I must just repeat what I was saying, when Judy and Zoltan arrived.

I've been directed to ensure your return to New York, without blowing my cover."

She looked over at Andrew.

"This includes you, Andy. I know it's mad, but we're all supposed to report to Brian Tutch at Marquetcom."

"They seem determined to pull my strings, whether in Oxford, New York or the boondocks," he observed ruefully.

"I can probably explain a minor delay," Gill continued. "As helping to keep an eye on Robbie, who was still having strange reactions to his experience and appeared too poorly to cope with New York City. Simon helped out. We can probably fly from Las Vegas, when he's..."

She tailed off, looking at Robbie, who was crouched over, playing with his shoes. Overhead, leaves rustled as a breeze started. I instinctively looked up, but there was no other noise.

"I think we ought to push on," said Andrew. "I'll stay with Mom for a couple of days and then make it to meet Tutch at Marquetcom's suite in about four days. Meanwhile..."

He held up his cell phone.

"Let's go. There's a lot of road waiting!"

I took the first turn at the wheel, Gill beside me and Robbie lying on the back seat. Some miles on, Gill said:

"Si, we're near Bluff. Pull over and I'll call Sheryl."

I marvelled at the night sky – admiring both her moonlit profile and the brilliance of the stars out here. She finished talking.

"Sheryl will help. She said that, rather than going through Monument Valley, we should continue south to a small settlement called Chinle. It's right next to a Navajo site called Canyon de Chelly. Apparently, there are several nearby motels, and she'll join us at breakfast time."

"I want to make pee pee," came an infantile wail from the back seat.

After Robbie finished, we set off, passing through the tiny settlements of Mexican Water, Rock Point and Many Farms, finally reaching Chinle and the relative comforts of a small motel. The restaurant would soon close and the hurriedly eaten Navajo tacos were a reminder this was not mainstream USA. I left the others at the table and went to sort out rooms. A whispered conversation with Gill confirmed my hopes, but requesting a separate single for Robbie made me feel like a parent with a dependent child.

The next morning, Gill wore a big grin over breakfast. The previous night had been a major respite from recent stresses and the cereals, sausage and Canadian streaky was like a banquet.

"You look thoughtful," said Gill, smiling while she buttered Robbie's toast.

"Thinking about Craig, Carl and Myleen," I said. "Good folk, all of them."

I couldn't contain myself. "And... remembering last night!"

She blushed, but I felt her foot rub my ankle under the table.

Someone had pulled up a chair. It was Sheryl.

"You've made good time!" Gill said. "This is Simon, and Robbie, whom I mentioned."

"You gonna be our guide, Miss?" Robbie asked, sounding quite the simpleton.

The Navajo woman smiled indulgently.

"You'll soon feel better," she replied, and then responded to Gill.

"Yeah, I took a short-cut over the Hopi mesas."

Robbie left for the toilet.

"I've contacted colleagues in San Francisco. From the description of plasters around his nose, they feel fairly sure Ute will have inserted a chip in his sinus cavity and probably added some other processing."

"Fiona told you that?"

"I believe you also met our colleague, Marji – who's an expert on this. She's 'Fed-exing' a package over that she hopes will help. It should arrive tomorrow, so I suggest you keep the rooms on for another two days, although we probably won't get back for tonight."

After I extended our booking, Sheryl led us to a four-wheel-drive. Robbie looked like a bandy-legged, toddler.

"We're going to enter Canyon de Chelly. I know someone who can help."

We entered the canyon's mouth, and Sheryl carefully picked her way alongside a sandy wash, fringed with cottonwood trees.

"Fortunately, I'm known and accepted here," she explained. "Otherwise, the only way in is accompanied by an accredited Navajo guide. This is sacred land to our people."

"Why is that?" I asked, amazed by the huge orange walls, rising higher with every turn.

"Navajos farmed here for hundreds of years, although, actually, we displaced the Hopi," she replied. "When the Spanish arrived, we were displaced too, and that followed attacks by the Utes, Apaches and the Comanches. There's been much bloodshed, including a horrible massacre in the canyon's other arm. Eventually, the white Americans stopped the fighting by removing the Navajos to New Mexico – supposedly to learn Christianity and agriculture!"

"Forcibly?" I asked.

"Naturally! Kit Carson rounded them up for the so-called 'Long Walk'. As for teaching agriculture, they instead destroyed their homes, livestock and prized peach trees. Some eventually returned and a few farm the canyon floor, right to this day. We're meeting one – a Navajo medicine man, called Nakei."

We rounded another bend, but stayed close to the stream, which meandered down the wash. Sheryl pointed towards an impressive stone dwelling built into a niche high on the cliff wall.

"Built by the Anasazi," she said, before I could ask. "We call them the 'Ancient Ones'. They were long gone, even when we first arrived."

We passed several Navajo dwellings, known as 'Hogans', and, around the next curve, I saw a majestic stone spire rising straight up from the canyon floor. Sheryl pulled up outside an octagonal Hogan next to a small peach orchard. On the other side, it had an enclosure with a handful of sheep and a small field growing some other crop. An old man emerged and waved welcome. Sheryl beamed.

"Hi Nakei, it's been a while."

The craggy face grinned.

"How's your momma, Sheryl?"

We climbed out and waited while they carried out a spirited conversation in what I assumed was the Navajo tongue.

Eventually, the old man shook hands and, using English, invited us in.

"Why are we here?" asked Robbie, but nobody answered.

We chatted a while, Sheryl exchanging gossip and periodically reverting to the Navajo language. Food with an unfamiliar aroma bubbled away in the corner.

"We take lunch," said Nakei, ushering them to a table and bringing over a steaming dish.

"Blue cornmeal mash," explained Sheryl. She lifted the lid of the other container. "Cabbage burritos," she said, with far more enthusiasm than I could muster. Even so, I had to admit a sense of satisfaction after the meal, which we washed down with tea. Sheryl said this was infused from the hohoysi plant.

As Robbie had complained of nightmares, the old man prepared a special infusion to help make sleep easier.

I looked on, fascinated, as Nakei laid down a bed of rugs. He opened a leather bag, and took out eagle feathers bound with Navajo beads and a series of leather pouches. Then he sprinkled two separate powders around the edge of the makeshift bed.

"White and yellow corn pollen," whispered Sheryl.

Nakei crossed over to the stove and, after stirring for some minutes, poured the infusion into a big earthenware drinking pot. He said something to Sheryl in Navajo, and handed the pot to Robbie.

"Drink, he good. Drink him gone."

Robbie lifted the pot and, despite a grimace, drained the vessel. The old man then began to chant. After about ten minutes, he pointed to the makeshift bed and they helped a woozy Robbie on, watching as his eyelids closed.

"An infusion of datura leaves and seeds."

Seeing my doubt, she explained.

"Made from the Jimson weed, and gives enough narcosis for small operations."

Nakei reached into his bag, extracted a small bone instrument and proceeded to insert it into the sleeping man's nostril. Five minutes later, we watched him wipe away blood and apply a paste around Robbie's nasal area.

"Eriogonum and snakeweed," explained Sheryl. "Helps healing. I told Nakei he'd probably find this."

I peered at the tiny chip, smaller than half a grain of rice, resting on a plate by the bed.

"Just like Marji described," said Sheryl, enthusiastically.

I felt rather queasy.

"What's up?" asked Gill, looking none too comfortable herself.

"Just felt a bit dizzy. Wonder how long before he wakes?"

"Probably about an hour," replied Sheryl. "It's still complicated, though. According to Marji, they don't just chip. Usually, there's additional programming deepened by specific electromagnetic fields and chemicals that are piped into the room's air and water. This helps increase susceptibility. Marji will send something that should help."

I felt chilled, recalling the humming and electrical activity at Yerba Buena and the room at Camp Ute.

"How long before he'll be ready to return to the motel?" asked Gill.

The old man didn't answer, but started chanting, and then left the Hogan, looking purposeful.

"We'll stay overnight," replied Sheryl. "In the morning, I'll go to the motel for Marji's package, and then let Nakei finish his work." She stood up. "Come and see."

I looked at the still-sleeping Robbie, and then followed Gill outside. Nakei was layering a bed of fine sand. He then started grinding different coloured stones.

"Sand painting, for healing," whispered Sheryl. "Traditionally, the medicine man brought the whole family in to sing and dance. That helped intensify the patient's healing and then the painting pulls the illness from the patient and into the image."

I watched an intricate pattern of coloured sand take shape. When it finished, Nakei carefully covered it up, for later.

"Want to see more of the canyon?" Sheryl asked. "Nakei will look after Robbie. He needs to rest."

The old man nodded agreement and soon we drove into the canyon.

"I'll show you an Anasazi petroglyph."

We drove on to see the ancient pictures scratched onto the cliff face.

"The Anasazi disappeared around 1300, so you're looking at something very old."

I looked at the stylised human figures and animals, wondering what the artists would think of the world now. We moved on, passing other Hogans and the remains of another Anasazi settlement. The she turned the vehicle around and headed further into the canyon, to the enormous stone spire we'd seen from Nakei's.

"It's called Spider Rock."

I held Gill's hand, and tilted my head to take in the huge monolith rising from the canyon floor, more impressive than many a skyscraper. For some reason, I recalled the time we'd held hands at the 'White Horse', looking onto beautiful English countryside, but that had but a fraction of the power of this elemental landscape. I tried imagining a childhood here, as Sheryl outlined their mythology, including the warnings to naughty children that 'Spider woman' might take them 800 feet up to the top!

We drove further on, alone except for the occasional ex-army flatbed trucks rattling by with tourists on makeshift seating.

"They call those 'shake and bakes'," said Sheryl with a grin.

By the time we got back to Nakei's, the sun was sinking. The strange evening meal must have satisfied, because I slept through the night, only waking as light filtered through the east-facing door.

Nakei prepared breakfast, and chattered to Sheryl in Navajo about unknown subjects. Outwardly, Robbie looked brighter than at any point since we'd left Camp Ute. After breakfast, Sheryl returned to the motel to get the package from San Francisco. Meanwhile, Nakei inspected Robbie's nose, applying more eriogonum paste. Robbie seemed happy with the old man, so I took Gill's hand and we walked to the wash to sit under the cottonwoods. It was extraordinarily beautiful, looking down the serpentine canyon, with cottonwoods, tamarisk and coyote willow set against the colourful cliffs. We lay holding hands, looking at a few puffs of white cloud set against a brilliant blue sky.

"I defy you to think of Oxford on a grey wet Saturday," he said.

"You made me now, you idiot," she said with a grin.

The peace was interrupted by an approaching vehicle and I rolled over to look. It was Sheryl, so we returned to the Hogan. Inside, Nakei and Robbie quietly talked. Sheryl opened the large jiffy bag, and took out a portable CD player, headphones, batteries, jewel boxes with discs and a handwritten note. We crowded around, but, looking over Sheryl's shoulder, I could only make out snippets.

"Play the enclosed soundtracks... they'll almost certainly have programmed in control sequences that will need undoing. Colleagues have developed a way of neutralising programming, through a method using whole-brain integration. Basically, beats of different frequencies are presented to each ear. The brain hears, or rather creates, a frequency equal to the difference between two tones. The brain gets entrained and follows the frequencies, which get progressively lower and lower. It helps foster hemisphere synchronisation and encourages connections between different brain structures."

"Do you get all this?" I asked, and scanned through the text... *Pulse stimulation... amplitude modulated standing waves meeting behind the brain stem.*

"In a very general sense," she replied. "Apparently, it helps communication between different parts of the brain."

"Exactly," said Sheryl. "Processing is often multi-level, causing a type

618

of splitting off in the mind. Similar, I believe, to what the shrinks call dissociation."

As she turned the page, I could make out further snippets.

... The theta brainwave state favours uncritical acceptance of material... if they have used drug/chemical-induced hypnosis, listening to this will help break up patterns at the neural level... also spending time in theta and delta brainwaves, produces neurochemicals – beta-endorphins, vasopressin, acetyl-choline and serotonin, that aid healing and stress release.

"Okay, Robbie, listen up," said Sheryl.

"Basically, you got totally stressed out by your experience in the camp. This will kind of bathe your brain, and help clean things up."

Already, he seemed brighter, since the tiny chip had been removed.

"Bathe the brain, eh? Not brainwashing, I hope!"

I caught Gill's eye and smiled. It was probably the most together thing we'd had from him in days.

Marji recommended several sessions. Apparently, helpful subliminal messages were included, which were only detected unconsciously.

By the third listening, it was obvious to everyone that he was coming back. Nakei said he was now ready for the next step. We went out for some air, leaving him in Nakei's care.

"Surely we don't have to continue with more mumbo-jumbo? Can't we leave it at that?" I said to Sheryl.

Her face said that I'd seriously erred!

"No! Nakei has a superb record of helping people through trauma. Traditional ways might seem slow, but they are very deep."

I apologised and we went back into the Hogan, where Nakei was busy preparing something else.

"'Potentilla," said Sheryl. "For mental difficulties and bad dreams."

The old man then led Robbie outside and carefully uncovered the sand painting.

He pointed and motioned for him to sit in the middle of the painting. Then, holding a medicine bundle, he started chanting.

Gill and I left Nakei and Robbie to their work, and Sheryl stayed to help. In truth, the place was so magical, I wanted to savour every moment.

We returned to the stream and lay under the cottonwoods, hearing Nakei's chanting in the background.

"Combining science with something so ancient is amazing," Gill remarked.

I pulled her close, savouring the warmth and wishing we could stay. After about two hours, the chanting stopped and we returned to the Hogan.

"Hi Si, how are you doing?"

Amazing. Robbie's appearance and voice seemed as clear and normal as at our first meeting in New York!

Time to move on...

100

PHILADELPHIA – BROOKLYN

ZOLTAN'S PERSPECTIVE

The small, white jet landed safely in Philadelphia. Zoltan quickly found an available hire vehicle and was soon on his way to the city. Mercifully, the traffic was quite light and, on reaching the historical area, he saw little activity. He found parking close to Judy's and entered the dark house. Pausing for a black coffee, he went into the lounge, wincing at the sight of Judy's clothing still folded on the sofa. Although the place had provided ideal cover, he hadn't intended getting so personally involved. She'd really got under his skin.

He went upstairs, packed his remaining clothes and placed his bags in the lounge doorway, wondering whether to remove the bug. Woods mentioning the possibility of later patching things up with her finally caused him to decide against it. He returned to the kitchen and picked up the torch kept in the corner cupboard. Moments later, he shifted the crates and suitcase to the vehicle, picked up his bags, and set off.

Traffic on the New Jersey Turnpike at this time was also light. He made good time to Linden, and then exited for the Goethals Bridge over to Staten Island. Fatigue was setting in and he just wanted to reach Abdullah's. His foot was hard down on the Staten Island Expressway until he passed over the graceful span of the Verrazano Narrows Bridge to Brooklyn. It was now just after 3am, and there were few vehicles on Shore Parkway at this hour. He headed towards New Utrecht, and focused on finding the quickest way to Abdullah's – oblivious of speed restrictions.

It had started raining and ahead the lights of an all-night diner reflected in the camber of the wet road. He glanced down to the streaked neon lights on the road's surface and then to the rear-view mirror. A car pulled out and he instinctively eased up as he saw a second car pull around the first. It was the police! Their car came close behind and then flashed for him to stop. He complied and then wound his window down. The car had two officers and one walked over.

"Good evening, officer."

A large, black officer holding a torch bent down and looked in his window.

"Your papers, Sir?"

His partner started their car, and moved it in front, to block his exit.

He fished around for the licence, heart hammering while the officer shone his torch through the rear window. The officer returned and bent down to face him again.

"We followed you for several minutes. What was your speed?"

"Not sure. Was I going too fast?"

The cop appeared to smile, although it was difficult to tell in the half light. His partner was busy in their wagon – probably running a vehicle check.

"What's in the back?"

"Just kit for my work, officer. Look, I'm sorry if I drove fast. It's just that I had mechanical trouble earlier, or I'd have been here hours ago. That's why this is a hire vehicle!"

"Yeah, I'm sure, but what we often find, pulling people over at this hour, isn't good news."

"These are boxes of IT-related kit that I'm delivering to Canvey Solutions. Do you know them? Like I said, without the breakdown, I'd have been here long ago."

"Isn't it closed at this hour?"

"Yeah, but there are night staff, who can receive stuff."

"Okay man, just checking. You're a little off the track here, though. You can follow us in a minute 'cos we're going near there. We still have to check in the back though. Routine practice."

His mind went into overdrive. He could jam his foot down and take off, but that would probably end in disaster. He could kill them and run, or show a service ID card and bluster – but that might compromise everything.

"I'll take a look."

As the cop moved towards the rear, he reached under his seat. Just then a racket started from behind and he heard the sound of smashing glass. He spun around and saw an old Corvette approaching with several youths. One leaned out of the window swinging a baseball bat, and breaking the windows of parked cars. As it got closer, he heard the bass from a sub-woofer pumping out aggressive rap that echoed from the surrounding buildings. A youth chugged a bottle of beer and he saw the driver's face register shock, seeing the cops. Two other youths were in the back and another swiftly pulled his bat out of sight.

The officer thrust his head down to the level of the still open window.

"Be sure to watch your speed in future. We've other business now."

He dashed back to the police car, which accelerated away, following the youths' car, as it screeched left at the next corner. He sat a moment, waiting for his heartbeat to normalise, and thankful for his luck.

Abdul's street was dimly lit and, other than a single light in the corner house, no-one appeared still up. He parked and rang the bell, hearing a faint sound from deep inside and then a light appeared. Abdul must have hair-trigger responses because he reached the door almost immediately. He wore an old-fashioned night shirt, and quickly beckoned him in.

"Why at such an hour, Hassan?"

"Because of an emergency. Judy now suspects me. I'd been in Utah helping her sons and friends. Everything went terribly wrong, and I had to return quickly and move the stuff from Philadelphia."

"Why not Baltimore? We still have the lease."

"If things go badly and everything's in one place, it could all be lost. This way the material for the operation should be safe."

He briefed Abdul, omitting the visit to Camp Ute and the side trip to Nashville. He described how they'd seen through parts of his story and it all ended in a physical tussle. He had to remove the materials before they got home.

Abdul nodded thoughtfully.

"Come through and take a coffee, but you can't stay until things settle down. Meantime, we'll keep the materials at my store. For now, communicate via the network."

"And the operation?"

"Soon, Hassan – very soon..."

101

ARIZONA

SIMON MAHER

looked over at Rob, almost expecting to see the childlike torpor again.

His return to normality was like the relief that comes after carrying a heavy load. When we told him about his earlier condition, he was incredulous.

"Honestly! They'd really messed with your head."

I reached into my pocket and then opened the matchbox. The chip sat on a bed of toilet paper.

"Nakei removed this."

"Ugh, revolting! And you say I was kind of childlike?"

"Yes, all of three, or possibly, four years old," said Gill. "It was only after Nakei removed that wretched thing and worked with herbal medicines, chanting and the sand painting, that you sort of popped out into normality. Of course, the material Marji sent played a big part, too."

He shook his head again in apparent disbelief.

"Honestly, it seems a dream, or rather a nightmare. It felt like I was stuck in a bag, or something."

"Well, you can thank Nakei and also Sheryl for getting hold of the deprogramming kit," I replied, looking at the little player and headphones.

"Remember to pack that, Si," she said.

There was a knock and I slipped the chain into the catch and looked out. Sheryl was there and quickly entered.

"I stayed with friends overnight at Round Rock," she explained. "Listen, I've had more information from our network – information you need to have, before New York."

"Thanks for getting me back to Planet Earth," interrupted Robbie – his voice adult and in control.

"You're welcome. Isn't Nakei fantastic? You know, he's my great uncle?"

"No, but that figures," I answered. "What's the information?"

Instead, she turned to Gill.

"As you know, the rogue element want you under their control and Brian Tutch's supervision."

"Simon and I have to return to the UK, so I don't know how that will work?"

"Hold your horses – I'm trying to explain. We've two friendly agent colleagues, plugged into the New York scene. Both well understand the Tutch/Marquetcom connection. One, Michelle Grantz, you already know – she's part of Tom Freison's crowd. The other," she paused. "The other is really good, and managed to get close and personal with Tutch. Actually, she assists Nina, whom you came to help. Her name's Corinne, and she..."

No-one could have failed to hear Robbie's grunt. His hands covered his mouth and his eyes closed tight.

"Yes, I do know Michelle," said Gill. "She sounded me out and told me about Fee. I don't personally know Corinne, but... Robbie, whatever is the matter?"

"She's, I... I mean, I thought..."

Sheryl looked concerned by his sudden deterioration.

"Sorry." Robbie took a deep breath.

"You see, Corinne and I were friends. Actually, it was far more than that. On the way down here, we got news that she was probably working for the other side. I... I, therefore, thought that our relationship was only pretence and was lost to me."

"Corinne's much smarter than you realised," said Gill.

"What do you think, Sheryl?" I asked.

"Corinne's a part of a group that is broadly sympathetic to your position. As part of her work, she got in close to Tutch. The way I see it, the intel community includes several factions, now."

"Factions?"

"Yes… this is only my description. See, some colleagues are excellent. Most are loyal professionals, though they also include the foot soldiers, 'yes men' and 'time servers'. Many don't even realise the things we've discussed! Basically, they say 'yes, sir' and pocket the pay. Secondly, it seems a small rogue group has developed. We don't know the full configuration – probably numerically small, but potentially deadly. Thirdly – our small but widely spread network, which opposes the way our profession has been and is being misused. We're committed to national security, but not empire building, shilling for corporations or becoming freelancers."

Robbie nodded his comprehension.

"So, Corinne's almost been like… a 'double agent'?" he asked.

"You could say that."

I asked, "Why is this relevant to us now?"

Sheryl's face took on the sort of expression reserved to convey news of a terminal illness.

"As you now appreciate, the rogue group have been developing mind-control technology. Of course, governments always want to control the public mind. In fact, over the years…"

"You mean the old governing by PR thing," I interrupted. "Historically, we know all about that, but how does this relate to us now?"

Sheryl held up her hands.

"Hold your horses and I'll explain. I'm not claiming what I'm going to say is done with the administration's blessing. It might be a project by the rogue group that they hope to sell on. For example, what do you know about the use of fluoride?"

"Only that I haven't cleaned my teeth yet and, if we want a New York flight, we have to move! No, seriously, I don't get the toothpaste thing?"

Sheryl appeared mildly exasperated as I gave a wink.

Gill playfully punched my arm.

"Don't be facetious, Si. Sheryl said fluoride, not toothpaste! Go on, Sheryl."

"Thanks! First, a quick overview. Fluoride is a toxic and often left-over waste product from the aluminium and fertiliser industries. Also, from producing nuclear weapons."

"Are you saying that industrial waste is put into public water supplies as a health measure?" asked Robbie.

"In a manner of speaking. Apparently, a scientist from the aluminium industry suggested the teeth-strengthening effect, though the evidence is somewhat mixed."

"We're particularly interested in water quality issues," I said, "but I still don't see where you're going?"

"Fluoride has more controversial qualities than just supposedly strengthening teeth. The Russians used it as a tranquilliser in their prison camps. Apparently, the Germans discovered that it calms certain areas of the brain, and promotes submission and compliance. Apparently, there were plans to medicate the water of occupied countries, to help with control. It's a major ingredient of some tranquillisers, even now."

"I've seen warnings on toothpaste here," said Gill. "We don't get that at home. To be honest, I didn't know any of this!"

"Shades of Aldous Huxley," I said. "Remember the warnings of a future where pharmacology helped people to accept their servitude? What a big seller that would be!"

"Well, you're on the right track," said Sheryl. "Chemists working for intelligence didn't give up. We think they've now developed something far more effective."

"Delivered via the water supply, by any chance?" I had a sinking feeling that I now knew where the discussion was heading.

Sheryl paused.

"Yes. As well as an obvious money spinner, we've learned that large-scale testing of a substance is planned, using ownership and the new private management of a water supply."

"Oh please, not Colombia! Nick described the coca spraying, but this sounds even more disastrous!"

Sheryl nodded, with a grave expression.

"Of course, without public consultation or agreement. That's why I thought you should know just what you're getting into, and why Tutch and Anson want you securely under their thumb." She opened her bag and passed a piece of paper to Gill.

"This is a private number for Michelle Grantz, if you need help. Don't give details on the phone – just say it's Diana. I take it you can do an American accent?"

"I think so," she replied, making a fair attempt.

"Michelle will acknowledge and, provided she uses the word 'build-ing' in the following conversation, you can meet at 8pm on the same day. The rendezvous will be the Stars diner near the A&T Plaza, Greeley Square. It's a stone's throw from the Empire State building, so you can't get lost. After the first meeting, you can make your own further arrangements."

Everyone agreed that it was now time to check out and make a move.

"We're almost equidistant between Denver, Salt Lake City and Las Vegas," I said, checking the road atlas. "I vote for Vegas – it should be more straightforward. What do you think?"

"Yes," replied Sheryl, "Vegas is probably the best bet – no pun intended! Contact me if you need further help."

After thanking Sheryl, we departed on Highway 264, passing through the Hopi Indian reservation. The map showed a link to US-89, via Flagstaff and the Interstate. I drove over the barren mesas, resisting the temptation to stop at the Hopi villages. Ahead, the San Francisco Peaks pointed the way to Flagstaff. After reaching the half-Hopi, half-Navajo town of Moenkopi, we joined US-89.

At first, everyone was preoccupied by the colours of the 'painted desert' and then by 'Humphrey's Peak', but eventually the chuff-chuff-chuff and a distinctive shadow caused Robbie to lower his window and look up.

"Shit – a helicopter."

The noise increased as the machine came dangerously close, whipping up clouds of dust. It moved ahead, hovering, as if waiting for us to catch up, and descended just feet from our roof. It moved ahead again and suddenly veered left at the next junction, following a small road signed 'Sunset Crater'.

"I'm stopping," I said. "I don't fancy getting buzzed again – it's downright dangerous."

I turned down the small road while the helicopter hung low, rippling the sage-brush. After pulling in, the helicopter landed on a nearby level patch. As the dust dissipated, three figures emerged and walked towards us.

"They must have attached a tracker to the vehicle while I was in the camp," said Gill. I did say we should change it!"

As there had hardly been the opportunity, I grunted agreement. The dust had now settled and I saw an Arm-Rite logo on the helicopter. The men finally reached us and the one in the middle removed his wraparound sunglasses to reveal Dick Riley's sly features. His tight mouth looked meaner than ever.

"Step away from the car, Maher. I mean right now!"

The window was down and, in the background, I could hear Gill urgently whispering something to Robbie.

"Why are you out here, Riley? Bored in Utah?"

The thin lips pulled into a dangerous smile.

"You know, that's pretty well what I intended asking you."

"Easy. We're on our way back and taking in the landscape, that's all."

The others exited and Robbie lolled around with a fatuous grin.

"I see the faggot's still trippin' then!"

"Hello Mr Riley," said Robbie.

"Simon, please take us to see Mr Biff," he whined. "Will we be there soon?"

In a flash, I realised what Gill whispered, concluding that Robbie had missed his vocation!

The men were armed, looked dangerous and we had no chance whatsoever of taking them on. Robbie's digital device was now concealed with the car tools, Gill's taped under the seat and mine pushed into the side of my shoes. It would probably take this lot all of five minutes to locate them.

"We're disappointed," sneered Riley. "Where should you be?"

We could only play for time.

"We're just going to McCarran Airport to fly back. Look, you've just flown over it so you know how exceptional this place is. Imagine living somewhere cold, grey and wet, like Gill and I do. We were returning to New York, as agreed, but wanted to see a few sights like the 'painted dessert' en route."

"Don't get clever, Maher. You're late. Stand over there."

Riley waved his gun towards a flat-topped rock by the side of the road.

"You two. Join him!"

There was nowhere to run.

"See what you can find," Riley said to the guards.

One opened the car door and rummaged in the car and one in the trunk. The first guard's search was desultory, but the one searching the trunk soon yelled 'got it' and held a device up.

Riley grinned.

"There, you don't need that. Anyhow, listening to a dead man is plain ghoulish. Listen up. Get yourselves back to New York City. You're expected by Mr Tutch in Marquetcom's suite at 6pm tomorrow. Don't miss that appointment for any reason!"

I wriggled my toes. The device was caught between the side of my foot and the inside of my shoe – uncomfortable, but, paradoxically, comforting.

"You've achieved nothing, Riley," I called. "There are arrangements for multiple copies to be sent to multiple locations. If anything happens to us, those will be activated."

Riley scowled and stepped forward. His body looked tight and ready to explode.

"Shut up, Maher! I disliked you from the start and you don't improve."

Without further word, they returned to the helicopter and took off in a cloud of dust...

102

PHILADELPHIA

ANDREW ALTON

I hadn't seen Mom like this since childhood and the distress over the marital breakdown. There'd been much weeping and periods of withdrawal, but then she'd recovered and had since remained resolute and strong. After our return from Utah, her distress was obvious again. Several new friends called by, but she'd stayed in her room and I'd had to make excuses for her.

"This is all because of Zoltan, isn't it?"

I'd tried to raise it several times before, but, uncharacteristically, she'd baulked. This time she nodded and the tears welled up.

"I hadn't felt love like that for years."

I touched her hand.

"I'm sorry to say it, darling, but I never felt quite so affected – even with your dad in the early days. Zoltan had qualities... or seemed to have qualities, I almost never expected to find in a man. Turned out I hadn't! I expect I must seem like a silly teenager."

"I understand, Mom."

"Zoltan seemed so genuine. How could he be associated with such a despicable place as that camp? I'm even doubting myself now. Usually, I'm such a good judge of people. He almost seems like two different people."

We'd been back two days, when another caller arrived. I went to the door, expecting another nice woman from 'Forward Together' calling to tell Mom about some meeting or coffee morning. Instead, I was confronted by a scowling man in a dark suit, flashing a security identification.

"Andrew Alton? Let's talk – inside!"

I hesitated, but he pushed by and entered the lounge.

"Where's Mrs Alton?"

"Upstairs, I think. Is that a problem? She knows pretty well everything."

"I know that. I'm Leonard Thurby, security agent and associate of Brian Tutch."

I'd half expected this.

"Brian's disappointed that you haven't been in touch."

"Much as I appreciate his hospitality, we've been rather busy. My mother has been unwell."

"Oh, I see. So, you're a humourist! Obviously, I was being far too obscure. The appointment with Brian isn't optional."

"You'd be a great asset in B movies, Mr Thurby."

"Don't be smart, Alton. Ask Maher and James about detention. Somehow, I don't think you'd cut it! In fact, you can ask them tomorrow evening at 6.30pm at Marquetcom's business suite. Don't mess up again. Incidentally, I assume you still have the return section of your flight home?"

"Of course."

"Good. Expecting a nice smooth departure?"

"I don't see why not."

Thurby showed some yellow, crooked teeth. A retort formed along the lines of: *You're a complete phoney, Thurby, who doesn't actually work for the great American public, at all!* Common sense prevailed and I kept quiet.

"Come and see Mr Tutch, Alton, or you'll get a ticket to somewhere else entirely."

Thurby stood and went to the front door. When it closed, I heard Mom descending the stairs. She was crying again, and asked who called.

"Someone from 'Forward Together' about a meeting. The Syrian situation, I think. I explained that you had a migraine."

"Thanks, darling. Andy, might we have misjudged Zoltan?"

I steered her into the lounge and a comfortable chair.

"Sorry, Mom, but no. Like I said, I watched guards salute him into the camp."

"But, you've heard him talk about social justice, poverty – in fact, most of the important issues, and he's been a good friend to Freddy. We may have got it all wrong. It might be a situation like Gill's and that, really, he's genuinely on our side? We won't know if we don't give him a chance to explain?"

"And his disappearance to Nashville?"

"Could be anything. Perhaps he was detailed to observe Nick, or to help. We won't know if we don't speak to him."

"But, you said he's taken everything, cleared his room and the shed. You must face it, Mom, it isn't going to happen. I know you can't imagine it right now, but I'm sure you'll meet someone else in time."

Her eyes welled up and I didn't have the heart to continue.

103

BROOKLYN

NICK MARTIN

Although just twenty-one days had passed since departing, morale at Canvey had almost completely plummeted. The first morning, I spent with staff requiring advice and preparation for redundancy counselling. The atmosphere choked with the sheer intensity of anger and despair. Apart from concern that was virtually wrenched from my soul, I had little concrete to offer workers. Not surprisingly, Canvey's help barely reached the legal minimum. More than one made reference to Tim Miles's suicide. I could have countered by mentioning my efforts to help Tim and his wife, but that would have been totally unprofessional.

Tom Phelan looked into my office, and made some cryptic comments about the length of my time away, but I didn't pursue it. Late in the morning, my secretary put her head around the door.

"Dan wants to see you at 2pm," she said, and arched her eyebrows.

This is what I dreaded most. She left and I used the remaining time to scan the headers of unopened emails. What with Dan Farlin's meeting and this evening's appointment with Tutch, much of it would have to wait until tomorrow. At least I'd see Nina tonight and we'd hopefully dine together afterwards.

The bolted sandwich felt stuck in my throat as I went up to Farlin's office on the top floor. My eyes felt sore from lack of sleep and nights plagued with memories of scraping off Richard Monroe's brains and bone from my hands at the edge of Old Hickory Lake.

"Come in," called Farlin's silky voice.

I opened the door, fully expecting to see one or more of the senior executives, but Farlin was alone. The unnaturally smooth face wore his trademark smirk.

"Do come in and sit down, Nick. We've been worried, because you've been ill. Feeling better, I hope, although, you do still look a little peaky?"

The mouth smiled, but Farlin's eyes were as cold and dead as ever.

"Thank you, Sir. I'm afraid, while exploring in the South West, I picked up the worst ever dose of food poisoning. Don't know how those diners get away with it."

Farlin smirked, raising his eyebrows.

"Really, Nick. When your call came with the problem, it apparently showed you calling from Nashville?"

I felt my colour rise.

"Oh that. Yes, I took a quick side trip to Nashville. Always wanted to see the Oprey and explore the country music thing. No, immediately before that, I'd been around Utah's National Parks and picked up something very bad." He grimaced. "That Tex-Mex stuff."

Farlin raised his eyebrows and the cold eyes looked right through me.

"Too bad, Nick, because it'll be Latin food again, real soon!"

"Bogotá?"

"Indeed. Your illness was a shame, because I'd been sending messages for you to come right on back. See, old Biff Anson wants the show on the road, right away. He's heard rabble-rousers might be planning trouble. He's got ideas to sort things out."

"When are you suggesting?"

"Day after tomorrow should do it – unless you can scoot off earlier?"

"I'll take the first option, please."

"Good! By the way," he paused, but the gaze stung like an ice-burn. "You are fully committed to this project, aren't you, Nick?"

"Of course," I croaked.

Leaving early on my first day back only heightened the anxiety. All my efforts to ease the long-hours culture had achieved little. I left at five, informing my secretary of an urgent doctor's appointment, and made my way to the subway. The roads had already filled and I was glad to have left the car behind. The train wasn't so bad, but, today, I was so preoccupied with Utah and Colombia on the journey back to Manhattan, I may just as well have been on the Columbia space shuttle!

I changed at Brooklyn Bridge-City Hall and then continued on to Herald Square. Emerging into softened light, I walked over to Thirty-Fourth Street and the Empire State building. Yesterday, an uninvited visitor called at my apartment, and stressed that my absence would be serious – although the whole situation still seemed totally perverse.

Busy looking up at the Empire State's spire, I accidentally bumped into another pedestrian and mumbled an apology. When I looked further up the street, I saw the familiar figures of Simon, Robbie and Gill ahead. I increased speed and called out.

"All prepared for this meeting?"

They turned, looking relieved to see me.

"You got back okay then?" asked Gill. "How's Nina?"

"Fine. We dined together last night. She should be here at any moment."

"We had an eventful trip," said Simon. "Took us longer than expected, including unwanted 'encouragement' en route."

"Yes, I had an unexpected visitor last night, renewing my 'invitation' to this meeting," I replied. "By the way, Robbie, you don't half look a hell of a lot better!"

He grinned sheepishly.

"Yeah, so they tell me! Fortunately, I had amazing help. I'll tell you later."

We entered the huge marble-clad lobby and took an elevator to the sixtieth floor. Andrew was already sat in Marquetcom's reception area, by himself. I checked my watch. Only minutes left, but still no sign of Nina. I sat beside Andrew.

"How is Judy?"

"Absolutely devastated... I hadn't actually twigged the relationship until we were down in Utah! I feel pretty stupid now!"

"I shouldn't beat yourself up. You're an academic, not a counsellor."

"Yes, but my own mom!"

"Wonder why Nina isn't here?"

Our conversation was cut short by the arrival of a young man.

"Dr Alton's party? I'm Mark Finkelstein, Mr Anson's assistant. Please follow me."

I noticed Robbie's colour rise. It must be difficult for him.

Finkelstein led us into the depths of the suite. Robbie whispered.

"This is one of the conference rooms."

Finkelstein opened the door. We filed in and I immediately saw the distinctive features of Tutch almost bordering on the colouring of an albino. Beside him sat Anson and a third man I didn't recognise. Tutch spoke first.

"Sit down, ladies and gentlemen. Better late than never. I want to start by clarifying your position."

I interrupted.

"Someone is missing!"

"That's right, Mr Martin. We'll explain after our meeting has finished. Firstly, you should understand, that you now fall under the provisions of anti-terrorist legislation. Your recent adventures settled that."

"Just for walking around that place?" asked Robbie.

"Don't be smart, son," said Biff. "I had more than enough of that when I made the mistake of employing you."

"Mr Anson means that you're known to be troublemakers," continued Tutch. However inflated and self-righteous you may feel, you actually work against the interests of your respective countries. Your actions in Utah made that situation even more serious. Aiding and abetting escape from that facility is the same as giving succour to terrorists."

"Sophistry," replied Andrew. "Illogical, and attempts to conflate quite different concepts. We well understand how legal weasels try to freeze out dissent. As Rob said, we only walked around and looked."

"Don't be totally unintelligent, Dr Alton. We know exactly what you were doing. Helping to break persons out from a restricted, secure environment is an extremely serious offence."

Tutch looked at me.

"As your experience in Nashville confirmed, Mr Martin."

Tutch then spoke directly to Robbie.

"Surely, you didn't think your daddy would hold out, did you?"

Rob paled.

"What does my father have to do with anything?"

A look passed between Anson and the third man and Tutch smirked.

"You kept your daddy completely out of the loop and let him walk straight into it. After you'd left, he and some friends attempted entry – but, by then, it was too late, wasn't it? Anyway, now he's enjoying a little country retreat, and – with a little help – he'll soon be happily talking!"

"Like what happened to me?" said Robbie with the kind of expression found on Gothic sculptures.

Tutch nodded with a grin.

"So, our first message is cooperation, because your own position is in jeopardy. You might also want to consider whether your behaviour affects the position of Mr James senior and, also," he looked at Nick, "the Parenda woman."

"Some of us have to get home," said Simon.

"That brings me to the second matter. Your stay will need to be extended for a while, until certain other arrangements are made."

Tutch looked at Gill.

"Your situation might be slightly different. We'll talk later."

"We all have commitments," said Andrew.

Anson leaned forward.

"I happen to know you can stay out at least another month. Remember, I have connections to your employer."

"I also have Anne to consider."

"Bring her over," replied Anson. "Don't know why you left the poor gal behind."

Anger flashed in Andrew's eyes.

"That's rich, coming from someone who, in fifteen years, has never bothered to meet her!"

Anson appeared to ignored the jibe, although his darkening face said differently.

"As you've been told, Marquetcom is going to facilitate your stay."

He continued addressing Andrew. "We can easily arrange for Anne to fly over."

Andrew looked thoughtful.

Tutch continued.

"The other thing is, you're expected to report to me every third day. In the meantime, continue your business in a low-key way. Of course, that won't include libellous or slanderous comments about Mr Anson, his business, or actions detrimental to his interests or any other legitimate US corporation."

I remembered my dream in Bogotá of Tutch morphing into a reptile.

"You're beginning to sound like a bloody lawyer," I said.

"Perhaps I am," shrugged Tutch.

"The demands appear very one-sided," said Andrew. "You seem to forget that we have material that could cause you extreme trouble!"

"You'd be somewhere very different if that wasn't partly true, but it has a limited shelf life, as you'll find out."

For several minutes, an outburst had been building.

"No, it won't," I snapped. "If anything untoward, and we mean anything, happens to any of us, including Nina, all that sad, sick information will surface so far and wide, you'll wish that you weren't just slippery sociopaths, but proper humans with hearts and proper jobs."

Surprisingly, Tutch looked amused.

"Temper, temper, our lonely, lovesick little puppy! You're in no position to be making threats. Think about it!"

A dozen responses filled my mind, but I stopped, recalling Nina's sweet face and kind eyes.

"Don't for a moment think you'll be out of mind or sight, between the times you're here," said Tutch. "Now it's possible that, on at least one occasion, I may be away." He pointed to the third man.

"Jack Klieberman here is an associate. Should I be away, Jack will meet with you, instead."

Klieberman, a dapper little, silver-haired man, looked in his sixties. He nodded and raised a hand.

"Hi, we'll probably talk later."

"One other thing," said Tutch.

He picked up a box from the floor, and tipped out smaller boxes containing cell phones.

"Always keep these with you. You must be reachable at all times. Also, keep them regularly charged – normally overnight. If, for some reason, that can't be done, you must stay near while it's charging. Is that clear?"

Tutch passed round boxes, which had names on them.

"Understand that we'll know if these aren't individually being kept with you! Okay, we'll leave things at that for today. Mr Martin and Ms Marney remain. Return here at the same time in three days. If you have material issues, or require other help in the meantime, please contact Mark Finkelstein in the first instance."

The others filed out, and Gill and I remained. Finkelstein appeared at the door.

"Ms Marney, go with Mark now and I'll call you back shortly."

Gill left, clutching her new phone, followed by Klieberman.

Anson spoke first.

"You've been here before for meetings, Nick. You seemed smart and committed, but I really don't care for the company you keep. What do you have to say about that?"

I knew that Anson had a lifetime history of messing up other people's lives. With his large, aggressive face and Tutch's unhealthy smirk, they seemed like two maggots in a pod. However, I knew discretion was necessary and further outbursts must be curbed.

"I'm really sorry to hear that, Sir. I first met Rob James while working on your Colombian water project. Rob negotiated with us, as you know."

Anson's nostrils flared and his face wore an expression of disgust.

"I know, but he was a useless little piss ant and I needed rid of him."

"As for your son and the others, I met them through contact with Rob. I gather they're interested in water management issues."

"Mismanagement, you mean," sneered Anson. "Andrew's no better than a socialist and quite clueless about real business."

"I'm sorry you feel that way, Sir. He seems very intelligent. The best thing now seems to get back on track and for us to work effectively together."

"Don't fucking try to patronise us, Martin," said Tutch with real venom.

"We well know that HR types are slippery bastards, but this just won't wash. Ten minutes ago, you virtually tried blackmailing us – remember?!"

With a lump in my throat, my mind seized up.

"I... we, everyone wants to stay safe. It's just that I was worried about Nina."

"You mentioned water supplies," said Tutch. "Which is exactly what we want to discuss. You return to Colombia tomorrow. Is that right, Biff?"

"So Dan tells me."

"Well, somehow or another, word about the change of ownership got out. Apparently, local idiots there want to make trouble. You asked about Parenda?"

My heart sped at hearing her name.

"She's gone ahead with instructions to use her contacts to sort it out!"

"You mean stop the protests? Have you seen her documentary?"

"Of course," laughed Tutch. "The woman is a complete pain, which is what makes it so funny. Smoothing matters instead of trouble-making will do her a power of good!"

As the two sets of shoulders heaved with laughter, I remembered Simon describe the frequent empathy bypass of sociopaths.

"You've actually asked her to help?"

"Oh, she'll want to. For some reason, she's suddenly worried about her precious charity – and the safety of some vulnerable contacts in Colombia and back home. I can't imagine why!"

Tutch sniggered. Anson leaned forward, and stared at me before speaking.

"We don't want you tempted to play for the wrong side down in Colombia. Neither would Dan. Still, I'm sure you'll want to keep cool to protect your little Latino lover. That is right, isn't it?"

I nodded miserably.

"Good," said Tutch. "We understand each other then. I'll personally see you down in Colombia in two or three days. Jack will supervise the others while I'm away – which is why we introduced him today."

104

MANHATTAN

GILL'S PERSPECTIVE

Gill waited in Finkelstein's room, wondering if this had been Robbie's old office. Finkelstein brought in coffees and gave her a sickly smile. It still amazed her that, after everything, they still believed her to be 'on side'. She checked her watch. If Tutch kept it short, she could still make the other rendezvous. She looked up and caught Finkelstein's gaze. He quickly looked away, but she noted a hint of rising colour. She considered engaging him about Colombia, but, at that moment, his phone rang. He grunted something and was on his feet, before she could speak.

"They're ready. Follow me, please."

She followed, praying that they'd continue to believe her.

Back in the conference room, Tutch and Anson appeared relaxed and Klieberman had left. Both tried smiling, but Tutch hardly presented as avuncular – more a Mafia Don!

"We're pleased to have you working with us, Gill. Our countries have a long tradition working together."

Inside, she could hear Simon's voice saying, 'Yes, a long tradition of resource grabs and unfair trade'.

She smiled back.

"Thank you, Sir. I'm rather concerned by what you said, about staying on? My time here should soon finish?"

"Don't worry," he replied. "I'll have Freison arrange things with

London. We need your help until we've decided on the best disposal for these characters."

Her adrenals squirted their distress and the mafia image suddenly seemed even more appropriate.

"Disposal, Sir?"

"You know – like 'a court's disposal'. In other words, how to deal with them."

Anson's shoulders rocked and he roared with laughter.

"Ah, I see you're meaning. 'Disposal'... very good!"

She laughed along with them.

"What do you make of Maher and Alton?" asked Tutch. "You've hung around them for a while now?"

"Typical malcontents. Anti-corporate, anti-capitalist bleeding hearts who happen to be more articulate than most of that breed. They have the potential to influence others, which is why we had them under observation."

"You Brits have 'pussy-footed' around with some issues," said Anson.

"For example, it was left to me to put the brakes on the sort of mis-education Andrew spreads. You should get the right people to sort your education system."

His face grew dark.

"Have you heard the slanderous crap they spout about successful business leaders?"

She shrugged.

"You mean, questioning their motives... that old nonsense? I assumed it was just envy. I was hearing good old-fashioned, father-son, or rather, son to father, rivalry."

She held her breath. For a moment Anson's eyes narrowed, but he swallowed it.

"You seem a sensible sort of gal. Perhaps I should have had a daughter!"

Heaven forbid, she thought – smiling sweetly.

"What happened about the trip back from Utah?" asked Tutch.

"You mean why did we take so long?"

"Exactly! You were told to encourage them straight back!"

His expression had turned sharp. She'd wondered when this would be raised.

"I know, but I had to play clever to avoid suspicion. Maher was absolutely blown away by the landscape and wanted to see more. He was also worried because young Rob James was still out of it, and feared he'd fall apart in New York City."

It sounded contrived even to her ears! She tried another tack.

"In the circumstances, a compromise made sense. Maher knows I love nature. We often walked together in England, so pressuring him prematurely would have been out of character."

Tutch relaxed a little.

"And the recording of Monroe's conversation... what did you find out?"

"Only that Martin made copies and then forwarded the file to several locations over the internet. Just before we split into separate groups, on the night of their release, Nick gave each group a copy. He'd bought several USB devices in Nashville."

"And gave your group one?"

"That's right. I knew where it was, but your guy in the helicopter almost went straight there! We hadn't the facilities to make copies and, anyway, had our hands full with Rob James."

"What about James?"

"He still suffered the effects of the camp and was acting like a retarded infant. We carted him around while Maher got his fill of Indian country, including a trip to Canyon de Chelly and across the Navajo and Hopi lands. After the incident with the helicopter on the last day out, James complained of feeling sick. Maher pulled over and Rob then started a serious nose bleed and threw up."

She shuddered.

"It was rather horrible. He seemed to pick up afterwards though – almost as if he'd got something out of his system."

Tutch smirked knowingly.

"Yeah, okay. Good job. Incidentally, you'll need to keep seeing Freison's crew weekly, to keep London happy. Call and see Matacic at 10am tomorrow. Meanwhile, continue the surveillance and let us or Jack know anything significant. I leave for Bogotá on Sunday and should be out for three or four days. Jack Klieberman will cover for me. If you or the others need something, Finkelstein will give it priority."

She escaped into the fresher air of Fifth Avenue, deciding that they likely topped her list of people not to get stuck in a lift with. She checked her watch, relieved to still have ten minutes before her other appointment. She turned down Thirty-Third Street to Greeley Square and the Plaza, and then quickly located the Stars diner. It was now almost five minutes to eight and exploring the Plaza would have to wait for another time.

She entered the Stars, ordered coffee and sat watching the world pass by. New customers kept arriving, but, after ten minutes, there was still no sign of Michelle. A classy-looking blonde arrived in a waft of expensive perfume and sat at the next table. Meanwhile, Gill looked out at the passing pedestrians, and admired the tiny lights strung through the trees here.

"You're waiting for Michelle?"

She turned. The attractive blonde smiled and then asked again.

"Expecting Michelle?"

For a moment, she wondered if Tutch had arranged to have her followed. Worse still, that Michelle's role had been uncovered.

"Sorry? I don't understand."

The woman held out her hand.

"I'm Corinne. My colleague Sheryl mentioned me while helping you out in the boondocks? Perhaps I can help here?"

They shook hands. Corinne was stunning and she recalled Robbie's reaction. Still, if anyone could help clarify his ambivalent sexuality, this was her. Disconcertingly, she recalled Fiona as Corinne slid over to the opposite seat.

"Where's Michelle?"

"We decided that I'd make the initial contact. Your dealings with Michelle at the office will then seem the more natural. We think it might be better if I'm your support contact."

It made sense.

"Did Brian or Anson mention Nina at your meeting?"

Feeling unsure, Gill paused.

"And Robbie – how is he?"

"Sorry Corinne, but I find what you are asking troubling. Sheryl said you had got in very close to Tutch. If true, you'd know all about it!"

"Yeah," she replied, her innocent blue eyes looking clear and untroubled.

"Brian and I often sleep together, so yes there's 'pillow talk'. I know Robbie was taken into the Camp and had started processing. I was sorry about that because he's really rather cute."

She tried concealing her shock. London would never expect such a thing of her. Trying to distance from her difficult feelings, she gave the woman an account of Robbie's healing experience.

"Good, I'm glad. I'd rather like to see him again."

"Corinne, we've been given special phones by Tutch and told to keep them with us at all times."

"You do realise that you can be tracked at all times and they can be remotely activated – so, bye bye privacy and watch what you say!"

"Yes, I thought so."

If you need privacy, get a faraday bag pouch thing – but use it sparingly or they'll soon realise."

"So, how close to Tutch are you? Sheryl told us that he's not exactly one of the good guys. Having met him, I certainly agree."

"Oh, Brian's a gorilla," she said cheerfully, "a total psychopath. Look, I know Sheryl explained to you that a faction in the service appears to be freelancing. Brian is high up in that grouping – that's why I've made myself close to him."

"Don't you resent... you know?"

"Resent sleeping with him? Good gracious, no – he's good. Anyway, it's totally my decision. My body is mine to enjoy as I see fit!"

She tossed her hair and laughed.

"I never have understood why people make such a fuss over these things."

Gill swallowed.

"It would be way beyond the call of duty, for me."

"Really? I thought it was exactly the same for you. You slept with your mark to get closer. Good job, I say."

Any sense of moral high-ground suddenly crumbled. She'd rarely thought of it that way. But this wasn't just a case of 'sleeping with the enemy' – she actually loved him. Her heart hammered as she built her defence.

"Actually, Corinne, I've been through ethical torments for months. You seem totally un-fazed. What's your secret?"

She laughed out loud – a pretty, musical laugh.

"You take it all far too seriously. At the end of the day, it's all just a game. Follow your heart, or, better still, follow your body."

"I'll have to take your word on that. Our worry now is staying safe. The group feels under threat because of what we know."

"Another reason why I wanted us to meet. Yes, potentially, the group are in danger, though not you, just yet. Nick is due to fly to Colombia again, tomorrow. As the water project will soon step up several gears, things could get nasty."

"Why?"

"The 'water medicating' experiment Sheryl discussed with you is being trialled in one of Colombia's outlying departments. Anson's outfit has links with ex-paramilitaries and military advisers there."

"Aren't Colombian paramilitaries notorious for executions?"

"I'm afraid so. Brian and Anson also have other business interests, including in a security outfit called Arm-Rite."

"They were at Camp Ute."

"Yes. Arm-Rite and Marquetcom are Brian's big conduits for inter-facing with the outside world. Successful corporations are an extremely effective cover. Getting private spooks embedded in the intelligence and military apparatus always had the potential for very profitable activities."

"I suppose so."

"They also plan involving Zoltan Heltay. I gather you know him?"

"I met him while at Andy's mom's. He later came down to Utah with her until eventually we realised he's big trouble. What exactly is his role?"

"Ha. You mean you met aspects of him!"

"What, you mean he's psychotic or something?"

"Not exactly, though you're on the right lines."

Corinne talked brightly, as though this was a chat about clothes or cosmetics. Perhaps Zoltan wasn't the only disordered one.

"People can confuse multiple personality disorder, you know the Jekyll and Hyde thing, with schizophrenia. Of course, they're actually quite different."

"He has a multiple personality?"

Gill began feeling odd herself. Corinne nodded, swallowed more coffee and smiled.

"These days, it's called 'dissociative identity disorder' and, in a way, yes that is what I'm saying. Apparently, Zoltan emerged from a small group who were given special processing in childhood. Apparently, he had more than a little help from the dark parts of the service, to acquire a splintered personality. The thing is, he can now be whoever his controller wants."

"You mean, he can be mind-controlled? My God, does he realise?"

"Almost certainly not! You see, he exists in split-off, separate parts. One can almost feel sorry for him."

The coffee in her stomach had curdled. These people were mad and had no limits. She excused herself and went to the rest-room at the far end of the diner. Maybe it was just accumulated stress, but her head spun. Feeling weak at the knees, she grabbed the edge of the washbasin and then slowly eased herself into a cubicle. It was mainly dry retching and she managed to keep her stomach's contents down. She struggled out of the cubicle, straightened her hair and took stock. Corinne had confirmed everything Fiona and Sheryl had explained – and more. They were to be put under the control of a rogue group, nominally embedded in intelligence, but which also sheltered behind a corporate face. A group that really wanted them dead, and which had access to, who knew how many, 'mind-controlled' operatives. To top it all, she was in the process of blowing a formerly safe job and future.

When she arrived back, Corinne was busy tucking into a serving of apple pie and ice-cream. A bowl waited in her place.

"I ordered for you too," said Corinne. "The apple pie *a la mode* here is the best."

Ignoring nausea, she thanked her.

"You didn't finish explaining why Nina's gone ahead?"

"No, I didn't. Well, Anson employed one of his clever strategies, but this time it backfired. He's had his people throw money around in Colombia and put together a phoney front group, clamouring for privatisation. All the usual nonsense – greater efficiency, an improved infrastructure, etc. There might also have been 'accidental' hygiene slip ups – bugs and upset stomachs – to help move things along! You know, to prove public bodies are incompetent and it would clearly be safer in private hands!"

Gill swallowed, upset stomachs were the last thing she wished to hear about, right now.

Corinne continued. "Paradoxically, the push for privatisation actually raised awareness. So much so that local activists are now up in arms and want the whole thing stopped. Of course, Nina's contacts with activist networks down there are unrivalled."

"Yes, apparently Tutch threatened her and the charity, if she didn't cooperate. Mightn't the activists also turn on her, though?"

"Tutch and Anson win either way! Like you, Gill, I've also changed my outlook and Nina proved to be a great teacher! As you're already in it up to your neck, I might share something with you."

"Go on then."

"Nina and I secretly helped with a little 'corporate espionage'. Nick arranged employment in Canvey's storeroom with our friend so that he could modify equipment earmarked for the new Colombian head office. Therefore, we should be able to monitor their plans and activities. He installed new chips that can use ambient electricity, even when the computers are off."

"Why?"

"I hadn't quite finished. This equipment can store millions of keystrokes. Information can then easily be transmitted to a van with a receiver, out of office hours. Simple really! At the time, Nick only knew about the privatisation plans, but not the water medicating scheme."

"So, what plans do they have for Simon, Andrew and Robbie?"

"Anson has put the screws on Andrew's college. Brian's highly amused by the whole thing. You see, their type of research already pushed boundaries and ruffled feathers. Amazingly, Alton's 'Ethical Trade and Development Unit' comes under the business school's umbrella – can you imagine?"

"I can, because I worked the Oxford area. But, I mean, what will happen to them now, here in New York City?"

"They'll be kept under surveillance. Believe me, mechanisms exist to disappear them, and squeeze the information out one way or another. Robbie would quickly crack, so Nick was clever to disperse that information. They really do fear that it could emerge anywhere. By the way, what actually are the arrangements?"

The question hung in the air, needing layers of deceit. She decided to sidestep the answer. She owed nothing to Corinne and, by choosing allegiance to Simon and friends, had made her own bed. She met Corinne's gaze.

"You're right, it really was a clever move. I understand that he made multiple copies, though I don't know in what format. I believe copies have probably left these shores, and are probably stored in cyberspace – the cloud – I don't really know. He kept the details secret."

Corinne nodded.

"Your ice-cream has nearly melted."

She reached across, delicately scooping the remaining curled petal with a forefinger and licked it.

"I genuinely think they haven't decided yet about your friends, so they're keeping them close."

Corinne reached into her bag and passed a card with her name, the charity and an address on the Upper East Side.

"Contact me if and when you need support. Come around for a meal anyway, later in the week. Give me a call when your schedule's free."

Gill's next action was obvious. She walked over to Sixth Avenue, and flagged the first available cab to Nick's flat on the Upper West Side.

She must quickly warn him of Corinne's information...

105

UTAH

ZOLTAN'S PERSPECTIVE

This was Zoltan's first time back at Ute since the humiliation of his rescue from the Abajo Mountains. He stayed silent as the car took him from the airstrip to the familiar gateway, but acknowledged the salute from the barrier guards. Moments later, the driver dropped him outside the administration building. He stood a moment on the steps, looking across the camp to detainees in the exercise area and beyond to the high-security section.

He entered the building, pleased to find the smiling Gerry on duty. She took him down and moments later opened the door to Forest's office. This time, it was Woods and the white-haired Brian Tutch. Tutch's grin was rather like some horror movie character. He'd seen him now several times since the Philadelphia bus episode – more than enough for his liking! Dr Farrow then joined them from the door at the far end.

"Hello, Major," greeted Woods. "Good trip?"

"I didn't expect to be here again so soon. You have a job for me?"

"Yes. You brought the materials as requested?'

"Direct from Kane and Field."

"Good, our friends in Columbia need additional chemicals."

On the other side of the room, Zoltan noticed the trolley piled with antique sound equipment, including an old Ampex reel-to-reel. His guts had noticed too and were clamping reflexively. He looked away, trying to quieten the sensations sweeping his body.

After tapping on the main door, Dick Riley scuttled in, looking even more rodent-like than usual. Woods didn't hide his displeasure.

"You're late, Dick. I thought you corporate people were supposed to be efficient!"

Riley's ultra-thin lips turned down as he nodded.

"Yeah. I had a call from Houston. Gotta dance when the boss calls, right? Anyway, I think you'll be pleased."

Woods sighed.

"If you say so. Let's start, shall we?"

He turned back to Zoltan.

"When you load up, also include four SAMs and more boxes of small-arm ammunition."

"What's with the SAM's, Sir?"

"For bringing down two spray planes, but no more. Of course, it'll be blamed on the FARC residues. Whatever the claims about ceasefires or disbanding, those ex guerrillas can still cause headaches."

"I thought Arm-Rite personnel were flying the spray planes?"

Woods' face hardened.

"That's why this has to be done right. Give FARC the kit to act, but this way we can choose where, who's flying and what spin is given."

"I don't get it."

"Think about it! It keeps things hot and increases demand for weapons. Meanwhile, the former paras can move peasants away from exploration areas and be around to mop up any trouble from rolling out the privatisation."

The logic was devastating.

"I thought the paras were supposed to be demobilising."

"'Supposed to' right, but some continue autonomously. Certain groups seem possibly for hire. FARC have also supposedly finished – but we don't know how long it will hold. Do you get the plan now, said Woods?" Look, I'll sum up: this way, there's still market for weapons, Arm-Rite continues the security for spraying, the water project gets a clear run in the Putumayo region, and additional territory is freed for exploration. Everyone's a winner!"

"Except the two Arm-Rite pilots," Zoltan replied.

"Don't worry," said Riley, looking unperturbed. "We've chosen a couple of completely dispensable, fucked-up smack-heads who've migrated to coke. Vets from South-East Asia who originally flew in stuff from the golden triangle. Anyway, it's now okayed and, given their state, they're probably far better off out of it!"

He smirked at Woods.

"That's why I was late – getting the final decision from Houston. I said you'd be pleased!"

Tutch spoke next.

"We have other worries, though. Canvey's Nick Martin opens the new operational centre in Bogotá soon and we've started trialling the product in Putumayo Department. Following the recent débâcle in Utah, you should avoid contact with Martin, although he won't yet know about the water experiment. Hopefully, the locals will soon be eating out of our hands!"

Riley sniggered.

"Parenda, Martin's woman, has been pressured to help calm the local protests, and she's well connected. Of course, if an accident somehow later happens to her, we won't exactly be shedding too many tears!"

As Tutch described how her work would be affected if she failed, Zoltan concluded that his reactions on the Pennsylvania roadside were right – Tutch belonged under a stone!

Time dragged on, as they ironed out details. He felt tired and wished these were leisure plans, not another assignment. Still, at least he'd have company this time – not that anyone here knew that little detail! He hadn't lost his touch. Judy eventually accepted his explanations! He told her that, realising Senator Monroe was in danger, and Nick planned to visit, he'd discretely ensured Nick was kept out of harm in Nashville! She'd been elated, saying she 'knew it'! He obviously was 'one of them', and shared their values! Not even Abdullah knew of his success bringing her around. With Andrew over in New York researching with his assistant, their subsequent 'making up' had been so sweet!

"Are you taking this in, Major?" asked Woods, breaking into his thoughts.

He looked up and saw concerned faces.

"Sorry," he said. "Yes. I'm sorry, it was a very early start today."

He suppressed a grin, remembering just how the day had really started!

Tutch left and the meeting wound down. Woods produced a bottle of whiskey, and offered him a tot. He took a glass, and then, unusually, another. Dr Farrow left by the inside door. Woods talked about Afghanistan, filling his glass again. Soon they were swapping tales. The bottle seemed to lower as he half-heartedly entertained, and then dismissed the old prohibitions about alcohol. His head swam and, at one point he fixed on the little trolley with sound equipment. He looked away, put the glass to his lips again, and started to drift. In the background, he heard distant humming, faint at first, though gradually increasing. His eyelids seemed oddly heavy and limbs felt wooden. He briefly resurfaced, noticing Farrow had come back into the room and his eyes closed again. He forced them open, though this simple action seemed to exhaust the last of his remaining strength. By the time he saw Farrow pull the trolley over and felt the headphones covering his ears – he was immobile.

A gruff and guttural voice growled in his ear.

"Your colour is Friesian... Your colour is Friesian......"

106

BOGOTÁ

NICK MARTIN

This time, Bogotá seemed less overwhelming. However, opposed as I was to the developments, I had to admit Canvey's advance team had performed well. Tomorrow, interviews for local staff had been arranged and the new IT equipment, with 'extras', had been installed without hitch or comment.

The cab bumped its way over to our rendezvous at Bar Suba. I reached into my wallet and quickly re-read Gill's note, explaining Nina's new set of local difficulties. Just thinking of the name, Miguel Hernandez, brought images of a cart-wheeling helicopter, smoke and orange flames. The taxi finally dropped me outside Bar Suba. The sun had almost set and the first diners of the evening were arriving. I entered the bar and saw Miguel at the far end. He waved and I ordered a beer and joined him.

"Hello Señor Gringo," said Miguel with a wink. "Hungry?"

"Yeah, starving. Do they serve American food? I might stay with the known, for tonight."

"They do everything," replied Miguel. "So, how's the new office coming on?"

"So far so good!"

The spicy aromas eventually convinced me to try another local speciality. Miguel seemed relaxed, but, for me, overlooking his former role was challenging. This time they only had taped music, though 'A

Horse with no name' was an old favourite and masked our conversation.

"How about the equipment?" Miguel asked.

"All installed and we open soon. A small advance team from New York has prepared over recent days. Local staff interviews are being held tomorrow."

Miguel's rather strange melange had now arrived and he started eating.

"Chosen yet?" he asked between mouthfuls. "This is a traditional country dish – called Bandeja Puisa."

"What the heck is it?"

His finger hovered over each ingredient.

"Rice, fried plantain, pork-scratchings, minced beef, frijoles, and a maize cake topped with fried egg."

Miguel called to the bar staff. "Pass the hot aji sauce, please."

"I'll try that then," I said, with faint enthusiasm.

"Good. You'll probably have lots more country cooking where you're going!"

I nodded weakly, but, when I looked up, I saw Miguel smiling at someone behind. Miguel asked:

"And for you?"

I turned and saw Nina's smiling face. We quickly hugged. She then pulled up a chair and confidently ordered something with an unpronounceable name she was sure I'd love. I changed the order.

"I gather Anson has pressured you to help calm protests."

Her eyes crinkled as she laughed.

"Anson doesn't understand how things work here. You probably haven't seen the graffiti around the city yet? Still, the brothers agreed to hold back for the moment. Thanks to your help, they'll get their moment later!"

"You haven't told anyone of my involvement?"

"Of course not! They'll do what I ask and trust that I have a plan."

She reached over and stroked my hand.

"Which is true, isn't it?"

I swallowed.

"All I know is that there are plenty of unhappy people. Just before you arrived, Miguel was saying how tired people were of fighting. He doesn't know if the peace will endure."

She nodded.

"He's right. After decades of discord, people have had it: government troops and paramilitaries fighting so-called guerrillas – when all most people wanted was peace."

I pictured the burning helicopter.

"I understand that some groups traded in narcotics. That makes me very uncomfortable."

"Some resorted to that, though the trade is global. Anyway, certain agencies in the north are said not to have totally fought shy of it, either."

"But, Nina, some of the reported things... I mean, kidnappings, murders, narco-trafficking, are beyond...?"

Miguel looked like he was about to burst. Nina held her hand up to stop him.

"I know. Some lost support because of those things. You have to realise that they have also been savagely hunted and repressed. Sometimes... it's a case of survival."

Miguel nodded, and took up the argument.

"You saw for yourself the damage from spraying! Colombia had huge sums from the US, to achieve what? Keep things safe for more corporate plunder and the status quo? Meanwhile, the cocaine keeps flowing."

I nodded, but felt unable to get beyond the helicopter and extinguished lives.

"Not all our helpers are active guerrillas," said Nina. "As far as the water privatising is concerned, that fight is supported by various civil groups, indigenous groups, socialists, Marxists and anarchists who stop short of fighting, but still want change. Haven't you seen anarchist 'circle As' all over the city?"

None of this sounded remotely reassuring and I suddenly yearned for home and my safe apartment on the Upper West Side. As if reading my mind, Nina slipped her hand over mine and stroked my wrist.

"It'll all be fine. Everything is under control."

The meal arrived and conversation changed to lighter topics.

"I took time out today and found a great shopping area called 'Chapinero' – between the centre and the ritzy barrios, higher up."

"Yes, I know it," she replied. "If you really want to do the tourist thing, don't forget to take the teleferico to Monserrate. The views are fantastic."

"Or the Gold Museum," added Miguel, rolling his eyes. "Look, can we get down to business? The van and equipment is ready. We can more or less start monitoring right away."

Nina nodded.

"The authorities have announced the city's water stays in public control for now, but not necessarily in the provinces. I gather that the launch is planned in two outer departments first, Tolima and Putumayo – where you visited last time, Nick."

"Your information is correct," I replied. "The consortium has acquired supplies in both places and others to follow. Our people have been down there in recent weeks."

Nina raised her eyebrows questioningly.

"Yes, while we were getting free from that mess in Utah, Anson's people have been here getting things in place. Unfortunately, Tutch arrives tomorrow, so I should soon know more."

I burnt to discuss 'medicating the public mind' via the water supply. With Miguel present, though, there were too many 'unknowns'.

"What are you thinking?" she asked.

"Just what an almighty mess this is. I'm expected to help coordinate the arrangements between the new Putamayo acquisition and the new headquarters. Meanwhile, there's Tutch to contend with."

Nina smiled.

"Let's meet tomorrow evening," she said. "You'll probably need to relax after seeing Tutch? I really like the Bar Teusquillo and I think you would, too."

I nodded.

"Incidentally," she said, "I also have to see Tutch, too, at 4pm. They certainly won't let me remain unsupervised, so you won't be the only one needing refreshment!"

"I expected repercussions after that mugging episode," I said. "Strange, with international coordination, like those dire warnings I was given in New York."

Miguel shrugged.

"I don't know. I thought it was obvious you'd been robbed. It happens here all the time."

"Meanwhile, we're back to the wilderness."

"But, before that," said Nina reaching into her bag for pen and paper. "You'll find the bar here. Does 7pm sound good?"

MANHATTAN

ROBBIE JAMES

It's really strange the way the mind regurgitates its material. Elements of my experiences in Camp Ute and in the desert kept ebbing back. My left-over feeling was of anger and wanting payback. Last night, I woke from a vivid dream in Nakei's Hogan as the old man prepared another infusion. This time, for manliness and courage! All day, powerful emotions had flooded my mind and body – as if new information was somehow roving around my system, making new connections outside conscious awareness. Sheryl claimed traditional healing methods were truly profound, often reaching deeper than many Western therapies. Now I understood! Occasionally the old urges for adult bookshops came to mind, but they soon left. Somehow, that just seemed rather sad and superficial. Even when Tutch's colleague visited my apartment, to urge cooperation and remind me that Terry was still held – I didn't buckle.

I tidied the apartment and then walked over to Dean and Deluca's, studiously avoiding my old haunts. Their food display, as usual, was mightily impressive and I returned to St Mark's Place with several bags of food to prepare lunch for the others. While waiting, I checked for a reply to my earlier email. It was there and Nancy suggested meeting at 6pm in the Stars diner, near my old office. I fired off a quick confirmation and, while scanning through the other headings, another message caught my eye – this time from Corinne.

Robbie, it's been a while. Miss you! Please call, or come around. C.'

The bell rang and I smiled and welcomed in Si and Andy.

"You look remarkably cheerful," Simon remarked.

"Yeah, feeling far more together," I replied. "My time with the old guy in the canyon really helped. In fact, I dreamt about him last night. Anyway, your lunch is almost ready, but, in the meantime, tell me how the research is getting on. Yes, Si, I absolutely do remember our time in the UN Library!"

Simon chuckled.

"Well, we've had some really useful interviews," replied Andrew. "Whatever stunts Dad pulls, one thing is for sure, the research will continue."

Simon nodded.

"Yes. Dr Gianavecci, the psychopathy expert I first saw over in San Francisco, proved extremely helpful. I wonder what Dr Farrelly will feel about us having his input?"

Andy grinned.

"Probably green with envy! Apparently, Gianavecci is big in the forensic world."

"Gill says that we must be careful with those phones that Tutch gave out. Not only can they be used track locations, but they can be remotely activated to listen in, record and read texts. I'm putting some stuff together for us about faraday bags – and a few tips on pausing location history, how to use airplane mode and a few other ideas that could help give some privacy. Whatever Tutch says, we might have to occasionally leave the phone somewhere – temporarily separate from it – to be completely 'off the leash'. Incidentally, on the theme of Tutch andAnson, we've had unexpected visitors – have you?"

I described yesterday's visit.

"The general message was: 'You'll need to toe the line, because we have your dad.' Little do they know how thin our connection is, although I suppose I'd like to prove myself to the old bastard. He's basically always thought of me as 'a bonehead' and a waste of space."

"I know the feeling," replied Andrew, "though I doubt if I'm as charitable as you. Heck, we sound like a convention of maudlin Freudians!"

"Continuing the theme of 'problem parents'," I asked, "how is Judy?"

Andrew sighed.

"Quite poorly. Pity I hadn't realised her feelings until it was too late."

"You don't suppose that she'd pick things up with Zoltan again?"

"No. Mom's far too smart."

We agreed that our lunch together was a sliver of normality in quite a bizarre situation.

"I'm blown away about those cell phones Tutch gave out."

"Yes," Andrew replied. "Remember they track your position. Mind you, from what Gill described about the facial recognition system, they pretty well know where we are anyway. It's no way to live!"

"A taste of the future, perhaps?" replied Simon. "Hard-line conspiracy buffs predict a future with a micro-chipped population, transparent to our political and corporate masters."

I remembered what had been concealed in my sinuses.

"I'll see them in hell first."

We finished lunch.

"We must soon leave."

"Seen much of Gill, Simon?"

"She's at her office today, but we'll meet this evening. Anyway, we'll see you tomorrow evening with Tutch or perhaps that Klieberman guy."

The others left. I cleared away the debris from lunch and remembered Corinne's email. Simon had the evening with Gill, so why not take up her offer? My hand shook as I tapped out her number, but I decided to take the bull by the horns.

"I got your email, Corinne. Are you busy this evening?"

"No, having a night in. Why not come over?"

"I'd like to, but I already have an earlier important engagement and don't know exactly how long that will take."

"Not a problem. Come as soon as you can. You'll find the place is still comfy."

My stomach turned over! What exactly did she mean...?

"I've such good memories of last time," she cooed.

No more ambiguities!

I rang off and, with several hours to kill, realised just how long it had been since I'd looked around my own doorstep. I stashed a small bag of necessary things for the upcoming task, left the apartment and turned down the Bowery. I whiled away the afternoon, first in Chinatown, moved on to Little Italy and then the Soho galleries. Late afternoon, I refuelled at Dean and DeLucca's fabulous delicatessen, and then headed for my mid-town appointment. Walking over to the Spring Street subway, the Empire

State building stood ahead like some monstrous phallus. I quickly intercepted the thought, and instead compared it to the staggering 'Spider Rock'. One thing that had become abundantly clear following Nakei's ministrations was just how much the interference by my childhood priest had affected me. Perhaps time with Corinne was just what I needed!

I exited the subway early, at Twenty-Eighth Street, and walked up Broadway before crossing to Greeley Square and the Stars diner. It was now 6.25pm. Nancy arrived exactly on half past – reliable as ever. She leant over, giving me an almost maternal peck on the cheek.

"Hello sweetheart," she said, sitting down. "I've missed our chats. Unfortunately, your replacement is a very stuck-up young man."

"Thanks for meeting at such short notice, Nancy."

We exchanged news for a few minutes. Nothing much had changed at Marquetcom. She said that Anson was as intolerable as ever – though, I knew that. Nancy, of course, didn't know of our enforced evening meetings. I excused myself and went into the toilet. I took a plastic bag and wrapped the cell phone given by Tutch. I unscrewed the cistern cover and carefully placed the little parcel above the water line and then taped it in place. It could stay there an hour and no-one would know I wasn't still in the diner. I returned and picked up the conversation.

"Unfortunately, Nancy, my termination didn't exactly end things between Biff and me!"

She raised her eyebrows.

"In the past, we supported each other, Nancy, but now I need your help again."

"I don't know, Robbie. I haven't any real influence. I don't think he'll take you back, though."

"That isn't it. You wouldn't realise this, but Biff is still making life intolerable for me and some friends. Do you remember the briefing paper I wrote about the human costs of water privatisation?"

"Of course. It was probably the final nail in your coffin!"

"Quite possibly. See, I've been involved with a small group of activists, fighting the damage of these projects. Unfortunately, Biff found out and now has his hooks into us. It's serious. People are losing livelihoods and worse."

She bit her lip.

"I know he's vindictive, with contacts in high and low places, but I don't think I can help – not realistically. Don't get me wrong, I have my own morality about these things, too."

"But if you could do something simple that would help me and the others fighting – would you?"

She stared into her coffee as though searching for an answer.

"I guess… I mean, of course, but how?"

"One of Biff's nastiest habits is misusing information."

She nodded.

"Well, two can play that game! I made copies of information that might be very helpful. I was marched off the premises, though, so it's hidden in my old office!"

Her face registered understanding.

"And you want me to get it for you?"

"Really, I need to do it, Nancy. I hid it really well. Also, I left something in Biff's office and need a few moments to retrieve it. Could you let me in?"

She suddenly looked old, as though an unwanted early retirement or worse was imminent. For a moment, I thought she'd refuse outright, but then colour returned to her face.

"No time like the present, I suppose. When I left, everyone had already gone. I can access the key box with my swipe card."

"Thanks. What about cleaners?"

"Also gone by now, but, if we wait another half an hour, there should definitely be no danger. She paused and picked up the menu. "Time enough to try the chicken fajitas."

"Good idea. I'll get them."

She coloured and raised a hand.

"No, no, I didn't mean that. I'm happy to get my own."

Given our age difference, it never occurred that she might be a bit sweet on me. I remembered her revealing her husband died about ten years back.

"No, don't be silly."

I touched the back of her hand, and repeated my thanks. She coloured again. Perhaps dining with a man was a rare event, these days.

Afterwards, I paid and we left, passing the Horace Greeley statue and taking W Thirty-Third Street to the building's entrance. We ascended to the sixtieth floor and entered the now deserted reception area. She entered the code and held my arm as we crept in the dark to find the light switches.

"Occasionally, I work late on special projects and come in at night. I bring a torch on those occasions."

She fished in her bag for the swipe card. Keypads opened most doors, but she also used a swipe card for a box of keys to handle secondary locks in several locations – including Anson's room. Although now deserted, we still crept once inside the suite and she reached for my arm to feel for the light switches in the corridor.

First, I went to my old office, and felt an irrational surge of anger towards my replacement. Finkelstein was obviously a tidy freak with nothing out of place. First, I took thin rubber gloves from my bag and then started the computer and scanner. Taking a screwdriver from my bag, I pulled the desk away from the wall and removed the hatch covering the heating. I lay on the floor and reached inside, taking out a green notebook and a sheaf of photocopied papers – including copies of the marketing plan for Kane and Field's 'Peak-Me'. I passed a range of papers through the scanner. Nancy tapped on the door and passed the key for the secondary lock for Biff's office.

"Don't tell me what you're going to do," she said. "I'll wait in my office. Come down when you're ready."

"Thanks Nancy. By the way, what's the Finkelstein guy's first name?"

"Mark."

"Okay. I'll join you very soon."

I opened the email system and then wrote a message, attaching several scanned documents.

Biff,

I believe my predecessor had concerns about ethical issues – notably your lack of them. I can certainly see why! The attached material concocted to justify interference in Colombia is a good example of your willingness to bend truth, and should be widely exposed. Of course, the real purpose of depriving people of their heritage is just to enrich the elite and predatory corporations – like Marquetcom.

The 'Peak-Me' campaign also well illustrates some aspects of your deviousness – though, of course, there are many more examples – are there not? Imagine the outrage of thinking people worldwide, should this cynical material find its way into the right hands! Ditto, your creepy deceptions on behalf of Big Pharma. Perhaps you should properly understand the effect of your actions on others and be more understanding of those who try to rein in your abuses.

As a small initial taster, a copy of your proposed marketing plan for 'Peak-

Me' has been forwarded to Spin Watch, the organisation that monitors slippery spin-meisters, like you. I'm sure they'll find it most revealing!

Best wishes,

Mark Finkelstein.

I wrote a covering note to 'Spin Watch', attached the copies and clicked 'send'. Picturing Anson's reaction, I then tucked the other papers into my bag and went to Nancy's office. She was fiddling with papers, and looked strained.

"I assume Biff still records calls and meetings held in his office?"

She nodded.

"Yes, the recorder is in the second drawer."

I moved next door to Biff's office, opened the secondary lock and went in. At first, I thought the drawer was locked. Perhaps all the desk pounding had distorted the runners. I pulled harder and, when it finally opened, I saw a device like an extra-large external hard drive. Its capacity would be huge! I pulled at it and the cabling had sufficient slack to let me rest the device on the desk. I found the port, and connected it to an external hard drive from my bag. As the data hurtled down the cable, I took out the remaining equipment. The funny little man in the shop off Canal St had felt sure that this would handle the task.

I went over to the seating area where Biff conducted discussions, and explored the space behind the large mahogany unit by the wall. I slipped the slim recorder behind and then checked the field of view from each chair. Nothing was visible, so I returned Biff's recorder to the drawer and my external drive to the bag.

I can do a bit of fishing too, I thought with satisfaction.

We left the building, and buying Nancy a drink seemed the least I could do. I went into the toilet and retrieved the cell phone. When I got back, the colour had returned to her cheeks and, after two gins, I noticed her gazing in a decidedly non-maternal way. I intuitively responded.

"Nancy, I remember you telling me about Biff's ex-wife, Judy? Well, it turns out, we've now met. I actually stayed at her home in Philadelphia with Andy – the older son, whom you also mentioned."

Her eyes opened wide in surprise.

"Really! What's she like?"

"Well, I can see why Biff would miss her. Lovely lady... still very attractive, though, of course, there is far too big an age gap for me to think of her in that way."

Her expression said that, despite the gin, she'd got the point. I felt awkward and rather guilty that I may have misused her.

"What would you say to an evening at the Met? Korngold's 'Das Wunder der Heliane' opens soon. It's a great opera and I can get another ticket?"

"Are you really sure? Yes, I'd like that."

We left the bar together and I made for the subway. Half an hour later, I pushed the bell at Corinne's apartment...

108

BOGOTÁ & PUTUMAYO
DEPARTMENT, COLOMBIA

NICK MARTIN

I wished our time at Teusquillo's and the night's subsequent events could have lasted forever, but, when I woke, Nina had already gone and left me a note. Strangely, Bogotá had rather grown on me and, in the light of morning, another trip to the steamy provinces seemed even less appealing. I read her note again. She'd join me later tomorrow. If only she wasn't in tow with Miguel and those damn ex-guerrillas – if, indeed, they were actually 'ex'. I recalled my previous flight in the little Cessna with Miguel and Luis – and shuddered.

After breakfast, I moved my belongings downstairs to a temporary storage room and put together a handgrip of essentials. I left the mobile phone, reasoning that I could explain that it wouldn't be necessary in the jungle. To pass the time, I thumbed through a Colombian guide-book in the lobby until reception called to say the taxi had arrived. The hotel seemed accustomed to the needs of a business clientèle and were happy to help charter a flight to Putumayo Department. Apparently, they had many business guests with interests in the south. I was told to rendezvous in the café with a Señor Tacho of Puto-Air, who would fly me to an airstrip near Puerto Asis.

The taxi pulled into the airport and I made my way to the café. A familiar figure with an impressive moustache lolled against a pillar. Oh no!

Moments later, Luis was pumping my hand, with a big grin.

"What are you doing, Luis? I thought you... you know, were with another outfit. Oh, I get it. You aren't by any chance the mysterious 'Señor Tacho'?"

Luis beamed and nodded.

"Nice seeing you again, Nick. Listen, our comrades have many roles. This brings revenue and keeps us linked with Bogotá. Nina arranged things with the hotel. Please follow me."

We went to a small hanger with a little Cessna outside. Soon we flew over impressive mountains and then Luis banked and headed south. Below was verdant and I didn't doubt it when he claimed the flora and fauna was probably more diverse and abundant here than almost anywhere. For how long, though, what with spraying, resource exploration and, now, messing with the water!

Eventually, we descended into an isolated valley at what seemed an impossible angle. Odd, because I'd assumed that we'd head for the main regional airport rather than somewhere so remote. I wanted to query it, but, given our current crazy approach, I'd rather Luis focused on landing. We bumped to a halt on a ridiculously short runway. Luis helped me out and we crossed to a small tin building on the perimeter.

"Luis, I assumed we'd use a proper airport near the town, because I've important business nearby."

Luis shook his head.

"All in good time, Señor. You need to meet your support. People who can help you get things right. Nina will join us tomorrow. Bad things have been happening and things are very wrong."

"The whole thing is wrong, Luis, which is why I agreed to have contact in the first place. I still haven't recovered from the last helicopter business and can't afford anything like that again!"

Luis wrinkled his nose and the large moustache twitched.

"You don't understand, Señor. Many strange things have happened since your colleagues came. People are strangely affected and we worry about the safety of our water."

We reached the tin building, and exited through a gate at the perimeter. Behind the building, I saw a shapely woman in battle fatigues and beret perched on the hood of an old jeep. It was Elsa! She grinned and I reluctantly smiled back, still struggling to reconcile her beauty with that deadly attack.

With a sinking stomach, I climbed in.

"Luis, I asked the hotel to arrange a charter flight to the main airstrip. How on earth did I end up with you?"

"Nina and Miguel have extensive contacts."

"What did you mean by, 'Strange things affecting people'?"

Luis curled a large arm around his shoulder.

"Let's not mess about, my friend. Miguel has contact with Nina and we know exactly what's happening."

I already knew they could kill without compunction.

"What's strange?" I persisted.

"Previously, we had influence, but the people around here have now become... become... well, they've lost their spirit. But, of course, that's the idea, isn't it?"

We immediately took off, with Elsa at the wheel, and I felt my face flush. I wanted no part defending that experiment, caught between rogue intelligence, corporate profiteers and guerrillas! Anyway, what was Nina's real position on all this? It seemed a literal and a philosophical landscape where power and deception had replaced any kind of moral compass.

We sped through a rich, green landscape. In various places, the jungle had been cleared for small banana plantations and what Luis said were pepper plants. A spine of emerald-coloured mountains wore a thin veil of mist and, in other circumstances, it could have been so perfect. We bumped along for miles until the vegetation suddenly turned brown, presumably following fumigation.

"Coca?" I asked, pointing to a brown patch.

"Yes, and, next to that, black pepper. Over there, vanilla... all ruined!"

"But they must destroy coca," I replied, despite recalling Nina's alternative explanations from one of our earliest meetings.

"Many of the brothers have tried to grow alternatives – medicinal herbs, papaya, coffee," said Luis. "You can see what happens. The coca growers just retreat further into the jungle and continue there. There's little else!"

"I see," I replied, beginning to feel concerned about another impromptu engagement with spray planes. "Where are we going?"

We joined another road and I saw a pipe that followed the tree-line.

"Not far now," Luis replied.

Elsa said something in Spanish and, as we turned the corner, I saw a small lake of oil lying where the ground fell away. Charred and shredded trees stood guard over a fractured pipe.

Luis said something angrily, but Elsa successfully managed to both shrug her shoulders and hold onto the wheel.

"I warned them to hold off," Luis exclaimed. "The place will be crawling with the military – as if we don't have enough problems!"

About seven miles further on, she swung the jeep into a side track. The overhanging trees here were rich with colourful fungi and tree orchids. We finally arrived in a small clearing with a handful of huts and tents. People were engaged with various chores. Some carried AK-47s, and others had pistols.

"Welcome," said Luis. "You'll stay here with us for the moment."

"You don't understand," I replied. "I have to meet with the manager and the team running the local water service. They expect me, later today or tomorrow!"

"Don't worry, my friend. You'll go tomorrow and we'll be close by. Depending on what you find, we'll stop their use of these chemicals!"

I followed Luis to one of the tents, worried by his words.

"You'll sleep here tonight, so get unpacked and join us in the main building for food."

Luis left and I pulled the tent into some kind of shape for what promised to be a long night. The tent was just about high enough to stand and had duck boards and a mosquito net. It was a far cry from last night!

I left the tent, and quickly surveyed the camp before joining Luis. Outside the second largest building, women prepared vegetables on a large trestle table covered in plastic. On the other side, men toiled over an old truck, hammering away, and legs protruded from underneath. Beyond that, several men unloaded long boxes from a van. I started crossing to the main building, but something tugged at me to look again. I squinted against the sun. One figure looked almost familiar as he bent over, reloading crates in place of the long boxes. Then they closed the van doors, and quickly drove away.

I walked to the main building where Luis and Elsa were serving themselves stew from a large pot. I joined them, feeling uneasy and barely able to return Elsa's smile.

"I you give food," she tried.

I thanked her, thinking, *If only Nina would hurry up and join us.*

I assessed the situation. I hadn't actually agreed to come here, so it was technically kidnapping – but, then, that's what they do. On the other hand, they were clearly friendly with Nina, who'd arranged the contact in the first place and probably had some part in Luis flying me. Perhaps it would all become clear after she arrived. I recalled her descriptions of visiting the Zapatistas and the literature she'd shown me. Despite hefty doses of Marxist dogma, that sounded a welcoming, even uplifting, experience. This felt quite different.

A large man holding an AK-47 hurried over and spoke in Spanish. Luis and Elsa were immediately up on their feet.

"Quickly Nick," said Luis, "we must leave immediately."

His tone was urgent and I ran behind. We scrambled into the jeep and I noticed that two of the long boxes I'd just seen taken from the van were in the back. Luis sped up the track to the road, and this time turned left.

"This is the way to Junin," said Luis.

"If you say so," I replied. It might be the road to Mandalay, for all I knew. "Why the indigestion? I was enjoying the stew!"

"A little task," Luis replied. "You'll see."

At that, Elsa, who was sitting beside Luis in the front, turned and gave me another dazzling smile. The road ahead forked and we took the left turning. I sat in the back again. These were indeed the same boxes, I now felt certain of that.

The jungle was thick, but, after about five miles, I saw a clearing ahead. Luis pulled off the main road, and proceeded down an almost imperceptible diagonal track leading to the clearing. We reached the edge of a field, and tucked the jeep back behind the tree-line.

With a sick feeling of impending disaster, I realised that the increasing noise was coming from above. I got out and the other two ran around to the back, slid the boxes out and quickly opened them like practised pit-stop mechanics. I looked across the clearing at moist crops and, in the distance, saw that a low-flying plane was approaching. I was about to call out to Luis and Elsa when I realised that another plane was coming from behind. The first crop-duster started to release its herbicide, and the toxic clouds billowed out over the plantation. I turned back to shout a warning, but saw they'd taken out a shoulder-mounted missile and were preparing to deploy. My guts turned to water. Not again! I couldn't just be a passive witness to murder. The second plane roared overhead and, through the mist raining down, I saw the flash as Luis fired. The slim missile streaked across the sky, swatting the plane down with a fiery impact, showering debris over the field.

My legs seemed leaden and, at first, wouldn't respond. I burst through an invisible barrier holding me back and ran, shouting, at Elsa, who was now shouldering a second missile. I yelled, rushing forward, waiving my arms, but she took no notice. I tripped over a tree root and a searing pain tore at my ankle. I broke the worst of the fall with my shoulder and rolled over, shouting again. The second plane had now reached the far side of the clearing and banked hard left to avoid the fate of his colleague. I had to prevent repetition, but it was too late – I saw another flash! The missile launched with an acrid whiff of propellant, streaking towards the second plane, which it knocked down in a star-burst of orange flame. I was almost certainly watching another life being extinguished. I lay mute as Luis and Elsa whooped and embraced. They saw I was shivering and came over to pull me up. Luis's eyes shone.

"Two less! These so-called 'military advisers' can be driven out!"

I perched on a fallen branch, caught up in terror and dismay.

"But you've just killed two people and destroyed aircraft!"

Luis shrugged.

"Mercenaries deserve it. Also, predatory corporations who fund paramilitaries to do their dirty work. In the past, ordinary union members have even been murdered. Yet, they allow mercenary 'contractors' to spray us. Not content with poisoning from the sky, now they want to mess with our water. You really believe we shouldn't defend ourselves?"

It was a mental and moral syntax that lay outside of my experience. I stood unsteadily, looking across the field at the smouldering fragments of hot metal. Further words failed me.

"Come," said Luis to Elsa.

"Zoltan certainly brought some good stuff. Let's get out before they see the smoke. Luckily, no helicopter guard today."

I hobbled back to the vehicle and Elsa guided it down the tiny track and then accelerated back towards the camp. Given the amount of destruction caused, they were watchful but quite relaxed.

"You know, Nick, after fumigation like that, the soil can take a year to recuperate," said Luis. "Soil, crops, livestock, water and humans, all contaminated with glyphosate."

I grunted, still assimilating their reference to Zoltan with astonishment. My neck cricked, from looking up in anticipation of swishing rotor blades. All too soon, we turned down the track to the encampment, and were back at their site.

"Hopefully, we should be okay here," Luis explained. "This camp is new and, despite the supposed disbanding, there's still a paramilitary stronghold at Chamaico. Most of the nearby towns – Junin, Orense, Concaran and Ayacucho – are friendly and support us. At least they did, before your people started messing with their water."

I nodded, unable to respond to something so outside my experience or comprehension.

"Why drag me along?"

Luis smiled.

"Why do you think?"

I felt a flash of irritation.

"I suspect, to get me as compromised as possible. Make sure I stay on what you consider is the right side. I've now witnessed the downing of three aircraft, and been indirectly involved with other things back in Bogotá. The fact I experienced a mugging directly after meeting Miguel now feels fishy. Particularly as the funds went towards something nasty, and for a while pointed to me!"

The smile became broader.

"Welcome to our world. Before being judgemental, remember Guatemala, Salvador, Chile, Iraq. Would these things have happened without the needs of corporations and the war machine that can eventually back them?"

I bit back a response, hoping against hope that Nina's eventual arrival would counter a growing fear I'd made one of my worst mistakes, ever.

Late that afternoon, I accompanied Luis, Elsa and two others named Gustavo and Aurelio for a drink, passing through beautiful countryside to the township of Ayacucho. Utah had been wonderful, but the countryside here was wild and totally foreign. Ayacucho was a sleepy town hazy with humidity, located between the forest and the mountains. Luis pulled up outside a bar on the main drag. Several villagers lolled against an outside wall, munching something. An old church appeared to be the best building in town, but a dilapidated, paint-peeled schoolhouse told of the general poverty.

We entered the bar and the exclusively male clientèle inside were chewing, drinking and smoking. I expected the usual buzz of a bar, but the place seemed unnaturally quiet. Realising Elsa had disappeared, I alerted Luis.

"It isn't suitable," he explained. "She's over the road with a woman friend."

A cheerful looking, bright-eyed man joined us. He slapped Luis on the shoulder and they spoke in animated Spanish. He then passed some leaflets around and everyone shook their heads in dismay.

"This is Pablo," Luis explained, as the man extended his hand. "Pablo's a trusted friend who followed our advice. His family avoided the piped water supply and took fresh water from the river near our camp. Do you notice anything?"

That question wasn't difficult. Pablo's face was alive and vital, while most others were dull – and almost zombie-like.

"I think so," I replied.

"These leaflets suddenly appeared in town, warning people against offering us support," said Luis. "You can see the result. Normally we're really welcomed when we come into town. Now look! Someone has a real hit on their hands with this chemical!"

It was indeed spooky finding a whole population just a few molecules away from compliance. I shivered. It had seemed bad hearing about it, but the reality was truly shocking.

"If this is the result of the additive and a few leaflets, imagine what a sophisticated delivery could achieve?"

"Exactly, my friend! Remember that tomorrow."

When we left, it was dark and we almost collided with a mother pig and her following piglets making unsupervised passage down the main street. The insects were now out in force and the blurred halo around every light would be an entomologist's dream. We returned to the camp in silence. After the evening meal finished, I refused Luis's invitation to join them and friends for drinks in the main hut and returned to my tent. The babble continued for hours, until eventually I fell into a tense sleep.

I woke shortly after dawn and, after dressing, spent time in the camp grounds. People moved about and I saw activity in the food preparation area. I sat on my haunches and allowed an old grey dog to sniff my hands. As the light increased, myriads of butterflies fluttered from the trees – blue, red, bronze, purple and brown. Some were intent on clinging onto the canvas and their jewel-like colours relieved the dull camouflage. I heard an approaching vehicle and then saw a jeep with two people enter the compound. Elsa jumped from the driver's seat, but the other figure was concealed by the passenger door. My heart sped as I saw Nina's profile and I ran over to take her in my arms.

"However did you get here from Bogotá. Luis didn't leave?"

At that moment, Luis arrived.

"I'm not the only pilot, my friend."

Luis embraced Nina with familiarity, and I found her apparent ease with their violence worrying. To see her embraced by someone who'd recently dispatched a fellow pilot – seemed almost inconceivable.

We went over to the cooking area and breakfasted together.

"You didn't tell me how the staff interviews in Bogotá went?" she said, as she slipped her hand into mine.

I grinned, remembering that we'd had rather more interesting things to do.

"Good," I replied. "You were right. There's no shortage of bilingual, computer savvy, young people in Bogotá."

Luis left after breakfast. I suggested to Nina taking a walk and we headed for a quiet place by the camp's edge. Despite the lump in my throat, I couldn't avoid raising the events of the previous day, or control my quivering voice.

"I don't understand it," I protested, "Luis a pilot, as well. Surely that wasn't necessary? It will probably bring retribution and more violence!"

She took my hand, looking directly into my eyes.

"If they'd killed your brother, would you feel differently?"

"What do you mean?"

"About a year ago, Rodrigo, Luis's brother, visited friends near Concaran. He played with their children by a new papaya plantation. From nowhere, spray planes turned up, so Rodrigo tried to get the children out of the way. There was a helicopter gunship above as he frantically searched for his friend's son, who'd been terrified and fled. The child later said that Rodrigo waved his AK-47 in the air, probably signalling them to hold back, but, as he ran across the field, they shot and killed him."

"Was the child okay?"

"Physically, yes, but real devastation has since been visited on the locals and their crops. They think they're being deliberately pushed around to suit exploration interests. Others have been harmed by the ex-paramilitaries, again to please business interests. It's a life and death struggle."

I explained to Nina what I'd heard about Zoltan bringing weapons.

"They must buy where they can. I'm told they've used him once before."

"But we know the guy is involved with US Intelligence. It doesn't make sense!"

"No, he's associated with a rogue outfit. Luis said they previously had a supply line from an ex-Russian military source. Probably Russian criminals, capitalising on the wonders of the free market, but that connection got busted."

I whistled, though was that really so different from business with this rogue group?

"Equipment previously came from Russia?"

"Yes. Apparently, quite a sophisticated arrangement. The Russian shipments stopped in Amman en route, refuelled, and then went on to parachute drops and remote landing strips here."

"I suppose it wasn't a charity operation?"

"Sadly, cocaine is an international currency."

I tried to mentally link Nina with what I'd witnessed yesterday. Her gentle face seemed as beautiful as ever. Surely, if some objective moral tally was even possible in this awful game, she'd be on the right side.

"Look, I have to go to the water treatment plant near Orense today, they expect me. Luis said something about being in the background?"

She placed her hand on mine and touched my shoulder with her other hand.

"Wait here a moment, Nick. I need a quick word with Luis."

She left and I wandered back to see the butterflies again, but they'd risen in the warmer air and now flitted around the perimeter instead. I watched a huge iridescent blue settle on a red fungus growing out of a tropical plant. It was so absorbing that her voice startled me.

"We'll leave in about half an hour. Luis and three others are going ahead now and will approach Orense from a different direction. They know of a secluded spot where they can keep watch on the plant."

I was about to ask if she'd come too, but she'd anticipated it.

"I'll pretend to be your assistant. You'll probably need help with Spanish, anyway."

We took coffee and, from the corner of my eye, I saw a jeep leave with Luis and the others.

"It truly is a beautiful country, Nina."

"The profiteers don't care about that!"

We walked the perimeter strip while she identified various plants and insects. About half an hour later, we set off.

Orense appeared a medium-sized town, little different from others in the area. We passed through the centre, and then turned north, to reach the water plant.

I found the admin office, and asked to see Señor Fernando Montesinos, the Manager. Montesinos had been kept on after the takeover and had good English. Nina duly introduced herself as my assistant, and we were taken to Montesinos's office.

"Some American colleagues will join us soon," he explained. "They helped with the new arrangements."

Canvey's advance team were still back in Bogotá, so this was unexpected. A short time later, there was a knock and then Anson's creepy new assistant, Mark Finkelstein, entered. For a moment, I almost expected to see Tutch following, but the second man was a pasty-faced tough with extremely greasy hair.

"Hello, Nick, hiya Nina," said Finkelstein. "Good to see you again. This is Frank Caher, Mr Tutch's assistant. By the way, Brian will see you when you get back to Bogotá."

I nodded, dry-mouthed at this turn of events. I glanced at Nina. We had no option but to continue the pretence for Fernando's benefit.

"We need to confirm operations, with Señor Montesinos and agree the plant's coordination with the Bogotá centre. Please take notes, Nina."

"No filming this time?" Caher said to Nina. Fernando looked up questioningly, but didn't pursue it.

We talked for almost two hours, but, afterwards, Finkelstein and Caher seemed keen to leave. Fernando, though, was a friendly character, who clearly wished to make a good impression. We talked infrastructure and the region's other water treatment centres.

"Now I'm here, could I see the treatment plant?"

"Of course, Señor," he replied. "It's right next door. Look, over there!"

He beckoned, and walked to the window to point to a collection of buildings.

"I'll briefly explain the process, and then we'll take a look. First, water gets piped from our upland reservoir. The levels of bacteria, protozoa and algae here are usually quite low, but purification is still necessary. Water is pumped to the holding tanks over there, and alkalised with lime. Come, I'll show you. It's easier to understand if we walk around."

We left the administration building and, as we walked next door, I wondered where Luis and the others were hidden. The wooded hillock across the road seemed the most likely place. Fernando then took us down to one of several low buildings.

"This is where we alkalise the water. After the pH is adjusted, it proceeds to the flocculation and then the clarification stage."

We entered a low building that contained a long basin.

"Treatment with aluminium hydroxide causes the impurities to precipitate and then coagulate," explained Fernando. "This appliance then pushes the flock from the basin. We'll go next door now."

We proceeded to a similar structure, next door. A paved area ran between the buildings down to a smaller building below. As we walked, some activity there caught my eye. I looked rather more closely and then stared. It very much looked like the vehicle I'd seen making deliveries at the camp. A man struggled with a crate, which he then carried down to the small building. Three armed men stood by the vehicle.

"Keep up, Nick," called Nina, from a distance. I looked up. She and Fernando were waiting outside the next building, looking puzzled. I quickly moved forward to join them.

"So, then the water passes to these sedimentation basins, before going on to the filtration unit," said Fernando. "Mr Finkelstein said the new investment plans might let us change from slow sand filtration to rapid models. Maybe," he said proudly, "even to units with polymer ultra-filtration membranes!"

Nina caught my eye.

"What is it?" she whispered.

"Back there! It looked like the truck I saw delivering to the camp. Hang on."

"Fernando, what is that little building at the end, between the flocculation unit and this building?"

"You mean where we fluoridate the water? Yes, Señor Martin, we'll get to that, but, before fluoridation, comes the disinfecting process.

Once we had an outbreak of cryptosporidium and, another time, shigella, simply because the..."

Outside, someone shouted and two shots rang out. Fernando gulped mid-sentence, and I grabbed Nina's hand and ran towards the end of the shed. We could hear the sound of feet running along the side of the building. Ahead was a door, but, before even reaching it, the handle twisted and a terrified Judy Alton ran in. It was difficult knowing who was the more surprised.

"They tried to get Zolt... Major Heltay," she gabbled. "He's on our side, you know!"

Nina produced a gun from somewhere and ran for the door.

"You know what he was delivering?" Nina shouted. "Luis and the others must have twigged the bastard, and taken action."

I'd never heard her swear before, but, with shots and armed guards outside, it hardly seemed relevant. The sweating Fernando joined us from the far end.

"What's happening, Señor?"

"I'm not sure, Fernando, but keep your head down. We seem to be under attack."

"They have guns," said Judy, her voice still trembling.

I moved to the door and looked out. Nearby was a still body with blood oozing from a wound to the heart area. A motor started and I looked up to see a vehicle accelerate and then disappear behind the end of the building. Zoltan was driving and had Nina sandwiched between two men in the back. I ran forward, but more shots came and I heard a vehicle with screaming tyres driving crazily around the perimeter. My heart pumped frantically as I ran full speed to the end of the building, as Luis and two others rounded from the other side.

"Look!" shouted Luis, pointing to the gate.

Zoltan's vehicle kicked up dust as it roared onto the main road and sped away.

"What the hell happened, Luis? They've taken Nina!"

He nodded sadly.

"Yes. Probably back to Chamaico. They have a camp nearby."

I ducked back into the building, where a shocked, trembling Judy waited with Fernando.

I ran back outside.

"What ever happened?" I asked a chastened Luis.

"I told you we'd act if we found how they affected the water."

"I didn't realise that meant crashing in and letting Nina be captured. Who are they?"

Luis looked towards the body.

"Obviously, the former paramilitaries. Can you believe that, after doing business with us, Zoltan also traded with them?"

"Very easily! Arms dealers don't worry about trading with opposite sides," he replied, remembering a discussion with Simon.

"What exactly happened?"

"When we saw him drop materials at the treatment plant, everything became obvious. The two men at your meeting went down to the fluoridation building and we could hear them talking. Apparently, Zoltan had delivered more chemical. They said a little went a long way and seemed delighted by its success."

"Just a minute."

He put his head back into the building. Fernando had found two chairs and sat with the shaking Judy.

"Fernando, remind me again, how many treatment plants are there in the province?"

"Three, Señor. One the other side at Huaraz, but the nearest is Chamaico. What about the body, Señor, because I must call the police. Does your colleague know who did this?"

Luis looked confused and shrugged before replying.

"No. The paramilitaries are pigs and don't care."

Fernando stood up, hopping from foot to foot.

"Go ahead, Fernando. We'll look into the office before leaving."

Judy came outside, still shaking uncontrollably, and averted her eyes from the body.

"I'd better go," said Luis, after Fernando left. "The others have gone back up there."

He pointed to the hillock.

"You're thinking Zoltan might deliver to other plants. Probably to Chamaico, because a former paramilitary camp is nearby."

Luis left and, when I slipped an arm around Judy for support, she clung onto me. I walked her out of view of the corpse.

"What did you mean about Zoltan delivering chemical?" she asked. "He told me he was here in a special role, giving support and equipment to the anti-narcotics operation."

I explained Corinne's information, as best as I could.

"This isn't only a lucrative privatisation. They're simultaneously trialling a product that induces compliance when added to the water. Guess it'll also make life easier for the oil people."

I'd have thought that, for Judy, registering any more distress was impossible – but no!

"Nick", she said, rubbing her forehead, "Zoltan explained everything. We got back together. I came with him because I was convinced we were still batting for the same team. I intended telling you all later. Zolt explained that, when he realised that you were onto the Senator Monroe situation, he went to Nashville to try and stop anything bad from happening. Remember, I said at the time that we should give him a chance? After he explained, it all made sense."

I looked into her anxious face, knowing that love can blind and just how desperate she was to believe in him – even now!

"Judy, Andy described watching Zoltan being welcomed at Camp Ute and saluted in. That operation has been corrupted and isn't what it seems!"

She stuck out her jaw in unconvincing defiance of the obvious.

"But, remember how well informed and committed Zoltan was to the important things to us. You can't fake that!"

I raised my eyebrows, but she wasn't about to capitulate.

"Zolt contacted me in Philadelphia. He wanted to explain things and, well, I… I wanted to hear. He's sickened at the way things are going and the corruption of it all. He's just been biding his time. When the time's right, he'll help to bring the whole rotten thing down. He has a detailed plan."

"Yes, but he…"

"No, wait, Nick. You already know that this is possible. You met an agent in Nashville who felt just the same way. Then there's Gill and Simon. Why couldn't the same be true of Zoltan?"

It felt brutal, but had to be done. I described Zoltan transporting boxes to the camp and their role in the aerial murder. She was trembling, but I continued, describing the compliance chemical, my evening visit to Ayacucho and the effects on the locals.

She shook her head with a pained expression.

"Zoltan said intelligence had information about possible attacks on the water infrastructure. He said we were bringing surveillance equipment for the plant – cameras and the like." She shook her head. "This is just awful. I can't believe I've been fooled again!"

Are certain women just more susceptible to being misled by their hearts? I recalled Nina's ready justifications for Luis and Elsa's actions – but shook my head and quickly shot the thought into outer darkness!

"Let's take a look in the little building where he took the crate."

We walked down the passageway to the fluoridation building. The door was open, though the place seemed empty. Drums labelled 'hexafluorosilicic acid' were piled on the floor next to the pipes, pumps and mixers. A metal staircase led to a small mezzanine floor, giving access to an overhead hopper and a small office.

"I'll look up here." I started climbing, and felt her hand support the small of my back as she followed. A light was on, although the office looked empty. Two bags were opened on a nearby bench. One bag contained a pale blue powder, and the other a white powder. Judy sniffed at the white powder and, before I could speak, took a little on a finger, and delicately dabbed at it with her tongue.

"I thought so – cocaine. The blue must be the chemical."

I was stunned.

"How did you know that? I don't get...?"

She looked shamefaced, but smiled and then seemed to decide something.

"Yes, we used it for a very short period when Biff and I were young and he'd started making big money. I haven't been back to it since – though I don't know about him. Please don't mention this to Andy, or anyone else."

I nodded.

"The mixing operation was probably financed with cocaine."

"I saw some boxes being taken away from the camp. We must ask who usually works the fluoridating operation. Do you by any chance have a matchbox?"

She took one from her bag and I filled it with the white powder.

"Any other containers?"

She emptied her compact case into a nearby bin, replaced it with some blue powder, dusted the case and put it back into her bag.

"Come on, let's go."

Back in Fernando's office, the little man looked shaken.

"The police will be here soon. No problems because you were with me all the time. I can vouch for that. Where are you staying, in case they want to speak?"

My heart sunk. After the mugging and fertiliser episode, I was probably still on record.

"A hotel in Orense... I've forgotten the name, but that's where we'll be."

We left and sped back towards the camp.

"Where did you and Zoltan stay last night?" I shouted over the noise of the jeep.

"Chamaico. Military advisers are still there and another group helping local forces."

"Paramilitaries," I said. "They've faced off for years against the guerrilla group I stayed with. There's supposed to be peace now. How the hell did we get mixed up in such an awful mess?"

She shrugged.

"Loyalty to son, heart and cause, I suppose. And you?"

"The same, except for the 'son' bit."

"What was that about a hotel in Orense?"

I glanced sideways, but quickly pushed the thought away.

"I don't know, it was silly. Somehow, I thought saying 'at a former FARC camp' might not be helpful!"

We found our way through Orense and I noticed at least two hotels, and more unhelpful thoughts. *Damn, was it the heat, a brush with danger, or what?*

I found the road back out of town, passing through incredibly profuse and exotic vegetation. The mist developed into rain and a heavy sky discharged huge droplets that pinged off the road. At the next crossroads, I turned down towards the camp. The wet vegetation seemed an even deeper green and it could have all been so beautiful. I slowed down before entering the track to the camp. People were now running for shelter and the entrance was slippery with red-orange mud.

Once inside, I looked around and saw Luis, who was sitting with Elsa and two men, Gustavo and Aurelio, from our evening trip to Ayacucho. They seemed strangely relaxed after their involvement with the treatment plant fiasco. Judy, though, still looked tense and pale as I tried explaining who she was and why she was here. Luis looked quizzically at Judy and then spoke to Elsa in Spanish. She immediately stood up.

"Go with Elsa. She'll show you the few comforts we have... things for women."

It sounded more a command than invitation.

"We have to rescue Nina," I said, sickened that fate had taken her yet again.

"That's why I sent the woman out," Luis replied. "Depending on this Zoltan guy's influence at Chamaico, perhaps we could trade the women."

"Sorry?"

"Zoltan gets the woman Judy back, if they return Nina to us."

"Luis, you don't understand. Judy now gets that he's totally untrustworthy scum. Hell, even you were pissed at finding he'd traded with both sides."

Luis bubbled air through his lips, and shrugged.

"I guess so. What do you suggest then?"

That was indeed the question, but my mind seemed about as empty as a monk's in advanced meditation. Most people here had weapons, and were still dressed in battle fatigues. Could we perhaps storm the paramilitaries' camp and seize her? No, it would be hopelessly dangerous. I caught Luis's eye, but he only shrugged.

"Could your people get her back?"

He gave a throat-slitting gesture and shook his head.

"Could I offer myself in exchange?"

"I'm sorry, Señor, but you're of no value."

"What if Arm-Rite's people discover that Zoltan brought the kit that knocked them out of the sky? Might they turn on him and let her go?"

Luis again shook his head.

"Why would they? They hate us, but Nina is a known activist. Neither the government troops, paramilitaries nor for-hire Yankee mercenaries have any love for her."

Gustavo had been chugging on some local concoction for several minutes. He pulled out a cigar and ostentatiously lit up, blowing guffs of sweet-smelling smoke over the table.

Elsa and Judy returned, prompting Gustavo to say something in Spanish. Luis nodded vigorously.

"Gustavo remarked how much our Elsa resembles Nina."

I looked up as they approached. Although Elsa's face was a little wider than Nina's perfect ellipse, there indeed was a strong similarity. If only I'd taken Elsa to the plant, instead.

The others were talking excitedly while I ran with a fantasy. What if Elsa somehow impersonated her. But how would that work?

The others gabbled on until my attention was captured by Gustavo saying in pretty fair English:

"Ask him about the parachute."

The bastard! So, all this time he could speak English and couldn't be bothered!

"Good English," I said, directly to Gustavo. "Ask who about the parachute?"

"You, of course, my friend."

"We have an idea…!"

109

MANHATTAN

SIMON MAHER

The city had become quite overpowering and secretly I yearned for the scale of a European town – somewhere, in fact, rather like Oxford! Despite its energy and excitement, New York City had started to grate. Gill's description of facial recognition on the transport system, and our attachment to Tutch's cell phones, didn't help. Andrew and I had recently moved to a B&B near Washington Square in the Village. Things seemed quieter here, though Andy had recently become agitated because Judy had disappeared. In fact, today, he'd taken a train over to Philadelphia to investigate!

I walked into Washington Square, to take advantage of sun after several rainy days. Dog owners exercised their charges in a specially roped off area, fascinating the local children. Perhaps this was as close to a circus as they got. I joined them to watch several breathless owners taking their dogs through a series of hurdles. It seemed such a shame that Gill had an office briefing today. With Andy away, we could have spent time together.

I was watching a clever German shepherd jump the hurdles when a vibration from my left pocket signalled an incoming call. At least it was my personal phone, and not Tutch's wireless manacle – which I always kept in my right pocket. The German shepherd finished his run, replaced by a contrived race between two Afghan hounds that seemed more important to the panting owners than the dogs.

I picked up the call, and Robbie's voice sounded urgent.

"Si, what are you doing? Could we meet?"

"I suppose so. I'm just kicking my heels in Washington Square. I only had one interview, which finished earlier this morning. Andy's gone to Philly because he's worried about his Mom and Gill has a briefing in her office."

"Wait there and I'll be with you in ten to fifteen. Let's meet by the dog exercise area?"

"Have you got me under surveillance? That's exactly where I am!"

"Funny you should ask that. I'll explain later!"

I walked over to the arch and, soaking up the atmosphere, followed the red-brick row houses around the northern edge of the square. I got back to the dog exercise area as a rather preoccupied Robbie arrived.

"Lighten up, Mr James! You know, this place always feels European to me."

"So you said the first time we came – the time in the bar I don't like mentioning! Perhaps it's all the ancient bones here! It's been a cemetery, a duelling site and they hung criminals just over there!"

"I'll have you know that not all we Europeans are ancient fossils! Anyhow, what's on your mind?"

He mouthed, 'Tutch's cell phones. Let's leave them charging at your B & B' At least that gives an excuse. If necessary, we can say that we briefly went into the square for a quick bite to eat."

We quickly dumped them and returned and walked a path beside the square's edge.

"So, again, tell me what's on your mind?"

Before his answer, 'jaw-dropping' had only been a cliché! Whatever happened to Robbie in Arizona should definitely be bottled! 'Courage' and 'Robbie James' had certainly never previously featured in the same sentence!

"You're actually telling me Nancy let you into the suite and then to your old office. Amazing! How on earth did you talk her into that?"

Robbie coloured.

"And faking a message from Finkelstein, copying Anson's recordings and bugging his office. I don't know whether you're totally crackers or a hero?"

"Go easy with the insults – I haven't finished yet. It seems that Nancy is kind of sweet on me. I feel a heel, but, you know, she's a little desperate and I know what that feels like."

"Don't beat yourself up."

"Since then, she's kept in contact. I've sort of seen her a few times, because, you know... I reckon I owe her."

"So, she's rather sweet on you. In a maternal way?"

Robbie's expression was hard to interpret.

"Don't give me that jive about gay or bi men often having complicated relationships with their mothers."

"No, I think she likes me in all sorts of ways. Anyway, I told her about the recording device concealed in Anson's office. Against all expectations, she downloaded the last two days' recordings, while Anson was out. Last evening, we ate together at Sardi's and she gave me the results. I've now had a listen."

"And?"

He whistled.

"Loads, but the biggest surprise came from Anson's meeting with that Klieberman guy. They also took a call from Tutch."

"What was said?"

"Look, there's a seat over there free. Let's sit a while."

"I'll throttle you if you don't hurry up and tell me."

We walked over to a seat facing the dog walkers. Two Alsatians decided to fight to the death and discussion was impossible in the yelping melee.

"Okay. Tutch was apparently calling from Colombia. From what I could put together, our old friend Zoltan is also down there – wait for it – hand in hand with your boss's mom!"

"With Judy?"

"Yes. Not only that. Something involving Zoltan and ex-paramilitary forces. It seems they grabbed Nina and then made off!"

"Shit! Nick will be beside himself. Was he mentioned?"

"Tutch said Nick Martin 'almost stumbled over the "operation"' – whatever that means. Finkelstein's down there, too, for some reason."

"You obviously had a lucky escape then."

"I don't think Anson would ever have sent me. I reckon the skids were under me for quite a while before I was actually axed! On my night in the office, I saw that Finkelstein had continued with some of the work I'd suggested."

"Which I assumed you planned to be substantially flawed?"

"Naturally! Presumably, Finkelstein will have other ideas."

"I bet he does – the creepy little squirt."

"The other fascinating snippet was a visit from that Woods guy at Camp Ute. My guts flipped just hearing his voice. If necessary, Marquetcom may be in line for a lucrative contract, soften up Joe Public for us taking an extended role in Colombia."

"What's the game? Did they elaborate?"

"Complicated. Resources figured, of course, but possibly a bigger military presence, to put the frighteners on next door, Venezuela!"

A large dalmatian broke from its owner and seemed obsessed at sniffing Robbie's leg. I held the insistent dog at arm's length, hooking fingers under its collar, until the owner arrived.

"Sorry, guys. Beautiful day, isn't it?"

His comment struck a chord. I looked around, seeing the mainly carefree faces of dog walkers, students and courting couples, envying their innocence – instead of all this nightmarish intrigue. Even the dealers trading on the edge of the square had it less complicated!

"Yes, it's beautiful. Your dog seems in good shape!"

The man and dog left, though it was difficult to know who was in charge. I reflected on what Robbie had said. In fact, this was probably dangerous information they shouldn't have. Information that could potentially lead to premature death! The scene before me suddenly took on a darker aura. Let's face it, an assassin posing as a phoney dealer or dog-walker could strike at any moment, here, or get us in the subway – especially with that tracking system. The man roller-blading over there could shoot point blank and skate away. When he turned, Robbie looked puzzled.

"What's up, man?"

"I was just thinking that we're actually very vulnerable."

Robbie nodded.

"Yes, but they don't know what arrangements we might have for the Richard Monroe material. Imagine a podcast released simultaneously to virtually every progressive site on the 'net! Actually, technically that wouldn't be so difficult!"

"They'll have already thought of it. I'm amazed if they couldn't somehow pull the internet, rather like the Burmese Junta did a while back."

"What, and disrupt e-commerce? Don't be silly, these guys worship money."

"Selectively filter keywords like the Chinese do?"

"Maybe. Listen, I haven't finished. The rest of the discussion between Woods, Anson and that Klieberman guy was really intriguing. They talked about 'Z'. I assume that means Zoltan. They said... 'Z will return in a couple of days and make a delivery to M to bring off the "big one"' – whatever that means. Actually, that should be very soon! Delivering to M is a puzzle. Somewhere prominent like the Met – maybe?"

"Isn't Corinne in contact with the people in Colombia? Might she know more?"

"Great minds, Si. I'm seeing her later today. Hey, you could come too." He grinned. "Though I might stay longer than you!"

"I get the picture! Listen, I really must tell Andy the news about his mom."

I punched in Andy's number. Moments later, an irritated voice answered, but the background noise made it difficult to hear.

"Sounds noisy. Where are you?"

"Just arrived at the station," came the strained voice. "Hold on a second. I'll go outside."

Andy's voice reappeared at full strength.

I passed him the news about Judy, but the line stayed quiet. When he eventually spoke, his voice sounded lifeless.

"Okay. I'll see you later tonight. Sorry, I just can't talk at the moment."

We quickly returned to the B&B and picked up the phones.

"I suppose I'd better get back," said Robbie, winking "Lot's to do and I must get spruced up for tonight."

"May see you over there."

I went back out into the square and wandered over to the fountain and then went over for a better look at the Garibaldi statue. A few minutes later, I felt the phone vibrating in my right pocket. Why, oh why, does the universe so love complications? It could only be one of those sick bastards. I nervously picked up and heard Klieberman's voice.

"I've missed our talks, Mr Maher. Please come to the suite at 5pm because I have something to discuss with you."

I could only agree, knowing refusal would be futile. Now I had the afternoon to kill. I returned to the B&B, picked up my little digital camera and made my way to mid-town, intending for a little sight-seeing before meeting Klieberman. I whiled away some time at Macy's and the nearby shopping plaza. Probably like most visitors, my eye kept being drawn to the graceful set-backs and spire of the Empire State building. I took shots from various angles. I hadn't yet visited the observation platform, though, so joined the queue and was disgorged moments later onto the eighty-sixth floor observatory. A crowd of mostly Japanese tourists milled around, seemingly more interested in photographing each other than the astounding views. Despite obtrusive anti-suicide barriers, the little camera coped well. The view extended to the north tip of Manhattan and beyond, though, disappointingly, the 102nd floor upper observatory was 'closed for security reasons'.

The descent was remarkably swift and I still had another twenty-five minutes before Klieberman's appointment. I crossed over to a hot-dog stand on the corner and, against my better judgement, decided to try one. Somehow, it seemed the day for touristy things. In fact, after Klieberman's appointment, I'd find the reopened Empire diner, and tick off another art-deco site. The vendor commented on my British accent while he dispensed a gut-defying squirt of mustard onto the obscene sausage. Over the road, a delivery van had pulled up and two men started to unload. I munched my prize, watching as they dragged trolleys of stationery to the trade entrance. A third man jumped from the back, dressed like his colleagues in light blue overalls. The lowering sun lit his face, causing the man to shade his eyes. I did a double-take and, even with mustard dribbling onto my shoe, I couldn't look away. Surely not! Undoubtedly, though, it was the figure and profile of Zoltan – now dressed as a delivery man. The figure appeared to squint across the street, and then set off for the hot-dog stand. I realised that the vendor was still holding out coins and repeating "your change". I mumbled, "Please keep it" and, with rising panic, quickly made for the nearest shop.

I'd entered a camera store and turned back to look from their front window. Zoltan, if indeed that was his figure, was buying a hot dog at the stand. That, in itself, seemed sufficiently out of character, but dressed in blue overalls as a delivery man for a stationery supplier?

I remembered the recording Robbie had heard. 'Zoltan would return for the "big one?"' I turned around to find an assistant looking enquiringly, so I purchased a new memory card and then returned to the entrance. 'Zoltan' still awaited his hot dog, so I held the camera to my face, framing imaginary shots. As a potential customer, this should seem fairly unremarkable behaviour. I hit the rocker on the zoom and Zoltan's face filled the screen – there was now little doubt! I clicked the shutter, and then repeated the action with the second delivery man. The third loaded a trolley and stubbornly refused to turn. After several shots, I toggled the controls back to wide angle, to show the whole of Zoltan in his overalls, wondering what Gill would make of this strange development.

Zoltan took his hot dog, crossed back over the street and then climbed into the driver's seat. I clicked again, noting the van's livery – Abbas Office Supplies.

I checked my watch, realising with a jolt that only six minutes remained until my appointment with Jack Klieberman. I moved further up the street and crossed, shielding my eyes from the low sun. On the other side, I turned towards the van and extended the zoom until the vehicle registration was clear, pressed the button and then set off at full stretch around the block.

I reasoned that Zoltan can't have contacted Klieberman or he wouldn't have risked me seeing the delivery – unless, of course, Klieberman also didn't know about it! I quickly walked on, when a familiar vibration came from my left pocket. What timing! I picked up to hear Andy's voice sounding even more stressed.

"I went over to Mom's and there's been a fire. That little shed at the back is completely destroyed!"

I made my most sympathetic response in the circumstances, and explained the imminent meeting.

"That must be terribly worrying, Andy, although it's difficult to do much right now. Poor Judy! We'll work something out when you get back. Call as soon as you arrive."

I circled the block. Wiping away a film of perspiration, I took the lift to Marquetcom's floor. As I entered, two men in light blue overalls exited the suite with large trolleys. One stopped at reception to ask for a signature.

"Thanks Abdul," said the girl. "See you next month."

I stood quarter profile, scratching my temple to conceal my face until I heard the doors close behind them. My mind flew into top gear. Zoltan, back from Colombia, Nina abducted, Judy's home burnt. Now Zoltan outside, dressed as a delivery man and a delivery had been made. I crossed to the desk. Everything was wrong. Every cell in my body screamed it – but what could I do?

"You're here to see Jack?"

I looked back to the smiling receptionist, dimly aware she'd asked the question for the second time and that I must present as being seriously distracted. I mustered my best smile.

"Sorry, I'm Simon Maher here to see Mr Klieberman and I'm four minutes late for our meeting."

She nodded.

"I know, please follow me."

My real impulse was to hail a cab and follow Zoltan. 'Bringing off the "big one",' Robbie had said. Zoltan was outside right now and, yet, I was wasting time with Klieberman.

I entered the office half expecting to see Anson's sneering face, but it was just the diminutive figure of Jack Klieberman. Thanks to Corinne, we now knew that Klieberman ran a long-established private investigation firm and had also added a security wing to his operation.

"Come in, Mr Maher. So glad you could join me."

I wanted to be sarcastic, but nothing clever came to mind.

"Finding people is your trade, isn't it?" I replied lamely.

"So, our researcher's done his homework – very good! I suppose you must miss 2a Bodleian Court?"

Hearing my address coming from the little New Yorker's mouth was another surprise I'd rather have done without.

"Maybe."

"And those chats with Professor Grotstein? How about adventures in Farrelly's high-security unit? Of course, that type of environment might well be a taste of your future – or not. I guess that depends on you! What kind of future would you like, Mr Maher?"

"Oh, I don't know – full plates and apple pie for everyone. World peace. Bent greedy sociopaths barred from public office – nothing too much!"

"Seeing you couldn't even keep a job in a shopping mall, how will our happy saviour achieve such miracles?"

Everything seemed to fall away. How could they know all this? Klieberman stood up, revealing a well-tailored suit.

"Let's get more comfortable."

He crossed to one of the well-filled leather chairs at the other end of the office. I sat opposite, reeling and willing myself to avoid looking at the cabinet where Robbie had secreted the recorder.

"So, your future, Mr Maher. We've been contacted by the 'Spin Watch' people. I suspect you might know who passed confidential and sensitive material, although that isn't entirely what I want to discuss."

"Why am I here?"

"Limited information was released within a very morally indignant article. While those people are a joke, it had an irritating effect, and caused some minor problems. In fact, Mr Anson is taking personal charge of neutralising it. The point is, that your work back in Oxford is finished. I'm sure you understand that. However, you're a good researcher and we'd like to offer you alternative employment here."

"You're joking! You think I'd work for a shark like Anson?"

"Hear me out. We're offering the opportunity to undertake paid research, exploring what you would term 'corporate malfeasance'. You'd have excellent resources and a generous salary."

"I don't get it. You're offering me paid work to expose corporate shits, even though we clearly put Anson and this outfit in that category?"

"Yes, but with an extra element. Your researches won't involve Mr Anson's interests, although the work can include competitors."

"Oh, I get it. Anson funds a phoney front organisation – some foundation or other with a slick name. I then get to do potentially useful work, but which Anson misuses to hurt competitors?"

Klieberman shook his head.

"Dear me. You really are a deeply cynical man, Mr Maher. This just makes good business sense. You continue with the work you believe is important, in the hub of things – here in New York. Surely, it's no surprise that you wouldn't directly work against your employer's interests. I'm afraid that's life. Think about it and do let's try to be realistic, shall we?"

The offer seemed so unexpected that I lacked any framework or reference point to understand it. Klieberman then opened up a photo album and turned it around to show me.

"Mr Anson keeps several apartments for the use of business associates and, occasionally, key members of staff."

I recognised the distinctive double towered Century apartment building on Central Park West. Klieberman slowly turned pages, showing interior shots of a luxurious apartment.

"Initially, you could stay here. It's very comfortable."

"Impressive too. Obviously, you know plenty about me, including my fondness for art deco and for Irwin Chanin's work. However, I'd expect you to also know that I don't compromise my values."

Klieberman shook his head and his sad expression almost seemed genuine.

"Values are an expensive commodity, Mr Maher. Sometimes fatally so! I'm not sure this generous offer is one you can afford to refuse."

"Neither can I accept its real cost. What about Andrew and Rob James?"

"I'll speak with them separately, soon, but we have something similar in mind. Mr Anson has excellent connections with the publishing industry."

"I'm not surprised, but the idea of Andrew working for him is absurd!"

"Families working together is good, Mr Maher. I've known Biff for years and, when Andrew was young, he always intended for him to enter the business. Anyway, given the college sponsorship, he's already partly working for Dad. Perhaps he hasn't quite realised or faced up to that."

Klieberman stood up abruptly.

"Anyway, please consider this offer carefully and the other things I said. We'll talk again soon."

I exited Marquetcom's suite and, within moments, was back on Fifth Avenue. I circled the block, but there was no van from Abbas Office Supplies and even the hot-dog vendor had gone. The streets were still busy and the tiny lights in the trees were turning on. My head felt full – Robbie's news, Andrew's discoveries in Philadelphia, and now even more complications, courtesy of Klieberman. I remembered that Andrew would soon return and need support. I stood trying to decide on the best course of action – hands fingering the cell phones in both pockets. Andy would call when ready, though who knew what delays might occur? Meanwhile, I should tell the others of the developments.

I hurried on, though now with something else on my mind. I passed the Rockefeller Centre, continuing up Fifth Avenue to Central Park South. Following the park's perimeter, I stopped to gaze at the unexpected new object of my imagination – the Century Apartments. I muttered to myself.

"You wouldn't sell out for a moment. Of course, this is tempting, but if the devil himself had an earthly address, it would probably be in New York City!"

These thoughts were probably predictable, but, nevertheless, as I continued up Fifth Avenue, I periodically turned to gaze at the Century

Apartments building, as I counted down the streets to Corinne's apartment.

It was just opposite the zoo that I first realised something strange was afoot. Police vans arrived and several large white trucks pulled up beside the park. Odd figures emerged wearing what almost looked like white spacesuits. Others wheeled a large box down a ramp and onto the ground. I stood trying to make sense of the scene against the scream of approaching sirens. Turning, I saw fire appliances, police motorcycles and more trucks sweep around East Sixty-Third Street. I turned back and a scowling figure in a 'Robocop' uniform advanced in my direction. The cop gesticulated for me to go.

"Leave now," he shouted.

"Why? I'm just going as far as the Frick collection, and then crossing to Lexington Ave."

"Anti-terrorist exercises will happen here, today and tomorrow. Just do what you're instructed!"

"What's with the spacemen?"

"Anti-radiation suits. Leave the Park area now. You could turn down East Sixty-Fourth Street and walk over to Lexington."

"Why can't...?"

"No, right now. Move it!"

I turned at Sixty-Fourth as another convoy of police and fire vehicles, all lights and blaring sirens, swept by and turned into Fifth Avenue. About ten minutes later, I reached Nina and Corinne's building and held the button down until Corinne answered.

"Hang on – someone's coming."

The door opened and it was Gill. We hugged and kissed.

"You'll never guess what I've just seen."

"Tell us upstairs. First though," she dangled a small key, "we're leaving the darned phones from Tutch – in the downstairs mailbox for an hour or so."

My phone joined the others in the box.

"Robbie contacted earlier and said you were coming over, so I came straight from the office. Things are frantic down there. I'll tell you about it upstairs."

"Look, I really wanted to see you, too, but I can only stay a while until Andy gets back. He's having a crisis"

We went upstairs and Corinne opened the door. Robbie held up a glass of wine and waved.

"I just saw something really weird by the park," I announced.

"Yeah, that often happens to me," said Corinne, raising her eyebrows and grinning. "You wouldn't believe half of the weird things I see!"

I started describing the scene by the park, but Gill interrupted.

"That's what I tried to tell you downstairs. Things have been completely frantic today because a full-scale anti-terrorism drill is happening in multiple locations, over the next two days. All the emergency and security services are included, radiation detection equipment – the whole works. To ensure a convincing exercise, no warnings were given."

"Whereabouts?" asked Robbie.

"Probably over most of Manhattan, though I haven't seen the actual plan."

"That wasn't the only unexpected thing I saw today," I said.

Everyone looked up expectantly.

"Klieberman called me in for a meeting late this afternoon. What he said was quite a surprise – though not half as much as what I saw, beforehand!"

"Tell us!" said Corinne.

I described seeing the overall-clad Zoltan.

"Gave me quite a turn. Remember the evening we all rushed him in the mountains? I keep thinking, Robbie, about what you heard on that recording, 'Zoltan's coming back for the "big one"'."

Robbie nodded.

"Exactly. Today would be his first day back, so why drive around in a delivery van?"

"Brian gets back soon," said Corinne. "So, I should hear more about what happened down there. Maybe he…"

"Oh no," said Gill, cutting across in a chilling tone.

She paled, and stared at the ceiling, as if in private torment.

"What is it?" asked three people simultaneously.

Gill shook her head, a grimace distorting her usually attractive face.

"What have we noticed several times about these exercises? 'Zoltan's coming back for the "big one"'. Perhaps what we should be asking is 'why would he come now?'"

Her meaning dawned on the others.

"You mean the exercises might be cover for an operation?" I asked. "We already know that Zoltan isn't who he seems to be."

She nodded.

"Exactly! Were you able to identify the delivery van?"

"I can do better," I replied, pulling the little camera from my jacket. "I was going to show you this anyway, but, look, this shows the company name and phone number on the van."

"You say that boxes of stationery supplies went up to Marquetcom's suite?" checked Robbie. "I don't get it. If Marquetcom fronts for the rogue group, surely they wouldn't want dangerous stuff on their premises?"

Gill was already speaking softly into her cell phone: "Meet me in about half an hour."

She looked up.

"I've just spoken with my friendly colleague. We're going meet at the office to try and find out more about Abbas Office supplies. Much as we hate Marquetcom, Anson and everything they stand for – they might actually be in real danger. If a spectacular is planned, they'll probably wait for daylight for maximum effect, so we've little time."

A familiar vibration came from my left pocket and I fished out my personal phone.

Andrew's voice sounded reproachful.

"I'm back and thought that you'd be waiting. We must talk. Things are hotting up and I'm worried Mom may be in danger."

"I'll be back in about a half hour," I replied. "Stay there."

Gill was already moving towards the door.

"That was Andrew," I explained. "He's back from Philly and worried about Judy. Our news won't exactly help. I haven't told you yet about the crazy job offers from Klieberman!"

"Klieberman? Jobs? What was that about?" asked Robbie, but I was already leaving.

"I'll explain next time. Must get the phone and then return to help Andy. I'll call you soon."

110

COLOMBIA

NICK MARTIN

Luis drove with Elsa beside him, and I sat with Gustavo in the back. He swung right at the next road, and headed to the airstrip. Even under headlights, the vegetation looked incredibly dense and the thought of battling through on foot made me shiver.

Eventually, I saw the outline of the little airport's tin shed and, moments later, we pulled up by the perimeter. A small plane stood on the strip. Luis turned, grinning.

"Got your 'chute? Come on, let's get you ready."

I picked up the pack, and my stomach lurched, as if the future plummet through the air had already started.

"Don't worry, Señor," said Gustavo, baring his teeth. "It really isn't so bad."

Luis helped to put my 'chute on, pulling at the straps before circling around Elsa and Gustavo to check their fastenings.

"Let's go."

The plane jolted down the primitive runway into the dark, gathering speed. The vegetation rushed closer and closer. I already knew the valley was tight, but, with no perspective in the dark, the damned plane seemed almost glued to the ground. I braced for impact, with my hands contracting into fists, but, at the last moment, the little plane miraculously lifted clear of the trees, and climbed into the inky sky. My stomach felt as if back on the ground as I quietly battled nausea. The others jabbered away in Spanish.

We climbed higher, clearing the mountains, and then Luis banked hard. Below, everything seemed dark except for occasional lights from small plantations. On the horizon, a smear of lights marked the edge of Juno. We flew on for another few minutes until pinpricks of light developed into the outline of Chamaico. The wing dipped and Luis flew parallel to the edge of the town before climbing again. Luis said something, and Gustavo and Elsa stood up.

"Jumping in about two minutes," called Luis.

"Where?"

"When we flew from Bogotá, you asked about flora and fauna," answered Luis with a grin. "Now you can take a closer look!"

"We're jumping out into the jungle?"

"Don't worry. We know the general direction."

I touched the holstered revolver at my side, unsure whether to be comforted or alarmed. I'd never carried a weapon before, but Luis was insistent. As if in warning, my mind unhelpfully reeled through jumbled shootings – probably images reassembled from newsreels. I'd only use it as a last resort if my life was threatened.

Gustavo opened the door and beckoned. As I felt the rush of air, a panic seized me and my legs wouldn't respond. Elsa looked over and smiled. I fought my paralysis, and took the slowest possible walk to the door. Luis yelled and pointed to his watch. Gustavo shouted instructions again and held out his hand. At that moment, Elsa jumped and I watched her body wrenched sideways by the wind and disappear into the blackness. Gustavo pointed to the wheel, then my feet, and grabbed my hand. The meaning was only too clear – I should stand on the wheel mounting and jump from there. I edged my way out, with a racing heart and the rush of air on my face. Gustavo's grip seemed firm, but, no sooner had I balanced on the wheel mounting, than Gustavo let go, and the rushing air forced me from the wheel to plummet into the night sky.

I touched down with a jolt, grateful that the night was windless. The target clearing wasn't large. Gustavo was already down and, as I turned around, the shapely, but lighter, form of Elsa floated down just a few yards away. We detached from our harnesses, and bundled the 'chutes up and hid them under brush at the clearing's edge.

"Come," said Gustavo, pointing. "There's a small road over there."

'Small' was an understatement. It was more of a track, but at least it gave us passage through the thick undergrowth. The others set off at a pace, leaving me lagging. As they jabbered, I noticed Elsa's small backpack and, remembering her previous actions, wondered about its contents.

We progressed down the track with the jungle coming close on each side. I was uncertain of the fauna, but was certain it would be different from New York City's! Already, I heard unfamiliar sounds coming from several directions. The guidebook had mentioned pumas, jaguars and boa-constrictors, so I picked up speed.

We walked for at least two hours, and then joined a small road. Gustavo turned around, raising a finger to his mouth.

"We must be quiet. Their camp is about two kilometres further down here."

I touched the metal lump near my thigh.

"What's the plan? I don't want to shoot anyone."

"Wait," said Gustavo. "You'll see."

Elsa had disappeared behind a tree and, when she reappeared, I could hardly believe my eyes. She was now wearing a skirt finishing far too close to her crotch and shiny leather boots. Her top was a low-cut blouse and shapely breasts spilled out of a push-up bra. I must have appeared dumbstruck because she grinned and, with her boots together, gave a little shimmy. There wasn't a straight man on earth who wouldn't have reacted.

"What the...!"

"Their camp is different to ours," said Gustavo. "No discipline."

About fifteen minutes later, we heard a vehicle coming from behind and Gustavo led us back into the vegetation. A high squeal of excited girls came from a people carrier and, as the vehicle passed, I saw the headlights illuminate clouds of butterflies or, more probably, moths. We pressed on, keeping just inside the undergrowth and saw a gentle glow ahead. Eventually, we reached a particularly huge tree, probably some kind of fig, and rested against it. This was growing close to the camp's entrance. Gustavo took his backpack off and started fitting together some kind of automatic weapon, previously carried in sections, and slung it over his back with a strap. I peered at the camp entrance, with the sound of laughing voices coming from behind the trees. Several women dressed like Elsa loitered outside and I watched men from the camp approach and then escort them inside. Suddenly, the plan became clear. There was a spirited discussion between the others and Elsa hitched up her skirt to show Gustavo a concealed knife, not to mention some shapely legs and unexpectedly exotic underwear. The fact that I fanned my face was quite involuntary, but she creased up with silent mirth, rather belying our situation!

"Elsa will find her way in," said Gustavo. "We'll make our way around the perimeter and hopefully meet up later."

Elsa embraced Gustavo in a decidedly non-sisterly way – unless that impression was just due to her clothing. She picked up her small bag after dropping a small pistol inside, and edged onto the road. Moments later, she stood outside the camp, leg forward and skirt perilously high in the classic pose of a night worker. After about three minutes, a man approached. They had a short discussion and she disappeared inside, holding his arm.

"She's brave," I said to Gustavo. "Naturally, I want to rescue Nina, but I also want Elsa safe."

He shrugged.

"Elsa is a survivor, but Nina's activities potentially benefit the continent."

After Elsa left, they slowly circled around the camp.

"What is this place?" I asked. "A military camp or the other lot?"

"Remnants of ex-paramilitaries," Gustavo replied. "Supposed to be disbanded, but some remain in business. Remember that damaged oil line? We suspect they now take the corporate dollar... vicious bastards!"

"I believe something like that happened in Nigeria," I replied.

Gustavo shrugged, and then went over to the fence and, with a pair of snips from his bag, cut a vertical slash to about three feet from the ground. The fence was a low-tech structure with no signs of alarm and seemed more suitable for dissuading animals than much else. Across the site, light glowed from several groups of tents and a few low structures that, in many ways, looked similar to our own encampment. We moved further around the perimeter and saw a man emerge from one of the buildings with a woman and walk to the far side. The light was poor, but, as she lay on the ground and pulled up her skirt, there wasn't much doubt about what was about to happen.

Gustavo pulled the cell phone from his pocket.

"Vibrating phones are a wonderful invention," he said with a wink. "Come quickly – we'll go opposite them."

He pointed to the couple on the ground and then, keeping low and behind the tree-line, we made our way around to the couple engaging in alfresco delight. I couldn't help thinking that a spot of unhealthy voyeurism seemed superfluous, and was unsure of Gustavo's plan.

"Look, it's Elsa," Gustavo whispered, pointing to the figures. He crawled over to the fence and snipped a new exit.

We could hear grunting, which, even at this distance, soon changed to an unmistakeable rhythm. I felt really awkward. It didn't seem quite decent...

The grunting changed to a gasp, and then a whimper. Abruptly, one of the bodies went limp and fell to the ground. Elsa, crouching low and mainly in shadow, ran to the fence, near to our hiding place. Gustavo moved to join her. The two Colombians whispered fiercely, while I kept my attention on the camp grounds. The paramilitaries seemed quite occupied by the 'joy division' whoring, although most of the action seemed under roof or canvas. Elsa passed her knife to Gustavo and he cleaned it on a nearby bush, and returned it. Even in the low light, he saw her quickly raise her skirt, and replace the knife in a sheath cleverly attached to a garter belt.

"Wait here," Gustavo hissed to me and, without further word, crawled through the slit made in the wire.

I lay flat on my stomach, keeping watch. Elsa had turned left, moving towards a small building opposite the first hole we'd snipped. Gustavo kept low and moved towards the body. On the other side of the camp, a sweep of light came from approaching headlamps and I realised we were now virtually opposite the camp's main entrance. For a moment, light filtered around a building, casting a brief illumination on the ground where Gustavo lay. Almost as abruptly, the light shut off and I heard the vehicle's door slam. Gustavo was up again and, reaching the body, hunched over it for a moment and then began dragging it back. He was panting by the time he reached the fence. He put the man face down by the slit, and started to push.

"Grab his arms," he hissed.

I fastened my hands onto sweaty arms, tugging at the body through the opening like some sort of crazed obstetrician. Eventually, it passed through and I could see a dark stain and a tear in the shirt that oozed blood. Gustavo followed the body through the fence and then, together, we dragged it into the undergrowth.

"We'll return to the other hole," said Gustavo.

"What's the plan?"

"Her new 'boyfriend' told Elsa where Nina was being kept," he replied with a wink and pointed to a small building, which Elsa was now nearing.

We made our way back to the other hole and I recognised the outline of a large tree. A noise came from further down. One of the ex-paramilitaries advanced in our direction, following the fence-line. He appeared relaxed and had his rifle slung across his back. He lit a cigarette and the glow briefly illuminated his face. We pushed back into the bushes as he got closer and passed beyond the small building. I feared the man would see Elsa lurking in the shadows and, for one gut-clenching moment, expected to see another killing. The man continued, and eventually passed us as he continued his casual patrol of the perimeter.

Gustavo touched my arm and pointed forward. Crouching low, we continued moving around the fence-line to get closer to the building that held Nina. We reached the point where the fence had originally been breached and waited in the bushes. After about five minutes, two female figures rounded the small building, advancing in our direction. Half way, one figure suddenly doubled back to the building again. The other figure continued, finally reaching the fence. It was Nina, who was now also dressed like a whore, a beautiful angelic whore and the most desirable vision I'd ever seen! At that moment, a shot rang out, followed by shouting, and Elsa came running around the building.

Gustavo held the wire open as Nina started to crawl through.

"Quick, take over," hissed Gustavo.

A light played across the ground by the side of the building.

I ripped wide the wire and was face-to-face with Nina.

"Elsa went back for my bag," she said. "She brought these clothes so that I'd fit in. Please don't say...!"

From the corner of my eye, I saw Gustavo pull out something. He bowled like a cricketer, but the subsequent explosion showed it was no ball. Lights came on all over the camp and Elsa could be seen clearly running the wrong way and heading for the main gate. Gustavo hurled another grenade in the opposite direction and, after this explosion, people appeared all over the campsite.

"Get under cover," said Gustavo. At that moment, a shot took down Elsa, who crumpled face down and didn't move. They retreated into the bushes and, when I looked again, two figures were standing over her body.

"Come on, we must leave," said Gustavo. "There's nothing we can do."

Even in the limited light, I thought that I detected a tear in the guerrilla's eye. I followed, hand in hand with Nina.

"Do you think they know where we are?" I called breathlessly.

"Elsa's bravery, running towards the gate, might have confused them, but don't rely on it."

The undergrowth got thicker as we doubled around to the north of the camp. My face stung from branches, pushing through a particularly dense pocket. We forded a small stream, scrambled up the bank and found ourselves on the edge of a small road. Gustavo reached into his bag, pulled out a small torch and shone the light in both directions. Almost immediately, a motor started.

I peered into the darkness as a vehicle reversed towards us. As it pulled level, I recognised two faces from our camp.

Gustavo opened the rear door and we jumped in. It moved off even before the door had fully closed, and Nina and Gustavo gabbled something in very fast Spanish. About six or seven kilometres further on, we came to a couple of low tin sheds. Beyond were three small planes and, on the edge of the strip, two helicopters. A gate was already open, so we drew up beside the larger of the buildings. A dozen or so men emerged and I made a rather odd braying sound, as the warning caught in my throat.

"They're ours," said Gustavo.

Nina leaned over and we kissed – the first opportunity since the breakout.

We crossed to the main building, and discovered the gruesome sight of two bodies and a mess of blood from their cut throats. My stomach understood almost before my mind and I turned away and started heaving. Nina squeezed my hand and gently stroked my back, until the nausea passed.

A plane engine started and Gustavo said something to Nina. We walked over to the Cessna and saw Luis waiving from the pilot's seat.

"I have to go," said Nina. "Farewell for now my love. I'll be in touch soon."

My stomach dropped, and I struggled to catch my breath.

"Going where?" I asked. "Can't I come?"

"You stay," replied Gustavo. "Miguel says you're needed back in Bogotá."

Nina leaned forward and threw her arms around me. Her lips were near my ear when she whispered.

"Luis will fly me to Bolivia. I'm going to stay with Richard Monroe's daughter and son-in-law near La Paz, until things quieten down."

We kissed, and then she climbed into the Cessna.

The plane taxied off and I followed Gustavo back across the strip, seeing Arm-Rite logos on the other aircraft. As we drove away, simultaneous explosions detonated and the sky was lit from the pyre of Arm-Rite equipment, disintegrating in fire.

111

MANHATTAN

GILL'S PERSPECTIVE

Gill slept extremely badly following yesterday's discoveries. She arrived early at the operations room to rendezvous with Michelle. Thankfully, it was empty, because their attempts last night had been disastrous. Unexpectedly, a special team had commandeered the room in order to review recordings of the exercise and check for any problems with the surveillance equipment. The team were tasked to make improvements and anticipated that this would take most of the night!

The flickering of the ethernet signalled the usual incoming information, but today Gill had her own material to input. Michelle also looked drawn and even her usually vibrant auburn hair appeared lifeless.

"Is anyone else here?"

Michelle shook her head.

"I put in a brief appearance on the street. Most staff are tied up with the exercise or coping with a civil liberties bunch demonstrating on Fifth Avenue. Of course, we should be with them, doing image capture."

"Funny you saying that, because that's just what I intend right now," she replied, taking out Simon's Olympus compact from her bag. She searched until finding Zoltan's image.

She described yesterday's sighting and pictures to Michelle.

"Corinne might have mentioned this character, who seems to keep popping up. A real enigma," she continued. "We can't imagine why the sudden deliveries to Marquetcom's office. We believe he has connections to the rogue element, but..."

"Gill, don't patronise me," Michelle snapped.

"I'm just trying to explain..."

"Isn't having a rotten group embedded in our service a disaster enough? If we're to have any hope of stopping them, we have to be honest with each other. I know that Corinne told you exactly who he is... or, more accurately, what he is. The problem with a mind-controlled operative is that only their controller knows which is the active part and its mission!"

"Sorry, Michelle. Until recently, I didn't know that such a thing really existed, outside of Hollywood. Okay, I agree and I need your help. Total honesty it is!"

She fiddled with the Olympus's controls, bringing up images of Zoltan and one of the other delivery men.

"As a start, I'd like to input these images to the facial recognition system. Would that be traceable to us?"

"I don't think so," replied Michelle. "Let's get them downloaded onto a workstation."

Images of Zoltan and his colleagues appeared on the monitor and Michelle set to work, enlarging, cropping and adjusting balance and contrast. She clicked the mouse again and the image became criss-crossed with multiple lines, and slowly rotated as the programme made a multitude of calculations.

"That should do it."

Gill had another idea.

"Could we access yesterday's recordings from the transit system and then retrospectively scan for these characters – just in case? That statement, 'Zoltan's coming back for the "big one"', is really bugging me."

"Possibly. Let's try."

Michelle played around and another image of Zoltan appeared on the monitor. Yesterday's date was showing on the information bar at the top of the screen. The location – the 116th Street/Colombia University subway station.

"Amazing, but rather spooky. I wonder why he's there?"

"Kind of depends on what 'the big one' means," replied Michelle. "Maybe scouting for a target?"

"What else is near? The university, of course, but does anything else obviously come to mind?"

Michelle looked puzzled.

"I'm a native New Yorker, but don't often get up that way. Let's think. Other than Columbia University, there's the Cathedral of St John the Divine, Riverside Church and a National Monument called Grant's Tomb."

"Nothing that immediately makes much sense," said Gill, "unless an attack on Columbia University sends a message. I don't know, protesting US involvement in Colombia?"

"Nah, that's a different spelling for a start," said Michelle. "Although, Columbia certainly educates some of our brightest and best. Nothing involving those churches either – unless they're somehow deliberately pushing the Islamic line?"

Michelle pursed her lips.

"I'll tell you what, though. The recognition system is being extended from just covering the transport system by installing security-cams at additional sites. It will work anywhere the new cameras are installed. It's still a work in progress, but let's give it try."

Michelle entered some additional commands. Within seconds, Zoltan's face appeared on the screen, against a background of highly polished marble. The information bar showed yesterday's date and the location – Grant's Tomb.

"What the... where the heck is that?"

"Not far from the University," replied Michelle.

"Would staging a spectacular at Grant's Tomb send any particular message?"

Michelle bit her lip, and slowly shook her head.

"Dunno. Not really. Grant was a civil war general who later became President. Unless they're signalling that our current divisions could eventually drive a wedge, even another civil war? There are times our red versus blue states or the conservative versus liberal situation are like squabbling between two different tribes."

"Sounds fairly abstruse... I can't imagine many people leaping to that interpretation. Bankers, plutocrats and corporations versus everyone else – more like it! Listen, Michelle, can you bring that van up on the screen?"

Michelle gave the software a further command. A second man was standing beside the van, so she cropped, enlarged, and entered his image.

"I wonder what they were really up to yesterday? I can't see Zoltan ferrying copy paper and toner cartridges around. Can you bring it closer?"

She brought up the details from the van's livery and then sensed something was wrong. Michelle had turned pale.

"What is it?"

"I happen to know that those people have the contract for our office supplies. Actually, we had a recent delivery!"

Michelle switched to another database and took down the details of Abbas Stationery – a business address in Brooklyn – and the owner's name – Abdullah Bim Ami. Within moments, she had his private address.

"The deliveries must have come from their stores. We should get over there to check it out," said Gill.

"If Zoltan plans planting something, that could be where it is, or was, stored."

Michelle nodded. "But the deliveries to our office? Tutch must know about it if he's with them. What's he playing at?"

"Where are your supplies kept?" asked Gill.

"On the floor above. Our office manager, Virginia, is an anal-retentive type. To get a new pen or notebook, we virtually have to jump through hoops of flaming fire. I think I should go up and check later. All the field staff, even Tom Freison, are on the exercise so there's no sense in panicking yet."

"I'll leave that one to you. I think I should get over to Brooklyn right now, and take Corrine and Robbie. Let's go live now, in case Zoltan's currently on the transit system."

A flagged person appeared almost instantly, at City Hall subway station. When Michelle panned back on the security cameras, though, they both caught their breath. Zoltan was in a wheelchair! Could the person pushing him be the other delivery man in the image entered earlier, but now with a beard? If so, the recognition system hadn't identified or flagged him! Michelle took manual control of the camera as the duo moved onto the platform for Brooklyn-bound trains.

She grabbed her cell phone and called Corinne.

"We must meet right away, there's an emergency. Have you seen our honorary Navajo?"

"He's with me now."

"Can we meet at the Thirty-Third Street subway, by the ticket office. Is 15 minutes enough? We have to get over to Brooklyn immediately!"

"Can do. See you then."

She turned back. Michelle was still manually controlling the camera and they watched the bearded man push the wheelchair onto a Brooklyn-bound train.

"I'm leaving right now. Keep in touch with any developments."

The others arrived at the subway and, once safely onto an R-line train, she filled them in on the last hour.

"This business of Abdullah's is near the Prospect Avenue station and his private home is a couple of streets behind the store."

They arrived at the Prospect Avenue stop, and set off for the store.

"Seen any more of Nancy, Robbie? Any more recordings?"

Corinne was holding Robbie's hand and answered for him.

"The opera, tonight!"

"Das Wunder der Heliane, by Erich Korngold," said Robbie, looking pleased. "She deserves something nice and, with some luck, might have another recording!"

Gill checked the map.

"The next left, but perhaps we ought to approach separately."

"Good idea," said Robbie. "I'll continue on the road parallel to this and then circle around from the other direction."

"I'll go ahead," said Corinne. "They don't know me, so, if they appear, I'll warn you on my cell phone."

The group separated, Robbie continuing straight on, while she turned left and Corinne walked further ahead. After the next bend, the store should be found on the left.

A car slowly drove by and her heart raced. The driver looked slightly familiar. Was he the second delivery person in Simon's photo? She tried recreating the image in her mind. It was possible, though she wasn't really sure. The phone in her pocket vibrated and Robbie's voice came through clear and strong.

"They both just left the store. It was Abdullah, who took a car heading your way – in fact, he probably just passed you. Zoltan continued on foot. I'll have to follow him. There's really no choice..."

112

BROOKLYN

ROBBIE JAMES

I kept well back, even though Zoltan set off at quite a pace. Apart from the Brooklyn Museum and the occasional trek to Coney Island, I didn't know much about the borough. I returned the cell phone to my pocket, not knowing where this would lead, but prepared to follow!

Zoltan walked to the waterside and looked out over the water back towards Manhattan. He abruptly moved inland, passing through something of an industrial wasteland, and I tried to follow unobtrusively. Eventually, we reached a green wooded area and Zoltan quickly ducked into an impressive gateway and seemed to disappear. I picked up speed, reaching what I at first imagined was a park, until seeing the sign *Greenwood Cemetery*. At the gate, an official conversed with an older couple. As I approached the gate, the man disappeared inside, so I smiled, quickly pushed past and rapidly moved to a clump of trees. I looked out and saw Zoltan walking ahead purposefully. The grounds were particularly beautiful, paying testimony to our fascination with death. I followed along carefully as Zoltan progressed through a landscaped park, passing mausoleums and statues, and I wondered why the dead got an environment denied to most of the living.

Zoltan briefly paused, so I sheltered behind a distinctive statue of an angel that had a single finger pointing skywards. Zoltan climbed a hillock, apparently called Battle Hill, and stood on a ridge looking over New York Harbour. He seemed to spend time contemplating and then moved off again, taking a different path down, making it even more difficult to keep up.

At the bottom of the hill were many more mausoleums. Surprisingly, he stopped outside a large structure with bronze doors, and then abruptly entered. About five minutes later, he emerged, wearing a black backpack, and secured the door behind him. After he'd rounded the next corner, I returned to the building. A small brass plate stated; *The Langley Family*, but there was nothing else that explained the strange development. I removed my lightweight jacket, pulled it inside out and rolled it into a hand-held bundle, cursing that I was so exposed. A nearby sign drew attention to historically important civil war graves, but, with no time to investigate, I hurried on.

Ahead, Zoltan rounded a small lake, and unexpectedly paused by a headstone set under a graceful ash. He slipped off the backpack and sat to one side, appearing to gaze at the headstone. At first, he was cross-legged, but later crumpled, hugging his legs and staying still for several minutes. The posture evoked a sense of sadness and I could only conjecture at his experience. He then seemed to touch the ground with his forehead and, although I couldn't be sure from here, I sensed there was a controlled sobbing. Eventually, Zoltan stood up, reattached his backpack and set off, slowly at first, and then purposefully striding towards the main entrance. This action seemed too significant to ignore, so I abandoned caution and quickly ran to a nearby grove while Zoltan continued on to the exit, without a backward glance. I watched his backpack disappear through the gate, and jumped over a flower bed and ran back to the headstone. A name, Colonel Wilhelm Gunther, was carved into it, plus a German inscription and verse, under a Maltese Cross. I wrote the name and verse on a scrap of paper, before running to the gateway and exiting the cemetery.

The figure with a backpack was briskly walking ahead, so I crossed the road and followed behind. We were soon back in civilisation. I called Gill, but her phone was off, so I tried Corinne, but couldn't connect with her either. Ahead, I saw Zoltan enter the Twenty-Fifth Street Subway, and once again had little choice other than to follow.

I entered the carriage behind Zoltan's, where I could observe passengers leave, and started the nerve-wracking return to Manhattan. When we arrived at the City Hall station, Zoltan abruptly left. I followed, jumping out as the train was about to move, to the considerable disapproval of fellow travellers. I kept my eyes fixed on the black backpack as Zoltan exited the subway, and then circled around the park, looking up to the Woolworth building and then to City Hall, like any normal tourist. At one point, he took out his cell phone and entered a number, though he didn't appear to speak. He left the park, crossed Broadway and then rapidly walked further on to the Chambers Street-Church Street subway station and joined another train. I could only enter the carriage behind, wondering where and when this unexpected tour of the New York subway system would finish!

The carriages here were more crowded, although this thinned out as we moved further up the island. I stayed by the door, recalling that classic scene from the movie *The French Connection*, wondering if fancy footwork would also leave me stranded, watching Zoltan wave from a departing train. Surely, after all this time, he must have noticed?

We eventually arrived at 190th Street subway, near the northern tip of Manhattan. This time, Zoltan alighted, ran over to the elevator and disappeared. I waited for the next lift, remembering that I'd once come here to visit Fort Tryon Park and 'The Cloisters' – the medieval art museum. The next elevator arrived, and I found myself stuck with several family groups, heading to the museum.

"...it was quite an explosion," I heard the man in front say.

"Yeah, just back from Sixth Avenue, behind the Rockefeller complex. Smoke drifted right over the East River."

Another adult queried something, but I couldn't make it out.

"Apparently, they don't know if it was a gas leak or something else. Anyway, we've waited a long time for this outing, haven't we, Deanna?"

We reached the surface. I caught sight of the backpack ahead and skirted around the museum group, to follow it through the park. I stopped behind a tree to send a brief text to Gill: *1.55pm – still following. Just arrived at Fort Tryon Park.*

Zoltan seemed to have a gift for picking picturesque spots and the view over the Hudson to the New Jersey Palisades was no exception. A visit to the nearby museum would make a welcome respite now, but, alas, that wasn't my choice to make. Instead, Zoltan made for a ridge overlooking the river, and stood still looking towards the George Washington Bridge. I felt completely out of my comfort zone. *What if I was spotted? What was the backpack about? Why...?*

I wasn't concentrating properly and stumbled over a loose rock. I fell heavily, twisting my shoulder and grazing my hand. I rubbed my ankle, and then slowly moved my shoulder. The muscles were already in spasm, as I slowly stood. I was shaken by the fall, but stumbled forward. Adrenalin acted faster than any conscious realisation that Zoltan and backpack were gone. Suddenly, someone kicked my feet and I collapsed into a jumbled heap of pain and started sliding down the bank. I reflexively closed my eyes and, with a momentary sense of *deja vu*, heard boots thundering after me. I crashed into a tree, as dirt from the pursuing boots sprayed my face and a hand fastened on my neck like a crab's claw.

"Another little tumble," hissed Zoltan. "After Utah, you ought to be a little more careful. I saw your attempts at trailing me within half a block. You were so amateurish in the cemetery, perhaps you need another visit."

I looked up. My vision had become grainy, though it was sufficient to see that the backpack was missing. I opened my mouth to speak, but the hand squeezed and something pressed at my neck.

I slipped from consciousness, thinking... *carotid artery!*

113

COLOMBIAN JUNGLE & BOGOTÁ

NICK MARTIN

I felt absolutely possessed by the memory of Nina waving goodbye. Parted again, so soon, hardly seemed possible. Although I now knew Gustavo had good English, we returned to the camp in silence. The combination of Nina leaving and the awful sight of the bodies extinguished any wish to chat. After arriving, Gustavo was approached by Emilio, one of the senior ranks. As usual, they talked in Spanish, but even someone deaf and blind would have realised something was afoot. After Emilio left, Gustavo told me word had come from Miguel in Bogotá. He said, "You and Judy must return to Bogata immediately."

We departed, flying through the night, and landed at a small strip somewhere outside the city. Miguel waited and then drove us back to the hotel in town. He seemed tense, but didn't offer an explanation.

"What is the rush, Miguel?" Not that I hadn't had my fill of jungle life.

"We'll take a quick detour and I'll show you."

"Could I get out at the hotel?" asked Judy. "Maybe I'm showing my age, but I'm all in."

"Sure, Señora. I'll let you out and continue on with the Señor. We shouldn't be long."

Miguel treated us almost as a couple, triggering more erotic thoughts that I immediately regretted. We drove through deserted streets until eventually I recognised the Avenida where the office was located. Moments later, we pulled up outside the blackened remains.

"Shit, what the hell happened here?"

Miguel looked as shamefaced as someone of his ilk could manage.

"The equipment worked well, Nick – too well as it happened! In the first 'broadcasts', we heard about proposed future price hikes."

"How did that lead to this, though?" I asked, nodding at the destruction.

"I'm sorry, Señor, but I told someone in our circle, whom I thought could be trusted. They let word slip, the rumour quickly spread, and… and this was the result. Probably only Nina could have calmed things, but she wasn't here."

"Where's the van and receiving equipment," I asked, sounding professional, even to myself.

"Somewhere way outside of town and remote", replied Miguel. "It won't be found."

"What about the IT equipment, and its 'extras'?"

"Just look at it," he replied.

"It looks like little survived, though I'll check in the morning. What action have the authorities taken?"

"The police tried breaking the demo up, but the fire had started and took hold before the fire service could arrive. A couple were arrested, but no wider investigation seems under way. The cause appears quite obvious – arson by an angry crowd."

"Check again in the light and, if necessary, remove anything incriminating, in case of further investigations. I'll have to report what happened to our office in New York, when it opens in the morning."

"Of course."

We drove back and arranged to meet in the morning. I entered the hotel and spoke to a sleepy female member of the night staff.

"I'm Nick Martin. Have you my key?"

She looked at the book and spoke without looking up.

"You'll find Mrs Martin in room 322. She said to say sorry, but she just couldn't wait up. Take the second key."

Surely, she hadn't! My mind whirled, though quickly re-anchored around the memory of Nina waving from the plane. That relationship was far too precious and I couldn't slip again!

"Actually, Mrs Martin had a very exhausting day, so I won't disturb her. Can I take another room?"

Nothing was said about the matter over breakfast. Heaven knows I'd often masked stress and loneliness – by mindlessly clinging to another's body. At least I still had Nina, whereas, for Judy, Zoltan really was a lost cause. I explained about the fire and then returned to the room to phone Tom Phelan, who agreed to update Dan. He encouraged me to return at the earliest opportunity.

Miguel arrived and we left together for the site. Although I'd long wanted the project to be derailed, I'd never expected this. Almost everything was burnt or mangled. Virtually nothing combustible remained and most pieces of kit were unidentifiable.

"Apparently, burnt electronics can be toxic," I said to Miguel with a wink. "I'll arrange through Sergio Fontibon to have the site professionally cleaned."

Six hours later, I settled my tired body into the seat and the thrust of jet engines propelled us down the runway for the haul back to New York City.

Judy's fingers briefly touched the back of my hand before she spoke.

"Thanks for looking out for me. Sometimes, I just get too emotional!"

114

MANHATTAN

BIFF ANSON'S PERSPECTIVE

Biff welcomed the others to his office. It was unusual for the 'Private Intelligence Consortium', as they now called themselves, to actually meet here. Now that Klieberman–Boss had a security division that provided more appropriate cover, meetings were generally held at Camp Ute or over at Jack's premises. Today was special though, and the culmination of more than a year's planning.

Biff resented Tutch's attempts to dominate – emphasising the intelligence aspect and neglecting the business contribution. Tutch really should respect the 'private' aspect of the operation. Even Jack seemed tense now. In fact, if the group hadn't had the backing of Marquetcom and Jack's input, none of this would have been possible!

"I guess we should start," said Tutch, yet again seizing the initiative. A particular welcome to Mr Woods and Dr Farrow from the southern grouping."

"First some news," interrupted Woods. "We've been concerned for some time over Colonel Forest's 'hang-ups' and traditional ways. He was 'sold' on our idea of a quiet destabilising in Colombia. Turns out, though, that his involvement proved too risky, so that's been taken care of."

Tutch smiled and nodded, but soon took the lead again.

"Let me introduce 'Abdullah', as Zoltan knows him – or, in reality, Yoel Herzog, an ex-Mossad friend who greatly assisted our plan."

"Hi everyone! We meet at last, Mr Anson. As you know, I've made a number of deliveries here in recent months."

Biff grinned. "Yes, the last delivery had exceptional whiteness. I believe your paper's pretty good, as well!"

Everyone laughed, and Woods continued.

"As you know, Dr Farrow programmed Heltay to set a series of explosions, which should encourage agreement by the authorities," said Woods. "Demands have gone to the mayor's office, to Security and Washington. As planned, Yoel arranged for the demands to originate from his network, so that will point to the Islamists."

Dr Farrow nodded agreement.

"Brian, do you intend to reel those guys in later?" asked Woods.

"Yep, the whole damn network," said Tutch. "While everyone is fretting over the pay-out, we should get the kudos for helping to knock out a terrorist cell!"

"Everyone's a winner," said Abdul/Yoel, rubbing his hands together like a manic grasshopper.

"Do we all still agree to hold back with involving the militia freaks for the time being?" asked Tutch. "They could still be a first-class diversion for our next event."

No-one disagreed.

Biff swallowed, and looked around the room before speaking.

"I'd also like Freddy kept out of harm's way."

The assembled company agreed.

"Family first," added Tutch slyly.

"That's clear then," said Biff. "Are there any worries about the payment… or more to the point, its repatriation?"

"No problems," replied Tutch. "Ways have been found around the changes with the Swiss system, so it will be safe. Yoel's payment takes the form of hefty samples of the compliance technology. The Palestinians might complain about water, but, after this, they'll lap it up! Results from Colombia suggest the potential of this product is huge."

Yoel grinned from ear to ear.

"Zoltan's brought a stash over to our Brooklyn store – quite close to the waterfront!"

Tutch checked his watch.

"Doc Farrow, Zoltan timed the explosions to start shortly after our demands are made. That should be fairly soon now?"

Farrow nodded.

"Yes, he'll need time to get the materials moved for the next op. Sooner or later, we'll need to use the suitcase. I let him believe it would probably be placed here, so I'll have to programme in fresh instructions."

"I reckon we should leave some of the biological materials behind," suggested Yoel.

"Good thinking," replied Tutch. "That should stoke the Islamo-phobia no end."

"Any chance that the authorities won't take the bait?" asked Klieber-man. "You know, mightn't believe that we mean it?"

Tutch smiled and shook his head.

"A little caesium is wrapped around the next one. Just a whiff to show that we mean business. That's the beauty of having our operation tied to the terrorism and radiation exercise. Just a trace will be released any time now, and should mostly dissipate over New Jersey. The sniffer units, of course, will already be on the scene because of that exercise!"

Initially, Biff thought his rush of distress and stomach acid might be because, until recently, Judy had lived in New Jersey, but as the others laughed and joked, he'd begun to feel strangely nauseous and unreal.

He opened the drawer, reaching for the antacid and, for the first time in decades, had absolutely no idea what to do next...

115

BROOKLYN

GILL'S PERSPECTIVE

Gill caught up with Corinne outside the Abbas Stationery store.

"With both of them out, we can probably afford to get a little creative."

Corinne nodded.

"Exactly. Play along with me, because I've an idea. Are you carrying picks?"

"Of course! What do you have in mind?"

"Best if we're spontaneous. Just work with me."

They entered the reception. A young woman wearing a hijab was at the counter and appeared to be occupied with a telephone call. She held up a hand, put the phone down and disappeared, mumbling:

"Sorry. Be back real soon."

A plastic folder of stationery samples and illustrations of office equipment was left on the counter. She looked on as Corinne scanned through it and then swept the folder into her bag and quickly zipped it up. The woman returned, relayed information about an order and replaced the phone. She looked expectantly, and opened her mouth, but Corinne spoke first.

"Hi, we're from the Andean council for children's welfare. Could we see your manager?"

"Sorry, he left a few minutes ago and won't be back today. If it's about supplies, I can get Mr Tammer to see you?"

Corinne nodded.

"Thanks, yes."

"Okay, in the meantime you can look at... hey, it's gone again! Sorry, I thought I'd put the sample book out again, because our catalogue is being reprinted. I'll get Mr Tammer."

"Thanks."

She phoned through to stores and, moments later, a young black man appeared, introducing himself with a southern twang.

"Hi folks, I'm Mark Tammer. How can I help you ladies?"

Corinne smiled sweetly and held her hand out.

"Hello, Mark. Actually, we're calling for two reasons. First, we represent a children's charity and are visiting local businesses about possible support. We hoped to speak with your manager, but, apparently, he's out. The other thing is we probably need a new stationery supplier who can give a good deal."

"Mark, the sample book's gone again," called the woman.

"Maybe you can show us what you have," said Corinne with a grin. The young man arched his eyebrows quizzically.

"There aint hardly no-one in today," he said. "Most everyone's caught that bug doin' the rounds. Folks are throwin' up, an all. I'll show you guys our range, and Miza can print a copy of anythin' interesting. Prices vary accordin' to volume."

They followed him through a door behind reception that led in to the main stores. Corinne touched Gill's arm, and mouthed instructions.

"In a couple of minutes, ask for the toilet and then take a look around while I keep him occupied."

Tammer took them up and down the racks of paper, envelopes and equipment, pulling out samples for them to see.

"This is the standard stuff, or we can supply non-standard to order."

They walked further up the store, passing boxes of printers, scanners and then racks of everyday office products, from paper and guillotines to staplers. A well-built young man passed, with a trolley piled with boxes. Tammer called out:

"Hi Fang, the folk here want to see our range."

The man raised an arm, revealing impressive biceps.

"There's only me, Fang and Miza that's left in. Everyone else has took sick."

Whatever she planned must be due soon.

"I'm sorry, Mark" said Gill, "Do you have a bathroom?"

"Sure," he replied, pointing to two doors on the right of the store. "Take the first door. The other door is locked. That's where we keep special accounting software and stuff. I can't guarantee the state of the toilet because we don't usually have no customers out here."

As Gill walked towards the toilet door, she heard a gasp followed by a cry of pain from behind. She spun around and saw Corinne crouched beside an exposed pallet, doubled up and rubbing a bloody ankle. Mark crouched beside her calling for Fang's assistance, so she quickly entered the toilet door. In fact, a passage led to the toilet and – halfway down – another locked door. That must be another entrance to the locked store. Gill fished around in her bag for the picks and soon had it open. Inside were a number of crates and a battered-looking suitcase. She started with unexpected recognition. The collection looked identical to what she'd seen in Judy's shed. In addition to that, half a dozen unmarked drums were stacked against the back wall. One was pulled forward, so, taking a penknife from her bag, she ran it around the seal and twisted off the lid. It lacked any packing information. She slit open the plastic inner liner covering the pale blue powder, took a matchbox and a packet of throat pastels from her bag. She emptied the pastels into the bag and covered several fingers with the cellophane packing. She slid the matchbox half open to make a scoop, filled the pastels sleeve with powder and put it into her bag. After replacing the drum's lid, she returned to a now empty storeroom and then made her way to the front office.

Corinne sat in reception, with Mark crouching at knee level beside her, pressing a pad of tissues to her ankle. His real focus of attention was obvious, as Corinne had allowed her legs to drift open. Fang sat opposite, looking somewhat bemused. He grinned, exposing a ruby set into a tooth. Corinne's face was out of their line of sight and she looked over and winked, before speaking.

"We mustn't hold these good people up, Gill, what with them being short staffed and everything."

"Are you sure you don't want us to call the paramedics, Ma'am?" asked Mark. I'm not really s'posed to take folks inside," he added.

"I'll be fine. Would you print off that price list, though? We'll take that and be back in touch later."

"Already done," said Miza. Corinne hobbled over to take it.

We left the store and retraced our way to the subway station.

"Zoltan's materials from Judy's shed were in the second side room.

At least we won't have to search Abdullah's home. By the way, did you gash your ankle badly on that pallet?"

Corinne grinned. "No, I always carry a razor blade."

Despite the look of innocence, Corinne seemed a bundle of deviousness. Before she could even joke about that, Gill's cell phone started vibrating. She picked up, to hear Robbie's breathless greeting.

"Did you see Zoltan?"

"Yes, but probably not what you imagine. I followed him to Fort Tryon Park, at the top end of Manhattan."

"What's he up...?"

"Gill, hold on a moment, and listen. I'd previously followed him through Brooklyn's Greenwood Cemetery. Oddly, he picked up a backpack there, secreted in a mausoleum, and brought it here. Unfortunately, I had an accident, a fall, and he sneaked up and half choked me. Just before losing consciousness, I saw that the backpack had gone. He may have only put it down to deal with me, but he might also have placed it somewhere to..."

The explosion at Fort Tryon Park must have been truly deafening. Despite quickly removing the phone from her ear, the sound still reverberated. She listened again, but the line was dead.

Corinne had moved ahead and beckoned frantically.

"Quickly! Remember Abbas's delivery to Manhattan 1 office. We still haven't heard from Michelle. Hurry, Gill. Whatever is your problem...?!"

116

MANHATTAN

SIMON MAHER

I looked at Andy, and then back to his notes. Interviewing the people from 'A Fairer World' was stressful, knowing Gill, Corinne and Robbie were trailing a dangerous, and probably deranged, agent. Andy still seemed only half present, and I suspected that wouldn't change until his mom reappeared.

"They were quite an impressive bunch, weren't they? Had really good ideas."

Andrew nodded with little enthusiasm. I tried to engage him again to take his mind off things.

"You know, developing strategies for a fairer system isn't easy! In their place, what would your priorities be?"

"I don't know. Maybe participatory economics? A crash diet for the Pentagon? How about proper funding for elections or keeping corporate money away from influencing foreign policy? No, they were nice guys alright, with good ideas, but way too optimistic. Until the last big crash, few really understood the 'big finance' stranglehold. Even after everything that's happened, they still pull the strings. To be honest, though, Si, I'm more than a little preoccupied right now – worrying about Mom and the others. I really need some air."

We left the B&B to go into Washington Square. An approaching fire engine's siren was deafening as it moved north. Andrew still didn't seem himself, so I tried another tack.

"Do you think a more productive type of capitalism is even possible, rather than coddling sociopaths and fraudsters who profit from gambling with other people's money? I say, the predatory, disaster and casino models should be junked for one that caters to genuine entrepreneurs and workers."

"Sociopaths can misuse any system," he replied. "People like Dad always find a way around the rules, or else re-write them!"

"That psychoanalyst I interviewed, Alberto Gianavecci, was a strange old bird, and, unusually for an analyst, had both a social and a political dimension. He said something that really stuck in my mind. He said our struggle now isn't the old class struggle and ideas of 'left' and 'right'. The system is now so pathological that you first must determine if the levers of power are in psychopathic hands. Usually, they'll be busy undermining truth and fairness, and callously seeking their own advantage! He referred me to a Polish psychiatrist called Lobaczewski, who, from personal experience, described life under what he called a 'pathocracy'. In other words, a parasitic minority that had taken control of society, perpetrated evil for their own interests, regardless of the effects on others. Sound familiar?"

Andrew looked up.

"But what then? Mandatory psychometric assessments to keep such people away from positions of power?"

"Slightly draconian! Raising public awareness of the way sociopaths operate, maybe? Teaching the signs that they're corrupting a political party or corporation. In other words, the very work that we're trying to do!"

"That sounds a little like the old joke about asking fish for alternatives to water."

Talking and walking around the square, we became aware of the frequency of sirens and, to the north, wisps of smoke hung in the sky. On the other side of the square, I heard a New York University student call out to his skateboarding colleague. Their words carried on the breeze.

"An explosion, come and see!"

The first student disappeared inside.

"Something odd is happening," I said to Andy. "Let's check on television."

Back in our room, the TV coverage was indeed frantic, as long-range lenses focused on a pall of smoke hanging over Fort Tryon Park.

"Traces of caesium are also detected," the commentary advised. "The mayor has issued a statement saying that the 'levels of radioactivity are very low and essentially meaningless'. No need for panic or an evacuation."

The cell phone rang – it was Gill. I listened to her news of the discoveries in the Abbas stores and then of Robbie's call. I updated her on the television coverage.

"Apparently, the explosion was quite small. Let's hope Robbie's okay!"

"I pray so," she replied. "Zoltan's still out there somewhere, and we also don't know what was delivered to Marquetcom's office. A delivery to M... Woods had said! Odd though it may sound, Andy's dad might be in danger, too. I know there's no love lost, but he is family and Marquetcom's headquarters is in a landmark building with other business suites, with tourists, and..."

"Gill, it's me you're talking to and I don't need convincing. Is there anyone in the service you trust?"

"Only one, but she won't pick up. Obviously, I must raise the alarm over what we discovered at Abbas. Trouble is, I don't know to what extent the rogue element might have penetrated our office!"

In the background, the television screen had changed to a view of City Hall Park and a macerated tree. The scrolling banner read *Small explosion in City Hall Park – no radiation detected.* As I listened to Gill, I watched as men in white suits with radiation equipment circled the tree. Andrew seemed fixated on the screen, with a look of horror, and then choked out:

"Simon, I think we should head for the Empire State building. Gill could be right. Zoltan might return to Marquetcom's suite."

The banner changed to breaking news.

New York: Islamic Group issues a threat of a nuclear explosion. Demands unclear.

I passed the news on to Gill.

"It's odd," she replied. "Remember those air force exercises that were already underway on 9/11. Also, the existing exercises the same day of the London tube bombings. I think there's a pattern..."

I interrupted to tell her that a small explosion was being reported in a wooded area close to Grant's Tomb.

"Okay, we'll make our way back to Manhattan," said Gill. There's a diner near the Empire State building called the Stars. Let's meet there and decide a way forward. Say about fifty minutes?"

I interrupted to describe the on-screen scene – damaged vegetation and a small crater – before the camera then panned back to show the side of Grant's Tomb.

"I actually know for a certainty that Zoltan visited there yesterday," said Gill. "I'll explain when we meet." She gave the directions to the Stars diner.

We watched the live broadcast for a few more minutes and then went out to the square again.

"How on earth did it come to this?" I asked, more to dispel stress than in the expectation of an answer.

"We identified some of the reasons earlier," replied Andrew.

Andy's cell phone rang. He answered and his face brightened.

"We're in the middle of a rather tricky situation, Mom. How are things at the airport? Really?"

I wandered off to give them privacy and, by the time I returned, Andy looked much better.

"That was Mom. She's with Nick at the airport. Apparently, security is going at full throttle and they're closing to incoming flights. Anyway, Mom's decided to stay overnight because she'd like to see me. I'll take her out for a meal."

He grinned. "Provided we're still in one piece."

"And Nick?"

"He'll join us at the diner place Gill described. He said he could be a little late…"

117

MANHATTAN & BROOKLYN

BIFF ANSON'S PERSPECTIVE

Biff's stomach growled and he sipped some antacid. The group were about to leave for a restaurant lunch when Zoltan phoned. Tutch took the call and his face quickly turned serious.

"Apparently, Zoltan's on his way. There was a complication and he needed to deal with Rob James. We may as well hang on 'til he arrives. Yoel, could you wait in the conference room, because we don't want him confused by finding you here? Really, I think we should eliminate the whole damn problem by just getting rid of them all!"

Yoel's grin looked positively dangerous. He nodded and left.

Things felt like they were slipping out of control. Biff's stomach growled again.

"They still have Monroe's transcriptions, though, Brian. After listening to the copy that Riley found, we agreed that stuff was dynamite!"

"Working on it," said Dr Farrow. "There's enough material to sample, synthesise and then digitally re-edit. The problem was providing an explanation for the incriminating context. We've now worked up a plausible script and virtually finished the 'new' recording.

"Biff, as our PR expert, perhaps you'd fashion a more innocuous context to Monroe and Martin's meeting – if needed?"

Biff nodded, though was now focused on this suggestion of eliminating the group. After all, whatever his shortcomings, Andrew was still family!

There was a knock and Zoltan was shown in. He updated them.

"I assume you eliminated James?" asked Tutch.

"No, but he'll have a husky voice for a time. Perhaps it'll make him sound more manly! I only needed him out the way until I'd set the explosion."

"Zoltan, we need a small business discussion," said Tutch. "Please wait in the room next to Mark Finkelstein's office. Dr Fallows will be down soon to see you."

When Zoltan had left, Tutch assumed control again.

"I reckon that settles it. As Rob James followed him – the others are bound to know about it. I suggest that Yoel does the necessary. They don't know him, which should allow an element of surprise."

"Who exactly do you mean?" asked Biff.

"The whole damn lot, including the British agent... we certainly don't want any loose ends."

Biff felt stunned.

"You mean Andrew, too? Surely not Judy?" he croaked.

Yoel re-entered the room before Tutch could reply.

"Just heard from the Wilmington cell, and they've had a response. It seems the city authorities and Washington are playing for time. Their formal response is that they aren't in a position to finalise agreement until tomorrow."

"You predicted as much, Brian," said Woods. "Probably hope we'll get careless and make a mistake."

"Then we'll up the ante and use the water option. Keep the threat of the explosion, but, in the meantime, send Zoltan up to Kensico reservoir with the infective agents," said Tutch. "You'd better prepare him, Doc."

"Yeah," replied Farrow. "The equipment's in the side room. I'll do it now."

"The materials are in my Brooklyn store," interjected Yoel. "He'll expect to find me there."

"Of course. While you were out, Yoel, we agreed time's up for this lot. We definitely need rid."

"I couldn't agree more," said Yoel.

"So, will you do the business? I suggest you start with the Marney woman. She's experienced and might try to pull something. Zoltan can help and then continue on for the reservoir job."

There wasn't a flicker of doubt and Yoel just nodded impassively.

The pressure in Biff's head was getting overwhelming. Normally, he called the shots, now everything seemed out of his control.

"Wait, Brian. Let's leave Judy out. It's not necessary because she isn't really a part of this. I mean, she just happened to put people up in her home."

Tutch's smile was derisive.

"She was there for Zoltan's fiasco in Utah, later accompanied him to Colombia, linked up with Nick Martin and they probably flew back together today. She's fully in the know and a definite threat."

It was ages since he'd felt out of control and his impulse was exploding or even hitting Tutch.

"It'll be quick," Yoel said, his mouth twisting into a narrow slit.

"Can't take chances," he added, grinning, "although many would be more than happy to lose their ex!"

The others looked at him. Time slowed, and he felt everything closing in.

Fuck it, though! No-one else was about to make decisions about his family. Secretly, he'd always known the family was his Achilles heel, but never imagined it being tested this way. The family never really understood he wanted to be seen doing well by them. As the other conspirators agreed that this was the only sensible course, he struggled towards a decision that earlier would have been unthinkable – but now required immediate action!

"Actually guys, I feel really bilious. Possibly food poisoning," he said. "I'll give the meal a miss and see you when you get back."

He poured some more antacid to emphasise the difficulty.

"I'll give it a miss too," said Yoel, with a grin. "I've lots that needs finishing before pay-out. I agree that taking out the British agent first makes sense. She'll know the tricks of the trade. In fact, I heard that someone sounding like her visited the store earlier. Probably, she'll return to explore more, so I'll leave right away, before Zoltan reaches the store."

After the others left for lunch, Biff leaned over his desk, resting his head between cupped hands. Was he actually going to embark on a course that he'd never, ever have imagined? The task ahead felt daunting. His speciality in PR had been explaining the inexplicable,

concealing the unpalatable and steering people to accept the unaccept-
able. He'd carved out an empire that way, but this demanded far more
from him than any marketing stunt or tricky contract.

He punched out the number for the phone assigned to Andrew and,
after several rings, it answered. In the background, he could hear
sounds of shouting and a siren.

"Where are you, son? I urgently need to see you – face-to-face."

"Biff, what a surprise! If this phone rings, it usually means a call
from Tutch or Klieberman. It's certainly one hell of a coincidence,
because I was on the verge of contacting you. I've received information
that you might be in real danger."

"Seems we're speaking the same language for once. What you just
said is true. I am in danger and so are you – that's why I'm calling. Have
you heard from Mom, son, because she's also at risk?"

"Yes, about fifteen minutes ago.

"We need to meet."

"Why? Meet about what? I'm in Washington Square at the moment
and I'm due at an appointment in mid-town, in about 45 minutes."

"Wait there. I'll bring a car and driver. Meet you by the arch in about
15 minutes, and I'll explain everything then. If you like, I can bring you
back to mid-town for your appointment."

"What about my assistant, Simon? He's with me now."

"I have to speak with you alone. He can take the subway. This really
is vital. See you soon"

Shortly afterwards, the Lexus drew up at the square and he
instructed the driver to return in about fifteen minutes.

He saw Andrew talking with Maher close to the arch. His next
action was unprecedented and felt quite strange. Their last encounter
had been entirely adversarial, following years with no direct contact.
He saw Maher walk off and watched his eldest child approach. The
flush of pride and tenderness he felt towards the stubborn young man
quite took him aback. Judy, he'd never stopped loving, but Andy
seemed always to despise things important to him and had spurned
attempts to bring him into the business.

Andrew reached the roadside. They stood face-to-face opposite
each other – his son looking him directly in the eye.

"This really is a strange day, Biff."

So, it was to be 'Biff'. Words caught in his throat, but a speeding
police car reminded him of the urgency.

734

"I have information... not to sound overly dramatic, that... that a professional killer is searching for you – and for Mom, too."

Andrew continued staring without blinking.

He gulped.

"If you like, a contract that involves all of you!"

"That sounds rather theatrical, Biff!"

"This isn't a game, son. Have you... seen what's been happening?"

Faltering like this hadn't happened since reporting to Pop, in childhood. Since, he'd always made certain of keeping control, but... He turned away from Andrew's piercing stare.

"It's you, isn't it?" Andrew said. "You've got something to do with the chaos and explosions? Zoltan is an associate and now you've let Mom stumble into some horrific plan?"

People said he was stone-hearted, but that jibe hurt.

"You're so wrong, son. I've kept an eye out for Mom ever since we broke up. In fact, I never stopped loving her."

"I think you're confused between love and control, and always have been. To you, love is some kind of sugary sentimentality that actually masks control and domination. It isn't what most people would call love."

"But, it isn't like that, son. Actually, I only ever wanted the best for all the family and planned that you'd join me in the business. You're bright, I'll give you that, but you never fully grasped entrepreneurship, the values of competition or the personal honour of reaping a justified reward. You never understood the nobility, either, of healthy self-interest or self-reliance. You didn't see just how corrosive collectivism and socialism can be."

"As a matter of fact, I do understand that there are some problems. Unfortunately, though, there's a type who won't or can't leave it at that – who dominates and accumulates with reckless disregard of the needs of others. Of course, that will force people to band together."

Inside Biff, some kind of mental filter or fuse appeared to be breaking down. As he listened to the young man, his own flesh and blood, he filled with memories.

"I remember you boys as children and I do wish some things had been different!"

In the background, he could picture Judy's smiling face. He'd pushed and bullied all of them and, in this moment, he suddenly knew it!

Police cars sped by with blaring sirens and, without warning, the world started spinning and his knees buckled.

When he came to, he found Andy's arms encircling and pulling him into a sitting position. He looked down to the trousers of his Italian suit, covered in dust, and slowly raised his eyes to the start of Fifth Avenue. Further along was the Empire State building – the site of many of his triumphs. If Tutch had his way, it was the probable site for planning the execution of the young man who was so tenderly brushing him down – and for dear Judy! Biff struggled to his feet. His world was disintegrating and decades of achievement were as so much dust in his mouth. Andy's words had found their mark – a tender spot where a heart still existed. He saw with disturbing clarity that his son's integrity made his own decayed existence seem like a festering pile of rubbish.

He felt shocked by his next words and heard them as though from outside. Andy looked shocked, too, but something urged him on.

"Son, I'm really sorry, really sorry for everything, but things haven't always been as you imagine. I do want to listen, hear and understand your views, if you'll tell me, but, right now, we have to act quickly. You said you spoke to Mom. Where is she, because she's in real danger? You didn't use the phone Tutch gave out to speak to her, did you?"

"No, we also have our own personal phones. I texted her. She's at the airport."

"Call her right now. Quickly! I'll explain."

Andy pulled out his phone and entered a number.

"Mom, hello, I'm actually with Biff, and…"

He snatched the phone from Andrew's hands.

"Judy, it's me. I've been a bloody fool and you're in grave danger. Turn around and return to Philly right now. I'll do everything I can at this end to protect you."

She cut him short.

"That isn't possible, even if I wanted. They've closed flights here and I gather it's the same at La Guardia and Newark. The trains are disrupted, too. Anyway, Andy and I planned dinner together."

"Then keep your rendezvous with Andy, same place, same time. The company has safe accommodation you can use. I'll give the instructions to Andy. Listen carefully. A man going by the names Abdullah or Yoel is actively searching for you. He has a medium build, light brown hair and a sort of Middle Eastern appearance. Please take care! He knows where you've been and where you live. I'll pass you back to Andrew now and I'll do everything possible to halt this mess."

Andrew took the phone with shock and incredulity.

"No, Mom, I don't exactly know, except that we all appear to be in danger. I should do what Dad says. We're really in the 'twilight zone' now – because, apparently, he's having a 'change of heart'! God willing, I'll see you later."

He heard that word 'heart' again and now 'Dad'. Yes, he did have a heart, even if it had become calloused over time. If only they understood that, in his own way, he'd struggled for them, too. Pop had been quite right – the world was a tough and unforgiving place!

He looked up and saw the Lexus by the side of the road. Simon Maher had gone.

"Quickly, son, over to the car!"

They climbed into the rear, behind tinted windows, and he checked his watch. Judging from their usual eating habits, there was probably only about ninety minutes before Tutch and the others returned to Marquetcom's office.

"What about the others of our group?" Andrew asked. "Are they targets too?"

He nodded, not even attempting justification.

"Can you communicate with them, son?"

Andrew nodded.

"Tell them to head to the San Remo Apartments on the Upper West Side. I have another apartment there. I'll call and instruct the doorman."

"Unfortunately, it isn't so easy. We discovered Zoltan's working with a guy called Abdullah, with a stationery business in Brooklyn. Of course, you know that because he delivers to Marquetcom. Our friend, Gill, and her colleague have gone over to check his store. Hey, you just mentioned someone called Abdul. You don't mean the same...?"

"I'm afraid so, yes!"

Andy pulled out his cell phone.

"I have to warn them!"

It felt like the final straw. It had gone too far, now. Applying pressure was normal enough, but killing family members was absolutely something else. This had never been the intention!

"It's complicated, son. Yoel plans starting his destruction with the woman, Gill, but I'm afraid there's more. Zoltan will collect an infective biological substance from Abdul's store and has been instructed to dump it into the city's water supply."

"But you'll also hurt people who merely need water!"

Andy's words hit hard. He recalled Rob James's briefings. Good God, this is just what the little fag said their planned privatisation would do!

Andy's face was a mirror that he couldn't bear looking into. Had he really descended to something quite so disgusting? Andrew's face said yes! His remaining armour was evaporating, like mist under sunlight. He turned away, unable to hold eye contact.

"You have to understand, son, this isn't at all what was planned."

Andy, though, was already tapping out a number on his cell phone. He listened, almost sharing the horror as Andy relayed the situation. When he finished, his son's face was grim.

"Gill's near a subway station in Brooklyn, but turned back because they've shut that part of the subway down."

"Good, she should hail a cab and head for the San Remo"

"No, when she heard the story, she insisted on going back to the store to wait for Zoltan and…"

He grabbed his son's wrist.

"She'll be a sitting duck for Yoel! The phones Tutch gave show your position to within yards, even if you aren't using them!"

"Shit! I'll call back and warn her to dump it. We must get over there. Simon will want to come, too. Turn back so I can run into the B&B and get him."

Andrew paused and then swallowed.

"Dad, you do realise that Gill will have to call in law enforcement, don't you?"

He nodded. They locked eyes and, in a moment of silent communion, there was a closeness that has been missing for decades!

118

MANHATTAN & BROOKLYN

SIMON MAHER

I changed my clothing, preparing to meet with the others at the diner. In the background, the television spewed out thin updates, mainly repeating the same sequences of the explosions' effects. A weapons expert speculated on the likely effects of a dirty bomb in Manhattan, but didn't venture into the possibility of a true nuclear device.

I turned off, ready to leave for the meeting, but, at that moment Andy arrived – red-faced and breathless.

"Come quickly, come. Dad has a car waiting outside. Apparently that Abdul character plans to kill Gill. We're potentially all targets."

"Fuck! Okay, coming. Why your dad's car? Gill took the train. In fact, she should be heading back now?"

Andrew interrupted.

"Apparently the subway's been closed."

"Got it. Hang on, those phones Tutch gave us. She could be tracked."

"Already onto it – I just called her. The phone's probably half way up Long Island, by now. She said she'd throw it on the back of the next open truck she sees. I'll leave mine here."

"So where is she now?"

He looked over, but Andy was struggling for words.

"What is it?"

Dad has had a change of heart. Whatever was the original plan, he says that now it's all spiralled out of control. Apparently, Zoltan is going to return to Abdul's store to collect biological materials. They plan to threaten infecting the city's water to crank up pressure for their demands. When Gill heard that news, she and Corinne decided to return to Abdul's place to stop him."

"Let's go!"

According to the driver, the traffic was far worse than usual because of the subway problem. I prayed and called Gill's personal cell phone, breathless with relief when she answered.

"Please don't go back, Gill – it's far too dangerous. Find a café, and then phone us with your location. We'll join you there."

She replied in a way I'd glimpsed once before and I knew that argument would be futile.

"Sorry, Si, it's my duty. With genuine security and public protection issues, things are different. Corinne feels the same, so don't worry about us. Listen, I was just about to call you! Will you personally talk to Tom Freison, my bureau chief, and explain what's happening? According to someone in our office, their last delivery of stationery from Abdul might contain... well, who knows what! Also tell him we need people over here with sniffer equipment. I can't seem to reach anyone else. Normally, I'm prohibited from revealing the location, but this is a total emergency."

She gave an address behind the Rockefeller Centre complex. I felt torn between needing to protect her and public duty.

"I tried to contact someone I trust there, called Michelle Grantz, but there's no reply. I know Freison's out on the exercise, but not where. You may have to find an FBI office and ask for help with locating him. In fact, do that. It's possible that explosives are hidden in the office stationery store. Michelle wanted to check that. They probably won't stop at anything, now. I found crates and an old suitcase that Zoltan previously had stored in Judy's shed. They are in an inner store room, about halfway down on the right side of Abdul's warehouse – next to the toilet. The next explosion might be far more serious."

"Gill, we're coming. You could be in real danger. Please take..."

"Simon, are you listening?" she snapped. "Corinne contacted Sheryl in Arizona. There may be no alternative but to release everything. Please see Tom in person, now, and tell him! We don't know yet whether other agents in our office have been compromised."

"Hang on a moment! You won't know this, yet, but Nick and Judy got back from Bogotá this morning. Nick's en route to a meeting, near the address you just gave me. He should arrive in about ten or fifteen minutes – far quicker than we can manage."

"It's vital…"

"No, listen. Nick's a far better choice for gaining quick credibility. After all, he's in a local Brooklyn business and was the one who actually spoke with Monroe!"

"I don't know, Si. Getting detection equipment down here to check out what's really in the stores and stopping Zoltan has to be the priority. Who knows what else he might have planted?"

"I agree, Simon – it's a good idea," came Corinne's almost girlish voice. "Nick's tackled several tricky things since all this started, and Gill needs her knight in shining armour. We probably both do!"

Gill spoke again.

"Okay, I agree. Listen, we've just reached the road leading to the store and should be there soon. Get Nick straight onto contacting Freison and please be careful!"

I hung up and then called Nick.

"Fucking terrible traffic!" shouted Biff from the front. "There's no way around until we get a bit further down."

The traffic thinned and eventually we were able to cut down some side streets. As we passed the subway station, the driver asked.

"We're almost there. Do you want me to park outside?"

"Drive by and we'll take a look first," Andy called.

Moments later we passed the store. Several cars were in the street, but nothing out the ordinary. We parked a little further along.

"Wait here, Henry," Biff told his driver.

"Best if at least one of us stays intact. If we're not back in an hour, phone Nancy and have her explain to Brian that I tried making a quick visit to Queens but the car's broken down."

I walked to the store, beside Biff and Andrew. After the past history, it seemed almost inconceivable that we were now joining together in common purpose – but life does take these strange turns sometimes! Even so, my stomach seemed alive with butterflies and my legs tight to the possibility that Abdul may already be back, and on home territory!

We entered the store, but the reception area was empty. I heaved myself over the counter and we could hear the sound of a flushing toilet from behind the wall. I then noticed the lump in my right pocket.

What a fool! In the rush, I'd brought along Tutch's cell phone. We could be tracked!

I half pulled it from my pocket and pointed.

"Dump it as soon as we get out," hissed Andrew.

I gently opened the door to the warehouse and the others followed. Almost immediately, we heard the crack of a shot come from inside. I reflexively flinched, crouched, and then waited. Gradually standing, I inched forward to allow Andrew and Biff passage through the doorway. Ahead, an eerie, horrible gurgling noise had started, which was immediately followed by another shot. To the left, another door opened and I saw a young woman wearing a scarf stick her head out. I looked back to the others, but Biff had moved with a speed quite belying his size. I froze, but inevitably the woman's head turned until she saw me and genuine shock registered on her face. Her mouth opened to shout, but, at that moment, Biff reached out from behind and covered her face with his hand, pulling her back into the reception area. Surprised by Biff's quick action, I crept forward into the main part of the warehouse with Andy following. Keeping low, behind racks of equipment, we reached an intersection and could either turn left, right or continue straight ahead. I turned left towards the building's far side, reasoning that there must be space on the margins for fork-lift access. With luck, we could work our way down the side, parallel to the site of the shot. There was still no sight or sound of the girls.

My neck was cricked from being stooped over. Ahead on the right, something moved. I turned, and mouthed to Andy 'Where's your father?' He shook his head, and showed empty hands. As I crept to the next bay, I could hear someone moving on the cement walkway. I froze, and then realised the sound was moving away. I peered from behind the end box and saw a man in a leather waistcoat and well-developed biceps clutching a gun, and moving forward with an anthropoid gait. Further on, a young black man in a business suit lay crumpled on an empty pallet. The blood pounded in my ears as I watched the figure in the leather waistcoat reach the store's right side and the two doors. The man put his head in the right-hand door and spoke.

"Mark overheard your conversation, but won't do it again."

The man entered the other door, and closed it behind him.

I wiped my brow and moved forward, stumbling over a piece of timber that had propped up a damaged pallet. Andy picked it up and brandished it like a makeshift weapon, managing to look rather absurd. We continued up the aisle to the body, but the mess oozing from the young man's shattered skull said it's too late – move along!

The sounds that were now coming from the side room suggested something heavy was being dragged across the floor. I approached the door with my heart thumping erratically and, although poised to quickly run, had no real destination or plan! Where on earth were the girls, anyway?

Something touched the side of my head and I looked down to see a crumpled ball of paper on the floor. A second piece landed nearby. I jerked around, and looked up into the tiers of racks that extended right up to the ceiling. Three racks up, wedged behind several boxes, I saw Corinne looking down. She waved and pointed over the aisle to where Gill peeped out from behind more boxes. Gill popped up and blew me a kiss. The noises from the side room got louder. Something was being dragged to the door, which could open at any moment!

I looked at Andrew and, in desperation, we turned and ran back down the aisle. A few yards on, I saw an empty slot in the racking and threw myself into the gap. Andrew clattered on down the aisle, but, at that moment, a voice called out.

"Fang, come here and help."

I heard the other door open, and then a voice cried out.

"Shit, someone's… Hey you, stop or I'll shoot!"

The running feet stopped.

"Come here right, now."

I heard Andy return and, as he passed, he threw the piece of wood into the gap, grazing my chest. Hopefully, this would just seem a random action after being caught out. I heard the other door open and another voice spoke.

"So, you've come to help us, Andrew – how kind!"

Wedged between boxes wasn't the ideal spot for observation. I'd only had a brief meeting in Philly and that night in the Abajos, but the voice was definitely Zoltan. Andy's reply confirmed it.

"Hello Zoltan! I see you're out on another IT consultation!"

"Very funny! Where's your assistant?"

"Simon, you mean? Back in the Village. He had an interview lined up for later, though – with all the commotion – who knows?"

I wiggled into a slightly better position. The boxes lined up regularly, forming a small gap at the end of the row. My field of view was slight, but I could see that Andrew was by the door next to Fang, who was holding a gun. Zoltan stood in the doorway. Zoltan then moved and another face appeared. It must be Abdullah, Yoel or whatever his name was. Zoltan said something softly and the other man nodded and grinned.

"Excellent. You've come to me. Where's the British woman?"

"I don't know what you mean."

"Yes, you do. She was up by the subway station not long ago, and then, unhelpfully, dumped her phone. Someone of her description came here earlier – isn't that so, Zoltan?"

"That's right."

"Never mind, with sufficient heat, she'll no doubt turn up! I do hope you like barbecues? Human flesh smells sweet when toasted. Your military cooked many in the Middle East that way – isn't that so? Zoltan, bring us some rope from the storeroom, and we'll fix a kebab!"

Zoltan disappeared and then emerged with rope. Andrew was then taken out of sight and secured to the end of the same rack where Gill was hidden. I surmised that, if the side room was where Gill saw Zoltan's equipment, the girls had hidden nearby to watch for activity.

A clicking noise came from the left. I'd heard similar sounds several times already, but facing my fear of rodents right now seemed a bridge too far. There came a sudden scraping noise, and then Biff's voice bellowed out.

"Let him go!"

I heard scraping, and twisted around. Anson was shuffling down the aisle with the young woman from reception, held out before him. Her scarf was tied over her mouth and Anson held a gun to her temple. I quickly turned back, to look down the gap between the boxes, and saw Abdul reach into his jacket. A shot sounded and I heard something fall. I couldn't stop myself and peered around the outermost box and down the aisle. The woman lay motionless. Meanwhile, Anson had moved further up and stood in front of his son, his bulk shielding Andy from Abdul and Fang.

"No, you don't, Yoel! I didn't sign up to have anyone in my family killed!"

"Stand aside, you stupid old man. Do you want to fry too? It's us or them, now!"

Anson had two guns pointed at him. Fang lurched forward and quickly pulled Biff's gun away.

"Tie them both to the racking," snarled Abdul. "Help him, Hassan. We must shift the stuff now. What a mess!"

I looked upwards. From here I could just about see Gill's hair, hidden behind a box.

'Hassan'? Why did he call Zoltan by that name? Did Gill have something planned?

Abdul and Zoltan returned to the storeroom. Now that Andrew and Biff were secured, Fang returned the gun to his pocket and sat on a box, smoking. More sounds came from the storeroom. Then the door opened and Abdul and Zoltan emerged with a trolley piled high with drums.

"Back for more soon," said Abdul. "Keep an eye on these two."

They trundled the trolley towards the far end of the store. I suspected there'd be a loading bay. After some minutes, they returned for additional drums and again trundled them to the rear of the warehouse.

"I gotta take a leak," said Fang, after the others had returned to the small storeroom. He left for the toilet.

I wriggled out of the crevice, removed my shoes and held them up as I ran to the rear of the building. Sure enough, a white van had backed up to the loading bay and was full of drums and crates. Being mildly obsessive sometimes had advantages and always carrying a pen was one such result. I copied down details of the van's livery and registration number. As the sliding front door had been left open, I climbed into the cabin and pushed the phone Tutch gave me right the way under the driver's seat. As I climbed out, a glint of metal caught my eye – the keys were still in the door! I quickly pocketed them and slipped back into the main building, this time turning right. I sped with bare feet to the outside aisle, still carrying my shoes, peering down each aisle to check as I moved down the building. Reaching the fifth aisle from the front, I stopped at the corner and peered down the length of the rack. On the other side of the warehouse, Abdul and Zoltan again pushed the trolley forward to the loading bay. This time, an old suitcase sat on the top, which Zoltan supported with one hand. As they passed out of sight, I crept to the next intersection, in alignment with the side storeroom and the rack where Andy and Anson were now secured. Reaching the corner, I lay on the floor, inching forward, and then gradually peeped over the top of a carton. I expected to see Fang, but, instead, Gill was crouched down pulling at the ropes securing Andy. The toilet door began to open and I clamped down against an impulse to shout a warning. Too late... Fang emerged and, even from here, I saw the coarse features register surprise. Fang sprang forward to grab Gill, but she stepped sideways, spun and then delivered a kick-box blow, causing him to gasp and double up. He recovered, and lunged forward with a winding punch to her abdomen. She doubled forward, and he lifted his gun, hissing:

"Say goodbye, charity girl."

I hurtled barefoot down the aisle, with no time to worry about shoes!

Whether it was my speedy approach or Gill's defence that saved the day was uncertain. I skated the last few feet with outstretched fists and delivered a kick, knocking Fang to the ground. The man rolled over, with a grimace that showed a ruby set in a yellow canine – but he still had the gun. I tried regaining balance to deliver another kick, but had far too much momentum. I saw a shadow as something hurtled through the air and smashed into Fang's head. The impact caused him to crumple and lie still, but Gill collapsed forward at the same time.

I looked up and into the racking. Corinne was standing beside an open carton with that damnably carefree expression again. She pointed to an empty box and then to the office guillotine now lying on the floor next to Fang, and climbed down.

I went over to Gill and crouched beside her, but she'd passed out.

As Corinne reached the last tier of racking, we heard the squeaking noise of the trolley. I ran back to the aisle, and wedged myself into the hiding place again.

"Oh, what have we got here?" came Zoltan's voice.

I heard an odd rubbing noise and peering out, saw Corinne being pulled over to where Andy and Anson were tied.

"Do you know her, Hassan?" asked Abdul.

"No."

"Fang said two women were here this afternoon, posing as charity workers."

"We must quickly move out."

"Put them in the storeroom," said Abdul. "Who'd have thought my task would be made so easy?"

"Zoltan bent down and took Fang's gun. Then they opened the storeroom and dragged the unconscious man inside. After Abdul emerged, he guarded the others, while Zoltan untied their ropes from the racks, retying them until their bodies were fully encircled.

"Get in," snarled Abdul, pointing towards the open storeroom.

"You too," he said to the hobbling Corinne.

Zoltan grabbed Gill's hands, and pulled her into the room. He reached the door before she could struggle, but it was too late – the door was locked.

"We'd better leave," said Abdul. "Anyone else will be in the main store for the fireworks! Pest control was due a visit, anyway."

I lay frozen in my hiding place as the footsteps moved towards the loading bay again. The sound of feet returned. Perhaps they'd discovered the van's keys were missing.

"It'll spread quicker if we start it at both ends," called Abdul.

The footsteps moved beyond me to the front of the warehouse. Soon I heard a crackle, faint at first, and smelt smoke. Feet ran towards the back of the building as the crackling intensified. I wriggled from the crevice as the sound of slamming bay doors reverberated through the building. The crackling soon changed to a roar and pieces of blackened paper whirled like deadly black butterflies through the darkened smoky air. I ran to the locked storeroom door and pushed at it. The others shouted and coughed. I ran at the door. Nothing whatsoever moved, but pain screamed from my shoulder. I fetched the guillotine that had felled Fang and ran it into the door – but it bounced off like a rubber ball. My heart was thundering with panic as I started to gasp. At the far end, a wall of flame had built and was now licking at the ceiling.

I rushed to the front and found my way into reception. Smoke had seeped in and I couldn't see out of the windows. My memory fetched up something, so I felt around in the corner, barely able to make out the red object through watering eyes. I picked up the heavy extinguisher and ran back into the main building, but then slipped over. The extinguisher would be useless against this wall of flame, but might make a good battering ram.

I ran at the door, holding the extinguisher at the lock's level. Nothing! I repeated the assault several times – but still nothing moved. Smoke burnt my airways and I was feeling dizzy. I hit the door again with a supreme effort and a tiny crack appeared. Moving back some yards, I charged at the door and this time the wood splintered. I repeated the process until, finally, part of the door broke away.

Gill was at the front of the room, but, as I extended my hand to help her, the lights went out. She stumbled forward, followed by Corinne and Andy. The girls had by then succeeded in getting the ropes untied and Biff helped to pull out the semi-conscious Fang by his ankles. I led them into the reception area, holding the extinguisher aloft, repeating the battering operation on the front door. Eventually, still gasping, we were out and into fresh air.

A crowd had gathered and I heard the whir of an approaching helicopter. I looked up, but the additional sounds of fire appliances and police sirens obscured the direction. I felt waves of relief that we were now out, and hugged Gill until common sense reappeared.

"Quickly, let's look at the back. They were loading a van behind the warehouse. I removed the keys and tucked Tutch's cell phone under the seat."

"Careful. Remember, they have weapons."

"I'll watch Fang," called Corinne.

Gill and I ran forward and, when I glanced back, Fang was on his knees, retching.

We reached the back of the building, and I slowly eased my head around the corner. A silver Mercedes stood beside the van and I saw Zoltan carry a box to the trunk. At that moment, the van started and Abdul's head popped up inside. He must have either hot-wired it or had another key. The van moved off, and then Zoltan slammed his car trunk and followed. The two vehicles drove to the rear of the lot and out through a back gate. We ran together through the gate and out onto the street, but both vehicles had by then rounded the corner and disappeared.

When we returned, fire appliances were setting up. The helicopter noise had stopped, so I assumed that it must have landed.

"What do we do now?"

119

MANHATTAN – BROOKLYN

NICK MARTIN

I struggled through the crowded streets of Manhattan. I was only just back from Colombia, and it almost seemed history was repeating itself. Just as happened in Utah, I was being diverted onto a side mission while Gill and the others got down to the real business! I wondered how things were progressing in Brooklyn? Here, the combined effect of the official exercise and the explosions meant confusion and barely controlled panic. Nevertheless, I located the mid-town FBI field office, and poured out my story. Mercifully, it was taken seriously and their officers helped locate Tom Freison.

Freison was apparently 'coordinating things' near the Plaza Hotel, though I wasn't exactly sure what might be involved. En route, I was told of an explosion that had occurred at his office. Objectively, it had been quite small, but, as soon as we arrived, it was obvious that the man was really quite shocked. Apparently, though, he'd paid attention to an earlier message from Gill's colleague, Michelle Grantz. I said:

"If necessary, Michelle will be able to verify what I'm going to tell you."

Freison shook his head sadly, and explained that Michelle and several admin staff had been casualties!

I tried telling him more, but Freison was besieged by cell phone calls, radio messages and requests from staff. A more awkward time to request his help would be hard to imagine. Eventually, I was able to tell him that we knew an agent in Arizona of his acquaintance, who would have further vital information. Freison took me to one side and then sprang into action, asking to be patched through to Sheryl. After they conversed, he passed me the receiver. I thanked Sheryl for her earlier support. She then spoke to my concerns.

"Nick, we're fairly certain Tom Freison is clean, but aren't sure if Manhattan 1 office has been penetrated. Tom doesn't think so, although Tutch did have a few dealings. Anyway, Tom intends to move quickly."

She rang off and Freison contacted colleagues in Brooklyn, requesting that FBI associates bring in Klieberman and Tutch. Tutch had apparently been closer to the other metropolitan Security offices, so there could be more concerns about infiltration there. I was still trying to put the various pieces together when a car screeched alongside.

"Get in," shouted Freison. "We've clearly no time to waste."

We drove at speed to the Thirty-Fourth Street heliport, with a helicopter ready to go. We were airborne almost immediately, crossing the East River and then flying over Brooklyn. Despite the circumstances, I couldn't resist turning to see the iconic Manhattan skyline. Freison caught my eye and grimaced.

"Gill's very worried about what's in this store and has requested radiation detection, so we have problems. Gill's an excellent agent and I trust her. I hope they can quickly bring those bastards in. Tutch probably won't crack easily, but Klieberman just might."

The radio crackled out a dispiriting message.

"It isn't surprising that the radiation truck is caught up in traffic," he said, pointing down. Below, the traffic snarls were obvious, though from up here, the harbour looked strangely serene and ahead a ship ploughed its passage beneath the graceful span of the Verrazanno Narrows Bridge.

We continued flying over Brooklyn. On the edge of a commercial area ahead, smoke rose from what looked like a burning warehouse.

"That's it!" called the pilot, and pointed to the smoke...

120

BROOKLYN – STATEN ISLAND

SIMON MAHER

I quickly followed Gill as she ran with her identification already in hand. She gabbled something to the first police officer, who pointed over to a car that had just arrived. Two men climbed out.

"Those are the security guys," said the cop.

Gill ran to their car. By the time I'd caught her up, another agent, who was on the phone, pointed to where Biff, Corinne, Andy and Fang waited. I watched as Fang was led away by the police. Another officer moved to take Anson's arm and Andy shouted.

"Gill, come quickly. Dad has important information!"

"Si, this is agent Rod Kelly," she said. "Wait with him here and I'll be straight back because it's vital that we catch Abdul's van up. Be back in a moment."

I climbed into the back seat, and watched Nick and two other men run from the direction of a helicopter that had just landed. Gill spoke with Biff and Andy, and, after waving and pointing, ran back and jumped in next to Rod Kelly.

I leaned forward to speak to Kelly.

"Go down the side of the warehouse, and the road behind should be clearer. That's where the van left from!"

We moved off and, as I looked back, I saw Nick and companions running at full speed back to the helicopter. Andy had stayed with Biff and the police, but then everything became obscured by water from the fire pump. Rod kept moving until we rounded the building, and then screeched out of the rear gate.

Gill turned around.

"Nick just arrived by helicopter with Tom Freison, my boss. They're going back to the chopper to find Zoltan. Biff says that Zoltan's been sent to target the city's water supply. Fortunately, I memorised his Merc's registration. An APB has now been issued and licence recognition cameras are active."

"Finding him sounds a tall order," I replied. "How extensive is the water system? It surely has to be..."

"Hang on, Si, you haven't heard the rest. Biff just explained that the phones they gave out to us have an additional feature. A small amount of explosive, that can be detonated just by a special incoming signal. In other words, Tutch, or whoever, could theoretically have blown our heads off at any time!"

"Yes, but they didn't know for certain that we had them at any one time. For example, they could have been placed in a left luggage locker, while we got on with something else! I can see why they'd want the deed actually witnessed. We now have another problem, though. I put my phone under Yoel's seat in the van! Yours is riding about in a truck somewhere. Andy has already heard that information from Biff and you told Nick already, so that leaves Robbie's phone somewhere. Nick still has his phone, but knows about the problem, so won't answer it. Do you know if they found Tutch yet?"

"No, he's totally off the map. Incidentally, they're radioing the helicopter to re-emphasise the phone danger to Nick."

"The phone I left in Abdul's van... I gather phones can be accurately tracked?"

"Exactly. Tom's seeing to that. Their position can be pinpointed, but activating the explosive apparently needs both a particular signal – and someone to answer it."

The radio crackled.

"Hopefully, it's what we want," said Rod.

"Brooklyn office," announced the voice. "Aerial observation says the target is nearing the end of Hamilton Parkway and looks ready to join the Expressway. He's probably heading for Verrazano Narrows Bridge."

"Thanks Jerry. Any word from Tom Freison?"

"Still above, and searching for the Merc, but no joy as yet. I'll call with any developments."

Rod picked up speed on Queens Expressway. We accelerated past most other traffic, and saw the bridge's superstructure rising dramatically ahead. We were close to the bridge's approach when we saw the traffic back up. I gripped my seat as Rod braked powerfully. Further up, the traffic swerved to avoid a white van that had pulled into the side. Brake lights flicked on and off as drivers braked and changed lanes. Rod skilfully weaved in and out of the honking traffic, but the start of a genuine snarl-up was obvious. As we got closer, a figure could be seen carrying a large suitcase-like object to the edge and then push it over.

"That's our man!"

The traffic struggled to find a way around the van and drivers up ahead honked and shouted. We were about five car lengths away when the figure, now clearly seen as Abdul/Yoel, rejoined the van. Taking advantage of the slowing traffic, he started manoeuvring out and had crossed two lanes. He suddenly stopped, leaned out of his window with gun in hand and waved down a nearby BMW.

We were hemmed in by blocked traffic. Rod cursed, started the warning lights and then jumped from the car. Gun in hand, he crouched low, and weaved his way around stationary cars, towards Abdul and the van. I looked on from the car, uncertain what part I should take. Abdul pointed his gun at the BMW's driver, and then suddenly ducked out of sight and reappeared with a cell phone pressed to his ear.

My warning choked in my throat, and became a silent scream. I'll never forget the sight of the exploding head, looking like an overripe tomato, as it painted the windscreen and side windows with blood and brains. My system protested, and went into overload. I flung open the back door, retching onto the carriageway, but, when I'd finished, found that I was now alone! Gill ran towards Rod and the van. I stepped over the mess, and followed Gill to reach the even greater mess in the van. When I arrived, Rod had covered the headless torso with his jacket and grabbed the steering wheel. Several nearby motorists positioned themselves to help push and, averting my eyes, I also helped push until the van was fully back in the slow lane.

A police helicopter arrived in a flurry of wind and noise, hovering parallel to the roadway, before veering away again. Gradually, the held-up traffic pulled out around the van and wailing sirens announced the arrival of more police cars. Rod pulled quickly away, before the police presence stalled the movement, and radioed control. I spoke as he was on air.

"Rod, can you have them check with Anson how Zoltan typically travels. For example, to and from Camp Ute. I just noticed signs saying Newark Airport."

"Will do, although the city's reservoirs are mostly up-state. Perhaps we should join with the search there, because at least you guys know his appearance…!"

121

BROOKLYN – VALHALLA – KENSICO DAM

NICK MARTIN

As the helicopter lifted, turned north, and crossed Brooklyn towards Queens, I looked back to the warehouse. The smoke had diminished, but, even from here, it was clearly wrecked. We continued flying over Queens, parallel to Manhattan's famous skyline and the pilot pointed down as we passed the site of the old Shea Stadium. We continued on, skirting La Guardia airport and crossed water, which I guessed must be the East River, before broadening out to Long Island Sound. Before I could check this with the pilot, the radio crackled into life.

"Tom. I've a message for Nick Martin. His colleague, Rob James, was picked up after wandering down from Fort Tryon Park. He was apparently found in the upper reaches of Broadway – dazed, but basically unharmed. He's now undergoing medical checks."

Freison, sitting in front, turned and gave a thumbs-up.

"Good news!" he shouted.

"Something else important," the voice continued. "It seems Martin's group were given cell phones and instructed to keep them handy at all times. I gather Nick Martin knows they were booby-trapped, but now there's been an incident. So, to re-emphasise, if that phone rings, don't on any account answer it. Hold it and forensics and bomb disposal will handle it later."

"Okay, Jerry. Got it!"

Goosebumps swept over me and, for the moment, my entire attention centred on the object in my right pocket!

"Couldn't we just turn over the water and then dump the thing?" I called.

"No can do," said Freison. "We couldn't guarantee its safety. Anyway, it's crucial evidence."

We were now flying above the Bronx and gradually the massive conurbation thinned out and the green of lower New York State began to unfold below.

"I think the Croton watershed in Westchester and Putnam county is the most likely place. We're heading there now," said Freison.

"The oversight of all three main watersheds has been improved, although it's still difficult. A complex system of interconnected reservoirs, underground pipes and aqueducts is virtually impossible to completely monitor."

The radio broke into our conversation.

"The Merc was spotted by a licence-plate reading camera out near Flushing airport."

"Thanks, Jerry. Had it crossed the bridge by any chance?"

"No, hang on, Tom. This guy's smart and he got off Whitestone Expressway at Twentieth Avenue and then seized another car at gunpoint... a light blue Toyota. We spoke to the owner, and fed details into the plate recognition system, but he's probably well beyond city limits by now."

"You mean he crossed Whitestone Bridge and went up through the Bronx?"

"I reckon so!"

"Thanks, Jerry. Repeat that plate for me and stay in touch."

"Will do. Patrols are searching the main roads north. Any clues where he's going?"

"We think the Croton watershed is the most likely. Of course, he may think he has a better chance at the Delaware watershed – or even continuing right up into the Catskills!"

"Okay, talk soon."

Below became increasingly green and attractive.

"Where to first?"

"I'm drawn to Kensico reservoir. It's both the closest and also the final holding area for about ninety percent of the city's drinking water, which arrives there from all of the watersheds. The water then enters tunnels to take it on to New York City."

A small town appeared below.

"White Plains," called Freison. "We're nearly there."

Ahead, wooded hills formed an attractive valley, with a lake and dam at one end.

"Kensico dam and reservoir," called Freison.

Below, I could see several boats as we circled above the lake. It reminded me of that fateful day at Old Hickory Lake.

"Apparently, the fishing is good," called Freison.

Without warning, a Boeing 737 suddenly lifted off from the lake's east side.

"What the hell," I shouted. "I wasn't expecting that."

"Westchester County airport," replied Freison. "Several airlines handle domestic flights from here and it also handles business traffic. This is dormitory territory for corporate bigwigs... and it's handy for them."

"Tom, mightn't this be Zoltan's escape point? I'd almost bet that someone's already waiting to get him away. I'd put money on him laying low at Camp Ute, before returning to Colombia. Cross-country driving would be far too dangerous. Could we put down and take a look?"

"Good thinking," replied Freison. "Anyway, we need a car to get us to Valhalla to check the reservoir out. We partner with Environmental Protection, for reservoir security, so I'll have someone meet us."

We radioed for permission to land and a car to meet us. As I looked down on water destined for thirsty New Yorkers, I reflected on the journey from a New Jersey meeting hall – to this!

"Apparently, there are some agents already there to help out."

We moved closer to the airport's edge and started descending.

"Valhalla – did I hear you correctly?"

"No connections to Odin or Wagner, though. It's just happens to be the name of the little town closest to the dam. Look."

Tom passed over a map and, astonishingly, he was right!

"Good, though, given our circumstances, I'd prefer other associations to the... 'home of the gloriously slain'!"

"You're getting a bit too imaginative, now," Freison replied, as we touched down.

A black SUV approached at speed and pulled alongside. The man in the passenger side sprang out.

"I'm agent Lance Gable, Sir. Agent Roy Mason driving. We've been briefed."

"We need to get over to Kensico," said Freison, "but first to airport security, please."

We hurried to the main building and located the security manager. Freison requested lists of today's flights and passengers, but there was no listing for Zoltan Heltay, Tutch, Klieberman, or anyone else relevant.

"I believe you also handle corporate flights?"

We huddled over the manifest, seeing flights to Boston, Milwaulkee, Chicago and Toronto. At the bottom was listed a private Lear jet flight to Utah, for the Arm-Rite Corporation.

I caught Freison's eye.

"Yes, I see it. Excuse me, is the Lear for Arm-Rite in yet?"

"Arrived about two hours ago."

"Where's the pilot now?"

"Probably in the corporate waiting area, with his other passengers, although I believe they're still awaiting Mr Anson."

"Anson! You mean Biff Anson? You know him?"

"Sure. He has a residence nearby and often uses us for domestic travel."

I felt a familiar vibration from my left pocket and retrieved the cell phone used by our group. I listened while Simon described the incident on the Verazzano Narrows Bridge.

"Where exactly are you?"

"Manhattan was totally gridlocked, so we turned back to Brooklyn and picked Andy up. We'll come and help with the search."

"Our idea is starting with checking out the Croton watershed. We're currently at Westchester County airport, quite near the Kensico reservoir. We've just discovered that a flight for the Arm-Rite Corporation is standing by – destination Utah. You know what that means! Gill's boss, Tom Freison, has requested more agents to help comb this area and is sending agents to other reservoirs. Tell your driver to head for Valhalla and the Kensico dam. Hope to see you soon!"

122

KENSICO DAM

SIMON MAHER

I squeezed Gill's hand as we sped through the massive conurbation and finally headed for Valhalla. Andy followed in another car with Rod Kelly. Freison, it turned out, was wrong. It hadn't been Klieberman who'd cracked but Dr Fallows, the military psychologist. Surprising! If anyone knew how to handle stress, it should be him!

We arrived at the dam and, a few moments later, a car with Nick and Freison, pulled up, having been delayed at Westchester. Two further cars followed with additional security agents. We were welcomed by Department of Environmental Protection staff, all sporting luminous hi-vis yellow safety jackets. Their leader, Hank Todd, passed out more jackets for us.

"Just remember that anyone you see not in one of these jackets won't be one of us!"

"Are there any other resources for reservoir security?" asked Freison.

"Your colleagues only take an advisory role," replied Todd. "Watershed police regularly patrol by foot and boat and a K9 team is available if needed, though that's only once been called for. If necessary, we can access a SCUBA unit and a contract gives access to a plane and helicopter – though that has never been called upon. Do you really think your man is planning to contaminate the water?"

"We believe so," replied Freison. "The four individuals with us here have direct experience of the guy and can visually identify him."

Feeling rather conspicuous, I said.

"Zoltan Heltay, the subject, is specially trained and can kill without hesitation."

"Simon's quite right," agreed Gill. "Consider him highly dangerous."

"Understood. We've temporarily closed the road over the causeway and access points to the reservoir have been closed. A boat patrol's been out and instructed fishing parties to leave immediately."

"Shouldn't we get started?"

"Agreed," replied Todd. "We'll split into four patrols. One of the four of you with each group."

I scrambled up the bank with Todd and his group of security and environmental protection men – all in their yellow safety jackets. Once at the top, I looked back across the dam wall and the now closed drive-way. To the right, the road from White Plains followed the edge of the reservoir and separated Kensico dam from Rye Lake. Todd's group moved ahead and turned left.

"We should check the aqueducts, too, in case he tries spiking them," Todd said to the group. "Mantle's patrol can check the Delaware aqueduct and Beck's to the far end."

The group set off, but, after a few minutes, the radio silence was broken as one of the watershed police reported back.

"Apparently Beck's patrol found the light blue Toyota pushed under trees at the top of Nannyhagen Road, Sir. No sign of our man, though."

"Keep behind the tree-line, and fan out as we go forward," said Todd. "Keep going until we meet up with Beck's group. This guy will eventually make a slip." He looked at me. "You stay next to me."

Todd and I stayed close to the lake just inside the tree-line, while the others fanned out from the water. Keeping in line, the group moved north.

The shoreline curved and, ahead, I saw a boat pull in. A tall, brunette woman dressed in navy, with a backpack, tied up and then climbed onto the bank. She had no yellow safety jacket and quickly disappeared into the trees.

"See that?" I whispered.

Todd nodded.

"Won't risk the radio – too noisy," he mouthed.

We crept forward, and gradually moved around the lake.

The woman had totally disappeared by the time we met up with Beck's group, but so too had Michael Childs, one of Todd's team. By the time it was established that Childs was furthest from the water, the panic was palpable. Todd radioed the news to the other patrols on the eastern side. Beck's team moved further west and then both groups headed back towards the dam. After about ten minutes, an agitated voice came over the radio. It was Beck.

"We just found Childs' body behind a tree, minus his safety jacket and car keys. He's dead!"

Everyone picked up speed, and Todd was now holding a gun. I saw the dam ahead and, by the water's edge, two figures in yellow jackets were talking. On the ground was a large navy-blue backpack.

Todd broke cover, and ran towards the pair.

I looked on in horror as the crack from the shot reached us, and I saw one of the figures fall into the water. The other picked up the backpack and disappeared, as the whole patrol ran towards the dam.

Todd asked for someone to call for an ambulance and another man dove in and pushed the body to the shore.

"I thought swimming was banned," someone said, but no-one laughed. I followed Todd onto the dam wall and we looked down onto the plaza below. No sign of the figure with the backpack!

The bank further along was less steep and everyone scrambled down and made their way to the area now immediately below. Someone in his team thought Childs drove a Chevy, possibly green, though no-one knew the registration. Several unsuspecting families were picnicking in the park below. One reported that a tall brunette with a backpack had passed them, probably heading towards the car park. The patrol rushed there, only to find a crumpled yellow safety jacket and an empty bay.

"Shit! Zoltan must have frightened a description of his car from him," said Todd. "Childs, poor devil, has… had… a couple of kids, too."

The others started arriving, including Freison, the security agents from the airport and Andy, Gill and Nick. People stared helplessly at the safety jacket, but it could give nothing more.

"Now what?" I asked. "Where might Zoltan go, to further his mission?"

"Could be anywhere," replied Todd. "The network is huge."

"But this reservoir holds the water before it travels underground to New York City?"

"True... well, apart from Hillview."

"Hillview?"

"A reservoir down in Yonkers. Water is piped here from the other watersheds, stays for a week or two to settle out. Afterwards, tunnels take it to Hillview, and the city draws directly from there. It would be harder for him to get at it there, though. Mind you, it'll be even harder when the proposed cover is finished!"

He looked over to Freison and their eyes met.

"I'll call for more agents to attend," said Freison.

"My car's over that way," said Todd, pointing. "Hillview is sometimes on my agenda so I know the way."

"I'll follow in a minute," said Freison, already phoning. As I left, I could hear him talking on the phone. "...possibly be disguised as a woman with a brunette wig. Last seen wearing navy blue..."

I jumped in beside Todd. The back door slammed and, when I turned, Gill and Nick had climbed into the back. As we sped away, Gill massaged the back of my neck and, by the time we reached just outside Yonkers, her phone rang. From the responses, the call was obviously Freison. I turned and her expression was grave.

"Okay, Sir. Let's hope that works." She rang off.

"That was Tom. It turns out that the psychologist guy, Farrow, that you saw in Ute, has control over Zoltan. He hopes to get him to abort the mission. Agents are already on their way to Yonkers. Let's just hope they're in time and it works!"

As we arrived at Hillview, however, action was already under way.

We jumped from Todd's car and ran across to the trees for shelter, but, in the first minute, a bullet whistled nearby and most people hit the ground. Police and agents were everywhere and, even with the gunfire, we could hear more approaching sirens and the sound of a helicopter. With the possibility of unknown contamination about to mainline an unsuspecting city – the stakes couldn't be higher.

I inched forward, willing the horror to cease and for everyone to be safe. In the middle of a fierce exchange, the scene suddenly became quiet after the returning shots from Zoltan abruptly ceased. A surprised agent who'd sneaked in close mumbled over his radio link:

"Weird. The target has now stopped firing and is taking a call on his cell phone!"

The agent then asked for permission to take Zoltan out, but whatever was said on the call must have somehow worked. The next moment, he shouted out his willingness to surrender!

I caught Gill's eye and we surged forward with the others to watch as the bizarre figure, complete with a woman's wig, was brought to the ground. As the oddly vacant-looking figure was pulled to his feet and cuffed, I had a momentary flashback to the night Zoltan had been overpowered in the Abajo Mountains. I refocused and peered over the agents' shoulders as they unfastened Zoltan's backpack. Explosives could be seen behind a row of phials. I realised with horror that, if things had gone differently at Kensico, Zoltan could have introduced toxins to the aqueduct and then blown the dam. That would have impeded the flushing out of bio-hazards and, for that matter, fighting fires. We watched Zoltan taken away, mumbling the word 'Fresian', whatever that meant, over and over again.

Tom Freison took us back to the city, to a different security office, where the surprisingly intact and together Robbie waited. A television played in the background, reassuring viewers. The perpetrators of a criminal plot to blackmail the city had now been apprehended and all was well.

THE WIG, Zoltan's dishevelled, odd appearance and the toxic backpack were some of the indelible images I mulled over during the subsequent week. The suitcase bomb had been safely retrieved and, on the surface, life gradually returned to normal. Debriefings continued for another three weeks, underpinned by the serving of gagging orders for the group. Additionally, legal papers came from the UK for Andy and me, amounting to the same thing. We realised that a massive cover up was under way and that the whole mess would be portrayed just as a simple criminal conspiracy for a ransom. No mention of any corruption in the intelligence community or the role that the outsourcing of sensitive functions to private business may have played. Neither would the tie-in to compromised corporations like Arm-Rite or Marquetcom be explained. As far as the public were concerned, a so-called Islamic terrorist cell had been broken up, and multiple arrests made.

Predictably, the military-industrial-intelligence complex quickly used the whole episode to ratchet up costly demands – supposedly to prevent anything similar ever happening again. Who could argue?

Increased surveillance of the public's communications would, of course, be necessary because the terrorists had misused cell phone and internet communications! Those of us who had uncovered this mess were prohibited from making contact with Marquetcom and neither the fate nor whereabouts of Biff Anson was revealed. Nick then heard that Canvey had reconsidered the business environment in Colombia and that the operation there would immediately cease. We were prohibited from sharing the details of what we'd seen, experienced and discovered in Colombia, until after an undisclosed period had elapsed. We were only told that this time would be substantial and that any details that were eventually released must in no way interfere with the peace!

There was really a lot that needed to be shared. The intel community that facilitated so much underhand nonsense also had people that could think for themselves and could be brought around. We had examples. Gill herself, Michelle, Fiona, Marji, Sheryl, Toby and many others whose names we didn't know. There was a desperate need for 'intelligence' to actually use some intelligence!

Freison disappeared from our lives, although, some time later, we heard he'd suffered a fatal accident. One day, we were told by our new supervisor that travel documents, for me, Andy and Gill, had been cleared and were now ready.

We returned to the UK. No hint of any of the events down in Putamayo had surfaced and that might very well have been the end of the episode. Deep down, though, I thought that eventually we'd act – we must act – on our discoveries.

There seemed a growing attitude of public disquiet and resistance, fears about a forthcoming financial collapse and a growing hostility both to elite and corporate manipulation. The problem was where and how to start – a problem that would soon be answered! Gill began her process of exiting the service. Andy and I learned that the planned contraction of our teaching unit had been rescinded and our former employment was available. Together with Farrelly and Grotstein, we started sifting through the interview materials to work out how the additional new material could be integrated into the research project. We debated the controversial knowledge of unjustified public surveillance, intelligence service misuse, corruption, and more details of the extent of sociopathic corporate behaviour. Not just that, but also governments supposedly committed to the public interest – in intensive partnerships with private interests that are not necessarily concerned with the public good, but clearly with profit and personal advantage. Given the entwined nature of government and corporate data collection, there now isn't any facet of life that escapes information sharing. If the government can't legally collect certain data, there are always data brokers who have the information and who'll sell it. Everything is now logged in private sector databases. Often there is a quid pro quo to this arrangement. For example, there is apparently a plan to copy GP health records onto a database. It remains to be seen, in practice, if will eventually be available to commercial third parties.

These debates continued and, perhaps, if we hadn't received Nick's email, our life may have returned to some semblance of normality, but that wasn't to be. I looked at Nick's message again, shaking my head.

N has now returned, and things have mostly quieter. However, she's discovered that some of the old players have turned up in Brazil. Game on again? Surely, we can't allow this? Maybe now the time to release the hottest recording ever made in Nashville. Do you agree? Are you ready?

Nick.

I looked over at the kitchen wall and the factory girls from my travels. For the first time in months, I thought of Miki at the children's home and the folk from Nina's documentary who, in many ways, had sparked the whole extraordinary episode. Surely, people of goodwill everywhere should metaphorically scream 'Ya Basta'.

Gill would arrive tonight. I knew that she agreed and we'd no doubt plan our strategy.

I typed *You're right. Yes, we are ready!* and clicked send...

EPILOGUE

Two agents huddled under a tree outside Maher's campus apartment, as wind-driven curtains of rain lashed the building. One pointed skyward.

"Maher's water struggles must have earned the support of 'upstairs'!"

Although, technically, Maher was still an employee, no-one in the campus administration had been told of this search. After picking the lock, the rain-soaked duo slid into the apartment.

Dick Hennessy slipped out of his soaking telecoms overalls and looked around in open dismay. Gill spent time here in those first months? The chaos would daunt a professional cleaner. Never mind. Maher, the little worm, had information of extreme sensitivity, making the services both here and in the US extremely jumpy. Now, Maher and Gill had disappeared. Even worse, they'd probably been colluding for some time.

His colleague, Gordon Downer, shrugged and pulled a face. "Surely the place has already been turned over, sir? Someone has beaten us to it!"

"No, I remember Gill describing this as normal for him."

Hennessy spotted notes on Maher's computer desk and struggled to cross the room, stepping over books and kicking over a pile of CDs in an involuntary hopscotch. He picked up discs of so-called 'world music',

Joe Jackson's 'Night and Day' album, Schoenberg's 'Gurreleider' and Szymanowski's opera, 'King Roger.'

Downer grinned and watched the gymnastics. Hennessy started reading the notes, leaving Downer to the search. The writing was heavy and polemical, but, with no leads, there was little choice but to wade through. A brief glance confirmed it would be irksome. Trouble was, he knew from past experience that Maher and Alton sometimes said things that were near to the bone.

"Typical, lefty, preachy bafflegab," he called to Downer.

He weighed the pile by hand, and took a deep breath. Downer was searching in the next room, so he read aloud – as much to share the irritation as anything. It appeared an anti-corporate rant, prefaced by lauding Nina Parenda's television documentary. That probably explained his later association with the wretched woman. The next section he saw was:

A Call To Action

Most are now convinced that our system as currently configured is unsustainable. Many yearn for alternative principles to organise economies and society with equitable principles – rather than just the mechanisms of private ownership, greed and scarcity. They want societies motivated by more than narrow economic criteria – particularly given our huge environmental challenges. Surely, we need a new outlook recognising the interdependence of life and the importance of sharing.

Unfortunately, an elite consisting of mega-corporations, international finance, assorted plutocrats and tech-owners think that they alone have the right to design your future. Having enriched themselves with the fruits of globalisation, privatisation and predatory trade deals – they believe that virtually everything is (or should be) considered a commodity and up for sale.

Some of it rang uncomfortable bells, and Hennessy continued with more in this vein for several pages. If only Maher would give some clues about his next move. He skipped to the next page.

...hence, we're presented with a succession of scapegoats and 'bogeymen' – terrorism, currency crises, pandemics, asylum seekers, immigrants, anti-social neighbours, sexual minorities, paedophiles on every corner – even mothers who dare to publicly breastfeed! Problems are invented that an unsuspecting public are told should concern them, and with demands for 'something to be done'! Of course, the politics of fear are often extremely lucrative! Politicians, think-tanks and business interests present themselves as having the 'solution'. The

'solution' is usually costly, requiring new laws that extend the state's powers, reduce civil liberties and justify dubious policies. Plans usually result in giving more power to corporations and, magically, put even more public wealth into private pockets...

Despite his protestations, Hennessy slowly began to think that Maher actually spoke some sense. He reasoned that the same must have happened with Gill. Downer then entered the room holding a photograph.

"A picture of Gill. It looks like Alton's with her?"

He took the photo. A sunburned Dr Alton stood beside Gill, on the rim of a canyon. Below, a wilderness of glowing red rocks and boulders stretched to the horizon.

"Probably Utah," replied Hennessy and continued reading.

Of course, the powers that be would prefer a passive, 'dumbed-down' global hive of consumers – to mature, thinking citizens. Rather: millions of juicy customers, programmed from infancy for a lifetime chasing brands and corporate logos. The same corporations that quietly buy political influence and set agendas committing 'democratic' governments to facilitate corporate wish-lists, rather than the will of a populace they've long ceased to serve.

Hennessy swallowed hard and then picked up another pile.

Rarely does unfiltered information get past the media's filters and many real issues are often buried by celebrity tittle-tattle or sensationalised personal behaviours. Little appears by chance! One exception, though, was a broadcast by International Cable Network Inc, describing the trend to privatising water supplies in the undeveloped and developing world. Images of hardship, sick children and a forceful commentary by child poverty advocate, Nina Parenda, played across Europe and the Americas, to considerable disquiet. Amazingly, her criticisms were broadcast without the usual bowing to business interests – due to a few courageous individuals who were, of course, quickly punished.

The following recounts activities that some saw as just another business opportunity – but, others, as an example of an insane system. The individuals concerned, however, hadn't expected to uncover a plan of depraved greed – potentially threatening millions, extending control, undermining free will and democracy.

So, Maher, did intend to release the information, then! This really would cause some bitter water!

Downer returned from the bedroom with a piece of paper.

"This appears to be our next point of enquiry, Sir."

Relieved to be pulled away from Maher's rant, and its awkward questions, Hennessy took the paper and saw the details for an online reservation for two – Heathrow to Sao Paulo, dated two days earlier. He clutched his head and groaned as his cell phone began to ring.

THE END

JOHN. J. King (c)

ABOUT THE AUTHOR

John previously worked as a social worker, trainer and psychotherapist. He also worked as a manager in a well known forensic establishment - from where he drew considerable inspiration for "Bitter Water." Further work is planned on similar themes.

Lightning Source UK Ltd.
Milton Keynes UK
UKHW010900141221
395640UK00001B/1